# RAG
# TRADE

# RAG TRADE

## Lewis Orde

St. Martin's Press
New York

**Library of Congress Cataloging in Publication Data**
Orde, Lewis.
  Rag trade.

  I.    Title.
PZ4.068Rag   [PS3565.R38]    813'.5'4    77-16737

ISBN 0-312-66241-6

Although this novel bears no intentional similarity to any real companies or individuals, it is dedicated to the many outstanding characters I have met and the many friends I have made in the European and North American men's clothing industries...particularly F. G. (Jim) Welchman, of Savile Row, London, who ranks among the elite of the world's custom tailoring fraternity, and Morris Gay and Jack Thornton, both of Toronto, two retailers who really know what it's all about.

# Part

# 1

# GELLENBAUM AND SONS

# 1

Jacob Gellenbaum felt that he was dissolving in a bath of perspiration. His skin was clammy. His glasses kept slipping down his long, straight nose. And the three-piece suit stuck to his body, turning even the slightest movement into an awkward maneuver. The stiff shirt collar did nothing to ease his discomfort, rubbing irritatingly against the folds in his neck despite repeated attempts to create some space between skin and celluloid.

Looking out through the window of the small tailoring shop onto Essex Street, in New York City's lower East Side, Jacob nodded sympathetically at passers-by who were trying to cope with the humid eighty-degree temperature. Men with open collars and rolled-up shirt sleeves, and women in light cotton dresses walked along the street, stopping occasionally to wipe their glistening faces; sweat stained their clothes, damp patches underneath the armpits spreading out to join those across the chest and back. Two children sauntered past, licking popsicles, tongues greedily seeking the cooling touch of the fruit-flavored ice.

Nobody hurried. To simply walk in the city's stifling heat required enormous effort. Speed was out of the question; wherever they were going would still be there when they arrived.

Inside the tailoring shop, the atmosphere was just as sultry and oppressive. A large electric fan revolving slowly from its mounting in the unpainted plaster ceiling did little more than recycle the humidity around the small area. Sometimes, if the wind was just right, the heavy blades succeeded in drawing a minute amount of air in from the street, past the narrow wood and glass door which was held open throughout the summer months by a heavy pressing iron.

Despite the strength-sapping heat, Jacob continued to wear the heavy wool suit, the vest buttoned tightly below his tie and stud-fastened collar, the pristine white handkerchief showing exactly one-quarter of an inch above the top of his breast pocket. In winter, when icy winds tore across

3

the city, turning streets into tunnels of freezing air, Jacob's preference for formal clothing was practical, insulating him against the chill temperatures. In the height of summer, as now, he perspired. But, he reasoned, if a little sweat, perhaps a small amount of discomfort, was the price he had to pay for being properly dressed, then it was a small price and one which he would pay willingly. Besides, without the pockets provided by the vest, where could he wear the heavy gold watch and chain?

Plucking the watch from its resting place in the right pocket of the vest, he opened it and examined its face. The hands stood at three minutes to twelve, the same time they had shown for the past twenty-five years, since 1910, when he had dropped it onto the deck of the steamer bringing him and his late wife from England on the last leg of their journey from Poland to New York. After inspecting the damaged mechanism, a jeweller had declared the watch to be irreparable. He had offered to buy it from Jacob for the gold value alone, but the then new immigrant to the United States had been reluctant to sell, despite the poverty in which he found himself. To Jacob, the watch represented the sole object of wealth he had brought out of his homeland, and its familiar presence soothed him in times of stress, the well-known shape and weight bringing reassurance in the face of problems.

Like now. Confronted by his only son, Jonathan, who was trying to make him give up the work of a lifetime and enter into a new venture.

America, Jacob thought wearily. How differently you make the sons from the fathers. What dreams, what ideas, what ambitions you give to children.

"Papa." Jonathan's voice was quiet but insistent. "Have you been listening to a single word I said?"

Jacob turned back into the shop, caressing the watch for a final time before slipping it into the vest pocket. Ensuring that the chain was straight across his stomach, preserving the air of dignity that he tried so hard to maintain, Jacob looked up into his son's eyes, marvelling as he always did at how he could have produced such a giant. A biblical lion. A Samson with powerful arms, a broad chest, a thick mane of black hair and a firm nose and jawline. And those eyes, Jacob thought. Deep brown, set wide apart. Surely the eyes of an honest man.

"I'm listening," he replied, the Polish accent giving a lilt to the language he had learned so painstakingly. "I'm listening, Jonathan. But I'm not sure I understand what you're trying to tell me."

"Papa, go to the mirror and take a long look at yourself. You're only forty-eight, and already you're beginning to look like an old man." Jonathan tried to soften the words with a warm smile. "When I bring friends home in the future, I'll have to introduce you as my *zayde*, my grandfather. They'll never believe you're my father."

Jacob snorted derisively. "So this is what your American education does for you. Teaches you to laugh at your father, make a mockery of his work and tell him he's been wasting his time all these years. Tell me, what else did the teachers fill your head with?"

Jonathan spread his hands in supplication. "You know better than that. I wouldn't mock you. I'm saying all this because you're my father and I love you more than anything else in the world. I want the best for you, can't you understand that? But right now I think you're banging your head against a brick wall. Tailoring might have given you a good living in the old country, even here many years ago when you first came over. But now"—he shrugged his broad shoulders expressively—"it's finished."

Without waiting for an answer, he pointed through the shop to the front window. "See all those people out on the street, Papa? They're all wearing clothes made on a production line, just like a new car or any other piece of machinery. If you want to make money out of clothing, you've got to run a factory. Everything's machine-made. Sewing, pressing—it's all done by machine.

"We'll soon be at a point where machines will be so sophisticated that all you'll have to do is stick a piece of cloth in at one end and you'll get a completed garment out at the other. Machines are taking over from the craftsmen. It's happening in every industry. Your kind of tailoring's on the way out."

Jacob reached out for a chair and sat down heavily, hearing the legs squeak as they scraped across the unvarnished wooden floor. "On the way out," he muttered dolefully, repeating Jonathan's words as though speaking to himself. "That's what my educated son tells me."

When he spoke again, his voice had taken on a more resolute tone. "My work is so much on the way out that it was good enough to pay for that precious education of yours. While other boys were leaving school early to try and find any job they could, bringing in a few dollars if they were lucky, to help out their families, you stayed on to finish. That made me very proud, Jonathan. And it made me very happy because you had a better chance at life. But now"—he waved his right hand forlornly—"when you come back and tell me that I've been wasting my time, I'm not so happy. Tailoring was good enough to pay for you to stay at school, and it will be good enough to keep me for a few years yet."

"That's right, Papa," Jonathan agreed patiently. "It'll keep you going as long as you work fifteen hours a day, seven days a week, for the rest of your life. What kind of existence is that?"

Jacob raised his eyebrows in surprise. "Seven days a week? And when have you ever known me to work on *Shabbes*? Have you ever seen me with a needle or a pair of shears in my hands on God's day?" He wagged a finger admonishingly at Jonathan. "You, you heathen! You work on *Shabbes*. But me? Never!"

An overwhelming sense of weariness enveloped Jonathan as he stared down at the older man, noticing the brown hair streaked with gray, the dandruff-flecked collar of his jacket. This is hopeless, he thought. It's just about impossible to win any sort of argument with my father, to make him see any point of view which differs from the way he has built his life. He's a wonderful man, but he's as stubborn as any army of mules.

Squatting down next to the chair, Jonathan leaned closer to his father. "Papa, you'd like me to work with you. Right?"

Jacob nodded eagerly, his eyes shining at the thought of such a thing. It had been his dream since Jonathan's birth that one day he would be in partnership with his son.

"I will," Jonathan continued. "But not here, not in this kind of business. I don't want to be a tailor."

Jacob opened his mouth to protest, but Jonathan held up a hand. "Give me a moment. Let me finish what I've got to say. Ever since I was a kid old enough to understand what was going on around me, I've watched you working in this shop, or in a place just like it. It used to break my heart. It still does. You bent over somebody's coat, always rushing to get it finished on time, wrecking your eyesight to make sure the stitches were perfect, worrying in case your customers weren't coming across with the money. You'd close up and rush home to make me something to eat when I got back from school, then you'd run straight back here to work for another few hours. The only time I ever saw you, had you to myself, was on *Shabbes*. Friday was the one night in the week when you'd lock up the shop and come home early and we could be together in the evening.

"Papa, you're an expert with clothing. You're an artist. There's nothing you don't know about making suits. All I'm asking you to do is transfer that knowledge to a factory. You'd run a fantastic place. I've seen the rubbish some of these other places are turning out, and you wouldn't lower yourself to do the alterations on those suits even if your best customer got down on bended knee and begged you to. I've already got contacts for machinery, for fabrics, for trimmings. It'll only be a small factory to begin with, maybe one hundred suits a week. But we can build on it, Papa." The words tumbled out faster as Jonathan's enthusiasm for the project carried him away.

"All you'll have to do is supervise production, look after the technical side, the designing, the pattern grading. I'm the one who'll worry about the selling. You'll work less than you've ever done, Papa, and you'll have more money in your pocket, a nice place to live, things you never could afford before. Can't you just see it now, Gellenbaum and Son, in letters ten feet tall?"

Jonathan looked up into his father's eyes, seeking some reaction. Behind the glasses, Jacob's gentle brown eyes were blank, showing nothing. Five seconds passed; then Jonathan stood up and walked to the door. Jacob also rose and followed him. At the door, Jonathan stooped and kissed his father on the cheek, a hurried action as if he did not want it to be seen by any person outside the shop. Then he went out into the street.

Jacob felt a twinge of jealousy as he watched his son walk away. He envied the ease with which Jonathan strolled along the sidewalk, the self-assured casualness as if he, and he alone, owned the city, the nonchalant greetings to people he passed, the simple action of kicking an empty cigarette pack into the gutter. That's the difference between us, Jacob thought. My son is an American, a native of this country, whereas I am still living in the Poland I fled twenty-five years ago.

As Jonathan turned a corner and was lost to view, Jacob went back inside the shop, locking the front door. Walking to the rear, he sat down at the small cutting table, absent-mindedly studying the pattern of the piece of fabric on which he had been working before Jonathan's visit. He pushed the cloth aside and rested his elbows on the working surface, supporting his chin in his hands. Jonathan was right, of course. He had the American education; he thought like an American. Just watching his son walking along the street had convinced Jacob of that. His whole style had exuded confidence. He was at home in this country as Jacob could never hope to be. After all, this was Jonathan's country, not Poland where Jacob had learned and first practiced his trade.

Twenty-five years after coming to the United States, Jacob sometimes still found himself yearning for the simple life he had known in Poland. Since his first day in New York—having been allowed to land after the traumatic experiences of the immigration procedure on Ellis Island—his life had been cloaked in confusion. He understood his tailoring and his responsibilities to his family. Beyond that, however, his new country had remained something of a mystery. For Jacob, America would always be a land where children grew to be bigger than their parents, where they shrugged off the old ideas, the established values which had held the communities together in the face of outside hostility. Even partially insulated by the Jewish immigrant community which surrounded the small shop, Jacob continued to feel twinges of unease, as if he did not belong. He had made friends. There were even men he had known in Poland; they would sit together in one of the many chess clubs which dotted the neighborhood, drinking tea, playing, reliving old times. But to Jacob, it was not the same; he remained a stranger in what was now his own country.

The small tailoring shop was the pinnacle of Jacob's achievements. He had worked day and night for two years to save the money for the rent, bent double, pushing and pulling on the needle in the little sweatshop factory where he had first found work, the day after landing from Ellis Island. He remembered well the look on Anna's face when he had returned to the small room they rented, telling her that he had found a job without even speaking a word of his new country's language. "Polish and Yiddish," he had told her. "Everybody in this country speaks either Polish or Yiddish." And she had laughed with him, the worries that had accumulated over the long, uncomfortable sea trip disappearing in the knowledge that there was a better life in America.

But the novelty had worn off. Fourteen-hour days in the factory, which barely paid for food and room rent, aged him, forming a permanent curve in his back, dulling his senses with the continuous rattle of machinery, the ever present damp mist in the air from the presses giving him cold after cold, one respiratory ailment after another which the crowded living conditions did nothing to ease.

Anna had also gone out to work, operating a sewing machine in a different factory, her legs tired after pushing the treadle up and down, eyesight dimmed by the closeness of the work, fingers pitted by needle marks where her concentration had wavered for the tiniest fraction of time. Together they formed a resolve—to sacrifice the few luxuries they could afford, which others might term necessities, in order to save for a tailoring shop of their own where Jacob could return to the world of craftsmen, be looked up to again as he had been in Poland among the small community he serviced. Week after week they put away whatever money they could. Cents turned into dollars; while others squandered, Jacob and Anna scrimped and saved... until that proud day when he opened the shop in Essex Street, its window half-covered by the handwritten sign in Polish, Yiddish and English that Jacob Gellenbaum was open for business.

Anna had continued to work, disregarding the pains in her legs and fingers, her eyesight cleared by the knowledge that tomorrow would be better, that Jacob was building up his business, gaining customers through recommendation. When they were ready, she left the factory and joined him, helping until her eighth month of pregnancy made further work impossible.

When Jonathan had been born, Jacob's joy knew no bounds. He had closed down his small shop for a complete day, revelling in the occasion, certain at last that he belonged in this country. He had a son who was an American, who would grow up to make him proud. Living, eating and sleeping three to the same room meant no hardship to him anymore; sharing the same outdoor toilet with the six other families that occupied the building was nothing more than a temporary problem. The business would prosper, Jonathan would grow, and they would find a place of their own. God would look after them.

Anna's coughing spasms had started when Jonathan was two, spending his days in the shop on Essex Street while his mother helped Jacob. At first it had been dismissed as a cold. Then, when it grew worse, with blood being sprayed up from Anna's tortured lungs, Jacob became worried. Savings they had put aside for the apartment they would one day own went instead for doctor's bills, a seemingly never-ending succession of visits that confirmed Jacob's worst fears—tuberculosis. Suddenly Anna was no longer in the shop to help him or at home to cook and look after Jonathan. She was in a sanitarium, gradually fading away. When she died shortly before Jonathan's fourth birthday, Jacob was so numbed by the loss that he hardly even realized that he was so far in debt. For the next three years, he worked five out of every six days for the sanitarium and for the doctors who had tried to save Anna's life. His dreams for everything lay like a shattered plate, strewn this way and that as he tried to reorganize his life. Only Jonathan mattered now, and Jacob was determined that whatever it cost him, his son would have every opportunity to make something of himself. Jacob did not want the journey to America to have been completely in vain.

Together they had stayed in the single room until Jonathan was ten, finally moving out in favor of a larger home where each could sleep in privacy. Through sheer hard work he had managed to make enough money from the shop on Essex Street so that neither of them went without, but it was a struggle, always a fight to find the money for the rent, the supplies he needed, the food that Jonathan consumed in greater quantities as his body grew at a rate that frightened Jacob. A giant, that's what his son was turning out to be; a giant who dwarfed his father when he was twelve years old.

For Jonathan's *Bar Mitzvah*, Jacob had pulled out a bolt of cloth he had been saving for seven years, plain blue of a finer quality wool than any of his customers ever had. He worked on it with loving care, disregarding himself in favor of his son. That Saturday in the synagogue, when Jonathan had stood alone before the ark, his already deep voice chanting the words of the Torah, Jacob had let the tears stream down his face unchecked—his son a man, dressed in a finer suit than any other member of the congregation. Somewhat self-consciously Jacob had spared time to look down at his own clothes, the five-year-old dark gray suit that he had carefully pressed the day before so that its shininess would not be so noticeable, its age not so apparent.

And now, he thought, staring gloomily at the wall in front of him, in many ways his own son was a stranger to him, a young man with ideas so divergent from his own that sometimes Jacob was frightened.

A factory, he thought. What do I know about running a factory? I'm a tailor, not an engineer. My life has been built around a needle and thread, shears—not machinery. God blessed me with a strong son. He gave him a good brain. And now America has turned him into a dreamer, a young man with his head in the clouds.

Since leaving school, Jonathan had worked in three men's clothing factories, beginning as a clerk before pushing his way up to the sales side. Depression or not, he had witnessed manufacturing companies begin operation and had become firmly convinced that the future was in the hands of the mass manufacturers, not with the small tailors.

During the previous year he had put out cautious feelers among machinery and fabric suppliers, trying to gauge their response should he request credit for beginning his own business. Their reactions had been encouraging; he had proved his value to the companies he had worked for, and the results had not gone unnoticed. Furthermore, the depression had cut deeply into the suppliers' business, as men who considered opening up factories were plagued by second thoughts. To make up for the loss in business, the suppliers were willing to take a gamble on any man they saw as a worthwhile prospect.

Jonathan had spent too many of his twenty-three years watching his father eke out a meager living, grieving as he grew older and began to fully understand the never-ending anxieties which surrounded Jacob. He was always the last in line for payment, never knowing from one month to the next whether the rent could be paid on either the apartment or the shop.

The money which Jonathan could have brought in by leaving school in an earlier grade and working full-time would have eased the situation considerably, but Jacob would not hear of it. We'll get by, his father had repeatedly insisted. And they had—just. And deep down, Jonathan had known the reason for his father's stubbornness, the desire that at least his son should gain from his leaving Poland. Now, when Jonathan believed that he could help his father, repay the sacrifices he had made, he was finding it difficult because Jacob was so frightened of change.

From Essex Street, Jonathan walked to Houston Street, stopping outside the empty two-story building with the sign outside that declared it to be for rent. The agent was waiting, eager to conclude the business; any empty building he could lease was a reason for celebration. His face broke into a wide welcoming smile as Jonathan approached, and he stepped forward to greet him.

Jonathan had inspected the building several times and knew it was ideal for his purpose. Unknown to his father, he had borrowed from whichever source among the community would listen to him to raise the money for six month's rent. The haggling over interest rates and a loyalty to the community's own people had often gone on far into the night as Jonathan fought to attain the best deal. His father's reputation had helped. He was Jacob Gellenbaum's son, hard-working, honest Jacob whose son had finished school. He had brains; he'd go a long way. Then he had taken up the offers of credit from fabric and secondhand machinery suppliers, leaving the actual selection of a factory site till last. When he presented the factory to his father as an accomplished fact, Jonathan knew there could be no further argument between them.

The agent opened one half of the double front doors, and Jonathan entered. He glanced quickly at the first floor, with its office layout, before running up the stairs, two at a time, eager to be at the top. Once there, he relaxed, hands on his hips, looking at the open expanse of the second floor, visualizing the sewing machines and presses in place, hearing in his mind the noise of a factory in full operation. He heard the hiss of steam under pressure, saw the racks of completed suits being moved to the service elevator on their way down to the distribution area which would be installed downstairs, and from there to the city's retailers. Those retailers whom he had befriended, taken into confidence that he would soon be opening his own place.

There was a warm feeling in Jonathan's chest as he turned to the agent. "Where's the lease?"

The agent had it ready. Jonathan scanned it briefly before signing. He dug into his trouser pocket and pulled out a rolled-up wad of money. Peeling off the correct amount, he handed it to the agent, waiting while he was given a receipt.

"Will there be anything else, Mr. Gellenbaum?"

Jonathan looked around the empty floor again before replying. "I don't think so. If anything comes up, I'll be in touch with you."

He cut short the agent's gratitude by walking away to the other end of the building, peering into corners, checking the placement of electrical outlets, looking at the position of lighting fixtures and steam pipes. When he returned to the top of the stairs, the agent had gone.

Outside in the street, Jonathan paused by the agency's sign. He noticed two men watching, curious about who would have business in the vacant building. To satisfy his own pride at going through with the deal, Jonathan made a grand production of ripping the sign from the window frame where it had been nailed. He broke the sign in pieces across his knee and discarded the debris in a trash can on the sidewalk. When he looked at the two men again, he was pleased to see that they were discussing his action. He viewed their interest as recognition, and it made him feel good.

The elation brought about by the unexpected audience deserted Jonathan as he walked away from the building. His mind raced over the tasks that would face him the following day. He had to supervise the delivery of machinery; minor carpentry work still had to be done, and fabric and trimmings for the first production had to be purchased. Then, when the last details were settled and the sign was in position, he would bring his father to see the building. That was the part to which Jonathan looked forward the most.

At dinner that evening, Jonathan made no further mention of the factory. He acted as if the meeting with his father had never taken place. After eating, while Jacob remained at the table smoking and reading a newspaper, Jonathan washed and dried the dishes. After putting away the last piece of crockery in the cupboard above the tiny sink, he turned to his father.

"Doing anything tonight, Papa?"

Jacob put down the newspaper and looked across the room at Jonathan, his cigarette sending up a tiny spiral of smoke directly between them. "I was thinking of going down to the club, play a game of chess or cards maybe. And you?"

"Nothing special. See a few of the guys, that's all."

"Your friends who think I'm your *zayde*, I suppose," Jacob smiled as he spoke, returning to the newspaper before Jonathan could think of a reply.

When Jonathan returned home after midnight, he was surprised to find his father still up, sitting in an armchair and smoking. The ashtray was almost filled to the brim with cigarette butts.

"I met Herschel Ackerman at the club tonight, Jonathan. He asked after you, how you were getting on."

Jonathan struggled to place the name, finally remembering the man as one of his father's friends from the old country. "So?"

"He told me he's heard you've been borrowing money, Jonathan. Lots of it. Is it for this factory idea of yours?"

"Herschel talks a lot," Jonathan said, an unintentional note of irritation creeping into his voice. "I didn't know they let old women into the club."

Jacob found the remark amusing. A faint smile crossed his face as he replied. "Perhaps you're right, Jonathan. Herschel hasn't spoken two words to me over the past month. But tonight he was waiting for me. As soon as I walked in, he rushed over to tell me what he had heard."

"And you're sore about it because I never told you," Jonathan concluded. "Does it bother you that I've been borrowing money? I had to get it from somewhere."

"I'm not angry," his father said. "Just a little surprised. Obviously this dream of yours is further along the road than I thought."

"You didn't answer the question. Does it bother you that I've been borrowing money, that I'm up to here in debt?" He raised a hand above his head.

"Borrowing only upsets me if you can't repay the money," Jacob said quietly, remembering how he had worked to pay off the bills after Anna's death, the shame burning deeply within him that he owed money. "What if you don't make a success of this dream, Jonathan? What if you can't pay the people back? There is nothing more terrible than owing money and being unable to repay."

Jonathan remained adamant in the face of his father's gentle questioning. "There are no ifs and buts about it, Papa. It's a sure-fire thing as long as you come in with me."

"First you tell me that I'm wasting my time by being a tailor. Then you try to blackmail me. What comes next?" Jacob asked.

"Papa, for Christ's sake! It's too late to play games. Can't we talk about this in the morning?"

Jacob smiled again. "Even him you've got to bring into it now. Believe me, Jonathan, there's one person who won't give you any help." He glanced down at the ashtray, tapping his cigarette carefully. "Please listen to me. A lot of people already know that you've borrowed a large sum of money, and they are going to be looking at you to see how honest you are, to see whether or not you pay it back. Do you follow me?"

"I follow you. You're worried that in case something goes wrong the name of Gellenbaum is going to stink."

Jacob pursed his lips as he digested Jonathan's comment. "I don't worry about my name. It's your name that concerns me. You're starting out in life, and if this deal that you're so crazy about falls down, you'll carry around a black mark for a long time. Everywhere you look companies are folding up. Why are you so certain that you'll be different from anybody else, that you'll succeed?"

"Because I've done my homework. I've been tapping the accounts I handle right now, seeing if they'll give me a chance when I start up."

"That's dishonest," Jacob complained. "While you work for a company you must remain loyal to them. By taking their customers this way you are stealing from them."

Jonathan made no attempt to counter the accusation. He did not want an argument with his father that he had no way of winning. How can you win a row with somebody who never raises his voice? he wondered. Every argument with my father is a gentle discussion that he always wins. He began to seek another approach, when Jacob held up his hand.

"I'll tell you what I will do," he said to Jonathan, realizing that he had made his son uncomfortable, and regretting it. "When this dream of yours is finished, take me to see it. Then I'll decide whether I should listen to you or to myself."

On the following day, Jonathan stayed in the factory on Houston Street for more than sixteen hours, showing the delivery men where to place the machines, inspecting each unit to make sure that it was in operating condition, overseeing the installation of storage lockers, checking electrical and steam connections. He arrived home exhausted, long after Jacob had gone to bed. After gulping down a light snack, he threw himself onto the couch in the living room, still fully dressed. The next thing he knew was his father waking him in the morning.

"And how is the dream today?" Jacob asked.

Jonathan yawned and wiped the sleep from his eyes. "Almost there," he replied, sitting up and swinging his feet to the floor. "When I come by the shop this afternoon, I want you to stop whatever you're doing and close up. Then I'll show you the place, and you can see for yourself."

When Jonathan walked into the shop on Essex Street that afternoon, grease marks and dust covered the front of his white shirt; his dark gray trousers were badly creased from kneeling in the factory, helping the workmen put in the finishing touches. Jacob stood at the rear of the shop, chalking pattern marks onto a piece of cloth; in deference to the continuing hot weather, he had removed his jacket but still wore the vest fully buttoned, the gold watch and chain stretched across his stomach. He smiled a greeting as Jonathan approached.

"Ah, my dreamer comes."

Taking his father's jacket from the hangar, Jonathan held it out to him. Jacob slipped his arms into the sleeves. "*Nu?*" he asked, pulling the bottom of the jacket straight. "So where is this wonderful dream of yours?"

"Remember the old Leamans factory on Houston Street?"

"Leamans?" Jacob thought for a moment. "Sure, they made women's dresses, didn't they? But the place has been empty for more than a year, ever since the company went out of business." He looked hard at his son, whispering, "Did you get a good deal on the lease? They've been trying to let the place for ages."

Jonathan laughed loudly, a booming, happy sound which filled the entire shop. "I got a hell of a deal on the lease, Papa. And on the machinery. And on the fabric. The only thing that hasn't come easy so far is you. And you'll come around when you see what we've done with this place."

While Jacob locked the front door, Jonathan waited impatiently, shuffling his feet in his desire to be started, needing to show his father what he had accomplished. Neither man spoke as they walked, each alone with his own thoughts—Jonathan happily anticipating his father's reaction to the factory, Jacob proud of his son's drive and ambition, yet fearful that he might have overreached himself.

A block before the factory, Jonathan stopped walking and gripped his father's arm. "What are we going to call this place, Papa?" he asked excitedly. "What name?"

"A miracle, please God," Jacob muttered. Or a curse, he added mentally, his imagination taking him on an unwelcome tour of what would happen should the business founder and Jonathan be unable to repay the debts.

Uncaring about the curious looks from other pedestrians, Jonathan hugged his father, holding him tightly in both arms. "You're incorrigible, you know that?" he said. Locked in Jonathan's grip, Jacob tried to shrug as though he agreed with the sentiment. Incorrigible? It was a word he had never heard before.

Then they turned the final corner and saw the building. Jacob stood and stared for several seconds, unable at the final confrontation to fully comprehend that his son had proceeded to outfit a factory which would make in hours what it took him days to produce.

Jonathan's voice bubbled over with excitement. "How do you like it, Papa? What do you think of it?"

Jacob continued to stare at the brown bricks, the windows, some with fresh putty where workmen had replaced broken panes. "It's a building," he said finally. "What's to like or not like about a building?"

"What can you tell from the side?" Jonathan asked. "Come and look at the front."

They crossed the road together and stood on the sidewalk, gazing at the façade of the building. Jacob studied the structure, letting his eyes roam from one end to the other. He was still stunned by the sudden reality of his son's dream. Then his gaze dropped to the main entrance and the large blue and white sign above the double doors.

"Gellenbaum and Son," he breathed out, his voice hushed, reverent. "You've really called it Gellenbaum and Son."

"I told you I would. And it's all set up, ready to go. Except for one thing—the Gellenbaum. It's got me, but I'm only the son part of the deal. Without the main Gellenbaum, the factory won't turn out a damned thing. I'm missing the technical man, the designer, but I don't know where to find him."

Ignoring his son's banter, Jacob continued to stare across the road, letting his eyes rest on the sign. The traffic which moved between him and the building passed by unnoticed. He had eyes only for the sign, the bold blue lettering, the white background marred in the corners by the pins fixing the board to the wall.

Gellenbaum and Son. Me and my son Jonathan, with his American ideas. Gellenbaum and Son—that I should have lived to see this day.

Jonathan watched his father cross the road, knowing that the battle was over. He was thankful that he was alone; there was a lump in his throat, and if his father had spoken he would have been unable to reply. Feeling the need to do something with his hands, he lit a cigarette, pinching the white tube tightly between index finger and thumb as he drew on it, all the time watching his father.

Tired eventually of examining the building's exterior, Jacob beckoned for Jonathan to cross the road and join him. "Where is the key?"

Selecting one from the bunch attached to his belt, Jonathan opened the double front doors, standing aside to let his father precede him. Jacob looked at the offices and distribution area on the first floor, passing through quickly as though there were nothing to interest him there. Then he walked slowly up the narrow flight of stairs to the production floor. When he saw the machinery all laid out, he stood silently, nodding his head every so often as he followed the layout of the operation.

"What do you think of the crazy dream now, Papa?" There was a tremor in Jonathan's voice as he joined his father, putting an arm around the older man's shoulders.

The tremor did not pass unnoticed. Jacob turned to look at his son, noticing the half-smoked cigarette held loosely in Jonathan's free hand. "Smoking does that to me as well sometimes," he said simply.

Freeing himself from Jonathan's grasp, Jacob began to walk along the row of sewing machines, stopping occasionally to try one. He looked at the cutting area, then the presses. Finally he turned back to face Jonathan, who had remained at the top of the stairs.

"Where is this production man of yours supposed to work?" he called along the length of the building. "You can't expect to stick me just anywhere and forget all about me."

It took perhaps two seconds for the import of Jacob's question to register on Jonathan. Then, with a wild yell of delight, he leaped forward, lifting Jacob high into the air, whirling him around exuberantly.

"Pick any place you like!" he shouted. "Everybody else will work around you."

# 2

Feet, Jonathan's middle-aged secretary had chided him repeatedly, belong on the floor, not on the desk. But she was out of the building for a few minutes, and Jonathan was taking advantage of the situation by having both feet planted firmly on the desk. He leaned back in the chair, hands clasped behind his head, his deep brown eyes studying the shining leather of his shoes, pretending he was looking into a crystal ball in which he could see the future.

The future. He chuckled happily at the thought of it. If the next three years promised as much as the last three years had given, he would be more than satisfied. Closing his eyes, he allowed himself the infrequent luxury of daydreaming during business hours, casting his mind back to the opening of the company. Everybody's doubts had proved to be groundless; his father's natural anxiety about the massive step he was taking, even his own never-admitted worry, had proved to be totally unfounded.

Those first three years, he decided, had been more than good. They had been fantastic, emblematic of the kind of success story which Americans claim can only happen in their country. Everything had fallen into place like a simple jigsaw puzzle, a natural progression of events, as if the good fortune of Gellenbaum and Son had been fated from the outset.

Vividly Jonathan recalled the first stroke of luck, the termination of a lease for a building on the same block. As the depression ebbed and money began to move again, the factory was having difficulty in coping with the orders which Jonathan was bringing in. He moved quickly, taking the lease on the second building and setting up additional manufacturing facilities. Following this, the original building with its now laughable initial production of one hundred suits a week had been gutted and renovated into a jacket-making unit, while the second factory had been tooled up to specialize in trouser production. Total production had risen to more than three hundred suits a week.

The new production units had been launched with one major advantage over the original installation—all machinery was fresh from the manufacturer. The secondhand sewing machines, working off a central power shaft with drive belts forming complicated geometric patterns, were replaced with modern equipment. The old-fashioned steam presses, with their constantly leaking valves, had also been supplanted. The money which Jonathan had borrowed to begin the venture was repaid, and the company's sole outstanding debt was to the sewing machine supplier. If he so wished, Jonathan could have paid it off. But the man had offered good credit terms, so he had accepted.

The majority of the three years' profits had been ploughed back into the company to pay for the expansion. The one indulgence which Jonathan had allowed himself was the construction of a well-appointed showroom and office which took up half the first floor of the original building. It was in this office that he now sat, listening with one ear for the return of his secretary so that he could remove his feet from the desk before she could tell him yet again that they belonged on the floor.

Hearing the sound of a closing door from the secretary's small adjoining office, Jonathan reluctantly swung his feet down, clearing away any dust they might have left with his hand. His own office door opened a moment later.

"Mr. Epstein's here to see you. Shall I send him in?" the secretary asked.

Jonathan grimaced. Epstein the union man, just when he was thinking that everything was going so well. "Show him in," he muttered.

Mike Epstein elbowed his way past the secretary, striding into the office as if he owned it. He pulled a chair up to the desk and sat down facing Jonathan.

"Have a seat," Jonathan offered. "Make yourself at home."

The sarcasm was lost on the union official. His red face remained expressionless, and the blue eyes stared blankly across the desk. A kiss curl of black greasy hair, which he occasionally brushed away, hung down on his forehead.

"I'll give you ten minutes," Jonathan said. "I've got an appointment at eleven o'clock, so make it quick." He had little love for the union man, having spoken with him in an official capacity twice during the past three months. Their argument was simple. Epstein wanted Jonathan's company to be unionized. Jonathan did not.

"We're into two more factories, Mr. Gellenbaum," Epstein began, pulling a dog-eared notebook from his jacket pocket, opening it and passing it across to Jonathan so that he could verify the increased union membership. "Gellenbaum and Son is one of the few holdouts."

"So?" Jonathan made no attempt to help the man along, leaving him to find his own openings.

"You're doing a disservice to your workers," Epstein said. "That's what's so."

"I told you before, I'll give you ten minutes. Don't waste it. What you're saying now you've said a million times already." Jonathan pulled out a cigarette and lit it, waiting for Epstein to continue.

"Are you against unionization?" Epstein asked. He had thought that telling Jonathan that two more clothing factories had agreed to let their workers become members would impress him.

"Damn right I am. I've yet to see how you can help anybody."

"We've established a minimum wage," Epstein pointed out. "Our members don't get exploited any more, so there's more harmony between management and the workers. Better work gets done that way."

Jonathan cut him off quickly. "We pay more than your minimum wage already. We don't need you."

"What do your people say?"

"They've said nothing about wanting to join a union. So I guess they're happy." He held up a hand as the telephone on his desk rang.

"Jonathan Gellenbaum here." The call was from Jacob, in his office on the second floor where he supervised the production department.

"Jonathan, I've got the rest of Mr. Gilbert's samples ready. Do you want to come up, or should I send them down with one of the girls?"

"I'm a bit busy at the moment," Jonathan replied, looking at Epstein. "Gilbert's due in any moment, and I've got to get things ready. Plus I've got somebody down here at the moment. Maybe you should send them down."

There was a pause, and Jonathan guessed that his father was looking for somebody to act as messenger. "All right," Jacob said at last. "They'll be with you in a few minutes."

Jonathan replaced the receiver and turned back to Epstein. "Your time's running out. What else do you want to say?"

"We're going to start talking to your people," Epstein said. To Jonathan it sounded like a threat. "Then maybe they'll want to join."

"Talk all you damned well want. But if you try force," Jonathan said slowly, "I'll break your head." He had heard enough of the methods used by the unions to increase their membership in the clothing industry. And now his factory was a prime target, a holdout.

Through the open office door, he saw one of the factory girls enter the showroom carrying some samples of the next season's ready-to-wear line. She looked around in bewilderment until Jonathan left his desk to assist her. Maybe this was a good time, he thought, to find out if Epstein's already tried anything.

"Thanks. I'll take them now." He lifted the suits out of her arms, smiling at her.

The girl's oval face, framed by short, curling auburn hair, was vaguely familiar to him, but he could not put a name to her. He kept his visits to the production departments to a minimum; any problems in that area belonged to either his father or the factory manager.

Hanging the suits on the rack with the other samples, he returned to the girl, taking her by the arm, leading her to the door of his office, looking in where Epstein sat. He turned as he heard Jonathan's voice.

"Ever seen that guy before?"

The girl shook her head, confused by the question.

"If he ever speaks to you, or if you see him speak to anybody else here, let me know. Got it?"

"Who is he?" she asked.

"Tell her who you are, Epstein," Jonathan said. Then, before the man could do so, he added, "Name's Mike Epstein. Works for the union. They think we'd be better off unionized." He let go of her arm, and she began to walk toward the stairs. "Thanks for the suits," he called after her.

Epstein stood up, hands thrust deeply into his jacket pockets, pulling his gray suit more out of shape than it was already. "I think you've made your position clear, Mr. Gellenbaum."

"I made it clear the first time you came to see me," Jonathan said. "I don't want you or your friends hanging around here. Any trouble and I'm coming after you with a baseball bat."

Epstein said nothing, his eyes half-closed as he weighed Jonathan's words. Finally he turned to Jonathan and gave him the benefit of a sly smile. "You'll be hearing from us again, Mr. Gellenbaum. When your machinists and pressers don't want to work for you any more, you'll come begging to us. I'll remember today."

"Door's that way," Jonathan said. "Close it on the way out."

He watched Epstein walk across the showroom, wondering how much of the man's threat was bluff. There was no way any union could improve the conditions at Gellenbaum and Son. Jonathan and his father had both seen the business from the bottom, and they agreed that exploitation such as they had witnessed would never occur in their own factory. Maybe other factories needed to have their people join a union, but not here.

As Epstein reached for the door, it opened inward and Al Gilbert entered the showroom, standing aside to let Epstein pass. Jonathan closed his eyes for a moment, trying to shut out the sight of Gilbert. From one piece of trouble to another. Gilbert owned five men's wear stores in the New York area—an account Jonathan had sweated blood to open; the man knew only too well the buying influence he wielded, and he used it at every opportunity.

Gilbert shuffled through the showroom, a short, overweight man wearing a navy and white chalk-stripe Gellenbaum suit. Nice touch, Jonathan congratulated him mentally, but I bet you didn't do it on purpose. He remained behind his desk, letting Gilbert search for him. Preparing everything for the man was one thing; fawning over him as a valued customer was totally alien to Jonathan's nature.

When Gilbert spotted Jonathan sitting in the office, he raised his right hand in greeting, the large diamond on the little finger sparkling in the glare of a spotlight. Jonathan lifted a hand in acknowledgment, studying the customer as he came closer, noticing the closely set pale blue eyes above the pudgy cheeks, the slicked-down fair hair with the precision parting.

Never trust a man if there's not enough space between his eyes to put a quarter, Jonathan remembered his father once saying. And here comes Al Gilbert.

Jonathan's secretary brought in coffee for Gilbert—double cream, double sugar—then left the two men alone. Without saying a word, Gilbert sipped the coffee, his eyes flicking left and right over the rim of the cup, missing nothing. Jonathan sat easily in his chair biding his time. He was in no hurry to push Gilbert into ordering; the man was in the office to do business, and pressing him would serve no useful purpose.

Waiting for Gilbert to finish the coffee, Jonathan lit another cigarette and idly watched the smoke drift toward the ceiling. He had taken only three puffs when Gilbert put down the cup, wiping his thick lips on a blue silk handkerchief. Picking up the fabric swatches which Jonathan had laid on the desk, he began to peruse them, rubbing each piece of cloth between his thumb and forefinger with a practiced motion to judge the quality.

"Making the rounds with union officials these days, Jonathan?" Gilbert asked, the pale blue eyes looking up from the cloth for a fraction of a second.

"You know Epstein?" Jonathan asked, surprised. He had no idea that Gilbert would be familiar with the glowering union man.

"We've met in the past. Another firm I was dealing with has practically been wrecked by union action."

"Tell me more," Jonathan said.

"About three months ago." He gave Jonathan the name of the company; he recognized it as one of the two names Epstein had showed him in the book. "About six goons waited outside the factory one night, beat up three of the workers. Two of them were in the hospital for a week. Now everybody's a union member, demanding this, that and the other. And they're not working even when they get what they want."

"What's the angle?" Jonathan asked, although he already had his own opinions.

"The company goes bust," Gilbert said simply, "and then it's snapped up for a song. Good business to be in, I'd reckon."

"Is that where Epstein comes into it?" Jonathan asked. Gilbert's answer had coincided with his own views.

"Epstein's as much a union man as I am," Gilbert said. "I reckon he's working for some mob that's controlling the union." He bent his head again, peering at the cloth. "How's that old man of yours?" he asked, changing the subject completely, leaving Jonathan still floundering with the problem of Epstein and the union.

"My father, you mean." Jonathan was irked by Gilbert's phrasing of the question. "He's very well."

Gilbert tossed the swatches back onto the desk. "You want to tell him to keep a close eye on that department he's supposed to be running. Some of the forty-fours in the last batch of ready-to-wear suits didn't fit too well. They were tight. My alteration tailors had to let them out, and that costs me money. I don't like it. My business wasn't built up on mistakes—mine or my suppliers!"

Jonathan pushed the visit by Epstein from his mind, promising himself to deal with it later. Elbows on the desk, he listened patiently to Gilbert, hearing him out. Many of his customers made him the butt of lighthearted complaints, gentle friendly digs, nothing more. With Al Gilbert, however, the words seemed to take on a different quality, an underlying nastiness, as if the man were trying to see whether he could force a concession from a supplier. Through the industry grapevine, Jonathan had heard countless tales of Gilbert's stinginess, his search for any excuse to knock down a price. Yet the man's business was too big to ignore. A sizeable order for the next season, covering all five stores in the Gilbert group, would keep the factory running for a few weeks, with the probability of repeats on the strong sellers.

"Nobody else complains about the sizing, Al," Jonathan offered.

Gilbert glared across the desk, his small eyes narrowed to slits. "Your other customers don't have the sophisticated clientele that I do. They're strictly rag trade operators, a bunch of schnooks. My places run on class."

While trying to maintain a diplomatic posture, Jonathan groaned inwardly. "What happened, Al?"

"A couple of my boys in the West Thirty-fourth Street store—you know, that's the Gilbert flagship—hit your bad sizes the other week. We carry your ready-to-wear and your made-to-measure service..."

"Get to the point, Al," Jonathan interrupted tersely. "You don't have to keep reminding me about what a big customer you are."

Gilbert grinned wolfishly, taking great delight in the power he carried. "Like I was saying, Jonathan, a guy comes into the store, and it's better for my salesmen if they can fit him straight off the rack rather than go through the business of ordering from your measure service. They throw a tape around this guy and find out he's a forty-four. So they pull a forty-four from the rack, only it fits him like it's a forty-two. I nearly called you up there and then to give you hell, but I figured it could wait till I saw you.

"After all," Gilbert smiled, an expansive beam which he believed would make Jonathan more receptive to the complaint, "we've got to scratch each other's backs in this business. We're put on this earth to help each other along. See,"—he jerked a thumb over his shoulder at the street door—"I even told you a couple of things about Epstein that you didn't know; help you be on your guard against him."

Jonathan was unmoved by either Gilbert's smile or his homespun philosophy. "Do your salesmen know how to measure a man properly?" he shot back. "Can they tell a forty-four when it's staring them in the face? Are you supplying them with decent tapes? Tapes distort a bit when they're old, give you all kinds of wrong measurements."

The smile dropped away from Gilbert's face, replaced by a belligerent scowl as he leaned forward in the chair. "What's that supposed to mean? Of course my boys know what the hell they're doing. The ones who didn't are out on their asses a million years ago. And there's nothing wrong with the tapes I give out. It's your old man's measurements that are no damned good."

Jonathan picked up the telephone. "Hold your horses, Al. We'll get my father in on this." He dialled Jacob's extension, drumming his fingers on the desk top while he waited for an answer. "It's Jonathan. Can you come down with some forty-fours and a tape? I want you to prove a point for me." He hung up and looked back to Gilbert. "Now we'll be able to see what's what."

Sitting back in the chair, Gilbert pulled out a silver and leather cigar case. Opening it, he looked inside thoughtfully before selecting a short, fat cigar. Jonathan watched the performance with concealed amusement. He had dealt with Gilbert for almost two years and had never once seen the retailer offer a cigar to anybody else.

Completely unaware of Jonathan's scrutiny, Gilbert snipped the end off the cigar, letting it fall unheeded to the carpet. Putting the cigar into his mouth, he sucked greedily to ensure that it drew easily. Lastly he pulled a gold lighter from his jacket pocket, flicked it into life and held the end of the cigar in the flame, watching intently until it glowed.

As Gilbert replaced the lighter in his pocket, Jacob entered the office carrying four jackets, which Jonathan took from him and laid across the desk. Gilbert remained in the chair, the cigar held casually between two pudgy fingers; he nodded briefly to Jacob, who continued to stand by the office door, staring stiffly.

Jonathan opened the top jacket and checked the label for the size. Removing his own jacket, he said to Gilbert, "I'm a forty-four chest. Check if you want."

Gilbert took a tape from Jacob and ran it around Jonathan's chest, grunting as he verified the measurement.

"Pick a jacket," Jonathan invited. "Any one will fit."

"Try that one," Gilbert said, pointing to a royal blue jacket at the bottom of the pile.

Jonathan put the jacket on; it fitted perfectly. "Want to see some of the others on me? See they fit all right?" he asked cockily. "Or will you take my word that the sizes are okay?"

Gilbert shook his head. "No. These seem good. But I'm telling you that some of last season's stuff was wrong." He removed the cigar from his mouth and looked at the chewed end, soggy with saliva. "Get this straight, Jonathan, and your old man's my witness. If any of the next lot gives my boys trouble, you're getting everything back, every damned last one of them. Either that, or you pay my alteration costs for me."

Jonathan flicked his eyes to the office doorway, wondering how his father was taking the criticism. Then he realized what Jacob was doing. Jesus, he thought, not now with the watch. His eyes followed the gold timepiece as it passed from Jacob's left hand to the right, partially mesmerizing him; his father was obviously distressed that the quality of his merchandise was being questioned. Quickly Jonathan looked back to Gilbert, wondering if the retailer had even noticed that he had upset Jacob.

"Does your last remark mean you're going to order, Al?" Jonathan asked, relieved that Gilbert was still staring at him, oblivious to Jacob's agitation.

"Sure I'm going to order. But any more screw-ups and I take my business elsewhere."

Jonathan laughed at him, knowing he was on certain ground. "You'd never get the same quality for anywhere near the same price, Al. Everybody else in our price range is turning out schlock. Buy that and your salesmen would have trouble—no matter what kind of tapes they used."

Gilbert made no reply, and Jonathan drove the point home. "Don't you believe me, Al? Ask my father. He'll tell you all about quality." He glanced again at Jacob, relieved to see that the gold watch had been replaced in his father's vest pocket.

"I believe you," Gilbert said finally, a condescending tone in his voice. "I reckon I must have caught a couple of bad ones, jackets that slipped past when nobody was looking." He held up the fabric swatches, waving them in the air. "This for next season?"

"That's what it's doing on the desk."

"Okay. Let's get down to some work." Gilbert riffled through the swatches a second time, stopping at certain fabrics, jotting down notes with a gold pencil. Jacob, seeing his presence was no longer needed, picked up the jackets and tape and left the office, thankful to be away from the commercial side of the business, happy that all those problems were handled by his son.

"Where are the samples?" Gilbert asked, finished with the swatches. Jonathan pointed into the showroom, watching Gilbert shuffle out toward the rack. He paused at the first suit, looking at the styling details, the cigar jutting out from the side of his mouth like a brown, malignant growth. He moved down the rack, pulling out garments, comparing them. "This is it?" he queried, coming to the last suit.

Jonathan nodded. "That's it for ready-to-wear suits. Topcoat and sports coat samples will be ready sometime next week. You're the first to see the ranges," he added, knowing how it would appeal to Gilbert's ego. Psychology played a hell of a big part in dealing with certain customers.

"What about your prices for fall?" Gilbert asked. "How much are you sticking on this time?"

"We're not. They're being held to last season's level. Our own costs haven't gone up enough to justify passing on any increases to our customers."

Gilbert favored Jonathan with a broad smile, his cheeks rising to almost cover his eyes. "Good," he said approvingly, drawing out the word. "Gellenbaum and Son is the kind of supplier I like to deal with."

Jonathan returned the smile with one of his own, but it held a subtle trace of mockery. "And what about your prices, Al? Are you holding them down as well, passing your good fortune on to your customers?"

The smile of Gilbert's face grew even wider. "Our prices are none of your business, Jonathan. We buy from you. You don't buy from us." He paused long enough for the comment to sink in and then added, "Now let's get down to some hard facts."

Pulling a book from the desk drawer, Jonathan prepared to take Gilbert's order. Although he was assured of the retailer's made-to-measure business throughout the season, the ready-to-wear order was more than he had hoped for. As he scribbled down the details, he reasoned that Gilbert must have cut one of his other suppliers; either that, he thought, or one of his manufacturers doesn't want anything more to do with him, which was probably closer to the truth. Unless—the visit by Epstein came to mind—he's handing me the order that he would have placed with the unionized factory, waiting to see what happens to me.

He read back the fabric, design and sizing specifications to Gilbert, who bobbed his head in agreement.

"What about delivery?" Jonathan asked. "When do you want them by?"

Gilbert checked the small calendar on the wall behind Jonathan. "How about the end of June? That gives you just over three months. Ship them to West Thirty-fourth Street, and we'll arrange to get them to the other stores."

Adding the delivery date to the bottom of the order, Jonathan said, "I'll be in touch with you when the other samples are ready, to make sure you get the first bite again in case there's something you want to order big enough to get it exclusive."

"You do that," Gilbert replied, standing up, preparing to leave. He laid the cold cigar in Jonathan's ashtray and moved toward the door. As he opened it, he called back, "Don't forget now, Jonathan. I want your forty-fours to fit my forty-fours."

Jonathan experienced mixed emotions as he watched Gilbert leave. He was exhilarated at the size of the order, but he longed for the day when he would no longer need the Al Gilberts of the world as customers. Jacob was upset, and that sort of aggravation was not necessarily worth the business. He waited until the door had swung closed behind Gilbert; then he walked upstairs to see how his father was feeling.

"Has he gone?" Jacob asked.

"Just left. Sorry about dragging you into it, but he was trying to beat me down. Claimed some of the forty-fours in last season's order were too small."

Jacob made a sign of disgust with his hands. "I know the type of man. A *schnorrer*. And the bigger they get, the bigger *schnorrers* they become. When I had the shop in Essex Street, I had too many customers like your Mr. Gilbert. They always had plenty of money for themselves, their vacations, their shiny cars. But when it came my turn they began looking for something wrong with the suit so they could knock me for a dollar. Does he pay on time?"

"So far. But I reckon he's always looking for the angle, the chance of an extra profit for himself by getting our prices down. I told him we were holding our prices for fall, no increase at all, so he's taking advantage of that by putting on a bigger markup. If his customers complain, he'll just shrug his fat shoulders and tell them it's the manufacturer's fault; they put up their prices, and he can't afford to absorb the increased cost." Jonathan grinned suddenly, patting his father on the shoulder. "Guess we just can't win, can we?"

"Retailers," Jacob grumbled. "Sometimes I think that *meshuggeneh* Karl Marx was right."

Marx—the name recalled Mike Epstein to Jonathan's mind. He wondered if his father knew anything about the union official's visit and decided that he did not. And best he should keep it that way. There was no sense in worrying Jacob about something that might never happen. He also remembered the auburn-haired girl who had brought down the sample suits, how he had used her in his threat to Epstein; he felt he owed her something of an explanation.

"What's the name of the girl you sent down before?" he asked his father.

A twinkle appeared in Jacob's eyes at the unexpected question. "Miriam. Miriam Helman, a machinist. Are you interested in her?"

Jonathan understood his father's expression. "Not in the way you'd like me to be. You're going to have to wait some more for your grandchildren. I just want to see her about something."

He began to move away toward the sewing room when Jacob pulled him back, refusing to let the conversation end. "You want me to put in a good word for you?" he joked. "Tell her what a wonderful son you are?"

"I can do that myself."

"Don't you go in there interfering with their work," Jacob said. "You belong downstairs, finding other customers to take the place of Mr. Gilbert."

Ignoring his father's words, Jonathan headed straight for the sewing room. Miriam Helman was seated at a machine, matching up the checks on a sports coat before joining the seams. Jonathan stopped a yard away, watching her. Unaware that she was being observed, Miriam lined up the pattern and began feeding the fabric into the machine, watching intently as the needle flashed up and down.

"Think that pattern will sell?" Jonathan asked as she came to the end of the seam, backtacking before she cut the thread.

Surprised at the intrusion, the girl turned around and looked up. The piece of cloth fell to the floor, and Jonathan stooped to pick it up, dropping it into her workbasket.

"I think you're due for an explanation and apology for what happened downstairs before," he began.

Miriam's hazel eyes opened wide in question. "I don't think I understand you, Mr. Gellenbaum."

"You know who that guy was before, the one I pointed out to you?"

She shook her head; the auburn hair bounced as if it had a life of its own. "Only what you told me before."

"You might get to meet him soon. Name's Mike Epstein, from the union. He's trying to push union membership here. You sure you've never seen him before?"

Miriam looked thoughtful, staring down at the sewing machine as she tried to remember. "Not him. Sometimes there have been a couple of men outside handing out leaflets as we leave or stopping some of the guys and talking to them. That's about all though."

Jonathan did not allow his surprise to show. Epstein, or whoever worked with him, had already started to infiltrate the factory. Maybe he had better look into it before it got out of hand, like other factories where the management woke up one day to find the union had taken over.

"Thanks," he said, rapping his knuckles on the machine in farewell. "Thanks a lot, Miriam."

# 3

Maybe his father was right, Jonathan mused. Maybe he was interested in the auburn-haired girl he had used to demonstrate to Mike Epstein that he would be ready for any union pressure. He seemed to have spent an inordinate amount of time walking through the production area during the past couple of weeks, stopping to talk with Miriam whenever the opportunity arose.

Jacob found the situation increasingly amusing. He purposely used Miriam for any errands to the showroom, continually ribbing Jonathan when they were alone.

"Did you put in a good word for me like you said you were going to?" Jonathan asked his father.

"Certainly," Jacob replied grandly. "I told her all about what a wonderful child you were, and how you wet your pants when I took you to Central Park, because you were scared of the policeman's horse."

Jonathan blanched at the memory of an event he thought he had forgotten. "You didn't, did you?" he asked incredulously.

Jacob just laughed and turned back to his work.

When the factory closed that evening, Jonathan waited outside; if he was interested, maybe it was about time he made a move, before she grew tired of his journeys through the sewing room and started seeing somebody else. What if she was already seeing somebody else? Am I going to make myself look like a fool? he worried, as he stood on the opposite side of the street watching people leaving.

A small group of people at the end of the block caught his attention, three men wearing topcoats and hats pulled down low over their faces. One of them Jonathan could swear was Epstein, his hands-in-the-pocket slouch recognizable anywhere. As Jonathan began to cross the road for a closer look, two factory workers were confronted by the group and stopped, listening to what the three men had to say.

Jonathan quickened his pace, worried about what the three men intended. As he neared, however, the two workers continued on their way. He stared after them blankly, feeling foolish as Epstein called his name.

"Worried that your people might want to join the union, Mr. Gellenbaum?" He turned to his two comrades and muttered something. All three men burst out laughing.

"I told you to stay away from here, Epstein. I won't warn you again."

Epstein made a show of looking up and down Houston Street. "You own the sidewalk? You make one move toward me while I'm on the street and I'll call a cop so fast you won't know what the hell happened."

Jonathan realized he had no right to accost the men while they stood outside his premises. Inside it was a different matter; here he was powerless. Nevertheless he was determined to have the final word.

"If I get one complaint from any of my people about being shoved around by your goons, you know what's going to happen to you."

"They'll soon be our people," Epstein said. "All union members. Then you're going to jump to our tune. See you around." They began to walk away, when one of the men touched Epstein's arm, indicating that he should look back toward the factory entrance where more people were leaving. Jonathan also looked and to his consternation saw Miriam walking toward him, her long green coat flapping in the light spring breeze.

Epstein waited for her to come closer; then he glanced at Jonathan, recognition coming slowly to him. "Isn't that the broad from a couple of weeks back, Mr. Gellenbaum? The one you told to let you know if we ever spoke to her?"

Jonathan said nothing; there was no need for an answer. The set of his face told Epstein all he needed to know.

The union man waited for Miriam to reach him, her eyes flicking from one man to the other, finally to Jonathan as if he could explain what the group was about. Then Epstein reached out an arm and stopped her.

"We want to talk to you about the union, Miss."

She glanced to Jonathan, seeking his help. He stood motionless, waiting for the situation to develop.

"I'm in a hurry," Miriam protested, trying to push her way past. "Please let me go."

"Let her go." Jonathan's command came out much louder than he had intended. Several passers-by stopped to stare at the confrontation, and he felt his face reddening, whether from embarrassment or anger he did not know.

"We're talking to the lady, Gellenbaum." The Mr. had disappeared; Jonathan sensed it signalled the beginning of a show of strength. Three on one—or would the other two turn tail and run if he punched Epstein out?

"Are they bothering you, Miriam?" He knew it sounded trite, like something out of a bad comic book, but he could think of nothing better. "Do you want to go home or do you want to listen to these goons?"

"I want to go home," she whispered, turning pleading eyes on Jonathan. "Please make them let go of me."

"You heard her," Jonathan said. "Let go of her arm before I break yours off for you."

Epstein smiled and his two henchmen closed in around him. He applied more pressure to Miriam's arm. She gave a quiet cry of pain as his fingers dug into her arm like a steel grip.

For a man so large, Jonathan moved with a quickness that amazed many of those watching. More important, it took Epstein completely by surprise. Within two strides, Jonathan was on Epstein, lifting him high into the air by his coat lapels, forcing him to let go of Miriam. She scampered away to watch from a safe position.

"I told you what was going to happen," he whispered. "You didn't want to listen, did you?" He felt Epstein's associates move in behind him; then Miriam screamed a loud warning.

"Watch out! He's got something in his hand."

Jonathan whirled around like a dancer, the struggling body of Epstein held in front of him. He saw the leather-covered sap rise in a threatening arc; then it was whipping down. Desperately he thrust Epstein forward, using him as a shield, wincing as the sap thudded down onto the crown of the man's hat, crushing it. The body in his hands ceased its struggling and went limp. Jonathan released his grip, letting Epstein fall to the sidewalk, and then he jumped forward.

The sap wielder was still stunned that he had hit Epstein instead of his intended target. He was looking stupidly at Epstein's body when Jonathan's bunched fist caught him full in the mouth, splitting both lips, knocking out two teeth and sending him sprawling into the road, the sap flying out of his grasp. Only the alert reactions of a motorist saved him from being run over as he lay in the road, blood pouring from his shattered mouth.

"What about you?" Jonathan asked, turning on the third man. "You want to try your luck as well."

The man looked down at Epstein, then to the body in the road. He held up his hands in a peace gesture, turned around and bolted down the street, his hat flying off in the rush; he made no effort to retrieve it. Jonathan walked slowly along the street, forgetting all about Miriam, about the crowd which had gathered, and crushed the hat with his foot, kicking it into the gutter.

The man in the road was the first to recover, holding a handkerchief to his mouth in an attempt to staunch the flow of blood. Warily he edged over to the body of Epstein, keeping one eye on Jonathan. Under his prodding, Epstein came to groaning, raising a hand to his head.

"Do you believe me now?" Jonathan asked.

"We'll be back," Epstein said. "We'll be back for you, Gellenbaum. Nobody's going to forget this."

"Bring the adults with you next time." He turned away from the two men and looked at Miriam. "You all right?"

"I think so." She looked flustered, the appearance of a woman who has her honor defended and does not know quite how to thank her champion. "That was very brave of you," she said.

"It was coming." He looked around, glaring at the people who had gathered. "You got nowhere to go?" he snapped. "Go on, beat it. Go on home."

The crowd departed slowly, leaving Jonathan alone with Miriam. "Where do you live, Miss Helman?"

She seemed surprised by the question. "Wythe Place, just off the Grand Concourse in the Bronx. Do you know it?"

"Come on, I'll see you home." He put an arm through hers and guided her toward the subway station.

"Can I ask what that was all about?" she ventured.

"You can ask, but I'm not too sure I know," Jonathan replied. "I think they were using you to test me, to see if I meant what I said about kicking their butts all over Houston Street if they started meddling in the business."

"Will they be back?"

"Probably. I'd better make some preparations for them." He tried to push the subject from his mind. He had been waiting outside the factory to meet Miriam, not to engage in an all-out brawl as if seeking to impress her that way. "My father's supposed to have put in a few good words for me," he said. "Have they helped?"

Despite the sudden change in subject, Miriam continued walking. There was the beginning of a smile on her face, but she stared straight ahead at the sidewalk. "Do you always work through your father, Mr. Gellenbaum?"

"Then he did say something?"

"He mentioned you just once. He brought in some pieces for me to sew and said how important it was for the samples to be perfect, as you had an important customer coming in. Then he asked me what I thought of you."

They passed the crushed hat in the gutter. Jonathan idly wondered how long it would lie there before somebody picked it up, reshaped it and kept it for his own. "And you said what?"

Miriam slowed her pace as they reached an intersection. "I didn't really get the chance to say anything—even if I could have thought of something to say. Before I could open my mouth, your father gave me his opinions." She stared hard at Jonathan, weighing him up against his father's views. "He thinks the world of you, you know."

Wonder what he'd think if he knew about today's episode, Jonathan pondered. That gold watch would come out in double-quick time, going from one hand to the other like a streak of lightning. "Don't mention a word about today," he said earnestly. "I don't want him worrying."

"Does he worry about everything?"

"Pretty much. It gives him something to do." The light changed, and they began to cross the road. "Did he mention anything about Central Park and the horse?"

Miriam's brow creased as she tried to remember her conversation with Jacob. "I don't think so. Why?"

"Nothing," Jonathan said hastily, relieved that Jacob had only been joking; he never knew with his father whether he was serious or kidding. "It's just a private joke between my father and myself. It's not important."

Reaching the entrance to the subway, Miriam walked down the stairs followed by Jonathan. He paid the two fares and stood with her on the platform, chatting generally about the factory. When the train came, he followed her inside, sharing a double seat.

"You don't have to see me all the way home," she said. "I'm perfectly all right. If anybody needed help, it was those two guys you laid out in the street."

"Don't worry about dragging me out to the Bronx. It's just part of our new company policy of getting to know our people better. You're the first. What easier way is there than to travel home with you, protecting you from the evils of the city? Like before."

"I think you were using my presence to make a point before."

"You're right. If you want the truth, I was waiting outside the factory for you. I wanted to speak to you, get to know you a little bit better. When Epstein grabbed you, it seemed like a pretty good way of killing two birds with one stone—getting a better look at you, and dumping Epstein on his ass, where he belongs—although his playmate did the job for me. It wasn't an accident, Miss Helman. I was really waiting for you."

Five seconds passed while Miriam tried to understand Jonathan's mood. "I hate being called Miss Helman," she confided, determined to match his friendliness. "It makes me sound like a middle-aged spinster, all withered and shrivelled up inside. Please call me Miriam."

"Miriam." Jonathan savored the name. "Only if you call me Jonathan. If you must call anybody Mr. Gellenbaum, give the distinction to my father. He's more deserving of the respect than I am."

"Your father's a very sweet man." She giggled suddenly, holding a hand to her mouth, embarrassed by her outburst. "Tell me, does he ever wear anything other than a three-piece suit, a stiff collar and a tie?"

"During the summer, when it gets really hot, he takes them off before he has a bath," Jonathan replied.

In other circumstances he might have been concerned by the faces which turned his way as Miriam burst out laughing. Now he ignored them, happy to be sitting next to this girl. Maybe he should send Mike Epstein a get-well card, he reflected; the presence of the union official and his two goons had made everything much easier.

Changing trains, they travelled together to the Bronx. When they reached their destination, Jonathan held her by the arm before she could join the rush through the turnstile.

"You don't expect me to go all the way back by myself, do you?" he protested. "I came out here with you, so it's only fair that you travel back with me."

Puzzlement etched itself across Miriam's face. "Then what would I do?"

"I'd drive you back here. That's what I was going to offer in the first place, before Epstein got involved."

Miriam glanced along the platform, then at Jonathan. "You're a nice guy, but can I take a rain check on the ride? My parents are expecting me for dinner. I'm late already."

Jonathan linked arms with her, moving toward the exit. "Then I'll see you right to your door."

She stopped abruptly, pulling him around by the action; they stood alone on the platform. "You don't have to see me home. You must have other, more important things to do. I can get there by myself, thank you."

"I've come this far, I'll take you all the way," Jonathan said firmly. "Haven't you heard that there are monsters loose on the streets, other than those we've already seen tonight?" He stood on tiptoe, his advantage in height magnified to immense proportions. Holding out his hands like claws, he advanced on Miriam. "Stop press. Stay indoors tonight, ladies. There's a vampire running amok in the Bronx."

Miriam did not bat an eyelid. She stood her ground, watching him come closer till his hands passed either side of her head. "Let me know when you've finished with the Bela Lugosi bit. I wasn't frightened by the movie either."

A train thundered into the station. Jonathan dropped his pose immediately. Taking her by the arm again, he said, "I mean it. I'll see you all the way home."

They walked for five minutes before reaching Miriam's apartment building. Jonathan looked at the front, thinking it resembled a thousand others he had seen in the city—a solid, respectable brown face and a sense of anonymity which protected its tenants.

"Just you and your parents live here?"

"And my young brother, Myron. He's just turned sixteen. Are you coming in?" she asked.

Jonathan balked at the invitation. "I've got to get back to the factory," he lied. "There's a stack of paper work to catch up on. Anybody who tells you the boss is the first to leave is full of the proverbial."

He sensed rather than saw the girl's disappointment, a sadness that the frolic was over, that they were picking up their own lives again after an interesting but all too brief interlude.

"Thanks for seeing me home," she said quietly. "And for the other thing as well."

The other thing? It took Jonathan a moment to realize that she meant taking care of Epstein and his friends, temporarily at least. "I still owe you that ride," he said. "How about I come in one evening after I've given you that and dinner?"

Miriam's face brightened immediately. "That sounds lovely."

Jonathan took her hands, enveloping them in his own. "I'll see you at work tomorrow." He turned and walked away, knowing that she was watching him. Reaching the end of the street, he waved to her, waiting till she reciprocated. Her face stayed with him for the entire subway ride back to the factory.

From Houston Street he drove his small Chevrolet to Jacob's apartment to see if he needed anything. The apartment was empty, and Jonathan began to visit the clubs his father frequented. He found Jacob at the third attempt, engrossed in a game of chess with one of his friends from Poland. Jonathan quietly pulled up a chair and sat down to watch the game, seeing his father move in for the kill.

After more than a minute of eerie silence, broken only by somebody coughing on the other side of the club, Jacob stretched out a hand and gravely moved a piece, strengthening his attack on his opponent's beleaguered king. Only when he had stopped the clock did he turn to Jonathan, acknowledging his son's presence for the first time.

"You ran away quickly tonight. Was it business or was it Miss Helman?"

Jonathan waved a hand at the chessboard. "That's where your attention should be. You might get jumped on." He breathed a silent sigh of relief that Jacob had learned nothing of the trouble outside the factory. From his second floor office on the other side of the building, he would have been hard put to hear sounds of the fight, but somebody might have told him.

Involuntarily Jacob checked the position of the chessmen to see if his opponent had moved. "He's not going to jump on anybody this time," he whispered to Jonathan. "Now tell me how Miss Helman is."

"Well, when I left her. Why the sudden interest?"

"Interest? Me?" Jacob frowned in disbelief that his son could have accused him of such a thing. "I thought any interest in that direction was being shown by you. I am just observing."

"And what do you see?" Jonathan asked, curious about what his father had to say.

Before Jacob could reply, his opponent coughed to signify that he had moved. Seeing that nothing had happened to alter his offensive strategy, Jacob moved the next piece. "Check."

Stopping the clock again, he resumed his conversation with Jonathan. "You ask me what I see. I see problems. Miriam is a lovely girl, but she works for you. Do you think it wise to mix the two things?"

Having made his opinions known, Jacob returned his concentration to the game. He raised his eyes to the other player, fixing him with a stare that declared it to be futile to continue the battle. Jonathan watched, fascinated, as he had done so many times when his father had played. He could see no escape for Jacob's opponent. The man could block the check with either of two pieces, or he could move the king. Either way, the ultimate result would still be the same, even allowing for best possible play—five moves at the most.

The other man saw it too. Almost listlessly he flicked out a hand and knocked his king off balance. It fell to the board with a clatter, rolling back and forth before lying still in defeat. Jacob beamed, shaking the hand that was offered to him.

"Nice game," he consoled the loser. "A very nice game. I enjoyed it. Thank you." The man walked away to another table, and Jacob pointed to the seat he had vacated. "Would you like to play against your father, Jonathan?"

"Not really. But I will just to keep you happy." With a feeling of resignation, Jonathan moved into the empty seat and began to arrange the white pieces. He had not played chess with Jacob in months; if he lasted twenty-five moves, he would classify it as a victory.

There had been a time when Jonathan was an avid player, learning under Jacob's skillful tutelage, grasping at any opportunity which was offered to improve his game. It was a cheap form of recreation, one which they both had enjoyed; after the board and pieces were paid for, there was no further outlay. Jacob had started him off with a queen advantage; then, as his skill increased, the handicap had been reduced to a rook, a knight, a bishop, until finally they had faced each other across the board on equal terms. Jonathan had resorted to every trick he could think of. He had studied the gambits of the masters, putting together combinations which he felt would sweep his father off the board like a routed army. He had even lowered himself to challenging Jacob when he returned home late in the evening from the tailoring shop, tired after a long, hard day. But his father had seemed to liven up when he saw the men set out, and Jonathan's record had remained abysmal. Tonight, he was certain, would prove to be no different, especially with the problems that plagued him. Nevertheless he began to move the pieces mechanically into an opening.

"When are you going to see this girl?" Jacob asked, positioning his own men in response to Jonathan's opening.

"I'll ask her out for Saturday night. Dinner and a show."

"Umm." Jacob deliberated over a move. "And how about our good friend Mr. Gilbert? How is his order coming?"

Jonathan moved a bishop into the fray, depositing it on the chosen square with a cavalier flick of his hand. "The larger sizes are well in hand. The forties can get going next week, and then we can get going with the smaller sizes. If we're lucky we'll have the whole order ready ahead of time, ship it early."

"Good. Good. Give the man no cause to complain." Jacob peered at the board, evaluating his son's last move. "You know something, Jonathan? You should sit on your hands till you decide what is and what is not the right move. Then you wouldn't make silly mistakes like you just did."

Jonathan looked glumly at the chessmen as his father forked the white knight and bishop with a pawn. Jonathan took the pawn with the bishop, only to have it taken in turn by the covering pawn; he moved the knight to safety.

"Even you shouldn't be this easy to beat," Jacob complained. "Your mind's not on the game."

Fifteen moves later, Jonathan's game was totally beyond redemption. He was two pieces down and struggling vainly to ward off Jacob's inexorable march to victory. He looked at the board for a final time, fully accepting the hopelessness of his situation.

"Settle for a draw?" he asked Jacob. "I'll give you one if you ask really nice."

Jacob pushed his chair back from the table and stood up. "And since when is absolute annihilation grounds to offer a draw? Not in my knowledge of the game, it isn't."

As they were eating in the small restaurant next to the club, Jacob put down his knife and fork and gazed solemnly across the table at Jonathan. "Just what is the matter with you? Are you thinking so much about this girl that it's even putting you off your food?" He gestured at the meal which Jonathan had hardly touched.

"No, it's not the girl." Jonathan shifted uneasily in the chair, trying to avoid telling Jacob what had happened outside the factory. He cursed himself for believing that he could keep anything of that nature from Jacob, even for a few hours.

"What is it then?"

Jonathan breathed out deeply, resigned to telling his father. He would hear about it in the morning anyway, so what was the point of keeping it from him any longer? "I had a run-in with three guys from the union," he mumbled, his head down, staring at the food. "They were waiting outside the factory tonight, stopping our people."

"An argument?"

"More. I decked two of them, Mike Epstein and another guy. The third one ran away."

Jacob sucked on his tongue, making a clucking noise. Jonathan was uncertain whether it was meant to convey worry, sympathy or astonishment that he should get into a fight. "You were all right?"

"Sore knuckles, that's all. It's been bugging me all night, wondering what they're going to get up to next. That's the way they always start, leaning on the workers, trying to persuade them gently, then making an example of a couple of them so the others all join. Next thing you know, the place is unionized and we're out of business because we've got nothing but a gang of troublemakers on our hands."

"I thought you said you saw Miriam tonight," Jacob interjected. "Did you, or were you using her name as a cover for all this?"

"I did see her. She was the cause of it. I was arguing with Epstein when she came along. He grabbed her, started pushing her around a bit to see what I would do."

"And you did it." Jacob sat back in the chair, a worried expression covering his face. "I don't like it, Jonathan. We've been lucky so far; they haven't bothered with us. Maybe it's because we were so small. Now we're getting bigger, they want a piece of it."

"I'll talk to everybody tomorrow," Jonathan said. "I'll find out what the feeling is. Even if it means bumping up their wages to double what the union can get for them, I'm keeping those crooks out."

After making an attempt to eat the meal, Jonathan drove his father home, seeing him safely inside the building before continuing to his own apartment. He sat down in the living room, listening to the radio for a while, going over in his mind the events of the day. Somehow he could not separate the disturbance outside the factory from Miriam; her face kept appearing, running across his mental vision as he tried to concentrate on Epstein, on figuring out what the man's next move would be. Finally he gave up, giving all his attention instead to Miriam, finding it more pleasurable to think about her than to relive the violence. Out of curiousity he picked up the telephone directory and looked up the name of Helman; there was no party of that name listed at the correct address. Closing the book, he tossed it carelessly onto the table, wondering what he would have done had the family been listed. Called her up at eleven-thirty at night? Hardly the way to make friends; her parents would probably force her to change jobs. He turned the radio on again, fiddling with the tuning control till he found some music. Then he sat in an easy chair and chain-smoked till past two in the morning.

When he arrived at work the following morning, he found that the fight of the previous night was common gossip, spread like wildfire by the workers who had witnessed it. Any hopes that Jonathan had of keeping it quiet and informing his people in his own time were rudely dispelled when he walked through the front door and was greeted with a scattered round of applause by four men who worked in the pressing section, and cries of "Joe Louis, here we come!"

Feeling his face reddening, but simultaneously liking the sensation of being a hero, Jonathan hurried past the men, waving a hand half in admonishment of their greeting, half in acceptance of their praise. In his own office, he called his secretary, instructing her to arrange a meeting for eleven that morning where he could speak to the staff of both production units.

For the first hour Jonathan stayed in his office, bringing correspondence up to date, scribbling replies to letters which his secretary could type later. Finally there was no valid reason for him to stay downstairs any longer; the meeting with his employees was not due for another ninety minutes, so he had time to spare. He walked upstairs and opened the door to the sewing room. Three girls were working inside. Two of them turned to look as the door opened, their eyes widening as they recognized the visitor, but Miriam remained bowed over her machine, concentrating on the fabric she was sewing. Only when she had finished the seam and dropped the piece into the workbasket did she turn around.

"See?" Jonathan exclaimed, moving close to her station. "I saved you from the vampires last night. Without me, you'd never have made it home in one piece."

She laughed delightedly as she remembered his platform antics of the previous evening. "Hasn't anybody told you that vampires don't really exist, Mr. Gellenbaum?"

A shadow crossed Jonathan's face at the unexpected use of his last name; she understood why. "You're still Mr. Gellenbaum at work," she whispered, so that neither of the other girls could hear. "Both you and your father."

Jonathan nodded, relieved that the girl was not seeking to take advantage of the situation. "How about I meet you seven o'clock on Saturday night? I'll pick you up on the corner of your street."

"Fine."

"See you then." Without making any reference to the meeting he had called for later that morning, he turned and walked toward the door, smiling cheerfully at the other two girls as he passed them.

Watching from the door of his office, Jacob saw his son leave the sewing room and head down the stairs. Jonathan made no sign of having seen his father.

Despite the problem which Jonathan had told him about, Jacob found himself smiling. Another dream, he thought. My son has found another dream.

**4**

At three minutes before eleven, when Jonathan entered the pressing room accompanied by his father, the area was full to overflowing with factory workers, all eager to hear what he had to say. Beginning as a hesitant cheer when he first appeared, the enthusiastic applause reached ear-splitting levels by the time he jumped up onto a small table and clapped his hands, trying for their attention.

"Please!" he shouted. "Can we have some quiet?"

The noise rolled on, sweeping over him till at last he gave up and just held his hands in the air as acceptance of the ovation. His eyes felt damp as he gazed over the crowd, their uplifted, welcoming faces bringing a lump to his throat. One worry, at least, was over; he had no need to tell them what had happened the previous night.

Slowly the applause died down. Atop the table, Jonathan picked out the faces of the people he knew best—his father, who stood off to one side, slightly frightened by the tumultuous welcome; Miriam in the front row, her hazel eyes shining at the sense of occasion; other people with whom he came into daily contact. Wherever he looked, the expressions were the same, like a sporting crowd cheering on their hero, willing him on to his next victory.

He clapped his hands again, and the noise fell away with a suddenness that took him by surprise, dying abruptly into an expectant silence as the crowd waited for its champion to speak.

"You've all heard what happened outside here last night," he began. "That was just the start of it. There's going to be more. And unless we make some plans for the next time, we may not always be so lucky."

"We're ready for them," a voice from the back shouted out. "They won't come back in a hurry again."

Jonathan tried to identify the speaker, wanted to show his gratitude for the support. He peered across the intervening space, but the faces merged into one festive crowd, all eager for the next step in the battle.

"I want a show of hands," he called out. "Who wants to keep the union out of here?"

A forest of arms was thrust up into the air.

"Now who, if anybody, wants the union in this factory?"

The pressing room went dead. Not a hand was raised, and Jonathan beamed triumphantly at his father. See, his eyes said, I've got an army behind me; what were we both so worried about?

"Okay! Just because I don't want the union here, and you don't want the union here, doesn't mean to say that the union doesn't want to be here. We're fighting a war with those people, and they're not going to stop trying to get in. You know what they've done at other factories, don't you?"

A chorus of jeers split the air, vague mutterings of what would happen to the union goon squads if they tried the same thing at Gellenbaum and Son. Jonathan began to feel like Napoleon rousing his troops before a big battle where the odds were against them but where they knew they would end the day victorious.

"They'll be back," he continued. "Last night wasn't the end of it. And when they come back I want us to be ready." He held up a hand for silence as cheering began to erupt again, killing it off before it gained impetus. "In the future, whether it's lunchtime or when we leave the factory, I don't want anybody going out of here by themselves. There's safety in numbers. Epstein's mob is going to try and intimidate us, rough some of us up if they get the chance. If we're together, they're going to think twice about it. By ourselves they've got an easy target. When you leave this building, make sure you've got somebody with you. And if there is trouble,"—his voice rose into a screaming crescendo—"make damned sure that we come out on the winning side."

Out of the corner of his eye, Jonathan saw Jacob beckoning to him. He dropped lightly down from the table and went over to his father while the employees stood watching. Jacob whispered a few words in his ear, and Jonathan nodded before resuming his perch.

"We've got to face the possibility that some of us might get a black eye or a split lip," he said. "Even the best armies in history had their casualties. I'm not going to say don't worry about it, because that would be a damned stupid thing to say. What I am going to tell you, however, is not to worry about losing time off work. If, God forbid, something does happen to one of us, he won't lose any money because of it. He'll get his pay till he's well enough to come back. And we'll take care of any medical expenses. If we can see this through, we'll come out stronger than ever before." Without waiting for any questions, he dropped down to the floor and pushed his way through the crowd to the exit.

Jacob followed him down, finding his son sitting behind the desk; there were tears in his eyes. "Did you see that?" he asked his father, choking back his emotions. "They're with us all the way. Can you ask for a better bunch of people than that?"

"Treat people decently and they'll treat you the same way," Jacob replied. "Can you wonder why the union had such little difficulty in getting into other places? They treated the workers like pigs, and they were repaid in kind."

"How long do you think they'll put up with harassment from Epstein's men?" Jonathan asked. "Even people like we have can only take so much. Then they break."

"While they see a leader, they will follow..."

"Until a few people get broken heads," Jonathan interrupted. "And after last night's episode, I don't think that will be long in coming. Epstein's going to be out for blood because of what happened to him last night. I made him look like a fool, and his goons as well. If that gets around, they'll lose all their power."

"Then you have to end this quickly, Jonathan. Finish it at the first chance you get."

Jonathan looked at his father, noticing for the first time that the gold watch had not left his vest pocket. It struck Jonathan as odd—over Al Gilbert's complaining about jacket sizes, his father had been worried; here he was acting as if there were nothing to concern him.

"No watch?"

For a moment Jacob looked mystified. Then he smiled. "Do you think that the watch is always a mirror of my feelings?"

"It's usually a pretty good barometer. When it's out, you're worried. When it's away like now, you haven't got a care in the whole wide world."

"I worry," Jacob said. "But I think that we have a situation here that can be determined by ourselves, as long as our people are not forced to go through a long period of trouble."

"Okay." Jonathan rose from the desk. "I'll finish it first chance I get."

A picket line formed outside the building just after lunchtime, eight men carrying placards which denounced Gellenbaum and Son as resisting union improvements to their workers' standard of living. A few pedestrians gathered to watch but moved on quickly when nothing happened. Jonathan was happy just to watch; the real test would come when the factory closed for the day and his people began to mix with the pickets.

During the afternoon he went upstairs to make arrangements to take Jacob home after closing time. From there he went into the sewing room; it was obvious from the expressions on the machinists' faces that his speech of the morning had had the desired effect. He could not keep himself from smiling as he crossed the floor to where Miriam sat.

"I'll walk you to the station tonight," he offered. "There's a bunch of pickets outside, and it might get worse by the time you leave."

"Would they pick on a girl?"

"They did yesterday. Or have you forgotten?"

"They were testing you," she reminded him.

"I'll still walk you to the station. Remember the talk this morning. Nobody leaves here alone."

She indicated the other two girls in the room. "I'll go with them."

"You'll be safer with me," he said and left the room.

By four-thirty the picket line had been strengthened by the arrival of Epstein and his two associates of the night before, one man wearing a strip of white plaster to cover his split lip.

"Come back for another dose?" Jonathan called out from the factory doorway.

Epstein made no reply. He continued to stand silently in the shadow of the factory wall, flanked by his bodyguards, watching the picket line circling on the sidewalk like a group of circus elephants.

When it came time to close up, Jonathan stood on the sidewalk outside the factory, nodding good night to factory employees as they trooped out of the building in groups of four or five, heading for the subway. From the other production unit on the same block, he could see a similar procedure being followed. Epstein also watched, making no attempt to interfere with the exodus, content to let his picket line obstruct the sidewalk so that the employees had to step out into the road.

Jonathan waited for the next group to leave his own building, then moved to its head, leading it into the heart of the picket line. The men with the placards glanced to Epstein for direction before stepping aside to let Jonathan's people through without harassment. First round to me, Jonathan thought, returning to his post by the door. But this is a championship bout, and they last for fifteen rounds. There are still fourteen to go.

When Miriam came down five minutes later, accompanied by the other two girls from the sewing room, he repeated the performance, driving a wedge through the picket line till the girls could pass safely through. Again no effort was made to stop him when he returned, and he began to wonder whether Epstein was prepared to wear him down in a waiting game, picketing the factory every day, constantly reminding the workers that the union was there without having to resort to the strong-arm tactics that had been employed at other sites.

When Jacob came down, the last person to leave, Jonathan sensed a tenseness beginning to form. The picket line broke up, letting Epstein and his two henchmen through to confront Jonathan as he helped Jacob into the car.

"I owe you one for last night, Gellenbaum."

Jonathan closed the door on his father, seeing him safely inside the car. "Tell me about it sometime. I'm going home." He began to walk around the car, stopping at the back to open the rumble seat. Across the seat lay a heavy starting handle.

"It's payoff time, Gellenbaum. We're moving into your place whether you want us or not." He stepped forward, trying to catch Jonathan by surprise as he bent over the open rumble seat. Through the rear window of the car, Jonathan caught a glimpse of his father's frightened face. The next moment he came up with the starting handle, swinging it in a wide arc toward Epstein's head, checking his swing at the last moment like a batter trying to save his strike on a bad pitch. The handle stopped inches away from Epstein's head, quivering in Jonathan's grip as the union man flung up a hand in futile defense.

"Do it again, Epstein, and it won't be a checked swing," Jonathan promised. "I'll take your head clean off your shoulders."

Epstein stepped back, his face paling as he fully comprehended the threat in Jonathan's hands. Jonathan followed, the starting handle held out in front of him like a rifle, jabbing the air, making his quarry retreat faster, and flinch each time the end of the handle flashed out toward him. "Last time, are you going to leave my people alone?" He changed his grip on the handle again, holding it like a bat.

Epstein licked his lips nervously, anticipating the swing so that he could duck underneath it and close in on his man. Jonathan did not swing. The sound of a door handle being turned froze him into immobility for a second; then he saw Epstein's goons dragging his father out of the car while the placard-carrying pickets stood still, witnessing the abduction.

With a bellow of fury Jonathan flung himself forward, knocking Epstein aside, the handle coming around in a low curve to catch the nearest man solidly behind the knees. His legs gave way underneath him, and he let go of Jacob's arm. The handle swung again, missing the man with the split lip as he darted out of the way, crashing into the fender of the Chevrolet, chipping paint, denting the metal. Jonathan turned back to the fray, gauging the threat posed by Epstein and the other man as they circled him warily, worrying that the men on the picket line would also join in. He feinted with the handle and Epstein ducked away.

Suddenly a loud whistle cut across the street, followed by the sound of pounding feet on the sidewalk and the sight of a navy blue uniform as the patrolman came running toward the three men, his nightstick out, the leather thong dangling from it.

"Drop that handle!" he yelled at Jonathan.

Jonathan eyed Epstein cautiously before laying the handle across the hood of the Chevrolet, leaving it within easy reach until the patrolman arrived.

"Just what the hell is going on here?"

"Ask him!" Jonathan jabbed a finger at Epstein, who was trying to lose himself in the picket line as it dissolved, its members hoping to leave the scene quietly.

"Hey, you!" The patrolman beckoned with his night stick. "Get your ass over here!"

While Epstein and his uninjured bodyguard walked slowly toward the policeman, Jonathan turned to his father, relieved to see that he was none the worse for being dragged from the car.

"Somebody want to tell me what's going on here before I put the lot of you away for the night?" the patrolman demanded.

"This is my factory," Jonathan said.

"You Gellenbaum?"

He nodded.

"And who are these characters?"

"Union pickets." Jonathan refused to give Epstein the title of union official. "They're trying to get my people to join the union, any way they can."

"What's your name?" The patrolman jabbed Epstein in the chest with the night stick.

"Epstein. Michael Epstein."

"You live here?" He indicated the street with a sweep of his hand.

"No. In the Bronx. University Avenue."

"Then get back where the hell you belong. And take your crippled buddy with you." Epstein bent down to pick up the man with the injured legs. "I see you on my beat again, I'll bust your head open." He stood juggling the nightstick while Epstein and the other man supported their injured comrade, helping him to a car parked along the street. The placard bearers dispersed.

"This the first time you had trouble with them?" asked the patrolman.

"No. I sent them packing yesterday. I might not have been so lucky today, though. Thanks for your help."

"That's okay. If they come round again, give a scream to the precinct. Bunch of cruds." Whistling, the patrolman moved off after Epstein, standing menacingly by the car until it drove away.

Behind the wheel of the Chevrolet, Jonathan sat for a long time without saying anything, his mind going over the scene in which he had just participated. It was just as well that patrolman had turned up when he did. Epstein and his two cronies I could have taken out, he reasoned, but what if the pickets had joined in? And my father! Trying to use Jacob in their fight against me! He gripped the wheel tightly in his fury, knuckles showing white as he realized how close his father had come to injury. And what will happen next time? Will they try to get hold of Jacob again? Or will they select Jacob as a prime target, working through him to get at me?

"I don't think that man will walk properly again for a long time," he heard his father say. "Did you have to hit him so hard?"

The complete farce of the question made Jonathan burst out laughing. "Who else but you," he asked, turning in his seat, his anger and anxiety dispelled, "would ask a question like that? He was attacking you, and you're only worried that I hit him too hard."

"He's still a person," Jacob said.

"They were trying to hurt you," Jonathan insisted. "Doesn't that mean anything? And they might try again."

"After that?" Jacob seemed dubious. "I wouldn't try anything again if somebody hit me like you did to that man."

"I belted the car as well when the other son of a bitch moved," Jonathan said. "It's still working."

Jacob dismissed the rationalization. "Now you're talking crazy. You won't have any more trouble with that man Epstein, not with the police offering to help you." He went quiet for a minute, then looked curiously at his son. "How come we're going this way? I thought you were taking me home. This isn't the way to Delancey Street."

"You're staying with me tonight," Jonathan said. "I'm not leaving you alone in your own place." He still found it curious how his father could want to remain in the section of the city he had inhabited before the factory had opened. Certainly his apartment was comfortable, but why stay there once he had the money to move out? Jonathan had moved out as soon as he could, taking a place on East Twenty-fifth Street, close enough to the factory, and far enough away from the poverty he had known as a child to be able to forget it.

The telephone was ringing as he opened the front door. Leaving Jacob in the hall, he trotted across the apartment to answer it.

"Jonathan?" It was a girl's voice, worried. "It's Miriam Helman. Did anything happen tonight?"

A slow smile spread across his face, and he glanced around to see if his father was close enough to hear the conversation. "A policeman came along and broke everything up," he said. "No trouble at all."

A sigh of relief passed through the earpiece. "I was so worried," she said. "They looked so ugly out there with their placards. And those three men from last night..."

"There was nothing to worry about," he assured her. "I wouldn't let myself get into any trouble. I've got to be in one piece to see you on Saturday night." He waited for her to say something, but no words came. "Look, I'll see you at work tomorrow," he said. "I have to go now because I've got to sort out some things with my father. Thanks for calling. I appreciate it." He waited for her farewell and then hung up.

"Your favorite machinist," he said in answer to his father's unspoken question. "She wanted to see if we were both all right."

"Beware," Jacob mocked. "She'll have you dancing to her tune in no time."

"That's what Mike Epstein told me as well. About the union," he added quickly, "not Miriam."

There was something about hospitals which sent a chill through Mike Epstein. Even when his seventy-year-old mother, with whom he lived in the Bronx, had been in the hospital with pneumonia, he had hated to visit her, dragging himself there each day, viewing it as a punishment to sit by her bed and watch broken bodies trying to heal. Now, as he left St. Vincent's Hospital after being told that his bodyguard had a broken leg, the familiar sickening emotion swept over him; he could not wait to get outside on the sidewalk.

The man with the split lip was waiting, smoking a cigarette, cupping his hand to protect it from the slight drizzle which had just started to fall.

"How long's he going to be in?"

"A week," Epstein replied. "Then they're going to let him out with a cast and a couple of crutches." He got into the car and started the engine, waiting for the other man to close the passenger door. "Gellenbaum's made us look like a couple of jerks. We've got to do something about him. While he holds out, other people are going to get the same idea."

"What have you got in mind?" the other man asked.

"If he won't let the union into his factory, then we're not going to let him in either." The man with the split lip looked mystfied, and Epstein explained further. "A nice warm fire. Then we'll see if all those people without jobs want the union or not. They're with him now because they're working for him. What's it going to be like when there's no work to be had there any more?" He chuckled humorlessly at his own logic.

Epstein drove up to the Bronx, turning off University Avenue at One Hundred Seventy-first Street, pulling up in front of a small, gloomy-looking apartment building. He got out and locked the door, then led the way inside. His mother, a frail-looking, white-haired woman, was reading a Yiddish newspaper in the living room when he entered with the other man. Epstein kissed her on the cheek as he hurried past on his way to the bathroom. When he returned, he was holding two empty bottles which he handed to the man with a split lip.

"Are you going out again tonight?" his mother asked, laying down the newspaper. Her voice was cracked, the words hard to understand with the guttural German accent she had retained.

"Yes, Mama. But we won't be back late." He turned to the other man and saw the half grin across his face which disappeared as soon as he realized it was there.

"What's the matter with you?" Epstein demanded roughly. "You ain't got a mother or something?"

The man thought it best not to reply. Epstein was out for revenge, and he wanted to make certain that Jonathan Gellenbaum remained the target.

Going back to the street, Epstein opened the trunk of his car and pulled out the five-gallon gas can he kept there for emergencies. Ensuring that nobody was watching, he started to fill the bottles with gasoline, slopping some onto the road. As he replaced the can, he noticed a small container of paint in the trunk, a special color he had ordered for touching up the car. He withdrew it, pouring some paint into each bottle of gasoline.

"What's that for?" the man with the split lip asked.

"Makes it stick when it goes off. Don't you know anything?"

Finally Epstein ripped up a rag and stuffed a makeshift wick into the top of each bottle. "Hold those and don't smoke," he said.

It took Epstein an hour to drive back to the Houston Street factory, his eyes continually flicking to his right, checking that the two bottles were being held upright. The smell of gasoline was almost overpowering, even with the windows open. Once he saw the other man clasp the bottles to his chest while he searched with his free hand inside his jacket.

"You looking for a cigarette?"

"Yeah. I'm dying for one . . ." His voice trailed off as he realized what Epstein had told him.

They drove past the factory three times, circling around the block, waiting for a clear shot at the building. The first two times too many people thronged the sidewalk. On the third time, it was almost empty. Epstein pulled the car into the curb, leaving the engine running, the gear stick pointing into first, his foot pressing down the clutch.

"Both through that window," he said. "That's Gellenbaum's office and showroom. The place will go up in a second." He revved the engine while he sat watching. The other man pulled a lighter from his pocket, got out of the car and looked around cautiously. There was a spark as he coaxed the lighter into life, then a brighter flame as he lit the wick of the first Molotov cocktail. It arced through the air as he raised his arm and let fly, followed immediately by the sound of breaking glass. The second bomb followed the first.

Before it had time to hit the carpet inside the office, the man with the split lip was back inside the car, and Epstein was gunning the engine, racing away from the curb, determined to catch the traffic lights one hundred yards in front of him before they changed to red. Above the roar of the engine, he heard the sound of the explosion from behind, saw the belch of flame through the window.

"Good," he whispered, speeding through the lights as they changed, holding down the horn to clear a path through the pedestrians who had already started to cross. "Let him get out of that one."

They were on their second game of chess when the telephone rang. Jonathan had lost the first one—not that he had expected a different result—but he was enjoying the second game, forcing his father to think over the moves, to deliberate more than usual.

"Make it a good move," he said to Jacob as he stood up to answer the call. "It could be your last of this game."

Jacob raised a hand in acknowledgment of the jibe, his eyes never leaving the board. He heard Jonathan answer the phone; then he looked up in concern as his son's voice took on an urgent note.

"How long ago?" Jonathan snapped. "Okay. I'll be down there in ten minutes."

"Who was that?" Jacob asked as Jonathan strode past him, snatching a coat from the hall closet, opening the front door.

"Fire department," he called back. "The factory's on fire."

"How bad?"

"They think they've got it under control. I'm going down there now."

"Should I come with?"

"No. You stay here. Figure out your next move." He slammed the door and took the stairs two at a time, running to where he had left the Chevrolet. Fire. It had to be Epstein. Too much of a coincidence to be anything else. Would the police or fire people be able to find evidence that it was arson? Would they be able to tie it in with Epstein? With his union recruiting campaign?

He jumped into the car and tore away from the curb with a screech of tires. The first light he passed through was red; he was too concerned with the factory to worry about driving. How badly was the place damaged? Had the fire department managed to save anything? No point in worrying, he tried to tell himself. You'll find out what's going on when you get down there.

He completed the journey in a partial daze, only half-aware of the streets he had raced through. Two fire engines were parked across the road in front of the factory, uniformed figures in hard hats dragging hoses along the sidewalk as they pumped water from the hydrants through the window of his office. He stopped the car at the police line and hurried out, brushing past the patrolman who tried to stop him.

"I'm Jonathan Gellenbaum!" he shouted at the officer. "That's my factory."

The man let him through. Panting, he reached the fire captain who was directing the operation. "How bad is it?"

"You the owner?"

"Yeah. I just got a call from the fire department to come down here. What caused it?"

"Couple of people"—he indicated two men who were talking to the patrolman who had broken up the fight earlier on—"say it looked like an explosion. There was a car parked in front of the factory. A man got out and threw some things through the window. He jumped back in the car and took off. Couple of seconds later there was a bang, and the place started going up."

"What's the damage?"

"Hard to say at the moment. We got here pretty quick, got it under control. You may be lucky and just get away with superficial damage, nothing structural."

"Is it just downstairs?"

"That's all. Isn't that enough?" He walked away from Jonathan, moving among his men, directing them to attack the fire from another angle.

Jonathan stood watching for a minute; then he moved to the patrolman who was interviewing the two witnesses. The patrolman recognized him immediately.

"Seems like it's arson, Mr. Gellenbaum. Two witnesses saw somebody throw something through the window. Got a look at the car, enough to identify it as a dark-colored Ford. But no license plate number. Two people in it, driver and the guy who threw the bomb."

"Thanks. I think I know who it was."

The patrolman looked interested. "Would you mind telling me, or do you figure it was those guys you were having trouble with this afternoon?" Jonathan said nothing in reply, staring sourly at the fire. "You're figuring on getting hold of your starting handle again, aren't you? Going to sort it out yourself, right?"

"Maybe I'll use a baseball bat instead," Jonathan said. "Don't worry about me. I'll look after it, deliver them right to you." He moved closer to the fire fighters, relieved to see that the flames were dying down.

Five minutes later the fire was completely out, and firemen were tramping through the ground floor of the building, checking the damage. Jonathan followed them in, appalled by the water damage; the whole of the showroom was flooded out, walls and ceiling smoke-blackened, his desk a charred ruin. Directly in front of the desk, the carpet was burned right through to show blackened floorboards. A similar spot was on the other side of the showroom.

"Two bombs," the fire captain said. "That's where they landed. Lucky you weren't sitting in here at the time." He went over to the desk and began scraping the surface with his fingernail.

"Found something?" Jonathan asked.

"Paint. Whoever made that bomb, or bombs, sure wanted the stuff to stick."

Jonathan followed the captain around the office, bending down with him as he scooped up pieces of broken glass. "Looks like it's from a soda bottle. We'll soon find out."

When he returned to the car, Jonathan was breathing easier. The damage was light, superficial. He would not be able to use the showroom for a couple of weeks, till it was refitted. But, thank God, the factory upstairs was still operable. Epstein had made his play. Now he, Jonathan, would reply.

First he drove back to his apartment, settling his father's worries. Then he picked up the telephone directory and began looking through the Epsteins. There were three in the area he wanted, but only one with "M" as the first initial.

"You can sleep in my room," he told Jacob. "I'll stay out here, listen for the phone in case anything else happens." He found fresh linen and made the bed for his father, closing the door quietly as the older man lay down. Jonathan waited for half an hour, to be certain that his father was asleep; then he left the apartment. On the passenger seat beside him as he drove northward, toward the Bronx and University Avenue, was the starting handle.

# 5

There was no reply, so he knocked again, scuffing his shoes impatiently while he waited. Finally a faint voice came through the door, asking who it was.

"I'm a friend of Mike's," he called back, wondering who the woman could be; she sounded too old to be his wife. "Is he in, please?"

"He's out," the voice came back. "Won't be home till late."

"How late?" Jonathan asked; the starting handle hidden underneath his coat was becoming uncomfortable. "It's very important that I see him."

"I don't know. Maybe you'd better go away and come back tomorrow. Or telephone him."

"Okay." Jonathan gave up, seeing there was no point in further conversation. He would wait downstairs for an hour, till midnight. Then, if nothing happened, he would be forced to leave it with the police. As if that would do any good!

He got back into the Chevrolet and sat outside the apartment building, smoking nervously. It crossed his mind to visit Miriam while he was in the neighborhood; she was interested in what happened.

Each time a car came toward him slowing down, he gripped the handle with a feeling of excitement, willing it to be a Ford, hoping for it to come to a stop by his own car, for the door to open and reveal Mike Epstein's slouching figure. He threw the cigarette out of the open window, replacing it with a fresh one, wondering if Jacob was still sleeping or was up roaming around the apartment, chain smoking as he was.

The familiar, square shape of a Ford appeared in his rearview mirror, its lights illuminating the curb as it slowed down and prepared to pull in behind the Chevrolet. Jonathan hunched down in the seat, hidden from view. He heard the engine of the Ford turning over before dying away; then a door slammed, and footsteps echoed past his own car. He pushed down on the handle and opened the door a fraction, looking out. There was no mistaking Epstein, hands thrust into the pockets of his topcoat, wide-brimmed hat pulled low over his forehead.

"Mike," Jonathan whispered. "You forgot something when you burned the factory."

The figure stiffened, head coming up as it began to turn, eyes widening as Epstein recognized Jonathan climbing out of the car, the starting handle swinging loosely in one hand. "You forgot that I'd be coming after you."

Epstein swung around and began running for the safety of the apartment building lobby. Jonathan swung his arm back and sent the starting handle whirling through the air. It struck the sidewalk with a loud clang and a shower of sparks, rising up as it rebounded, cutting across Epstein's legs, tripping him into a squirming heap. Before he could regain his feet, Jonathan was standing over him, the metal bar again in his hand, swinging threateningly.

"Get up," he ordered.

Epstein rose slowly, arms in the air in an attitude of surrender, the skin on his hands scraped and bleeding, his trousers torn from the fall.

"Who was the other guy with you tonight?"

"When?"

Jonathan swung the handle toward Epstein's head. "You know when. When you tossed two fire bombs into the factory." The handle whistled through the air an inch from Epstein's right shoulder.

"I've been to a club all night—after putting my friend in the hospital, the one whose leg you broke."

"What was the club?"

Epstein paused to think of a name. He opened his mouth to speak, then screamed in pain as the starting handle came down across his right arm.

"Who were you with?"

"You broke my goddamned arm!" Epstein wailed, clutching his injured limb.

"You've got another one left. Who were you with?" Jonathan looked up and down the street, certain that Epstein's cry would bring attention. He saw nobody.

"Solly Kaye."

"Where does he live?"

"Jerome Avenue." Epstein's eyes followed the metal handle as it swung back and forth. His arm was not broken, just badly bruised, but he was in no doubt that Jonathan would swing the handle hard enough to break a bone. He had already done it once today.

"Who's in your apartment? Your wife?"

"My mother."

"Let's go up and see her."

Epstein was about to protest. How could his mother see him like this? Then he remembered the pistol he kept hidden in the dresser in his bedroom, bought years earlier, never used. Did it work? Would he get the opportunity to use it? "My mother's an old lady," he said. "She's ill. This'll kill her."

Jonathan prodded him with the starting handle. "Get moving, before I really break your arm."

Pushing Epstein ahead of him, Jonathan entered the building again, waiting while the union man fumbled in his pocket for his key.

"Is that you, Michael?" a voice called out. "You're home so late. There was a man here before looking for you. Said he was a friend, but I wouldn't let him in."

"It's okay," Epstein called back. "He's here with me now."

"You'd better believe he is," Jonathan whispered. "You act reasonably, and your mother won't see you get your head kicked in."

From the bedroom walked Epstein's mother, wearing a long woollen dressing gown. She eyed the starting handle in Jonathan's hand warily.

"You're the man who called before?" she asked. "You said you were a friend of Michael's. Why are you pushing him around with that bar?"

"Ask him why he tried to burn my factory down tonight instead." Jonathan shot back. "Or don't you know what he does for a living?"

"Michael!" The old woman's voice grew faint.

"It's a mistake, Mama," Epstein said. "We'll have it sorted out in a few minutes. Why don't you go back to bed?"

She remained standing where she was, staring in horror at Jonathan, at the starting handle, at the murderous intent in his eyes.

"Do as he says," Jonathan ordered. "Otherwise you're going to stand there and watch me bust every bone in his body."

The threat decided her. She gave a final lingering look at her son, then turned and walked slowly back to her bedroom, closing the door. Jonathan thought he heard the sound of a key in the lock.

"Whereabouts on Jerome does your pal Solly Kaye live?"

"I don't know the number, only the building." Epstein saw the handle start to rise and backed away, trembling. "I'm telling you the truth. Aren't there places you know how to get to, but you don't know the number?"

The handle dropped. Without thinking hard, Jonathan could not remember the number of his father's building. He knew the apartment well enough, but what was the number?

"I've got it written down in a book," Epstein volunteered. "It's in my dresser. I'll get it out for you."

The words seemed too eager for Jonathan's liking. He followed Epstein into the bedroom, watching carefully as he opened the top drawer of the dresser and scrabbled around for the book.

"It's here," Epstein said. "I know it's here somewhere."

He continued rummaging around the handkerchiefs and socks, pushing things one way, then the other, in his frantic search for the address book. The heavy Colt .45 automatic lay next to his right hand, a clip inserted, but the chamber empty. Would Jonathan have time to swing before he could pull back the slide and jack a round into the chamber?

"Come on," Jonathan grated. "Find the damned thing. I want that guy's address. Then you and me are going for a ride to the precinct house."

That's what you think, Epstein muttered to himself, his right hand closing around the butt of the automatic. You might be going down there, but not me, pal. Burglar shot by apartment owner. Very sorry, he'd say to the police, but what else could I do? Aren't I allowed to protect my property?

His left hand worked the slide, and then both hands were bringing the pistol out of the drawer, swinging it around to bear on Jonathan's head. Jonathan saw the sudden action and swung wildly with the starting handle. It missed Epstein completely, crashing into the dresser, knocking over the framed photograph of his mother and late father. He tried to bring the handle back; his senses slowed as he saw Epstein's finger squeeze back hard on the trigger, harder still as the hammer remained cocked.

"Fire, damn you!" Epstein screamed.

The handle came around again, knocking the gun from his grasp. It sailed through the air and crashed against the wall which separated his bedroom from his mother's. Before he could move after it, Jonathan brought the handle down a final time, cracking him across the side of the head, knocking him senseless to the ground. He stepped over the still body and picked up the gun, curious as well as thankful that it had not fired. Unloading the clip and emptying the chamber, he squeezed the trigger. The hammer stayed where it was. Then Jonathan sat down on the bed as he spotted the small button on the side of the butt, feeling weak as he pressed it upward, faint as he squeezed the trigger and the hammer dropped.

He pocketed the gun and ammunition while he waited for Epstein to come around. When he did so, the first thing he saw was Jonathan's shoe; he looked up the trouser leg, past the coat to the face which stared down dispassionately.

"Better tell your mother you're going for a ride and you won't be coming back tonight," Jonathan said softly. "Otherwise she's going to worry about you."

The same patrolman was coming off duty when Jonathan marched Epstein into the precinct house.

"The other guy's name is Solly Kaye," Jonathan said, pushing Epstein to the desk; the union man's bruised head was turning an evil-looking purple. "You'd better see about this as well," he added, pulling out the gun. "He tried using it on me."

"You could have saved yourself a lot of trouble," the patrolman said, taking the gun, examining it. "If you'd have let us handle it, you could have been home in bed, nothing to worry about."

"He didn't try to burn your house down," Jonathan replied. "I took it sort of personally."

"I bet you did," the patrolman said, taking a close look at Epstein's head. "You still using a starting handle, or did you go in for a baseball bat after all?"

"Starting handle. My batting average was never that good." And both men laughed, leaving the pitiable figure of Epstein alone for a moment.

When he arrived home, it was after three. Opening the apartment door silently, he crept into the hall, hanging up his coat and tiptoeing onward like a housebreaker. It was to no avail; he caught the smell of tobacco and saw his father's outline by the window, sitting upright in a chair, staring out onto the street.

"I thought you'd be in bed," he said to Jacob.

"Who can sleep? While you're off chasing bandits, how can I rest?" Jacob stubbed out the cigarette and turned on a table lamp. "What happened?"

"Epstein's at the police station. And we've got the name of the other guy. Police are picking him up now. They'll both be charged with arson, Epstein with attempted murder as well."

Jacob's eyebrows rose. "Who did he try to murder?"

"Me. Pulled out a gun, but the safety was on and he never knew it. That was when I hit him."

"Hard? Like you hit the other man?"

"Harder. And across the head. He took ten minutes to come around."

"You're all right though?"

Jonathan looked down the length of his body. "Everything's where it's supposed to be. Can I ask for any more than that?" He tried to sound lighthearted, knowing that his father was worrying and would probably stay up all night.

"A real gun?" Jacob sounded amazed.

"A real gun," Jonathan said. "One with bullets in it. And I know what you're going to say next."

"What?" Jacob lifted his head in defiance. "How would you know what I'm going to say next?"

"You're going to say, what kind of thing is that for a Jewish boy to do, pull a gun on somebody, try to shoot them?"

Jacob nodded in agreement. "The son knows the father better than the father thought he knew the son," he said quietly. "A business like you have, and we must mix with gangsters."

"Not through my choice." Jonathan began to undress. "Are you going back to bed? Or are you going to make a cup of tea?"

"You want tea, I'll make you tea." Jacob puttered off into the kitchen, leaving Jonathan alone in the living room smiling as he heard the sound of water rushing into the kettle.

"You sure you don't mind going out with a tough guy like me?" Jonathan joked as he stood over Miriam's sewing machine. "Might get you a bad reputation, being seen in my company."

She smiled up at him. "I'm willing to take my chances on that. Anyway, according to everybody around here, you're a regular hero, not a tough guy."

"Unfortunately you don't get to be a hero unless you're prepared to be as tough and nasty as the next guy." He raised a beefy hand to his mouth, covering a yawn.

God, he was tired. It had been past four when he had finally crawled onto the living room couch the previous night, still half-dressed. He had sat up for an hour drinking tea with Jacob, smoking, telling his father everything that had happened at University Avenue, going over it again and again as questions were raised. Then, at seven o'clock in the morning, when he would have gladly given up the factory to stay in bed for another two hours, the police had telephoned, wanting extra information for his statement. He was kept at the precinct house till almost midday, answering more questions, identifying Epstein as the man who had tried to shoot him, pointing out Sally Kaye as Epstein's accomplice during the earlier fight.

At least that was one problem off his mind. Epstein wouldn't be around bothering anybody for a long time. Now all he wanted to do was forget the whole episode, drive it out of his mind for good. He wasn't pleased with the memory of wielding the starting handle, cracking it across Epstein's arm and his head, or breaking the other man's leg with it; he wished it had never happened, that they had never tried to start with the factory. But it was done, and there was nothing he could do about it. Epstein and his cronies would get sent up on his testimony, and that was the end of that. The only person Jonathan felt the least degree of sympathy for was Epstein's mother, the elderly woman whose belief that her son held a respectable position within the union had been rudely blown apart.

"You sure your parents don't mind either?" Jonathan asked Miriam. "Maybe they'd like you to go out with somebody a little milder."

"They don't know I'm going out with you. Do you think I tell them everything?"

"Guess not." He winked at her and walked away toward his father's office, knocking once and entering. Jacob was hunched over an adjustable drawing board, busily at work grading a pattern, using scales and instruments that never seemed to make any sense to Jonathan.

"You must have gone up in Miriam's estimation," Jacob said, laying down his tools. "After last night she must believe she has a real Sir Galahad."

"You as well, eh?" Jonathan chided him. "Wherever I go this morning I'm getting it. People clap me on the back, call me vigilante, say they wish they'd had the guts to do the same thing. I wish it was a year's time already. Epstein would be behind bars, and we'd have forgotten all about this business."

"My own son," Jacob grumbled, "fights a man with a gun, and I can't even talk about it. Give me grandchildren to talk about instead, and I'll stop already with last night."

Jonathan grinned hugely. "Don't hold your breath too long," he told his father.

# 6

The theater doors burst open, and the crowd spilled out onto the Broadway sidewalk. People congregated in small groups, talking excitedly, laughing as they remembered parts of the show. Others stood alone as they waited for friends to pick them up.

Jonathan elbowed his way unceremoniously through the mass of people, clearing a path for Miriam, who clung desperately to his hand, her purse dangling from the crook of her arm, banging against her side with every movement. When they reached the edge of the crowd, Jonathan slowed down, giving them the chance to catch their breath.

"It's like a stampede," he gasped. "I thought we'd get crushed to death before we made it outside."

Miriam laughed gaily, her hand remaining clasped in Jonathan's. "It was worth it. It was a wonderful show, and I've had a lovely evening. Thank you very much."

"It's not finished yet," he said. "I don't go to the theater that often, but I know that you're supposed to eat something after the show."

They walked north for a few minutes, Miriam leaning against Jonathan, feeling secure in his embrace. At the junction with West Fifty-third Street, where Jonathan had left the Chevrolet, they entered a restaurant. Jonathan pulled out a chair for Miriam before he sat down himself; seeing a waiter approach, he slid the menu across the table.

Miriam pushed the menu away. "Whatever you have will suit me fine. I'm still full from dinner."

The waiter hovered by the table, pad and pencil at the ready. Jonathan ordered coffee and cheesecake for two, waiting till the man had left before giving his full attention to Miriam.

"Do you ever get any comments from the other girls?" he asked.

"Somebody did ask me once whether I was seeing you outside the factory," Miriam replied. "You've been coming into the sewing room often enough in the past two weeks to create some speculation along those lines."

"What did you tell them?"

"No. Very sweetly and very simply."

"Thanks for lying."

"I wasn't lying at the time," Miriam said.

"Good enough, but from tonight you are. It might put you in an awkward position if any of the other girls found out."

The remark brought a wide smile to Miriam's face. "Not to mention the position it might put you in, Jonathan. You'd have every single girl in the factory making eyes at you."

"How do you know they don't already?" Jonathan was enjoying the repartee.

"I listen to the factory gossip," Miriam replied mischievously. "Every lunchtime while I eat my sandwiches I point my ears in a different direction. And they don't—at least not in the jacket factory."

Jonathan did his best to look crestfallen. "And that blows the whole reason for starting the business. My father was hoping that I'd find a wife among the girls. He has this tremendous fear of me remaining single all my life, something about tucking me into bed and reading me a story when I'm sixty. Looks like I've let him down."

"What did your father say about the other night?" Miriam asked, becoming more serious. "About Epstein, with the gun and the way you went up there?"

"If you can imagine a man being proud and worried sick at the same time, you've got him. He couldn't get over the fact that it had been a real gun." He shook his head, brushing back the thick black hair which dropped over his eyes. "Truth is, neither could I. I don't think I could move a muscle when I realized that he had left the safety catch on, how close he came to pulling that trigger." He saw Miriam's frightened frown and added, "I'm going to get that starting handle gold-plated and mounted on my office wall—when everything's redecorated, that is."

The waiter returned with their order. Miriam took one look at her portion of cheesecake and broke it in two with the pastry fork, pushing the larger part onto Jonathan's plate.

"You need it more than I do. You've got a lot more to fill up." She added a spoonful of sugar to the coffee and stirred it. "Who do you take after, Jonathan? Your father's not a big man. Where do you get your size from? Your mother's side of the family?"

Jonathan finished chewing a mouthful of cake, washing it down with the coffee. "My mother's dead. I never really knew her. She died when I was a kid, but from the old photographs my father's got, she was a very small woman. Guess I must be a throwback to some Cossack ancestor that nobody wants to talk about."

"Your father's nice," Miriam said, changing the subject abruptly to cover her confusion at causing Jonathan to reveal that his mother was dead.

"I'm surprised he's working in such a hectic business."

Jonathan wondered whether Miriam should be told the story behind the factory. Finishing the coffee, he ordered a refill. While he waited for it to cool, he began to talk about the small tailoring shop on Essex Street, glossing over the many problems, concentrating instead on the few warm memories he had of the place. Miriam listened attentively, her hazel eyes never leaving Jonathan's face.

When he had finished, she sat thinking about the tale. "So it's really Gellenbaum and Father. Gellenbaum and Son doesn't tell the whole truth."

"It does. Without my father, the place would never have got off the ground. He's forgotten more about suit construction than most manufacturers ever learned. He had to come in with me; otherwise there'd have been no factory. It was just a question of setting up the whole deal so that he couldn't refuse."

"And he couldn't say no if he thought you'd fall flat on your face without him," Miriam concluded. "Is that it?"

"Right on the nail."

"That's a lovely story, Jonathan. And the way you tell it, giving all the credit to your father, makes it even lovelier. I wish I could help my father in the same way."

Jonathan took a gulp of coffee. "What does he do?"

"Salesman in a furniture store. He's been there the past ten years, right through the worst of the depression, so we should be grateful about that, I suppose," she said. "It must have taken a lot of courage for you to open when you did."

Jonathan made light of the timing. "What better period was there? Everybody was going so crazy looking for business that I was able to pick up some good deals. And if you can make a dream come true during bad times, think how well you'll do when the sun comes out again."

During the drive to the Bronx, Jonathan continued to talk about the factory's history. He answered Miriam's questions, trying not to become too technically involved for fear of boring her. Parking the Chevrolet outside the apartment building, he cut the engine and sat back.

"Tomorrow?" he asked.

"Aren't you coming up? That was your condition on taking me out. Remember?"

Jonathan looked to his right at the building, wondering which windows belonged to Miriam's apartment. "Who's up there?"

"Just my parents, I imagine."

"What about your brother?"

"Myron's away for a week with some friends. Some tournament from the club he belongs to—baseball, I think."

"Don't you know?"

Miriam shot back an answer without thinking. "I don't know one ball from the other."

Jonathan chuckled deeply, the sound magnified in the confines of the car. Realizing what she had said, Miriam turned scarlet, thankful for the darkness which hid her blushing face.

"Come on," Jonathan said, not wishing to prolong her confusion. He got out and moved around to the other side of the car, holding open the door for her.

The lobby of the building was in semidarkness, two of the four bulbs in the lighting fixture having burned out. Miriam pointed to a flight of stairs to the right of the entrance.

"No elevator?" Jonathan sounded disappointed.

"Walking's quicker. The apartment's only on the second floor."

Standing outside the apartment door, Jonathan heard the sound of music from a radio. He watched Miriam fumble in her purse for the key, searching in the near darkness. Frustrated, she snapped the purse shut and rapped sharply on the door with her knuckles. The noise of the radio died down, and a woman's voice called out, demanding to know who it was.

"It's me, Miriam."

The voice from behind the door came a second time. "Forget your key again? One day you'll walk out of here without your head." There was the sound of a lock being turned, and the door swung open to reveal a middle-aged woman in a pink wool dressing gown, her harshly bleached hair in curlers. When she saw Jonathan, her mouth dropped open in amazement which changed to acute embarrassment as she realized how she was dressed.

Miriam's voice faltered as she made the introductions. "Jonathan, this is my mother." She saw the woman looking expectantly and added, "Jonathan's a friend of mine. He took me out tonight."

Jonathan stepped into the open doorway, his right hand held out. "Good evening, Mrs. Helman. Glad to meet you." The woman hesitated before taking Jonathan's hand in her own.

"Likewise," she responded. "You coming in?"

Jonathan entered the long, narrow hallway. Behind him, the woman closed the door, giving her daughter the benefit of a puzzled glance. "Why didn't you say you were bringing somebody back here?" Jonathan heard her whisper. There was no reply from Miriam.

Walking through into the living room, Jonathan came across a man whom he assumed to be Miriam's father. He was sprawled in an easy chair, eyes closed, shirttails outside his trousers, fast asleep. A newspaper was clutched loosely in his hands, spread across his chest as though he had been reading when sleep overtook him.

"You'll have to excuse us," Miriam's mother began to apologize. "We weren't expecting anybody." She walked across to the sleeping man and shook him roughly by the shoulder. "Sam! Sam! Wake up! We've got company. Miriam's brought her young man home."

Instead of feeling uneasy about the unforeseen reception, Jonathan had to fight hard to suppress a laugh. He found the whole situation vastly entertaining and felt that he had stumbled unwittingly onto the set of a Marx Brothers farce. At any moment he expected a closet door to fly open and a short figure with moustache and cigar to come bouncing out, offering to act as defense counsel for the sleeping man. He looked around to see how Miriam was taking it; she stared at him helplessly, a bemused expression on her face. He winked to reassure her.

Under his wife's proddings, Miriam's father awoke, blinking rapidly as consciousness returned. His hands tightened on the newspaper as he tried to figure out what it was doing on his chest. Then his eyes focussed on Jonathan.

"Sam, this is Jonathan, Miriam's friend," his wife said.

Sam stood up unsteadily, tucking his shirt back into his trousers. The newspaper fell to the floor, its pages separating around his slippered feet.

"Sorry," he said to nobody in particular. "Reckon I must have dozed off. What time is it?"

"Just after eleven, Mr. Helman," Jonathan offered. "How are you?"

"A bit ashamed of myself, if you want the truth," Sam admitted, shaking his head to clear the sleep. He smiled sheepishly for being caught asleep, and Jonathan took an instant liking to the man. "Miriam finally brings home a boy, and he finds me sacked out with my shirt hanging outside my pants." He shook his head, the rueful smile still on his face. "Can I get you a drink, Jonathan?"

"Coffee'll do fine, thanks."

Sam turned to his wife. "Fanny, where's your sense of hospitality? Jonathan wants a cup of coffee. While you're about it, I'll have one as well."

While Miriam went with her mother into the kitchen, Sam invited Jonathan to sit down. He picked a seat on the sofa, looking hopefully at Miriam's father, waiting for him to open the conversation.

"Miriam's never mentioned you before, Jonathan. Where do you know each other from?"

"We work at the same place," Jonathan replied easily.

"Oh, Gellenbaum's. You're in the factory."

Jonathan corrected him. "I'm on the sales side, the hard part of the business."

"Hard is right," Sam said sympathetically. "Selling's a damned hard life. You can never satisfy the customers; it just isn't possible. They're always thinking that you're trying to pull the wool over their eyes, pull a fast one on them, cheat them for a buck. Complaints, complaints and more complaints. If God himself came down and tried to sell some of my customers a piece of furniture, they'd reckon he was lying."

Jonathan recognized the sentiment and appreciated it wholeheartedly. He listened, genuinely interested, as Miriam's father recounted the things which had gone wrong in the furniture store that day; he appraised the man as he spoke, taking in the warm brown eyes, the thinning brown hair sprinkled with gray, the friendly, open face. When Miriam returned with the coffee, Sam was in the middle of describing a customer who had spent two hours deciding on a footstool, and Jonathan was thinking about Al Gilbert, wondering whether he could get his order finished in time while the repairs to the showroom and offices were taking place.

Miriam placed the tray on a table, passing coffee to her father and Jonathan.

"Where's your mother?" Sam asked.

"She'll be out in a minute." Miriam took a cup for herself and sat down next to Jonathan.

Sam sipped the coffee before laying the cup and saucer down on the arm of his chair. "Miriam's very happy at that factory," he told Jonathan. "Says the guy she works for is a real fine man."

Feeling Miriam's thigh press lightly against his own, Jonathan shifted his position slightly. "Jacob's a wonderful fellow," he agreed. "But the best one there's got to be the son. He's the brightest thing to hit the clothing industry in years."

Miriam had the cup to her lips when Jonathan made the remark; she spluttered violently, spraying the coffee over everything within a yard radius. Jonathan grabbed for the cup and placed it on the carpet while Miriam dabbed ineffectually at the damp stains on her dress. Sam stared wide-eyed at her, then at Jonathan, seeking an explanation for the outburst. Jonathan returned the look with a blank expression.

"What's the matter with her?" Sam asked. "Nobody said anything funny—leastways, not so far as I could see."

Miriam pointed a finger at Jonathan. "He is the son," she explained to her father. "It's his factory. The Mr. Gellenbaum I work for is his father."

Sam's reaction was very simple. His eyes resumed their normal shape, and he muttered, "Oh."

Jonathan apologized. "I should have said something earlier. Maybe I was just curious to see what Miriam had said about the place. It wasn't a very nice thing to do, and I'm sorry."

Sam took the apology in his stride. "If you were waiting for something bad, you'd have had to wait all night. The only time Miriam ever talks about the factory, she talks about your father. And it's all good." He stopped talking as his wife entered the room. Jonathan noticed she had brushed out her hair and put on a dress. She sat down, taking the remaining cup of coffee, and looked around for somebody to bring her up to date.

"I understand your son's away," Jonathan ventured, "playing baseball or something. Miriam couldn't remember what." He looked at her out of the corner of his eye, and she began to blush again.

"Myron the ballplayer," Miriam's mother said sarcastically. "He's got this big ambition that one day he's going to play down the road at Yankee Stadium. And his father encourages him yet."

"Sure! Why not?" Sam said, defending his absent son. "What's so terrible about playing baseball for a living? The boy's got a good arm and a good eye. Why not make money doing what he enjoys?" He looked to Jonathan, his chin stuck out belligerently. "His mother wants him to become a doctor or a lawyer, something boring like that. If the boy's a natural ballplayer, why shouldn't he make his living at it?"

Amused at being brought into what he could see was an argument of long standing, Jonathan was about to reply, but Miriam's mother got in first. "You only want him to become a ballplayer so you can get into the games for free and hang around with all those other bums. But what's going to happen when he gets older?"

Miriam threw both hands into the air. "Please!" she cried. "Can we not go into this now? We have a visitor, so can we leave Myron's career out of it for once?"

"Why?" asked Jonathan, grinning happily; he felt the evening was reaching a good climax, unlike any other time he had met a girl's parents. "It's a lively conversation, and I'm enjoying it. I like to watch a good game, and if your brother can make it in the big leagues, more power to him."

Miriam turned to him, her face flushed. "You're as bad as the rest of them," she said hotly. "You and Myron would get on like a house on fire."

"I'd like to meet him. He sounds like a kid who knows what he wants out of life."

Sam relaxed in the chair, nodding contentedly, happy at finding an unexpected ally late on a Saturday night. His wife, however, was not prepared to let the subject drop. "Knows what he wants all right!" she snapped, glaring at her husband's peaceful form. "Wants to be a sporting down-and-out. The Yankees!"

Jonathan stayed for another fifteen minutes, realizing that Miriam's parents—certainly Mrs. Helman—were not about to go to bed and leave him alone with their daughter. As he stood up to leave, Miriam joined him.

"I'll see you to the car," she offered. "You might get lost going down the stairs with the lights out."

He shook hands again with Sam, who seemed to be on the point of returning to sleep, said good night to Miriam's mother and left the apartment. Outside, he leaned against the side of the Chevrolet, arms folded across his chest, looking at Miriam.

"Well?" she asked pensively. "What do you think of the family, the Helman ogres?"

"I haven't had much experience of judging mothers, but I like your father. He and I have a lot in common. We both sell for a living."

Miriam began to apologize for the way the apartment had been when they arrived, but Jonathan silenced the excuses by laying a finger across her lips. "If the place had been decked out with ribbons and your parents dressed up in their best clothes with a band playing, I'd have been worried. They were better this way, more natural."

"No regrets about coming in then?"

"Only that I didn't get to meet the notorious Myron," Jonathan replied. "It seemed incomplete without having the cause of the argument around to stick up for himself."

"You'll meet him next week," Miriam said. "He'll be back from his baseball tournament then."

"Sure it's baseball?" Jonathan teased.

"I'm sure. Could it be anything else after that scene upstairs?"

Jonathan put his arms around Miriam's shoulders, bringing her closer to him. The top of her hair came up to his chin, and he had to bend sharply to bring their faces level. "See you about three tomorrow," he said.

Kissing her lightly, he released his grip on her shoulders and got into the car. Miriam watched him start the engine; he waved to her as he swung the car around and headed for the Grand Concourse. After the rear lights disappeared around the corner, she walked slowly back to the building entrance.

Sam Helman was still in the chair, leafing through the newspaper which he had salvaged from the floor, when Miriam reentered the apartment. His wife was in the kitchen washing the coffee cups.

"He's the big boss?" Sam asked, lowering the newspaper so that he could see his daughter.

"The nicest boss I've ever known. Do you like him?"

"Sure. Anybody who agrees that there's nothing wrong with a Jewish ballplayer must be one hundred percent okay."

His wife, returning from the kitchen, caught the last sentence and shot him a scornful glance. "You could have told us you might be bringing him in after your date," she said to Miriam. "God knows what he thought of me in curlers and a dressing gown, and your father fast asleep in the chair. Thank God he wasn't snoring his head off like he usually does."

"I never snore," Sam said indignantly.

"You do so!"

Miriam had to shout to make herself heard. "He's coming back tomorrow! Can we put on a better show than this?" Her parents forgot their dispute over snoring; as one, they turned to look at her. "He's picking me up at three, and we're going out," Miriam said. "No curlers, please."

Jonathan awoke just after eight the following morning. He tried to phone his father but received no reply and assumed, correctly, that Jacob was at the synagogue for morning prayers. After eating a light breakfast, he drove to his father's apartment, letting himself in with the spare key he kept for emergencies.

He was about to light his third cigarette when he heard his father's key in the lock. Dropping the unlit cigarette into the ashtray, he walked into the hall calling his father's name. Jacob stood framed in the doorway, a black Homburg hat set squarely on his head.

"Something wrong that you should be up so early on a Sunday?" Jacob asked.

Jonathan kissed his father on the cheek. "Nothing wrong. I called you earlier, but I figured you were at *shul.* So I came round to see you instead."

"I know. I saw your car outside." Jacob removed the hat and put it carefully on the top shelf of the hall closet. "And you rushed around to tell me about your evening with the Helman girl, right?"

Jonathan followed his father into the kitchen, where Jacob filled the kettle and placed it on the stove, taking two cups from the cupboard above the sink.

"I had a good time," Jonathan said. "I'm seeing her again this afternoon."

Jacob pulled a wry face. "Twice in two days? Here,"—he placed the palm of his hand on Jonathan's forehead—"let me see if you're running a fever. Maybe I should call the doctor. No," he said, removing his hand, "it feels cool. So what's so special about this girl that you should want to see her again so soon?"

"I don't know," Jonathan confessed. "But there's more to it than that. I want her to work downstairs with me in the showroom, when we get it back to normal. I don't want her in the factory any more. I think she's wasted up there."

"So why are you telling me all this? It's up to you."

"I want your opinion, that's why. I want to hear what you think about the idea."

Pouring boiling water into the teapot, Jacob thought over his son's proposal. "What would you have her do, Jonathan? Sit around all day and make conversation with you? That way nobody would get any work done around the place."

"We could do with somebody else in the showroom, full-time," Jonathan argued. "I'm getting too tied up in there when I should be out on the road. We need a proper, full-time showroom manager."

Jacob stirred the tea and replaced the top on the pot. "Jonathan, I've never been nosy about what you do. It's your affair, none of my business. I only know that having to run the showroom has never bothered you before. You've always taken it as part of your work. All I ask is that you think of the embarrassment if things don't work out." He returned his entire attention to the tea, spilling the first drops into the sink to clear any dust from the spout.

"Think about that, will you?" he asked. "Remember the chess games. Sit on your hands till you are absolutely certain that the move you are going to make is the right one. Don't let yourself get pushed into a corner you can't get out of."

Jacob poured the tea into two cups, handing one to Jonathan, who led the way into the living room; when they were seated, Jacob turned to his son, regarding him fondly.

"Do you know what really bothers me about this idea of yours?" he asked.

"Tell me and I'll know."

"You're taking away my best machinist," Jacob complained. "You could have had your pick of all the girls, yet you take the best. That's what really upsets me."

# 7

As the Chevrolet turned the corner into Miriam's street, a baseball bounced crazily across Jonathan's line of vision, spinning away past the car. He braked hastily as the ball was followed by a running youth, his chest heaving with exertion, oblivious to anything but his quarry. Jonathan leaned on the horn angrily, sticking his head out of the open window to shout at the boy. Remembering Miriam's brother, he dropped his voice.

"You Myron Helman?"

The boy did not stop running. "That's him up the street!" he yelled back. "The cripple who can't throw straight to save his life."

For a moment Jonathan continued to watch the boy as he caught up with the ball, gasping for breath as he stooped to retrieve it from the gutter. Then he put the car in gear and carried on toward the apartment building.

Myron was standing in the middle of the road, punching the pocket of his baseball mitt with a savage determination, completely unconcerned about the chase he had given his friend. As Jonathan came to a stop and got out of the car, the glove pummeling stopped.

"You must be Myron, right?" Jonathan felt that the question was unnecessary; the boy shared Miriam's hazel eyes and auburn hair, although his nose was far straighter than his sister's bob. His chest and shoulders had a look of strength about them which belied the age of sixteen that Miriam had quoted to Jonathan.

"That's me," the boy replied, affecting an air of swaggering toughness. He sauntered across to the car, studying Jonathan as if deciding whether he should be allowed any further. "You must be the boyfriend, the Casanova they're all going crazy about up there."

The choice of words set Jonathan back. Miriam's friend he could have expected, possibly even boyfriend, but the Casanova they're all going crazy about was too strong. "Something like that," he muttered at last, uncertain how to reply.

"Well I don't know if I'm any too crazy about you," Myron volunteered. He looked past Jonathan, his eyes narrowing. "Better watch your head or you'll lose it."

Jonathan ducked instinctively. A split second later the baseball flashed past two feet to his left. Myron put the glove across and snagged it backhanded, the leather closing around the ball the moment it connected with the pocket.

"Nice catch," Jonathan said, straightening up and looking back down the street to Myron's partner, wondering how confident the boy was of his aim.

"They're all nice. Doesn't matter how they go in as long as they go in." Myron appeared to take more interest in Jonathan. "You play at all?"

"If I did, would you be crazy about me as well?"

Myron's face split in a wide grin. "Could be. You'd have something going for you if you did."

"Sorry to disappoint you. I don't have the time to play, but I watch occasionally."

Myron's next question was short and sharp. "Who?"

Remembering the argument which had taken place on his first date with Miriam, eight days earlier, Jonathan had his answer ready. "The Yankees, of course. Who else is there?"

Dropping the ball into his glove, Myron thrust his right hand out at Jonathan. "Put it there. I'm getting to like you already. You know how to make the right impression on people." Jerking the gloved hand toward the second floor, he added, "She's waiting for you, if you're interested. They've all been going mad, running around with brooms and mops. Of course, if you'd rather stay down here and play ball, we could always find you an extra mitt."

Jonathan pretended to think over the offer. "Thanks all the same, but I think I'd better go on up. If they've been cleaning up in my honor, it's the least I can do."

He began to walk toward the building entrance, stopping after a few strides. "Let me have the ball," he said, swinging around to face Myron. "See if I can do any better than you." Cocking his right arm, Jonathan threw the ball mightily at the other boy. It sailed five feet over his head and disappeared down the street, bobbing unevenly as the boy gave chase again.

Myron's voice was loaded with sarcasm. "Pretty good, coach. Maybe you'd be better off upstairs with the old folk."

"I'm going. Just make damned sure you don't put any dents in my car," Jonathan warned.

Myron eyed the small Chevrolet speculatively. "How about a ride in the rumble seat?"

"Only if there are no dents in the bodywork when I come down."

"You got it, coach." Myron looked away from Jonathan as the baseball came rocketing back from the other end of the street. He held the glove out in front of his face; the ball hit the pocket with a satisfying thud.

Jonathan rapped once on the apartment door, wondering while he waited for an answer if Myron had been serious about the preparations for his visit. He heard the lock being turned; then Miriam stood in front of him wearing a pale blue dress, her eyes sparkling with anticipation. Looking past her into the hall to see if either of her parents were watching, Jonathan kissed her and entered the apartment. Closing the door, she turned to follow him.

"I finally met your notorious brother," he said. "Quite a character."

"That's one way of putting it," she answered, smiling. "We thought we'd lost you for a moment there. Saw you talking to him and figured you'd be down there all afternoon."

"I was just showing your brother how to throw. He almost took my head off when I drove around the corner."

"You didn't do much better," Miriam said. "I was looking out when you made your spectacular attempt."

"But it's not my life's ambition to play for the Yankees."

"Don't start that again, for God's sake," Miriam said quickly. "You'll have my mother jumping onto her high horse."

Walking into the living room ahead of Miriam, Jonathan saw her mother sitting down, a pair of knitting needles flashing busily in her hands. Sam Helman stood by the window watching his son's progress. The older man shifted his position as Jonathan entered.

"Quite some arm you've got there," he said in greeting. "Made my son's friend run a few yards."

Uncertain whether he was being offered a compliment, Jonathan inclined his head modestly. "Good to see you again, Mr. Helman." He acknowledged Miriam's mother, who laid down her knitting and smiled up at him.

"They're going to get into trouble, Sam," she said, moving her eyes to her husband. "Mark my words, they'll smash a window or put a dent in somebody's car, and the police will be round here in a flash, just like last time. You'll see." She looked back to Jonathan. "Is your car downstairs?"

"It'll be okay," Jonathan assured her. "Myron gave me his word that he'll look after it." He felt Miriam's hand on his arm, drawing him off to one side.

"Let's get away before we're waylaid," she suggested. "Everybody means well, but I want to be with you. I don't want to share you."

"Five minutes," Jonathan whispered. "Let me be polite." Remembering what Myron had said, he added, "Your brother claims that you've all been cleaning up like mad. I feel like an honored guest."

Miriam bit her lower lip as she felt her face redden. "I'll kill him. He knows better than to say things like that." Seeing the smile on Jonathan's face, she relaxed. "We didn't do it for your benefit," she pouted. "Sunday's our regular day for cleaning the apartment."

Jonathan chatted with the Helmans for a few minutes before excusing himself and Miriam. They walked out of the building into the sunlight where Myron and his friend were examining the Chevrolet.

"Thinking of buying it?" Jonathan asked.

The boys spun around, surprised by Jonathan's voice. Myron began to say something in reply, but the look on Miriam's face stopped him. As she advanced, determination in her every step, he retreated rapidly.

"I'm finished with you, Myron Helman," she snapped, surprising Jonathan with the vitriolic quality of her tone. "Don't ever ask to borrow money off me again. Don't even speak to me or come near me."

Laughing, Jonathan grabbed her arm as she closed on Myron. "Leave him alone. That's what kid brothers are for, to annoy older sisters."

Seeing a supporter, Myron stopped backing away and began to toss the baseball into the air, smirking cockily. His friend stood off to one side watching warily, leaving open an avenue of escape; he was quite prepared to let Myron receive his sister's wrath by himself.

Jonathan felt Miriam loosen under his grip. "I suppose you're right," she said. "But just once, I'd love to clip him round the ear."

"He'd probably clip yours right back. He's bigger than you are and a lot stronger. Now how about making up with him?"

While Jonathan and Myron waited, Miriam debated the suggestion. Myron's friend continued to hover on the periphery, uncertain whether to stay or run for his life.

"Go on," Jonathan encouraged her. "Ask if he'd like to come for a ride with us."

Unable to believe what she had heard, Miriam pivoted sharply to face Jonathan. He nodded slightly. "I promised him a ride in the rumble seat if he didn't put the ball through a window."

Miriam looked up at the sky, at the clouds which were becoming heavier, threatening to blot out the sun. "What if it rains?"

"What do you think? Your brother gets wet."

Miriam's smile held an impish quality as she regarded her brother. He watched cautiously, his weight balanced on his right leg, ready to flee at the first sign of a resumption in hostilities.

"Would you like to come for a ride with us, Myron?" The voice oozed sweetness. "Jonathan says he promised you one."

"Serious?"

"Serious."

Myron's earlier bravado returned. "Sure. Why not?" He pulled the glove off his left hand, tossing it and the ball to his friend, dismissing him in favor of the preferable opportunity. "Rumble seat?"

Jonathan walked to the rear of the car and opened the occasional seat. Myron hoisted himself in grandly, clowning, waving to the second-floor window where the Helmans were watching. "Drive on!" he shouted.

As Jonathan opened the passenger door for Miriam, she walked past him to the rumble seat. He watched as she stood behind Myron, who, unaware of his sister's presence, was still playing to the gallery his parents provided. Without warning, Miriam playfully clipped him across the back of the head; then she ran back to where Jonathan was standing.

"I had to do it," she giggled breathlessly. "He's never been that defenseless before."

Closing the passenger door, Jonathan walked to the back of the car. Myron was glaring indignantly through the rear window at his sister, muttering to himself.

"Behave yourself," Jonathan said. "One wrong word and I'll fold you up for the rest of the day."

Myron swivelled in the seat, looking up at Jonathan. "I think you would," he said slowly, appreciating Jonathan's build. "I really think you would."

Winking to confirm the fact, Jonathan walked to the driver's side and got in, slamming the door. "Where to?" he asked Miriam.

"How about Central Park Zoo? We might be able to lose Myron."

Jonathan started the engine. "He won't cause any trouble back there. If he does, I'll reverse into a wall. Were you really mad at him before?"

"It's a game. He calls me all the names imaginable, and a minute later he comes to borrow money, claiming that nobody ever had such a sweet, wonderful sister. Perpetually broke, that's my brother. He spends every cent on baseball, watching the Yankees, buying magazines, equipment. If Lou Gehrig was charging twenty bucks just to say hello, Myron would somehow find the money to be first in line." She sat quietly for a moment while Jonathan laughed, happy that she had said something intentionally funny.

"I've lost count of how much he owes me, but he's a good kid really. Helps around the apartment with whatever he can. Works part-time to bring in some money."

Jonathan caught a glimpse of Myron in the mirror, making faces at them through the window, crossing his eyes and sticking out his tongue. "I think you scared his friend more than you scared him," he joked.

"Story of my life," Miriam said. "I always scare off the wrong people."

Jonathan looked at her curiously, not asking her to explain. "What was that your mother said before about the police coming around if Myron broke something, just like last time?"

"Oh, God," she said. "I was hoping you'd missed that line. He and a couple of friends were playing stickball out in the street one day, and they put the ball right through somebody's front window, one of the houses opposite. You've never seen such a commotion in your life."

"Who hit the ball?"

"Who do you think?" she replied blandly, as if the answer should be obvious. "Myron, who else?"

"What did the police do?"

"Nothing. Especially after Myron told them it was the best line drive he'd made in ages and it was a damned stupid place to put a front window anyway. My father had to pay to replace the glass."

"Must have loved that."

"Myron could demolish the building, but as long as he did it playing some form of ball, my father would never complain. Only my mother gets upset, and she goes too much the other way."

Parking near Columbus Circle, they walked into the southern end of the park. People thronged the walkways and crowded the lakeside, throwing bread to the birds, strolling, watching, enjoying the day of rest. Myron picked up a flat pebble and skimmed it across the water, watching in fascination as it bounced three times on the surface before sinking; widening ripples marked the place of its demise. He bent down, searching for another suitable stone. Miriam hissed at him and he stood up, scowling at her.

Jonathan watched the brother-sister duel with a feeling of amusement. He was in two minds—thankful that he had no elder sister, yet curious how it would have felt. Simultaneously he was realistic enough to know that his emotions for Miriam would hardly have been the same had she been his sister.

Discouraged from skimming more stones across the lake, Myron put one hand in his trouser pocket, pushing his free arm through Miriam's. "Better take the other one, Jonathan," he suggested. "I don't suppose anybody's told you yet, but she suffers from dizzy spells, fainting fits where she does strange things. Last time we came down here, it took four cops to get her out of the lake." He rolled his eyes for emphasis.

Miriam breathed in deeply. "You'll get it, Myron," she whispered. "Just keep going."

Arms linked, they walked across the park to the small zoo. As they neared the buildings, Myron let go of his sister's arm and ran off.

"Now what's he up to?" Jonathan asked.

"Gone to see his twin. Whenever we went to a zoo as kids, he'd run off and fool around at the monkey cage."

They continued walking, following the direction taken by Myron. There was a crowd in front of one cage, and Jonathan, looking over people's heads with ease, could see that Myron had pushed his way to the front. He was standing opposite an ape, inside the safety bar, jumping up and down and making faces at the animal. The ape stared back blankly, occasionally scratching itself.

Jonathan watched the performance, as amused as anybody else until he saw a zoo attendant walking toward the cage, quickening his pace as he neared, intent on learning the cause of the abnormally large crowd.

"Myron!" Jonathan yelled. "Time to leave."

Warned in time, Myron spotted the attendant pushing his way through the crowd. He dropped his hands, bent underneath the safety bar and made his way back to Jonathan and Miriam. Some of the spectators applauded as he passed them; grinning hugely at the acclamation, Myron bowed from the waist.

"You're an embarrassment," Miriam grumbled as they walked away. "I feel ashamed to be seen with you. Why"—she turned to Jonathan—"why you ever invited him to come along is beyond me."

"I was curious about your tolerance level. It's low."

It began to rain as they drank coffee, safe underneath the canopy of a restaurant in the park—not heavy rain, a light drizzle which, nevertheless, had a piercing quality to it. Thirty minutes passed as they waited in the restaurant, hoping that the bad weather would blow over, watching the park become deserted as people left in search of shelter.

"Make a run for the car?" Jonathan suggested eventually, resigning himself to the rain lasting all afternoon. He stood up and put some money on the table; then the three of them ran back to the car.

"What about me?" Myron asked as they reached the Chevrolet. "Where am I supposed to sit?"

"The same place you sat on the way up here," Miriam replied immediately. "It'll pay you back for that disgusting display at the monkey cage."

"Great!" Myron exploded. "Just great. I'll catch pneumonia, and you'll rob the Yankees of the best second baseman they're ever likely to have. The name of Miriam Helman will be blackened for eternity in the legend of Yankee Stadium." He tried Jonathan. "Can't you squeeze me inside the car?" he asked hopefully.

"Only two seats inside." It was difficult to look genuinely sorry for Myron's predicament, but Jonathan managed it. "Rumble seat or nothing. Sorry."

"How about I sit in front with Miriam on my lap?" Myron suggested, beaming at the simplicity of the solution. "I guess I could put up with her under the circumstances."

His elation was short-lived. "Not so likely," Miriam told him. "You can sit in the rumble seat or take the subway home. Make your mind up."

"I haven't got money for the subway."

"Enough!" Jonathan held up a hand to stop the argument. "I'm getting soaked listening to the pair of you. Look, I live near here. We'll go up to my place till the rain finishes. You won't get too wet during that ride."

"I suppose not," Myron conceded, slumping his shoulders in an exaggeratedly weary fashion. "But if I die of exposure, be it on your head." He waited for Jonathan to open the rear, then climbed into the seat.

Inside the car, Jonathan looked back. Myron was sitting very straight, arms folded resolutely across his chest, staring ahead, a look of martyrdom on his face as the rain, now much heavier, coursed down his skin and flattened his auburn hair.

Jonathan nudged Miriam; she slid around and looked at her brother.

"I feel almost guilty sitting in here," Jonathan said. "I'm bone-dry and comfortable, and Myron's getting a soaking."

"Don't feel guilty. My brother's an actor, hamming it up for our benefit. He's also as strong as an ox. Rain won't do him any harm; it never stopped him from playing baseball."

Jonathan headed out into the traffic, glancing at Myron's reflection every few seconds. "I'm sure your brother can take it. I'm just wondering what damage the rain will do to the rumble seat."

"Myron's more important than your rumble seat."

Jonathan took his concentration off the road long enough to squeeze Miriam's hand. "That's what I knew you'd say."

He was not certain when the decision was made. Perhaps it was while he watched Miriam protectively insist that her brother remove his wet clothes and wear Jonathan's dressing gown, the arguments forgotten. Or maybe it was while he watched her at the stove, preparing omelettes for the three of them, making herself at home immediately in the unfamiliar kitchen. Jonathan was not sure of the exact time of the decision; all he was certain of was that he would marry this girl, this little slip of femininity whose fragile slightness made his own bulk look even more ponderous.

While Miriam cleared the plates after the meal, Jonathan sat at the table mulling over the decision. Even the sight of Myron, threatened with engulfment by the oversized dressing gown, did nothing to distract him. I'm twenty-six, he thought, and the only deep relationship I've ever had with anybody has been with my father. He surveyed the apartment, furnished well but with little taste, wondering how it would look if Miriam had been responsible for its appearance. He looked back to the kitchen, seeing Miriam drying the plates before putting them away, his eyes resting on her face. Then he switched to Myron, noticing again the family likeness.

"Nice place you've got," Myron said, a moustache of milk framing his mouth.

Jonathan only half heard the statement. Myron repeated it, uneasy about conducting a conversation with Jonathan, the youthful bluster of the afternoon having disappeared.

"Thanks," Jonathan said. He snapped into full awareness abruptly. "How would you like to do me a favor and see yourself home, Myron? It's still raining hard, and you'd only get wet again in the rumble seat. Plus I want to be alone with your sister for a while."

The knowing grin which began to form on Myron's face dropped away as he realized how out of place it was. "Sure, so long as you spring for a subway token."

"You're a bum, you know that?" Nevertheless, Jonathan dug into his pocket and flipped a quarter across the table. "Keep the change," he said generously. "Just make certain your clothes dry quickly."

Balancing the coin on his thumbnail, Myron flicked it high into the air, catching and dropping it into the pocket of the dressing gown in one fluid movement. He pushed himself away from the table and walked into the bathroom where his clothes were hanging. As he passed Miriam, he patted her on the rear, speeding up as she spun around; the dishcloth in her hand flashed spitefully at his ear, but he was gone.

When he returned two minutes later, he was fully dressed, with Jonathan's dressing gown folded over his arm.

"They dry?" Jonathan asked.

"Dry enough. I'll take my chances on pneumonia."

Miriam looked from Jonathan to her brother, anxious to learn what was taking place.

"Got the money?" Jonathan asked.

Before Myron could reply, Miriam cut in. "What money?" she demanded. "Has he been bumming off you, Jonathan?" She turned on Myron. "Have you?"

"Forget it," Jonathan said. "I'm paying him for services rendered."

"What services?" Miriam asked suspiciously.

"Leaving us and going home by himself. That's one hell of a service rendered."

Myron pulled the quarter from his pocket and held it up for Miriam to see. "Two bits," he said, mocking his sister. "A lousy two bits, and that includes the subway fare home. Obviously he doesn't think you're worth any more."

Jonathan suppressed a grin. "You're wrong there. I think Miriam's worth a lot more. But you,"—he pointed a finger meaningfully at Myron—"that's all I think you're worth. Now beat it."

Dropping the dressing gown over a chair, Myron kissed his sister good-bye. As he opened the apartment door, he called back, "Jonathan, I hope you haven't wasted your quarter." He laughed hugely at the joke and closed the door hurriedly.

"What was all that about?" Miriam asked, still mystified.

"I wanted some time alone with you. Your brother's a nice enough kid, but there's a time and a place for him. My apartment, right now, is neither the time nor the place."

Miriam finished clearing up, then walked to where Jonathan sat at the table. She stood behind him, her arms around his shoulders, caressing his lightly. "Why did you want him to go?"

Jonathan craned backward to look into her face. "I had a date with you, not with the New York Yankees infield."

"Why did you ask him to come for the ride?"

"To make friends. I thought he'd get bored and we'd be able to ditch him in an hour." He pointed to the chair which Myron had been using. "Sit down, Miriam. I want to speak to you." He waited while she made herself comfortable.

"Wasn't much of a day, was it?" he said. "Maybe we should give each other a rain check."

"I enjoyed it. Didn't you?"

Jonathan nodded slowly, the huge head moving back and forth. "It was a good day for making my mind up about certain things."

Miriam's interest quickened. "Such as?"

He stared straight into Miriam's eyes, noticing the green flecks on the pupils for the first time. "There's a couple of things. I need somebody to work with me downstairs, running the showroom. Would you like that?"

Miriam cocked her head to one side; it was not the question she had been expecting, and she needed time to think. "What would I have to do?"

"Run the showroom. Simply that. It's better than playing tunes on a Singer sewing machine."

"That's all?"

"You'd have to marry me as well. That's part of the deal. Everything has its price, even advancement."

"Marry you," she repeated quietly. Picking up the glass Myron had been using, she toyed with it, watching the white dregs slopping around the bottom. "Jonathan, I've always lived with the idea, foolish as it may seem, that the man I married would propose in a more romantic way, not include it as part and parcel of a job offer." She replaced the glass on the table and laughed lightly. "After all, any proposal has got to be more romantic than the one I just received from you."

"I never had the time to see romantic movies," Jonathan said, feeling it to be an ample explanation. "I only say what I think is right."

Stretching her hands across the table, Miriam laid them on Jonathan's, feeling his knuckles underneath her fingertips. "What will your father say? Does he know?"

"He has an idea. And he's upset about me taking away his best machinist."

"After only a few dates?" Miriam was smiling.

"I think we know each other a bit better than that. And my father would like nothing more than to have you as his daughter-in-law."

"I couldn't think of a nicer father-in-law."

Jonathan jumped on the words. "Is that a yes, or is it just something nice to say about my father?"

"I can't give you a yes, Jonathan—not until you ask me a question. All you've done so far is state that I'd have to marry you as a condition of becoming showroom manager." The smile gave way to a look of intense seriousness. "Do you think you could do a little bit better, Jonathan?" she pleaded.

He stood up and walked around the small table. Bending forward, he brought his face to within inches of Miriam's. "Will you?"

Two words, she thought. And she smiled, knowing that those two words were about as close as she was going to get to the hoped-for, romantically phrased question.

"Yes." Barely was the word out of her mouth when Jonathan pressed his lips down hard on hers, bruising them with the urgency of his feelings. She pulled away slightly, shocked by the sudden pressure. Then she responded, standing up, her arms snaking around his neck, pulling him closer, pressing the length of her body against his, feeling him straining against her.

Slowly she relaxed her grip and drew away, creating space between them, her face red, skin hot. Jonathan stood silently, his arms still around her waist, refusing to let her move any further.

Frightened at the sharpness of her own passion, Miriam sought a refuge, a hideaway where she could gain time to put her thoughts together. "Jonathan, at the zoo this afternoon, I remembered something you said that evening you took me home from the factory after Mike Epstein tried to stop me."

Jonathan barely kept his tone level. "What was that?"

"You asked if your father had ever mentioned Central Park and a horse. What did you mean by that?"

"He took me there one Sunday afternoon when I was about four years old, not long after my mother died. A policeman on a horse came toward us. My father gave me a piece of sugar—God only knows where he got it from—to give to the horse. Only when I held up the sugar and this great ugly beast stuck its head down, I got scared." He shifted uneasily as the memory became clearer.

Miriam became genuinely curious, no longer playing for time. "What happened?"

Jonathan cleared his throat before he spoke again. "I wet my pants. My father and the cop thought it was the funniest thing they'd ever seen. They were hysterical, falling all over the place. The cop had to get down off the horse before he fell off. And I was standing there dripping. Even the damned horse was laughing."

Miriam kissed him again, a light, brushing touch of the lips which held none of the frantic urgency of the earlier kiss. "I hope you've grown out of it by now," she whispered.

"I thought I had, but it feels as if I've just succumbed to a related problem."

A narrow shaft of sunlight found its way through the window of the bedroom, gently caressing the bottom of the bed, bathing Miriam's calves in a soft light. She gazed at the band of light for a moment before laying her head back, reaching out for the crumpled pillow next to her. Through the open door she could hear Jonathan moving around the apartment, the sound of water running in the bathroom, then the closing of a door. When he reentered the bedroom, she began to draw the sheet over herself, an instinctive defense, until she realized how out of place it would seem.

He stood in the doorway wearing only a pair of gray trousers, a shirt held in his hand as he gazed down at her, taking in her whole body. "How you feeling?"

"How should I feel?" she replied dreamily.

He began to slip into the shirt, doing up the buttons from the bottom. Miriam had never seen it done that way before.

"If I told you I felt marvellous, what would you say?" she asked.

"I'd say, how else could you possibly feel?" He gave her a huge grin as he turned back into the living room looking for his tie.

Miriam lay on the bed for another five minutes before getting up and putting on the dressing gown Myron had been wearing. If it had been big on her brother, it was like a tent on her. She had to fold the sleeves over twice; even then the hem reached well past her feet, and the shoulder seams came almost down to her elbows.

"Coffee?" Jonathan asked as she stepped carefully into the kitchen, taking care not to trip over the dressing gown.

"You make coffee for yourself?" She tried to sound astonished.

"Proper little cook I am. Long as it's in a can, I can cook it."

She sat down at the table and prepared to be waited upon. When the coffee arrived, half of it was slopping around in the saucer.

"Pour it back into the cup," Jonathan suggested, doing so with his own. "Doesn't make it taste any worse."

"You really do need somebody to look after you, don't you?" she said. "Do you ever cook anything, seriously now?"

"Eggs occasionally. They're like eggs Florentine, but you don't get them so often."

She leaned back in the chair and giggled. "Jonathan," she gasped. "You're absolutely precious."

"You really think so?"

She nodded happily.

"No regrets about before?"

"Regrets?" she repeated, puzzled by the question. "Why should I have regrets?"

He looked down at the coffee for a moment, taking his time in answering. "Whenever you lose something, there's always some degree of regret."

"No regrets," she assured him. "There are some things in life that are meant to be lost."

"Good." He seemed genuinely pleased. "Now you'd better get out of that ridiculous dressing gown and into your own clothes. If we don't get back to the Bronx soon—what with Myron and his big mouth—your parents will send out the police."

Saliva glistened wetly on the heavily chewed end of the cigar as Al Gilbert
leisurely removed it from his mouth. He studied the cigar for a moment
before replacing it, gripping the end with his teeth, biting hard but not with
sufficient pressure to disintegrate the leaves completely. A small flake of
wet tobacco became detached from the cigar, and Gilbert picked it off his
lips with a fingernail, wiping it on his open vest.

He sat behind a desk in the office at the rear of the West Thirty-fourth
Street store—the main one of his chain—his jacket on the back of the chair,
tie undone, shirt sleeves rolled up above his elbows to expose fat, white,
hairless arms. In his hands were the figures for the preceding week, black
and white evidence of the difficult times his group of five stores was facing.

The depression's over, he thought grimly; that's what people keep
telling me. And I'm having a harder time now to maintain profits than I was
during the worst years. He looked up and down the columns of figures
again, hoping that he might have missed something, a small detail which
would have brightened the dismal picture. But nothing changed. With a
sense of desperation, he laid the sheets of paper on the desk top and stood
up to ease the cramp of prolonged sitting.

Gilbert's office was well furnished. The mahogany desk and his high-
backed chair dominated the room, squatting in the middle of the rich,
green carpet like a monarch's throne. Although Gilbert's own chair was soft
and padded, the two chairs facing the desk were conservative and less
comfortable, a psychological touch by which the retailer could feel above
whoever entered the office to speak with him. Around the stained wood
walls were two easy chairs, a sofa, and Gilbert's personal executive toy, an
aquarium.

It was to the aquarium that he now walked, watching the tropical fish
dart through the clear water, play hide-and-seek among the ornaments,
seek the algae on the inside of the glass. Gilbert reached up for the box of

fish food which was kept hidden on a small bookshelf and began sprinkling it onto the surface of the water, watching spellbound as the fish forgot their previous interests and concentrated on the offerings. He dipped a finger into the water, just breaking the surface, feeling his pets nibble at the skin thinking it to be another source of food.

Tired finally of playing with the fish, Gilbert withdrew his finger. He straightened his silk tie and rolled down his shirt sleeves before donning his jacket. Inspecting his appearance in the mirror by the door, he grunted approvingly; then he opened the door and stepped out into the store. It was a moment he always enjoyed, when the vastness of the group's major outlet beckoned to him like a woman's welcoming arms.

Only now the store was empty of customers, the clothing displays looking as neat and contrived as when they had been arranged that morning. Salesmen stood around, pretending to be busy as they heard the door open, not wanting to meet Gilbert's eyes. They knew only too well that he had cut staff mercilessly at the other four stores as sales had declined; they were fearful that similar action would follow at West Thirty-fourth Street if trading results did not improve.

Clasping his hands behind his back, Gilbert strode forth. He relished the sensation of being king, pushing it to the extreme with his salespeople, knowing that there were not enough positions available elsewhere for them to defy him. Taking his time, he walked across the store to a rack of ready-to-wear suits, the first of the new shipment from Gellenbaum and Son that he had put on display. As he neared the rack, he thought about the change which was taking place within the industry, how the traditional made-to-measure service was losing popularity to these ready-to-wear styles. He had no trouble envisaging the situation in twenty years when ready-mades would dominate the market. Customers would no longer have to wait six weeks between ordering a suit and receiving it; in the future, they would be able to see what they were getting immediately. Gilbert had been a men's wear retailer long enough to know that a salesman had to sell a made-to-measure suit twice: once when the customer placed the order, a second time when it was returned from the factory fully made up, and the customer shook his head and said he didn't think it would turn out like that. Now the approach was changing. Ready-to-wear clothing was the coming way of doing business. No more fabric swatches lying around the store for customers to dither over, no more problems in taking and relaying measurements to the factory, where somebody else would put his own interpretation on them. Nothing other than a straightforward transaction, money for goods, not a deposit for a promise. Gilbert was pragmatic enough to realize that with ready-to-wear he would have to carry a larger inventory with more money tied up in stock, but that one disadvantage was outweighed heavily by all the positive factors. Shirts come ready-made, he thought, so why shouldn't suits?

He stopped in front of the rack, looking in amusement at the back of a salesman who was still trying to look busy by checking the sizings of the suits to ensure they were hanging in the correct order.

"Give it up, Len," he said. "You're not fooling anybody, least of all me." He watched the man stiffen as he heard the voice. "If you want to do something useful, go out into the street and drag in a few guys with empty wardrobes and full wallets."

The man turned around, shamefaced at having been caught in the pretense. "Sorry, Mr. Gilbert. Just thought I'd see that the sizes were in sequence. Makes them easier to find that way."

Gilbert examined the salesman, the half-hidden blue eyes running lazily over the man from top to bottom, verifying that he was clothed completely in store merchandise. It was a hard and fast rule which Gilbert had laid down years earlier that all his employees buy from the store; they received a minute discount as an incentive, and Gilbert wanted each man to act as an unpaid advertisement.

"What do you think of them, Len?" Gilbert asked, gesturing at the suits.

The salesman fawned over Gilbert. "I think they're great, Mr. Gilbert—fashion details, construction, price, everything. Just great. Fantastic."

Gilbert silenced him with an imperious wave of the hand. "Cut the crap, Len. I'm not a customer. I want to know if you think we're doing the right thing by getting involved so heavily in the ready-to-wear market. Or should we stick solely with the measure trade?" He waited impatiently for the answer, eager to see if his employees agreed with his trend of thought and, even more important, whether they could see the coming changes which he could.

The salesman thought carefully before answering. "I guess we're doing the right thing, Mr. Gilbert. Out of ten customers who come in to buy a suit, if we can fit three, even four off the rack, we're doing ourselves a big favor. We're saving time, and we're getting the dollars quicker. Saves waiting around for the finished suit to come back from the factory and taking the money then."

Gilbert nodded, inwardly pleased that the man was bright enough to know which way the market was heading. "What about the styling details, Len? And don't hand me that line of crap you did before."

"I like the suits, Mr. Gilbert. They've got a clean line which makes a man look good. But..."

"But what?" Gilbert snapped, annoyed by the salesman's reticence. "Say what you think."

"I don't know about the lapel buttonhole."

"What about it?"

For answer, the man pulled a jacket from the rack, poking a finger through the buttonhole to emphasize his point. "Are these things really functional, Mr. Gilbert? Who needs a buttonhole any more? Nobody wears flowers these days. I think they tend to break up the line of the lapel. They detract from the jacket, not add to it."

Gilbert reached out for the jacket. "Here, let me see that." The salesman yielded the garment to Gilbert, who poked his own forefinger through the hole, an idea forming in his mind.

"Is there anything else you want, Mr. Gilbert?"

Gilbert looked up from the jacket, seeing the salesman's worried face. "Yeah," he said sharply, "about two dozen big spenders." Putting a hand into his pocket, he withdrew a fistful of silver. "Here," he added, thrusting the money at the salesman. "Buy the boys some coffee with my compliments."

He walked back to his office, the jacket hanging over his arm. The salesman watched, stunned by Gilbert's uncharacteristic show of generosity. Inside the office, Gilbert sat down behind the desk and began to search through his files for the delivery notes and confirmation of order from Gellenbaum and Son. Buttonholes, he thought, looking for the documents. Buttonholes. Simple little things—a work of art, some manufacturers say. Why the hell didn't I think of something like this before? It has to be some dumb jerk of a salesman who puts me on the right track.

Locating the documents, Gilbert began to read the details. Eight hundred suits had been delivered so far, two hundred for the main store and the remaining six hundred split between the other four stores; there were two hundred suits still to come. And that meant eight hundred left-hand lapels had been delivered so far, each with its own little buttonhole, its own useless piece of ornamentation.

The salesman was right. Who needed a buttonhole any more? Who wore flowers these days? Lapel buttonholes were nothing more than a useless frippery, a throwback to an earlier era, which added extra cents to the cost of each jacket.

Grinning malevolently, Gilbert reached a pudgy hand across his desk and picked up the telephone.

The diamond ring sparkled with fiery life as Miriam looked at it for the hundredth time that morning, watching how the main stone and then the cluster caught the light, breaking it up and relaying it as a myriad of colors, each seeming more brilliant than the last display.

Two months had passed since Jonathan had proposed to her on that rainy afternoon after the aborted visit to the zoo, and still she had difficulty in believing that it had happened. It was not the fact that he had proposed, but the speed with which he had accomplished it. Nothing that fast had ever happened to any of her friends. None of them could boast of a proposal after only eight days. And deep down she had known it would happen that afternoon; she could not explain the origin of this knowledge, but to Miriam that was unimportant.

When Jonathan had driven her back to the Bronx that night, timing it before the Helmans went to bed, her parents had been stunned into silence by the suddenness of the news. Her father had been the first to recover, kissing her, hugging Jonathan enthusiastically, shaking hands with him over and over, calling him son. Her mother had remained in the chair for a full thirty seconds, as if refusing to believe what she had heard. Then she, too, had congratulated them, albeit not with her husband's fervor. Even Myron, fully dried out from the soaking he had received in the Chevrolet's rumble seat, had been happy for her; she smiled, remembering how he had said that she would have to lend him some money if she expected a wedding present. And had her parents known anything, could they have guessed what had happened in Jonathan's apartment after Myron had been bribed to leave? The shine in her eyes must have betrayed her—or had her happiness at making the announcement disguised her other joy?

And Jacob—perhaps that was what had given her the most pleasure. He had looked horrified when she had first called him Mr. Gellenbaum after revealing the news of the engagement.

"My son has no respect for his father," he had joked. "He calls me Jacob unless he wants something. My daughter should do the same. Perhaps then I would not feel so old." How overjoyed he had been at the tidings, how proud to see his son settle down!

Working now in the renovated showroom—which showed no evidence of the fire bomb attack—Miriam missed Jacob; there was no reason to see him regularly during the day. Being with Jonathan, however, when he was in the office, more than made up for any sense of loss brought about by the move.

She heard the telephone ring in Jonathan's office and waited for the secretary to answer it. It rang a second time, then a third, growing increasingly insistent as each summons remained unanswered. Miriam walked to the partitioned area where Jonathan worked; he was out, and so was the secretary.

"Gellenbaum and Son," she said, picking up the phone on Jonathan's desk. "Miss Helman speaking; can I help you?"

She listened as the speaker identified himself, asking for Jonathan. Checking the desk diary, she saw that Jonathan would not be returning to the office till late afternoon and relayed the information to the caller.

"Tell him to get in touch with me the minute he gets in," the voice at the other end of the line said brusquely. "Have you got the message straight? It's Al Gilbert and it's important."

"Yes, Mr. Gilbert," Miriam replied before realizing she was talking into a dead phone. She left a note on Jonathan's desk, placing a copy of it on the secretary's typewriter.

When Jonathan returned just after five, Miriam passed on the message before the secretary could do so, adding that Gilbert seemed upset. Jonathan listened, his mind racing as he tried to think what the problem could be. But he could think of nothing. Gilbert's order was all up to date; there could be no complaints about that.

Expecting something out of the ordinary, Jonathan shut himself in the office and dialled Gilbert's number.

"Al Gilbert." The voice which answered was gruff.

"Al, it's Jonathan Gellenbaum. I've got a message to call you. What's your problem?"

"You, Jonathan. You're my problem—you and that damned bunch of garbage you sent me for fall."

Jonathan screwed up his eyes in disbelief. "What the hell are you talking about, Al? You're not making any sense. Do you mean those ready-to-wear suits we're delivering to you?"

"That's exactly what I mean. They've all got buttonholes on the lapel. I never asked for buttonholes. I never wanted the damned things. Yet you've gone right ahead and given them to me."

"For Christ's sake, Al!" Jonathan yelled. "All my suits come with lapel buttonholes."

"I'm not interested in all your suits, Jonathan. I'm only worried about the ones you send to me. Those buttonholes break up the whole line of the jacket. My customers don't like that. And the one thing I do know is what my customers like or dislike. That's what my business was built on, an understanding of my customers' tastes. That's why I specified no buttonholes."

Jonathan gripped the receiver fiercely, pressing it hard against his ear. "Listen to me, Al. You made no such specifications. You wanted the merchandise just the way the samples were. You saw the lapel buttonholes when you ordered." While he spoke, he thought back to the meeting with Gilbert when the retailer had placed the order. Had anything been said about lapel buttonholes? No; he remembered the meeting distinctly. No change to the sample specifications had been suggested. Besides, what the hell was Gilbert playing at, complaining when the bulk of the order had been delivered, not when the first suits had arrived in the store, which would have given time to change some of the following merchandise?

"Al." Jonathan dropped his voice, seeing no sense in indulging in a shouting contest. "What's taken you so long to phone me? If you wanted to raise the roof, how come you didn't do it with the first delivery a few weeks back?"

"I never noticed," Gilbert explained glibly. "The store managers check the deliveries for their respective stores. I don't get myself involved in mundane operations like that; my time's too valuable. One of my boys at West Thirty-fourth Street brought it to my attention today. He distinctly remembered us deciding that we wanted to break away from the lapel buttonhole, and he thought it worthwhile mentioning."

"Is he there now?" Jonathan interjected. "I want to speak to him."

"Of course he's here now," Gilbert replied sharply, "but I don't see what difference it makes. You're speaking to me, and I'm being straight with you. Those suits are useless to me."

Jonathan looked through the office window into the showroom and saw Miriam peering in, curious about the earlier shouting. He lifted a hand and waved at her.

"What the hell am I supposed to do with those suits, Al?" he demanded, still looking at Miriam. "They're your order, and you've got to pay for them."

Gilbert's voice became conciliatory. "I'll pay for them, Jonathan. Don't get yourself in a turmoil over that. But I'm not paying for your mistakes. I want a discount, something to make it worthwhile for me to keep the suits."

With Gilbert's last words, the whole meaning of the complaint became clear to Jonathan. So that's what he's up to, the sly, conniving bastard. He's got me over a barrel because I can't shift the stuff anywhere else; he knows it and he's capitalizing on it.

"You've had eight hundred delivered so far, right?"

"Yeah. Eight hundred. That's across the five stores. I'm still owed two hundred. Say, is it too late to stop the buttonholes on those?"

"I think so," Jonathan said. "I'd have to ask my father, but I think the suits have already been cut. They're probably being sewn right now. Anyway, what do you reckon your discount's worth?"

The answer came back without the slightest hesitation, confirming Jonathan's suspicion that Gilbert had engineered the whole situation.

"Five bucks a suit."

Jonathan whistled quietly. Five dollars a suit, five thousand dollars in all—a nice round figure which would knock the stuffing out of any profit he hoped to make—and more.

"That's a lot of discount, Al. I'm in business for myself, not just for your benefit."

Sensing that he was winning, Gilbert pushed the point further. "Take it or leave it, Jonathan. You've still got my business on measures. You'll make enough profit on that to compensate for this mistake. I reckon I'm being nice about the whole thing, offering to keep the suits. If I refused to, you'd be stuck but good."

"I know that," Jonathan grunted, stalling for time, trying to think his way around the problem. "It's a decision I can't make on my own. My father's got to have a say in the matter, Al."

"Your old man!" Gilbert bellowed. "What's it got to do with him? You run the show, Jonathan, not your old man."

The prospect of losing five thousand dollars blotted out the reference to the old man. "What time will you be in the office till?" Jonathan asked. "I'll speak to my father and then I'll get back to you."

"Better make it tomorrow, Jonathan. I'm leaving in a minute. Besides,"—Gilbert laughed coarsely—"there isn't much you can do about it, unless you want to try eating a thousand suits, all with buttonholes in the lapels, for dinner over the next few months. You'll see. My way's the only way. You should be thankful I'm being so easy about the whole thing. If I didn't think so much of you, Jonathan, I'd tell you where to shove the lot."

Jonathan waited till Gilbert cleared the line; then he smashed the receiver down onto the rest, his eyes blazing, the veins on his forehead standing out like ropes. When he looked up, Miriam was standing in the doorway, frightened by the fury on his face.

"Al Gilbert," he rasped, as if that explained everything.

Miriam stared, uncomprehending. "What's he done?"

"Us! He's pulling a fast one, and I can't see any way out of it." Giving himself a few seconds to calm down, he explained the situation to Miriam, adding how much it would cost the company.

Miriam refused to share Jonathan's pessimism. "Is there nothing we can do?" she cried. "There must be some avenue we can take."

Jonathan shook his head, the heavy locks of black hair falling onto his forehead. Irritated, he brushed them back roughly. "Nothing I can think of at the moment," he said glumly; the position looked worse to him with each passing second, as the skillful simplicity of Gilbert's swindle became even more apparent.

"We could sue," he said, "but what good would that do? The most critical time is the immediate future when we'll need the money to pay our own costs. Even if a court found in our favor, we'd be bankrupt and out of business by the time the case came up. We could take the suits back. That'd hurt Gilbert, sure, but he'd overcome that by buying inferior merchandise from elsewhere. Whichever way you look at it, we come off hurting the most." Forgetting that Miriam was in the office, he let his anger out by slamming a clenched fist down onto the desk top, making papers jump into the air.

"Take it easy," she whispered. "Everything'll work out."

Her calmness made Jonathan feel foolish at the display of temper. "See if Jacob's in, will you?" he asked. "Let's see what he's got to say about it."

Miriam dialled Jacob's extension, passing the instrument to Jonathan when his father answered. "We've got troubles with Gilbert," he said tersely. "Can you come down for a few minutes?" He replaced the receiver, more gently this time.

"Think you could make us some coffee?" he asked Miriam, forcing himself to smile. "We're going to be here for quite a while."

Miriam disappeared into the small kitchen behind the office, returning five minutes later with three cups of coffee. She placed them on Jonathan's desk, using cardboard mats to prevent the surface from being stained. Then she sat down, saying nothing, leaving Jonathan alone with his worries.

With Jacob, Jonathan's explanation was brief. He rattled off the highlights of the conversation with Gilbert, describing how a five-dollar discount would affect the company's financial standing.

Jacob stroked his chin thoughtfully. "What else can we do?" he asked eventually. "It seems that Mr. Gilbert has put us into a position from which there is no escape. You know and I know that there was never any mention of lapel buttonholes when he made the order, but that means nothing now." Jacob's voice held a note of utter resignation as he continued.

"We both knew the type of man we were dealing with, Jonathan. We had heard enough about him, seen with our own eyes what he was like. Perhaps we should have made him sign the order and not dealt with him as trustingly as we deal with our other customers. Possibly his business is not all it should be, and he's looking for a way to ease his difficulties. Five thousand dollars from us might go a long way in that direction. Now I fear that we will have to cut our losses, take his offer and never deal with him again."

Jonathan listened to his father's opinion, feeling it in line with his own thinking. He looked to Miriam, more out of politeness than from a hope that she would have a plan of action.

"Have you got anything to add?"

"Yes, I have." Miriam's voice was sharp, reminding Jonathan of the Sunday afternoon when she had taken off after Myron outside her parents' apartment. "I don't know that much about the business side of the industry, but I think you're both making a big mistake by letting this crook run roughshod over you." She paused long enough to take a breath, carrying on before Jonathan had a chance to say a word.

"You fought back like a madman only a few months ago when you were threatened by the union thugs. You didn't take *that* lying down. Why are you acting so differently now? This man Gilbert's doing the same thing as Epstein was, only he's going about it in a different way. They're both trying to take your hard-earned money out of your pockets."

"This is nothing like the same situation," Jonathan tried to explain. "Epstein was a gangster, nothing else. Al Gilbert's just trying to pull a sharp piece of business. I can't go after him with a starting handle. I'd finish up in jail. What he's trying to do..."

"What you're letting him do, you mean," Miriam cut in.

"What I'm letting him do," Jonathan said, taking a deep breath, "is done every day by a hundred different businesses. But he'll only do it once with us."

"And that once could be enough to put us out of business. Once, Jonathan," she said heatedly, "is all it needs." She switched her attention to Jacob, who had been watching the exchange with a bemused expression on his face. "You're both splitting hairs about this. Gilbert and Epstein are the same, only they go about their crooked business in different ways. One keeps a faint cloak of respectability about his operations, while the other one didn't give a hoot what anybody thought of him."

Despite the seriousness of the situation, Jonathan could not help smiling at Miriam's spirit. "What do you reckon we should do?" he asked, an unintentional note of condescension in his voice. "Spring Al Capone from jail on the condition that he does away with Gilbert? It wouldn't work. There's supposed to be honor among thieves."

Miriam sat with her lips pressed into a thin line, waiting for Jonathan to finish. "You're picking an unfortunate time to make jokes," she reprimanded him.

He held up both hands in a peace gesture. "Sorry. But what would you do? I'll grasp at any reasonable straw."

"See if you can rent a store for a week," Miriam suggested. "There's plenty of space around. You must be able to find an agent who'll help."

"What good would that do?" Jacob interrupted, mystified by the course the discussion was taking.

"Let her finish," Jonathan said. "I think I can see where she's heading." He nodded at Miriam to continue.

"We take all the suits back from Gilbert, every single one. That'll hurt his business to begin with because he'll have to compromise to fill up the gaps in his stock. Then we sell the suits ourselves," she said triumphantly.

Jacob's look of mystification became total. "How will we sell them?" he asked faintly. "We're manufacturers, not retailers. We don't know anything about dealing with the public."

Jonathan cut in before Miriam could answer the question. "We don't have to sell them. They'll sell themselves because they'll be on offer for almost wholesale prices," he said, supplying the logical ending to Miriam's argument. "That's what you had in mind, right?"

"Exactly. We take our normal selling price and add on an extra margin to cover the cost of renting the shop and publicizing the sale."

Jacob remained unconvinced. Without even thinking about it, he pulled the gold watch from his vest pocket and began to toy with the chain. "I don't know," he muttered. "I still think we should let Mr. Gilbert have his victory this time."

"No," Jonathan said firmly. "And will you stop calling him Mr. Gilbert? The man's a pig; he doesn't deserve the respect of being called Mr. anybody. We can kill two birds with one stone here, get rid of the suits and give Gilbert a smack in the eye at the same time. I like it. I think it's a great idea. What kind of advertising do you think we'll need?" he added, to Miriam.

"Handbills, circulars. Saturate the area—offices, stores, residential— the lot. I'm sure Myron could get together some of his friends and spend a day passing out the handbills." She sat upright in the chair, her fists clenched in excitement.

"I've got it!" she enthused. "We take a shop on the same block as Gilbert's. And we make it a big one-day sale, the same suits which Gilbert's has been selling, but at considerably reduced prices. We must get rid of most of them, and if he's pulled this trick because business is bad, maybe we can finish him off."

The desire for vengeance made Jacob see his future daughter-in-law in a new light. The sweet, obliging girl who had worked for him in the sewing room had disappeared; in her place was a sharp-minded young woman. "That's not a very pleasant attitude to take," he scolded her gently. "I thought we were trying to rescue ourselves, not drown somebody else."

Jonathan glanced sideways at his father, marvelling at the older man's charitable stand. "I don't think any of us is feeling pleasant as far as Gilbert's concerned," he said. "Right now I'd like to stick the point of my shoe in his fat face. But you're making a good point. If we can give Gilbert a fat lip at the same time, all well and good, but getting rid of those one thousand suits is the main objective." He turned to Miriam. "How about taking a ride uptown this evening, seeing what stores are available?"

"Good idea. We'd better get going as soon as possible."

"Want to come?" he asked Jacob.

"I'll leave this sort of thing to you, Jonathan. You handle it a lot better than I do." He stood up to return to the second floor. "Just let me know what happens."

On the block where Al Gilbert's main store was located, Jonathan and Miriam found three empty stores. The interiors were in darkness, but he estimated that they were the same size as the Gilbert operation, and each would offer suitable space for stocking and selling the suits he intended to pull back. Making notes of the agents' names, he took Miriam home to the Bronx.

The following morning, he telephoned the agents, beginning with the one responsible for the store only four removed from Gilbert's. The man was not interested in a short-term arrangement; neither was the second agent Jonathan called. As he dialled the number of the third on the list, he decided to offer a large lump sum for the use of the store, not wait till the agent told him that the premises were not available for a short time.

The immediate mention of money had its desired effect. The agent explained at great length that it was not his company's policy to let on such short terms, but as Jonathan was willing to pay in advance a sum well above the normal rent, he was quite certain that normal procedures would be waived.

Satisfied, Jonathan put through his call to Al Gilbert. The phone was answered on the third ring, and Jonathan could picture the fat retailer sitting in his office, trying to appear completely unconcerned.

"Al, Jonathan Gellenbaum here about those eight hundred suits we've delivered, plus the two hundred you've still got on order." He decided to let the man enjoy his false position. Jonathan was risking everything by taking back the suits, and he was determined to extract the greatest possible pleasure from the situation.

"Glad to hear from you, Jonathan. Did you talk it over with your old man?" Gilbert asked.

"I had a big discussion with my father about it last night."

"Is that so?" Jonathan could almost see the man drooling into the mouthpiece as he anticipated agreement on the five-dollar discount. "What did you come up with?"

"My father agrees with me one hundred percent, Al. Say,"—Jonathan paused as if an idea had suddenly taken shape—"none of your stores has sold any of those suits yet, Al, lapel buttonholes and all?"

Gilbert laughed at the question. "No, Jonathan. Sorry, but we haven't sold a single unit." He had taken them out of the selling areas, placing them in storage until he heard from Jonathan. "If we had, I'd have given you full price on anything that went. I'm a fair man, you know that. But I think we're going to have to drop our own price to get rid of them. I'm doing you a big favor by keeping those suits, really sticking my neck out for you. Anybody else, I'd tell them to come round and pick everything up. But I value our relationship."

I bet you do, Jonathan thought sourly. Anybody you think you can take for five grand must offer a valuable relationship. "That wasn't what was bothering me, Al. I just wanted to make sure you still had all the suits."

There was the faintest hesitation from the other end of the line, as if Gilbert had suddenly become aware that all was not as he had envisaged it. "What do you mean by that, Jonathan? I don't follow you."

Grinning openly, Jonathan resisted the temptation to shout into the mouthpiece that he was pulling back the whole order. Instead, he drew out the conversation, relishing the shock he was about to hand the retailer.

"I also value our relationship, Al. You're a good customer, one of our best. You must be, because you keep on telling me that you are."

"Glad you see it that way," Gilbert responded, lulled once again into a feeling of security. "These things happen to everybody once," he added patronizingly.

"Guess they do," Jonathan agreed. "And we wouldn't dream of doing anything that might inconvenience you."

The sensation of doubt nagged at Gilbert again. "What are you trying to say, Jonathan?"

"I reckon you're doing us a big favor, Al. But if things don't work out for you, and you get stuck with the suits because your customers don't like buttonholes, I'd feel pretty bad about it."

"Don't worry about that, Jonathan. I'm a good enough merchandiser to shift them."

"No. I won't hear of it, Al," Jonathan said resolutely. "I don't want you to take a chance of being burned because of our incompetence, so I'm taking all the suits back."

He heard nothing but Gilbert's labored breathing. Then the receiver exploded with such sound that Jonathan was forced to move it away from his ear.

"You're doing what!" Gilbert screamed.

Jonathan's voice was cold, unemotional; the charade was over. "You heard me right, Al. I'm taking them back. I want every last one of those eight hundred suits. Pull them back from your stores, and we'll arrange to pick them up Thursday afternoon."

Gilbert's voice maintained its screaming pitch. "You won't get away with this! You're welshing on a deal, Gellenbaum! I'll sue you, your company, your old man, everything!"

"What deal?" Jonathan asked caustically. "You claimed yesterday that the deal wasn't worth a damn because the styling specifications weren't as they should have been. I'm doing the honorable thing. I don't want to see you get stuck with our garbage." His voice took on a harsh, grating tone. "Just make damned certain those suits are ready to pick up by Thursday afternoon, Al—every last one of them. No damage, nothing missing, just the way they were delivered to you. There'll be hell to pay if anything's missing or damaged."

"You can't do this to me, Gellenbaum!"

"Al baby, I can and I have. Tough." He cut off Gilbert's continuing protestations by hanging up. Sitting back, Jonathan felt the tension which he had been concealing finally escape in the perspiration which sprang to his forehead.

Hearing the end of the conversation, Miriam entered the office. "How did he take it?"

"Get that worried look off your face and I'll tell you."

Miriam's lips, which had been pursed in anxiety, curved upward into the faintest of smiles. "Well?"

"He wasn't very happy. And he wasn't entitled to be, having just been given a massive kick in the teeth. All we've got to worry about now is that we come out smelling like roses. Otherwise..." He let the word hang in the air.

"Otherwise what?"

"Otherwise we'll all be wearing a rose in our buttonholes for the next century, you included."

Miriam walked around the desk, sitting on the edge, facing Jonathan. "Do you really think we've done the right thing, Jonathan? Jacob's very worried about it."

"What's wrong with you all of a sudden?" he asked. "When you came up with the idea yesterday, thirsting for Gilbert's blood, you were all excited about it. Now you're hedging around. What's going on in that mind of yours?"

Miriam swung her legs back and forth, watching them. "Of course I'm concerned. I'd be stupid if I wasn't. But what happens if the whole thing goes sour on us and we can't get rid of the suits? Gilbert gets egg all over his face, and we come up holding the broken shell."

Reaching out his left arm, Jonathan encircled Miriam's legs, pulling her along the shiny desk top toward him. "It won't go wrong," he said soothingly. "Have some faith in your own ideas."

She bent forward and kissed him, the touch of her lips warm on his own. "You're right, Jonathan. It's a brilliant idea from a brilliant person. How could it go wrong?"

# 9

Late Wednesday evening, as the last workers left their Manhattan shops and offices, a large gray Gellenbaum and Son delivery truck drew up outside the empty store on West Thirty-fourth Street, just east of Sixth Avenue. Jonathan jumped out of the driver's side while Miriam and Myron clambered out of the passenger door. They met at the rear of the truck, where Jonathan opened the double doors. Inside was a collection of clothing racks and full-length mirrors borrowed from the factory. Taking a key from his pocket, Jonathan passed it to Miriam, who unlocked the front door of the store, holding it open with a toolbox which Jonathan brought from the truck. Then he and Myron began the task of unloading.

When the racks were in the store, all standing against one wall, Jonathan helped Myron to bring in the mirrors and a length of curtain track. While Miriam watched, they installed the track across the rear of the store, hanging up mismatched lengths of suiting fabric to form hastily improvised changing rooms.

"What do you think of your brain wave now?" Jonathan asked Miriam as he replaced the tools in the box by the door.

Miriam looked around the store; apart from the fixtures they had brought, it was completely empty, nothing but plain wooden flooring and a faded, embossed paper covering the walls. "I don't know. I don't think I'd buy a dress in a store that looked like this. But then, I'm not being asked to," she added with a smile.

"How about you, Myron? What have you got to say?"

Myron shrugged his shoulders. "Suppose you know what you're doing," was his noncommittal comment.

"What about your side of the operation?" Jonathan asked. "Are your pals all geared up to go?"

"What a question," Myron shot back. "Of course they're ready. When I drop my hand, they'll hit the whole neighborhood, stuffing flyers into the mailboxes of every office, every residence, every store other than clothing stores in the area. This time tomorrow night, the whole area will be three feet deep in paper."

"How many flyers did we get printed up?" Miriam asked.

"Twenty thousand," Jonathan told her. "Myron's friends have got their work cut out to deliver that many, no matter what he says."

Miriam began to estimate the cost. "Anything else?"

"We've got signs going into the window on Friday, and we're paying four people to come in from the factory to help sell. Oh, and there's two private cops we've hired for the day."

At the mention of police, Myron became more interested in what was going on. "What are they for, to keep the crowds back?"

"Nice thought," Jonathan said. "But do you know how much money we'll finish up with if we're lucky?"

"Hadn't thought about it."

"Myron, we're trying to get rid of one thousand suits. We'll need some protection if it all goes right."

Myron narrowed his eyes to slits as he had seen gangsters do in the movies. "Wow," he whispered. "I think me and a few of the boys'll knock over this joint come Saturday night."

Jonathan grinned at the antics of his future brother-in-law. "Just make sure you don't get knocked over in the rush when we open the doors on Saturday morning," he warned. "Otherwise six of your friends'll be carrying you by the handles. And I don't think you've got six friends."

"Okay, coach. You got it."

Much to his parents' disapproval, Myron cut school on Thursday afternoon. He arrived at the factory shortly after one, gulping down a sandwich with Jonathan before they drove to the empty store. They went inside just long enough to take a rack apiece, which they wheeled along the sidewalk to Gilbert's.

Pausing outside the store, Jonathan faced Myron. "Ready? If you want to back out, now's the time to do it. This is where the fireworks might begin."

"Ready whenever you are, coach. Let's go see the man."

"Knock off the gangster act, Myron. Word might get out that I've got a spotty-faced, teen-age hoodlum working for me."

"You're going to have one for your brother-in-law," Myron laughed. "That's even worse for your reputation."

Jonathan pushed open the door, allowing Myron to precede him into the store. There was no sign of Gilbert. Telling Myron to wait with both racks, Jonathan walked through the store, ignoring the salesmen's curious looks.

"Al," he said, stepping unannounced into Gilbert's office. "I'm here for my merchandise. Where is it?"

Gilbert remained behind the desk. "Sit down, Jonathan." He waved at the chairs facing the desk. "Let's talk about this misunderstanding, work it out like two sensible businessmen. We must be able to come to some sort of arrangement."

"This is my arrangement," Jonathan said evenly. "I've got men waiting outside to take delivery. Now where are the suits?"

Gilbert eased himself out of the chair and padded across the carpet toward Jonathan. "I was only kidding about that discount. You know how I am, trying to shave a cent here, a cent there. I'll pay your full price."

"Five bucks a unit isn't a cent here or a cent there," Jonathan said. "Now tell me where my goods are before I get mad."

Gilbert opened his mouth to add something, but the set of Jonathan's face stopped him. He pointed meekly at the door. "Out there. Some of it's in the store, the rest is in the basement."

"In good condition, I hope."

"In good condition, just like when it was delivered. You realize I'll never deal with your company again."

Jonathan allowed himself the faintest of smiles, a curling of the lips which contrasted with the hardness of his eyes. "Maybe that's the reason I'm doing it this way, Al. You'll run out of suppliers long before I run out of customers." He left the office, whistling for Myron to join him with the racks.

Comparing against the initial order for size and cloth specifications, Jonathan wheeled the suits two hundred yards along the sidewalk to the empty store, returning to Gilbert's with fresh racks. The whole exercise took the best part of three hours, while Gilbert watched with mounting fury, and his salesmen with worried eyes, knowing that the removal of most of the chain's ready-to-wear stock could bode nothing but ill for their future security.

As Jonathan wheeled the final rack out of the store, it occurred to him that Gilbert did not even know what the suits were going to be used for. He had taken it for granted that the retailer would have heard about the impending one-day sale, but Myron's friends had purposely missed all clothing stores when circulating the handbills.

"Aren't you even interested in what I'm going to do with these suits, Al?" he asked. "Surely there must be some curiosity underneath that double-dealing hide of yours."

Gilbert spat the words back. "I don't give a good goddamn what you do with them. Just get out of my store."

Deliberately Jonathan delayed the final exit. Myron stood in the doorway, eager to see what would happen, unconcerned for Jonathan's safety; his size alone would prevent any problems.

"I feel obliged to tell you, Al. As you were such a good customer, it would be unfair to keep anything from you." He pulled a sheet of white paper from his pocket, unfolded it and held it out to Gilbert. "You know the empty store down the road, just before Sixth Avenue?"

Gilbert nodded fractionally, his head moving no more than an inch, a fearful comprehension dawning. "What about it?" he rasped between clenched teeth.

"Listen to this, Al. You'll love it for its sense of business acumen." Clearing his throat, Jonathan began to read.

"This Saturday, for one day only, treat yourself to the same top-quality suits you used to find at Gilbert's, but at substantially reduced prices." He looked at the retailer, grinning maliciously. Then he told him the prices.

"You cheap son of a bitch!" Gilbert screamed across the store. "You double-crossing pig! I'll..."

Jonathan drew himself up to his full height, dwarfing the chubby retailer. "You'll do what, Al?" he asked softly. "Tell me what you'll do. I want to know." He waited, left hand still holding the flyer, his right hand clenched into a hamlike fist. Gilbert made no move to do anything, much to the disappointment of Myron, whose estimation of Jonathan had just increased to the level he usually reserved for Yankee ballplayers.

"Here, Al. Read the rest of the information yourself," Jonathan said. "It's not the greatest advertisement you'll ever see, but it tells the story." He stuffed the sheet of paper into Gilbert's breast pocket, crushing the blue silk handkerchief. "Keep it as a souvenir, Al, in case you want to buy something from us on Saturday. Maybe next time you'll be honest with your suppliers."

He turned around to help Myron push the final rack onto the sidewalk. As they walked away from the store, Myron was staring at Jonathan with unbridled admiration.

Jonathan arrived at the store shortly after seven on Saturday morning, relieving two of Myron's friends who had slept overnight on the premises as a security precaution; a similar arrangement had been operated on Thursday night.

He busied himself for an hour checking that the one thousand suits were arranged by jacket size and fabric pattern, and that the makeshift changing rooms were as clean as could be expected under the circumstances.

The two policemen from the private security agency arrived as he finished. They discussed the forthcoming sale with Jonathan, suggesting that the rear entrance to the store be locked permanently; that way there would only be one exit to guard against shoplifters. One man would stay on the front door the whole time to control the crowd outside, while his partner would wander around the store keeping an eye open for irregularities.

Shortly after, the additional help from the factory arrived. Jonathan talked to them as a group, advising them how to act during the sale. He knew that the environment was alien, but they would be able to measure and fit customers correctly; he doubted that there would be any need for hard selling tactics.

"Don't let a customer take more than one suit at a time into the changing room," he advised. "Don't listen to arguments about seeing which one looks best—just one garment at a time. It'll be pretty confusing around here today, and shoplifters thrive in those conditions. We're all rookies on this side of the business. We're facing a whole gang of problems we never even knew existed. If we can keep tabs on what goes into the changing rooms, we won't get any merchandise walking out of the front door. And keep an eye open for people with large shopping bags or clothing that seems too big. While your back's turned, one of these characters can do the disappearing trick with a couple of suits." He looked around to see if there were any questions.

"I don't have to stress how important today is to the factory, to all of us. You've stuck by me once before, when we had that little bit of trouble with the union"—somebody in the audience laughed at Jonathan's description, and he was forced to smile himself—"and now I'm asking you to stand by me again, to help me out of another mess. We're in a big hole at the moment because of our fat friend down the street. But if we get through today, and I know damned well that we will, we'll be in better shape than we've ever been. We'll have a better company, and everybody's job will be more secure." He studied each man fondly, placing them in the different sections of the factory where they worked. "Take care, and good luck to you all."

The queue began forming at eight-thirty, ninety minutes before the advertised time of opening. When Miriam arrived just after nine, she had to fight her way through the crowd of people lined up outside the store. She was rescued eventually by the guard at the door after one of the factory helpers recognized her. From time to time, Jonathan looked through the window at the mob of people outside and smiled as he pictured each man in the line wearing a Gellenbaum suit. It gave him a warm sensation, and, as he watched the line grow even longer, he knew it would soon be a reality.

He looked back into the store to see Miriam busying herself sweeping the floor in final preparation. "Do you want to take all the credit for the way today's going to turn out?" he asked. "Or am I allowed to keep some of it for myself?"

Miriam held the broom upright, leaning on the end. "I'm happy with the way it's going already," she answered, "and we haven't sold a single thing yet."

A sharp rapping noise on the window made him swing around. The guard at the front had the door open and was talking earnestly with a patrolman who was tapping his nightstick against his leg.

"What's the problem?" Jonathan asked.

"You're causing an obstruction," the patrolman replied, pointing with the nightstick to the queue which stretched for more than twenty yards. "People can't get into other stores or walk along the sidewalk. What time do you plan on opening?"

Jonathan pointed to one of the signs in the window. "Ten."

"Sorry, sir. You'll have to open up right now. Otherwise I'll break it up."

Jonathan checked his watch; nine-fifteen, still forty-five minutes left until the advertised opening time.

"What are you going to do, sir?" the patrolman insisted. "You'd better make a decision quick, before somebody phones in a complaint to the precinct house."

Jonathan nodded to the security guard. "Let 'em in." He turned into the store and clapped his hands loudly. "Get ready back there. We're opening early."

From behind came the sound of sudden movement, the noise of people surging through a narrow opening, scrambling to be first at the merchandise. They burst through the door, holding together in a tight bunch as they got their bearings. Then they exploded like a bomb burst, shooting off in all directions. The sales staff stationed themselves strategically, ready to help, watchful for shoplifters.

"See if you can keep it down to twenty or thirty at a time!" Jonathan yelled at the guard on the door. Then he grabbed the nearest customer by the arm and pulled him around. "What are you looking for, sir? Perhaps I can help you."

"Sure. What have you got in plain blue, my size?"

Jonathan waited until the man had unbuttoned his jacket, then ran a tape around his chest. "You're a forty, sir. We've got just the thing for you over here." He gripped the man's arm and led him over to a rack.

Miriam went out just after midday, returning with cups of welcome, steaming coffee and an assortment of sandwiches which Jonathan and his people digested as best they could. Twice during the afternoon, Miriam broke away from the crush and walked along the block, peering through the front window of Gilbert's. Jonathan was pleased when she reported that neither time had she seen any customers in the store.

As arranged, Myron arrived at five in the afternoon to help clear up and remove any leftover stock. When he walked in, only three customers remained in the store, looking through the last eighteen suits, trying to find something in their sizes.

Jonathan saw him and beamed expansively. "Not much left to carry out, Myron. Just the racks, mirrors and curtains."

"What about the suits?"

"We'll get rid of those," Jonathan replied confidently. He called across to the two guards. "See if there's anything you like in what's left. You can take a suit each."

Myron walked to a rack and selected a suit with a strident plaid. The jacket fitted perfectly, but the trousers were too big around the waist. Jonathan offered to get them taken in at the factory.

"And while you're there, see if there's anything in your father's size," he added. "His taste, not yours!"

As soon as the customers had left, Jonathan locked the front door and began to collect the money from his staff. He did not try to count it, knowing the task would be impossible; he simply tossed all the bills into a small suitcase, showing the contents to Miriam before he closed the lid. After he paid off the staff, he asked the two guards to watch over the suitcase.

"I'll be back in a minute," he told Myron and Miriam. "I've got one more score to settle with Al Gilbert."

Moving from rack to rack, he picked up the remaining dozen suits. Unable to carry them all by himself, he asked Myron for help. "Just follow me," he said, "and do exactly what I do. No fancy variations of your own."

The guard unlocked the door, and Jonathan and Myron walked out, arms loaded down with the dozen unsold suits. Jonathan swung right and began to march toward Gilbert's store.

"Where's the boss?" he demanded, barging through the front door, glad to see that the store was still empty of customers; he also noticed, with a distinct sensation of pleasure, the glaring gaps in the suit racks. Obviously Gilbert had been unable as yet to replace any of the merchandise which Jonathan had withdrawn.

One of the salesmen pointed through the store toward the office in the rear.

"Come on, Myron," Jonathan said. "Let's finish this job and go home." He walked past the salesmen and pushed open the door to the office. Gilbert was on the telephone; he looked up in surprise as he recognized Jonathan.

"What the hell do you want now?" he gasped, only remembering to place a hand over the mouthpiece after he had spoken.

"We had some over, Al. Just to show there's no hard feelings, we thought we'd give them to you."

Straightening his arms abruptly, Jonathan tossed the suits across the office. They landed on Gilbert's desk, sliding across the top onto the floor. Gilbert stared incredulously, still astounded by the intrusion. Myron's six suits caught him full in the face, knocking the telephone out of his hand. It crashed onto the desk, scratching the polished surface.

"No charge, Al," Jonathan said, "not even for the buttonholes." Ushering Myron in front, he slammed the door and walked out of the store.

After locking the money away in his apartment, Jonathan took Miriam and Myron out for a celebratory dinner, making the meal last till after the summer night fell, when he knew his father would be home from the *havdala* service at the conclusion of the Sabbath. They drew up outside

Jacob's apartment shortly after ten, and Jonathan gave two long blasts on the horn of the gray truck.

Jacob was waiting for them by the apartment door, listening for their footsteps in the hallway. "I've just made some tea," he greeted them. "Will you join me?"

"Tea? Did you hear that?" Jonathan asked Miriam and Myron. He threw back his head and laughed. "Al Gilbert's drinking tea right now. We're due for a bottle of champagne." He gripped his father by the shoulders, hugging him. "Jacob, you should have been there. It was like a herd of cattle gone berserk; we couldn't keep them away."

"Did you sell out?"

"We had a dozen or so left over from the thousand, so we gave them to Gilbert as a souvenir—a final touch."

Over the tea which Jacob insisted on, Jonathan proposed a toast to Miriam. "I'm marrying a bright girl, a girl who's got more business sense in her little finger than the rest of us have got together. She's shown us the way we've got to go."

Jacob put down his cup and looked inquisitively at his son. "What do you mean, the way we've got to go?"

"Look on today as a trial run," Jonathan explained. "Think what we could do if we opened our own shops, sold our own merchandise directly to the public. We'd have no more Al Gilberts to worry about. We'd be our own suppliers and our own customers. We'd get a share of both the manufacturing and retail profits. And, at the same time, we'd be giving the public a fair shake because we could afford to be competitive."

There was a dubious expression on Jacob's face. Events were moving too quickly for him. He remained a technical man, at home with a production problem, unused to the quick decisions of the business world. If he was honest with himself, he still doubted the wisdom of taking the one thousand suits away from Al Gilbert. And that was all over now, a fine success according to Jonathan. "Is anybody else doing this type of operation, Jonathan?"

Jonathan leaned across the table. "Remember when I went up to Toronto a few months back for that meeting with the Canadian manufacturers?"

Jacob remembered it vaguely, a discussion of fashion trends to which he should have gone but decided not to because of the travel involved. "What about it?"

"They were telling me about a clothing organization up there, Tip Top Tailors. And they're doing exactly what I'm saying we should do—retailing what they manufacture. They've got a lot of stores across Canada, all supplied from the one factory in Toronto, measure goods. They're almost an institution in the country, part of the Canadian way of life. The guy who founded them built up a reputation for a one-price made-to-measure suit, and the idea took off like a rocket. I'm saying we could do the same sort of thing down here, made-to-measure and ready-to-wear. We could also make our name on a one-price made-to-measure suit, and while the factory's on down time on the measure side, we could make ready-to-wears to fill the stores up with."

Jacob held up a hand. "I leave it all to you. You represent the business brains of this family. Rather, you and Miriam do." He smiled warmly at her. "Just tell me what it is you want from me, and I'll look after it." He glanced around the table, from Miriam to Jonathan to Myron.

"Would anybody like some more tea?"

# 10

Moments after the ceremony finished, Myron rushed blindly from the small private ward, his face changing color from white to green, a hand clapped across his mouth, his eyes bulging. Jonathan chased after him into the washroom and waited outside the commode until his brother-in-law emerged, breathing deeply to settle his stomach.

"Christ almighty, that's a barbaric tradition," Myron groaned, a feeble grin covering his embarrassment at being sick. "And to think I went through the same thing."

"You feel better now, good enough to go back inside?" Jonathan asked, laying a comforting arm around Myron's shoulders.

Still sucking in deep lungfuls of air, Myron nodded. "You got a cigarette first? I need something to take away the taste."

Jonathan took a pack from his jacket pocket and shook out a cigarette. Myron accepted it gratefully, waiting for Jonathan to provide a light. He inhaled cautiously at first, then more deeply, blowing the smoke in a thick column toward the ceiling.

"That's what you get for being godfather," Jonathan told him. "It's a big honor holding the boys for their *bris.*"

Myron took another deep pull on the cigarette, letting the smoke out more slowly, his nerves steadying. "I believe you, it's an honor. But did you and Miriam have to go in for twins? It's bad enough seeing it happen once, but who needs the repeat performance? Christ almighty," he muttered again.

Jonathan waited for Myron to stub out the cigarette; then they walked back into the ward. Apart from the initial spasm of concern, Myron's disappearance had passed almost unnoticed. The family was clustered around the twin boys watching as Jacob, his face glowing with pride, dipped a finger into a glass of wine, then into the babies' mouths. Miriam stood behind, her face still pale and drawn from the exertions of the double birth eight days earlier. Her mother stood alongside, protective, while her father shared the happy role of grandfather with Jacob, drooling over the twins, laughing, trying to make everybody believe that the boys could understand what he was saying.

"You've got some heirs to the business now," Myron remarked, again in full control of himself.

Jonathan smiled at the thought. "That offer's still open to you, Myron. When you want to come in with us, just say the word. You'll be more than welcome."

Myron made no comment. He stood for a moment staring at his father and Jacob bending over the babies, now serene as if the intrusion into their future manhood had never taken place. "Even after today, Jonathan, I want to be a doctor." He laughed suddenly, a cynical sound which seemed oddly out of place coming from such a young man.

"It'll make my mother happy when I graduate from medical school. She'll be able to tell all her friends about her son, the doctor. And my father will still have to pay to get into Yankee Stadium."

"Talking of Yankee Stadium, whatever happened to that glorious baseball career you had all mapped out?" Jonathan asked. "I thought you had your heart set on being the best third baseman the Yankees ever had."

"Second baseman," Myron corrected him. He flexed his right arm, pressing the biceps with the fingers of his left hand. "It's a good arm, but it's not good enough. It was a nice dream, nothing more—something to see me through the worst years of adolescence. But don't worry," he added quickly, "I won't take any patients when the Yankees are playing at home. I've still got my priorities in the right order."

"It's all coming clear," Jonathan said. "Forty-five heart attacks waiting outside the surgery, and a big sign saying that Doctor Helman will be back after the final out. Isn't that sort of attitude against the Hippocratic oath?"

Myron was unfazed. "When Hippocrates was alive," he answered blithely, "there were no New York Yankees—as difficult as that may be to believe."

"It is," Jonathan said, playing up to Myron. "I thought somewhere in the Bible it said that God created the Yankees in between the water and the light."

"And in his own image," Myron rejoined.

One by one, the visitors drifted away, leaving Jonathan and Miriam alone with their sons and Jacob.

"*Mazel tov* again," Jacob said, kissing Miriam on the cheek. "Such lovely boys. May they be as strong as Jonathan and as good-looking as you."

"What's wrong with my looks?" Jonathan complained lightly. "They've served me pretty well these past few years."

He examined his father while he spoke, noticing how much more relaxed Jacob looked, the worries of the small tailoring business now nothing more than a distant memory. Even the concern which Jacob had expressed over the opening of their own retail outlets, and the simultaneous cutting off of their regular customers, had been forgotten. The initial store in midtown Manhattan had shown beyond a doubt that their marketing approach was correct. Since then, two other stores had been opened in the city—one in Queens and one in Brooklyn—and a fourth in Albany, the state capital. Plans were in hand to extend the vertical operation further along the East Coast.

"There's nothing wrong with your looks," Jacob conceded. "They've served their purpose in the past, scaring away people like Mr. Gilbert."

The comment amused Jonathan. The incident with Gilbert, which had been directly responsible for the opening of their own stores, had happened more than two years ago; yet only six weeks earlier Jonathan had heard that the retailer had gone bankrupt and had left the city to work as a store manager for a men's clothing chain in the Midwest. Even Jacob had laughed when he was told about the man's downfall.

"That's all my looks are good for?" Jonathan said. "Scaring people?"

"Your looks are fine," Jacob told him, "but Miriam's are much nicer." He turned to her, smiling. "See how I stick up for you?"

Miriam sat down on the edge of the bed, arranging the covers over her two sons as she waited for the nurse to take them away. "Thanks, Jacob. I need all the support I can get these days. Even Myron thinks that Jonathan's some kind of minor god; he agrees with everything he says or does. I'm afraid I'll have to disappoint you, though. They won't both take after me. Simon has my color eyes, but Gerald's are deep brown, almost black, like Jonathan's. I guess we'll have to settle for one apiece."

One of the babies began to whimper, faint cries which gradually became louder. Miriam bent down to comfort him. "It's Simon," she whispered. "Maybe he's missing his little piece already."

Hearing Jacob suck in his breath in shock, Jonathan exploded into a roar of laughter. Miriam looked up crossly. "Sssh!" she hissed. "You'll wake Gerald as well."

No sooner had she issued the warning than the other baby began to move. Soon the room was filled with the sounds of crying.

"Go on, blame me," Jonathan exclaimed, seeing no point in trying to establish his innocence. "It's all my fault."

"Who else's fault would it be?" Miriam retorted. "You woke them, now you get them back to sleep."

"Easy," Jonathan boasted. He leaned over the bed and tickled his sons under the chin, one hand for each. Instead of easing the noise, however, his actions only served to exacerbate the situation; the babies cried even more furiously, flailing their legs, pummelling the air with tiny fists. Jonathan was glad when the door opened and the nurse came in to take charge.

Miriam returned home with the two boys a week later. Jonathan had converted the second bedroom of their new apartment on the East Side into a nursery, to which he insisted on going at every opportunity, to see that his sons were all right. Jacob spent all his spare time at the apartment, ostensibly to discuss the business with Jonathan, but really motivated by the chance to spend time with his grandsons; the chess games and the clubs were forgotten, paling into insignificance beside the new attractions.

As the three of them sat down for dinner, Miriam brought up the subject of her brother. "Did you ever get around to talking to Myron about joining the company?" she asked Jonathan.

"Nothing doing," he replied. "He's got his heart set on becoming a doctor. Wants to please your mother, I think. The idea of being mixed up in the retail business doesn't mean a thing to him." He stopped talking long enough to fork some food into his mouth, chewing thoughtfully.

"Anyway, I think all this talk about expanding the company is hypothetical at the moment. The way things are going in Europe, we'll be making uniforms soon, the hell with suits."

Jacob nodded glumly. He removed his glasses, wiping them on the table napkin. "Do you think we'll get involved, Jonathan? You know there's a very strong movement to keep America out of the war, let the Europeans sort out their own problems."

Jonathan chuckled, looking at Miriam. "Listen to my father," he joked. "The American talking—let the Europeans sort out their own problems." He became serious again, thinking over Jacob's words.

"It's everybody's problem," he said eventually, "not just the Europeans. We have to get involved. Look at the number of guys who've run off to Canada so they could get into it."

"And lost their citizenship," Miriam broke in. "What did that prove? How did they help anybody by doing that?"

Jonathan shifted his position so that he could look directly at Miriam, who sat beside him. "They're doing it for their principles, Miriam. They'll worry about citizenship when it's all over and they come back. What they're doing now is making clear their stand on what they think our government should be doing. Do you ever read Winchell's column or listen to him on the radio? He's the only one in this country with the sense to know what's going on and guts enough to speak out against it."

"Miriam," Jacob said gently, "you don't know Europe. You were born in America; so were your parents. You can't fully understand what's going on over there. If that madman wins—and God forbid, he looks like doing it—the whole of Europe will return to the Dark Ages. The outcome must affect the United States, far more than the last war did."

"The world's not big enough for us to play isolationist," Jonathan said, supporting his father. "We've got to look after everybody else. That's how Britain got involved. She declared war on Germany because she had a treaty with Poland. She didn't have the equipment, the arms or anything you need to fight a modern war. She only had the obligation. And you can see what's happening. With all their empire, all their resources, the British aren't even scratching the Nazis. It was only by good luck they rescued most of their men from Dunkirk."

"And you're trying to say that we haven't got anything either," Miriam concluded dubiously. "A country the size of the United States can't put together an army that would take care of Hitler?"

"He's got thousands of tanks," Jonathan explained. "He's been preparing for this for years while everybody else has been sitting on their backsides watching. What do you think we've got? I heard one story that from the end of the Great War to 1939 America built precisely six tanks, all of which were experimental models. We still have generals who think the horse has a valuable part to play in modern warfare. We're not even in a position to make war on"—he hunted mentally for the smallest country he could think of—"on Cuba, let alone a highly mechanized army like the Germans have." He took a deep breath, steeling himself for what he had to say.

"When we're ready, Miriam, properly ready, we'll go in—when we have the tanks, the planes, the guns. And when that day comes, I'll be one of the first to join up."

Jacob said nothing. His son's feelings contained no surprises for him. But Miriam sat up sharply, the expression on her face one of horror.

"Why you?" Her voice shook. "You have children. You're an only son. You own a factory that can make uniforms. Why does it have to be you who rushes off to fight other people's battles?"

Jonathan refused to let himself be drawn. Tenderly he took hold of Miriam's hands, soothing her. "This is a fight which involves us all, Miriam. We can't leave it to Britain, and I can't leave it to some poor guy who's got less to lose than I have. If Hitler conquers Europe, do you think he'll stop there? Of course he won't. He'll be looking west at us."

"But there's an ocean between us," Miriam protested. "How's he going to get across that? By walking?"

Jonathan ignored Miriam's stilted humor. "Time has a way of helping technology overcome natural obstacles. Germany's the most advanced nation in the world. They've proved it by the way they've smashed aside half the armies of Europe, like so many toy soldiers. Give Hitler time, while we sit back leaving it to the British, and he'll find a way. The Atlantic isn't insurmountable. It's just like a mountain, unconquerable till it's conquered."

"I don't believe what I'm hearing!" Miriam cried. "How can you talk like this, running away to fight? What about your responsibilities here?"

Leaving his meal half-eaten, Jonathan stood up and began to walk toward the door.

"Where are you going?" Miriam called after him. "Rushing off to enlist before it even starts? Are you that desperate to be the first one in uniform?"

"I'm going out for a walk and a cigarette. I don't want to argue with you."

Miriam turned to her father-in-law, a look of complete helplessness on her face. "Jacob, please say something. He's your son; maybe you can make him listen to reason."

Jacob heard the door slam behind Jonathan and shook his head sadly. "Miriam, there is nothing I can do. Jonathan is Jonathan. He does what he thinks is right. Isn't that one of the reasons you love him as much as you do?"

The words took an instant to register on Miriam's brain. When they did, she whispered, "Yes."

"Then forget about it till it happens," Jacob said. "When he comes back, don't mention it again. Just leave it alone. In the meantime," he added, forcing a smile onto his face, "you have two wonderful sons to think about. Your days should be filled with happiness, not with bickering over the foolishness of some little Austrian clown who wears a funny moustache."

# 11

Man, Jonathan decided in a sudden philosophical moment, is a complex mixture of conflicting emotions. When I sailed out of New York three years ago, there were tears in my eyes. Now that I'm completing the return journey, when a big fat smile should be pasted across my face, the tears are starting all over again.

Leaning against the ship's rail, he tried to blink back the first tears, but to no avail. They squeezed out, hanging motionless for a fraction of a second before beginning the journey down his cheeks; the trail they left felt cold in the brisk wind which battered against the ship. To his left stood a grizzled sergeant staring blankly across the water, not seeing the famous skyline, the boats of welcoming, waving people, the banners proclaiming him. Hearing the sergeant sniff loudly, Jonathan felt better, glad that he was not alone in his emotions.

Through the veil of tears, Jonathan watched the familiar landmarks slide past, everything unchanged since he had last seen them three years earlier. Has it really been three years, he asked himself, since I sailed in the other direction? Does so much time go by so quickly? And can so much horror be packed into it?

That final parting from Miriam had been heartbreaking; three years later the memory of it still caused him to choke. To the end she had insisted that his job at the factory, making uniforms, was crucial to the country's war effort. She had thrown the names of other men in the clothing industry at him, men who were using their positions to stay at home with their families. But he had rejected every argument. He remembered pointing to Jacob and saying that he was the man who could make the uniforms. We don't need any salesmen, he had told her. We've got a good steady customer now—Uncle Sam. He won't try to welsh on any deals because of a dispute over lapel buttonholes.

Disregarding the tears, he managed a weak smile at the thought of that final argument, but he recalled feeling little amusement as the ship had sailed out that foggy morning into a submarine-infested ocean, bound for God only knew where. Now, like Saint George of legend, he and millions of others were returning to the castle, their brows wreathed in victory, their swords and lances laid aside. The dragon lay dead in its Berlin lair, and the future was anything but clear.

From the desire to do something with his hands rather than from the need to smoke, Jonathan stuck a cigar into the side of his mouth, lighting it with the dented Zippo he had carried throughout the war. Puffing contentedly, he rested his elbows on the rail again, watching the buildings of Manhattan loom closer with every revolution of the ship's screw.

"Looks pretty, huh?" a voice rasped.

Turning, Jonathan saw the sergeant pointing across Manhattan to where the Empire State Building's radio mast caught a narrow beam of sunlight through the heavy overcast.

"Right now that looks more inviting than a broad with her legs spread wide open just for me." The sergeant laughed drily.

Jonathan's face broke into a grin at the comparison; he wondered idly how Miriam would view such a comment.

Two tugs came out from the dock, bobbing up and down on the gray, wind-disturbed water. Jonathan leaned out to watch the lines being taken up as the small boats prepared to guide the ship to its berth. The cigar was clamped comfortably between his teeth, and he could feel a choking sensation rising in his throat.

So this is what it's like, what he had dreamed about for three years, what had kept him going through the worst of it—the homecoming. Postwar America, the strongest power in the world, taking over from a battle-shattered, bankrupt Britain. Now we're the champs; the sun hasn't set on the British Empire, it's just moved three thousand miles west to shine on us.

Over his thoughts, he heard a band playing from the dock and recognized Sousa's "Stars and Stripes Forever." He began to hum the tune, tapping his right foot in time with the melody, the cigar jumping up and down in his mouth like a conductor's baton.

As spontaneously as he had begun to hum, he stopped, grinning self-consciously at other men on the rail who had turned to stare at him. Lifting a foot, Jonathan placed it on his duffel bag, taking his weight on the other leg. He tried to describe the sensation of returning home and could not. He could think of nothing more definitive than "good," and he felt satisfied with that simple, honest adjective. It was good to be coming home, and it would be good to see Miriam, the kids and Jacob. Let the poets render superlatives; he was happy with the genuine feeling which enveloped him.

And the business, he thought. Miriam and Jacob had mentioned in letters that the stores had been allowed to slide, but who really cared? They'd pick up again. Besides, he'd had plenty of time to come up with new ideas. He thought about the uniform he was wearing. That's probably one of ours; it fits too well to be anybody else's. Too bad the company was not allowed to put its own labels in the uniforms. He remembered some of the officers taking advantage of being stationed in London prior to the D-Day landings by having their dress uniforms custom-made. But Jonathan reckoned that the uniforms which came out of the Gellenbaum factory were just as good.

As the tugs busily maneuvered the ship into its berth, he peered down over the crowd of uplifted faces, searching for his own welcoming committee. All the faces seemed like shapeless blurs, white blotches gazing upwards, with ill-defined holes for eyes and mouths. He wanted to shout Miriam's name, but he knew that his voice would be swept away in the general din. Looking left and right, he saw that many of the soldiers on the rail were weeping—men who had gone through the worst horrors, whose chests were covered with decorations for bravery; they were sobbing, wiping tears from their eyes, unashamed of their sentimental displays.

A burst of movement from the dock made Jonathan look down again. A soldier was waving up, directly at him, it seemed. In his arm was a brown-haired child, its head snuggled against his uniform. Jonathan strained his eyes trying to identify the man, but the cap shaded the soldier's face. Then, with an almost physical jolt, he recognized Miriam standing next to the soldier, both arms waving frantically. To her right, standing stiffly upright as though on a parade field, was Jacob, the familiar Homburg hat jammed solidly on his head. He bent down and lifted up Simon, waving the child's arm in greeting.

Jonathan pulled off his cap and waved it wildly, shouting at the top of his voice, not worrying that the words were lost in the overall rush of sound. The band continued to play. Streamers went out from the dock to the lower decks of the ship. People shouted and screamed. Everywhere was pandemonium, but Jonathan saw little of it, heard none of it. His whole being was focussed on the small group waiting for him—his two sons, Miriam, Jacob, and the soldier who had to be Myron.

Pulling back his arm, Jonathan flicked his cap toward the group, watching it sail over the heads of the crowd and descend through space like a flying saucer. It missed the intended target by ten yards. An elderly man stuck a hand in the air, snagging the cap, throwing it up in triumph as he joined in the welcoming celebrations, not caring whose cap it was, nor for whom it was meant.

As the ramps went down, Jonathan hoisted the duffel bag on his shoulder and raced toward the nearest disembarkation point, disregarding the fact that without the cap he was out of uniform. He stood impatiently in the queue to get off the ship, watching jealously as the first men ran down the gangplank, the lucky ones into the waiting arms of their families and friends. There was a space as a man hesitated. Jonathan darted into it, past the disembarkation officer and down the ramp. His legs felt wobbly as he hit the firm ground of the dock, unused to solid surfaces after ten days at sea. The thought flashed across his mind that he would have to get his land legs back.

He continued running, feeling his legs strengthen with every step, moving swiftly past groups of people embracing their sons, their husbands, their fathers, their brothers, past others still waiting for their men to disembark. Then he was in Miriam's arms and she in his. He hugged her, swinging her off the ground, kissing her excitedly, the years of tension, loneliness and fear being swept away in seconds.

"God," he breathed. "I can't begin to say what this feels like." He put her down gently, tears springing to his eyes again as he looked at his sons, bending down to hold them close to him. "Simon. Gerald. How big you've both got." His tongue tasted salt as the tears reached his mouth.

"Say hello to your papa," he heard Jacob say, the gruffness in his father's voice hiding his feelings. "Kiss your papa. He's been away a long time."

Simon turned away, shy, confused. Gerald put his arms around Jonathan's neck in an experimental gesture, wondering who this strange man was, why he was making everybody so upset and at the same time so happy.

Jonathan stood up holding a son in each arm, his face wet from the tears which now ran unchecked. He looked into Jacob's eyes and saw a reflection of his own. Then he turned to Myron, who stood slightly apart from the group; his brother-in-law was wearing a medic's crest and buck sergeant's stripes.

"Do you really expect me to whip out a sharp salute for you, Captain?" Myron joked, trying to make light of the situation, cause the others to laugh.

"Don't bother. When do you get out?"

"I'm out already. I just haven't had the time yet to steal a suit from the factory."

Jonathan did not fully understand Myron's answer. He was too busy looking around the dock, watching other men off the ship reacting in the same manner as he. There were enough tears to relaunch the ship which had brought them home.

Holding his sons tightly, rejoicing in their closeness, Jonathan strode toward the dock exit. Myron followed, carrying the duffel bag, while Miriam and Jacob, arms joined, brought up the rear.

Still in uniform, Jonathan leaned back in the chair at the head of the table. Gerald sat balanced on one knee, Simon on the other. Around the table sat Jacob, Myron and Sam Helman, while Miriam and her mother busied themselves in the kitchen preparing the next course of the homecoming dinner. Playfully Jonathan bounced the boys up and down, listening to them squeal in delight as they accepted this stranger into their young lives.

"Jonathan, they should be in bed," Jacob said, tapping his wristwatch for emphasis. "It's almost half-past nine."

"Who cares what time it is?" Jonathan replied. "This is my day, and I'm doing what I want to do." He looked down at the boys. "We've got to get to know each other again, isn't that right?"

Miriam's voice came from the kitchen, cutting across the murmur of conversation around the table. "Your father's right, Jonathan. It's long past their bedtime. If they don't go to bed right away, you'll have two hellions on your hands in the morning. Simon's a bad-tempered monster if he doesn't get enough sleep, and Gerald's not much better."

Jonathan eyed Simon with mock seriousness. "Is that true?"

The boy blinked his hazel eyes and looked away. Jonathan switched his gaze to Gerald, noticing the likeness to his side of the family; whereas Simon, as Miriam had predicted, took after the Helmans. "What about you, Gerald? What are you like in the morning? Do you wake up with a hangover?"

Gerald giggled shyly and buried his face in Jonathan's chest.

"Come on," Jonathan said, rising. "To bed for the pair of you before your mother's nagging drives me back to the army." He left the table, one son held under each arm, and went to the boys' bedroom, undressing and tucking them into bed. Before turning out the light, he kissed each one good night.

"That was quick," Miriam said in surprise when he returned. "Did you wash them properly?"

Jonathan looked puzzled. "Wash them? Why?"

Everybody laughed as Miriam stared unbelievingly at Jonathan, whose confusion at the question was doubled by the reception to his answer.

"Because they're supposed to have a wash before they go to bed," Miriam said slowly, the exasperation in her voice tinged with laughter. "Oh, never mind," she added helplessly. "Let them sleep now."

"I see." Jonathan savored the moment, an instant of time to treasure in his rehabilitation. "You'll have to teach me all these things over again." He sat down and began to eat, talking between mouthfuls. "We never bothered washing before we went to bed. We didn't have the time or the facilities. Mind you, I've also forgotten what a bed looks like." He looked across the table at Myron, who had shed his uniform in favor of a pair of dark slacks and a white shirt.

"Where did you get to, anywhere interesting?"

"Training cadre at a medic school," Myron said. "No overseas duty, nothing. I might just as well have stayed in New York."

"Uh-huh." Jonathan moved to Jacob. "Does anybody mind if we talk shop, or do you want to keep it to army stories?" There were no objections, so he continued. "I know the stores didn't set any records during the war, but what's happening to them now?"

"Men were in the army, the navy, the air force," Jacob said. "Our customers were wearing our uniforms, not our suits. It's beginning to pick up a little, but nowhere near as good as it was before you went away."

"But the factory was busy right through?"

"If you can wait till tomorrow, you can go through the books and get the proper picture."

"I'm only after a rough idea," Jonathan said, "something to show me the situation. By the way,"—he began to laugh—"whose idea was that advertisement, the one Miriam sent me?"

Jacob looked blank. "Advertisement? What advertisement are you talking about?"

"The one that showed the column of marching soldiers," Jonathan explained. "It was an advertisement for Gellenbaum and Son, and the copy read, 'These styles will soon be seen in Berlin.' Who dreamed that one up?"

Miriam began to turn scarlet. "We borrowed it, you might say," she admitted, her voice faltering. "A Canadian company was using it, and we thought it would look good for ourselves."

Jonathan pounded the table in delight, making the cutlery jump. "Don't be ashamed of it. If you can't borrow from your allies, who the hell can you borrow from? It was a beautiful thing to send. We were the only Sherman in the whole Third Army with a taste for fashion. Everybody else had a photograph of Betty Grable stuck up on the inside of the tank. We had an ad for Gellenbaum and Son."

"What did you call your tank?" Myron asked. "What nickname?"

"What else?" Jonathan said. "Gellenbaum's Gehenna." Seeing Myron's look of bewilderment, he added, "Look it up in the dictionary when you get home."

After midnight, when the guests had left, Jonathan slumped down on the edge of the bed brooding, the gaiety of the evening drained away. In his hands was the jacket of his uniform, the red, blue and yellow triangular armor patch staring up at him, the bold, black figure four at the apex seeming to jump out with a life of its own.

"Want to tell me what you're thinking about?" Miriam asked tenderly.

Jonathan held up the jacket. "I'm going to ask Jacob if he can make this into a suit. It'll be different. I'll be the first kid on the block with one."

Miriam sat down on the bed next to him. She took the jacket from his hands and tossed it onto a chair. "Forget about the jacket, Jonathan. Forget about everything associated with it."

"Wish I could, but it's not that easy."

"Then talk about it. Tell me what it was like."

Jonathan shook his head wearily. "I don't think you'd understand. And I'm not sure I'd want you to."

Miriam looked at Jonathan's profile, at the lines which had appeared around the mouth and eyes; the soft curves which had been there before he left for Europe three years earlier had disappeared, replaced by a granite hardness. "Are you going into the factory tomorrow?" she asked.

"Guess so. May as well get back into the swing of things."

Miriam laced her fingers around Jonathan's neck and leaned back on the bed, pulling him down. "We've got a lot of time to make up for," she whispered huskily. "Right now is as good a time as any to begin."

Almost lazily, Jonathan let his left hand stray to Miriam's stomach, fingering the fine fabric of her negligee, tracing delicate patterns.

"Hello, Empire State Building," he muttered.

"Mmm?" Miriam did not open her eyes. "What's that about the Empire State Building?"

Jonathan chuckled softly. "Some sergeant's coarse joke. It doesn't matter."

He felt Miriam's hand on his thigh, touching, moving higher, exploring, fingers undoing his belt, feeling inside.

"That's my Empire State Building," she moaned. "The finest erection in New York City."

Jonathan pretended to sound dejected. "Only in the city?"

He cut off any further conversation by placing his mouth over Miriam's, forcing her lips open with his tongue.

Long after Miriam had fallen asleep, Jonathan lay awake, staring in the darkness at the ceiling, feeling the warmth of Miriam's body in his arms, her light, even breathing contrasting so strongly with his own labored gasps.

Tell me what it was like, she had said.

Where do you begin? Where do you start a horror story which you wouldn't have missed for anything in the world? How do you tell somebody, even your wife, about the friends you made and lost, about how, as time went by, you tried not to get too close to anybody in case they were next in line? How can you explain what it feels like to gather up the pieces of what was once an American soldier, searching for his dog tags amidst the mess so that his parents could receive a polite telegram from the Department of Defense?

And above all, how can you possibly describe the gut feeling, the animal instinct which fires a burning hatred and a desire for revenge a thousandfold—where you want to smash, to maim, to kill, to get even for the deaths of people you never even knew existed in countries you'd never heard of?

Dear God, Jonathan thought, will I ever be able to forget that night in the Ardennes when I appointed myself your judge and executioner?

He began to sweat as the events of that night became clear. The weather, that was the first thing—a real witches' brew of snow and low cloud, freezing cold and poor visibility, as hospitable as the inside of an icebox with the light turned out. How many miles had the division covered from the jump-off point? How long had it taken them?

They had been all set to head east for the drive into Germany when they had received news of the German breakout in the Ardennes; orders had come down almost immediately from Third Army headquarters, making them pivot north to smash von Rundstedt's offensive.

It didn't matter about ground covered or time elapsed. All Jonathan remembered was his company breaching the outer perimeter of one of the German divisions surrounding the besieged airborne troops twenty miles outside Bastogne. Initially they had encountered an infantry unit taking a break in the mistaken belief that its rear was secure. He remembered snatching the machine gun from the surprised tank commander, pushing him aside roughly. The words that he had screamed frenziedly into that cold December night came ringing back to haunt him.

"Try to kill me, you kraut bastards! I'm a Jew! See what you can do with me!"

The machine gun had danced in his grip as he aimed indiscriminately into the mass of wildly fleeing German infantrymen, watching them collapse in agony as bullets slashed into them, seeing others fall under the tracks of the advancing Sherman, knowing the same situation was being repeated all around him as the division smashed its way through to the encircled defenders.

And when it was over, when the tanks had rumbled to a halt among the relieved defenders, he had felt nothing but a savage sense of satisfaction—satisfaction at the success of the mission, certainly, but even more at the number of German soldiers he had seen fall under the machine gun's relentless pursuit.

There had been a look of respect in the tank commander's eyes, but the awe had been tempered with a fear of being with this madman, this company commander who rode up front, screaming at the enemy, daring them to kill him, shouting gleefully as his bullets found their mark, revelling as the tank rolled over bodies, its tracks crushing any life that was left.

Tell me what it was like, Miriam had said.

I couldn't. Even if I wanted to.

He was still reliving that night when Gerald pushed open the bedroom door and walked in. He stopped momentarily, frozen in shock at seeing a man in his mother's bed. Then he remembered the excitement of the day before; his father had come home.

"I can't sleep," he whimpered. "I can't sleep."

"You too, huh?" Jonathan rolled over to make room in the bed and pulled the boy in. "Come and join the club."

# 12

Seated behind the desk of his Houston Street office, Jonathan felt anything but relaxed as he watched his father pace agitatedly around the office, the thin body stooped as he stared down at the gold watch, trying to find the solution to yet another problem in its mute face. Jonathan dearly wanted to say something, to find some words of comfort to ease his father's distress, but he knew that this was a situation where his father would have to accept an inevitable event.

The pacing continued for another minute without a word being said. Then Jacob sat down opposite Jonathan, snapping the watch closed with an air of finality.

"Why?" he asked. "What makes you want to do a thing like this? Are you so ashamed of the name of Gellenbaum?"

Jonathan let the air come out of his lungs in a long, painful sigh. "You know I'm not ashamed of the name. I'm just thinking about the future of the business. We got along fine before the war with the name of Gellenbaum and Son, but what were we selling?"

"Good suits," Jacob broke in. "That's what we were selling. Good clothing at reasonable prices. Our name never stood in the way before."

"No, it didn't," Jonathan conceded. "But did you ever stop to think that it may not have done us much good either? Things have changed from the days of the old tailoring shop on Essex Street, when all your customers were compatriots. I did a lot of thinking on that boat ride home, trying to make up my mind what I wanted to do with my life, with the business. I was hoping you'd understand my point of view."

Jacob fiddled with the watch chain, counting the links with his fingers while he thought of a reply. "Many times I didn't understand you, Jonathan—when you first wanted me to come into the factory with you, I was scared then because I thought you might be reaching for too much; then when you wanted to risk everything by taking the suits back from Mr.

Gilbert and selling them yourself. Always I went along with you, though, because this was your country. I thought you knew best."

"And didn't I?" Jonathan asked triumphantly.

"You did, Jonathan. You did," Jacob agreed, slipping the watch back into his vest pocket. "But now, when it comes to changing your name, this I oppose strongly, because I am no longer certain that your ideas are the best ideas."

Jonathan took the conversation onto a different tack, trying to make his father realize the importance of the action he planned to take. "Have a look at some of the other big stores in this city," he said, "the really high-class ones. Not necessarily men's clothing stores, but places that have built their names on quality—Brooks Brothers, Abercrombie and Fitch. Look at those names. Listen to how they sound. Then try to compare how a name like Gellenbaum and Son is going to stand up when we're selling merchandise in that category.

"I'll tell you how it's going to stand up," he continued, without giving Jacob the chance to reply. "We're going to sound like the poor relations, the *schnorrers*. Call it another of my dreams if you like, but I want to open a really top-class men's store, not the bargain-basement, one-price-suit operation we were running before the war. And when we make the change, it's got to be a complete change, not a compromise where we upgrade our quality and keep the old name. The name's a damned big thing."

"And what, tell me, is so wonderful about this *goyishe* name you've dreamed up?" Jacob asked.

"Chestertons." Jonathan drew the name out, separating the syllables, revelling in the pronunciation. "It's got that certain ring to it. A name like that oozes class."

Jacob was far from impressed with his son's description of the proposed name. "Ring of class," he muttered sarcastically. "To me it sounds like a cigarette brand. Jonathan, I can see a man walking into a cigar store and asking for a pack of Chestertons, but a men's clothing store by such a name?" As if the thought had an effect on his subconscious, Jacob pulled out a pack of cigarettes, offering one to Jonathan, who refused.

"I forgot," Jacob apologized. "You don't smoke cigarettes any more. Did you take up cigars because you felt they would go with the new name, ooze more class than cigarettes?"

Jonathan ignored the double dose of derision. "Something to chew on," he answered. "It wasn't always wise to light up a cigarette, so we chewed on cigars instead. It gave me a taste for them."

Jacob made no further comment on the change in his son's smoking habits; he reverted to the discussion on the new name. "Have you spoken to Miriam about it? After all, it's her name as well, or have you forgotten that in your haste?"

"She's with me."

"Of course, she would be," Jacob said resignedly. "And do I have to change my name as well to benefit this scheme of yours? Or can I remain a Gellenbaum?"

Jonathan stuck an unlit cigar into his mouth, rolling it around. "Be serious, will you?" he pleaded. "I'm trying to take the business a step further, a big step, and all you can do is make jokes because I want to change my name and use it for the new store."

"You don't have to change your own name," Jacob pointed out. "Just call the store Chestertons."

"No. No good. I want to be known as Jonathan Chesterton of Chestertons. The two things go hand in hand."

"What about the four Gellenbaum stores?" Jacob asked. "What happens to them? Do they also come under the new name?"

Jonathan smiled. "Relax, will you? The four Gellenbaum stores remain exactly as they are now. They still bring in money. We'll supply them on the same basis as we've always done, from our own factory, with shirts and other accessories brought in from outside suppliers. But the factory has got to be enlarged and tooled up to make top-quality garments for Chestertons. Also, we'll have to put together a proper buying group for the Gellenbaum stores.

"A buying group?" Jacob asked. "What for?"

"If we come across any cheap clearance lines, we can knock the prices right down and get rid of them through Gellenbaums, use the four stores as clearance outlets for a good profit. Plus we can push through goods we can't sell at Chestertons."

Jacob stiffened visibly. "I don't like this idea one little bit," he protested. "First you want to change your name. All right! That's your privilege. You believe it will help you get the new store off the ground. But when you want to use the stores which bear my name for running clearance merchandise, garbage, that's when I say enough. We built our reputation on those stores, and now you want to do this, to . . ." He searched for the right word. "To prostitute the Gellenbaum name when it won't even be your name any more."

Jonathan heard him out patiently. "Have you quite finished?" he asked softly. "We're not prostituting anybody's name, and heaven knows where you, of all people, come up with a word like that. We're simply moving ahead with a logical plan of operation, keeping abreast with the times. I can't afford to have the Gellenbaum stores competing with the new Chestertons stores once we get them going. I've got to draw a distinct barrier, and I can see no better way of doing it than this. Unless," he added sharply, "I close down those four stores, and I don't want to do that."

"Thank you for your consideration," Jacob said icily.

Jonathan sat back, tired, head lolling, eyes staring up at the ceiling. He tried to remember the last time he had disagreed strongly with his father. Certainly it had never happened during the eleven years since opening the factory. Fatalistically he reasoned that it had to happen sometime; no business partners ever got on perfectly all the time, even though they might be father and son. Recalling some of the partnerships he had witnessed in the clothing industry, he hurriedly amended the last sentence: especially if they were father and son.

Deciding to drop the tactful stance because it was getting him nowhere, Jonathan fixed his father with a hard, level stare. "Jacob, if we didn't have the money put away from the government contract work, I'd think seriously about closing down those four stores to pay for the first new one." He knew the words were blunt, painfully so, but it was a course which Jonathan believed had to be taken. If he was ever going to make it clear to his father that he intended carrying the plan through, bluntness was perhaps the best weapon.

There was no immediate reply from Jacob; his son's frankness had hit him hard. He sat thinking over Jonathan's words, wondering if there was any point in continuing the argument.

"All right," he muttered eventually. "I can see there is no use in arguing further with you. Tell me what it is you want from me, and I'll back you up like always. Just leave me alone in the factory and do whatever you want. Gellenbaum, Chesterton, whatever you feel like calling yourself, it's your business."

Leaning closer, Jonathan tried one last time to persuade his father of the advantages of the plan, using words he would be able to appreciate. "Remember how you used to say that life is like the chess games we used to play, that I should sit on my hands till I was sure of where I was going? Jacob, if you had the opportunity to really get a jump ahead in the game, wouldn't you sacrifice a piece or two? Wouldn't it be worth it to get into a winning position?"

"It would," Jacob agreed softly. "But I never dreamed you'd look on me as a piece to be sacrificed for your own ends."

"You are not the sacrifice!" Jonathan shot back, his voice rising despite his desire to stay calm. "The four stores are. All we'll be doing is using them to unload cheap goods for a nice profit if and when we get the chance. It'll be merchandise on special promotion so people will know what they're buying. The regular measure service and off-the-rack suits will still be available from the factory. And the factory will be making two levels of merchandise, the usual suits for Gellenbaums, and top-quality suits for Chestertons. Can't you understand that?"

"Not really, Jonathan. But I'm an old man living in a young man's world. Like I said before, do what you want. I'll be here to help you as always."

Jonathan was in a foul mood when he arrived home. Even the twins, who greeted him ecstatically at the front door, failed to cheer him up. They ran toward him as he entered the apartment, but his obvious preoccupation with other matters soon persuaded them to look elsewhere for their entertainment.

Over dinner, Miriam began to scold him for ignoring the boys, but there was no fire in her words; she could imagine the problems he was encountering in persuading Jacob of the necessity for taking another gigantic step.

"He told me to do whatever I wanted to do," Jonathan muttered, pushing the plate away, the food hardly touched. "It seemed like he was washing his hands of the whole affair."

"It'll be like the factory all over again," Miriam said soothingly. "When he sees the first of the new stores, he'll be as excited as a child. Wait and see."

"If the name of Gellenbaum was splashed across the front, there'd be no trouble," Jonathan replied. "It'd be like you say. The problem is that he's mad at me because I'm changing it to Chestertons. And the worst thing is, I can see his point. He's proud of the name. Christ, I am as well. But you try getting a top-quality men's clothing store to appeal to the rich *goyim* when it's got a name like Gellenbaum and Son out front. We've got to present an Anglo-Saxon exterior."

He pulled the plate toward himself again, nibbling at the food but hardly tasting it. "You know, Miriam, when I was over in England before the Normandy invasion, we used to go into the West End of London a lot. They've got all the good custom tailors there, centered around Savile Row. You must have heard of the place." He waited till she nodded.

"They call it the Golden Mile of men's tailoring. Anyway, you know damned well that maybe a quarter of those companies are owned and operated by Jews, men who started out like my father did. But did we ever see a Cohen or a Levy on the sign? Hell no! Of course not. The people who patronize those places are the upper-class *goyim* all the way on up to the Royal Family, King George VI and the rest of them. And like it or not, we've got to do the same thing in New York. You know the saying," he added, grinning slightly. "If you can't beat them..."

"But did you have to take it out on the kids?" Miriam asked.

Jonathan felt ashamed of his earlier behavior. He stood up and went to the boys' bedroom; they were both awake, talking in whispers across the narrow gap which separated the two beds.

"May I come in?" asked Jonathan, standing in the doorway. "Or is it for little people only?"

He entered the room and sat down on the carpeted floor between the beds, leaning back against the wall. The boys looked at him hopefully, Gerald on the left, Simon on the right.

"Want to hear a story?"

"Tell us what you did in the war." The demand came from Gerald.

"Stayed out of sight," Jonathan replied quickly.

"No, you didn't," Simon chimed in. "Uncle Myron told us you killed all the Germans."

Jonathan let a broad smile creep across his face, the bad feeling resulting from the argument with Jacob disappearing. "That's not quite true," he said. "I had to leave a few for the other men; otherwise they'd have got jealous."

Gerald nodded sagely, his deep brown eyes wide open in admiration. "That's right," he said, directing his words over Jonathan's head to Simon. "He'd have been greedy if he killed them all by himself." Then he looked down at his father.

"Tell us how you killed them all."

"Sold them suits that were too tight," Jonathan replied flippantly. "They choked to death."

Simon sucked in his breath, marvelling at the revelation, but Gerald refused to be overawed. "That's silly," he told Jonathan.

"I suppose it is. But you should be asleep anyway, so how about it?"

"You said you'd tell us a story," Gerald reminded him.

"What do you want to hear?"

Both boys answered simultaneously. "Goldilocks and the three bears."

Making himself comfortable against the bedroom wall, Jonathan glanced left and right to make certain that both boys were paying attention. If I have to go through this one again, he thought, they'd better stay awake to hear it out.

"Once upon a time," he began, the book clasped in his left hand, "there were three bears..."

The bedroom door swung open and Miriam tiptoed in. She stood motionless for a moment, waiting for Jonathan to finish the sentence. "Can I listen as well?" she asked, when he looked up.

Jonathan tapped the carpet with the book. Miriam walked past the bottom of Gerald's bed and sat down next to Jonathan, stretching out, resting her head on his chest. He put his free arm around her and continued with the story, changing his voice to fit in with the characters.

Skipping the parts he thought he could get away with, he soon came to the end of the story. "Goldilocks was never seen again, and the three bears lived happily ever after," he said, dropping the book onto the carpet.

He looked up at Gerald, who lay fast asleep, clutching a small teddy bear. Simon was turned away, bent almost double, a thumb stuck into his mouth.

"You did it to me again, you horrors," Jonathan muttered, shaking his head in disgust. "Come on, Mrs. Gellenbaum-Chesterton, née Helman. Time to leave."

Then he realized that Miriam, too, was sound asleep.

# 13

Opening the heavy briefcase full of work from the office, Jonathan extracted a thick sheaf of documents, laid them on the walnut desk of his den and began to sort through them. As he checked the sales figures on the store reports, his left hand automatically unwrapped a cigar from its cellophane wrapper and thrust it into his mouth. For a while he sat chewing the cigar thoughtfully, running his eyes down the columns of closely scrawled figures, comparing the performances of the different merchandise categories against the previous week's figures, seeing how they matched up.

He paused from the work while he searched for his gold Dunhill lighter, feeling through the pockets of his jacket till he found it. As always, he glanced at the minutely engraved inscription which completely covered the face and back of the lighter. "To Jonathan. Thanks for ten wonderful years. Just don't you dare smoke your rotten cigars in the house! Miriam."

And, as always, he grinned hugely.

Miriam had never complained about the cigars during the years they had lived in the East Side apartment; perhaps it was because they had paid rent. Now, in their own home in Great Neck, it was a totally different story. Almost from the day of their moving into the four-bedroom, Georgian style house, she had been at him. The drapes will reek of stale smoke, she complained; the carpet will stink, the furniture will smell like the inside of a cigar store, or worse, like a longshoreman's bar. Eventually they had compromised. Jonathan could smoke in the den, or in the spacious back garden which gave him a view toward Long Island Sound. But nowhere else were his cigars allowed in the house.

Still smiling at the thought of the inscription, Jonathan returned his attention to the store reports. Halfway through the spring season, the four Chestertons stores were showing an average increase over projected sales of thirty-eight percent. That was cause enough for celebration, but the greatest joy in Jonathan's eyes came from the success of the main store, a two-story operation on West Fifty-seventh Street, just off Fifth Avenue. Opened five years earlier, over all of Jacob's objections to the name change, it was moving ahead in a way that was no less than spectacular. The three other stores, in Boston, Washington, D.C. and Philadelphia, were all pulling their weight, but the New York outlet—closest to Jonathan's heart because it was the first—was by far the most successful.

Even Jacob, who at Miriam's and Jonathan's insistence had given up his own apartment and was living with them, had gradually come to terms with the new stores and the strangeness of the name which adorned the fronts. Twice a week he left the house with Jonathan to visit the West Fifty-seventh Street store, ostensibly to check the quality of merchandise coming in from both the company's own factory and from outside suppliers, but really to alleviate the encroaching boredom—because for Jacob, working in the factory was now nothing more than a memory to be treasured.

A year earlier, taking advantage of a more plentiful labor situation and cheaper real estate values, Jonathan had closed down the manufacturing operation on Houston Street and transferred it to Buffalo; the decision to do so had caused a flood of soul-searching on his part, like the emotions of a fledgling bird leaving for the first time the nest it has come to know so well. With nothing left in New York that required his full-time attention, Jacob had been forced to take a back seat. He visited the new plant twice a year, at the beginning of each selling season, just as he regularly toured the four clearance stores which still carried his name. They were courtesy calls, however, nothing more; merely a way of keeping in contact with the operation he had helped to launch.

Jonathan emerged from the den into the wide hallway leading in from the front door, the reports clenched in his fist, the cigar, forgotten, still in his mouth. He walked past the doors to the living and dining rooms into the bright, airy kitchen, creeping up behind Miriam, who was busy at the sink, savoring the knowledge that she was unaware of his approach. He grasped her around the waist, lifting her up, feeling elated that her figure was almost the same as it had been when he had first met her.

She screamed in fright, dropping the empty saucepan she was holding, spinning around to face him; the saucepan fell to the floor with a loud clatter, bouncing away.

"You scared the life out of me!" she gasped. "I never heard you come out of the den." Then she saw the cigar in Jonathan's mouth and pointed threateningly at it.

"Okay," he said placatingly, realizing he had unwittingly broken her one concrete rule. "I'm going, I'm going. I only wanted to know where the kids were." He retreated along the kitchen floor, back toward the den.

"Myron came round earlier this afternoon and took them over to the park," she replied. "He wanted to see you about something, so he took the kids out instead of hanging around the house waiting for you. He was scared I might give him something to do."

"What did he want?"

Miriam shrugged. "Didn't tell me. Now get out of here with that thing." She sniffed, wrinkling her nose in disgust at the smell of burning tobacco. "You've only been in the kitchen for a few seconds, and it stinks already. Out! Get that stinking piece of weed out of here."

Wickedly Jonathan took a deep draw on the cigar and blew the pungent gray smoke across the kitchen at Miriam. She coughed as the cloud enveloped her. Waving her hands to clear the smoke, she looked for something to throw, but Jonathan was already back in the sanctuary of his den, his private fortress which Miriam entered only to dust.

Myron brought the boys back from the park half an hour later, their impending presence announced by excited shouts as they wriggled free of their uncle's grip and raced toward the front door. Inside the house they made straight for the den, bursting in on Jonathan as he ploughed through the paper work, telling him of all the things they had done during the afternoon. From there, leaving their baseball mitts, bat and ball on the floor of the den, they rushed into the kitchen to find their mother, leaving Jonathan alone with Myron.

"If you want a smoke, you've got to do it in here," Jonathan said, sweeping his hand around the den. "Your sister's on another one of her clean air kicks, God help us all." He pulled out a folding chair for his brother-in-law, waiting till he was seated before closing the door.

"How's the folks?" he asked.

"Not bad. My mother still nags and my father carries on like he can't hear a word she's saying."

Jonathan chuckled quietly at the answer. He, Miriam and the two boys went over to the Helmans' home about twice a month, and nothing much seemed to have changed since he had first met them—except there were no longer any arguments about Myron's future.

"How's the medical profession?" Jonathan asked. "Any good offers for an aspiring sawbones?"

A sour look crossed Myron's face at the question, a combination of a smile and a painful grimace, like the joining of the theater's two faces.

"That's what I came round to see you about," he replied. "You could say prospects are looking up a bit. I got the offer of a position today."

Jonathan's interest quickened. "Great! Congratulations. You must be thrilled. Where is it?"

Slowly Myron pulled an envelope from his pocket, a familiar-looking envelope with a government seal on it. "Place called Korea. Ever hear of it?"

The feeling of pleasure left Jonathan abruptly and he slumped back into the chair. He sat numbly, unable to speak, staring stupidly at Myron.

"Guess there goes my dream of flashy cars, padded shoulders and one-hundred-dollar bills in every pocket, for the time being," Myron said philosophically. "My country calls me yet again, and I must go."

Jonathan reached out a hand for the draft notice and looked at it, reading the words mechanically. "Too bad," he muttered, knowing that the words conveyed nothing. "You should have got married and had a couple of kids, done something smart like I did."

"Wouldn't have helped," Myron said. "I'd have been better off playing third base for the Yankees."

"Second base," Jonathan corrected him, and both men laughed for an instant. "You're lucky you didn't. Uncle Sam would have had you pitching grenades instead of firing off double-play relays. This way you'll be in some safe, secluded place, and you'll get in valuable surgical experience."

Myron leaned down and picked up the ball which the boys had left behind, tossing it from one hand to the other. "The kind of experience I'm going to get out there won't stand me in good stead when I get back—not unless the rate of bullet wounds and guys with shrapnel in their guts takes a big rise in New York."

"Does Miriam know?" Jonathan asked quietly.

"Nobody but you. I knew it was coming, so I've been intercepting the mailman for the past couple of weeks. I take my physical, then it's good-bye Charlie. Frozen Chosen here I come, or wherever the hell they decide to send me."

"You'll be commissioned this time," Jonathan reminded him, desperately seeking something optimistic to say. "That's some comfort at least. No KP or guard, none of that happy horseshit."

"Suppose it's some consolation. Maybe when I get back—if I get back—I'll be so sick of the world of medicine that I'll take you up on that offer you made a few years back."

"No ifs about it," Jonathan said. "And don't speak like that in front of Miriam, for God's sake."

"Yeah. I'm feeling sorry for myself. Every minute of the past couple of weeks I've been saying why me? I did it last time, let some other dumb bastard pull his weight in this one."

"You didn't do anything last time," Jonathan reminded him, "unless you call guarding the home front and seeing which wives were feeling lonely, fighting a war."

Myron dropped the ball and slapped Jonathan across the knee. "You're right. I didn't do a damn thing last time, and I'll probably do the same this time. But I still might take you up on that offer when it's all over."

"It's still open to you," Jonathan said, happy at having cheered Myron up. "Even more so now, with the Chestertons stores going the way they are. Go on, go tell your sister. I'll take the kids out for a walk while you do it. And remember—you use the word when, not if." He stood up to let Myron walk past, watching from the door of the den as he moved, heavy-footed, toward the kitchen. Just great, Jonathan thought. Just what we needed—

somebody back in uniform again, getting his butt shot off for no apparent reason.

"Simon! Gerald!" he called. "Come here. I want you."

He heard the sound of running footsteps as the boys raced through the living room on their way in from the garden. Opening the front door, he took them by the hand, leading them outside.

"Where are we going?" Gerald asked.

"For a walk. Just a short walk before dinner." Jonathan began to stroll aimlessly in the direction of the main road, dragging his sons behind him.

"But we've just been out," Gerald complained. "We spent the whole afternoon in the park with Uncle Myron. Why do we have to go out again?"

"Because I say so," Jonathan answered brusquely.

Simultaneously he cursed himself for being a coward. But under no circumstances did he want to be present when Myron told Miriam his news.

# 14

The new Chestertons store in Chicago was something special. A self-satisfied smile stretched across Jonathan's face as he watched the shopfitters putting in the finishing touches, setting up the interior display units for the grand opening on the following day.

The foreman wandered across the carpeted floor to where Jonathan stood, checking the progress of the men he passed. "What do you think, Mr. Chesterton?" he asked. "Up to your expectations?"

"Right up there. Reckon your men will be finished by five this evening?"

Looking at his watch, the foreman furrowed his brow as he made some rapid calculations. "Should be if there are no holdups. When are you expecting your stock to come in?"

"There's some in the basement already," Jonathan told him. "The rest of it, the big stuff, is being held in storage at the warehouse. Soon as you give us the word, we can call them for delivery."

"I'll let you know soon as I can." Stepping away from Jonathan, the foreman looked around the store, letting his eyes sweep lazily across the expanse. "You've got a crack spot here, Mr. Chesteron," he complimented Jonathan, mentally transforming the scene of disorganization into a finished store. "I wish you luck."

"Thanks." Jonathan walked away, leaving the man to get on with his work. Avoiding display units which lay helter-skelter across the floor as they awaited attention, he headed for the stairs leading down to the basement. Bending his head to miss the top of the doorway, he walked carefully down the stairs, seeing the piles of cartons at the bottom. The man who was sorting through them looked up as he heard Jonathan's footsteps.

"Found anything that looks like it might belong to us yet?" Jonathan joked.

"So far we've got a wonderful line in all the latest fashion boxes," the man replied, grinning broadly. "Give me your size and I'll see if I can fix you up."

Jonathan laughed; the sound echoed across the basement. "Very large, as my wife would say. And I'll take it in blue if you've got it, Brian."

"Can't help you there," Brian Chambers replied. "Any color you like as long as it's beige."

"You're too young to remember lines like that," Jonathan said, studying the man who, on the following day, would become the manager of the newest Chestertons store. Brian Chambers was young, certainly, only twenty-five. But Jonathan was a firm believer in the power of youth; he remembered how young he had been when he had opened the Houston Street factory.

To Jonathan, Brian Chambers represented an outstanding catch from Marshall Field. When word had gone out in the men's wear trade press that a Chestertons store was being planned for Chicago, the first outside the East Coast, Brian had written a comprehensive letter to Jonathan at the New York office, detailing his retail experience, limited though it was, and asking to be considered for a selling position with the new store. On his first trip out to Chicago after receiving the letter, Jonathan had taken Brian out to dinner. He had been impressed with the young man's intensity and his knowledge of the direction in which the retail industry was heading. They both shared the belief that retailing—no matter what the area of merchandise—would become a matter of the big getting bigger and the small existing precariously at best, or going out of business altogether.

And Brian, in firm agreement with Jonathan, was convinced that Chestertons was going to be very, very big.

"How long do you plan on staying?" Jonathan asked, watching his new manager rip open a box and check the contents.

"Till it's done, I guess." He put the box aside and eyed the pile which still confronted him, undismayed by the task. "When can we begin to shift some of this stuff upstairs?"

"Shopfitters say they reckon to be finished about five. Right after they pack up, we can begin setting our stuff up."

Brian scratched his head, disturbing the short, light brown hair which had remained well groomed despite his exertions in the basement. "Ask them if we can bring up some of the stuff now. Even if we only put it in the vicinity of where it's supposed to go, it'll save us time later on. Then I'll put in a call to the warehouse to arrange a time for the suit and sports coat delivery."

Jonathan retraced his steps up to the store. One of the shopfitting crew was vacuuming the deep brown carpet—with the almost invisible Chesterton name woven in black—picking up the debris which was distributed generously across the floor. He found the foreman standing at the front of the store, talking with the window dresser whom Jonathan had brought with him from New York.

"Any chance of us setting out the shirts, ties and knitwear?" Jonathan asked the foreman. "Looks like your men have finished in that area, and we can save some time by getting started now."

"Okay by me, Mr. Chesterton, but try to stay out of my people's way. It's for your own good. If the job goes after five, you'll be paying overtime."

Jonathan clapped the man on the shoulder. "And don't I know it," he said humorously. He walked back to the basement stairway and called down to Brian; less than a minute later, the first cartons began coming up the stairs.

It was almost one o'clock in the morning when Jonathan and Brian left the store, satisfied that everything was in order for the following day's opening; there were still a few jobs that needed doing, but they could be finished in the morning. The shopfitting crew had departed just after five, leaving Jonathan and Brian to set out the merchandise. By the time the trucks with the outerwear had arrived, the smaller goods had been arranged. Four hours later, after sorting out the suits, sports coats and trousers by design and size, the job had been completed. Now, as they walked to an adjacent parking lot where Brian had left his car, each man felt the excitement of the following day in a different way—Brian because he would manage a store for the first time (and what a store!), Jonathan because the opening of a store in Chicago symbolized an immense geographical stride for the company.

"Hungry?" Jonathan asked, getting into the car. He was starving, but he did not want to eat alone.

"Famished," Brian replied, "only there aren't too many places open this time of night that I'd trust my digestive system to."

"Come back to the hotel," Jonathan invited. "You're running me back there anyway. I'll get somebody in the kitchen to make something for us."

Brian turned the ignition key, listening to the engine stutter into life against the December cold, playing with the choke control till it was idling smoothly. "People at your hotel would love you at one in the morning. If you were lucky, you might wind up with a glass of lukewarm milk and a stale cheese sandwich. I've got a better idea. Come back to my place for a while. We can talk about tomorrow while I make something hot."

"You cook?" Jonathan asked, surprised.

"Not cordon bleu, but passable. Nobody's ever sued me for ptomaine poisoning yet. How about it?"

"What are you hanging around here for? Drive on."

Brian pulled into the parking lot of an apartment building on Lake Shore Drive, facing Lake Michigan. As the icy wind ripped off the lake, Jonathan pulled the heavy topcoat tightly around himself, trying to find some warmth in its depths. Despite the weight of the fabric, he shivered violently as the fierce gusts tore through him like a solid force.

"Now I know why they call this place the windy city," he stammered. "Get us inside quick."

Brian's laugh was whipped away by the wind. "This is nothing," he replied, fumbling in his coat pocket for the key. "It's only the beginning of December. You should try it in January or February."

"You stay here and try it," Jonathan said. "Just let me get back to good old, damp New York."

Brian led the way to a fourth-floor apartment. Opening the door, he flicked on the lights and invited Jonathan inside. As he removed his coat, Jonathan surveyed the apartment, curious about the life-style of this young man with whom he was entrusting the welfare of the new store. The apartment was papered in a pale blue shade which toned in well with the deeper blue coloring of the living room suite. To offset this, the carpet was a deep, rich rust color, a combination which Jonathan found appealing. Several ornaments were scattered around the living room, casually placed, it seemed at first glance. Yet Jonathan sensed an underlying note of precision. Overall, he decided that he approved of the layout, even if some of it was a bit too chintzy for his own tastes.

"Like it?" Brian asked.

"Looks a damned sight better than the store when we left it. I think we'll hold our Christmas special promotion right here."

Brian laughed appreciatively. "What do you want to eat?"

"Better make it something pretty light. I still want to get some sleep tonight."

"I'll do some omelettes," Brian decided. "They won't take too long. Make yourself comfortable while I'm fixing them."

Jonathan dropped heavily onto the dark blue couch, feeling the springs sag beneath his weight. Must do something about that, he thought absent-mindedly. At the last checkup, to which Miriam had almost forced him to go, the doctor had pointedly told him that he was putting on too much weight. But what does a doctor know? had been his initial reaction to the news. Nonetheless he felt an occasional barb of worry, having a heavy build to begin with. He grinned suddenly, remembering that the doctor had also told him to cut down on his smoking, give it up altogether if possible. Yes, I will. Miriam must have paid him to tell me that. I pay him to get the truth about my body, and Miriam's probably slipping him money on the side to say what she wants me to hear. Some doctor. I'll be glad when Myron gets back from his field hospital in Korea. He'll tell me what I want to hear, none of this don't-do-this and don't-do-that garbage.

Brian returned from the kitchen ten minutes later, carrying a tray which he laid gently on the table. Jonathan whistled loudly in admiration as he saw the two fluffy omelettes, accompanied by toast and hot chocolate. "Brian, you sure you want to manage one of my stores?" he asked lightly. "Because you'd make somebody a lovely wife."

A red tinge suffused Brian's face, spreading from his cheeks up to his forehead, finally to his ears. "The modern bachelor knows how to look after himself," he said quickly, hoping that Jonathan had not noticed the blush; it didn't do for a store manager to show embarrassment. "We've come a long way since the living-out-of-cans routine."

"Watch it," Jonathan warned, scooping up some of the omelette. "You're making fun of the happiest days of my life."

He cleaned the plate quickly, taking his time over the chocolate, which was still too hot for his taste. "Are you going to run me back to the hotel?" he asked hopefully, waiting for the drink to cool.

Brian tried to answer with his mouth full, finally pointing to the blue couch on which Jonathan was sitting. "That pulls out into a bed. If you want, you can sack out there, and I'll run you back early in the morning, in plenty of time for the opening."

Jonathan agreed with the suggestion. "That's fine. I don't really want to drag you out again. We don't open till midday, so there's plenty of time." He yawned, covering his mouth with a beefy hand.

After clearing away the dishes, Brian brought in a set of bed linen which he dropped on the couch next to Jonathan, pale blue, matching the rest of the apartment decor. Good sense of color, Jonathan noted; well worth remembering for the future. He pulled out the bed, threw the linen across it in a haphazard manner and undressed, crawling in between the sheets in his underwear.

For a few minutes he lay awake, listening to the sound of the shower as Brian prepared for bed. For some obscure reason, Jonathan found the whole situation vaguely amusing; the life of the bachelor had certainly changed since he had tried it.

Early the following morning, Brian drove Jonathan back to the hotel, waiting while he cleaned up and changed. Then they drove to the store, where Jonathan got his first chance to see the new sales staff as a complete unit. He had met them, one at a time, several weeks earlier when he had made the hirings on Brian's recommendation. Seeing them now, as a team, made Jonathan feel even more confident of his new manager's efficiency.

The salesmen were all young, clean cut and immaculately groomed. Even more important, they were already thoroughly conversant with the Chestertons merchandise. He watched with ill-concealed interest as the first customers entered the shop, eager to see the selling techniques of the new people. Posing as a customer, Jonathan strolled across the store and began to examine a display of ties, holding them against his plain blue suit to check the contrast. Simultaneously he eavesdropped on a transaction which was taking place at the next counter, listening delightedly as the salesman traded the customer up to a more expensive suit than the one he had enquired about originally, confidently suggesting accessories such as shirts and ties to turn a normal sale into a far more profitable multiple sale.

Pleased with his observations, Jonathan replaced the ties and started to walk toward the shirt units, when he felt Brian tap him on the elbow.

"Telephone, Mr. Chesterton."

"Did they say who?"

"Your wife."

Mentally Jonathan kicked himself. In all the excitement of the new store opening, he had forgotten to call Miriam, something he normally did every night when he was out of the city. Annoyed at his neglect, he walked quickly to the cash desk, picking up the receiver.

"Hi, Miriam. Sorry about last night but we were so busy getting things straight that I clean forgot to call. You have to come up here and see this place; it's out of this world." He listened for her reply, hoping that his enthusiasm would carry across the hundreds of miles separating them. But there was nothing, no sound other than a faint buzz which could have been interference on the line.

"Miriam?" He began to get anxious about her lack of response. "Are you there? Say something. What's the matter?"

Then he realized that the slight noise he was hearing was not interference. It was the sound of somebody crying, tight pain-racked sobs as Miriam choked back the tears.

"It's Myron," she burst out, the words finally coming in an unstoppable torrent. "Come home, Jonathan, please. Myron's been killed."

Jonathan felt behind him for the cashier's chair and slumped down, the strength draining out of his body. Oh, Christ. Not this, not to us.

When he spoke again, the words were only half-formed, the ends trailing away in his throat.

"I'll be back on the next plane. Don't do anything till I get there."

He listened for a reply, but there was only silence. Slowly, as if in a dream, he replaced the receiver and stood up, his legs shaky. The store did not matter any more, the clean-cut salesmen who were carrying his name, nothing. He beckoned to Brian, who, sensing that something was amiss, came running over.

"Get me to O'Hare. I've got to get back to New York."

"What's wrong?"

The composure began to return as Jonathan forced himself to accept the news. "My brother-in-law's been killed in Korea, and I've got to get home. If you run up against any problems here, call Head Office. Somebody there'll sort you out."

During the journey to the airport, Brian concentrated on his driving, not talking, listening with half an ear as Jonathan reminisced about Myron.

"Never saw a thing in the last war. Spent it as a medic teaching other guys how to patch up chest wounds. Now he goes out as a doctor, a captain, and catches it. Doesn't make any sense, does it?" He glanced at Brian, taking the younger man's silence as affirmation of his own words.

"When I first met him—when was it?—in 1938 he had his heart set on playing for the Yankees. You follow baseball?" he asked suddenly. Brian shook his head, never for one moment taking his eyes off the road. "Never mind," Jonathan continued. "He reckoned he was going to be the greatest second baseman who ever played in the majors. I used to kid him about it, telling him he was going to be a great third baseman. Got to be a joke between us. He had it all worked out, only he never made it. Decided to be a doctor instead, to please his mother. A nice safe profession. Respected. Good money. A pillar of society." Jonathan's eyes watered as the memories of Myron came flooding back.

"A nice safe profession," he repeated. "Only now they're going to ship him home in a wooden box with a flag to keep him warm." He swore softly, then lapsed into silence, watching the snow-covered buildings slide past as Brian ignored the posted speed limits in his haste to get to the airport.

At O'Hare, Jonathan grabbed his suitcase and ran toward the reservation desk, not sparing a glance for Brian, who remained in the car, stunned by the sudden turn of events, his mind trying to reconcile the jovial man who had opened the store that morning to the tearful man he now watched, the suitcase swinging from his right hand like a lead weight.

His voice breaking, Jonathan cancelled the flight reservation which would have returned him to New York at the end of the week and asked for a seat on the next flight, explaining the urgency of the situation. Forty minutes later, he was sitting on an aircraft, the seat belt done up, watching Chicago drop away beneath the wings.

As the taxi dropped him off in front of the house in Great Neck, Jacob opened the door.

"Where's Miriam?" Jonathan asked his father.

"Upstairs talking to the Helmans."

"The kids?"

Jacob pointed to the next house. "The neighbor took them in when they came home from school. She said they could stay there overnight."

Jonathan shrugged off his coat, letting it drop onto a chair. "What happened?" he asked flatly, the frantic rush from Chicago catching up with him.

"The Helmans got a telegram this morning. You know..." Jacob broke off, his face a mask of helplessness.

"How did it happen?"

"Who knows how these things happen? The telegram said it was ten days ago."

"When's the... when's Myron being flown in?" For some reason, he could not bring himself to use the word body.

"Two days' time," Jonathan replied. "They're bringing him into McGuire Air Force Base in New Jersey."

"Do you know if anything's been done about the funeral?"

"I spoke to Sam," Jacob said. "He mentioned something about the arrangements being made through his *shul*. But I think you should look after it, not leave it to Sam."

"I'll see to it." He turned away from his father and ran up the stairs, stopping outside the bedroom door for a moment while he listened to Miriam's voice as she spoke to her mother. She looked up as he entered; her eyes were red, her cheeks stained with dried tears. Jonathan stood by the bed feeling absolutely powerless to do anything. I never had a brother, was the one recurring thought. How the hell do I know what it feels like to lose somebody that close?

Vaguely he heard Miriam tell her mother that he had arrived, flown straight back from Chicago on hearing the news. He sat down on the bed next to Miriam and put an arm around her shoulders, feeling the need to comfort her but not knowing what to do.

"Give me the phone," he said, taking it gently from Miriam's hand. She relaxed her grip on it, leaning her head against Jonathan's broad shoulder, trying to find spiritual strength in his physical strength.

"This is Jonathan." He waited for Miriam's mother to reply, then offered his condolences, knowing how futile they sounded. "Look, I'll bring you and Sam over here after the funeral. You can stay here for the week while the *shivah's* on, longer if you like, as long as you want."

He passed the receiver back to Miriam, levered himself off the bed and left the room. Outside on the landing, he clenched his fists so tightly that the fingernails bit painfully into the palms of his hands. He felt useless in the situation, and frustrated and angry with himself because of it.

Sam Helman seemed most affected by the tragedy. The friendly face was lined heavily. Black shadows framed the tired brown eyes, and he was stooped as if struggling under a heavy load, his shoulders slumped, his back bent.

Next to him stood Miriam's mother. Her hair was bleached and rinsed to a harsh, platinum shade, pulled back severely from her face, which wore a stiff mask, a set expression to hide her grief. She stared straight ahead, not seeing the other mourners, suffering her loss in silence, in self-imposed privacy.

Miriam stood beside Jonathan, her hand in his, fingers entwined, holding him for support. She had taken tranquilizers the previous night to help her sleep, and the effects were still evident. Every few minutes she closed her eyes as she fought off the drowsiness, leaning against Jonathan.

Off to the side stood Jacob, nervously fingering his watch chain, fidgeting as he looked at the family, then at the friends of the Helmans who formed a somber group.

Following his father's suggestion, Jonathan had taken over the funeral arrangements from Sam Helman, contacting the Military Air Transport Service to find out when the body would be arriving. Disregarding the tradition of having the body begin its last journey from the home, he had arranged for it to be transported directly to the cemetery, feeling such a decision to be in the best interests of the family.

The apartment doorbell gave a short, urgent ring, the unexpected sound seeming strangely sharp in the depressing atmosphere. Jacob looked around to see if anybody would answer it before he walked into the hall. A soldier wearing captain's bars stood outside, his finger on the bell push ready to ring again. In his right hand was a small, brown, imitation leather suitcase. Stamped in gold on the top near the handle were the initials M. H.

"Yes, can I help you?" Jacob asked.

"My name's Ben Cantor," the soldier replied. "I was with Myron in Korea." He lifted the suitcase so that Jacob could see it better. "I came home a couple of days ago and found out the time of the funeral. I brought back..." He stumbled on the words. "I brought back Myron's personal effects."

Jacob stood aside. "Come in, come in. You're just in time." He led the man into the apartment, pointing out Myron's parents and Miriam. Leaving the suitcase on the floor, the soldier approached the Helmans, shook hands with them, then turned to Miriam.

"Myron spoke about you often," he said quietly. "I'm sorry that we couldn't meet in happier circumstances."

Sensing that Miriam was unable to reply, Jonathan spoke for her. "We're very grateful that you came."

During the long journey to the cemetery, Jonathan sat next to the soldier, questioning him in hushed tones about Myron.

"Were you with him when it happened?"

The soldier's mouth dropped as he recalled the event, and he nodded glumly. "Our boys were having a big push to regain lost ground. The day before, the Chinese had driven a wedge into our front, penetrated about five miles. We were mounting a counterattack, and the hospitals were picking up the pieces as usual. Myron was pulling shrapnel out of a guy's stomach when a round landed short in our compound."

"One of our own?" Jonathan asked incredulously.

"Yeah, one of our own—and it wasn't the first time either. Theoretically we were safe, about two miles behind the fighting. If it looked like coming closer, we'd clear out quick."

"And Myron got hit by the shrapnel," Jonathan concluded, seeing it happen in his mind's eye—Myron in a doctor's gown being felled by a friendly artillery shell.

"No." The soldier's voice cut into Jonathan's thoughts. "Myron was killed by a freak accident. Nobody was hit by the blast, but a tent support snapped and dropped down onto the table. Myron was bent over the patient, trying to keep the dust and crap out of the wound, and the broken support ploughed straight into his back like a spear."

Despite the car's heater, Jonathan shuddered in horror. An accident, just like the soldier said—a goddamn freak accident.

"What happened to the patient?" Jonathan asked, not caring whether the man has lived or died.

"Dead. It was a hopeless case, nearly every vital organ destroyed. A grenade had gone off almost underneath him, and the guy had half a ton of scrap metal in what was left of his gut. But Myron wouldn't give it up. As long as there was the faintest sign of life, he had to keep on trying." The soldier leaned against the side of the car, fixing Jonathan with an even stare. "Great story, huh?"

Jonathan shuddered again. "Yeah, just great. Do me a favor. Don't tell anybody else how it happened—not like that, anyway."

"I wouldn't believe it myself," the soldier said, "except I was there to see it. I was operating on the next table. I don't think any of us moved for ten seconds, the shock was that great."

The coffin was waiting in the cemetery chapel, a flag draped across it. Six soldiers and a young second lieutenant stood at attention, forming an honor guard. Jonathan watched sourly as the lieutenant saluted Myron's friend.

You're getting a great send-off, Myron, Jonathan thought. No baseball pennants, no World Series trophies—just a red, white and blue flag for which you died by accident, and a snotty-nosed young shavetail and six fuzz-faced recruits who probably volunteered for this gruesome detail to get out of doing KP or guard duty.

It began to snow as the funeral procession moved from the chapel after the short ceremony, drifting white flakes which stood out starkly as they landed on the rabbi's black robe. Jonathan felt the wet flakes on his face, melting quickly under the attack of his body heat. He walked slowly, holding Jacob with one hand, his father-in-law with the other, following the coffin and its guard of honor to a far corner of the cemetery where the graves were recent, unmarked as yet with memorial stones. The column of mourners stopped by an open grave, a yawning black hole contrasting crudely with the settling snow.

The Hebrew words of the ceremony meant little to Jonathan; they soared over his head like a passing breeze, words jumbling into each other, although he could see his father's lips move as he made the responses.

As the rabbi ceased praying, two of the soldiers carefully folded the flag and passed it to the lieutenant, who presented it to Sam Helman. Sam nodded his thanks, taking the flag, holding it close to his side. It dropped from his nerveless fingers to the ground, lying in the snow; nobody made any move to pick it up.

Jonathan could watch no longer. He closed his eyes, screwing them shut to keep in the tears and keep out the sight of Myron's final journey.

Then the coffin was in the ground and the mourners were filing past, each shovelling a token spadeful of cold, damp earth into the gaping pit, covering the box from view; the pieces of earth rattled like the sound of death as they bounced onto the wood of the coffin, scattering against the sides of the grave.

Jonathan picked up the spade, bent down and dug into the pile of earth displaced by the gravedigger. He heard the rabbi's urgent whisper to cover the head of the coffin. Straightening up, he cast the earth into the pit, digging again, showering more earth onto the coffin, angry that Myron was lying there because of an accident, a miscalculated powder charge in an artillery shell, and a desire to protect a man already marked for death. Why weren't the Yankees playing at home that day? Jonathan thought bitterly. Myron wouldn't have opened surgery till after the final out. And he'd still have been alive.

Fiercely he thrust the spade into the ground, leaving it for the next mourner, bitter, hating the soldiers who stood at attention around the graveside, hating the rabbi whose meaningless words were supposed to bring dignity to a man's passing and comfort to those who loved him, hating himself as he remembered that December night in the Ardennes so many years before, hating everybody.

He heard Jacob's footsteps, soft on the settling snow, and shook off the comforting arm, stepping away from the grave, heading back toward the chapel.

# Part
# 2
# CHESTERTONS

# 1

The map was a cartographer's dream. Featuring the United States mainland, it was hand-painted and set in an eight-foot-square varnished frame, occupying a place of honor behind Jonathan's desk in the Chestertons boardroom. Next to it was a color blowup of the front of the main store on West Fifty-seventh Street, which fronted the Chestertons head office.

Thirty-eight small red flags dotted the map, showing the locations of Chestertons stores throughout the country, while seven blue flags denoted cities where the company was thinking of opening new outlets. Looking at the map never failed to arouse Jonathan. Whenever time permitted, he studied it leisurely like a general planning military strategy, moving his forces this way and that, marshaling them for a complete take-over of desirable territory. It was his dream that one day soon every major city in the United States would show a red flag.

The map had been bought six months after the Chicago store opening, twenty-four years earlier, when Jonathan had followed the initial move away from the East Coast by expanding the group as far afield as Seattle to the west and Atlanta and Dallas to the south and southwest. As yet, California was represented only by blue flags, but that was also slated for change.

Tired eventually of looking at the encapsulated Chestertons empire, Jonathan sat down behind the desk and picked up the Monday morning store reports, ready to launch himself into another week. He spared a moment to glance at the family portrait on his desk, taken three years before at Gerald's wedding. The sight of himself in a tuxedo with buttons threatening to pop made him wince. Miriam stood to his right in the photograph, the rich auburn hair now kept that shade with the assistance of a hairdresser's expertise, and Jacob was to his left, the snow-white hair fastidiously combed to one side. In the center of the group stood Gerald and his bride, Marilyn, a tall, willowy girl with ash-blond hair and candid blue eyes, while off to the side stood Simon, his arm around a girl whose name Jonathan could not even remember; whenever he saw Simon outside the office, he seemed to be with a different girl.

Pushing the thought of Gerald's wedding to the back of his mind, mainly because it reminded him that age was creeping up, Jonathan began to leaf through the thick stack of papers, his practiced eye picking out the important figures immediately. He fell into the Monday morning routine, comparing the figures for each store against the season's projected budget, then breaking down the figures into the respective merchandise categories. The results looked good, ahead in all categories except leisurewear, which had taken an almighty hammering. And Jonathan intended to get to the bottom of that costly problem during the afternoon's merchandise meeting.

After a few minutes, his eyes drifted back to the wedding photograph, singling out Simon.

"Bum," he muttered. "How come you made such a mess of the leisurewear this season?"

The face in the photograph grinned back, the expression which had been pasted on for the photographer now saved solely for Jonathan, the rich auburn hair and hazel eyes reminding him so uncannily of Myron. With the face, however, all resemblance ended. Myron had been stocky, mad about sports, muscles rippling every time he moved. Simon was slim, a perfect hanger for anything he wore, never exerting himself unless there was no other alternative.

"Bum," Jonathan muttered again, pushing the reports aside, tearing his eyes away from the face which mocked him. "You've wrecked what should have been the best season we ever had."

He picked up the telephone and dialled Gerald's extension. "Got five minutes for me? I want to see you."

Less than a minute after the summons, Gerald entered the boardroom, closing the door quietly behind him.

"Good weekend?" Jonathan asked, waving at a chair.

"Fair. We had some people over Saturday night for dinner—and spent most of Sunday recovering."

"Ah, to be young again," Jonathan said wistfully. "You're making me jealous what with the restricted life I have to lead because of your mother's nagging about my welfare." Gerald began to say something, but Jonathan cut him off, knowing that his son's words would be in support of the measures Miriam took to make Jonathan look after himself. "How's Marilyn and the baby?"

"Making a lot of fuss over each other," Gerald replied. "I think I'll have to move back in with you and Ma. I'd get more attention that way."

Jonathan laughed. "No way that's going to happen. We got rid of you once, and we're not letting you back in. So forget about that idea. Now what did I want to see you about?"

"The designer label angle?" Gerald guessed.

"My mind reader. What's happening with it?"

"I've got all the data back in the office," Gerald answered, referring to the company's interest in signing a top European men's wear stylist to design a range of suits exclusively for Chestertons. "I thought we could go over it after the merchandise meeting. Or is it going to be another one of our marathon sessions?" he added slowly.

"End of season—and you've seen all the figures, same as I have. You tell me how long it's going to be."

"Leisurewear?" Gerald asked.

"Leisurewear," his father grunted. "How would you like to switch places with Simon for a while, see how it works out? You become general merchandise manager, and he takes over as operations manager."

"Thanks, but no thanks," Gerald said, rising from the chair. "I've got no taste for fashion. Just give me cold facts and figures, that's all I ask from life."

"Okay. I'll speak to you about the designer thing after the meeting."

Jonathan rapped his knuckles sharply on the table. The quiet murmuring in the boardroom ceased, and those attending the merchandise meeting turned to face him.

"Right! You all know the rules. If you want coffee, go out and get it now. I don't want any interruptions during the meeting."

Finished with his customary opening to the Monday afternoon merchandise meeting, Jonathan leaned back in the seat, looking down the long mahogany table which dominated the boardroom. He fidgeted for a few seconds until he found a comfortable position, knowing that the session would be lengthy, signalling the end of one selling season and heralding the start of a new one.

At the far end of the table sat Jacob, wearing a blue, lightweight three-piece suit, the gold chain across his stomach lending a distinctive appeal to the garment. Jonathan smiled inwardly, remembering the watch, knowing it still showed three minutes to twelve. He looks good, he thought; the skin's sagging around his chin and neck and the hair looks like snow, but the eyes are bright and he's enjoying his senior years. What is he now? Eighty-eight, eighty-nine? He must be; I'm sixty-four. The revelation shocked Jonathan. God, where do all the years go? It seems like only last week that I was trying to talk him into giving up the tailoring shop on Essex Street. And it's more than forty years ago, a lifetime almost.

His eyes moved from Jacob to Miriam, admiring how she had kept her figure; maybe she's put on a bit of weight, but it's hardly noticeable. Miriam saw him looking and smiled back, the hazel eyes twinkling, still full of love for this man.

The two seats between them were empty, pushed back as Gerald and Simon had disappeared into Jonathan's secretary's office in search of coffee.

The only other person present was Gerald's secretary, who possessed the best shorthand note in the company; she sat away from the main table beyond Jacob, her head bent over the note pad, ready to take down the minutes of the meeting.

While he waited for Simon and Gerald to return, Jonathan pulled out a cigar from his top pocket and placed it in his mouth, rolling it speculatively between his lips, longing to light it but knowing he dare not. He spotted Miriam looking at him hostilely, ready to say something.

"Just chewing," he said defensively. "Just chewing."

Miriam sniffed disparagingly. "Everywhere you go smells like a wet cigar, this place especially. I don't know what's worse, the cigar smoke or the smell of wet, chewed cigars since you had to give them up."

The secretary looked up from her note pad, her mouth curved in amusement as she listened to the argument she had heard so many times before.

Jonathan took the cigar out of his mouth and looked at the already heavily mutilated end, smacking his lips exaggeratedly. "Him," he said, pointing the cigar at Jacob, "he can smoke as many cigarettes as he likes and nobody says anything. But me, I have to chew these darned things. Would you please tell me why?" He saw the secretary's grin and added, "This isn't for the record, got it?"—a reference to the time that she had mischievously included one such argument in the minutes of the meeting.

"Because the doctor said you've got to give them up," Miriam replied. "You've got to take care of your health."

"And what about Jacob's health? How come he gets away with it?"

Jacob lit a cigarette to prove the point he was about to make. "I'm too old to worry about my health. It's never bothered me, so in return I shan't bother it."

They stopped talking as the door opened. Simon and Gerald reentered the boardroom, each holding a white polystyrene cup filled with coffee, walking carefully to avoid slopping any onto the deep blue carpet. Jonathan waited for them to sit down; then he picked up the reports, signifying that the meeting was in progress.

"Okay, Simon, on your way. Let's hear your piece."

Simon cleared his throat, coughing into his hand. He looked at the others, favoring his mother with a faint smile before he began to speak.

"We've just finished week twenty-six, the final week of the spring season. Overall, we're above budget by 7 percent." He stared down at the report, studying the figures for several seconds before continuing.

"The biggest increase throughout the season has been in clothing—suits, sports coats, trousers, and so on—where we're seventeen percent above budget."

"Which means we're still down a hell of a lot in some of the other categories," Jonathan concluded, preparing the drag the whole problem of the poor leisurewear season out into the open.

"We had some difficulties with leisurewear," Simon explained easily. "We bombed out, in fact, didn't even make budget once during the whole twenty-six weeks."

Jonathan checked the leisurewear category on his copy of the report, although he knew already that it was forty-three percent below budget for the season. "Why?" He rapped out the question, making it sound like a rifle shot.

Simon pushed his long auburn hair off his forehead in a nervous gesture, becoming aware that his father was about to make a scene. "We bought the same merchandise right across the chain. It sold well on the East Coast but flopped badly in the Midwest and the Seattle region."

"What's happening to the stuff we're stuck with?"

"We're getting it shipped back east," Simon replied. "We'll put it on special promotion to get rid of it before the new season really gets under way and before the cold sets in."

Jonathan already had the information, but, once started on his crusade against poor buying, he was in no mood to withdraw his horns. The same situation had happened before—identical merchandise being bought for chain-wide distribution—and any clothing retailer with the vaguest knowledge of his trade knew that men in Seattle had different dressing preferences from men in New York; each region of the United States represented entirely different fashion spectra. Additionally the leisure-wear was summer stock—cottons, polyesters—and with the warm weather coming to a close, the company would be hard put to move the merchandise, even in the east where it had sold well during the hot months.

"Did you check with the regional managers before you turned your buyers loose?" Jonathan asked.

"Of course we did!" Simon retorted hotly. "We always ask for feedback from the stores to find out which way the market's going."

"But did you listen to what they said?" Jonathan spaced his words out. "Asking for comments is one thing, but it's valueless unless you utilize that information."

Gerald pushed a slip of paper across the table to his father. Jonathan picked it up, scrutinizing the short message. He looked meaningfully at Gerald, nodded, then turned his eyes back to Simon.

"Don't even bother trying to answer that last question. I've got a memo here from Brian Chambers. He claims the buying group never listened to a damned thing he said about the Midwest leisurewear market. Here, see for yourself." He passed the memorandum to Simon, who eyed it quickly, reddening.

"Who's managing the buying?" Jonathan snapped, without giving Simon time to say anything about the memorandum. "You? Or are you letting the buyers get in whatever they feel is right? The running of the buying group is your ultimate responsibility, right down to approving the cuff buttons on jackets."

Before Simon could reply, Miriam broke into the conversation. "Don't raise your voice, Jonathan. We can't be right with every range we buy."

"Of course we can't!" Jonathan shot back. "But when we're wrong, do we have to be this far out? This leisurewear category has cost us more than one hundred thousand retail dollars this season, what with markdowns and transfers to other stores. That's a hell of a big chunk." He looked down the table at Jacob as he finished speaking, but his father said nothing. His position in the company was nothing more than a courtesy; he did not get involved at all except to make occasional comments on the quality of merchandise. Jonathan still believed, and rightly so, that his father's technical knowledge surpassed that of many younger men in the industry.

Gerald raised a hand in question, waiting till his father nodded before speaking. "Why are we bringing this leisurewear back to put on special promotion here? We're far too late in the year to make any sort of worthwhile impact with it now."

"What do you suggest?" Jonathan asked. "We've got to get some of our investment back."

"What about the renovation of the Atlanta store? We're moving in a load of slow merchandise for the renovation sale, and we could either get rid of that leisurewear as renovation specials or use it as a low-price attraction for the reopening of the store."

Jonathan mulled over the proposition, agreeing with Gerald as, he admitted, he always seemed to. Was it just that Gerald looked like him, with bushy, dark brown hair and those deep brown eyes? Or was it that Gerald always seemed to be keyed into his way of thinking? Both, if he was honest with himself. Gerald possessed none of the airy characteristics of Simon; he saw problems in clearly defined black and white, and made his decisions quickly and accordingly.

"What's the renovation date?" Jonathan asked.

Gerald's eyes flicked down to the papers neatly arranged on his clipboard. "It's due to start on October 15, in seven weeks' time. That's the date the architect's given us. According to his schedule, it should take no more then two weeks."

Jonathan sat back, eyes closed, thinking. Renovation sales and reopening special promotions—where would clothing retailers be without them? Modernize a store, and use the last weeks before work started and the weeks immediately following to promote all the poor sellers you cannot move at regular price elsewhere. He found it mildly surprising that the public had never caught on that they were not getting the bargains they thought at these events.

"How much of that leisurewear do you think we could push through Atlanta when the store reopens, promoting it as a reopening special with thirty-three percent off regular price?" Jonathan asked. The question was directed at the whole table, but he hoped that Gerald would answer. While he waited, his eyes caught those of Miriam; he understood that she continually supported Simon because of his resemblance to her dead brother, but he challenged her to stick up for him now. She held his gaze for a brief moment before turning her eyes away.

"Maybe one thousand pieces," Gerald guessed. "We either run them as you suggest, one-third off, mixed in with regular-price merchandise, or we run a spiff on them and try to sell them for their full retail value."

Spiff. Jonathan hated the word, and he hated what it conveyed. A spiff was a special incentive, over and above a salesman's normal salary and commission, push money which was put into operation when certain goods were selling badly. When an item was spiffed, salesmen would steer customers towards it, knowing they would make extra money on the sale; the customer was unaware that he was being persuaded to buy a piece of merchandise which had been written off by the company as a buying error.

"What kind of spiff have you got in mind?" Jonathan asked.

"Two dollars a unit. That should get the salespeople interested." Gerald began scribbling on a note pad attached to his clipboard. "That would work out at two thousand dollars, plus shipping costs from the West Coast. But it will help to clear that category. It's a lot cheaper than knocking off a straight thirty-three percent."

"And if we ship the whole lot to the Gellenbaum stores and push them out as clearance items?"

"It'll cost us much more," Gerald answered immediately. "We'll have to retail at a much lower price, and we'll still have shipping costs. Either way," he added, "we come out smelling like anything but a rose." There was no hint of humor in his voice; it was a cold, factual statement.

"All right," Jonathan conceded, wearying of the discussion. "If nobody's got any objections, we'll push all the outstanding leisurewear into Atlanta with a two-dollar spiff per unit. Whatever's left over will go into the Gellenbaum stores. Is there anything else we can pile into Atlanta to capitalize on the renovation?"

Simon's voice was clear, untroubled by the poor buying policy in which he had been involved. "We've had an offer of three hundred suits which we can put on special promotion when the store reopens," he said.

"Who's the manufacturer?" Jonathan asked.

"Brenson and Selman."

Jonathan nodded, then looked past his son to Jacob. "You tell him about that manufacturer," he said to his father.

"Simon." Jacob's voice was gentle as if speaking to a child. "Brenson and Selman specializes in making schlock, garbage that won't last six months. Dry clean their suits two or three times, and they fall apart."

"But they're fashionable," Simon argued, his eyes still on Jonathan. "Those suits have got fantastic styling details."

"Fashionable be damned!" Jonathan roared across the table. Miriam jerked upright in shock while Gerald and Jacob remained calm, unmoved by the outburst. The secretary's head stayed low over her notepad.

"We're a quality company," Jonathan continued, lowering his voice. "We don't sell garbage, so we don't buy garbage. Your leisurewear fiasco was one thing—you didn't research your market properly—but I will not tolerate poor-quality merchandise in Chestertons. We've got thirty-eight stores across this country, and we've built our reputation by selling the best merchandise available at competitive prices. I don't give a sweet damn if those suits are the most stylish things in the world. If they don't give our customers value, I don't want to hear about them."

Simon stared at his father. "I've already ordered the suits," he said stubbornly.

"Then you pick up the phone and unorder them. Right now. I want to hear you do it."

Simon walked slowly to the telephone on Jonathan's desk. He lifted the receiver and dialled out, his back to the table, ignoring everybody. Jonathan looked at Jacob; the old man smiled slightly, nodding in approval of the action.

"This is Simon Chesterton of Chestertons," Jonathan heard his son begin. "Something's come up, I'm afraid, and we won't be able to take those suits from you after all." There was a pause; then Simon continued.

"Of course I can see how this is putting you on the spot, but there's nothing I can do about it. Our Atlanta store won't be finished when we expected—trouble with the unions. Yes. Yes, I'm sorry you feel that way about it."

Jonathan tuned himself out of the conversation, waiting for Simon to finish the phone call and rejoin the meeting.

"They won't deal with us again," Simon said, sitting down.

"Good!" Jonathan exclaimed emphatically. "That's the best news I've heard all day. I don't want to deal with *shmatte* merchants like that. Where the hell did you ever get the idea of doing business with that mob?"

Simon chose to ignore the question. "Do you want me for anything else?" he asked, acid in his voice.

Jonathan jumped to his feet, looming over the table, completely dominating the assembly. "You're damned right I want you for something else! Sit down!" He jabbed a finger savagely at the chair from which Simon was in the process of rising. "Maybe if you listen, you might learn something about the way this company should be run. I don't know whether you think the whole thing's a big game, just for your amusement. Let me assure you it's not. We're in business for two reasons—to make money and to keep our customers happy. We are not in business to help out garbage suppliers who should be in the bankruptcy courts, which is where they belong because they're a disgrace to our industry!"

The meeting lasted for another ninety minutes, during which time Jonathan chewed his way through two more cigars as he listened intently to Gerald outline plans for the expansion of two existing stores. Jonathan felt a sense of satisfaction as he digested the information. Why isn't Simon like his brother? he wondered. Then I'd have two retailers on my hands instead of one retailer and one idiot.

When the meeting broke up, Gerald stayed behind to discuss the designer project.

"Well?" Jonathan asked when the others had left. "What do you think about today's effort?"

"I think you shouldn't lose your temper so much," Gerald said. "It's bad for your blood pressure."

In jest, Jonathan wagged a warning finger at his son. "Don't you get in on the act. I get enough of it from your mother. Seriously, do you reckon we could persuade one of our competitors to take Simon in? We could kill two birds with one stone that way."

Gerald began to laugh, then stopped abruptly. "It's not funny, I know. Simon doesn't belong in a company like Chestertons. He should be in a boutique somewhere; that's his level. If he had his way, we'd be selling all the latest high-fashion clothes and nothing else. We'd have every avant-garde manufacturer lining up on our doorstep, confident of getting orders because they had an extra detail on the garment, no matter how absurd. And the hell with quality. Pa, be honest with me. Why do you leave Simon in as general merchandise manager?"

Jonathan spat out a piece of tobacco from the ragged end of his cigar. "Your mother, God bless her. She thinks the sun shines out of his rear end. You want to know something? Every night before I go to bed, I look up to heaven and say, thank you, God, for at least giving me Gerald."

Letting the compliment pass, Gerald pulled a sheaf of correspondence from the clipboard and showed it to his father. "Here's the rundown on the designer project, what we've done so far."

Jonathan took the letters and scanned through them, familiarizing himself again with their contents. "What do you think of this idea, Gerald? This sort of operation is more your generation than it is mine."

Clipping the letters back to the board, Gerald said, "We've surveyed the work of three top European men's clothing designers, and they've all intimated that they'd like to work with us, let us carry their name exclusively in the States. Now it's a tossup among the three."

"What about money?"

"Fairly comparable, within a few thousand dollars of each other," Gerald replied. "I don't think it's really a question of money. I'd like to be able to get the best man."

"What kind of research have you done on the market?"

"Quite a bit," Gerald said, collecting the facts in his mind. "We covered every city where we have stores and where we're thinking of opening, interviewing the Chestertons type of customer. Results show that the public is aware of these European designers. And, even more important, they would rather buy a suit which carries the label of an internationally acclaimed designer than a suit which has an ordinary store label inside it."

"So what's stopping you?"

"Time," Gerald said simply. "We have to make the time to go over to Europe and see these people. I've seen them once; now I'd like you to come with me."

The thought of both himself and Gerald being away horrified Jonathan; he had immediate visions of Simon running amok, changing the chain overnight into a string of airy-fairy boutiques.

"I can't come with you," Jonathan said, rubbing his hand across his eyes, suddenly very tired. "You make the arrangements. Go see these people and pick a good one. Otherwise I'll start screaming at you on Monday afternoon instead of your brother."

Miriam said nothing during the first part of the journey out to Great Neck. Seated in the back of the chauffeur-driven Rolls Royce, Jonathan suffered her silence, knowing what was troubling her. But he had enough problems of his own to worry about. Exclusive designer-labelled clothing—he began to feel as Jacob must have felt those many years ago when he saw the work of his life changing. Again Jonathan silently thanked God for Gerald, a boy with a fine brain and a keen appreciation of the retail industry.

"Jonathan." Miriam's voice finally broke the long silence. "Did you have to be so hard on him?"

"What did you want me to do? Pat him on the head and tell him what a bright boy he is? Miriam, he goes berserk in the office. I've given him and Gerald identical opportunities. They both started out in the stores, selling, getting a feel for the business once they left the university. They've both had the same breaks. And you can see for yourself what's happened."

"But did you have to shout at him in front of the secretary?"

"She's heard it all before," Jonathan muttered. "It'll come out in the minutes tomorrow that an offer of three hundred suits by Brenson and Selman for the Atlanta renovation was turned down. Simon won't go into the records as having been bawled out."

Still clinging to Simon's defense, Miriam said, "He's made differently from Gerald."

"As if I didn't know."

"There's no need to be sarcastic," she complained. "Gerald's a dour, conservative boy. You know we used to say he was too levelheaded. Simon's just the opposite. He can't see the business in the same light as you and Gerald can. He's a free spirit, an artist."

"So buy him a painting outfit for his birthday," Jonathan grumbled. "Look, Miriam. That's not the truth, and you know it. Gerald's a worker. He'd do well in whatever part of the business I put him in. Look at store operations; he's running thirty-eight stores, and he's doing a damned good job. Everything's under control; he's got the situation at his fingertips. But if I stuck him in as financial controller tomorrow, he'd slot into the position like he was born for the job. Simon's just lazy. He's not stupid, not by a long stretch. But he refuses to accept the responsibility that goes with the job. He likes the title, the money, the prestige, everything. Only he doesn't like doing the work. That's why we've had this foul-up with the leisurewear category all season. You were there during the meeting; it's going to cost us about one hundred thousand dollars for the season on markdowns and additional expenses to clear that merchandise. And we're still not sure of getting rid of it all."

"That's the buyer's responsibility," Miriam interjected.

"Of course it's the buyer's responsibility. And after this episode, I've a damned good mind to kiss that buyer good-bye. But Simon is over the buyers, all of them, and he has to okay their initial plans and their orders. Right now he just leaves it to the buyer concerned, doesn't get himself involved at all. He's not interested in the input from the regions. He does just what he wants to do. And on top of that, he agrees to buy a bunch of garbage for the Atlanta renovation and reopening. If those suits had gone in, we'd have lost all credibility in that city."

"All right!" Miriam's voice turned sharp. "So he's not as diligent as Gerald is. But he's still your son, just the same as Gerald. You don't have to come down on him as hard as you do."

Glancing to ensure that the partition behind the chauffeur was closed firmly, Jonathan raised his voice to match Miriam's tone. "If he was honest with himself and admitted he wasn't a merchandising genius, I'd treat him differently, try to help him get to grips with the problems. But he refuses to see it. He still thinks he's the only one with the answers, the one person in the boardroom who knows where the market's headed." Jonathan breathed out heavily, wondering how he had let himself get caught in yet another argument about Simon. Once he had started, however, there was no holding back.

"And look at his private life. Is that such a thing for a father to be proud of?"

"That's right," Miriam said caustically. "Bring that into it as well."

"Sure! Why shouldn't I? Gerald's married and settled down with a baby, and what's Simon doing? He's a bum, shacking up with this one for a few weeks, that one for another month or so. Has he ever told you about the money he loses gambling?" He waited in vain for an answer. "Well? Has he?"

"No," Miriam replied sullenly.

"Ask him about it sometime. He used to be proud of it, boasting to the office staff about how much he dropped at the track, at cards, on his Vegas junkets. He's nothing but a bum."

"Jonathan, I won't hear you talk about Simon in that manner. Not another word, do you hear me?"

Jonathan turned his attention to the back of the chauffeur's head, staring at the man's long hair which curled up beneath the cap. He sat fuming, unable to understand why Miriam could not see Simon as he could—a shiftless, worthless loafer who had the good fortune to have a rich father with a highly successful business.

God alone knows what'll happen when I retire, he thought bitterly. Even with Gerald's common-sense approach, the business will fall apart.

Simon—Midas in reverse. Every piece of gold he touches turns into a hunk of rotten cheese, an apple core, a piece of dirt. Everything he even looks at turns into a lump of shit.

# 2

Walking from the boardroom along the narrow corridor to his own office, Simon Chesterton pushed the scene with his father to the back of his mind. It was one disagreement in a series of many, nothing, as far as he was concerned, to be unduly worried about. His father belonged to the past generation, those businessmen who had become so immersed in their own importance that they had forgotten how to run a business. And on top of that, he continued to look to old Jacob for guidance, for advice when he was checking technical specifications of a garment. Simon laughed silently at the thought, finding it ludicrous that a company as large as Chestertons could still find a use for the services of his grandfather, a man who should have been put out to pasture years earlier, sent away to a senior citizens' home where he could spend his last years with his contemporaries—not left to interfere with the running of a modern company.

Even Gerald, Simon's twin brother, could not tell his left hand from his right. He agreed with everything Jonathan said, and vice versa. Gerald and Jonathan should have been the twins, not the father and son. They thought alike, even looked alike—the Tweedledum and Tweedledee of the rag trade.

Why, Simon wondered as he closed the door of his office, could nobody else see what he could see? Were they all blinkered, unable to see anything unless it lay straight ahead, using only five percent of their visual powers? Clothing's like cars. It should have a built-in obsolescence factor. What use are customers who only come back to you because their suits look as good after two or three years as when they first bought them? Men today are after fashion. The money is in the hands of the country's youth, and young people are not interested in stodgy, conservatively styled clothes which will last forever. They're not interested in quality; they don't give a damn about it. All they want is whatever style is in right now, and to hell with how long it lasts before the stitches start falling apart, or the cloth rubs through because it's made from some garbage fibre that even a rag manufacturer would not touch. Sell them a suit made of cardboard; they'll buy it happily as long as the fashion details are just right. But my brother and father can't see this. They've got their heads stuck so deeply into the quicksands of quality that they're incapable of seeing a thing in any other direction. So we'd lose a few customers. But who cares about these idiots who boast about their clothing's staying power? For every traditional Chestertons customer we lose—and good goddamned riddance to them— five young, fashion-conscious men with wallets full of money will step in to take their place. All because we'd be selling the right kind of merchandise, their kind of high-fashion clothing.

Fully convinced that his reasoning was correct, Simon sat down behind his desk, pushing aside buyer appointments, memoranda and store reports till he found what he wanted. Picking up the racing form, he dialled the number he knew by heart, tapping impatiently with a pencil on the desk top while he waited for a reply.

"Harry? Yeah, it's Simon Chesterton. I've got some business for you. Two hundred dollars on the daily double at Aqueduct tomorrow, Molly's Boy and Winnie." He paused, chewing the end of the pencil while he waited for the bookmaker to confirm the bet. Instead, the words he heard made him throw down the pencil in disgust, his bland expression changing to one of fury.

"Don't give me that crap, Harry, you son of a bitch!" he hissed into the mouthpiece. "I've never tried to stiff you on a bet before. Sure I'm into you for a few bucks, but it's not the first time. You know I always come across. Now take that bet, damn it, or I place my business somewhere else."

The telephone clicked in his ear, followed by the mechanical hum of the dial tone as the bookmaker broke the connection. Simon sat staring dumbly at the receiver for a moment; then he slammed it down on the rest.

Two rebuffs in one afternoon! That was just a bit too much. His father, with his antiquated ideas about fashion retailing, was one thing; he could live with that. But when the bookmaker—and Christ alone knew how much money he had put into that man's pocket over the years—told him to take a powder, that was the final indignity.

Still angry with the bookmaker, Simon sorted roughly through the correspondence on his desk, initialling it, then pushing it aside for his secretary to file later, after he had gone home.

He stood up abruptly, pushed back the chair and walked out of the office. "There's some stuff on my desk you can take care of," he snapped at the secretary, not caring whether she could make head or tail of the confusion. "I won't be back today." He walked through the main store and onto West Fifty-seventh Street, looking for a taxi.

By the time the short journey to his East Sixty-eighth Street apartment was over, Simon was in a better frame of mind. He prided himself on the ability to forget unpleasant events, and he'd be damned if he would allow the bookmaker's rejection to upset him. Life, he often claimed, was meant to be enjoyed to the full, with as little aggravation as possible; his father might have added, with as little work as possible, but Simon never saw himself in a lazy light. In his own estimation, he was the unrecognized genius of the company, and when hard times struck—as he was certain they would if the company maintained its present marketing policies—it would be he who rescued it. It would be his imaginative ideas, his innovative flair which would see it through.

Big deal if they were stuck with a load of leisurewear they couldn't sell. Either it had not been advertised properly, or the salesmen had not tried hard enough to sell it. From his own experience in the stores, Simon knew it was more profitable for a salesman to talk a customer into buying an expensive suit than to waste time in trying to sell cheaper leisure clothing.

And as for Brian Chambers in the Midwest complaining that the buying group had not taken into consideration any of the input received from the stores—well, that was nothing but stupidity. Simon bridled as he thought of the complaint. Brian Chambers is nothing more than a regional manager, a glorified store manager, and I'm general merchandise manager. What possible use could his input be to me? Buying's a skilled job, forecasting the market, trying to spot trends before they develop so you can buy early and possibly get a two-week jump on the competition. It's far too complex for the people out in the stores. We bought that merchandise because we felt it was right. And that's all there is to it.

Suddenly Simon remembered the Ford Edsel of his adolescence, finding it a comfort that even Henry Ford could be wrong sometimes.

Letting himself into the luxury one-bedroom apartment a few buildings removed from busy Park Avenue, he walked quickly to the telephone in the living room, picking it up, flicking the dial. "Hi, Della. It's Simon." His tone was soft, seductive, none of his personal aggravation coming through into his voice as he used New York Telephone as a method of foreplay. "I'm at the office at the moment, stuck in a meeting, but I should be free in a couple of hours. How about coming around then, and help me to unwind?"

He listened to the reply, grinning, self-satisfied. "You know how it is with our company, Della. I'd make it sooner, honest I would, but we're a one-man show. No kidding. If I didn't get down on my hands and knees and do some work, you'd see us with empty windows from coast to coast."

He held the telephone loosely in his left hand as he spoke, his right hand fiddling idly with a gold table lighter, turning it end over end. The lighter was nothing more than a decoration, never fuelled since the day he had bought it. Neither Simon nor his brother smoked, having been turned off the habit before they ever started by their father's endless chain of cigars.

"Okay," he agreed. "Eight o'clock it is. Be good till I see you." He blew a lingering kiss into the mouthpiece before hanging up, feeling very pleased with himself.

After placing a bottle of Dom Perignon champagne in the refrigerator to chill slightly, he undressed and showered, admiring his slim, elegant figure in the full-length mirror of his bedroom closet as he stood barefoot on the expensive broadloom. Running his fingers through the thick red hair which covered his chest, Simon recalled how a former girlfriend had once referred to it as her personal welcome mat; he smiled, recalling how many other girls it had welcomed since then. Turning sideways, he glanced at the reflection from the new angle, dropping his gaze to his penis, swaying slightly as he breathed in and out.

Tearing himself away from the mirror with an effort of will, he donned light gray slacks and a gaily colored sport shirt, eagerly anticipating the evening that was to come.

Gerald Chesterton carefully eased the dark brown Ford Thunderbird into the two-car garage of his Colonial style home outside Manhasset, glancing sideways at his wife's red Alfa Romeo sports car as he turned off the engine and stretched his arms and legs. Sitting still, he listened to the sounds of metal contracting as the engine parts began to cool, hearing it as a lullaby dulling his senses more with each click and creak. He yawned, covering his wide-open mouth with a hand, feeling the desire to stay in the womblike comfort of the Thunderbird and sleep. He felt cozily relaxed and tired—especially tired after the mental stress of the merchandise meeting which had included yet another of those endless rows between his father and brother. Although Gerald had come to expect the arguments as part and parcel of the merchandise meetings, they continued to leave a sour taste in his mouth.

If only, he dreamed, opening the car door, Simon had wanted to be an accountant or a doctor or a lawyer. The thought of his brother as a lawyer appealed to Gerald's sense of humor; if he defended the villains, New York City would be a safe place to walk the streets at night. But if he prosecuted them instead . . . The idea did not even bear thinking about.

"Marilyn!" he yelled, entering the house through the communicating door from the garage. "I'm home. Where's my drink? The service in this place is going to the dogs."

His wife appeared from the kitchen, holding a silver tray in front of her. Balanced on the tray was a tumbler of whiskey and soda. She stood in front of him, bowing her head formally, the ash-blond hair tumbling down to hide her face. "Refreshment for my lord and master. And if you've just woken Karen up with your yelling, you can spend the next two hours persuading her to go back to sleep again."

They listened quietly, but there was no sound from upstairs, no crying as the baby awoke and made her presence known. Gerald plucked the glass from the tray, experiencing an enjoyable warmth in the odd evening ritual he shared with Marilyn. She had started the ceremony of bringing him a drink on a silver tray as a joke, the first night he had returned from work after their honeymoon. He had liked it and never suggested that she should stop.

He let go of the briefcase, hearing it hit the floor with a resounding thud from the stacks of paper work inside. Lifting Marilyn's head, he stared into the sparkling blue eyes.

"You forgot the stirred-or-shaken bit," he ribbed her.

She stood on tiptoe to kiss him. "That's a martini, nut," she laughed. "And you're Gerald, not James Bond."

"Mind the medicine," he warned, holding the tumbler out of harm's way. "Believe me, I need it tonight."

Taking Gerald's hand, Marilyn led him into the living room, pushing him down into a rocking chair. Placing a hand on each arm to stop him from getting up, she leaned over him, her face inches from his own. "It was that bad, worse than usual?" she asked.

Instead of replying immediately, Gerald drank deeply from the tumbler, clenching his teeth at the last minute to stop the two ice cubes entering his mouth. "The worst," he said eventually. "My father decided to go scalp hunting over the leisurewear. And then Simon did some grandstanding with a load of garbage he bought for Atlanta."

"Poor Simon," Marilyn murmured. "He tries so hard."

"Poor Simon," Gerald echoed sarcastically. "He belongs in a boutique and doesn't even try to relate to our kind of merchandise. I think the last time he and my father agreed on anything was when we were *Bar Mitzvahed;* they both agreed to go to the same temple for the service."

Marilyn giggled, finding the remark funny. She pecked Gerald on the lips, a quick brushing kiss which held the hint of something more.

Gerald finished the drink and laid the tumbler gently on a nearby table. He patted his knees invitingly. "Sit down and tell me all about your day."

Marilyn perched herself on Gerald's lap, the movement sending the chair rocking back and forth. "Well," she began, ticking off the events on her fingers, "after you left this morning, I played nine holes of golf. Then I had lunch in the club with the golf pro. By the way, he says my putting's improving beyond all recognition. In the afternoon, I played three sets of tennis and finished off with a sauna to get myself all relaxed for you. How does that sound?"

"Sounds marvellous," Gerald replied, putting his arms around Marilyn's waist and burying his face in her shoulder. "Now tell me what you really did."

"I took Karen out in the stroller, did some shopping and made dinner for that big ox of my husband. Does that sound any better?"

Gerald lifted his head. "Sounds worse, if you want the truth. The fiction was more interesting."

"Married women," said Marilyn, standing up and pushing Gerald back into the chair as he tried to follow her, "lead very boring lives—especially if they've got a nine-month-old baby daughter to look after as well."

"Still feeling tied down?" he asked sympathetically, seeing the mood descending, hoping it would be a brief one.

The gaiety dropped from Marilyn's voice. "Sometimes," she said quietly. "It's a big house, and it gets awfully lonely."

"What about your clubs?"

Marilyn made a face at the mention of the organizations to which she belonged. "They're all full of boring people who want you to hear about their problems. I'd rather stay at home and play with Karen, but she wants to sleep all the time. I'll be glad when I can get back to school and teach."

Gerald looked deeply into his wife's eyes. "Kids aren't that bad, you know."

The smile slowly came back to Marilyn's face. "I know. When I was small, I even used to go to school with them."

Gerald laughed at the joke, happy to see that the mood had disappeared as quickly as it had come. There had been times, especially during the final months of her pregnancy, when Marilyn had been almost unbearable to live with, withdrawn, worried that she was bidding farewell to the active life she loved. When Karen had been born, Marilyn's life had centered around the child to the extent that Gerald was frequently left to fend for himself. But he remembered not minding the disturbance to his way of life, as Marilyn appeared to be emerging from the shell she had built around herself during the previous months. Still, the moods came and went, often instantaneously, like a light being turned on and off. And Gerald had learned to accept them, hoping that they would soon disappear altogether as Marilyn became completely adjusted to the fact that being a mother in no way deprived her of leading an active life.

"I'm hungry," he said. "You mentioned dinner before. Is it worth being hungry for?"

"Roast chicken," Marilyn replied. She leaned over Gerald again; he felt her lips covering his face with quick kisses, the tongue darting in and out as she found his mouth. "Do you want me for the appetizer, or would you rather have me for dessert?"

There was a stirring in his loins as he clasped her close. "How about with the chicken? As a side dish."

Simon lay back in bed, hands clasped behind his head, staring up at the ceiling. He felt Della's hands gliding across his stomach, the heels digging in, massaging gently. Lowering his gaze, he stared at the girl who sat astride him, eyes down, intent on her self-appointed task. This one was some girl, he marvelled—the greatest bang he'd ever had, and extras like the teasing massage she was now giving.

Shuddering in delight and anticipation, Simon reached up to touch her head, running his fingers through the short black hair. Leisurely he drew her down till their lips touched, her brown eyes fading into indistinct blurs as they came too close for focus. He bit her lips gently before moving his mouth down past her chin till he was directly below her small breasts. His tongue came out, tantalizing an erect nipple, feeling it harden even more under the probing touch, a ruby embedded in a hillock of pale, soft, warm flesh.

Ignoring the whimpering sounds she made, Simon transferred his attention to the other breast. Then, without any warning, he rolled over, trapping her underneath his body, being snared himself as she wrapped her legs around his back, squeezing him with a wrestler's grip.

She cried out, and her hands dug savagely into the back of his head, pressing his face down into her breasts, suffocating him. Each movement a carefully measured action, Simon moved upward, kissing her neck underneath her chin, stifling her cries as he placed his mouth on hers, pushing roughly inside with his tongue, feeling her teeth clamp down.

He heard the sudden intake of breath as he entered her, moving slowly at first, then with an ever increasing rhythm of urgency, feeling her respond, her back arched, nails clawing into his own back, urging him on, words that made no sense being whispered into his ear.

When he climaxed, it was like a dam bursting, a release of violently angry floods which cascaded into a quiet valley, calming as the furious energy was spent. Impetus carried him on before he fell away drained, feeling Della lying limp in his arms, a fine sheen of perspiration covering her body, her breath coming in short, uneven gasps.

Later, they lay side by side, his arm curled underneath her back, a hand resting on her breast.

"Unwound?" she whispered.

"Almost."

She snuggled closer to him, a hand on his chest, fingers toying with the thick red hair, twisting it playfully. "Why do you stay there?" she asked. "Surely you'd be better off opening for yourself. Your father would soon realize how much the company needed you. They'd ask you to go back, and you'd do so on your own terms—if you really wanted to."

"Why should I leave?" Simon asked in return, picturing his father's expression of delight if such an occurrence took place. "They'll come around to my way of thinking in the end, hopefully before it's too late."

As he lay there, the realization came that he knew next to nothing about this girl who had shared his bed for the past four months. She worked for an advertising agency, and he had met her in a singles bar on Second Avenue after an unsuccessful outing to the track. Unsuccessful, he thought sourly; he could not remember the last time he had a successful trip.

Della had been sitting at a table talking to a friend. He had entered the bar, spotted the pair sitting alone and made a beeline for the table. After he introduced himself, Della had asked if he had anything to do with the clothing chain. He remembered that her friend had asked, what clothing chain? Hell, he could not even remember her face or name now, the stupid bitch. But Della, as soon as she had asked the initial question, had received his full charm. He had explained that he was Chestertons, a claim that she had first taken as bluff, looking at him in disbelief. So he had suggested they go to the West Fifty-seventh Street store there and then. When he had opened the door and taken her to his own office, she had been contrite, apologizing profusely for doubting him.

Never one to let a golden opportunity go to waste, Simon had taken advantage of the situation by taking her right then, on the carpet in front of his desk. There was a small table over that spot now, and it would stay there to make certain that nobody ever defiled the area with their feet.

"Where are you from, Della?"

"Minneapolis. Ever hear of it?"

"Of course I've heard of it. We've got a store there, opened it three or four years ago."

"I know it," Della said.

"How come you're from there?" Simon asked. "I thought the place was full of Swedes. What are you?"

"American," she replied dreamily. "That's what it says on my passport."

"Originally," he persisted, striving to remember her last name. Christ, was he that unwound that he could not even recall the name of the girl he had just laid? Sanchez. It finally came to him.

"What are you, Spanish?"

"Puerto Rican. My father was."

"I thought all Puerto Ricans lived in New York City," he said, trying to be clever.

She rolled over and put her head on his chest, nuzzling the red hair with her tiny nose. "I do," she said.

"Only for the last couple of years," he began, before deciding that there was no point in continuing the conversation. "Forget it. I don't really want to know anyway."

She stopped nuzzling and began to kiss him, moving her head down, over his stomach, lower still, feeling his muscles tense.

"You're right," she murmured in a voice so low he could hardly hear the words. "You don't really want to know anyway."

As Della's lips closed around him, a bizarre thought occurred to Simon. He had completely forgotten about the bottle of champagne in the refrigerator.

Ah well, it would do for next time.

# 3

"The truth now. How do I look?"

The question came from Jonathan as he stood in front of his desk, pulling down the jacket of his light brown suit in an attempt to straighten out the creases where he had been sitting.

Miriam eyed him with mock criticism. "Too many gray hairs, and too heavy around the middle." She reached up and brushed the hair off his forehead; it dropped back again the moment she removed her hand. "Other than that, you'll pass inspection."

From his position near the door, Gerald watched the performance, smiling affectionately. "You're not going to the White House to meet the President of the United States," he told his father. "You're meeting Nino Viscenzi. He's a man, just like anybody else."

"Sure," Jonathan agreed somewhat sceptically. "But what's he going to think if I turn up at Kennedy Airport to meet him dressed like slob number one? I'm the chief executive of a major clothing company that he's going to sign a design contract with. I have to make a good impression on the guy." He turned from his son to Jacob, who sat alone at the boardroom table, watching the scene with unconcealed amusement; the cigarette in the ashtray in front of him sent up a gentle spiral of gray smoke. "Come on," Jonathan said. "You're dying to say something as well. Let's have your two cents' worth."

"You act like you did when you first went out with Miriam," Jacob told him. "Fidgeting and fussing, making sure your shoes are shined, your pants are pressed. Do you really think this man deserves the same consideration?"

"Have your fun, all of you," Jonathan said patiently. He pulled back his jacket cuff and glanced down at the face of the solid gold Rolex wristwatch. A worried frown crossed his face. "Has anybody seen Simon?" he asked.

161

Silence greeted the question. Jonathan looked from one person to the other before picking up the telephone and dialling his son's extension. The secretary answered, saying that Simon had not been in the office all afternoon.

"Some vice-president," Jonathan muttered, replacing the receiver. "Now he doesn't even bother coming into the office for a full day. I say we go without him. The amount of interest he's shown in this designer label project has been zilch. Nobody's going to miss him." He waited for Miriam to come back at him, knowing that she would support Simon.

His wife did not disappoint him. "Give him another five minutes," she pleaded. "Mr. Viscenzi should be met by all of us this time."

Jonathan tapped his feet in annoyance, stopping only when Miriam glared at him. Gerald, seeking to ease the tension caused by his brother's absence, ventured some comments on the previous week's business, but nobody paid any attention to him.

Finally Jonathan checked his watch again, making a great performance of pulling back his cuff. "That's it," he decided. "We've waited long enough for his highness to show up. Viscenzi's plane is due in forty-five minutes, and it's murder getting out to Kennedy this time of the afternoon. We're going without Simon." He held open the office door for Miriam to pass through, waiting while Jacob and Gerald followed.

In the Rolls-Royce on the way out to the airport, Gerald discussed the meetings he had held in Paris with Nino Viscenzi, when the designer had agreed to style a range of men's suits and coats exclusively for Chestertons, giving the company sole rights to the use of his name throughout the United States.

"No matter what you've heard about designers, Pa," Gerald began, "forget it. This guy's no *faygeleh* who switched from making women's dresses because he saw there was money to be made in the men's clothing market."

Jonathan chuckled deeply as he looked at Miriam to see if any expression showed. She stared straight ahead, her thoughts on Simon.

"Go on," he prompted. "Bring us up to date. Things have changed a lot since Jacob's day."

Gerald shifted to a more comfortable position, leaning closer to his father. "This guy is men's wear through and through, and it shows in his designs. He doesn't come up with the kind of creations that would look better on women, like some designers we could all name."

"Careful," Jonathan kidded. "Don't mention any names. You might get sued."

Gerald smiled. "You know damned well who I mean without mentioning names. Viscenzi turns out styles that make a man look good. He's slightly ahead of the mass market, but at the same time he's taking the exaggerated styles and toning them down to suit our type of customer."

"Good old Mr. Middle America," Jonathan said, nodding.

"And for God's sake, don't try any of your mock Italian on him," Gerald said earnestly. "When he left Italy, he worked for a long time in London before opening his own business in Paris. He knows the markets, from our end to the cloth and yarn manufacturers. He's on top of the whole operation, from start to finish."

Jacob, remembering an old radio commercial, spoke for the first time during the journey. "You mean he can negotiate directly with the sheep?"

"That's about it, Grandpa. You'll get on well with him. You can spin yarns about the business fifty years ago, and he can tell you how much it's changed since then."

The patient humor which only the elderly can adopt successfully showed itself on Jacob's face as he regarded his grandson. "Don't worry about your grandfather, Gerald. I can still take care of myself in any discussion on clothing design and technology."

Simon walked away from the daily double cashier's window, a thick wad of fifty- and twenty-dollar bills clutched in his hand. He gripped the money exultantly, his fist crushing the new bills.

Finally. Finally the luck's changed, he thought. The daily double had paid forty-eight dollars and forty cents, and he had gambled one hundred dollars on the winning horses. Two thousand, four hundred twenty dollars—not bad for an afternoon's investment. And that was just the first two races.

With a spring in his step, he made his way back to the seat in the clubhouse, intent on getting back to the scratch sheet and handicapping the next race. He took no special notice of the two men closing in on him, taking it for granted that they were other racegoers. As they came abreast, one man gripped him tightly by the elbow, pressing on the nerve, while the second—memorable because of a misshapen left ear—adroitly lifted the roll of bills from Simon's weakened grip.

"Hey! What the hell's going on?"

"Shaddap!" the man who had taken the money snapped. "We're in the debt collecting business." He leafed through the bills, tossing the odd twenty dollars back to Simon. "There's your fare home. You still owe Harry twenty-six hundred. You've got two days to come up with it, or else we go to your old man."

Simon stood speechless as the two men hurried away toward the exit. The single twenty-dollar bill in his hand meant nothing. He opened and closed his mouth like a fish out of water as he tried to yell after the men, but no sound came. Two men walked in front of him, going to the window to place their bets for the next race. They glanced casually at Simon, his mouth open, eyes staring indignantly, then carried on, totally oblivious to anybody's troubles but their own.

Gradually the shock passed, anger taking its place as Simon crumpled the single bill in his hand. He stuffed it roughly into his trouser pocket and looked around for a public telephone. Dropping a dime into the slot, he dialled the familiar number.

"Harry? It's Simon Chesterton. Did you send two of your goons after me at the track? I just got hit for the money I won on the daily double."

He heard the bookmaker's laughter, and it made him more furious. "Lucky for you it came up. How much of the debt did they recover?"

Bastard, Simon thought. Stinking, miserable bastard, laughing about it. Without knowing why, just prompted by the all-consuming fury, he shot back, "Forty-eight hundred bucks. I had two hundred on the double. They let me keep forty bucks as cab fare."

"Your luck's in, getting up a big one like that," the bookmaker said. "Now you only owe me two hundred to clear up the five grand you were behind. Pay that off and I might take your business again."

"You cheap bastard!" Simon screamed into the telephone, unaware of the inquisitive stares which came his way. "I needed that damned money, Harry. I've got a goddamned good mind to call the cops onto you, let them bust you."

The bookmaker's voice came back quiet and level, all trace of laughter gone. "You go right ahead and do that, kid. I'll buy them off like I always do. But that Sanchez broad you've been sticking the old salami into won't be interested in you for a hell of a long time."

Simon gasped incredulously. "How do you know about her?"

"I've been keeping a fatherly eye on you till you came up with the money, you stupid jerk. You're too valuable for me to let you run around loose. What the hell do you think I'm running down here, a Salvation Army hostel or something?"

The knowledge that he had been under surveillance knocked the wind out of Simon. "Okay, Harry. I'll get straight with you."

"You do that, Simon. Just get the other two hundred together and we can be friends again, just like old times."

Miserably Simon trudged back to his seat, wondering what he could do with twenty dollars. Picking the same two letters he had used successfully for the daily double, he bet the money in an Exacta. One of his selections came in first by eight lengths, paying seventeen dollars and thirty cents; the second selection in the Exacta came one from last.

He tore up the tickets in disgust, scattering them on the clubhouse floor as he walked toward the exit.

"My other son would be here as well," Jonathan said apologetically, giving the excuse he had formed during the ride out to Kennedy Airport, "but unfortunately he had some urgent business with one of our suppliers and couldn't make it back in time."

Nino Viscenzi raised a hand in the air, brushing the explanation aside. "Please do not apologize, Mr. Chesterton. I will meet him when the time is more appropriate. That I have met you charming people is sufficient for the moment."

From his position at the end of the boardroom table, Gerald watched the exchange between his father and the Italian designer; he felt totally relaxed, happy that Viscenzi had not let him down. After being assigned by his father to conduct the negotiations on his own in Paris, Gerald had built up the Italian as an unequalled expert on clothing taste. Now Viscenzi stood before them, a man in his mid-forties, impeccably dressed in a deep brown chalk-stripe suit which toned perfectly with his dark brown, wavy hair and soulful brown eyes. In profile Viscenzi reminded Gerald of the prewar Italian movie heartthrobs—a straight nose flaring slightly above a wide, generous mouth, and a firmly chiselled chin with a deep cleft.

Seeing a pause in the conversation, Jacob walked across to Viscenzi. "Excuse me," he said, taking hold of the designer's jacket. "Is this from your factory, Mr. Viscenzi?"

"From my own factory, Mr. Gellenbaum," the Italian replied, thinking nothing strange about the difference in family names. "It's one of our new season's ranges. Do you like it?"

"Would it be too much trouble to ask you to take it off?" Jacob asked.

"Certainly." Viscenzi shrugged the jacket off, watching with interest as Jacob began to examine it.

Turning the garment inside out, Jacob scrutinized the seams, noticing the close spacing of the stitches. He turned the jacket the right way out and began to check as much as he could on a cursory inspection. While he worked, Viscenzi walked to where Jonathan stood.

"How old is your father?"

"Eighty-nine," Jonathan replied out of the side of his mouth. The answer made him feel proud.

"Marvellous," Viscenzi muttered. "Marvellous." He returned to Jacob as he finished the inspection, taking the jacket from him. "And your verdict, Mr. Gellenbaum?"

"Excellent work," Jacob enthused. "Beautiful cloth and wonderful workmanship. But I don't think we can make to those standards without putting our prices far beyond the reach of our traditional customers."

Viscenzi put the jacket on, slipping into it with an easy, fluid movement. "If my name is to be associated with your company—and I would very much like it to be—I expect certain high standards to be maintained. Obviously I have to protect my own reputation. But the suits which Gerald showed me in Paris would seem to meet the expected quality." He looked at Jonathan. "When can I tour the factory?"

"We've arranged to fly up to Buffalo tomorrow morning, if that's all right with you."

"Good." Viscenzi turned back to Jacob. "I don't expect you to make this quality garment for the prices you anticipate charging, Mr. Gellenbaum. If your technical staff could, they would be working miracles. I would ask them to come to Paris and work for me, in fact."

"Who sells that suit?" Gerald asked. "What level of men's wear retailer?"

"This is exclusive to my own store in Paris," Viscenzi answered. "The store is really a couturier-level operation, short runs and almost guaranteed exclusivity. We'll make, perhaps, one dozen of this style and color, that is all."

"What sort of price would you ask?" Gerald inquired.

The phrasing of the question amused Viscenzi. "Ask? What sort of price would we ask? We do not ask. We get."

"Okay," Gerald said, grinning at the answer. "What sort of price would you get for that suit?"

"For something like this," Viscenzi said, stroking the front of the jacket, "five hundred and fifty dollars."

The involuntary whistle which escaped from Gerald's lips was half shock, half admiration. "Five hundred and fifty! After I met you in Paris, I went to London for a week to look around. Even the tailors in Savile Row, the really top houses, are only getting three hundred pounds sterling. What's that in dollars?" he asked his father.

"This morning's rate or last night's rate?" Jonathan quipped, making fun of the country's tortured currency. "About five hundred and fifty, the same as he's charging in Paris."

"But everything's handmade in the Savile Row operation," Gerald said. He addressed Viscenzi again, still amazed by the physical enormity of the sum the man was charging for a factory-made suit. "How can you justify those sorts of prices," he asked numbly, "even taking into account your exclusivity?"

The designer answered with disarming simplicity. "Because," he said smiling, "I am Viscenzi."

When Viscenzi flew to Buffalo the following morning, he was accompanied by Jacob, Jonathan and Gerald. Instead of being merely satisfied with viewing finished garments, the designer insisted on touring the factory, seeing the complete operation. He began in the cloth receiving area where the fabric was treated chemically, passing through the cutting room where different sections of the clothing were cut out and the sewing department where he watched machinists deftly join the pieces of cut fabric, using the latest automatic machinery which saved precious seconds on each operation. As he watched the canvas which gives body to the front of the jacket being heat-fused into place on the inside of the top fabric, Viscenzi turned to Jacob.

"How long have you been fusing your canvases, Mr. Gellenbaum?"

"Quite a few years now," Jacob replied. "We began with the cheap, low-end suits which are sold in the Gellenbaum stores. Then, after we ironed out the bugs, we used fusing for the Chestertons suits as well." He looked intently at the suit Viscenzi was wearing, a navy blue three-piece with a pattern so faint that from a distance the fabric appeared solid. "That suit of yours is not fused, is it, Mr. Viscenzi?"

The designer's brown eyes twinkled in merriment. "You don't miss very much. No, it's not. None of the suits which come out of my factory are fused. We stitch the canvases in, just like traditional tailors have always done. Many times we have debated going over to fused foreparts, but we feel we would be cheating our customers." He appeared deep in thought for a moment, resting his chin on his hand. "Tell me something, Mr. Gellenbaum. If price was no object, would you rather stitch your canvases or fuse them?"

"Stitch them." Jacob did not even have to think about the answer. He remembered when the company had first switched from the traditional stitching to heat-fusing the canvases; the advantage had been that the fused canvases could not slip inside the jacket and would give a firmer feel and look to the garment. On some of the finer fabrics, the company had encountered strike-through where the adhesive from the fusing came through to the surface of the cloth. Other times, the heat or pressure had been insufficient, and the canvas did not fuse properly. "Yes," he said, recalling some of the problems, "stitch them."

Viscenzi laughed heartily and put his arm around Jacob's shoulders. "We think alike. One day my factory in Paris will go over to fusing, but I hope I am old and gray when that happens. I am too much of a traditionalist to suffer change gladly."

As Jacob and Viscenzi entered into an animated conversation on the industry, Jonathan and Gerald wandered away to where they could watch the discussion without being a part of it. Gerald shook his head in wonder, watching how the mutual interest could bridge both continents and generations. Recalling a part of the conversation he had overheard, he asked his father, "What was Nino saying about Pfaff?"

"Oh, the sewing machine manufacturers," Jonathan said. "He spent some time with them in Germany at their research and development center. Kaiserslautern, I think it was. Apparently he's very impressed with the strides they're making with automation. Said something about sewing machines taking the world over one day." He thought back to a conversation which had taken place forty years earlier.

"You know, Gerald, when I first talked your grandfather into the factory, the old one on Houston Street, I told him that one day you'd put in a piece of cloth at one end and get a finished suit out the other. I didn't believe it myself at the time. I was just trying to hustle him into coming in with me. Now it looks as though I may have been right."

Gerald nodded in agreement, but his thoughts had drifted away to his twin brother. Despite trying not to think of Simon, the trip to Buffalo had been blighted by his absence. It rankled Gerald that Simon had neither turned up at the airport to welcome the designer, nor come to the factory as courtesy dictated. They had not even been able to contact him at the apartment; five times they had tried to reach him, and each time the telephone rang on into infinity.

"How do we keep explaining Simon away?" Gerald asked his father as they waited for Jacob and Viscenzi to rejoin them.

Jonathan frowned. "Maybe it's better that Nino doesn't meet Simon just yet." He changed the subject swiftly as the other two men approached.

"You know what I can't get over, Gerald? It's the way your grandfather gets on with Nino. Just look at them," he said joyfully. "I think that's what he's been missing with just us for company."

# 4

Her heels clicking loudly on the tiled surface of the floor, Della walked briskly across the small lobby of Simon's apartment building on East Sixty-eighth Street, stopping in front of the tenants' directory. Taking no notice of the two men who had followed her into the building and who were now standing by the door while one searched through his pockets for a key, she pressed the buzzer to Simon's apartment, holding it down till he answered.

"Who is it?" The voice sounded tinny, distorted beyond all recognition by the building's security intercom.

"Della. Let me in."

"Come on up."

The automatic lock clicked several times as Simon held down the switch. She walked toward the door, passing between the two men, who stepped aside politely to make room for her. She looked quickly at them, shuddering slightly as she noticed the misshapen left ear of the man looking for his keys, hoping that he would not be offended by her obvious revulsion at the abnormality. Pushing open the door, she walked inside, hearing the two men fall into step behind her. At first nothing struck her as odd, nothing stranger than people who could not find the door key using her to gain access to the building; she had done it herself plenty of times, slipping in on somebody's tail. Then a chill iced its way down her spine, making her shudder again as she suddenly sensed that the two men represented a threat.

"Keep going, baby," the man with cauliflower ear whispered. "Don't do anything stupid and you won't get hurt."

Petrified by the quiet menace in the man's voice, Della stopped walking abruptly, her hands shaking with fright; the purse she was carrying dropped to the floor. Cauliflower Ear stooped down to pick it up, shoved it back at her, then pushed her toward the bank of elevators.

"Press the nineteenth floor," he ordered. "That's where your boyfriend lives, apartment 1918."

"Hey, that's funny," the other man crowed. "World War I ended in 1918. Looks like we're going to start it all over again."

Once the elevator was under way, Della held out her purse to the two men. "Take it," she offered, ashen-faced. "There's more than a hundred dollars in there, all the money I have on me."

The man who had made the joke about the apartment number took the purse and opened it, peering inside. "Guess what?" he said laughingly to his partner. "This chick doesn't carry a quarter of the shit my old lady lugs around with her." He snapped the purse closed and thrust it back at Della, eying her scornfully. "Keep your pennies, baby. We just want to talk to your boyfriend, nice and friendly. Ain't that right?" he asked the other man.

Cauliflower Ear nodded, a benign look on his fleshy face, which made the coarseness of his deformity even more grotesque. He looked up at the floor indicator, watching the numbers flick on and off as the elevator rose. On the nineteenth floor, it stopped. The two men got out, pushing Della in front of them.

"Ring on the bell like you normally would," Cauliflower Ear ordered. "We don't want to hurt you, but if we have to, we'll make a damned good job of it. I promise you that." He squeezed Della's arm savagely, making her cry out as he pushed her toward Simon's door. "Now ring."

Hesitantly Della pushed the doorbell, aware that the two men had stepped away to the side, out of the view of the spyhole. She heard the sound of the lock being turned, and the door swung open a few inches, held by the security chain. Simon peered through the narrow opening, saw Della and released the chain, opening the door wide.

The man on Della's right stepped in quickly, smashing against the door with his shoulder, sending it flying out of Simon's grasp. Simon froze as he saw the two men, recognition coming immediately. He flung an accusing look at Della, who remained rooted in the hallway.

Cauliflower Ear shoved her roughly into the apartment ahead of him, kicking the door closed behind. The other man had Simon pinned against a wall, lifting him by the jacket lapels, so that his feet barely touched the floor.

"Shitbag!" the man shouted at Simon. "How much did you tell Harry we took off you?"

Simon tried desperately to reply, but pure terror made him unable to control his speech. Words became jumbled, streaming out in a torrent of incomprehensible gibberish. Della watched, horrified, held in a firm grip by Cauliflower Ear. She tried to shut her eyes and block out the scene, but the lids refused to lower.

"How much?" the man repeated. He brought his right knee up savagely into Simon's groin. Simon's eyes rolled upward as he gasped in pain; he would have fallen to the floor had not the man retained his grip on the jacket.

"Forty-eight hundred," Simon spewed out, the muscles in his face and neck contracting in agony. "I told Harry forty-eight hundred." The voice was a harsh whisper trailing off into a groan as another spasm of white-hot pain shot through his body from his injured groin.

"Pick up the phone and call Harry," the man said, letting go of the jacket. Simon slumped to the floor retching, hands clasped to his groin as he curled up trying to ease the unbearable hurt. The man kicked him as he lay there, the toe of his shoe connecting solidly with Simon's back. Then he walked casually across the apartment to the telephone and dialled the bookmaker's number, leering at Della while he waited for an answer.

"Harry? We've got our boy here now. He wants to speak to you, something he has to get off his chest." He laughed loudly. "That's what I said, Harry. He feels confession's good for the soul. Might even help his nuts." Laying the receiver down on the table, he walked back to Simon, grasping the writhing figure by the arms and dragging him over to the telephone.

"Speak to Harry. He wants to hear what you've got to say about our meeting yesterday." He held the receiver out for Simon to speak into.

"Harry," Simon croaked, "they're telling you the truth. They only took twenty-four hundred bucks off me. I still owe you twenty-six hundred."

The man took the receiver away from Simon's mouth and held it to his own. "You hear that, Harry? What do you want us to do now?" He listened for a few seconds. "Consider it done," he said, hanging up.

"Harry says you've got till tomorrow night to come up with the rest. Otherwise we'll break both your legs." He bent down and picked Simon up, holding him by the back of the jacket. "And just in case you think we're kidding, sonny, here's the trailer for the main feature."

He began to walk toward the wall where Simon had been pinned, picking up speed with every step. When he was two yards away, he put one hand behind Simon's head and smashed him face first into the wall. Simon hit the solid structure with a crunching sound and rebounded before dropping like a brick, blood from his smashed nose and mouth staining the wallpaper.

The two men turned to leave. As they were going through the door, Cauliflower Ear turned to Della. "See if you can fix him up, sweetheart. He's got to be in shape to pay some money tomorrow. Otherwise you can buy him a set of crutches for his birthday."

Released from the spell, Della ran over to Simon, who lay unmoving by the wall. She held his head tenderly in her lap, forcing herself not to throw up as she looked at the smashed face.

"Simon," she whispered, the tears beginning. "Simon."

The hazel eyes opened slowly, blinking as recognition came. "You stupid bitch," he mumbled, the smashed mouth making speech difficult. "What the hell did you bring them up here for?"

"I couldn't help it. They were waiting downstairs. As soon as you opened the main door, they grabbed me and forced me to do it." She closed her eyes momentarily, the sight of Simon's battered face horrifying her. "Let me call the police."

"That's all I need." He tried to stand up, but the effort was too much; his legs collapsed under his weight, and he crashed back to the floor. Della ran into the bathroom, returning with a soaking wet towel which she held to his face. As she touched his nose, he recoiled sharply.

"Careful, for Christ's sake. I think it's broken." Gingerly he touched his face, feeling the cut lips and battered nose. Snatching the towel from her, he dabbed at his face, carefully avoiding his nose and mouth.

"Just get the hell out of here," he grated. "I'll call you if I ever want to see you again. Now get out!"

Della lingered for a second. Then she picked up her purse and ran crying from the apartment.

# 5

With a stylish flourish, Nino Viscenzi put his name to the three copies of the design contract, adding a swirling line underneath each signature. Replacing the gold Parker fountain pen in his jacket pocket, he turned in the chair and looked up at Jonathan.

"I am delighted to be in partnership with you, and I trust it will be a long and mutually rewarding alliance," the Italian said. "Together we shall show the American man all he has been missing over the years."

He shook Jonathan's hand warmly, then gazed at Jacob. "If I was asked to state the one single reason why I look forward to working in the United States, I would point to you. You are a delight to discuss manufacturing techniques with, a pleasure to talk to."

As Jacob began to blush under the Italian's sincere praise, Jonathan chuckled quietly, winking at Gerald. Jonathan was happy to see his father at the center of activity again; frequently he had worried about how Jacob felt being on the periphery of the business. Thankfully he was still an active man, in full control of his faculties, wanting to be involved, aching to be at the hub of things. But when the factory had been transferred to Buffalo, he had become like a man without a limb. Now this Italian designer, through a shared love, had brought him out.

"Nino, on the flight back from Buffalo you were talking about shops within shops," Gerald said, reminding him of the conversation. "Could we go into that a bit further? It sounds interesting."

Viscenzi made himself comfortable, crossing his legs, hands clasped underneath his chin. "It's a fairly recent concept in Europe," he began, "perhaps eight or ten years old. Take, for example, a chain of stores like yours, Chestertons. You have defined your market—fairly conservative in style, better end in quality. Fine. You have the formula for success. But suppose at the same time you want to offer a new outlook, a different

173

direction to bring in a more fashion-conscious customer." He looked at Gerald to be certain he was following closely.

"There are two ways you could go about this," he continued. "One would be through the normal operating conditions of your stores, only it would be a compromise. You would have a foot in both camps, and, quite possibly, you would upset your regular customers. The other way is to take one section of your store and separate it completely from the main area. In it you stock merchandise for the younger man, more exotic if you like than the garments you sell in the store. And to draw a distinct barrier, you call it by another name entirely, something which will appeal to the new customers you are trying to entice.

"For example," he looked meaningfully at Gerald, "if you were going to run such an operation, you could call it Mr. Gerald at Chestertons, or just Gerald—anything you like, as long as there is both an association and a strict dividing line. Even Young Chestertons. It's a simple concept which pays off well."

Gerald listened intently, the germ of an idea forming in his mind. When he looked across the boardroom at his father, he saw Jonathan staring back at him, a similar gleam of enlightenment in his eyes.

"Are you thinking what I'm thinking?" Gerald asked.

Jonathan nodded almost imperceptibly, feeling at one with his son, thinking along the same lines as always.

Confused by the interplay between Gerald and his father, Viscenzi asked, "Am I missing something?"

"Sorry," Jonathan said. "It's just that your description of shops within shops fits the bill for something we've been looking for. My other son, Simon, doesn't see the business in the same light as the rest of us, and we've been searching for something where he'll fit in better."

Viscenzi pursed his lips pensively. "Mr. Simon. That sound as good a name as any."

Simon walked out of the hospital, surgical tape covering his smashed nose, sutures in his lips and chin. Large Elton John sunglasses hid his blackened eyes. Waving down a cab, he instructed the driver to take him to West Fifty-seventh Street, sitting back during the journey, biting his lips gently to see if the anaesthetic was wearing off.

Where the hell am I going to come up with twenty-six hundred bucks in a hurry, he wondered miserably. Where do I find that sort of money without going to my father? The combined totals of Simon's checking and savings accounts came to less than fourteen hundred dollars, and any money he had put away was tied up in bonds and share issues, all unrealizable as cash at such short notice.

Fearfully he looked down at his legs, imagining them broken, wincing as his mind's eye saw a baseball bat come crashing down across the shins and splinter the bones, smashing them to smithereens.

Only when the cab jerked to a halt outside the store did Simon think of Della, cursing her for being the tool of entry for the two men, yet feeling a twinge of remorse at the way he had thrown her out. Everything had gone rotten in hours, and none of it would have happened if he had not tried to cheat the bookmaker. *What made me do it?* The question nagged at him, refusing to fade away although he could find no satisfactory answer. *What stupid logic made me tell him that his cowboys had taken twice as much as they had? Did I really expect him to believe me, and not them? Now I've got to come up with the rest of the money by tonight, or I'll be pushing a wheel chair for six months.*

Instead of using the separate office entrance, Simon walked through the first floor of the store, ignoring the curious looks from sales staff and customers which his appearance aroused. Inside the office complex at the rear, he removed the glasses and inspected his reflection in a mirror. *I look like the adult version of the battered baby,* he thought; *this'll shock them enough to come up with the money.*

Marching along the corridor toward the boardroom, he stopped by the secretary's desk.

"Is he in?" he asked brusquely, interrupting the girl in the middle of typing a letter.

"Yes, but..."

Simon heard only the first word, choosing to ignore anything which followed it. He opened the door and walked in.

In the middle of discussing the shops-within-shops concept with Viscenzi, Jonathan stopped talking abruptly as the door to the boardroom opened. He spun around, immediately furious that anybody should barge in unannounced, and curious to see who would have the gall to do so.

The figure in the doorway stopped in surprise at seeing a meeting in progress and looked around, bewildered.

"Nino," Jonathan said slowly, "I think this is my other son. He's doing his impersonation of the Mummy."

Viscenzi slid around in his chair, smiling to greet Simon. The expression changed abruptly when he saw the blackened eyes and the tape. He looked back to Jonathan. "I thought you said Simon was in the business with you, not a boxer."

Gerald quickly took the initiative. "Come in and sit down, Simon. Tell us what happened."

Closing the door behind him, Simon said, "I was attacked by two men."

"Mugged?" Viscenzi asked hopefully, having heard much about the streets of New York and finding it difficult to believe.

"Just attacked," Simon replied, guessing that the unknown man was

Nino Viscenzi, the designer he was supposed to have been meeting while he was at the track; he found himself wishing he had gone to the airport with the rest of the family that afternoon.

"Do you think we're entitled to an explanation for this interruption?" Jonathan demanded.

Simon moved his feet uncomfortably. "Pa, can I see you for a few minutes? Alone."

Jonathan shook his head in exasperation, then looked at Viscenzi. "Would you excuse us for just a moment, Nino? It's at times like this"—the voice was laced heavily with sarcasm—"that a boy needs his father."

He followed Simon out of the boardroom. The silence which greeted their departure lasted for more than half a minute as each man wondered what could have caused the injuries.

"Do you think it could be an angry husband?" Viscenzi asked finally, feeling that somebody had to speak.

Gerald grinned at the question, while Jacob looked confused and worried about what could have happened to his grandson.

"Anything's possible," Gerald replied. "Simon leads the life of the carefree bachelor. Only I thought he'd have had more sense than to chase women with husbands bigger than he is."

Jonathan returned five minutes later, his face white with barely suppressed fury. The unlit cigar in the corner of his mouth jumped up and down as he chewed vigorously on it, shredding the tobacco in his anger.

"I apologize for that interruption. Simon had a small personal problem which had to be taken care of." He saw Jacob about to speak and made a small motion with his hand; the meaning was obvious—later.

"Something to do with the supplier he was seeing?" Viscenzi asked lightly.

Jonathan's anger disappeared in the presence of this likeable Italian. A faint smile flickered across his face as he answered. "Not really. It had something to do with Simon's other business interests. He's been the victim of a run of bad decisions lately, and his partners didn't take kindly to it." He took the cigar out of his mouth and looked at the chewed end.

"Someday," he said to nobody in particular, "I'm going to light one of these things again. And the hell with what the doctor says about it." He looked up again, as if remembering that other people were present.

"Now what were we talking about?"

Gerald and Jonathan sat alone in the boardroom. It was seven in the evening, and Jacob had been driven back to the house in Great Neck by the company chauffeur, while Viscenzi was at Kennedy Airport awaiting his flight to Paris.

"How much did it cost you?" Gerald asked.

"Twenty-six hundred," Jonathan muttered. "That was to stop him from getting his legs busted."

"Take it out of his salary."

"What the hell good would that do?" he shot back, dismissing the suggestion. "You know what makes me really mad? None of this would have happened if he hadn't tried to get smart with the bookie and tell him that the collectors had taken twice as much as they actually had. The bookie didn't want Simon beaten up; he just wanted the money that was owing to him."

"How much was Simon into him for?"

"Five grand, would you believe?"

"Jesus!" Gerald gasped. "How did he run up a bill like that?"

"Clever handicapping."

"So the bookie cut off Simon's credit and demanded payment?"

"Yeah. He had a couple of muscle men keeping an eye on Simon, and when he picked up a bundle at the track, they took it off him. After he'd claimed they'd taken more, they wanted a piece of him for trying to make fools out of them. All the bookie was going to do was call me up and ask me to settle Simon's debt. And on top of that, your brother threatens to holler 'Cop' if the bookie comes near me."

"Smart guy," Gerald said. "Bets illegally and then wants to call the cops. I think we should get him a copy of Dale Carnegie's *How to Win Friends and Influence People.*"

Jonathan gave a short, sour laugh. "What the hell for? He wouldn't take any notice of it. Thinks he knows all the answers already. But talking about Simon, what do you reckon on the Mr. Simon idea? Be honest with me; don't say yes because it means getting Simon out of our hair for the time being."

"If it covers itself financially, it would have served its purpose," Gerald joked.

"Don't be flippant," Jonathan admonished him. "If we go into something like this—even with the ulterior motive of getting Simon out of the way—we've still got to work it out on a dollars-sales-per-square-foot basis. It's just like any other new store. Be objective about it."

"Nino says it works in Europe," Gerald said. "Therefore it should work here. We'll take an unproductive area of the stores, get the shopfitters in and set up a boutique. It should be profitable, but we've got to take the Simon factor into account. If you turn him loose in an operation like that, you could be asking for trouble."

Jonathan jammed another cigar into his mouth and began the chewing process all over again. "Leave that part of it to me. We'll make Simon general manager of the Mr. Simon operation, and he'll be so up in the air about having the damned thing named after him that he'll allow us some leeway when we check the merchandise he's buying. And I'm sure there's enough management potential in the chain to run the boutiques. We'll just be giving him a tactful shove sideways." He shifted the cigar from the left side of his mouth to the right. Watching, Gerald thought his father looked like a bulldog, Churchillian even, the way his heavy jowls drooped.

"There's only one place the money can come from," Jonathan said, having found a comfortable resting place for the cigar. "I can't go to the bank, so we'll have to sell off the Gellenbaum stores. But what I want from you is a recommendation on who takes over Simon's position as general merchandise manager. Give it some thought, Gerald, will you?"

# 6

Jonathan sat quietly in the old-fashioned rocking chair as he watched his father walk slowly from the living room and go upstairs. He waited till he heard the bedroom door close; then he looked at Miriam.

"What do you think? Is he upset or not?"

Miriam answered him with another question. "How would you feel, Jonathan, if something like this was happening to you?"

"Lousy, I guess."

"Try heartbroken," she suggested. "Isn't there any other way you can find to finance these Mr. Simon shops, any alternative to selling the four Gellenbaum and Son stores? Can't you think of something else?"

"Of course I can—not have the Mr. Simon shops at all, and let your son sort out his own affairs in the future. Then I wouldn't have to keep worrying about where I could put him so he couldn't do any harm."

"That's no answer," Miriam retorted angrily. "Couldn't you sell one of the Chestertons stores to pay for the changes? Why does it have to be the four Gellenbaum and Son stores that get the axe?"

Jonathan put a hand to his top pocket, ready to pull out a cigar before he remembered that Miriam would disapprove; he could not even chew them in the house any more. "Tell me another way," he said. "If it wasn't for that half-wit Simon, I wouldn't have to do any of this."

He saw Miriam's lips tighten as she prepared to defend her son. Christ, he thought, why the hell can't she see him the way he really is?

"Just because you helped him out when he got into trouble with those terrible people doesn't mean you can talk about him that way," Miriam said, the words coming quietly but carrying across the whole room.

"Don't give me aggravation about Simon now, Miriam, please. I'm not in the mood for it. I'm worried about Jacob and how losing the four Gellenbaum stores will affect him." He stood up, stretching. "I'm going for a walk to clear my mind. If Jacob's still awake when I come back, I'll try to speak to him, make him understand."

"Don't forget to wear a coat," Miriam called after him. "It's turning chilly."

Jonathan walked out the front door, inhaling the night air hungrily. He felt the bite of impending winter and hoped it would be a severe one. Topcoat sales had fallen well below budget for the previous two years, what with central heating and comfortable cars; let's have one lousy winter, he prayed, below freezing for five months. Maybe we can make enough money on topcoats to pay for the Mr. Simon launch.

Pulling out a cigar, he clamped his teeth around the end, licking it to get the taste of the tobacco. Feeling in his jacket pocket, he found the gold Dunhill lighter which Miriam had given to him on their tenth wedding anniversary. He wondered if there was any fuel in it. He could not remember the last time he had used it; he carried it simply because it was from Miriam. Flicking it with his thumb, he was happy to see the small flame dance in the darkness.

Feeling guilty, like a small child caught raiding the icebox, he bent down, cupping his hand around the flame while he lit the cigar. At first the taste of smoke seemed strange, a pungent, cloying sensation, and Jonathan was tempted to crush the cigar under his foot. But he persevered, drawing again, cautiously breathing in the smoke, feeling lightheaded as the first wisps reached his lungs and began to enter the bloodstream. He leaned against a tree while the dizziness passed; then he inhaled the smoke again, familiarizing himself with the sensation.

The hell with chewing them. The hell with doctors. The hell with everything, he thought, drawing heavily on the cigar. I buy them to smoke them, not to suck them like a lollipop. Damned doctors don't even know what they're talking about.

He continued walking around the block, the cigar stuck jauntily in the corner of his mouth, the end glowing red, brightening and fading as he puffed contentedly like a man renewing an old and dear friendship.

Staring down at the face of the gold pocket watch, Jacob saw again that moment on the ship when he had dropped the timepiece, setting the hands forever at three minutes to twelve. A tear began to form in the corner of his left eye; he made no attempt to block its path as it rolled down the side of his nose, stopping for an instant as if uncertain about the fall which faced it. Then it splashed down onto the watch glass, its perfect globular shape shattering, spreading out into a small pool, blurring Jacob's view of the hands.

When did I last cry? he thought. Was it when Anna died? No, it was when Jonathan—a young, ambitious Jonathan—insisted that I give up the tailoring shop because he wanted me to go into partnership with him; he didn't want me to work myself into an early grave. He wanted me to be a part of Gellenbaum and Son. And I cried because I realized how much my son loved me. Now, these many years later, I cry the tears of a foolish old man because the last part of our business with a Gellenbaum name is to be sold to pay for a new group of high-fashion shops.

Jacob wiped the glass dry with a handkerchief before replacing the watch in his vest pocket. He took a cigarette from the pack on the bedside table and lit it, watching the smoke drift lazily toward the bedroom ceiling.

He remembered his opposition to Jonathan changing his name, but that had passed, and his son had been right. Now Jonathan was taking away the last vestige of his identity. Not that he had been highly involved with the small group of clearance stores; since the big change after the war, they had been nothing special. As Jonathan had once joked, the Gellenbaum stores made their profits from the Chestertons mistakes.

Sitting back in the chair, the cigarette dangling from his fingers, Jacob tried to recall every event which had taken place since he had closed the tailoring shop. But the memories became confused; dates, events became jumbled in his mind. With a feeling of resignation, he stubbed out the cigarette and began to undress. He stopped when he heard the knock on the bedroom door and looked around inquisitively.

"It's Jonathan. Can I come in?"

"Come in, come in."

Jonathan entered the room and sat down on the edge of the bed, looking helplessly at his father, wanting to say something but unable to find the words.

Jacob said it for him. "I know. If there was any other way, you'd do it."

Jonathan nodded wretchedly. "You still read my mind pretty well. What can I say?"

Jacob went to the closet and took out a hanger, draping his jacket carefully over it. "Is there anything to say?" he asked Jonathan. "You have to go your way, and that's all there is to it."

"You're making me feel like a louse, Jacob. Don't do it." Jonathan's voice held a warning note. "I have to get the money from somewhere, and I can't go to the bank. The clearance stores are the only thing I can liquidate."

"It's all right," Jacob said sympathetically. "I understand everything. I understand the responsibilities that go with running the company, all the people across the country relying on you for their money. You have to do whatever you think is best."

"That's not the reason I'm going ahead with the Mr. Simon operation, and you know it," Jonathan said. "I'm doing it to keep some peace within this family. Whichever way I turn, I get it smack in the back of the neck." He looked up to see whether Jacob was listening or had continued undressing; he was gratified to see that his father was paying attention.

"If I keep Simon in his present position at Head Office, the dissension will be so great that it will wreck the company. Gerald can't work with him, nobody can. If I give him some money and kick him out, Miriam will come back at me for deserting him. This way, by setting up a high-fashion chain within our own stores and letting Simon run it, because that's where he belongs, I can just about balance everybody's feelings."

Jacob nodded slowly. "I told you, Jonathan, do whatever you want to do. I am eighty-nine years old, so it's safe to say that I've had my best days. Simon—please God that he settles down one day—needs your help more than I do. Sell the stores. Do whatever you think best. *Gei gezundheit!* Go in good health."

Jonathan got off the bed, feeling lost. "You don't have to translate that for me," he said. "That much Yiddish I understand. I'll see you in the morning."

Reaching the door, he looked back. Jacob stood by the bed, taking the watch from his vest pocket and laying it lovingly on the table; he did not even notice Jonathan's parting glance.

Entering his own room, he found Miriam already in bed reading a book, which she laid down as she heard him enter.

"What did he say?" she asked, as Jonathan sat down heavily on his twin bed.

"*Gei gezundheit,*" he repeated disgustedly. "He gave me his blessing, told me to go in good health."

Lifting his right foot, he kicked off the shoe, following the same procedure with his left foot. Rolling up his socks, he threw them fiercely at the wall, watching them bounce back toward him.

"Why the hell couldn't we have had just one son?" he asked himself angrily. "Why did we have to get twins?"

But his voice was loud enough for Miriam to hear.

For the second time that night, Marilyn Chesterton got out of bed. She moved gently to avoid waking Gerald, who slept on his side, one arm trailing across the bed. Closing the door quietly, she walked to the nursery to see why Karen was crying. She picked up the baby, cuddling her, hoping that she would go back to sleep.

The baby's cheeks were red, sore from the teeth which were coming through and causing the pain. But under Marilyn's gentle touch, the crying changed to a quiet whimper, then ceased altogether as Karen stuck a thumb in her mouth, sucking happily.

Marilyn held her breath as she replaced the baby in the cot, pulling the light wool blanket up to her chin. She tiptoed out of the nursery, leaving the door ajar.

Gerald was sitting up in bed when she returned, the reading light next to him throwing a bright circle onto the bed. His chest was bare, the thick black hair lying flat against his skin.

"She all right?" he asked.

Marilyn nodded. She sat on the bed and swung her feet up, sliding down underneath the sheet. "Teething. It must be rotten being a kid. We should be thankful we've got all the teeth we're ever going to have."

"It's not all that bad," Gerald contradicted her. "They get fed and clothed for nothing, just an occasional smile. If I had a toothache, you wouldn't get out of bed to see me."

Running her hand underneath the sheet, Marilyn pinched Gerald playfully on the thigh. "You're big enough to look after your own teeth." She removed her hand and lay back on the pillow, her blue eyes half-closed. "Tell me more about this scheme for Simon. It sounds interesting."

Gerald related the discussion with his father. Marilyn lay quietly, listening. "That's all?" she asked, when he had finished.

"More or less. What else do you want to know?"

"How many Chestertons stores will have these boutiques?"

"We'll start it off just in the local area—New York, Philadelphia, Washington, Albany. We might push west a bit, possibly as far as Chicago, but it's hit or miss to begin with."

"Have you told your father who you'd like at Head Office to replace Simon?"

"Not yet. I wanted some time to think about it, to make sure I was sure."

Marilyn pondered the last sentence, trying to identify why it irritated her. "You're repeating yourself. Two sures made an unsure."

"Idiot," he said, laughing.

"Do you think your father will agree that Brian Chambers should get the general merchandise manager position?"

"I've got a gut feeling that Brian's the man my father will go for. But he wants to see what I think before he makes his own recommendation. It's a little game he plays, seeing how often he agrees with me and how often he disagrees with Simon."

"I don't think I've ever met Brian," Marilyn said. "What does he look like?"

"Of course you've met him."

"When?"

"Last year," Gerald reminded her. "Remember when we brought the managers and regional managers into New York for the sales meeting? He's got light brown hair, going a bit thin in the middle and gray at the sides. About forty-eight or so."

"I've got him now," Marilyn said. "He's got a bit of a receding chin, hasn't he, like British royalty?"

"That's him," Gerald said, laughing again. "But he's no chinless wonder. He's done a hell of a job with that region."

"Isn't he the one who's always complaining about the lack of communication between Head Office and the stores?" Marilyn asked.

"Every week. He's continually having a go at the buying group because they ignore input from the stores and go their own sweet way. Mainly he's launching attacks on Simon, but nobody else ever backs him up."

"Why doesn't Simon listen to suggestions from the stores? Surely they know which way the wind's blowing in their own part of the country," Marilyn said.

"Simon figures he knows best. That's one of the reasons we have to get him out of that slot. During one meeting, he had the *chutzpa* to stand up and say we could knock at least three weeks off the seasonal budgeting sessions if we by-passed the stores completely," Gerald said, remembering the incredulous looks of those who had been present at the meeting. "That's one of the reasons why I reckon Brian will do well in the job; he knows how important store feedback is to the buying plan."

Marilyn rolled over, pulling herself closer to Gerald, her head nestling against his shoulder. "How long's Brian been with us?"

"Since we opened the Chicago store. When was that—'51, '52? It was the same time that Uncle Myron was killed in Korea."

The mention of death made Marilyn shiver. Here, in bed with Gerald, with the baby in the next room, she felt so alive, so vibrantly warm, that even the thought of death was oppressive.

"Are you getting out of the house at all?" Gerald asked, changing the subject purposely.

"Trying to," she replied sleepily. "I'm determined to get in some time on the courts before winter comes. I can put Karen in the portable cot and leave her in the clubhouse to sleep. I want to get back into shape before you start looking at other women."

Gerald placed the flat of his hand on Marilyn's stomach, feeling the muscles tense in anticipation. "I wish I had the time to look at other women," he said.

# 7

"New York's a filthy, disgusting place! I don't want to live there, and you can't make me go."

The woman's strident voice pierced the temperature-controlled atmosphere of the apartment, bouncing back off the walls to hammer at Brian Chambers from every angle. Angrily he spun around to face her.

"You think Chicago's such a Garden of Eden?" he snapped at his wife. "One city's the same as any other, Thelma. I've had a damned good deal with this company over the past twenty-some years, and I'm not passing up an opportunity like this. If you want to stay in Chicago, you're welcome to it. But I'm going to New York, and you can do whatever you damn well like."

Thelma Chambers wilted under the verbal barrage. She sat back on the couch, the hem of her blue dress clutched tightly in her hands, dragging it up past her knees.

The same argument, at one level or another, had been going on for the past two weeks, ever since Brian had been offered the position of general merchandise manager at the Chestertons Head Office, succeeding Simon as he laid the groundwork for the Mr. Simon boutique operation. Thelma, with a display of temper to match her red hair, had opposed the move from the beginning, claiming she would be leaving behind all her friends and business contacts and going to a city that was a stinking pit of obscenity.

Initially Brian had shrugged off her objections. But hour after hour, day after day of arguments had worn down the veneer of patience and understanding he tried hard to affect. He had begun to respond in kind, turning the apartment into a heated battleground of slanging matches and abuse.

There were tears in Thelma's blue eyes as she looked up from her dress, seeking Brian. "If we had children, it would be different," she said,

186

the sharpness displayed moments earlier yielding to a pleading tone. "I wouldn't be so lonely then."

"Don't start that again," Brian shot back. "Every goddamn time, you bring up the fact that we haven't got any kids. You didn't want any and neither did I." His voice grew louder as he gave vent to his feelings. "You'd have been a lousy mother anyway," he jibed, looking for a way to hurt his wife. "The kids would never have got fed till I got home at night, because you'd have been too damned busy working and seeing your friends all day long."

"You're a bastard," Thelma hissed. "A one-hundred-percent, twenty-four-carat bastard."

"Damned right! Just what a bitch like you deserves." He flung a final, disgusted look at his wife and stormed out of the living room, out of the apartment. Outside in the hallway, he leaned his head against the cool wood of the door, not caring if his neighbors saw him; they must have heard the argument anyway, so what did visual contact matter? He would go to New York, and if Thelma did not want to join him . . . tough. Maybe she would divorce him . . . even better. There would be no support to pay; she looked after herself very well with all those stupid love stories she wrote for the pulp publishers.

Brian still found it difficult to understand how Thelma could write about how it felt to be in love. What love had she ever given? What genuine affection had she ever shown toward him? Yet she had at least four of her short romances published every year under the laughable nom de plume of Louise Duvalier. Often he walked into a drugstore and saw her latest simpering novel on the rack under the French name. Thank God she used it, he thought. If she ever used the name he had given her by marriage, he would have taken her to court. What could he have sued her for? Defamation of a surname? Never mind, it was a hypothetical question anyway.

He remembered reading somewhere that comedians are supposed to be unhappy people, hiding their sadness in humor, losing their own cares by making other people laugh. The same yardstick, in his eyes, applied to romantic novelists; he and Thelma had slept in separate rooms for the past four years, meeting each other over the breakfast table in the morning like two guests in a hotel. Since the break in marital relations, he had entered into four affairs, all of which were unsatisfying, leaving him with a feeling of debasement. He often wondered if Thelma had followed the same course. If she had, he thought, she probably put it down to research and charged any expenses against her tax return for the year. After all, you have to know how something feels before you can write about it; you need the experience to get it down on paper. Otherwise you need a damned good imagination, and he was certain that Thelma did not possess one.

Remaining outside the apartment door, Brian cast his mind back to when he had met Thelma. How about a blind date with a journalist? a friend had asked. Sure, he had replied. I'm game for anything. But in those days, Thelma had been an attractive cub reporter with the *Chicago Tribune*, eight years younger than himself, funny to be around, always full of amusing gossip. Brian had been overcome by her vivacious personality, laughing delightedly as she recounted the latest tidbit of privileged information.

With marriage, however, had come realization—too late, it seemed to Brian. Gossip was the major part of Thelma's conversation. Occasionally it could be fun, but rammed down his ears all night long was a different story. One of the mayor's secretaries was having an affair with so-and-so from the municipal legal department, she would whisper, giggling as she recounted the rumor; a leading light in the police department—can't say who, but he's in the running for chief of police—is supposed to be receiving payoffs from a certain bookmaker. And even when his interest had waned, she had been too thick-skinned to see that the rumors were boring him to distraction. She was too damned thick-skinned and self-centered to see anything outside her own little world of a telephone and a typewriter.

Returning to the living room, he saw that Thelma had not moved. She remained on the couch, staring morosely at him; it appeared to Brian that she was hoping for some sort of reconciliation, but he had no intention of providing the opening.

"Made your mind up yet?" he growled.

"About what?"

"About whether you're coming with me to New York or staying here. Even easier, we can get a divorce and undo the mistake we made fifteen years ago."

"I'll go with you." It came out painfully, the hurt of abject surrender.

Brian could have accepted it gracefully, but he made no attempt to do so. "Don't do me any favors. Just make sure that's what you want to do before we leave Chicago. Once we're there, that's the end of it."

Walking past her into his bedroom, he realized that in New York he would see her every night, whereas in his present position as regional manager for the Midwest he was often away for a week at a time, spending time in the stores which came under his responsibility—that, and sending in recommendations to Head Office which were disregarded by that idiot Simon Chesterton.

Well, that was one problem which would no longer occur. He would listen to what the regions had to say, treating their feedback on local market trends with the respect it deserved. Besides, it made a lot more sense than the garbage he heard from his wife.

Simon studied the architect's plans for the first Mr. Simon boutique, which would be incorporated on the second floor of the main Chestertons store on West Fifty-seventh Street. The artist's impression of the boutique which accompanied the architect's plans pleased Simon; the entire look was aesthetically correct for the image he felt the Mr. Simon shops should portray—elegant, stylish and, most important of all, young and aware.

Picking up the plans, he walked the short distance to the boardroom and knocked on the door, awaiting the summons to enter. Not since he had barged in on the Viscenzi meeting had Simon entered without the courtesy of knocking. And now—especially now—when he wanted his father to give the nod and open the purse for the project, he was walking on eggs.

As he waited for Jonathan's answer, Simon touched his nose tenderly. It was still slightly sore, but the ugly swelling had subsided and the bone had almost straightened out to its original shape. Whereas before it had been perfectly straight, there was now a slight kink, which a plastic surgeon could fix in good time. The only lesson Simon had learned from his encounter with the two thugs had been to change bookmakers.

"Come in." Jonathan's voice was gravelly, a change which Simon had noticed during the past week, as if his father had a sore throat which refused to yield to medication.

Entering the boardroom, he sniffed sharply. There was something strange about the atmosphere. He had become accustomed—as had everybody else at Head Office—to being assailed by the smell of chewed cigars, yet this aroma was different, more acrid.

"Have you been smoking?" he asked Jonathan.

For reply, Jonathan removed an unlit cigar from his mouth. "See?" he said triumphantly. "I'm just chewing it. What are you doing, spying for your mother?"

Simon sensed that his father was in an infrequent good mood—at least, an infrequent good mood toward Simon—and decided to capitalize on it. "I thought I smelled cigar smoke when I came in," he said almost apologetically. "Guess I was wrong."

"You were right, but it wasn't me. Somebody was in here about ten minutes ago. They were smoking," Jonathan lied smoothly. "The smell hangs around for a while." He motioned to the papers Simon was holding. "What have you got there?"

Unrolling the plans, Simon laid them on the desk. Jonathan got up and stood next to him, listening intently as Simon explained the display and selling areas.

"What's the cost?" Jonathan asked when he had finished.

Simon handed him the architect's report and estimate. Jonathan perused it, multiplying it by the number of Mr. Simon boutiques they planned to open in the first wave of the operation, subtracting the final figure from the offer he had received for the four Gellenbaum stores. He knew the figure was at best a very rough approximation, but he stood to make a profit of almost two hundred thousand dollars. But there was still merchandise to be ordered for the boutiques, staff to be hired and the thousand-and-one other things which went into the launching of a retail chain; all that would eat up another healthy chunk. If the shops-within-shops idea took off, Jonathan intended to skim the profits straight off the top and expand the project till every store in the Chestertons chain carried a Mr. Simon boutique.

"How do you like the idea of running your own operation?" Jonathan asked.

What a question, Simon thought. "What do you think?" he asked in return. "It's the opportunity I've been praying for. It gives me the chance to show that my ideas are the right ones. At least," he added quickly, seeing his father's head turn, "right for a certain segment of the market. Where did you get the idea from? You never told me that."

"Nino Viscenzi. We were kicking it around that afternoon when you busted into the boardroom with your head in your hands. Have you talked to any suppliers yet?"

"Some," Simon replied. "I didn't tell them what we were planning to do. I just mentioned that we might be expanding our market slightly, no details of the boutiques."

"Good. What are you looking at?"

"Suits first of all. Once I've got that worked out, I'll build up the accessories around them."

"Reasonable," Jonathan concurred. "Just remember to clear every purchase through me. I'm still signing the checks around this place."

Simon's voice took on an almost unnoticeable trace of hostility. "I'll remember. After all, you never let me forget."

Jonathan let the comment pass. He rolled up the plans and handed them back to his son. "Look after them. You've got your big chance to prove yourself now. Do a good job of it. And don't forget to listen to feedback once you get started."

Simon returned to his own office in a dream. The first hurdle had been cleared—approval of the plans by his father, plans he had worked out with the architect and shopfitting people. They were his plans, nothing to do with Gerald, nothing to do with his father other than the matter of financing. Next would come the stocking of the boutiques, his decisions again. Do a good job of it, his father had said. He'd do more than that; he'd turn the Mr. Simon shops into a more profitable operation per square foot than Chestertons had ever been.

Still feeling elated at the success of the meeting with his father, Simon picked up the telephone and called Della at her advertising agency. He had forgiven her for that night, for bringing up those two goons, letting them use her to gain entry. She was still the best bedmate he had found, and when they were out together, he continually drew envious looks from other men. Talents like that, he decided, listening to the ringing of the telephone, bore a lot of forgiveness for other shortcomings.

Jacob sat in the front room of the house in Great Neck looking at the street outside, trying to find interest in people as they walked by. He had not been into the city for more than a week, and—if he was truthful with himself—he did not care if a month passed without him visiting West Fifty-seventh Street. Besides, as he had told Jonathan, an old man needs to rest more; he has to conserve his energy.

He felt in the pockets of his jacket for a cigarette before remembering he had left them upstairs on the bedside table. Standing up to go to the bedroom, Jacob suddenly felt his legs threaten to give way underneath him. The moment of panic passed as he clutched the chair for support, slowly lowering himself again.

Strange, he thought. My legs have never felt weak before. Is this the way old age catches up on a person, so quickly and so insidiously?

Is the relinquishing of an interest really the first death, followed at a later stage by the true death?

Marilyn Chesterton made a desperate attempt to return the service, but her racket missed the ball by a foot.

"That's not good enough, Mrs. Chesterton," the club coach called out from the opposite end of the court. "You're getting caught flat-footed. That was a lousy service, and it should have come back like a bullet."

Grinning foolishly under the rebuke, Marilyn walked toward the net, swinging her racket lazily in the air. "Enough, enough the maiden cried," she called across the court. "I've had it for today, Stan."

Stan Jarvis, the coach, laughed at her words of surrender, his white teeth gleaming like an advertisement for toothpaste. In fact, every part of Stan Jarvis's face could have been used in an advertising campaign for one product or another. His short brown hair, free from any trace of dandruff, seemed to cry Head and Shoulders, while his clear blue eyes looked as if he bathed them once a day in Optrex. And both Wilkinson and Gillette would have been proud of the perfect shave he always had.

"Your game's improving, Mrs. Chesterton," he complimented her. "But it's still nowhere near as good as it should be."

"I've got a good excuse," Marilyn replied.

"I know," Jarvis agreed. "I know all about your good excuse. It's sleeping in the clubhouse."

"It," Marilyn corrected the coach, horrified to think that anybody could classify her daughter as a neuter, "is a she."

"Got time for a drink?" Jarvis asked hopefully.

"Can we make it a quick one? I want to be home by four."

Jarvis led the way into the clubhouse, holding open the door for Marilyn. While he walked to the bar and helped himself, Marilyn looked at Karen, seeing that the baby was still asleep in her portable cot, her thumb implanted firmly in her mouth, sucking happily. For a moment, Marilyn thought of her father-in-law, Jonathan, and his cigars; there was a trace of him in the way Karen sucked on her thumb. When she straightened up, she was laughing, so absurd was the idea.

"What's so funny?" Jarvis asked, returning with the drinks. He peered into the cot to see if he could spot the source of Marilyn's amusement.

"Nothing I could explain," Marilyn replied, feeling embarrassed by her outburst. She felt her cheeks reddening and walked away quickly toward the washroom.

"Hey!" Jarvis called after her. "I've got your drink."

"Put it on the table. I'll be back in a minute."

Setting down the two drinks, Jarvis lit a cigarette and sat back to await Marilyn's return; although he always advised his pupils not to smoke, Jarvis rarely believed in heeding his own counsel. Other club members passed by the table, and he acknowledged them, recalling the familiar faces of people he had coached during his five years with the club.

Tennis was Stan Jarvis's world. It had always been his world, especially during the idealistic days of his youth when he had dreamed of playing in the annual Wimbledon grass court championships. The dream had come true, but it had been a once-only effort with a far from dreamlike conclusion. The promise he had shown at fifteen had failed to keep up with his physical growth, and he was completely outclassed in the one match he played, losing in straight sets to a far older player.

The experience of having his hopes shattered at Wimbledon taught Jarvis a valuable lesson. It knocked the streak of fantasy out of him, replacing it with a desire to utilize the considerable skill he had to the best advantage, but never to aim too high again. Coaching at private clubs offered the perfect solution. He still played tennis all day long during the summer, moving to indoor courts when winter came, passing on the benefit of his own skill to people who were willing to pay handsomely for the tuition—and getting to know rich, bored women.

Rich, bored women. He relished the description, knowing that the icing on his cake came from such sources. When he was fourteen and living with his parents in Oil City, Pennsylvania, he had gotten a nineteen-year-old girl pregnant because he was too inexperienced to take the proper precautions and she was too simple to know any better. The girl's father, after beating his daughter almost senseless to find out who was responsible, had stormed around to Jarvis's house, prepared to strangle the violator of his daughter. Jarvis's own father had called the police for protection, a move which was welcomed by the girl's father, who demanded that Jarvis be prosecuted. A wry local police chief had pointed out that the only charge which could be brought would be against the girl, for contributing to the delinquency of a minor. When the crisis had died down and the girl was married off to a local shopworker—who thought the pregnancy was his work, she was that generous with her affections—Jarvis had been told by his father that his brains were hanging between his legs. If that was the case, and Jarvis happily admitted it was, he would capitalize on that as well.

Playing tennis and servicing rich, bored women—it paid well, exceptionally well sometimes when grateful pupils, in both categories, showered him with gifts. And what could be better than job satisfaction and satisfied clients?

He watched Marilyn reappear from the washroom, admiring her legs and her body as she walked toward him, finding it difficult to believe that the baby in the cot was hers. This was one woman to whom he would like to extend his extracurricular coaching activities. He had been trying to judge her during the three coaching sessions he had given; she was rich, he knew that, but the continuing appearance of the baby made him wary. The first time she had brought Karen to the club she had explained that it was preferable to leaving her in somebody's care. Still, Jarvis was not too certain about his chances one way or the other.

"Your drink's still waiting for you, Mrs. Chesterton." He laid emphasis on the formality, seeing if she suggested that he use her first name.

"Thanks, Stan." She lifted the glass and took a sip. Jarvis watched her hungrily, eroticizing every gesture she made, fantasizing, mentally undressing her, letting his imagination run riot.

"How much do I owe you?" Marilyn asked, picking up the purse from the chair next to her.

"You've paid already, Mrs. Chesterton." Again he accentuated her last name, looking for the opening.

This time he found it. "Call me Marilyn. Everybody knows I'm a Mrs. because of that." She pointed at the cot. "How much do I owe you for the drinks, not for the coaching?"

"You don't owe me anything, Marilyn. I have to dig into my own pocket sometimes. If too many members insist on buying me drinks, I'll lose my independence."

"Are you that independent, Stan?" Marilyn asked, turning to look at him.

He laughed, waggling his arms like a bird in flight. "As free and as independent as the birds. I go where I please when I please." He went quiet, allowing what he considered a reasonable interval before he asked the question.

"Wouldn't you like to be the same way, Marilyn?"

Marilyn found the question disquieting. She looked away from Jarvis, stirring uneasily in her seat. When she turned back, he was staring across the clubhouse, his attention riveted by something that was happening at the bar. Was he trying to say something? she wondered; was there an underlying meaning to the question? Yet now he was ignoring her, looking elsewhere. Maybe it was just her, she decided, seeing things that weren't there.

Losing interest in the event at the bar, Jarvis returned his attention to Marilyn. "What kind of work did you do before you got married?" he asked, genuine interest in his voice.

"I was a teacher," Marilyn answered.

"Any interesting subjects, or boring stuff like math?"

Marilyn smiled at the question. "What would you consider to be interesting?"

"Mechanics," he replied. "Sports."

"Sorry to disappoint you. I taught English, mainly literature."

"That's boring," Jarvis declared decisively.

"Not at all," Marilyn argued, defending her profession. "It's a beautiful subject which covers an absolute wealth of knowledge."

"What's beautiful about..." Jarvis tried to remember names of authors, searching the deepest recesses of his memory. He had not read a book since leaving school unless it concerned tennis. "About books?" he finished lamely, having failed to think of any name other than William Shakespeare, and he was not even certain that it belonged in the conversation.

"Everything." Marilyn warmed to the subject. "Absolutely everything. Books are the world about us. They inform, they amuse, they thrill us. And sometimes they bring tears to our eyes."

Jarvis crouched forward against the table, trying desperately to hide the erection he was getting from looking at this woman; tennis shorts were not noted for their ability to disguise such events. "You talk about beauty," he said, fervently wishing he had something to lay across his lap to hide the telltale bulge in his shorts. "I'll tell you what beauty's all about. It's old man Rosewall returning a serve, just killing it dead on the other side of the net. It's Jimmy Connors covering the court. It's Nastase throwing a fit because he's not getting his own way, Rod Laver's top-spin lob. Those are the things that beauty's all about."

"That might be beauty to you," Marilyn conceded. "We all see it differently." For the first time, she noticed the awkward position which Jarvis had adopted.

"Are you feeling all right?" she asked, concerned.

Jarvis thought quickly. "It's an old back injury. It'll go in a minute or two. Slipped during a grass court championship a couple of years ago and wrenched my back."

"You should have it looked at," Marilyn suggested. "These things often get worse as you get older."

Christ! What was this broad trying to do to him, talking about getting older? "I hate doctors," he said. "They scare me because I don't think they know what they're doing."

Feeling the erection begin to diminish, probably as a direct result of being told that even he would get older, Jarvis straightened up slowly, peeking down surreptitiously to be certain that nothing showed.

"What sort of work does your husband do, Marilyn?" he asked, confidence returning.

"He's in the men's clothing business."

Jarvis snapped his fingers. "Of course. Chestertons. I should have made the connection. That's quite an operation they've got."

"Thirty-eight stores," Marilyn said proudly.

"He must put in a few hours," Jarvis said. "It's a wonder you ever get to see him."

Despite the casual friendliness of the remark, Marilyn began to feel uneasy again. She pushed the glass away, still half-full, and stood up. "I have to be going now. Thanks for the drink. I'll see you next week."

Jarvis made no attempt to detain her any longer. He walked with her to the door of the clubhouse, evaluating his chances as he watched her drive away in the small, red Alfa Romeo sports car. They were good, he decided. And he could not remember being wrong before.

Picking up his racket, he walked outside to the parking lot where the silver-gray XKE Jaguar beckoned to him seductively. He got in, started the engine and left the parking lot to the sound of rear tires protesting as they spewed gravel, trying to get a grip on the ground.

He passed Marilyn's red Alfa within a mile, giving a short blast on the horn as he pulled out to overtake. She flashed the Alfa's lights in response, and Jarvis waved. He snuggled down in the seat, making himself comfortable for the forty-minute trip to his Manhattan apartment. Automatically his eyes flicked over the Jaguar's gauges, checking the car's performance. He smiled, recalling how the coveted automobile had come into his possession. It had been two years earlier—a forty-year-old woman whose avaricious sex drive was not shared by her much older husband. During the coaching sessions, Jarvis had offered a sympathetic ear to her problems, following it shortly afterwards with the rest of his body. The XKE had been a token of her appreciation. And even when he had grown bored with the relationship, seeing he could milk it for nothing more, the woman had not resented him. What had he said to her? "Find yourself another stud, lady. You're interfering with my game." And, Jarvis admitted grudgingly, she had done just that. The last he had heard of her, she was enrolled in a judo school. The thought of the woman learning self-defense made him laugh; he was damned sure that she was defending herself with little effort against any advances the instructor might make. Perhaps that was what she needed—a black belt in the right place.

Traffic was heavy on the Van Wyck Expressway as Jonathan sat alone in the rear of the Rolls-Royce on the way to Kennedy Airport to meet Nino Viscenzi. The Italian designer was returning to check the first production of suits which would bear his name exclusively in the United States, and Jonathan was looking forward to meeting him again.

He puffed contentedly on a cigar, confident that the chauffeur would not report him to Miriam; ever since that afternoon when Simon had come so close to catching him smoking in the boardroom, he had been extremely careful where and when he lit up.

Pity that Gerald's not here as well, he thought; but he had been called away to inspect a group of three stores, in the San Francisco area, which Chestertons was contemplating buying. Jonathan looked down at his watch, estimating that his son would soon be breaking for lunch, three hours behind on the West Coast. And Jacob was also missing, having elected to stay at home in Great Neck. When Jonathan had asked him if he was coming to the airport to welcome the designer, he had begged off, pleading weariness.

My father never gets tired, Jonathan told himself, rejecting the older man's argument. He's got the constitution and energy of a two-year-old. But deep down, Jonathan knew that he was lying. Jacob was beginning to show distinct signs of his advanced age, and he was acutely aware of the reason why. Or, he corrected himself, the four reasons why. Since the sale of the four clearance outlets—the original Gellenbaum and Son stores— Jacob had seemed to withdraw into himself a little more each day. At the house he continued to eat with Jonathan and Miriam. But after dinner, instead of watching television, talking, or even playing an infrequent game of chess, he would excuse himself politely, saying he was tired and wanted to go to bed. On occasion Jonathan had looked in and seen his father sitting in an armchair by the window, still fully clothed, staring out into the darkness, his eyes unseeing.

Whenever he had tried speaking to Jacob, the older man had gone strangely quiet, muttering sometimes about his contemporaries who were all long dead, feeling alone in a world which had passed him by, left him as a relic of an earlier era to fend for himself among strangers. Jonathan had spoken gently to him, argued with him to get a response, even the faintest spark of animation. Nothing had helped. Jacob had virtually become a hermit in a house full of people, a lonely man in a crowded room. He no longer came into the office; he sat at home all day, occasionally reading the Yiddish newspapers which Jonathan bought for him in the city.

I suppose it happens to all of us, Jonathan mused; old age catches up eventually, and my father has been lucky that it's taken this long for it to search him out. Despite the forced rationalization, Jonathan continued to feel guilty about the sale of the Gellenbaum stores, the removal of his father's final interest. Ah, but what can you do? Take away Jacob's last traces of identity within the company, or split the family completely by either putting up with Simon's inadequacies or throwing him out altogether?

He entered the terminal, seeing that Viscenzi's aircraft had landed ten minutes earlier. Estimating that it would take the Italian at least fifteen minutes to clear immigration and customs, Jonathan went to the washroom, relieving himself of some of the countless cups of coffee he had drunk that day—something else the damned doctors frowned upon.

Leaving the washroom, he was pleasantly surprised to see Viscenzi standing in the reception area, a leather suitcase at his feet, looking around in bewilderment at not being met.

"Nino!" Jonathan bellowed across the area. "Over here."

Hearing the familiar voice, Viscenzi spun around and saw Jonathan striding toward him. He waved happily.

"Jonathan, it is so good to see you again," he cried, embracing the American. "But where is the rest of your family?"

"The boys are busy," Jonathan explained, picking up Viscenzi's suitcase and walking toward the exit with it.

"And your dear father, Jacob? Where is he?" There was anxiety in Viscenzi's voice, fear that something might have happened.

"He's at home resigning himself to getting old." Jonathan was surprised at how callous he sounded. He sensed Viscenzi staring at him in surprise and felt he had to add something. "Maybe your visit's what he needs, Nino. He thinks the world's forgotten him."

During the ride into the city, Jonathan explained how Jacob had been affected by the sale of the four stores. Viscenzi listened sympathetically, his head moving back and forth as he appreciated the predicament in which Jonathan found himself.

"I regard your father very highly," he admitted when Jonathan had finished. "It disturbs me to hear that he is not well. When we go up to Buffalo tomorrow, we will take him with us. Do you think that will help?"

"I've already asked him," Jonathan said gloomily. "He doesn't want to come."

Viscenzi smiled knowingly. "When I ask him, Jonathan, he will come. Wait and see." Leaning forward, he tapped the partition which separated the passengers from the chauffeur. "We are not going into the office after all," he said. "Please take us instead to Mr. Chesterton's home in Great Neck."

The chauffeur muttered a few words under his breath, swung the Rolls-Royce skillfully across two lanes of traffic and took the last exit off Grand Central Parkway before he had to cross the Triborough Bridge into Manhattan. Then he swung around to get back onto the parkway, heading out toward Long Island.

Listening as the Italian gave the new instructions to the chauffeur, Jonathan felt himself overwhelmed by a sense of mystification. How did Viscenzi, a friend, hope to achieve what the son could not?

Viscenzi rotated slightly in the seat to look at Jonathan, the gentle brown eyes still smiling, as if he had read Jonathan's thoughts. "The office will still be there when we return from Buffalo, my friend. Your father's well-being is far more important to me. Jacob is one of a disappearing breed, a true craftsman." He bent down to straighten his trousers before the knife-edge creases could be distorted by his new sitting position.

"I will tell you why I respect your father, Jonathan. But first let me explain what is happening in Europe; then you will be able to appreciate my feelings more fully. We have fashion colleges for men's and women's clothing designers, and they all turn out graduates who can draw pretty pictures." He spread his arms wide to emphasize the point, like a fisherman describing the biggest catch of his life. "Beautiful pictures they draw, Jonathan, but can they be made up into garments?" He shook his head sadly.

"Of course they can't be. These pictures are the figments of an imagination which the colleges have fostered. Imagination is important, the teachers tell the students. Imagination is everything. Jonathan, they are wrong, criminally wrong to put across this point of view. These colleges are ruining young people who, quite possibly, have a genuine aptitude for clothing design. For when these students graduate with their diplomas in imagination, they are crucified by the technical staffs of factories, laughed at if they get jobs. Otherwise they receive grandiose-sounding appointments from avant garde clothing manufacturers who are here one season and out of business the next.

"The good clothing manufacturers," Viscenzi continued, "used to wait for a boy to finish his apprenticeship with a bespoke tailoring house..."

"With a what?" Jonathan interrupted. "What's a bespoke tailoring house?"

"What you Americans call custom tailoring, handmade on the premises," Viscenzi explained. "As I was saying, they used to wait till a boy had finished his apprenticeship; then they would offer him more money than his employer could and lure him away onto their design staffs. But those days are ending. Bespoke tailors are becoming fewer in number, a craft threatened by its own high prices, and they want to hang on to the people they have trained; they want to get some benefit out of their endeavors. So now the manufacturers, most of whom are notorious for not going to the trouble or expense of training their own employees, are going to the colleges for their designers. They are stooping low in many cases and coming up with nothing. That"—he wagged a finger in Jonathan's face— "is why I respect your father so highly. He began life as a tailor, learning all the basics, finding out about making a suit, a coat, anything by hand. He is a craftsman who, if necessary, can finish a job with his own two hands, should the electricity break down. Do you follow so far?"

Jonathan grunted an affirmative reply; he followed Viscenzi's argument only too clearly.

"He is a man to be respected," the Italian carried on. "I loved speaking with him about our industry during my last trip. When I visit other manufacturers during my travels and meet their design staffs, I find myself getting bored because I have to lower the level of my conversation. But your father is my peer, at the least. Probably he knows even more than I do, but he has been polite enough not to push it down my throat and show up my shortcomings."

With a physical effort, Jonathan tore his eyes away from Viscenzi's face. He stared out of the car window, going over what the designer had said. Never before had he heard any man pay such a tribute to his father, let alone a man who had met him perhaps three times during the last trip—and such a knowledgeable man. He felt an uncomfortable lump begin to form in his throat and swallowed hard. How could anybody possibly reply to what he had just heard?

Viscenzi stretched out an arm, laying a hand on Jonathan's shoulder. "When we see your father, you will find that what I have said is true."

Instead of using his key to open the front door, Jonathan rang the bell. He and Viscenzi waited for several seconds till Miriam opened the door, looking in surprise at her husband. Her mouth dropped even further when she recognized Viscenzi. Before she had the opportunity to speak, Viscenzi stepped into the house, kissing her warmly on the cheek.

"Instead of going to the office," he said, "we thought we would pay a social call. Is your father-in-law here?"

Miriam looked to Jonathan seeking an explanation, then back to Viscenzi. "Upstairs in his bedroom," she began. "It's the..."

"Don't worry," Viscenzi interrupted. "I will find it myself." He strode across the hall and began to climb the stairs. Seconds later, Miriam and Jonathan heard his voice booming across the second floor of the house as he called Jacob's name.

Dragging one foot behind the other, Jonathan entered the house. He took hold of Miriam's arm and pushed her into the living room. "What on earth's going on?" she asked. "I thought you were taking Nino to the office, not bringing him here."

"He's giving us all a lesson in family life," Jonathan replied, still feeling emotionally drained from the ride with the designer. "Without meaning to, he's made me feel like a first-class louse about Jacob."

"What do you mean?" Miriam asked anxiously.

Jonathan was trying to think of a reply when he heard footsteps coming down the stairs, two pairs of footsteps. He put up a hand for Miriam to be silent. Together they watched the living room door open, and Viscenzi walked in, holding Jacob by the arm.

"What do you mean, you're not coming with us to the factory tomorrow?" Viscenzi was demanding. "Without your opinions, there is no reason in any of us going."

Jacob was fully dressed, as though he made a point of looking formal for sitting alone in his bedroom reading newspapers. He looked to Miriam and Jonathan, embarrassed that he had been brought down.

"Perhaps if I feel better tomorrow I'll come," he said noncommittally to Viscenzi.

The designer made a show of looking at Jacob, running his eyes over him. "You look well to me. There is no excuse for you not to accompany us. What time in the morning is the flight?" he asked Jonathan.

"Eight o'clock."

"Book another seat. Jacob will be coming."

"If you say so," Jacob muttered.

"No," Viscenzi contradicted him, "only if you say so."

Jacob shrugged helplessly. "All right, all right. I'll come with you to Buffalo."

Thelma Chambers looked around the two-bedroom apartment on Central Park West and sniffed contemptuously.

"It's small," she complained. "Much smaller than our apartment on Lake Shore Drive."

Determined to make an attempt to reconcile their differences, Brian walked to the window and let up the blind. "Look at that view, Thelma," he marvelled, casting his eyes over the park. "It's magnificent."

Thelma looked out, totally unconvinced. "It'll be especially magnificent at night," she remarked sarcastically. "We'll be able to see the muggings, rapes and murders in Central Park as they happen—just like being on hand when the eleven o'clock news is put together." She sniffed again, turning away from the window. "I preferred the view of Lake Michigan. At least it was clean."

Brian ignored his wife's grumbling and inspected the apartment again. He liked it, especially after the apartment hotel they had been living in for the past two months, and realized how lucky he had been to get the lease.

The new apartment was fully furnished and serviced, recommended by Gerald Chesterton, who, Brian was certain, also had a hand in having the application for tenancy approved. If the new position of general merchandise manager worked out—and the first two months had pointed that way—to the hinted-at vice-presidency, he and Thelma would be looking at houses in the New York area; well, he would. Thelma could do whatever she wanted.

"I'm going to drop by the office," he called out to her. "May as well get used to the short walk." There was no reply, not that he expected any, so he walked into the hall and rang for the elevator.

Thelma returned to the window, looking down at the people scurrying along the sidewalk four stories below. Then she strolled leisurely into the den which Brian—in a rare gesture of generosity, she thought—had said was for her own use. The red IBM Golfball typewriter was already in position, dominating the center of the desk, a sheaf of yellow copy paper next to it, waiting to be used for the first draft of her next romantic novel.

Robotlike, she pushed a sheet of paper into the typewriter, watching it jerk into position as she depressed the paper advance control. She sat looking dumbly at the paper, her fingers poised above home keys, but no ideas came. The outline of the story was fixed firmly in her mind, the characterizations, everything. But she could put nothing down on paper, just as she had written nothing during the past two months.

Frustrated, she ripped the piece of paper out of the typewriter and flung it into the trash can. Then she went back to the living room, stopping by the liquor cabinet. Pulling out a full bottle of gin, she poured a generous measure into a tall glass and went back to the den.

Seated again in front of the typewriter, with another piece of yellow paper in place, Thelma tried to concentrate. Still nothing. She picked up the glass and looked at the clear spirit, seeking inspiration there. Then she tilted it back and drank deeply.

Simon lay on the bed, looking down his body to where Della sat astride him. It was a position they had adopted, one which he found extremely pleasurable.

"Tell me how Mr. Simon's coming," she said.

"The stores or me?" Simon quipped.

Della giggled at the answer. Using her right hand, she squeezed his erect penis, feeling the blood-swelled organ pulse under her gentle touch. "I'm probably a better judge of your comings than you are," she replied. "Tell me about the shops."

"Later. Think of it as a reward if you do a good job."

Sensuously she stretched out on top of him, rubbing herself lightly against his body, taking the greater part of her weight on her elbows. Simon eased himself into her slowly, not wanting to rush, simultaneously frightened that he would lose control and climax before he entered.

Sensations intermingled as she gripped him, squeezing, sliding, gradually drawing him on. He dug his fingers into her buttocks, gripping her flesh as if it were a pair of handles, bruising her with his roughness. And still she continued her slow, rhythmic motion, interlocking with him until they erupted together, gasping as the strength left them in one almighty detonation.

Afterwards, they lay quietly, spoon in spoon, her back pressing against his chest, buttocks tucked into the curve of his stomach. His hands reached around and spread themselves over her breasts, soft now, the earlier urgency dissipated.

"Simon?"

"Mmm?" He nuzzled the back of her neck with his nose.

"Tell me about Mr. Simon."

"Why do you want to know?"

"Because you promised."

"We've opened four of them so far," he said sleepily, his eyes closed. "The others which are planned so far will open during the next couple of months."

"How are they doing? Are they showing a profit?"

Something seemed wrong. Simon could not identify the threat, but a doubt nagged at his mind, putting him on guard. His hazel eyes opened as he became alert.

"Why are you so interested in the boutiques all of a sudden?" he asked. "You never cared about anything before except getting laid."

Della pressed backward, rubbing against him, tantalizing his senses. She removed his left hand from her breast and pressed it down between her legs, feeling his fingers caress the short black hair, driving deeper till they found flesh.

"A wife should be interested in her husband's work."

Simon's fingers froze, then withdrew. He released Della and sat up in bed, the lethargy which had been overtaking him disappearing in a second.

"What was that?" he asked incredulously.

She rolled over to face him, the impish smile making her seem even more attractive to Simon. But there was no laughter in her voice, no teasing quality to match the facial expression.

"I think we should get married," she said earnestly. "As I can't see you ever asking me, I'm doing the proposing."

Simon leaned back against the headboard, feeling it sway slightly under the pressure. Marriage? To Della, of all people? What the hell was going on?

The first thought that came to his surprised mind was about his family. What would they say? Not that he really gave a damn about anything they said. He understood that it was part of Jewish folklore to disown a child who married out of the religion. But that dated from the old country, not here in modern-day New York. He had even heard of extreme circumstances in ultra-Orthodox circles, like those nut cases down in Williamsburg, where the family had sat in mourning for a week after such a marriage, signifying to the world that their relative had died.

Being disowned, if it should ever come to that—and Simon was certain that it would not—would mean the end of the Mr. Simon operation, or his part in it anyway. There would be no grounds for a lawsuit if the company continued to use his name for the chain, certainly not for a first name. And yet the idea of being married to Della began to appeal to him, if only as a means of annoying his family.

Ignoring Della, who continued to stare at him waiting for an answer, he closed his eyes and weighed the pros and cons. Would he be disowned, cast out like a leper? No. The idea was too farfetched. His mother would veto such a suggestion, for a start. He realized how she doted on him because of his resemblance to her dead brother; he had used the affection to good purpose in the past.

"How about it, Simon?" Della interrupted him. "I don't normally ask questions like this. Do I get the thumbs up or thumbs down?"

Very slowly, without opening his eyes, Simon extended his right hand, fist clenched. He turned it sideways and stuck out the thumb, enjoying the suspense.

Then he raised it.

# 9

Once his mind was made up, Simon Chesterton wasted no time in putting the plans of the previous night into operation. While Della concocted a speedy breakfast, he called the office, telling his secretary that he had come down with a fever and was waiting for the doctor to arrive; in all probability, he explained, he would be unable to return to work for two or three days. Grinning smugly at the deception, he walked into the kitchen, coming up quietly behind Della, putting his arms around her waist, feeling the warmth of her body through the shirt she had borrowed from him to take the place of a dressing gown.

"How long will it take you to call your office and pack a few things?" he asked.

"Buy a few things," she said, "not pack. When I get married, I do it in new clothes. Four or five hours at the most."

"When you're ready, come back here," Simon said. "We'll stay in the apartment tonight and catch a flight out tomorrow morning. We'll be in Vegas and married by the evening. Think you can stand the pace?"

Della continued to scramble eggs in the frying pan. "That's a question you should be asking yourself, Simon. Are you up to marrying me?"

"What's that supposed to mean?"

"I don't have a family to worry about," she explained. "Like I told you before, we were well rid of each other a long, long time ago. But what's your family going to say? What will their reaction be to you marrying a Catholic? A lapsed Catholic admittedly, but still a Catholic."

"That's something we'll find out about after the event. But I don't think they'll be too upset."

"No disinheritance?"

"Of course not," he said confidently. "I'm too important to the company. Besides, that attitude's old-fashioned. Those things only happened in the old country." Simon wished he felt as positive as he sounded.

Della scooped the eggs onto two plates and took them to the kitchen table, where the toast and coffee were waiting. "You'd better believe you won't get this sort of service when we're married," she said. "I'll expect breakfast in bed on a silver tray from you—every single morning, and twice on Sundays and holidays."

Simon dug his fork into the eggs. "That's not the only thing you'll get in bed on a silver tray," he mumbled, his mouth full.

Nino Viscenzi sat elegantly, legs crossed, in an office in the Buffalo factory. He held a jacket from the new designer label range of suits, inspecting, pulling at the seams.

Across the office from him sat Jonathan, waiting to hear the verdict on the garment, and Jacob, who sat upright in his chair, staring at the designer, his eyes exhibiting more interest than Jonathan had seen in recent months.

"Very good," Viscenzi said eventually. "Very good indeed. And well up to our contract stipulations." He laid the jacket across his knees and stared at Jonathan. "Tell me, have you given any thought to your advertising campaign for the Viscenzi suits? Where you are going to advertise the line, and what kind of photographs you should use?"

Jonathan shook his head. "It's something nobody ever seems to have the time to get involved in," he answered truthfully. "We tend to let our agency handle it. They've done a good job in the past, so we leave them alone. I believe in letting specialists do their jobs without any interference."

Viscenzi looked thoughtful after Jonathan's answer. "Maybe my own business in France is different, but I always get involved in the promotion. See," he grinned suddenly, before Jonathan could get the impression that he was being criticized, "we are two completely different people. What's good for you is bad for me, and vice versa."

"Do you want to be involved with the photography session for the Viscenzi line?" Jonathan asked, regretting that he had not thought of it earlier. Of course this man would be interested in the advertising; he lived, breathed and ate his work. He would want to be a part of everything to do with it.

"I would very much like to," Viscenzi agreed. "What model will you be using? The same man you use for the normal Chestertons promotion?"

"Yes. Fletcher Austin. What do you think of him?"

"He's good," Viscenzi enthused. "Very good. But would you be offended if I made a small suggestion?"

"Go ahead." Jonathan was willing to listen to anything the Italian had to say.

"Your normal advertising is very conservative," Viscenzi pointed out, "and that is right because it reflects your customers. But for the Viscenzi line I would like to see something a little more flamboyant, something that moves away from your regular promotion. Perhaps"—his brown eyes lit up—"a woman or two in the picture? Not just the straighforward fashion plate that Chestertons always has, but something where the model—this Fletcher Austin—is engaged in an activity, even if it's nothing more exciting than holding an umbrella for a pretty girl...or two."

"Let me make a phone call," Jonathan said. "You have to leave for France in the morning, so I'll see if the agency can arrange something at short notice—like tonight." He picked up the closest extension and asked the switchboard operator to put him through to the advertising agency in New York. A hurried conversation followed where he explained the urgency of the situation, the need for a session to be arranged that evening. Hanging up, he turned back to Viscenzi.

"They're going to call back when everything's set up. We can take some suits back with us from here, as long as they let us know Fletcher's measurements—if they can get hold of him in time."

Viscenzi held up a hand in acknowledgment. "Very good. If it can be done, fine." He picked up the jacket across his knees, inspecting it one more time before passing it across to Jacob, intent on drawing him into the conversation. "Here, what do you think of this? Is the quality high enough for you?"

Jacob took the proferred jacket eagerly and began to examine it in the same manner Viscenzi had done. While he concentrated, the Italian glanced at Jonathan, smiling, his eyes flashing a clear I-told-you-so message.

"What do you see in that jacket that is different from the normal Chesterton production?" Viscenzi asked, turning back to Jacob.

Jacob put the jacket aside and looked up. "The fabric design is slightly ahead of the normal Chestertons ranges. So is the styling of the garment. But this we knew about already."

"Nothing else?" Viscenzi asked in surprise. "There is nothing else in the garment construction that strikes you as different from American production?"

"Oh," Jacob said, as if it were not worth talking about, "you mean the full lining. I was wondering if you had noticed it." His brown eyes sparkled behind his glasses as he poked fun at the designer. "My son would never have noticed it, Nino."

"Your eyes are sharper than his are. Jonathan's eyes are only good for looking at cash receipts, not the finer points of a garment, like you and me." He took the jacket and tossed it casually across the office to Jonathan. "That is how the inside of a jacket should look—fully lined, unlike your normal production which, in common with most North American manufacturers, is only half-lined."

Jonathan caught the jacket one-handed, draping it across his knees, where he looked at the lining, nodding appreciatively. "I've got to admit that it looks better than the half-lined jackets we normally put out."

"Looks better?" Viscenzi queried. "Is that all you can say? It is better. The full lining which you American manufacturers seem to believe is unnecessary, nothing more than an additional cost factor, gives the jacket a better finish, more body. It hangs better and helps resist creasing when the wearer is sitting for a long time. Everything about it is superior."

"And there speaks a *mavin*, an expert," Jacob said to his son. "Listen to him. You might learn something about the business you make all your money from." He stood up and walked toward the washroom.

"It's a complete transformation," Jonathan whispered to Viscenzi after the door had closed behind his father. "He's a different man."

"It's simply a question of making him feel involved," Viscenzi explained. "In New York you're only concerned with the retail side of the industry. Jacob knows nothing of that; he doesn't want to know anything about it. He's a technical man, and he draws a distinct line between where his interests start and finish. When you return to the city, he will probably go straight back into his shell. The making of clothes is his life. Without it he is lost."

"How would you like him as your guest in Paris, running your factory for you?" Jonathan joked.

"No, I think not. As I mentioned before he might show me up," Viscenzi said. "That would never do for my image. But somehow you have to get him involved again. Give him some sort of responsibility in the manufacturing side. Create a position for him where he feels he can be of use. Otherwise he will really talk himself into believing that he is excess to requirements and just fade away. Even if you only send him up here once a week, take him to the airport in the morning and meet him at night, it might be enough to rekindle the spark that has been missing. Make a once-a-week job for him up here. Make him feel needed."

He ceased talking as Jacob reentered the room. Viscenzi greeted him while Jonathan remained seated, full of thoughts about his father, thoughts triggered by the family-based philosophy of the clothing designer. He watched while Viscenzi helped Jacob to a chair, searching for an ashtray as the old man pulled out a pack of cigarettes.

The telephone rang, and Jonathan answered it quickly, hoping it was the agency in New York. After a brief conversation, he hung up and spoke to Viscenzi.

"The agency's arranged it for seven o'clock this evening. We're going to use the Fifty-seventh Street store, rope part of it off to keep the customers out of the photographer's way."

"Let them mingle," Viscenzi said. "If your customers see a fashion photography session taking place as they shop, it will strengthen the identity they have with the store. And they might even start asking about the suits that you're photographing, why they are not on display?"

"You're right as usual," Jonathan admitted. He glanced at his watch, noticing that it was almost time to drive out to the airport for the return flight to New York City. If he and Viscenzi were to have time together at Head Office and witness the photography session before the designer caught his return flight to Paris the following morning, they would have to hurry.

With the advent of winter, Marilyn Chesterton took her tennis coaching indoors, using the club's wooden court to get her game in tune for the coming spring and summer.

She knew that her game was improving steadily, although Stan Jarvis continued to defeat her with what she considered sickening ease. But she would not be going up against any player of Jarvis's caliber when spring came. On the plus side, her scores were becoming more respectable as she employed guile against Jarvis's forcing power; women's cunning, as he had termed it jokingly, against a man's brute force and ignorance.

She looked forward to the two-hour sessions each week, finding in them a chance to work herself out of the lethargy she had been experiencing, the strenuous exercise bringing her back to the peak of physical condition which, in turn, dispelled the worries about her freedom. Jarvis had even begun to pass an occasional compliment, an attitude far removed from the days when he had started coaching her. Then he had virtually sneered at her every mistake; with hindsight, she realized he had been needling her into playing better, but at the time she had wanted to break her racket over his head and throttle him with the gut. Now she had to ruefully admit that his ruse had worked. She had bitten back her temper, letting it out in play, allowing her initial hostility toward Jarvis's attitude to be converted into scoring strokes.

Since that afternoon when she had sensed that Jarvis was showing a more than professional interest, his behavior had been exemplary. Although she had been exceptionally alert for his advances, there had been no cause for concern. He offered advice, pointing out her weak spots on the court—and that was all. Marilyn was beginning to see him as nothing more threatening than a tennis bum who made money—good money, she surmised, judging by the car he drove—from doing what he enjoyed.

"My turn to buy the drinks this time," she offered as they left the court at the end of the session. "You must have paid for them the past three weeks."

"I'm not keeping count, Marilyn," he said, wiping the handle of the racket with his towel. "But if you insist, I can hardly object. Rule number one in the club's handbook of employment regulations is that the member is always in the right and the coach is always wrong."

Marilyn laughed, joining happily in the lighthearted mood. "Except when it comes to coaching," she said. "Then the coach is always right."

"Don't bet your last dime on it," he warned.

They entered the clubhouse, and Jarvis indicated an overweight young woman sitting by the picture window, looking out at the snow-covered courts. "I gave her lessons last year, after spending two hours explaining the rules, which she didn't even know. Aften ten weeks, she still couldn't get a service across the net, let alone return one. And she had the gall to say it was all my fault and that I had no business being a coach because I didn't know how to play. That's how right the coach always is."

"But she still comes," Marilyn observed.

"She tried golf this summer," Jarvis explained, laughing quietly. "The golf pro told me that he got bawled out by her because she thought he was doing a bad job. He claimed she held the club like a tennis racket."

Marilyn slumped onto a chair, utterly exhausted but managing to find enough energy to laugh at Jarvis's description of the woman; she remembered seeing her during the summer dressed in a short skirt, wandering around the club's nine-hole golf course like a lost child.

Taking a five-dollar bill from her purse, Marilyn handed it to Jarvis. He returned from the bar with a beer for himself and a bloody mary for Marilyn.

"Where's the tiny tot these days?" he asked. "I seem to remember you bringing her with you during the fall. Scared she'll understand the game soon and laugh at you?"

Marilyn eyed the coach derisively. "I leave Karen at home now. We've got a housekeeper at long last. Besides, it wouldn't be fair bringing out such a small thing in this cold."

Jarvis listened with half an ear, his mind on Marilyn's body, not her words. He envisioned her undressing, picturing that last piece of clothing falling away to reveal the ivory white body underneath. Was her ash blond hair the real color, or was it dyed? There was only one way to find out for certain. He figured it was worth another try; surely he'd have better luck, with the damned kid at home instead of in the clubhouse to remind its mother of her maternal and familial responsibilities.

When Jarvis had coached Marilyn on her service, he had gripped her wrist, standing close behind as she raised her arm, demonstrating the proper motion. Memories of the haunting smell of freshly bathed skin spiced with a simple touch of cologne still made him feel giddy. But he was content to bide his time, waiting patiently until the proper opportunity presented itself.

Success had spoiled Stan Jarvis. He had yet to want the woman who did not want him in return. At least that had been the case before Marilyn Chesterton had come looking for his help. Now she was beginning to work her way underneath his skin, digging in like an irritating thorn that could only be removed one way. And Stan Jarvis was certain that the cure—that one way—was not far off.

The chauffeur was waiting at La Guardia Airport when Jonathan arrived back from Buffalo with Viscenzi and Jacob. "You going to watch the photography session?" Jonathan asked his father. "Or do you want to be taken back to Great Neck? Nino and I can grab a cab into Manhattan."

"I'll come with," Jacob replied, surprising his son. Jonathan believed that the journey and the visit to the factory would have exhausted his father. Maybe, he reasoned, Jacob was picking up strength from Viscenzi. "I'll watch what happens."

Jonathan gave the chauffeur instructions, then leaned back against the opulent upholstery, closing his eyes. Jesus, maybe Jacob wasn't tired, but he sure as hell was. The day had been a killer—get up early, fly four-hundred-odd miles, spend the day in the factory, then fly back again. This game was for youngsters; what the hell was he doing playing at it? With an effort he opened his eyes again, looking over the span of the Triborough Bridge at the East River, feeling ashamed of falling asleep as Jacob and Viscenzi regarded him with amusement.

The first thing Jonathan did on entering the store was to give the four suits he had brought back from Buffalo to his alterations tailor, telling him to press them immediately. Then he, Viscenzi and Jacob settled themselves in the boardroom, sending out for coffee and sandwiches, eating and talking till the photographer arrived.

Jonathan went out into the shop with the photographer, following him around as he sought the best place for the session. Customers and salespeople in the store followed the two men with their eyes, attracted by the cameras hanging around the photographer's neck.

"We need it to be near the dressing rooms so your models can change," the photographer told Jonathan. "How about we use the second floor, near the Mr. Simon shop? That's not too busy up there."

"Suit yourself," Jonathan told the man. "Just give me a call if you need anything."

"Okay, I'll get it set up." Disregarding the curious stares, the photographer completely covered the back wall with a roll of white paper. Then he began to set up his lights, calling one of the salespeople over to help him.

"Stay right in the middle there. I just want to see if you're casting any shadow."

"Here okay?" the salesman said, grinning at the thought of being in the spotlights.

"That's fine." The photographer took two shots with a color Polaroid, waiting as they developed. When they were ready, he looked at them critically for any sign of a shadow. They were perfect. Thanking the salesman, he handed the photographs to him.

"What was that all about?" the salesman asked, slipping the pictures into his coat pocket.

"I wanted to make sure everything was perfect for when the models got here," the photographer replied.

"Couldn't you have done it with them?"

"I don't have to pay you a hundred bucks an hour," the photographer said, slapping the salesman on the shoulder in a friendly gesture. "You're happy with a couple of Polaroid shots."

The taxi pulled up outside the Chestertons store, and Fletcher Austin stepped out, striding across the sidewalk, a small suitcase swinging freely from his right hand. People he passed on the short journey to the store stopped to stare at him, wondering where they had seen the face before. Television? Films? Fletcher acknowledged the inquisitive expressions with a broad smile, revelling in his fame. From the storefront an image of himself peered back into the street, a black and white blowup of an advertisement for topcoats. Some of the pedestrians were quick enough to make the connection, realizing where they had seen this tall, good-looking man before: in the Chestertons advertisements ... and staring out at them from newspapers, television screens and countless billboards throughout the country, advertising anything from clothing to suntan lotion.

Well-built, Fletcher had strong blue eyes set wide apart in an open, honest face, now deeply tanned from a working vacation in Mexico, where he had been posing for a series of swimwear shots for a national men's leisure magazine. His light brown hair was crisply cut, a departure from the long-haired era, and parted neatly on the left side.

He walked into the store, nodding to those salesmen who looked his way, and made for the back where the offices were located. Outside the boardroom, he picked up the telephone on the desk of Jonathan's secretary and buzzed through.

"Yes?" Jonathan's voice was brusque; it was well after six o'clock, his secretary had gone home and he was not expecting any calls.

Fletcher raised his voice about two octaves above his normal level, trying for what he hoped was a passable New York woman's accent. "There's a Mr. Austin out here to see you. Looks awfully lost, just wandering around." Without waiting for an answer, he hung up and leaned against the desk, watching the boardroom door.

It opened about ten seconds later as Jonathan looked out, perplexed at the call. When he saw Fletcher looking expectantly at him, he grinned foolishly and invited the model into the boardroom.

"Was that you on the phone?"

"Of course. I was doing my castrati impersonation."

"Come again?"

Viscenzi, who had risen from his chair at the model's entrance, explained for Jonathan. "An Italian term. Boy sopranos who want to keep on being sopranos. Castrati, you understand?"

"I do now. Thanks. Fletcher, I don't think you've met Nino Viscenzi."

"No, I haven't. But I've sure heard a lot about him. Those are his suits I'm modelling tonight, aren't they?"

"Yes." Jonathan waited while Fletcher shook Viscenzi's hand before continuing. "I think everybody's already upstairs waiting for you, using the second floor of the store. Anything you need?"

"I don't think so," Fletcher replied. "I've six shirts in here and a few ties, plus two pair of shoes."

"We would have supplied the shirts and ties," Jonathan protested. "What do you bring your own with you for?"

"Professionalism, I suppose," Fletcher said disarmingly. "I'm like the Boy Scouts of America—always prepared. Now where can I get changed?"

"Use my washroom for your make-up," Jonathan offered. "Otherwise you'll be using the dressing rooms upstairs. Sharing them with two girls," he added. "Aren't you the lucky one?"

Fletcher just rolled his eyes at the comment, causing Jonathan and Viscenzi to break out laughing.

"See," Jonathan said, pointing at the case after Fletcher had taken out his make-up kit and gone into the washroom. "The true professional. Brings along everything he thinks he'll need. One of the old school, is Fletcher."

"Like somebody else in this room," Viscenzi said quietly, nodding toward where Jacob sat, his eyes closed as he dozed.

"I knew we should have sent him back to Great Neck," Jonathan said. "Today was too much for him."

"Maybe," Viscenzi said. "And then again, maybe he'll wake up later and have dinner with us."

Attracted by the bright lights from the second floor of the store, a group of customers and salespeople gathered around the area which the photographer had roped off, watching intently as Fletcher Austin went through his repertory of poses, some with, some without the two girls the agency had sent along.

"The trousers don't look right," Viscenzi whispered in Jonathan's ear as they watched the shooting. "They're not hanging properly, as if they're a size too big."

"The photographer already pinned the back," Jonathan explained. "What else can we do?"

"Wait. I'll show you." Stepping out into the field of focus, Viscenzi held up a hand for the action to stop. First he knelt down and tried to drag Fletcher's errant trouser leg down to its proper level so that the crease showed straight. It did not help. "How far down are you shooting?" Viscenzi asked the photographer. "From the feet or from the knees?"

The photographer checked his viewfinder again. "Just above the knees, Mr. Viscenzi."

"Good. In that case the problem is solved." To everybody's surprise, Viscenzi dropped full-length onto the carpeted floor, holding a cuff of Fletcher's trousers in each hand, dragging them straight down so that the crease was perfect. Some nervous laughter erupted from the crowd of onlookers but died away as soon as Jonathan swung around to glare at the culprits.

"Perfect!" the photographer shouted. "Right on." The strobe began to flash again as he finished off the roll, Fletcher continually changing his position while Viscenzi stayed on the floor holding the trousers straight. When the shot was over, Viscenzi returned to Jonathan, dusting down his clothes.

"Nice trick," Jonathan complimented him. "I'm glad I asked you along."

"Good, eh? Would you do the same thing?"

"I'm not sure I'd be able to get up again."

They both laughed and turned back to the photographer, who was loading new film into the camera, waiting for the models to reemerge from the changing rooms.

The small dressing room which the two girls used to change in was filled with laughter as they busied themselves, getting ready for the next filming sequence. One of the girls, a brunette with shoulder-length hair, was pulling on a pair of brown leather boots, while the blond model was studying herself in the mirror, touching up her make-up.

"I tell you," the blond said, giggling infectiously, "if that guy gets down on the floor again like last time and tries to peek up our dresses, I'm going to demand time and a half for this job. Christ, what a way to make a living."

"Don't worry about it," the brunette said, standing up, banging her feet on the floor to make sure the boots fitted properly. "He's probably a fag anyway. Most of these designers are."

"Oh, no. Not that one," the blond contradicted her. "That one's as straight as they come. Mind you, he's rather cute—if you like the soulful Italian lover type."

"Don't you?"

"Not really," the blond admitted. "I go more for Fletcher's type, the all-American football player kind of man with the bronzed skin. Pity he's queer." She said the last sentence wistfully, as if she really believed it was a pity.

"Fletcher?" The brunette's voice was shocked. "Fletcher Austin gay? Don't be crazy. Where did you hear that?"

"Here and there. You can't keep something like that under wraps in this business. Everybody knows he goes for men."

There was a knock on the dressing room door. The photographer's voice bellowed through the wood that everybody else was ready and the girls were holding everything up. They hurried out.

All through the sequence, the brunette's mind was on what her colleague had said. She could not believe that somebody as gorgeous as Fletcher could be gay. It had to be gossip. She leaned closer to him for one of the shots, holding him around the waist, going beyond her professional duty. He turned to grin at her, the wide smile that had won him fame throughout the country acting on her like one drink too many. She felt faint as he squeezed her hand, unaware of the strobe flashing or of the photographer's shouted instructions.

Back in the dressing room, the brunette confronted the other girl. "You're crazy," she accused her. "He's no more queer than I am. Didn't you see what happened out there before, him giving me the eye?"

The blond model was unimpressed. "He's keeping up appearances, darling. Do you think he wants to advertise the fact that he's bent?"

Her mind suddenly made up, the brunette stood defiantly in front of the second model. "How much are you making from this job tonight?"

"Same as you. Why?"

"A hundred dollars. Okay, I'll bet you that one hundred dollars that I can get into bed with Fletcher Austin tonight and he'll perform like the stud I know he is."

The blond girl burst out laughing. "Being pretty crude about it, a hole is a hole is a hole. Whether it's your twat or somebody else's ass isn't going to make much difference to him. Of course you'll be able to get into bed with him, if that's what you really want. But no bet. I come by my money too hard."

"You're chicken."

"I'm not chicken. I've just got Scottish blood in me. I hate to see money wasted. But be sure to let me know what happens," she added mischievously as the knock came on the door again. "Jesus Christ!" she shouted. "We're coming. Can't you wait a goddamned minute?"

When the shooting was finished and the photographer packing away his equipment, the brunette sidled over to Fletcher Austin, who was folding his shirts back into the suitcase. "Doing anything later on?" she asked innocently.

"What have you got in mind?" Like the rest of him, his voice was strong, a vibrant quality that held the listener.

"Well," she said coyly, "I made a roast before I came out, but it worked out enough to feed an army. How about helping me make sure it doesn't go to waste?"

Fletcher appeared to hesitate for a moment, and the girl felt instant defeat; her friend was right, the guy was queer. Then he smiled again, bathing her with his glow. "I'd love to," he said, "on one condition."

"What's that?"

"You let me buy the wine to go with the meal."

Out of the corner of her eye, the brunette saw her friend preparing the leave the store. As she looked back, the brunette raised her hand into a triumphant, if concealed, V-sign.

"Well, what did you think of the show?" Viscenzi asked, as he stood with Jonathan on the now deserted second floor.

"I enjoyed it. I suppose that means that I should get more involved in the advertising side. Or maybe it was just your suits that gave it the extra sparkle."

"You are too kind," Viscenzi said, putting an arm around Jonathan's shoulder, guiding him downstairs toward the office. "Let us see how your father is."

They found Jacob still dozing, his head back against the chair. Jonathan prodded him gently, once, then again till the eyes slowly opened and the old man looked around himself in surprise.

"I must have been tired," he apologized. "How long did I sleep for?"

"Three hours," Viscenzi answered. "Now you should feel fit enough to come out with us for dinner."

Jacob yawned, trying to catch it with his hand. He was too late. "And to think I laughed when Jonathan fell asleep in the car on the way from the airport," he mused. "That's what you get for making fun of other people." He stood up, pulling his clothes straight, checking that the watch chain was straight. "How did the photography go?"

"Like a dream," Jonathan said. "Gave our customers a show they didn't expect. And, like Nino said earlier on, it helped us to establish a better link with them for the future." He began to narrate the events of the photographic session, and his father laughed when he got to the part about the designer stretching himself out on the ground to hold Fletcher's trousers straight.

"I'm wondering if that was such a good idea after all," Viscenzi said, laughing with the older man. "Perhaps your customers will think that a Viscenzi suit comes complete with a man to lie on the ground holding the trousers straight. Come,"—he put an arm around the shoulders of Jacob and Jonathan—"let us find somewhere to eat. I think we have worked enough today to deserve the finest cuisine we can find."

The brunette model lived in a small apartment on East Twenty-fifth Street, a second-floor walk-up that reminded Fletcher of a botanical garden. As soon as he stepped through the door, he was assailed by the sight of plants—standing in pots on the floor, hanging from hooks in the ceiling, dotted around small tables. He managed to identify a rubber tree and a spider plant. After that he was lost.

"What happens when you go away on a job?" he asked, laying his suitcase down on the floor.

"My neighbor comes in to water them," the brunette replied. "Or I give the superintendent five dollars to look after them."

He stood in the middle of the living room, hands on his hips, looking around. "Do you talk to them?"

"Only when there's nobody else to talk to. Tonight they'll have to look after themselves."

As she had promised, there was a roast. Together with the bottle of red wine that Fletcher had bought on the way to the apartment, they shared a pleasant meal, taking their time, sitting back afterwards over coffee.

"How long have you been modelling?" the brunette asked, wondering if Fletcher was going to make a pass at her or if she would have to make the first move. She was beginning to feel slightly embarrassed at having asked him back to the apartment for dinner; the earlier challenge had worn off, that moment of daredevil curiosity about Fletcher's sexual inclinations. Now she felt unsure.

"Fifteen years," he replied. "Since my early twenties, when I found out it was the only way I was going to make any money."

"That's a good career span," she said. "How did you break into it?"

"How did you?" he asked in reply.

"Modelling school. They got me a few small jobs when I graduated, and I worked on it from there. But I'm still nowhere near as well known as you are."

Fletcher inclined his head modestly at the compliment. "I owe my own success," he said, imitating a man making an acceptance speech for an award, "to sheer hard work. And, of course, my unique good looks."

The girl burst out laughing, holding a napkin to her watering eyes. "You are in a class of your own, you know. You're the..." Her voice faltered. "What's the word I want?"

"Doyen?" he suggested.

"That's the one. You are the doyen of the New York male models."

"I think you're after something," he guessed. "First an excellent dinner. Then a row of compliments. How"—he spread his hands in a grandiose manner—"can I repay all this?"

Her immediate answer set him back. "Come to bed with me. Right now."

Fletcher's years in front of the camera caved him from exposing the shock he experienced. "What about the dishes?" he asked quickly. "We can't leave dirty dishes on the table. It's uncouth."

The brunette hesitated. Was he backing away? Was her friend right? "They'll look after themselves," she whispered huskily. "Surely you wouldn't deny a dying woman this final wish."

"Dying?"

"Yes, dying for you. I've finally got you to myself, and I don't want to waste a single second of it." She got up from the table and walked behind him, running her fingers over his neck, opening his shirt, thrusting her hands inside, down his chest and stomach till her long nails were digging into his trouser waistband. He leaned back in the chair and gazed up at her, the smile that had launched five million American smokers onto a certain brand of cigarettes spread across his face.

"You're doing a pretty good job all by yourself," he said. "Do you want me to join in?" The picture had become clear to Fletcher; he could even guess the words that had passed between this girl and her friend back at the store on West Fifty-seventh Street. It was nothing new; he was aware of what was said about him in the business, that his good looks and physique were reserved for men only. So she wanted to have her little hour of fun finding out. Let her.

"It takes two to tango," she reminded him.

"And you've elected yourself as the leader. Just tell me the steps and I'll follow," he said.

"You know exactly why I'm doing this, don't you?" she said sharply, removing her hands and stepping back.

"Do you really think I'm going to let myself be seduced?" he shot back. "Of course I know what you're up to. You want to find out if all the rumors are true."

"Are they?"

"If I said no, you'd want me to jump into bed with you straightaway. And if I said yes, you'd still want to jump into bed with me because you'd see it as a bigger challenge. Right?" There was no answer from the girl. "Okay, so let's go to bed. And afterwards you can try to figure out whether you've just shared in a normal, healthy relationship or whether you've guided a gay model back onto the straight and narrow."

It took a few seconds for the brunette to understand what he had said to her. Then her eyes blazed. "You're a shit! Do you know that? You've been sitting here laughing at me the whole time, knowing exactly what I was up to and letting me think I was getting away with it."

"What else do you expect me to do?" he laughed. "It's been tried before by better seductresses. Everybody's got to find out if these rumors about good old Fletcher are true. There's only one person who knows the answer to that, and it's staying with me. I'm the only one who needs to know. And when I can find somebody rich enough to make the wrong decision, I'll sue him for every last cent and retire for life. People like you I'll just take for a free dinner." He did his shirt up, picked up his suitcase and walked toward the door.

"If anything," he called back, "the roast was a little too rare—just like your subtlety." He closed the apartment door just in time; a split second later, a potted plant smashed against it.

# 10

Passengers scurried through the terminal at Kennedy Airport looking for their baggage, their friends or information on their flights. Jonathan and Viscenzi stood alone in the confusion, watching the people around them, marvelling at all the activity.

"What time does your flight get in?" Jonathan asked.

Viscenzi looked at the clock above the checking-in desk. "About six o'clock this evening, New York time. Eleven at night in Paris."

"Short day," Jonathan commented sympathetically. "You're spending all your working hours in an aircraft."

"Far too short to be of any use," Viscenzi agreed. "But by limiting the trip to only a couple of days, I shan't have any jet lag to worry about—the latest of the modern illnesses."

"Was the trip all you expected it to be?" For some reason which he could not understand, Jonathan was having difficulty in conducting a conversation of any depth, feeling himself limited to mundane remarks to a man with whom he normally felt at ease.

"A very useful trip, Jonathan. I am pleased that your factory is keeping to the quality standards we agreed upon, even if I did cheat a little bit at the photography session last night. I am certain that the range will be a tremendous success when you launch it in the spring. But more important than my designs, did you speak to your father last night about going to Buffalo once a week?"

Jonathan's face brightened immediately. "He jumped at the idea. Wanted to know what he had to do. Even the thought of flying alone doesn't bother him."

"See!" Viscenzi exclaimed. "That's all you had to do to spring him out of his depression. Tell the factory manager to let Jacob wander around the plant, and he'll be happy. As long as he thinks he can still do something useful, he'll live to be a hundred."

"From your mouth to God's ears," Jonathan said, and Viscenzi laughed heartily at the expression.

Jonathan searched for another topic, trying desperately to fill the gap while they waited for the Paris flight to be called.

"What did you think of the Mr. Simon boutique in the West Fifty-seventh Street store?" he eventually asked.

Viscenzi pulled a slight face, biting down on his lower lip. "So-so. Please don't be upset by my remarks, Jonathan, because you expect the truth from me. Anything else would be an insult to our friendship. The layout, the decor of the Mr. Simon shop is quite standard, just the type of thing you would find in Europe. But the overall merchandise picture lacks a theme, a central story. Some of the styles are far more extreme than others, and that tends to give an unbalanced picture."

"I don't think I'm following you."

"The secret of these small specialty stores is that they tell a complete story. Single sales," Viscenzi explained, "are no good for the business. The idea is to stock merchandise carefully, and whenever you buy, always keep in mind what other inventory you will have. A shop like Mr. Simon must portray an atmosphere that will induce multiple sales. The customer—in this case, the younger, moneyed man with avant garde fashion ideas—should be able to see himself in a completely accessorized outfit the moment he enters the boutique. Your Mr. Simon operation lacks this totality."

"Initial results haven't been encouraging," Jonathan admitted quietly. "You reckon it's bad buying?"

"Not necessarily bad buying. I would rather say that it's disorganized buying, brought about by a lack of specialty experience. It's far easier to buy for a Chestertons store than for a boutique operation. For a large store, you can buy under an umbrella. And if something does not sell, you can knock it down, promote it off-price as a special attraction. After all, you build a certain amount of markdown dollars into your budget each season precisely for that purpose. For a Mr. Simon shop, however, there is very little margin for buying error. Everything has to be immediate; you have no space for promotional merchandise. If an item does not sell, it has to go. Every square foot of space is much more valuable."

Gloomily Jonathan wondered how much of what Viscenzi found fault with was Simon's doing. Now even those boutiques are going to cost us money, he thought. Everywhere Simon goes, he leaves a sick-looking bottom line, a story of what might have been but never was.

Over his thoughts, he heard the Air France flight being called and was aware of Viscenzi picking up his hand baggage.

"Jonathan, you know I wish you everything that is good. I will be in touch when I return to my office, and I look forward greatly to the first Viscenzi suits at Chestertons." He paused, holding Jonathan's hand gently in his own. "Look after your father," he added quietly. "Do what you can for him." Then he released Jonathan's hand and walked toward the boarding area.

Jonathan watched him go, the tall figure disappearing into the crowd of passengers assembling for the Paris flight. When he was lost to sight, Jonathan turned away and walked out of the terminal to where the Rolls-Royce was waiting, the chauffeur lazily smoking a cigarette.

"Office, Mr. Chesterton?" he asked, flipping the half-smoked butt out of the window.

"Office," Jonathan repeated. He lit a cigar, expelling the gray smoke in a column at the roof of the car, watching it spread out as it hit the fabric.

The Rolls-Royce moved slowly away from the terminal, picking up speed as it joined the main traffic stream from Kennedy Airport toward the city. Jonathan leaned against the side of the car, staring idly out of the window, watching cars pass in the other direction on the opposite side of the crash barrier, guessing where the passengers were going. Somewhere warm, no doubt; out of the New York winter for a two-week break, if they had any sense. A Yellow cab cruised by in the outside lane, heading toward the airport, its side only a few yards from the Rolls-Royce. Jonathan gazed at the two passengers and wondered where Simon was heading for. To see Viscenzi off? He's a bit late for that.

Simon! Jonathan sat bolt upright in the seat, the dreamy mood shaken off in a flash. What the hell was Simon doing out here? He'd called in sick the previous day, and there he sat in a Yellow cab on the way to the airport, a dark-haired girl by his side. Now what the hell was going on?

He leaned forward and hammered urgently on the partition. "Put your foot down!" he ordered the chauffeur, the confusion in his voice giving way to anger. "Get us to Fifty-seventh Street quick. I'll square any speeding tickets."

"Right, Mr. Chesterton. Will do." Obediently the chauffeur pressed the gas pedal down to the floor, feeling the surge of power as the big engine responded willingly to the increased ration of fuel. Jonathan slipped back into the seat, not feeling the acceleration, only concerned with what Simon was up to and how much it would cost him this time.

"Does it feel any different?" Simon asked.

"Different?" Della echoed. "Why should it?"

"We're legal now," Simon said. "Man and wife, and we've got a piece of paper to prove it."

Della raised herself on an elbow, looking in the darkness at Simon. "We were never illegal. If you're playing semantics, the word you're looking for is immoral. And I never considered us to be that."

Feeling the covers pulled aside as Simon moved, Della snuggled further down into the bed, luxuriating in the warmth generated by the two bodies. "We've got to celebrate," she decided. "What can we do?"

"A cable," Simon answered softly, the idea forming as he spoke.

"We're going to send a cable to the Chestertons Head Office. And we'll time it to arrive during the Monday afternoon merchandise meeting. That'll give them something extra special to include in the minutes."

The delighted chuckle which began in his throat turned within seconds into hysterical laughter. He lay back on the pillow, face red, eyes streaming as he saw the perplexed faces which would greet the cable. They would all be going frantic by then, wondering where he was, whether he was dead or alive. And the sudden announcement of his wedding would be a fantastic climax.

Through his tears and aching sides, Simon wished that just once he could be truly schizophrenic—in bed with Della, enjoying the pleasures of her body, and sitting at that long mahogany table in the Chestertons boardroom when the cable arrived.

# 11

Acutely aware that his left shoe was squeaking, Brian Chambers walked through the merchandise control area toward the Chestertons boardroom. The brown slip-ons were new and needed breaking in; each step he took seemed to be attracting attention to the creaking squeal as he took his weight on his left sole, raising the heel of the shoe. Office staff turned to look, and he grinned absurdly, pointing unnecessarily to his feet.

He knocked once on the boardroom door and entered. Jonathan was sitting at the main table, looking lost against the expanse of polished mahogany with nobody else to keep him company. In front of him were a cup of coffee and the latest weekly store reports.

"Sit down," he invited, waving a hand in the general direction of the nine other chairs which surrounded the table; the cuff of his navy jacket slid back slightly to reveal the small, solid gold, monogrammed cuff link.

Brian selected a chair opposite Jonathan, looking expectantly at his company president.

"Read the reports?" Jonathan asked. Brian nodded. "What do you think of the season so far?"

"Fair," Brian replied. "All categories are making budget. We're not setting any records, but there don't seem to be any bombs lying around either."

"If there are, they're camouflaged," Jonathan said. "We'll find out about them as a nasty surprise." He fingered the table top, smearing the shiny surface. "You're doing a good job, Brian. Between you and me, it's a far better job than Simon ever did in your position."

The unexpected praise took Brian by surprise. "Thanks," he said, beginning to blush. "By the way, where is Simon? I heard he wasn't well, had taken a few days off."

"Some bug or other," Jonathan muttered, knowing from his own investigation, however, that his son was in Las Vegas doing God alone knew what with God alone knew whom. "How long have you been with us at Head Office, Brian?"

"Three, four months."

"You like New York?"

"It's lively," Brian replied, tongue in cheek. "And it's where the job is."

Jonathan's face broke into a smile; he knew how many outsiders felt about the city. "Both Gerald and I wanted you here, Brian, because we felt that your knowledge of merchandise and operation procedure would strengthen the Head Office setup. I'm glad to say we were right." He narrowed his eyes, seeing how Brian was taking the compliment. "When you accepted the position of general merchandise manager, you were thinking about the future, right?"

Brian was puzzled by the question. "I'm always thinking about the future—a future with Chestertons, I hope."

"So do we," Jonathan concurred. "With Simon, the general merchandise manager spot was a vice-presidential position. No doubt that's also entered your mind."

"I'd be a liar if I said it hadn't," Brian replied truthfully. "I was thinking about that possibility if the job worked out well."

Jonathan took a drink from the coffee cup, leaving Brian to ponder over what was coming next. When he spoke again, he chose the words with great care. "You've been with us ever since we broke away from an East-Coast-only position, Brian. You took a chance on us by leaving a job with a bright future. Your work in helping us get established in the Midwest and your continuing loyalty have been invaluable. Now we'd like to repay that faith by offering you a seat on the Chestertons board."

Brian was stunned by the offer. He had seen such an event in the future—the distant future—coinciding with his success at Head Office. But to have it offered so quickly, and in such a spontaneous manner, took him completely by surprise.

"I don't know what to say," he began.

"A simple yes will suffice."

"Well, yes. Of course yes."

"Good," Jonathan said, beaming across the table. "That's all settled then. We'll have the papers drawn up so that you can become the first nonfamily VP." He stood up, signifying the end of the conversation. "Go home and tell your wife. Then you'll be all straight for this afternoon's merchandise meeting, so we can start taking potshots at you."

Jonathan walked out of the boardroom with Brian, leaving him as they passed Gerald's office.

"Have you got five minutes for me?" he asked his son.

"Sure. Ten if you want them. Have you told Brian?"

"Just now. He's still in a state of shock."

"That'll wear off when you start crucifying him," Gerald said. "Any word on my brother yet?"

"Only what I found out after I saw him at the airport. I couldn't believe my eyes when he went past in the cab with that girl next to him. He was so busy staring at her that he didn't see the Rolls. And I was so shocked that it didn't hit me for about twenty seconds or so."

If the situation had not been so serious because of the work that had to be done on the Mr. Simon shops, Jonathan could have seen the funny side of it—Simon running off for a quiet vacation with a girl. "I had a friend at Kennedy Airport check the airline passenger lists," he told Gerald, "and we found out he was off to Vegas." He tried to remember why he had wanted to speak to Gerald, having been led astray by two other subjects. Then it came back to him.

"The Belsize chain in San Francisco, that's what I came in for, Gerald. What's happening with it?"

Gerald picked up a typewritten report from his desk and passed it to his father. "It's all there. But in brief I've decided to let the three stores carry on pretty much as they have been doing. I've arranged to have a clearance promotion during the next three weeks; the local advertising agency which handled the Belsize account is looking after that. Architecturally they're good stores and shouldn't need much work. So when the present inventory's gone, we can take our time about turning them into Chestertons stores."

"What about the Belsize people?" Jonathan asked, concerned about the feelings of staff members who had been with the stores before the take-over. "How do they feel about working for a large company like Chestertons?"

Gerald pulled back the report and scanned through the pages. "The older employees, those who've been with the group for anything up to thirty years, are understandably worried about their future. But the younger ones, especially those with a feeling for retail, are glad about the change. I spoke to them all, and they see it as a good opportunity for advancement with a big, forward-looking company."

"Good, good. Who's still down there?"

Gerald gave his father the name of the Chestertons personnel manager who had remained in San Francisco.

"Get onto him and tell him to tread carefully with the older people," Jonathan said. "We don't want anybody leaving us just yet. We want those stores to run just as they have been running till we can get a good grasp on the situation."

Turning the key in the lock, Brian Chambers let himself into the apartment on Central Park West. He called Thelma's name, softly at first, then louder when he received no answer. Walking through the apartment, he checked all the rooms, coming finally to the den. It was also empty, although the desk bore witness that somebody had been working there. Curious about his wife's latest offering to America's middle-aged romantics, Brian went over to the red typewriter and looked at the sheet of paper inserted in the carriage. A sentence had been started and left unfinished, a beginning looking for a middle and an end. Next to the typewriter stood a tall kitchen glass, empty, with Thelma's lipstick making a red smudge around the rim.

From the den, Brian went to the kitchen, opening the **refrigerator** to make a sandwich for lunch. He felt annoyed that Thelma should be out. For once he had some news which even she would appreciate, and she had to be out.

Taking the sandwich and a glass of milk to the kitchen table, he sat down and began to eat, all the time thinking about Jonathan's sudden offer. Brian Chambers, vice-president of Chestertons—he decided the title sounded good, a fair reward for the confidence he had shown in Jonathan Chesterton so many years before by leaving Marshall Field. He had got into the Chestertons operation on the ground floor before the up button had been pushed really hard. As new stores had opened in the Midwest following the success of the Chicago venture, it had become clear that some form of operational supervision was required for the region. He had been the natural choice for regional manager, another step up the corporate ladder. And while his career in retail prospered, his marriage had rotted away.

Finishing the sandwich, he placed the dirty crockery in the sink, rinsing it and leaving it to dry in the rack. He put on his topcoat, checked that he had left nothing behind and walked into the hall. As he reached for the door handle, he heard a key being inserted in the lock on the other side of the door. Dropping his hand, he waited for the door to open, glad he would be able to tell Thelma of the appointment before he returned to the office.

Thelma entered the apartment, a thick coat wrapped tightly around her to ward off the outside cold. Her face was flushed and her walk, so Brian thought, unsteady, as if the bitter cold had driven clear through to her bones. She was carrying a shopping bag which weighed down her right shoulder.

Unseen by Thelma, he waited silently as she turned to close the door. Then he stepped up behind her, placing his hands over her eyes.

"Meet the newest vice-presdient of Chestertons, Thelma."

She screamed sharply in fright and dropped the shopping bag. There was the noise of breaking glass as the bag hit the floor. Liquid splashed against the cuffs of Brian's trousers, staining the fabric.

"You stupid bastard!" she shouted, spinning around to face him. "See what you've done."

Brian knelt down, sticking a finger into the running liquid which was soaking into the hall carpet. Tentatively he touched his tongue with the fingertip, recognizing the taste as gin. When he looked up from the carpet,

Thelma was leaning against the wall, crying hysterically at the mess on the floor.

It took Brian ten seconds to realize that she was quite drunk.

Miriam got out of the Rolls-Royce outside the store on West Fifty-seventh Street, watching while it pulled away toward its permanent daytime parking space in the underground parking garage on the same block. Then she walked the few yards across the sidewalk, hurrying, needing time to speak to Jonathan before the Monday afternoon merchandise meeting started. Entering the store, she smiled warmly at those salespeople who glanced her way, but never lessened her pace.

"Well, look who's the early bird," Jonathan remarked as Miriam stuck her head around the boardroom door to see if he was in. "Scared you might miss something? Or are you trying to catch me doing things I'm not supposed to?"

"Has there been any further word on Simon?" she asked urgently.

"Nothing," Jonathan replied. "For all I know, he could be putting the Mr. Simon shops down on the blackjack or craps table at this very moment. Who knows, maybe he'll hit a lucky streak and come back with more real estate."

The flippant remarks did nothing to ease the concern on Miriam's face. "Jonathan, I'm worried sick about what's happened to him, and you sit there making jokes. He seemed to have settled down these past few months, after that incident with the bookmaker. Now he runs off like this."

"Of course I'm making jokes about it," Jonathan said. "What else do you want me to do? Cry? I told you he was with a girl. He's probably cleared off to get some R and R."

"Some what?"

"R and R. Rest and rehabilitation. It's something the army gives to soldiers who've been in the front line too long—although how the hell Simon could ever hope to claim it is beyond me." For the first time, he realized that Miriam had entered the office alone. "Couldn't you persuade Jacob to come?"

"Do you know what your father was doing when I left home?" Miriam asked. "He was in the kitchen with an iron, sponging and pressing a suit to wear on Wednesday when he goes to Buffalo."

Jonathan burst out laughing. "You should have given him that blue striped suit of mine at the same time, the one I got caught in the rain with last week. What time did he get up?"

"About nine."

"Did he eat anything?" Jonathan asked, knowing that his father's appetite had been like that of a bird.

"Couple of slices of toast and marmalade, orange juice, coffee," Miriam answered. "Then he went out for a walk. When he came back, he asked me for the iron and complained it was nowhere near as good as the heavy ones he used to have in the shop."

"He remembers better than I do," Jonathan said, still amazed by the change his father had undergone since Viscenzi's visit. On Wednesday, Jacob was due to go to Buffalo for the day, where he would be met at the airport by the factory manager and put to work in the design department grading patterns till the late afternoon, when he would fly back to New York.

Miriam went silent for a moment and Jonathan sensed she was holding something back. "Say it," he prompted. "Say what's on your mind."

"It doesn't really matter any more," she said. "But before you had this idea of sending Jacob up to Buffalo once a week, I was going to suggest that it might be better if he went into a home. A trained staff might have been able to care for him more than we could."

"He's in a home already," Jonathan replied, not overly surprised by the confession. "Ours. And it's also his. Do you seriously think a bunch of nurses and doctors could do any more for him than his own family could? But like you say, it doesn't matter any more, because we've found the part that's been missing."

Miriam sat silently, thankful that the suggestion had only been a hypothetical one. She should have known how Jonathan would react to it. She wondered if Myron, poor dear Myron, would have felt the same way about their parents, cared for them as deeply as Jonathan cared for Jacob. Of course he would have, but the opportunity to do so had been taken away so cruelly. After Myron's death in Korea, her father had tried to carry on, but the loss of his only son was too great to bear. He had suffered two heart attacks, one after another. A third attack, two months later, killed him. Her mother had stayed in New York for three years before moving south to Florida, where she had met and married a widowed real estate salesman. They lived now in Saint Petersburg, where her new husband had maintained his business before retiring. Occasionally Miriam received a letter; once she and Jonathan had visited the couple, but it was like meeting complete strangers.

Seeing that Miriam was becoming upset, Jonathan walked around the desk to stand behind her, laying a hand gently on her shoulders. "We don't have to worry about anything like that now," he said. "Jacob's found his second childhood. I just hope I don't get complaints from the factory that he's driving them crazy up there."

Brian joined the merchandise meeting five minutes after the scheduled two o'clock start. Still shocked at seeing Thelma drunk, he muttered an apology to Jonathan and took his seat, trying to clear his mind for the business ahead.

"Something wrong?" Jonathan asked.

"Bit of a headache, that's all." Brian forced a grin. "Must be the excitement of being adopted by your family."

The meeting began with the routine coverage of categories of merchandise carried by the stores, breaking down the results into geographic areas. Moving to the acquisition of the Belsize chain in San Francisco, Gerald suggested transferring some of the slow sellers in the Chestertons West Coast stores to the new group, running them as specials when the stores reopened under the Chestertons name.

Jonathan gave the idea some thought before shelving it temporarily. "I'm more concerned about what we can do with those stores before we change the name." He looked at Brian. "Do you think we can get any cheap promotional goods into the Belsize stores before the name change? We may as well get away with murder while they're still under the old name."

Brian gave him the name of a West Coast supplier who imported sport shirts from Taiwan and Korea. "He's been trying to sell us some goods ever since Chestertons moved out West," Brian explained. "He was on the phone to me this morning, first thing, about doing some business with the Belsize stores."

"What's he got? Anything interesting?"

"He was talking about two hundred dozen polyester-cotton sport shirts," Brian said, "$3.59 each, delivered."

Jonathan heard Gerald's whistle of surprise and looked at him. "American manufacturers can't compete with prices like that," he told his son. "Our factory's lucky that it's got a captive market—us. But one day our manufacturers will have to band together and really do something about clothing imports, not the hemming and hawing they have been doing, but something really solid. Otherwise they'll all go out of business." He turned back to Brian. "If the stuff's any good, what sort of retail price could we get?"

"Maybe $9.99, depending on the quality. But I think we should settle for $7.49. Use them as a draw to the public, closing-down sale and all that. We can probably get rid of some of the other slow sellers at the same time, like Gerald mentioned earlier."

"Fine," Jonathan said. "I'll leave it with you. But the moment our name goes up over those storefronts, those shirts come right out. See if you can get them sale or return, get the supplier to take back what we don't sell."

"He won't do it," Brian said. "He's strictly a one-lump delivery merchant. If they look slow when it's getting near name-change time, we'll cut them right down, to our own prices if necessary."

"Okay. You see to it." He was about to add something when the telephone rang. It was his secretary.

"Telegram for you, Mr. Jonathan."

Jonathan shook his head in annoyance at the interruption, wondering irritably what was so important about a telegram that it could not wait till the meeting had ended. "What does it say?"

"I think you should read it," the girl's voice came back.

Jonathan sighed. "Okay. Bring it in."

The other people around the table took advantage of the unexpected break to relax and gather their thoughts for the next item on the agenda; the stenographer, having difficulty in reading back the last of her shorthand, decided to switch to a fresh pencil. The boardroom door opened, and Jonathan's secretary came in, dropping the cable in front of him. She was about to leave when Jonathan grabbed her by the arm.

"What's so important that you can't say it over the phone?"

The girl was clearly embarrassed. "I think you should read it," she repeated quietly.

Something in the girl's voice troubled Jonathan. He let go of her arm and picked up the cable, flicking his gaze over the capitalized words, uncomprehending at first, then astonished as his brain registered what his eyes saw.

"What is it?" Miriam asked. "Is it Simon?"

"Yes. It's your son," Jonathan said, his voice trembling as he passed the cable to Miriam. He waited while she read it, still incapable of believing the contents.

"Oh, my God," Miriam whispered. "He's run away to get married."

Gerald lifted his head from the report he had been studying and unintentionally began to laugh. "Married? Who'd marry him?"

Miriam continued staring at the cable, mouthing the words over and over again silently. Jonathan answered for her.

"A girl named Della Sanchez. Ring a bell with anybody?"

Looking to his left at Brian, Gerald toned down his laughter to a broad smirk. "If our newest VP wasn't here, I'd say that Simon's run off with a *shiksa*."

"He's here, and you just said it," Jonathan told him sourly, failing to find any humor in the situation. He took the cable away from Miriam and read it again.

"Does it say where the happy couple's honeymooning?" Gerald asked. "Maybe we could send them a card."

"Just the message, nothing else," Jonathan said. "Congratulate us. I have married a girl called Della Sanchez. Do you approve?" Disgusted, he crumpled the piece of paper into a small ball and flung it hard into the corner of the room.

"Is there any more business?" he asked.

After dinner, Jonathan helped Miriam to clear the dishes from the kitchen table, standing behind her as she washed them. He felt tired, hardly able to keep his eyes open. Either everything had happened too quickly, or he was just getting old. It was supposed to have been a nice, simple day, highlighted by telling Brian of the decision to make him a vice-president of the company. Instead, the day had turned into a farce. Brian had returned from lunch looking like a man with a hangover; then the cable had arrived from Simon, informing everybody of his happy news.

All right, he couldn't give a damn who Simon married; maybe it would do him the world of good, make him act up to his responsibilities. But what a way to go about it. Didn't he ever take the feelings of anybody else into consideration?

Miriam had not spoken about the cable, but Jonathan could see that she was distressed. And Jacob, he thought bitterly—he had taken the news badly. He had been sitting downstairs watching television, eager for Wednesday to come, when Jonathan and Miriam arrived home. Proudly he had shown Jonathan the perfectly pressed suit, boasting that he had not lost his touch and that he could still press a suit better than any machine. Jonathan did not have the heart to tell him immediately. He waited till after dinner, during which Jacob had talked incessantly about what he would do in Buffalo. Jacob had stared stupidly at first, reflecting Jonathan's own emotions when he had read the cable. Then his face had dropped, the eyes blurring behind the glasses. He had stubbed out the cigarette he was smoking, excused himself and gone upstairs to his room, saying nothing more, the happy mood at the prospect of visiting the factory shattered completely.

Jonathan waited till Miriam had placed the last dish in the rack, watching as she cleaned out the sink and straightened everything perfectly.

"Is this where we're supposed to ask each other what we did wrong?" he asked.

Miriam gave him a tired smile. "I don't think Doctor Spock would be much use in this situation. What are you going to do when Simon comes back?"

"What you'd want me to do. We'll accept this girl just like we accepted Marilyn when Gerald got married. I only hope she's as good."

Miriam walked past him and sat in the living room, resting her feet on a low stool. "I was praying you'd say that, Jonathan. What kind of girl do you think she is?"

Jonathan thought back to the brief glimpse he had caught of the girl as the Yellow cab had passed the Rolls-Royce on the way to the airport. Short black hair, that was all he could see. "If Simon knows her, you can be damned sure that she's good-looking, with expensive tastes," he replied. "Women are the only area where Simon never lowers his standards. I wish he was so quality-conscious at work."

They sat for half an hour, neither talking. Miriam thought about Simon, about the girl he had married, why he had chosen to do it so suddenly. Jonathan's mind jumped from Simon to Brian to the three new stores in San Francisco, finishing up with Jacob. What had Viscenzi told him about Jacob? Do all you can, that's what the Italian designer had said when they had parted at Kennedy Airport. Get him interested in life again by shunting him off to Buffalo for a few hours each week where he can feel useful again. Make it a high point of his week, something for him to look forward to. Then when he gets all psyched up, destroy the illusion completely by telling him that his grandson has run away to marry a *shiksa*.

Finally Miriam stood up and said she was going to bed. She bent over Jonathan's chair, kissing him good night. He continued to sit, listening to her footsteps above him as she prepared for bed; he knew from their years together the exact routine she followed each night and closed his eyes, picturing her actions.

Fifteen minutes later, when it was perfectly quiet, he went into the den. Locking the door, he opened the window slightly, just wide enough to let in some air without disturbing the thermostat for the central heating. Then he lit a cigar, the first he had smoked in the house for many years, blowing the smoke toward the partially open window while he chewed down angrily on the end.

Pulling his coat collar tightly around his neck, Brian Chambers left the office at nine o'clock. He was late leaving for two reasons. There was a mountain of paper work that had to be taken care of, and, secondly, he did not relish the prospect of going home to face Thelma, whatever state she was in.

He searched for an empty taxi for ten minutes before yielding to the futility of such a quest on a cold, miserable night. Bowing his head against the driving, freezing rain, he walked the few blocks to the Central Park West apartment; by the time he arrived, he was soaked through and frozen. In the elevator, his teeth chattered despite his efforts to stop them.

"Thelma!" he yelled, slamming the apartment door. "Thelma! Where are you?"

He heard nothing. Walking into the living room, dripping water onto the carpet from his soaking wet coat, he found his wife stretched out on the couch, one leg hanging over the side touching the floor. Leaving her, he took off his coat, hanging it to dry in the bathroom. Then he went into his bedroom to remove the rest of his wet clothes, changing into a heavy wool dressing gown.

Thelma had not moved when he returned to the living room. As he stood watching the inert form, the jeans and blouse in disarray, his fury mounted till the blood seemed to froth in his veins. He stormed around to the back of the couch, took hold of the top and rolled it savagely forward. Thelma toppled onto the carpet, her eyes opening in bewilderment. She stared stupidly at Brian, blinking rapidly as he came into focus.

"What's wrong?" she cried. "What are you doing?"

"Get up, you drunken slut!" he shouted at her. "What the hell's the matter with you?"

Thelma got to her feet unsteadily, her fiery red hair awry, eyes still sticky from sleep. Seemingly unaware of his insults, she rubbed her face with her hands. "What time is it?"

"What the hell time do you think it is? How long have you been sleeping it off? Since lunchtime? Or did you go out and buy more booze?"

"Go away, Brian," she whispered. "I don't think I can take you just now."

"You can't take me!" he yelled incredulously. "Just think yourself goddamn lucky that I'm not throwing you out into the cold with just a couple of bottles for company."

Thelma staggered away toward the den. Brian followed a step behind, waiting to see what she would do. On the desk was a glass, the same one he had seen at lunchtime, but now it was a quarter full with gin. Before he could stop her, she lifted it and swallowed the contents, breathing heavily as she replaced the glass on the desk top.

"That's better," she gasped. "Now I can see what you look like."

Brian gripped her by the shoulders and shook her roughly. "What the hell's gone wrong with you?" he snapped. "I came home at lunchtime to give you some good news, and I found you plastered then, with more booze in your shopping bag. What's got into you?"

"You have," she replied, slurring the words like a comic drunk, giggling as she caught the double-entendre of the statement. "No, not that way, Brian. You haven't got into me that way for years and years and years." He turned his head away, nauseated by the combined smell of alcohol and sour breath. She pushed herself out of his grip and pointed at the typewriter; the same sheet of yellow paper was in it, still featuring the same half-written sentence.

"You've got under my skin," she cried. "You. This whole stinking city. And . . . and this!" She snatched the sheet of paper from the typewriter; the platen buzzed angrily at the unnecessary force.

"I've written one goddamned manuscript since we moved to New York," she began to weep, tears streaking her cheeks, "and that was bounced. I hate this place. I hate everything about it. And most of all I hate you for making me come here. I've got no friends in New York. Even you're not here often enough for me to argue with. I have nothing"—she began to space the words out, raising her voice a pitch higher with each syllable—"to goddamned well do!"

She dropped the sheet of paper. Before it had time to flutter down to the floor, she was on Brian, pounding his chest with her fists, punching him strongly at first, more weakly as her strength drained away. Finally she fell against him, sliding down. He grabbed her before she hit the floor, catching another waft of her gin-laden breath, almost gagging on it.

"Now you can see what I'm looking for in a bottle?" she wailed, slumping against him. "Can you? Can you see anything at all outside that stinking company of yours?"

# 12

The dream was still vivid in his mind when he woke up at five minutes after five, every moment of it playing back in front of his eyes as he stared at the wall of the darkened bedroom. Sitting on the edge of the bed, bare feet flat on the carpet, Jonathan thought about the dream, going over the scenes as they had occurred. Behind him, Miriam slept peacefully, unaware that he was up.

He never dreamed as a rule, not dreams that he remembered, certainly. This one exception made him irritable. Why now? Was it the cigar he had furtively smoked before going to bed, locking himself in the den, blowing the smoke toward the open window? Was he suffering from a guilt complex about smoking in the house, going directly against Miriam's wishes? Despite the aggravation caused by the dream, he managed a weak smile as he thought about what Miriam would say if she knew he had been smoking in the house—or anywhere, for that matter.

But it was neither the smoking nor Miriam's probable reaction which perturbed Jonathan. It was the dream. Even now, the events covered by his subconscious remained as clear as if they were happening all over again.

The dream had started in the old tailoring shop on Essex Street. Jacob had been sitting cross-legged, bent over a jacket as he stitched carefully, his face wearing the patient smile which Jonathan remembered so well. Then the scene had switched to University Avenue, Mike Epstein and the starting handle. But when the handle had made contact with the side of Epstein's head as he scrambled for the gun, the face that had contorted itself in pain had been Jacob's. From there the dream had taken him to Al Gilbert's shop on West Thirty-fourth Street—only when Jonathan and Myron had thrown the suits at the fat retailer, it had been Jacob sitting behind the desk, a look of confusion and hurt on his face. Finally the location had changed to that December night more than thirty years earlier in the Ardennes. If I should dream about anything, Jonathan mused, it should be that. Again he had seen his Sherman tank rolling forward—Gellenbaum's Gehenna, he remembered telling Myron the name was—plowing into the fleeing German infantrymen as he had aimed the machine gun insanely, knowing that he would find a target wherever he sighted. Only the tank commander who had stared at him fearfully after the battle had again been Jacob.

Jacob. Jacob. Jacob. Christ . . . can't I think of anything else? It's as though Viscenzi's visit has touched off a guilt reaction about selling those four stores. But it doesn't make any sense at all. Jacob wasn't really involved in them. It was just his name that was used. And besides, he's happy again, off to Buffalo tomorrow for the day. He's going to work again.

Then Jonathan remembered the telegram of the previous day and realized that his father was anything but happy.

Treading quietly to avoid waking Miriam, he left the bedroom and looked in on his father, who occupied the next room, the second largest of the four bedrooms. Jacob was turned away, facing the window, the blankets pulled up to his neck as he slept soundly. Going downstairs to the kitchen, Jonathan made coffee and sat down to drink it, deciding that there was no point in going back to bed.

He followed the first cup with a second, feeling the fatigue begin to slough off as the caffeine took effect. Putting down the news magazine he was reading, Jonathan looked out of the kitchen window into the garden. It was still dark, but he thought he could see snowflakes. He turned on the outside light, watching the garden instantly bathed in brightness. One glance confirmed his worst fears; the lawn was white, already under one inch of snow, and more was falling steadily, heavy flakes drifting down sluggishly to join the carpet already there. Despite the coziness of the kitchen and his warm dressing gown, Jonathan shuddered violently, imagining what it would be like on the outside.

When he next looked at the clock it was six-thirty, the time he arose normally. Reheating the percolator, he made coffee for Miriam and a third cup for himself.

Miriam stirred slightly as he turned on the bedroom light and put the cup on her bedside table. He looked down on her tenderly while she continued to sleep, recalling the little girl who had brought him the suit samples for Al Gilbert. Then he touched her gently on the shoulder, dispelling the illusion as she awoke.

"What time is it?" she asked, blinking in the light.

"Six-forty."

"I didn't hear you get up."

"I was quiet. I didn't want to wake you, because you looked so beautiful." He did not want Miriam to worry that he had been kept awake by a dream. "I've got to leave early," he added. "It snowed a couple of inches during the night."

He watched while Miriam sipped from the cup, her auburn hair partially hidden by a net. Turning on the hall light outside the bedroom, he carefully opened the door to Jacob's room and peeked inside again. His father was still sleeping. Just as quietly Jonathan closed the door and returned to Miriam, taking his cup of coffee over to her bed, sitting next to her.

"When do you think Simon will be back?" she asked.

"Who knows? When he feels the honeymoon's gone on long enough, I suppose." He remembered what Viscenzi had said about the boutiques before his departure to France. "In the meantime I'm having Brian check over all the purchases for the Mr. Simon shops. There are a couple of areas where we're pretty weak, and Brian's input can be valuable."

"Do you really think that's a wise thing to do?" Miriam asked dubiously. "Those shops are Simon's special project."

"So they are," Jonathan replied, a tinge of sarcasm in his voice. "But that still doesn't mean he's got a license to lose money on them." Then he laughed. "Don't worry so much about Simon's ego, Miriam. He won't mind a little bit of well-meant assistance. The more successful those boutiques are, the more he can puff up his chest and shout what a clever little boy he is."

"I just hope you're right," was Miriam's quiet reply.

After showering, Jonathan dressed in a conservative blue suit with a matching pale blue shirt and wine-color tie. He made a light breakfast, reading the newspaper while he ate. Part of the outside sheet was wet where the delivery boy had left it half in, half out of the mailbox, but Jonathan was glad to get it in any condition on a day like this. Looking out at the garden again, he decided that the weather was too severe to drive into the city; he telephoned the company chauffeur who normally picked him up at seven-thirty every morning and instructed the man to drive straight to the office. He would make his own way by rail.

At seven-thirty he went upstairs for the last time to say good-bye to Miriam. Sticking his head into Jacob's room, he saw that his father still slept in the same position, head turned away from the door, facing toward the window. Putting on rubber overshoes and a heavy coat, Jonathan began to walk toward the bus stop, hoping that the bus service would be operating, not welcoming the prospect of walking all the way to the Long Island Rail Road station.

Gerald reached the office on West Fifty-seventh Street ten minutes ahead of his father. The journey from Manhasset—also by rail—had taken the better part of two hours because of the snow. He sorted through his mail quickly, wanting to speak to Jonathan as soon as he came in. He had just received the latest figures for shoplifting losses, and he was horrified at the amount of money the company was losing.

Merchandise losses through shoplifting were an occupational hazard and came under the general heading of shrink, which also included losses through improper documentation and inadequate inventory control. Since computerizing the stock control system, however, and doing away with the human error as much as possible, the main cause of shrink within Chestertons had been shoplifting. And the figures were increasing quarterly.

Gerald's secretary called through as soon as she saw Jonathan arrive. Giving his father a couple of minutes to settle in, Gerald rapped sharply on the boardroom door.

"Have you seen these?" he asked Jonathan, showing him the shoplifting figures. "They're downright disgusting."

Jonathan looked hurriedly at the figures, his mind only half taking in the information they contained. He was still too wrapped up in the dream about Jacob. "So?"

"Do you know what they work out to be?" Gerald asked. "An average of a thousand dollars per month per store. We've got forty-one stores, including those three Belsize stores in San Francisco, and we're getting hit to the tune of almost five hundred thousand dollars of retail value a year across the whole chain."

Jonathan passed the figures back to his son. "That's what you get with inflation," he said lightly. "Everything goes up. Blame it on the Arabs and their oil price increases if you like."

"Do you know where the worst spot is?" Gerald demanded, after permitting himself a small smile. "It's right out there." He pointed in the direction of the two-story main store which fronted the offices. "They lost almost five thousand dollars worth of merchandise in November alone. Shopping early for Christmas is fine; I love it. But shoplifting early for Christmas is something we can't afford."

"What sort of stuff's walking?" Jonathan asked. "Any particular styles in demand this year, or aren't the boosters that selective?"

"Leather coats and jackets obviously. They're always displayed near the front of the store to pull people in. Instead, people are pulling them out. Even with all the safety devices we've installed—the magnetic door alarms, safety chains, everything—we're getting hit. The better our security gets, the smarter the boosters get. Knitwear's another big thing that walks by itself. I reckon somebody's put together a school for boosters out there. They're getting hold of all the latest literature from the security companies and teaching their pupils how to outwit it."

"So what do you want me to do about it?" Jonathan asked. "And don't give me that line about catching the boosters. If we do, the courts are too crowded and too lenient to do any damned good."

"Educate our people to cut down on shrink," Gerald said simply. "Get a security agency in."

"Wait a minute," Jonathan interrupted. "We're not having any Brink's or Pinkerton men walking around our stores. Never mind about scaring away the boosters; they'll frighten our legitimate customers off."

"Not in that way," Gerald said, grinning as he pictured the scene. "Just get them in to lecture our people about guarding against shoplifting. The next time we have a manager's conference we can hold a session on it. Even you and I can learn a thing or two about it."

"Especially me," Jonathan said wryly. "Sometimes I reckon I'm getting too long in the tooth for this kind of work." He sat back in the chair and thought over his son's proposition. "I'll give you a better idea," he finally said. "Get a cop's uniform jacket and drape it over the back of a chair out front. It'll look as though we've got a cop in the store buying clothes. That'll scare the bad guys away."

"No way. It might work for the first day—and on the second day that would get lifted," Gerald said. "The best thing is what I suggested already. Include a session of guarding against boosting as part of the next manager's conference."

"Do whatever you think is right," Jonathan said. "This sort of thing comes under your jurisdiction anyway. If we can cut our shrink by twenty-five percent, we'll be looking very healthy. But strictly off the record, Gerald, I'd just love to get my hands on one of those thieving sons of . . ." He broke off in mid-curse as the telephone rang, head inclined as he waited for his secretary to take the call. Seconds later, her voice came through the intercom.

"Your wife is on the line, Mr. Jonathan."

"Thanks." Before picking up the receiver, he looked helplessly at Gerald. "See what your mother's like? I only left her a couple of hours ago, and already she's chasing me. Probably wants to know if I made it in or whether I'm stuck in a snowdrift somewhere. What would women do without somebody to nag?"

He lifted the receiver. "Yes, Miriam. What did you forget to tell me before I left?"

Gerald watched his father with a sense of amusement. Talk about an old war horse, he thought; my father's got to be the most aggressive man I know. He had to be, to build up this empire. God help the booster my father gets his hands on; jail will seem a better alternative. Gerald had heard many times from his mother and Jacob how Jonathan had kept the union out of the factory on Houston Street.

Then, with a feeling of deepening anxiety, he noticed that his father's expression had altered dramatically. The smile which had illuminated his face moments earlier had given way to a troubled frown; the casual tone had changed to one of strict urgency.

"Did you call a doctor?" Jonathan was asking sharply. "Okay. Now keep a hold of yourself. I'll be home as soon as I can get through the snow." He hung up and sat immobile in the chair, staring ahead, seeing nothing.

"What's up?" Gerald asked.

"Jacob. Your grandfather."

"What about him?" Gerald already knew what the answer had to be before he asked the question.

"Your mother says he's dead."

Disregarding the hazardous driving conditions, the chauffeur kept the Rolls-Royce's speed up as he made the journey out to Great Neck. Jonathan and Gerald sat in the rear, silent, watching the city recede as the car headed out toward Long Island. Gerald passed no comment when his father lit a cigar, sucking in the smoke, forcing it out between compressed lips.

Scenes from the previous night's dream flashed before Jonathan's eyes like rushes from a movie. Had it been an omen? No; he dismissed the idea as absurd. Thoughts like that were for superstitious idiots. Omen indeed. It had been a coincidence, nothing more. He had been worried about Jacob's health, and it had affected him.

And, as it had turned out, he'd had damned good reason to worry about his father's health.

The chauffeur braked the Rolls-Royce to a halt outside the Georgian style house, sliding an extra yard in the snow, the wheels bumping solidly against the curb, which was almost invisible. Without waiting for Gerald, Jonathan flung open the door and jumped out, walking quickly down the path to the house. Opening the front door, he stamped his feet on the mat to clear the worst of the snow from his overshoes and went inside. He found Miriam and the doctor sitting in the living room, talking quietly.

"What happened?" His voice was flat, missing the usual resonance.

The doctor answered. "I'm afraid your father has passed on, Mr. Chesterton. It must have happened during the night, while he was asleep—a very peaceful ending."

Jonathan blinked hard to hold back the tears that he knew were developing. He had felt bad during the journey, but hearing the news from the doctor gave it an air of desperate finality. Feeling his strength going, he slumped down into an easy chair, unaware that he still wore the topcoat and overshoes; puddles formed around his feet, soaking into the rich broadloom. Miriam walked across to him and sat on the arm of the chair, her hand on his shoulder.

"I'm sorry," she whispered. "I loved your father as much as you did. He was a wonderful man."

"I know," was all Jonathan could think of in reply. He took a handkerchief from his coat pocket and blew his nose loudly, dabbing his eyes at the same time. "Is there any specific cause of death?" he asked the doctor.

"Anno Domini, Mr. Chesterton. Old age. A tired body unable to carry on. There are medical terms to cover it, but I think they would mean little. How old was your father?"

"Eighty-nine," Jonathan replied, thinking to himself, if he says marvelous, I'll throw him out on his ear. "He'd never been ill a day in his life." He saw Gerald enter the living room, standing in the doorway, fidgeting, unsure of himself. "Gerald, call up the office, please. Get hold of Brian and tell him what's happened. He'll look after that end of things."

He leaned back in the chair, taking Miriam's hand from his shoulder and holding it to his face; the cooling touch of her skin on his forehead felt comforting. "How did you find him?" he asked.

Miriam's voice began to break as she spoke, the shock of recalling the morbid discovery weighing down on her. "I went in this morning, shortly after you left. I had a cup of tea for him, the same as every morning. He was lying facing the window, and when I went around to that side of the bed, his eyes were open, staring like two marbles. There wasn't any shine in them, nothing. He wasn't breathing. He was just lying there, staring at the window. Oh, Jonathan." She burst out sobbing, burying her face in his shoulder, shaking. "It was horrible. His mouth was open, and his skin was cold when I touched it."

Absent-mindedly Jonathan patted Miriam gently on the back. "I looked in on him during the night," he said. "He was lying that way then. I thought he was sleeping, and he must have been dead all the time. You know something? I dreamed about him last night. It was a stupid dream, but I couldn't sleep because of it. All the tough things I've ever done—Epstein, Gilbert, everything—and always the guy I hurt was Jacob."

"What did you do?" Miriam asked.

"That's when I got up and made coffee. I looked in on him on the way down, about ten after five. Just after I brought up your cup, I had another look—and a third time before I left for the office. He must have been dead all that time, and nobody knew a thing about it."

He stood up carefully, moving Miriam tenderly into the chair. "May I go upstairs and see him?" he asked the doctor.

"Of course. Before I go would you like me to prescribe a sedative for either yourself or your wife?"

Jonathan looked down at Miriam slumped in the chair, her eyes closed. "No. I think we'll be all right. Thanks all the same." He left the room, folded his topcoat over a chair in the hall, kicked off his overshoes and began to climb the stairs, his legs feeling like they were handicapped by a ball and chain.

Outside Jacob's room he paused, willing himself to open the door and step inside. His hand rested on the doorknob, fingers clasped around it. But the knob refused to turn.

He did not hear the footsteps coming up the stairs behind him. Only when another hand was laid on top of his own was Jonathan aware that he was not alone.

"Come on, Pa," Gerald said. "We'll go in together."

He turned the knob and pushed the door open, continuing to hold his father's hand as they walked toward the bed. Jonathan's grip tightened as he looked at Jacob's face. The body was on its back and the eyes were closed, a considerate cosmetic touch by the doctor. The sheet was pulled up to Jacob's chin, and if Jonathan and Gerald did not know otherwise, they would have assumed he was sleeping.

"He looks peaceful," Gerald said.

"Yeah. He's left all the loneliness behind him. No more worries now. It's all over for him." Jonathan sniffed again, feeling the pressure mount behind his eyes. "He's with his friends now."

He began to shake as the tears he had been trying to hold back flooded out, spilling over his cheeks as he stared down at the body of his father. He felt Gerald's arm around his shoulders, but he wanted to be alone, to share a final, private moment with this man who had given him so much.

"Gerald, go downstairs and look after your mother. She needs you as well."

Alone, Jonathan sat on the edge of the bed, seeing his father's face through a veil of tears. Taking one of the worn hands in his own, he caressed it, trying to pretend that the stiffness, the coldness did not exist.

"Jacob, I'm sorry," he muttered. "I wish you could hear me say this." His voice broke, the words seeming to strangle him, to suffocate him, because he knew they were not enough.

When did I last tell him I loved him? When I wanted him to come into the factory with me? Why do I wait till he's dead before I tell him again? Why couldn't I have told him when he was alive, not just let him think it? He knew I loved him, but that wasn't enough. I should have told him more often. Maybe, just maybe, he wouldn't have faded away then.

Jonathan stayed on the bed for almost an hour, holding the lifeless hand, thinking of all the things he should have done and had not. The tears had stopped, as though the ducts had dried up, unable to supply any more visible evidence of his grief.

Slowly he let go of Jacob's hand, laying it with an exaggerated tenderness on the blanket. Standing up, he noticed the gold watch and chain on the bedside table, neatly positioned next to a pack of cigarettes and an old lighter. Jonathan picked up the watch and opened it, looking down at the hands which showed three minutes to twelve. Snapping the face closed, he dropped it into his own pocket, feeling the weight pull down that side of the jacket.

The filigree-embroidered blue and white silk skullcap was perched on Jonathan's thick hair like an ornate leaf; only the bobby pin inserted at the front prevented it from falling off his head. He sat uncomfortably on the low wooden chair lent by the local temple for the one-week mourning period. Following tradition, he was unshaven and his tie was cut, the torn clothing signifying bereavement.

He looked around the living room, at the mirrors covered with sheets, at his family, at his friends who had come to pay their respects—everybody except Simon. Gerald had tried to trace his brother, but with no success. He was somewhere in Vegas enjoying his honeymoon. Or maybe Reno. Or maybe anywhere.

Jonathan's glance fell on Brian, who had arrived after the conclusion of the evening service—a sound decision, Jonathan concurred, as he would have been unable to understand a word of what was going on. Brian was proving to be more than a top merchandise man within the company. He was almost one of the family, always at your side when you needed him. He had come alone to the house, which Jonathan found mildly surprising. At other, happier occasions which they had shared, Brian had always brought along his wife. Maybe she did not want to come because of the unfortunate situation or the atrocious weather. He could not blame her; it was understandable in the circumstances.

Atrocious weather—that had to be an understatement of gargantuan proportions. The funeral that afternoon had been like a bizarre adaptation of White Christmas, produced and directed by a lunatic. The cemetery had been blanketed with snow which swirled up into a white fog in the fierce wind. People had slipped following the coffin to the graveside, their scrambling efforts to regain a foothold deadened by the snow. A silent movie of the passing of one man, no sounds except the prayers of the rabbi, who had acquitted himself as quickly as decency would allow—also understandable under the circumstances.

The initial flood of grief had passed, leaving Jonathan dead inside, completely drained of all emotion. It was as if the whole thing was happening to somebody else and he was nothing more vital than a spectator. Except Jacob was sleeping in a wooden box under six feet of cold, inhospitable earth, unable even to appreciate the beauty of the pure snow which covered him like a white, crystallized sheet.

He remained sitting in the chair while he drank a cup of coffee given to him by Marilyn, his daughter-in-law. Fervently he wished he could smoke a cigar, watching other people jealously as they smoked. But, grief or not, Miriam would object. Idly he wondered if Gerald had told her about the cigar he had smoked during the journey from the office to the house; he gave his son the benefit of the doubt.

Drinking the coffee, Jonathan resigned himself to spending the next few days sitting on the little chair. He would be kept up to date by Gerald. Perhaps there was even a silver lining to the cloud of Jacob's death—he would be out of the office for a week, and God alone knew how much he could do with the rest.

# 13

Simon returned to New York wearing a handsome tan on his face and a plain gold band on the third finger of his left hand. After staying for four days in Las Vegas, he and Della had flown on to San Francisco, spending three days there before returning to New York; a longer, proper honeymoon would follow later.

Once Della had left the apartment to return to her job with the advertising agency, Simon ventured out. Marriage agreed with him, he decided, taking the elevator to the ground floor of the apartment building. It was just a question of finding the right partner, whether his family was in favor of his choice or not. Della made no demands on him other than those in bed, to which he acquiesced joyfully. She was bright, personable, and looked good on his arm. They looked good together; more than that, they were good together, a perfect couple.

Shivering at the unaccustomed sight of snow in the street, he hailed a cab, directing the driver to take him to West Fifty-seventh Street. Not wanting to be noticed walking through the store, he used the side entrance, reaching the Chestertons Head Office through the stairway at the rear. Entering the office complex, he instinctively looked at the wedding band, shining it on his coat, eagerly anticipating the reception he would get. Good or bad, it did not matter as long as he was the center of attraction.

Then, in the long corridor which connected all the top management offices, he came face to face with his brother.

Simon's smirk reached from one ear to the other as he held out his left hand, flashing the gold ring at Gerald. "You heard the news, I suppose. How about offering some fraternal congratulations?"

Gerald dropped his eyes to the ring, bringing them up again quickly to Simon's face. "Congratulations. Now you'd better go see your father."

"Oh?" Simon's high feelings began to diminish slightly. "Where is he? In the boardroom?"

"No. He's at home."

"What's he doing there?" Simon asked, becoming irritated that his homecoming was not turning out to be the triumphant surprise that he had planned.

Gerald mimicked his brother. "We thought you would have heard the news. He's sitting *shivah* for Grandpa."

Simon stopped dead, unable to immediately comprehend his brother's words. "Grandpa dead? Jacob?" he asked slowly. "When did this happen?"

"The night we received your telegram." Gerald's voice turned rough, accusation mixing with sarcasm. "He must have died from being overjoyed at the news, couldn't stand all the happiness of seeing his grandson marry a *shiksa*."

Simon's confusion turned to belligerency. "Don't try to blame the whole thing on me. It had nothing to do with my getting married. He was an old man; it could have happened at any time."

For an instant Gerald felt ashamed of himself. "I'm sorry," he muttered. "I had no business making a crack like that. We're all a bit overwrought. We tried to find you in Vegas to come back for the funeral."

"We were probably in San francisco by then," Simon said.

"Well, whatever. It was funny at first—you were spotted by your father on the way out to Kennedy Airport, you and the girl in the Yellow cab. He was seeing Nino Viscenzi off and passed you on the Van Wyck on the way back. Your story about being sick didn't hold up for too long."

"Never mind all that," Simon cut in. "I'll make my peace with him when I see him." He began to walk past Gerald, who grabbed him by the arm.

"Aren't you going out to Great Neck to see him right now?"

"Afterwards," Simon replied. "But first I want to see what's been happening with the Mr. Simon operation while I was away."

Shrugging off Gerald's arm, he walked past his brother toward his own office. Gerald turned around to stare after him, wondering what his father's reaction would be to Simon's return.

Shortly after midday, Simon travelled in the company Rolls-Royce to his parents' home in Great Neck, stopping first to pick up Della at the agency. He was unusually silent during the journey, huddled up in his brown sheepskin coat despite the car's heater, thinking deeply about the short meeting he had held with Brian Chambers during the morning. The general merchandise manager had said that he had been checking all purchases for the Mr. Simon shops, and the more Simon thought about it, the more furious he became at his father for being unable to keep his meddling fingers out of the operation.

Had he been talkative, however, Della would have proved a poor conversationalist. Beneath the cool, sophisticated surface, she was as tight as a fully wound watch spring, wrapped up in thoughts about meeting her husband's family for the first time.

Miriam opened the front door for them, throwing her arms around Simon's neck in a lingering, fond embrace before stepping back to look at Della.

"Are you going to introduce me to your wife, Simon?"

"Sorry." He turned to Della, who was dressed warmly and smartly in a pale green coat with a mink collar. "Della, my mother. And vice versa."

Della took a hesitant step forward, gravely clasping Miriam's outstretched hand. "I'm very pleased to meet you, Mrs. Chesterton. I just wish it could have been under happier circumstances."

Miriam's eyes began to cloud. She dropped Della's hand and placed her own hands on her daughter-in-law's shoulders, holding her, saying nothing. Simon watched, wondering what was going through the minds of the two women.

"We're very happy to have you in the family," Miriam said finally.

With Miriam leading the way, Della stepped into the hall, followed by Simon, who helped her remove her coat. From there they walked into the living room, where Jonathan was seated on the small wooden chair reading a newspaper. He looked up as Simon and Della entered, noticing Miriam hovering nervously behind them. Dropping the newspaper to the floor, he stood up, eying the visitors speculatively.

Simon was shocked to see how his father looked. The deep brown eyes seemed sunken, and the small growth of beard added years to the heavy face. He crossed the room and shook Jonathan's hand formally. "I wish you long life."

"Guess we've all got to go sometime," Jonathan replied stoically. Inclining his head toward Della, he added, "One leaves the family and another one joins, eh?"

"I'm sorry the surprise comes while you're sitting *shivah*."

"So am I." Jonathan turned his full attention on Della, his eyes lighting up as he looked at her properly for the first time. For once, his son had not disappointed him. The girl was lovely—petite, demure, and very, very feminine. With no feeling of impropriety, he nodded his head in approval. Then he smiled at Della.

"Sit down," he invited, pointing to the couch set into the deep bay window which looked out onto the front garden, now bare of everything but an even covering of snow. "Tell me what made you marry this son of mine."

Della felt the tension begin to drain away. Simon had spoken often of his family, hardly ever in complimentary terms. He had always claimed that he was the moving force behind the company's present success, and she had taken the boasting as fact, having no reason to believe otherwise. Now, finally meeting the family was a traumatic experience, especially under conditions which were totally alien to her almost forgotten Catholic upbringing. Inquisitively she looked at the covered mirrors and the memorial candle burning in a small glass on the table. Understanding her puzzled glances, Jonathan explained the significance of the objects, certain that Simon, whose lack of consideration was almost legendary, had not.

"How long have you known each other?" Jonathan asked.

"Seven, eight months," Della replied. "Is that long enough?"

Jonathan was uncertain whether her question was a genuine response or she was trying politely to tell him to mind his own business. He decided to be charitable and choose the first alternative. "I reckon it's long enough," he said. "My wife and I only had three or four dates before I asked her to marry me. Time's not a concern as long as you're both sure of what you're doing." For some contrary and unfathomable reason, Jonathan decided to make his son feel uncomfortable.

"It just beats me that you got him to propose. We all reckoned that he was a bachelor for life and that no woman would budge him from his chosen path." Deep down, Jonathan was gratified to see Simon wince; a faint blush began to spread out underneath the West Coast tan.

"May I tell your father?" Della asked Simon.

"Sure. Why not?" A faint edge appeared in Simon's voice.

"Tell me what?" Jonathan asked.

"I proposed to him," Della said. "One of us had to make a move, and I figured that if I waited for Simon I'd be an old maid."

Jonathan put his face in his hands and laughed, finding it ludicrous that Simon should have been proposed to. "That's beautiful," he said. "Something you only read about in books."

"Don't laugh so loudly," Miriam reprimanded him. "If you hadn't asked me to marry you that day after the zoo, I was going to do the same thing." She was pleased at the way the encounter was going. Jonathan had promised that he would treat Della as he had treated Marilyn, and he was keeping his word.

Jonathan continued to laugh. "You?" he spluttered. "You were scared of your own shadow in those days."

"Who wouldn't be, confronted by a hulking giant like you?" she retorted. "You filled every place you went back then."

"Does that mean I've lost weight?" Jonathan quipped, knowing that he had not; it was a point which always annoyed Miriam, as she nagged at him constantly.

Della watched the interplay, relating it to her own family in Minneapolis—or wherever they were now, not that she cared a damn. In a moment of candor, she had revealed to Simon that her relatives had been nothing to write home about; if she did not see them for fifty years, it would be too soon. With two older sisters, she had been at the end of the receiving line for everything. And when her father had died fifteen years earlier, the situation had become even more difficult. While her sisters both married immediately after graduating from high school, Della had worked to put herself through university, determined that she would not fall into the same rut as her sisters—three kids each by the time they were twenty-five, and husbands who spent more time with their friends than they did at home. When she had finished university, Della had fled Minneapolis, ecstatic at seeing the last of her family and the people she had known since childhood. New York had offered many attractions—a career, a place to lose herself while she searched for her own identity, and an opportunity to mix in circles which would have been inaccessible in her own city. When Simon had appeared in the singles bar that night, she had seen in him a route to the plateau she craved. Through Simon she saw a way to advance herself, to banish forever the memories of her childhood poverty and shame. As Brutus had claimed about Caesar after participating in his murder, Della was ambitious.

Losing interest in his verbal fencing with Miriam, Jonathan turned back to Della. "What sort of work do you do?"

"Advertising. I'm an account executive with a small agency, Marc and Richard Ross. Ever heard of it?"

"Can't say I have. Any men's clothing clients on your books?"

"Not at the moment. But there's one I know we'd be interested in."

Jonathan smiled at the forthright attitude. "We shall see," he said. "I've never been one to avoid nepotism where it's applicable." Dropping the subject, he addressed Simon. "Did you get into the office before you came out here?"

"Yes. I spoke to Brian to see what's been happening since I went away."

"And?"

Glancing at Della, Simon hesitated, uncertain of the wisdom of discussing company business in her presence.

Waiting for an answer, Jonathan understood his son's reticence. He had obviously learned of Brian's investigation of the Mr. Simon purchases and, if past performances were anything to go by, he would be burning up inside. Jonathan was curious to see whether he would want Della included in any discussion of the topic, although her knowledge of the subject was zero, apart from what Simon might have told her about his role at Chestertons. His other son, Gerald, never objected to his wife being present during any conversation about the company. Now Jonathan was interested in seeing Simon's stand on the same matter.

As if sensing Simon's uncertainty, Della stood up and walked to where Miriam stood. "Can I see the rest of the house?" she asked. "It looked lovely from the outside."

Smiling inwardly at the girl's tact, Jonathan watched Miriam lead Della from the room, closing the door quietly behind them.

"Nice girl," he said to Simon. "Pity you couldn't have done it all above board, though."

The hostility which Simon had been cultivating during the journey to

Great Neck spilled out. "If I'd told you about Della before—getting married, that is—I'd have been involved in a stand-up row, just like everything else."

"Don't be so damned stupid!" Jonathan shot back. "You're big enough to make up your own mind about what you want to do. We welcomed her when you brought her in just now. We would have welcomed her before."

Not wanting to be drawn into a discussion on his sudden decision to marry, Simon switched to the meeting he had held with Brian that morning, his stomach tightening as he recalled being told that his purchases were under scrutiny.

"Did you tell Brian to go through my records?" he snapped at his father. "He's exceeding his authority, poking his nose where he's got no goddamn business."

Jonathan stood up to relieve the cramp he was getting from sitting on the small chair. He walked around the couch where Della had been sitting and stared out of the window, looking at the ruts which car tires had left in snow missed by the plow; a slight chill hung around the window frame. "Yes. I told him to check what you were doing. The figures from those shops should be much higher. We're not realizing anything near the full potential of the space we've allocated to the Mr. Simon shops."

Simon's voice rose in anger. "How would you or Brian know if I'm doing anything wrong? You're both completely out of touch with the young fashion market. I'm the only one in the company who understands it worth a damn!"

Jonathan forced himself to remain calm in the face of Simon's anger, letting his son expend his temper. "Neither Brian nor myself is out of touch. We probably know a lot more about the Mr. Simon customer than you do. But what's happening now is not being done at our instigation."

"Then who told you to do it?"

"Nino Viscenzi. He thought that a poor job was being made of the boutiques. Neither the merchandise nor the displays were telling a complete story; a lot of the stuff was too way out, far too extreme. The whole environment was wrong. What it boils down to, Simon"—he paused to let the words sink in—"is that the management of those shops is lousy."

Simon leaped up from his seat, shaking with fury. "What the hell does he know about the American market?" he shouted. "It's your business that you've brought him in as a fancy name designer, but he's got no call sticking his face into my side of the operation."

Jonathan turned away from the window and wiggled the little finger of his right hand under Simon's nose. "Nino has more knowledge of the industry in that much of his body than you'll ever have in your whole head. You should be damned grateful that he's taking an interest in the operation, not letting it go down the tube like every other thing you touch."

Simon paled as he heard the words. Blood drained from his face, leaving it ashen. "You have never given me the chance to turn any operation into a success," he said, his voice low, the words spaced out. "I'm pushed this way and that like an orphan, into any job that you think will suit me for the time being. If you gave me as much attention as you give Gerald, I could show you what I can do."

Jonathan looked out of the window again, his back to Simon. "I've seen what you can do. You fouled up the buying program when you were general merchandise manager because you wouldn't listen to anybody else. And no matter what you say, you're doing a poor job with the Mr. Simon shops. You haven't changed at all. You won't take any advice, even from experts. And on top of all that, you run away like a thief in the night to get married, as though you're ashamed of the girl. Or maybe you just wanted to spring it on us as a big surprise—look everybody, look how I married a *shiksa*. All right, you gave us all a big surprise. For once in your life you succeeded in doing something. Congratulations."

Losing interest in the scene outside the house, Jonathan turned back to his son. "As good as Gerald is, you're lousy. Gerald works his butt off to get results while you sit back in the hope that it will all fall together. Well it won't. You've got to work at it. If you want things to turn out right, you've got to bend your back. So from now on, Brian is going to check every proposed purchase for Mr. Simon. And he's even going to put in a few of his own ideas. You'll remain general manger, but everything goes through him. Do I make myself clear? Absolutely everything."

Tears of rage glistened in Simon's hazel eyes as he confronted his father. He felt helpless and sought frantically for a way to hurt Jonathan.

"It's you who doesn't know how to run a company!" he yelled. "You're always listening to advice from other people, following the last suggestion you heard—from anybody but me. You bring in Brian from Chicago, and you listen to him. Viscenzi, with his fancy European ideas which have no standing in the States, you listen to. Even your father, who was fifty years behind the times if anybody was, used to occupy a seat of honor at the meetings. And you all used to look up to him. Yes, Jacob. No, Jacob. What do you think, Jacob? Three bags full, Jacob."

Jonathan had been prepared to listen to his son's tirade, but when Jacob's name came up he flinched, remembering that he had buried his father only days earlier. "Leave Jacob out of it," he growled warningly. "He doesn't belong in this."

"Why not?" Simon shouted, totally ignoring the danger signals. "Is his memory so sacred that we can't criticize him? He was out of his depth in those meetings. We could all see that, but you still showered more respect and attention on him than you ever gave me." The voice reached a crescendo, words running into each other as frustration and anger drove Simon on.

"Instead of listening to the ideas of youth, you gave in to the mumblings of a ranting old fool!"

Jonathan's right hand came up sharply, catching Simon across the left cheek with such force that he staggered sideways, falling onto the couch. His brain slowly registered the fact that his father had hit him, something he had never done before.

In the kitchen, Della and Miriam sat drinking coffee and learning something about each other. During the few minutes they had been together, a warm bond had been established between the two women, despite the trepidation they had both felt about the initial meeting. Realizing her son's mercurial way of rushing into things, Miriam had not known what to expect. Della for her part, had heard stories from Simon about his family and was pleasantly surprised to find that neither his mother nor his father was as bad as he had painted them.

The sound of raised voices reached them, carrying from the living room into the kitchen. Della glanced at Miriam, worried by the angry words, fearing that she was the cause. But Miriam paid no attention to her as she tried to hear what the argument was about. The voices became more heated, then dropped off, leaving only Simon's to be heard. The words were indistinct, blurred by the wall between the two rooms.

"Is it me?" Della asked nervously.

"No," Miriam assured her, suddenly realizing what the row was about; she had warned Jonathan that Simon would not take kindly to his purchases being checked. "It's probably the business. They both get very heated up about it, but it usually boils down to nothing. Don't worry, Della. You'll get used to it."

Miriam's calm words did nothing to ease Della's concern. "Are you mad at Simon for marrying me?" she asked quietly.

"Not at all. If you and Simon are in love, that's all that matters." Miriam fell silent for a long moment; then, "It would have been nice, though, to have had a wedding to go to, although it would have had to wait for a while because of his grandfather's death."

Della lapsed into silence, thinking about the unfortunate timing of the runaway wedding; the old man's death had dampened everything. The return to New York and meeting the family had been anticlimactic, finished almost before it had started. And Simon was obviously having difficulties with his father over the business; but did they have to shout at each other like enemies, not father and son?

Although the words of the argument were indistinct, there could be no mistake about recognizing the ringing sound of the slap. Both women jerked upright, frightened by the clear report. Della began to stand, until she felt Miriam's restraining hand on her arm.

"Let them be," she advised. "It's private."

Looking into the older woman's face, Della recognized the sincerity behind the request. She sat down again, waiting for the argument in the living room to cease, knowing that the blow signified the climax.

One minute later, Simon walked unsteadily out of the living room and entered the kitchen. His left cheek, where Jonathan had hit him, was still red, the blurred outline of finger marks standing out sharply on the skin.

"What was that all about?" Miriam asked.

"He's a bit touchy today." Remembering Della's presence, he added quickly, "I jumped on a bad nerve. Maybe I should have gone easier, seeing the circumstances."

Watching the mother-son relationship, Della realized that Simon's affection toward Miriam was much deeper than toward his father, if any existed in that direction at all. Jonathan represented too much power for Simon to handle; she had sensed it earlier in the living room. Jonathan's presence had filled the room, completely overpowering and dominating lesser personalities around him.

She waited patiently while Simon continued talking to his mother glossing over the cause of the argument, making no mention of the slap. Finally she tugged at his sleeve till he looked around.

"Remember me?" she asked, forcing a smile on her face. "I came here with you."

After Della and Simon had left to return to the city, Jonathan resumed his position on the *shivah* chair, scratching his beard from time to time, annoyed by the discomfort it brought.

Miriam entered the room, pulled up a footstool and sat down beside him. "Was that row really necessary?" she asked. "In front of the girl as well."

Jonathan continued to scratch his beard as he replied. "Why don't you ask that imbecile if he had to be so stupid and uncaring about anybody else's feelings? That's a much better question."

Miriam remembered the sound of the slap and how it had shocked both herself and Della. "You never lifted a hand to either of them before. Why now?"

"Maybe I should have done it years ago." Jonathan's voice was tired, echoing the mental fatigue he felt. "He called Jacob a ranting old fool. I'm sitting on this chair in mourning for my father, and your son comes up with a line like that. What did you expect me to do?"

There was no possible answer. And Miriam also saw that there was no point in dwelling on the subject. "What do you think of your new daughter-in-law?"

Jonathan let out a short, humorless laugh. "From the few seconds I spent with her, she looked fine. You tell me. You spoke to her."

"She seemed like a very sweet girl," Miriam said. "Very gentle, very quiet."

Jonathan felt a wave of self-disgust creeping over him. Now, alone with Miriam, he was ashamed of the scene that had taken place. "I'm going out for a walk," he muttered, standing up and heading toward the door. "See you later."

The front door slammed behind Jonathan as he trudged up the path toward the road. Miriam rose and stood by the window, watching his overshoes kicking up the snow as he reached the sidewalk. Her eyes followed as he walked away from the house, seeing him stick the cigar into the side of his mouth and light it, puffing the smoke angrily into the cold winter air. With a deep sigh, she sat down on the footstool, closing her eyes, thinking about Simon and his new wife, and about Jonathan going out into the cold to sneak a smoke.

What's happening to us? she wondered. A week ago, everything was fine, just the occasional argument at the office. Now it's all gone berserk. Jacob's dead, Simon's married, and Jonathan's acting like a little boy.

# 14

Sleep refused to come. Brian had been in bed for more than two hours and still felt wide awake. Agitated, he turned over yet again seeking a comfortable position, but nothing seemed to help. His mind was too busy reviewing problems, trying to find solutions, dissecting them, then starting all over again as no realistic answers appeared.

He turned on the bedside lamp and glanced disgustedly at the clock radio. Two-thirty. Jesus, he thought, I've got to be up in five hours. I'll be like walking death tomorrow. Nevertheless he arose, slipped his feet into the shower shoes which served as slippers and padded across the carpet into the hall. Light showed under Thelma's door, and he could hear sounds of activity from within. He thought of knocking to learn why she could not sleep, but he was honest enough to know that he did not really care. If she had insomnia on top of everything else, that was her problem, and she could sort it out for herself. He had had more than enough of her; with all the booze she had been putting away, she should be out like a light.

In the kitchen, Brian poured some milk into a saucepan, standing over the stove while it warmed. Taking the drink to the table, he sat down, picking up a magazine to read while he drank. He heard the door to Thelma's room open but paid scant attention to the sound. Only when she walked into the kitchen and stood over him did he look up.

Her appearance shocked him more than he thought possible. The red hair was bedraggled and her eyes bloodshot. In a moment of bizarre humor, they reminded Brian of the American flag—red, white and blue. The light brown dressing gown she wore did nothing to hide the uncontrolled slouch of her body, so different from the erect posture of which she had once been justifiably proud.

"I heard you walking around," she began.

"So?" Brian was not inclined to start a conversation. All he wanted to do was drink the warm milk in the hope that it had a soporific effect on his system.

With a deep, wheezing sigh, Thelma sat opposite him, slumping forward against the edge of the table. On closer inspection, Brian could see that she had been crying, but no sympathy stirred within him. He had gone through enough emotional traumas since moving to New York; hardly a day had passed without some flash of the friction between himself and Thelma. She had been unable to write, claiming that the city affected her. Because of this, they had been living on his salary alone, which, although more than ample, took away any form of independence from Thelma, something she had always boasted about. Now she had to depend on him for everything, and it was even more galling when he lectured her about drinking while giving her housekeeping money which he knew would be used for just such a purpose.

"Can't we talk?" she asked, her voice choked with sobs. "Can't we speak to each other just once without having a fight?"

Brian sipped the milk, deliberately taking his time before replying. "What about? The weather? The New York Rangers? Crime on the subways? Give me a subject."

"About us," she said, ignoring his sarcasm. "Or are you too blind to see that something's happening, that our marriage isn't as rosy as it should be?"

"Was it ever rosy?" he asked softly. "Did we ever have anything approaching a perfect marriage?"

She stared at him for five seconds, holding his eyes, trying to see behind them. "Maybe it wasn't. But we're living in purgatory right now. And it's your fault as much as mine."

Brian dropped his eyes to the glass, seeing the thin film of skin which was forming on top of the milk. When he looked across the table again, Thelma was still staring at him.

"What would your pulp book characters do about it?" he asked. "Or don't they ever get into situations like this?"

"We're not talking about fiction," she said. "We're talking about us, you and me, why it's all gone wrong."

"I never asked you to become the town drunk," Brian said. There was no malice in his voice, no emotion at all.

"And I never asked to come to this God-forsaken place," she snapped back. "I had a career where I was, friends, everything. Here I've got nothing. God knows how much I've tried to write while I've been here, but nothing comes together, nothing works."

Brian felt his tiredness change to anger, and he pushed away the glass, slopping milk onto the Formica tabletop. "What the hell do you want me to do?" he snarled. "My life is here now, in New York. I've forgotten Chicago ever existed. I'm a vice-president of one of the top clothing companies in the United States. I've adjusted. Why can't you?"

"You bastard," Thelma whispered viciously. "You rotten bastard. Of course you've adjusted. You had to because your work's here. You know people here. But everything of mine is back in Chicago, everything I hold dear."

There was an inference in the sentence and Brian grabbed it. "Which means you don't classify me as something you hold dear. Go on, say it out loud."

"All right. I'll say it. I want to go back to Chicago, and I want a divorce from you. Now you've heard it."

"On what grounds?"

"Grounds?" She gave a short, brittle laugh. "You're talking about grounds? How about mental cruelty for openers?"

Brian's face split into a grin as he listened to his wife's words. He picked up the glass and, with a contrived air of casualness, carried it to the sink, where he washed it, rinsing it thoroughly, taking his time, every movement measured. When he had replaced the glass in the cupboard, carefully dried, he picked up a sponge and began to wipe the spilled milk from the table.

"Mental cruelty," he repeated lightly to Thelma, who had remained sitting, following his actions with her eyes. "You've been reading too much of your own garbage, Thelma. This isn't going to be decided in a penny dreadful. It's going to be decided right here, right now." The mirth fell away from his face and his voice took on a hard, grating tone.

"I'll tell you what divorce grounds are, Thelma. They're having a wife who's a stinking drunk if not a downright alcoholic; a wife who hasn't been to bed with her husband since before Noah set sail in his little wooden boat; a wife tries to stand in the way of her husband making a success out of life. That's what you call grounds for a divorce, Thelma. If anybody brings the action, it'll be me. And right now it seems like a damned good idea."

He strode away, leaving her in the kitchen, head resting on her clenched fists as she sobbed quietly. Back in his own room, Brian picked up the book from the bedside table and began to read, knowing he would not fall asleep.

Using a small part of his concentration, he listened to the sounds of Thelma leaving the kitchen and returning to her room. Through the separating wall he thought he heard her crying, but he could not be certain.

Neither could he care; he had suffered quite enough.

Gerald and Marilyn Chesterton were also awake, but the state was of their own choosing. They lay snuggled together, Gerald's left arm beneath Marilyn's neck, holding her head to his shoulder, his lips feeling the soft caress of her hair.

"What's she like?" Marilyn whispered.

"Who?" Gerald asked dreamily. "Simon's wife?"

"Yes. Della." Marilyn's voice became less distinct as she burrowed deeper into her husband's shoulder.

"Don't know. I've only heard from my mother." He had also heard about the argument between his father and Simon, but declined to mention it.

"I think we should ask them over," Marilyn suggested. "We've got to meet her sometime, so it might as well be at our instigation. Show her she's welcome."

"All right. You figure out the best night for yourself, and I'll speak to Simon about it," Gerald said.

The ash-blond hair brushed across his face as Marilyn raised herself up to look at him. He was certain that his wife's clear blue eyes were luminous; they seemed to glow at him in the dark.

"Men," she said teasingly. "That's not the way to go about it, you asking Simon."

Feeling himself becoming lost in the steady, tranquil gaze, Gerald murmured, "Why not?"

"Because you've never asked him before. If you can find out the name of Della's agency, I'll call her up and invite them both over for dinner one night."

With Marilyn's blue eyes taking complete control of him, Gerald agreed, happy to be relieved of the responsibility of asking his brother. He clasped his hands behind Marilyn's neck and pulled her down on top of him, feeling the electric tingle as their bodies joined.

"Do whatever you like," he said.

# 15

The fresh smell of menthol assailed Jonathan's nostrils as he rubbed the shaving cream vigorously into his face, feeling the seven-day beard begin to soften under his fingertips as he worked in the foam. Rinsing his hands, he picked up the safety razor and began to shave, using an upward stroke, wincing as the blade met resistance.

For a few seconds, as he had gazed into the mirror before applying the cream, he had considered leaving the beard to grow. It had itched maddeningly during the first three days, but after a week he had become accustomed to its feel. Staring at the reflection, he thought the heavy beard quite suited him; it was liberally flecked with gray, as was his hair these days, but he felt it lent a certain dignity to his appearance. Miriam, however, would never approve. With that in mind he regretfully began to rub the cream into his face.

Thank God the *shivah* was over. The small chair had been returned to the synagogue offices to await the next unfortunate who needed it. No matter how fervent his desire to show respect for his dead father, Jonathan had been at his wit's end as the days had passed with nothing to do but read and greet well-meaning visitors. Additionally he regretted deeply the argument with Simon, realizing the impression it must have made on Della. He knew that he could not blame the period of enforced inactivity for his action in striking Simon. He thought about apologizing, but the best course seemed to be to forget the episode completely. Bringing it all up again, even in the form of an apology, would serve no useful purpose.

As he shaved, watching the heavy stubble come off on the razor blade, his mind meandered back to Della. He had known other families where the son had married a gentile girl and had often wondered what his own reaction would be should either Gerald or Simon do the same thing. Well, now he knew. He accepted the situation with the sincere hope that Simon and Della made a success of their partnership. True, there was some validity in the old traditions, not that he had ever observed them strictly; three times a year in the synagogue kept him going for all the other times he missed. As long as Della was a nice girl—and she certainly seemed to be that—he could not care less what religion she was.

Rinsing the remainder of the cream from his face, Jonathan studied his skin to see if he had missed any patches of hair. Satisfied, he dried himself, then returned to the bedroom to dress, choosing a dark gray, striped suit for his first day back at the office. Remembering the weather, he took a heavy Crombie topcoat from the closet, draping it over his arm as he walked downstairs.

Breakfast—two pieces of toast and marmalade and a cup of coffee— was waiting for him on the table, placed there by Miriam, who was busying herself at the sink.

"Glad to be going back?" she asked.

"You can say that again." He tasted the coffee, grimacing because it was unsugared, another misery which Miriam subjected him to in the interests of his health. "I want to see if we've got any stores left at all."

Miriam joined him at the table, picking up her own cup. "The business isn't that bad, and you know it. The stores will have carried on while you were away."

"Maybe," Jonathan said grudgingly. "Mainly I want to see how Brian's getting on with his involvement in the Mr. Simon operation. We've got a bundle tied up in that, and we're getting nowhere near a fair return on our money." He looked up quickly from the table, catching Miriam in a candid stare. "No matter what you say about Simon, he's not a retailer. That's the simple truth, Miriam. He hasn't got a retailer's gut feeling for the market."

"But he's getting better," Miriam said earnestly.

Jonathan choked on the coffee, spluttering helplessly. He took a napkin and wiped his mouth, looking in disgust at his tie, where the coffee had left two small stains. "Miriam, for God's sake! He couldn't get any worse. Believe me, I'm thankful he got married. Maybe this girl will help straighten him out."

Finishing breakfast, he stood up, ready to leave. Bending over Miriam, he kissed her on the lips, still taking enormous delight in such a simple action after all the years of marriage. Her response was to run her hands along his cheeks, feeling the smooth skin appreciatively.

"Go easy on him," she whispered. "He's just not as clever as you are."

Jonathan snorted. "You give me honors I don't deserve. I'm not that clever. If I was, we'd only have had Gerald and called it quits right there." He walked out of the kitchen quickly. "See you this evening," he called from the hall, opening the front door.

"Don't forget to change your tie," Miriam called after him. "You can't go in with breakfast all over it."

Jonathan clapped a hand to his forehead. He let the front door swing closed and went upstairs, pulling the stained tie off as he went.

They had argued again during the night, and the memory left a bitter taste in Brian's mouth. He did not bother making breakfast, knowing he could eat on the way to the office. He just dressed and left the apartment, feeling tired from another sleepless night, unable to relax while the recollection of the most recent argument with Thelma plagued him.

He had returned to the apartment past nine the night before, his head whirling after yet another day of going over purchases with Simon. And Simon was not proving to be much help either; he was going out of his way to complicate matters, forcing Brian to drag information out of him instead of volunteering it. As every small piece of the puzzle fell into place, it became increasingly obvious to Brian that Jonathan had good cause to be worried. The whole ordering procedure seemed like a bad joke, as if Simon had accepted merchandise from any supplier who had the courtesy to knock on the office door and introduce himself. The man was even ordering qualities of clothing which would not have been used in the four Gellenbaum stores when they had acted as clearance outlets for Chestertons.

As a beginning, Brian had ordered Simon to stop delivery on whatever merchandise he could. Tell the suppliers whatever he liked, but just stop delivery. Then, when Jonathan returned, Brian would try to find a permanent solution to the situation.

Burdened by these problems, he had arrived home hungry and tired. He had found Thelma in tears, although she always seemed to be in tears these days, it seemed to Brian. She was crying and as drunk as he had ever seen her—crying over her inability to find her feet in New York, drunk because she could think of nothing else to do.

More from a desire to clean up the apartment than from genuine anxiety about his wife, Brian had picked up Thelma and carried her to her room, putting her gently on the bed so she could sleep it off. This she did for two hours, but as he relaxed in front of the television set watching the main news program, she had reappeared, demanding again that he give her a divorce and allow her to return to Chicago.

Still staring at the television program, Brian had yelled back, "Go to Chicago, for Christ's sake! Do whatever you damn well want to do, but just leave me alone!"

"I don't have the money," she wailed.

"What about all the money you made on those crap books? Didn't they ever pay anything? Of did you do them for love?"

"It's in a savings bank in Chicago."

Angrily he had thrust a hand into his hip pocket and pulled out his billfold, throwing it at her, feeling a savage sense of satisfaction as the small leather case struck her in the mouth. She had staggered back two paces, more from shock than from pain. Then she had looked down at the billfold, her eyes narrowing slyly as she recognized it. Picking it up, she had counted the money inside, wetting her fingers with her tongue to separate the bills.

Brian knew there was more than three hundred dollars in the billfold, and he waited to see what Thelma would do with the money. When she dropped the billfold onto the floor and left the room, he retrieved it, seeing the two ten-dollar bills which remained. With a feeling of resignation, he had stuffed the billfold back into his hip pocket, wondering if she would be true to her word and use the money to return to Chicago, or whether she would stock up the liquor cabinet like it had never been stocked up before.

Stopping at the small restaurant on the same block as the store, Brian ordered scrambled eggs and a glass of milk, reading the newspaper while he waited. He ate quickly, left the newspaper on the counter top and walked to the office, feeling the blood begin to move in his veins.

Jonathan was in already and had left a message that he wanted the meeting to begin at ten sharp. Brian sorted through his mail, dictating a cursory reply to a supplier who was looking for business and whom he would never dream of using. Simon might, he thought wryly. Then he prepared a series of memoranda to be sent to all Chestertons and Mr. Simon stores, setting out—for what he felt was the millionth time—the correct procedure for reordering merchandise from the company's distribution center.

When he had taken over the general merchandise manager slot from Simon, Brian had found great gaps in the communication between Head Office and the stores, a situation which was aggravated by the enormous distances involved in some cases. Subsequently he had spent a great deal of time and effort in trying to rectify the situation. But old habits were hard to break, especially when some of the stores were three thousand miles removed from Head Office and functioned with a large degree of autonomy. Orders for resupply continued to arrived in New York on anything but the right forms, and it took the merchandise control department extra hours to sort out the confusion. Even the Chestertons house magazine, *Store Talk*—a four-page monthly newsletter which Brian had advocated as an important communication tool—had been watered down after the first two issues because the majority of salesmen found the simple stories and features to be too highbrow for their tastes. During his years in the Chicago store and as a regional manager, Brian had never realized that to get a message across to the average store salesperson meant believing he had a mental age of fourteen and writing down to that level. The journalist hired by the company to produce the magazine had quit in a huff of righteous indignation after being requested to write so that fourteen-year-olds could understand. Brian could not find it in himself to blame the man for resigning.

Finally he was ready for the meeting. With copies of the orders Simon had made for the boutiques—his own notations on cancellation marked clearly on them—he walked into the boardroom ready for another round of those endless meetings. As if he did not have enough troubles on his plate already, he thought wearily.

Simon was seated in his customary spot, a steaming mug of coffee in front of him. Brian sat down at the opposite end of the table from Jonathan, realizing as he did so that he was occupying the seat which had been kept traditionally for Jacob should he choose to attend the meetings. He began to stand again, but Jonathan waved at him to stay where he was.

"Don't bother moving," he said, sensing Brian's predicament. "We don't believe in ghosts around here."

Gerald arrived a minute later, leaving the door slightly ajar behind him. Jonathan noticed, pointing to it. "Better close it tight," he suggested. "That way we can shout and scream at each other in peace and quiet."

Not knowing of Brian's findings on the Mr. Simon operation, Gerald grinned uncertainly. "Is that likely?"

"Anything's likely," Jonathan replied gruffly.

While Simon remained strangely quiet, staring morosely at the mug of coffee, Brian opened the meeting, covering the changes he had made in the ordering. As he mentioned each item, he elaborated on the measures taken, passing photostats of the orders to Jonathan so he could check them. An hour later, they had finished; the pile of cancelled orders in front of Jonathan was more than three inches high.

"How much will it cost us to get rid of the garbage you couldn't stop?" Jonathan asked quietly, still stunned by the results of Brian's investigation.

"About forty thousand dollars spread across the four Mr. Simon shops already open and orders taken from the two we plan to open this month." Brian consulted his figures again before continuing. "That's rough, of course, because we won't know the exact figure till we can find out where we can shift the junk we couldn't stop and how much we'll get for it."

Jonathan swivelled in his seat. "Forty thousand dollars, Simon," he whispered. "That's your wedding present from all of us. Enjoy it."

Simon shot to his feet, red in the face, embarrassed at having the whole thing dragged out like so much dirty linen—and furious. As he opened his mouth to speak, Jonathan roared at him to sit down, the sound reverberating around the boardroom like a clap of thunder, stunning the other three men. Simon dropped down, his hands feeling shakily for the chair, no longer certain it was there.

"That's better," said Jonathan, reverting to his normal voice. "I am now going to read the riot act, and it will benefit you to listen very carefully to every word." He leaned across the table, sticking his chin out at Simon.

"You will continue to concern yourself with the Mr. Simon operation. Ostensibly you will remain in the position of general manger, seeing suppliers, running the show. As far as anybody outside this company is concerned, nothing has changed. But you will not order one cent's worth of merchandise without first clearing it through Brian. You keep telling me about how much you know, how the young market is your market and only you can see what's happening. Now let me tell you something. I don't think you have the faintest clue about the young market; you can't tell it from a fish market. You don't know how to buy for the boutiques any more than you knew how to buy for Chestertons. And even if you had the right merchandise at the right price, I'm certain you wouldn't know how to go about selling it. Get the picture?" He waited for Simon to nod weakly.

"Good. As far as staffing your shops is concerned, Gerald will look after that. Any staff problems you have, refer them to him. He will have complete control over the operations side. You'll still have a vote at the meetings, and you still hold a seat on the main Chestertons board. But you have no power to act independently. Do you understand that? And I want a straightforward answer without any of your synthetic rages. We've all had them up to here."

Slowly, deflated, his ego squashed, Simon nodded in agreement. Jonathan looked from Brian to Gerald, staring at each man, registering their expressions, knowing they agreed with him wholeheartedly.

"Good," he said. "Now we all know exactly where we stand."

While Gerald sat in his office thinking about the scene he had just witnessed, another stage in his brother's humiliation—or was it education?—his wife was calling Simon's to arrange a dinner date. The first words, as always between two people who have never met, were tentative, but the feeling of wariness soon dissolved.

"You're a part of the family now," Marilyn said. "We'd like you to come over to get the chance to meet you. After all," she added brightly, "if we don't know you, how can we possibly talk about you behind your back?"

Della laughed into the phone. "I'm not sure if you're joking when you say that. Seriously, I'd love to meet you and Gerald. Simon's mentioned you all, and like you said, I'm family now. When's a good date for you?"

Marilyn looked at the pages of her diary, open in front of her on the telephone table. "How about Wednesday of next week? I've got a tennis session in the afternoon, so I should be tired enough in the evening not to talk too much. Okay by you?"

"That sounds fine," Della replied. "But you'd better let me clear it with Simon first, although I'm sure I can get around him. He'll just have to leave the office early for once, that's all."

Without thinking, Marilyn rolled her eyes upwards as she heard Della's remark. Oh my God, she thought. What's he been telling her? Nevertheless, she said nothing about the Simon she knew; that was for Della herself to learn.

"Unless I hear from you to the contrary, Della, we'll make it for Wednesday next week, about seven. Look forward to seeing you then." She pressed the receiver rest lightly, clearing the line, then dialled Gerald's office number.

"Guess what?"

"No surprises, Marilyn," Gerald pleaded. "We get too many around here of late."

"Della and Simon are coming over here next Wednesday..." Marilyn drew the sentence out, "...if she can get him to leave the office early for once." She waited, delighted to hear Gerald chuckle at the other end of the line. "Beautiful, isn't it?"

"I think she means if he leaves the track early enough," Gerald said, still laughing. "How did you get on with her?"

"Nice enough to speak to. Maybe opposites really attract."

"We'll see," Gerald said dubiously. His other line rang and he answered it, asking the caller to hold. "I have to go, Marilyn. I've got another call on hold, and I've got to make a report on staffing recommendations for the Belsize stores. I'll give you a call before I leave the office." He blew a kiss into the mouthpiece and hung up, turning his attention to the other line.

Marilyn continued to sit by the telephone, wondering who else she could speak to while the baby was asleep. Nobody worthwhile, she decided finally. Life seemed very tedious to her, especially in winter when she could not get out that easily.

Ah well, she dreamed, roll on the next tennis lesson. At least Stan Jarvis's brashness relieved the monotony for a while.

After the Mr. Simon meeting finished, Brian stayed behind with Jonathan, wanting to talk more about the changes he had instigated.

"Do you think Simon will go along with your proposals?" he asked Jonathan.

"I don't remember making any proposals," Jonathan replied. "I ordered him to go along."

"What if he doesn't?"

Jonathan considered the possibility. "My son or not, he'll be in a bind. I'll be honest with you, Brian. Sometimes, usually about once a day, I wish to hell he wasn't my son. Then I could throw him out without the slightest pang of conscience and let him go plague somebody else with his crazy ideas of retailing. But enough of that." He began to search through his desk drawer, coming up with a red, white and blue folder which he held triumphantly in the air. "What are you doing at the end of February?"

The end of February? That was seven weeks in the future, and Brian was living a day-to-day existence, what with the challenges in the office and trouble at home. Who ever had time to plan a month in advance?

"What's happening then?" he asked.

Jonathan tossed the folder across the desk. "Read it yourself. I thought you might be interested in the trip."

Brian scanned through the folder, seeing an advertisement for a week-long men's and boys' clothing exhibition in England.

"What do you reckon?" Jonathan asked. "Is it worth the plane fare?"

Brian studied the folder more closely, taking note of the impressively large number of exhibitors, both British and overseas manufacturers. "Have we ever gone before?"

"No. But that doesn't mean we shouldn't go now. Those Europeans can still show us colonials a thing or two."

"We've already got Viscenzi," Brian countered.

Jonathan waved the argument aside. "That's for one thing and one thing only. Look, the pound's cheap these days, so let's go see what these limeys have. It'll give us the chance to get out of New York for a few days." He looked hard at Brian before continuing.

"From what I've seen of you lately, you look like you could do with a break from the action."

The bluntness of the statement surprised Brian. He looked up sharply, forgetting all about the proposed trip to England. "What makes you say a thing like that?" he asked, trying to read something in Jonathan's face.

"Who are you trying to kid?" Jonathan came back. "For the past few weeks you've been running around like you've got ants in your pants. It can't be just trying to clear up Simon's mess. There's got to be something else that's bothering you."

Brian remained silent, wrapped up in his own thoughts, wondering how much, if anything, he could tell Jonathan. He decided to be completely frank; if he could share the problem, perhaps he could find the solution which had so far eluded him. "How about a wife who can't or won't adjust to New York and keeps looking for the answer in a bottle?"

No surprise showed on Jonathan's face. He had guessed something was wrong since that afternoon when Brian had returned from home for his first meeting in a vice-presidential capacity.

"Have you tried talking about it?"

"Very often—and in very loud voices," Brian replied with grim humor.

"You miss Chicago?"

"I'd be a liar if I said I didn't. But I make my home where my work is. It's a sacrifice, but a worthwhile one."

"Your wife obviously doesn't think so," Jonathan said. "What was your marriage like before you came here?" Seeing Brian hesitate, he added, "Be honest about it."

"It was a marriage. Nothing more, nothing less," Brian replied. "About the same as a million others, I guess. We lived together."

Jonathan's face contained a trace of sadness as he listened. "I must be a lucky guy," he admitted. "Same goes for Gerald. I don't think I've ever seen two people more in love than Gerald and Marilyn. Simon? Well..." He gestured helplessly. "We'll have to find out about that as time goes by. He's got to be good at something, so it may as well be marriage. But what do you plan to do?"

Brian's voice was firm. "Stay right here."

"What about Thelma?"

The look on Brian's face made his words superfluous. "She can do whatever she likes. I've had enough."

Jonathan stood up and made to leave the boardroom, patting Brian gently on the shoulder as he passed. "Think about it," he advised the younger man. "It's a big step. Make sure you don't fall flat on your face while you're making it."

Brian remained in the boardroom for another ten minutes. He stared at the chair where Jonathan had been sitting, envying the man for his happy union, knowing that his own had never been, could never be the same way. He thought over his reasons for unburdening himself to Jonathan. The need to confess? Perhaps. But why to Jonathan? Gradually the question began to rephrase itself, making more sense as its new form became clearer. Why not to Jonathan? He was the person to whom Brian was closest; they had been together since almost the beginning of the Chestertons empire.

For the first time, Brian realized that there existed a very strong bond between himself and Jonathan, stronger perhaps because of their totally different backgrounds. Jonathan was first-generation American, whereas Brian's ancestry could be traced almost to the Mayflower. There was not a thing the two men possessed in common except the chain of stores which they had helped to build.

In a blinding moment of clarity, Brian became aware that Jonathan was the only real friend he had, the one person he could trust enough to reveal his inner soul to.

# 16

Feeling delighted that her game was improving with every coaching session, Marilyn Chesterton closed the press on her tennis racket and placed it carefully on a chair, waiting while Stan Jarvis brought two cold drinks from the clubhouse bar.

As she watched the coach help himself, Marilyn wondered why she had ever felt uneasy about him. Jarvis was a loafer, full of his own ego—nothing more. Anything which she had seen behind his casual if inquisitive conversation had been a product of her own imagination, she was certain of it. The man was harmless; it was even an entertaining diversion to play up to him occasionally, watching him react positively to a mild flirtation.

Jarvis returned to the table, offering her the choice of two glasses. "Is one poisoned?" she asked.

"Tempered with a potent aphrodisiac," he countered. The cheeky grin on his face made him seem like a small boy to Marilyn, reminding her of the children she had once taught.

She smiled mischievously in return. "If it's all the same to you, I'll take the one without."

"Damned if I can remember which is which now," he said, handing her one of the glasses. "Too bad you're giving up your coaching for a while," he said, sitting down, watching as she sipped the drink. "Your game's coming along quite well."

"Quite well?" Marilyn raised an eyebrow in astonishment. "That's praise from Olympus, indeed."

Jarvis shot her a questioning glance. "Praise from who?"

"I forgot," Marilyn said. "You're not interested in the classics; the only Olympus you're ever likely to hear of is the camera." She laughed as the quizzical expression remained etched on his face. "Six weeks off won't kill my game. I'll be back at the beginning of March to tune up for spring."

"Any reason for the break?" Jarvis asked. "Or can't you take what I'm handing out?"

The ambiguity of Jarvis's statement was evident to Marilyn; she decided to play along. "I can take anything you can hand out, Stan. Don't worry about it."

Jarvis grinned knowingly. "Don't be too sure of yourself."

"Down, boy," she warned him. "You're in a public place. If you must know, I'm just too busy during the next six weeks to come here. It's that simple. I'm not two-timing you by going to somebody else for lessons."

"Fair enough. But don't blame me if I have to charge you double when you come back. It'll take me extra time and effort to straighten your game out," Jarvis said. "We'll have to take it from the beginning all over again."

"We'll see," Marilyn said, standing up, reaching for her racket. "We'll see what happens in six weeks' time."

"Guess we will." But Jarvis was thinking ahead, and his thoughts were far removed from those of Marilyn, planning how he would make this snotty broad want him, get down on her knees and beg for him to take her. His ego had been bruised more and more as each of his cautious advances were rejected jokingly by Marilyn. Having her was assuming greater importance in his mind than a mere sex act; he had to prove something to himself.

The meeting between Della and her husband's brother and sister-in-law began as a success in the art of diplomacy. Before Simon and Della arrived, Marilyn had forced Gerald to promise that he would not mention the stores; he acquiesced reluctantly, with the rider that if Simon introduced the subject, he would feel obliged to reply.

Still seething inwardly about the restrictions placed on him by his father, Simon was unusually quiet during the meal, only picking at the beef Wellington that Marilyn had prepared specially for the occasion, leaving Della to break the ice by herself. Knowing that she was in advertising, Gerald steered the conversation toward that subject, showing a sincere interest in her professional opinion of the Chestertons advertising program.

"Are we making the right sort of presentation?" he asked. "Do you think it puts the Chestertons viewpoint across, or are we missing something?"

Della thought for a while before answering, looking quickly to Simon as if seeking guidance. "I think your image is ultraconservative, if you want the truth. All your ads ever seem to do is state over and over again that Chestertons is a top-quality men's clothing store, dedicated to dressing the man who wants to wear the best. Creatively, they do absolutely nothing for me." She stopped abruptly, looking crossly at Simon as he began to laugh. "What's so funny?"

"Chestertons is ultraconservative," he explained. He would have said more, but Gerald held up a hand.

"Let Della finish what she was saying."

Waiting a few seconds to ensure that Simon would not interrupt again, Della continued her critique. "I think your sales figures would take a big jump if you did special promotions on a regular basis, say once a month."

"I'm listening," Gerald said encouragingly.

Della smiled appreciatively at his interest. "Do a four-day promotion using one line of your merchandise. Cut fifteen percent off the price for four days only. Obviously you can't run the same ad right across the chain because of varying style preferences in different geographical areas. But you could do an East Coast promotional program, for example, using the same suits. Or maybe you could feature topcoats or sports coats. Who knows?"

"What part of the week would these four-day promotions cover?" Gerald asked.

"The ad would come out in the Wednesday paper and take in Wednesday, Thursday, Friday and Saturday," Della answered immediately. "The busiest section of the week."

"And what about our regular customers who buy a suit on Tuesday at the normal price and find it the following day being offered for fifteen percent off as a promotional special?" Gerald asked. "They're going to be wild at us, with good reason. We're going to lose them because they'll feel they've been ripped off. We built our business by being honest with our customers. Don't get me wrong, Della. I can see your reasoning all too clearly, but if we started pulling strokes like that, we'd lose a lot of friends."

Seeing an opportunity to make his own views known, Simon butted in, cutting Della off before she could reply to Gerald's argument. "Her ideas are too far ahead for you to understand, Gerald. Right now Chestertons is making a reasonably good profit from a traditional customer. But that sort of customer represents only a small part of the total market. If we used promotions like the one Della just suggested, we'd pull in a new brand of customer."

Gerald felt the light touch of Marilyn's hand on his arm, a clear warning gesture which he decided to ignore. He had kept to his side of the bargain; now that Simon had thrown down the gauntlet, he was going to pick it up.

"Your Mr. Simon shops are supposed to be pulling in a new brand of customer," he said accusingly. "What's happening there?" Gerald watched his twin brother intently, knowing that he was digging into an exposed nerve. Simon started slightly at the question, but Gerald found Della's reaction far more interesting.

"I thought those shops were doing very well," she said suspiciously, turning in her seat to look at Simon.

Knowing that he had just pulled the rug out from under Simon's feet, Gerald suddenly felt sorry for his brother. He realized only too well the way that Simon must have built himself up in Della's eyes and knew that he could destroy the façade completely if he chose to.

"They are," he told Della, answering for Simon, who was fidgeting uncomfortably. "But we think they could do even better. Under Simon they're moving in the right direction, but you know the way it is. Retailers are never satisfied. Give them one dollar and they're immediately grasping for two." As he spoke, he glanced sideways at Marilyn; the expression in her vivid blue eyes was clearly forbidding. He dropped the subject, reverting to the earlier discussion on Chestertons' advertising.

"Say we agreed to do one of these limited-time promotions, what else would you have us do?"

Forgetting the flash of tension which had arisen over Gerald's mention of the boutiques, Della quickly regained familiar ground.

"I'd insist that you hire our agency as your first step. We don't like to give away too many trade secrets for nothing." She waited till Gerald stopped laughing, then added, "Perhaps we should put together a presentation for Chestertons, just a few ideas to show you what could be done."

Gerald lifted both hands high in an attitude of surrender. "Wait just a minute! You came here tonight to meet us and have dinner, not to sell us your services. All I want to do is pick your brains—for nothing."

"All right. I would suggest that you move away from the institutional type of advertising which you have been doing. Have no more of these reminders to people that you're the best in whatever town you're located. Liven up your ads a little bit. Say something special each time. You won't lose your regular trade. You'll enlarge it." She looked around the room, letting her eyes eventually rest on the magazine rack by the color television console. "Do you have any copies of your recent ads over there?" she asked.

Gerald got up and walked to the rack, sorting through the newspapers and magazines till he found a sports coat advertisement which had run the previous week. He handed it to Della, who held it at arm's length staring at it.

"Well?" Gerald asked, puzzled by the lengthening silence as Della continued to study the ad. "What do you think of it?"

"Do you know what the biggest thing wrong with this advertisement is?" Della asked in return, turning the sheet around for everybody to see.

Gerald and Marilyn looked at the advertisement, uncomprehending. Simon paid little attention.

"Looks fine to me," Gerald said eventually. "It shows what it's supposed to show."

"Look at the model," Della prompted him. "He's wrong, completely wrong for this shot."

"But that's Fletcher Austin," Gerald said in amazement. "He's the top male model in New York City—in the entire United States. We've got some shots of him for the Viscenzi suits, and he looks terrific. Nobody else could have done it like him. He's the tops."

Della took little heed of Gerald's enthusiasm for the model. "Make that past tense," she advised. "Fletcher Austin was the top model in New York, but now he's way over the hill."

Gerald refused to believe what he was hearing. "That man typifies our Chestertons customer," he said slowly. "Whenever a man sees Fletcher Austin in an advertisement, he automatically thinks of us. We've been using him for ten years."

"And that's precisely the trouble," Della responded. "He's as stale as a week-old loaf of bread. Everybody else is dropping him like he's got bubonic plague, but Chestertons is hanging onto him like he's made of solid gold. Drop him for your own good. Get somebody younger. Otherwise you'll only get middle-aged men identifying with Chestertons. If that's what you want, fine, but I ought to tell you that the disposable income is in the hands of America's youth, not its middle-aged men."

While Marilyn served coffee, Gerald thought over Della's suggestions. He admitted that her comments contained positive ideas, but he was still dumbfounded that she could find fault with the company's choice of model. Although he had little to do with the twice-yearly advertising photography sessions, he had met Fletcher Austin several times and had always been impressed with both the person and his photographic image.

For as long as Gerald could remember, the Chestertons advertising had been dealt with by an old, established agency, a small company which believed the way to successfully promote a client's product was to keep pounding the same message into the public's collective brain. All that mattered was that the Chestertons name and its synonymity with top-quality men's clothing was kept in the forefront. Fletcher Austin had been the agency's choice of model, and Chestertons had always been happy enough with the results to keep the arrangement.

Gerald tried to remember if a survey had ever been conducted on the success of the advertising program. No, not to his knowledge. Advertising was looked upon by the company as something that, while necessary, was part of the business which did not require too much attention; it was not directly related to profit and was therefore relegated to the back seat, to be looked at when somebody had the time, or, better still, to be sent to an outside agency. Consequently, the decisions on what to run and whom to use had been left to the agency's discretion. No proper budget had ever been made out for it. Nobody really cared about it as long as the regular advertisements appeared. Now here was Della with ideas—possibly good ones—for revitalizing the whole program.

He finished his coffee, waiting for the others to follow suit, an idea forming. Then he spoke to Della.

"How would you like to make a presentation to Chestertons on behalf of your agency? I think we'd be very interested in hearing exactly what you have to offer."

The dinner party broke up just before midnight. Gerald held the front door open long enough to see his guests drive off in Della's yellow MG Midget; then he helped Marilyn to clean up, putting away the crockery as she passed it up to him from the dishwasher.

"Well?" she asked, handing him the final plate and pushing the dishwasher door closed with her foot. "Let's hear the expert opinion. What do you think of your sister-in-law?"

Gerald took the plate and looked at it reflectively. "I'm at a loss for words," he admitted.

"How come? Even I never make you lose the power of speech."

"She is a very bright girl," Gerald replied. "As shrewd as they come. What I can't figure out is what a girl like that sees in my brother. And, even stranger to my mind, what makes her marry him?"

Putting both arms around Gerald's neck, Marilyn hugged him tightly. Disregarding the plate he was still holding, she pressed her lips hard against his. "Maybe she married him for the same reason I married his brother—because I was in love with him."

Gerald disagreed. "No way. Nobody falls in love with Simon—nobody other than Simon."

# 17

While Jonathan slept soundly on the six-hour flight from Kennedy to London's Heathrow Airport, Brian Chambers remained wide awake, twisting and turning in the wide first-class seat every few minutes, listening disgruntledly to the rhythmic hum of the Boeing 747's engines. He wished fervently that he could fall asleep like Jonathan, but somehow rest evaded him; he knew he would be fit for nothing when they arrived in London at the beginning of a brand new day.

Already dawn was breaking. Brian could see the first glimmerings of light peeking shyly through the aircraft's ports no more than a few hours after he had watched the sun set into the gray, late February sky over New York.

As soon as the aircraft had reached cruising altitude and the seat belt signs had been switched off, Jonathan had downed two stiff Scotches and fallen asleep almost immediately, his face turned away from Brian, hands clasped across his stomach. Brian had tried the same technique, willing it to work for him as it had for Jonathan. But all the spirit seemed to do was sharpen his thought process, and whenever he thought, the subject was always Thelma.

Seven weeks had passed since he had made known his marital problems to Jonathan. Since that time, his relationship with Thelma had become even worse. It was now the rule rather than the exception to arrive home in the evening and find his wife sleeping after a day of heavy drinking. Her typewriter lay untouched, gathering a fine layer of dust where she had neglected to replace the protective plastic cover. Brian was certain that she never even made an attempt to enter the den. Any money he gave her seemed to go toward replenishing the stock of gin she kept; there was never any food in the house unless he bought it, even such basics as milk and bread. Frequently he wondered how she managed to survive without seeming to eat anything, but he remembered reading somewhere that alcoholics—had his wife really turned into an alcoholic?—got their calories from their drinking.

Because of the worsening situation at home, he had been spending more and more time at the office, which was just as well considering the amount of work that had to be done to set the Mr. Simon operation properly on its feet. That, at least, was seeing the light of day now; suppliers had been trimmed ruthlessly by Brian, and a realistic merchandise plan had been laid down which was being adhered to strictly.

Jonathan had never made any further mention of the domestic problem, but Brian knew that its effect on him was only too obvious. He realized that something would have to be done, and soon; otherwise Thelma would drag him down with her. Maybe he could think of a solution during the time in London.

He must have dozed off eventually, because he was surprised to find a stewardess tapping him on the shoulder, reminding him to fasten the seat belt, as they would be landing soon. Jonathan was awake already, an unlit cigar gripped firmly between his teeth, champing on it impatiently as the aircraft descended slowly over London preparatory to landing.

"All set for the big expedition?" Jonathan asked.

Brian shook his head to clear it. His mouth felt like a piece of dried, shrivelled leather as he worked his tongue around, trying to spread moisture. "I'd rather be home in bed," he muttered incoherently.

Jonathan grinned, switching the cigar from the left side of his mouth to the right with a practiced movement. "You're on vacation," he said jovially. "An all-expense-paid vacation, courtesy of Chestertons. Look happy about it."

Brian held a hand over his mouth to stifle a yawn. "Some vacation. Who else walks miles around an exhibition center when they're on vacation? Tell me that."

Affectionately Jonathan laid a beefy hand on Brian's shoulder. "Take my word for it, we're on vacation. If we see something we like, maybe we'll take a trial order. Otherwise we're here to enjoy ourselves. I reckon we deserve it, don't you?"

The 747 banked into its final approach, zeroing in on the runway, tires shrieking in protest as they bit into the concrete. Dimly Brian heard the sound of seat belts being unfastened and undid his own. His legs felt cramped as he stood up, reaching for his raincoat in the rack above the seat.

Clearance through immigration and customs was speedy, and soon he and Jonathan were on the airport bus heading into central London. A taxi took them from the terminal to the Hilton Hotel on Park Lane, where they checked in. While Jonathan chose to walk around the West End window shopping, Brian went to bed, needing to catch up on the missed sleep. He awoke just after noon, showered and dressed, then went into the hotel lobby. There was a message from Jonathan suggesting that they meet for dinner.

The following morning, the two men took a taxi to Earl's Court in west London where the exhibition was being held. Showing business cards to the security guard at the turnstile, they began to walk along the narrow aisles, stopping every now and then to inspect a display which attracted them. As they stopped by one stand, Jonathan suddenly felt himself clasped from behind by a powerful pair of arms, and a familiar voice echoed in his ears.

"Jonathan! What a wonderful surprise!"

He broke out of the grip and spun around to face Nino Viscenzi, a huge, delighted grin beginning as he recognized the Italian. "Nino! Great to see you. But what are you doing here?"

"The same as I do every year," Viscenzi replied. "I always spend the opening day here. It's an important exhibition, and I get the opportunity to discuss business and bump into friends like yourself."

"What's so great about opening day?" Jonathan asked.

"It's not busy. Take my advice, Jonathan. Stay well away from this place on Wednesday and Thursday afternoons. Many of the London shops have a half day then, and this hall"—he waved an all-encompassing arm— "is crawling with junior sales assistants who have no power to buy anything, but they manage to get in everyone's way. But you, this is a new step." A humorous glint appeared in Viscenzi's eyes. "Are you not satisfied with your European designer, and wish to look elsewhere?"

Jonathan's face wore a look of outraged innocence. "Nino, when you have the best there is, can you look for something better?"

Viscenzi clasped Jonathan fondly, embracing him. "Say no more. I know that you would never go behind my back. Tell me, how is the rest of your family? Miriam? Your sons? And Jacob, is he well?"

The Italian felt Jonathan stiffen as he mentioned the old man's name. "Is there something wrong with Jacob?" he asked quietly. "I want to know."

Jonathan's face reflected his sadness. "He died a few weeks ago."

Aghast at the news, Viscenzi dropped his hands from Jonathan and stepped back. "Died? How did it happen? Why did you not tell me?" He switched his gaze to Brian, who stood off to the side feeling awkward.

"What was there to tell?" Jonathan asked, unable to offer a better reply. "It was my father, a matter we kept in the family."

Viscenzi regarded Jonathan piercingly, the soft brown eyes turning hard, accusing. "I know he was your father. But he was also my friend. How could you not tell me?" There was outrage in Viscenzi's voice, a cry of pain that he had not been informed of Jacob's passing. Then, remembering that he was in a public place, he lowered his voice. "Forgive me. The sudden news is upsetting." He moved uncomfortably from one foot to the other, scuffing the toes of his shoes on the floor.

"I believe in your religion that one wishes a mourner long life, Jonathan."

"That's right." Jonathan could not get over the extent of Viscenzi's reaction.

"Then I wish you long life, my friend—a long happy one." He shook Jonathan's hand firmly, then turned to Brian, putting an arm around the shoulders of both men. "Now let us see what this exhibition has to offer us. I think you will agree that the steps being taken by some of the European manufacturers are very interesting."

The three men walked around the exhibition for more than three hours with Viscenzi introducing people he knew to Jonathan and Brian. As they drew abreast of a combined display which featured leading British manufacturers, Viscenzi pointed out one man, urging his companions to take notice.

"Like yourselves he is an American," Viscenzi said, "but he is also the best men's clothing manufacturer in Britain."

The combination aroused Jonathan's curiosity. "How come?"

"He has been living over here many years, during which time he has made his company's name on a word you will undoubtedly appreciate— quality, Jonathan. Nothing but the very best. This company uses only the finest quality British wool cloth, and even then they buy only enough to make perhaps six suits from each pattern in each size range. That way, with their business all over the world, the people who buy their suits are unlikely to meet themselves coming around the corner. On top of that, every one of the garments you see on their stand is made by hand, just like a proper tailor would do the job. I think you would do well to look at this exhibit, study the merchandise. Perhaps you would do even better to place an order, as long as it did not clash with an existing customer in the areas your stores cover. These people are highly principled. They will not sell to more than one store in the same area."

Jonathan continued to stare at the manufacturer, watching as he talked to a group of buyers visiting his stand, hearing Viscenzi's words like a commentary.

"There is not another men's clothing manufacturer in the world who makes ready-to-wear garments to that man's standards," Viscenzi continued. "They cost a lot more, but his company's successful history proves that men will pay gladly for superb quality."

Led by Viscenzi, Jonathan and Brian walked onto the stand. Viscenzi pulled a jacket off the rack and began pointing out the details. "I believe Jacob would have appreciated this more than you, Jonathan, but watch and you will learn."

He opened the sleeve buttons and rolled back the cuff, exposing the inner lining. "Surgeon's cuffs," he explained. "Did you ever see surgeon's cuffs on a ready-to-wear jacket before?"

Jonathan shook his head, turning to look at Brian. The younger man was fascinated by Viscenzi's knowledge and stood watching avidly.

"What use are they?" Brian asked.

"It goes back a long way," Viscenzi said. "When a doctor was out on a call and had to wash his hands, it saved him the time of taking off his jacket. He rolled up the sleeves instead. Call it a gimmick, if you will, but it is a gimmick of quality." He straightened the sleeve, doing up the buttons. "To use Jacob's words, these things are for the *mavin*, the connoisseur."

"From my father I would have expected such a word," Jonathan said. "How come you know it?"

"I've been involved in the clothing industry too long not to know such words. Here," he added, pushing some fabric samples at Jonathan, "feel that. That's what you call *ponem*, right?"

Jonathan ran the cloth through his fingers, feeling the luxurious softness of pure wool. Looking at the selvedge, the outer strip of cloth on which is woven the mill's name, he saw that it came from a company in Langholm, Scotland, an exclusive mill which dealt only with the top end of the top end. "That's *ponem*," he agreed. "A beautiful face." He passed the fabric samples to Brian, letting him assess the quality. "Another word for your clothing vocabulary. *Ponem* means face in Yiddish, but it's also used to describe the feel of a piece of cloth. The Wool Board, or whatever the hell they call it over here—International Wool Secretariat, I think—is right in everything it says. There's no substitute for the stuff, it's the finest fabric in the world."

Listening to Jonathan, Viscenzi nodded his head approvingly. "Now you know why I am so adamant that any range of clothing which bears my name must be all wool. Believe me, I have received handsome offers from chemical organizations to promote their synthetic fibers, but I will have nothing to do with them. For me, natural fibers are all there is for our end of the market. And now that you have been introduced to this company, are you thinking of ordering their merchandise?"

"Would you advise it?"

"I would advise anybody who is quality-conscious to buy this label," Viscenzi said. He took the fabric samples from Brian and replaced them on the display, nodding politely to the stand representative who was hovering nearby in case he could be of assistance. "But it might conflict with my suits in your stores, Jonathan. If you buy from this company—if they will sell to you, to be more correct—it is not something you market under the Chestertons label. It must be sold under its own name as an attraction to the customer—snob appeal if you like."

Jonathan took the point. "Any other British suit manufacturers you'd recommend?"

"For a Chestertons store?" Viscenzi mused. "The answer must, regrettably, be no. If you have to buy British for your level of operation, it must be this man or nothing at all. Everything else you can make just as well in your own factory."

"What about knitwear?" Brian asked.

"An altogether different story," Viscenzi replied. "There the British manufacturers have everybody beaten. Come, I will show you some firms I know well. Perhaps they are to your taste; we shall see."

By the time they returned to the Hilton that evening, Jonathan was almost asleep on his feet. He estimated that he had walked at least five miles during the day, following Nino Viscenzi—who had seemed indecently sprightly—up and down the aisles from exhibitor to exhibitor, continuing to marvel at the man's knowledge of the industry and the people he knew.

While they had been together during the day, they had gone over the changes taking place in New York, particularly the new responsibilities for the Mr. Simon operation. Viscenzi had listened attentively to the steps Brian had taken, approving overall but offering his own carefully thought-out ideas. As the day progressed, Brian began to wish that he had a notebook or, even better, a cassette tape recorder to take down the Italian's suggestions; they all seemed so relevant.

Jonathan and Brian ate dinner in the hotel, discussing the merchandise they had seen, debating which items would be suitable for their own market. Viscenzi had been unable to join them, having arranged to return to Paris that evening, but his presence remained with the two men.

"There goes somebody who really knows what the hell he's talking about," Jonathan said, as he and Brian mulled over the Italian's ideas.

"He knows more about clothing than any man I've met," Brian agreed. "Mind you, he seemed a bit upset when he heard about your father."

Jonathan chewed his food wistfully for a while. "He was well within his rights to bawl me out. He and my father got along like a house on fire. I'll be honest, it never occurred to me to let him know that Jacob had died. I should have. I know damned well I should have." He stopped talking long enough to fork another piece of meat into his mouth, swallowing it hurriedly, anxious to be finished with the meal. The jet lag, combined with the strenuous day, was catching up with him and he needed sleep in the worst possible way.

"You going out this evening?" he asked Brian.

"Thought I'd look around the shops, see what the displays are like. Maybe we can pinch a few ideas."

"Good idea. If I wasn't so tired I'd join you."

Brian declined the offer of an after-dinner brandy. He left the table, went up to his room to collect a raincoat as protection against the cool night air, and walked out of the hotel, heading left toward Piccadilly. He found little to interest him till he reached Piccadilly Circus, where Piccadilly joins Regent Street and Shaftesbury Avenue. There, the windows of the men's wear stores were more brightly lit and better displayed. He stopped in front of each one, taking note how the displays had been built around a single theme, a central piece of clothing which was expanded into accessories such as shirts, knitwear and shoes.

When he looked at his watch, he was surprised to find it was past nine-thirty. He began to look for a taxi to take him back to the hotel for a nightcap, followed by writing down whatever he could remember of the conversation with Viscenzi. Then he stopped. Why should he return to the hotel for a nightcap? What was wrong with all the public houses he had heard so much about?

Giving up the quest for a taxi, Brian put his hands in the pockets of his raincoat and strolled along Shaftesbury Avenue, swinging left toward Soho Square. He passed two public houses, hearing the sounds of raucous laughter from within. At the third he stopped, looking curiously at the frosted glass windows; it was quieter than the first two, emitting a muted hum of conversation which barely reached outside to the sidewalk. He pushed open the door and entered, walking across an almost threadbare rug to the highly polished bar, paying little attention to the other patrons.

The bartender, a balding man in his mid-fifties, with long silver sideburns, nodded a greeting, asking Brian what he would like. Brian surveyed the row of bottles behind the man, grateful to see familiar shapes and colors.

"Scotch on the rocks. Johnny Walker Black."

"Coming right up." The bartender turned his back on Brian and reached up for the half-empty bottle. While he poured, Brian looked around the pub. Two men sat on barstools to his right, one talking, the other staring moodily into his drink. There was a third man to Brian's left who returned the glance openly, as if judging him. When Brian swivelled completely on the stool to look at the people behind him, he felt the first pangs of apprehension, the emotions of a man who has stumbled unwittingly into a situation he does not fully understand. There were no women in the pub; all the patrons were men.

The surprise must have shown on his face as he turned back to the bar. "Everything all right, sir?" the bartender asked innocuously.

"Yes. Just fine, thanks," Brian muttered, taking a pound note from his pocket and pushing it across the bar. He added an equal amount of water to the drink, waiting while the bartender made change.

Sipping the Scotch, Brian felt the uncertainty drift away as the smooth whisky ran down his throat, warming him. He took another swallow and relaxed completely, making himself comfortable on the stool, an elbow on the bar's surface, hand propping up his chin. Somewhere behind, a jukebox burst into life, a soft ballad which Brian recognized as Sinatra's "Love's Been Good to Me"; he found it vaguely intriguing that a record which was at least seven years old was still featured. The gentle strains wafted across the public house easing his mood, a hypnotic sound which lulled his brain.

It was not until the record was finished that Brian realized he was no longer sitting alone at the bar. The man who had been to his left had moved next to him. The eerie sensation which had asserted itself when he had first realized there were no women in the pub returned to Brian. He put down the drink and turned to the man.

"Something I can do for you?" he asked abruptly.

The man looked back at him through sensitive brown eyes, long eyelashes curling slightly upward, almost feminine. Wavy brown hair covered his ears. Brian judged him to be in his late twenties, early thirties.

"Something I can do for you?" he repeated, annoyed that no answer had been forthcoming.

The man smiled, friendly, disarming. "We both seem to be alone. I thought you might be looking for some company."

Then it hit Brian—a savage realization which smashed into him like a physical force, stunning him, knocking the air out of his lungs, making him shake. *Of all the places in a city of ten million people, I have to pick a fags' nest to walk into. If Thelma could see me now, she'd bust a gut laughing.*

Ignoring the remaining Scotch and water in the glass, Brian pushed back from the bar and stood up, his legs trembling. "Sorry to disappoint you, but we're both suffering from a case of mistaken identity. I've got all the company I can use, thanks—my own." He walked toward the door, his stomach tied in knots, praying that his legs would not collapse before he made it, willing himself not to look back at the man, remembering the biblical story of Lot's wife, who had been transformed into a pillar of salt. Had he glanced over his shoulder, he would have seen the man crack a joke with the bartender before they both broke into laughter.

Outside, Brian sucked in the cold air, striving to contain his labored breathing. His eyes swam, and his heart pounded like a jackhammer, sending the blood flowing into his head with such force that it throbbed audibly. He started to walk toward Shaftesbury Avenue, then broke into a panic-stricken run, knocking into a young couple, spinning around, almost losing his balance as he sought to reach the bright lights ahead which beckoned to him like an oasis to a man wandering in the desert.

He heard the violent squeal of tires followed by a man's angry curse as he ran across the road; he was only vaguely aware of the car that had missed him by a yard, its tires screaming as the driver jammed on the brakes. Then he was on the other side of the street leaning his head against a shop front, feeling the cool stone ease his fever. Thoughts cascaded through his mind, tumbling into each other, none making any sense. A minute passed as he stood there, his heart slowing, vision becoming clearer as he regained control of himself. Straightening up, he saw a cruising taxi come down the street, the yellow for-hire sign glowing brightly in the black bodywork, its driver looking for a fare. Stepping toward the road, Brian hailed it. He climbed in, gave the driver instructions and folded up on the rear seat, unaware of the journey, conscious only of the biting need to get as far away as possible from that public house in Soho.

In his room at the Hilton, Brian sat on the edge of the bed, the raincoat still buttoned. Christ almighty, he thought, why did I have to pick a place like that? The question hammered away inside his head like a recurring nightmare, demanding an answer and getting none, becoming more insistent the longer it was denied.

And why couldn't I recognize it for what it was before I made myself good and comfortable?

Angry and disgusted with himself, he tore off the raincoat and slung it fiercely at a chair, watching disinterestedly as it slid to the floor in an untidy heap. He dropped back heavily onto the bed, feeling the mattress bounce, then sag beneath his weight. Realizing that he still had on his shoes, he kicked off one, then the other, hearing them crash to the floor.

Again his mind concentrated on the visit to the public house, associating it with an earlier occasion, an event a million years before which had slipped into the farthest recesses of his mind, never, he thought, to be resurrected—until now. A college caper, that's all it had been, nothing more. He could not even remember what the man had looked like, although the happenings of that night became clearer as he dragged them out from his subconscious.

It had been a stunt, a show of bravado by a group of college kids with nothing better to do with their time. They had all drunk too much that Saturday night and had gone into town looking for excitement. Interest had centered around a small bar which was frequented by a clique of homosexuals, outcasts in the war years who kept to themselves, only entering into any form of communication when approached. For a twenty-dollar payoff jointly put up by his friends, who had watched gleefully from the other side of the bar, Brian had become friendly with the group, inquisitive in a naive manner, going so far as to leave the bar with one of the men. When he returned to college on Monday morning, he was adamant that nothing had taken place; they gave him the twenty dollars anyway for providing entertainment. It was only Brian who knew the truth of that night. He had earned the money.

Self-reproach kept him company for many years as he struggled to form relationships with women, always uncertain, worrying how that one night might affect him. Then he had met Thelma, the first time in his life that he had participated in a steady union with a woman. After he had married her, he began to philosophize about the incident. Everybody has a brush with homosexuality, he had reasoned, safe in the knowledge that he was married and living a completely heterosexual life; it's part and parcel of growing up, experimenting.

And then tonight—accidentally choosing that one public house instead of all the others he could have entered. Had he subconsciously been trying to find such a meeting place because of his troubles with Thelma? Had he been unknowingly searching back to what he had once known before Thelma, using London because nobody knew him there?

The idea was ludicrous. He had walked out of the pub immediately on recognizing it for what it was.

Why the hell hadn't he stayed at the hotel with Jonathan, had a brandy or two and gone to bed?

# 18

Simon sifted through the advertisement layouts spread across his lap, picking out the ones which appealed to him, laying them carefully in a separate pile on the coffee table next to the reclining chair he occupied.

"This," he said, showing one to Della, who sat in an easy chair on the opposite side of the table. "This is the best of the bunch—if you can get those squares in my family to go along with it," he added as a qualifying statement.

She took the advertisement from her husband and sat studying it. The layout was simple—a blowup of a man wearing a three-piece suit, the Chestertons logo at the top of the page, and a bold heading which declared fifteen percent off the regular price for four days only. The space where the copy would go was filled in with wavy lines. It was one of the layouts she would use in her presentation the following day, when Jonathan and Brian returned to the office from their European trip.

"This is the theme I discussed with Gerald when we were there for dinner," Della recalled. "But he was worried about the Chestertons regular customers feeling ripped off if they should buy a suit for the regular price shortly before the promotion." She continued to stare at the layout, turning it this way and that as if she was not completely certain. Laying it aside finally, she glanced at the others which Simon still held.

"What do you think of the one where we've used women as a backdrop?" she asked. "It's lively. Should be a good eye-catcher to somebody in the market for buying a suit."

Picking up the layout to which she was referring, Simon held it away from himself, taking in the overall effect. "Fantastic," he enthused. "But with the Chestertons way of thinking you've got to learn to crawl before you're allowed to walk. My father or Gerald—even Brian, come to that—would take one look at this ad and jump ten feet into the air, doing a dance and screaming that the concept's pornographic and will scare away our customers." He laid down the layout, sparing it a final glance before turning his hazel eyes back to Della. "Better save it, though. It might come in useful for the Mr. Simon shops, or perhaps later for Chestertons, once we've got them warmed up to the idea of a full-scale advertising program with some creative copy for a change."

Della looked thoughtful for a moment, her lips pulled inward, biting down gently on them. "Didn't Gerald say that they were using a couple of girls for the Nino Viscenzi suit ads?" she asked.

"Viscenzi's a special case," Simon remarked sceptically. "My father thinks that greaseball's the best thing he's ever seen. Viscenzi suggested women for the ads, so my father's going against his ingrained conservatism to oblige him. But for advertising our regular Chestertons production, he'd have a pink fit about using a woman in the ad."

Della filed away the information for later use. "What do you think your father will do when he finds out that the agency has entrusted me to make the presentation?" she asked, dropping the layout she was holding onto the pile. "It seemed the obvious thing to do, but how do you think your father will view it? Bad ethics? And the remainder of the board?"

"You'll get my vote," Simon assured her confidently.

"What about the others?"

Simon looked up sharply, his eyes narrowing. "What about the others?" he repeated brusquely. "They're no more important than I am."

Although her associations with the company were still sparse, Della had learned enough to know that Simon's position was nowhere near as powerful as he had described it during the first heady days of their affair. She had seen the tension which had arisen during the dinner with Gerald and Marilyn. Gerald, admittedly, had backed down qualifying his earlier statement about the Mr. Simon shops not doing well, trying to make it sound like a joke. Della had been content to let it pass then, possibly because she had noticed how tactfully instrumental Marilyn had been in making Gerald change the subject. The opportunity which now presented itself to talk about the power structure within the company seemed far better.

"Simon," she began slowly, "if I'm going to be involved with Chestertons at a professional level, where the results of my work are directly affected by the proficiency of your company, I think it would benefit us both if I know who really holds the reins. It's not you; I'm awake enough to see that. So who is it?"

Remembering the lies he had told her, Simon thought carefully before answering, debating whether to continue the pretense and try to bluff it out or soften his line. He decided on the latter course.

"My father's the top man as president," he said. "Then come Gerald, myself, my mother and Brian, all equal partners as vice-presidents although our functions differ." He decided the lie sounded believable, a delusion which lasted for less than a second.

"Simon, don't give me that crap!" Della snapped, shocking him; he had never heard her use any form of profanity before. "I wasn't born yesterday. I know what's going on to some extent. I used to believe all those stories you told me because I had no reason to think otherwise. But now I have to know the truth."

Simon stood and walked to the window, staring out across the street at the lights of the building opposite. He could make out vague shadows moving behind the curtains in some of the rooms. "My father." He said it so quietly that Della had to ask him to repeat it. "My father. He runs the place like it's his own little family. He's got to make every decision. He won't delegate responsibility because he feels the company can't run without him at the helm. When my grandfather was alive, it was even worse because he kept running to the old man for advice." He swung around to face Della.

"Remember that first day we got back from San Francisco and I took you over there, when my father was sitting *shivah?* That row I had with him? That was about old Jacob."

"You could have chosen a better time," Della said. "Tact isn't one of your strong points."

Simon ignored the comment. "My father thinks that every person at Chestertons—Head Office, stores, everywhere—is his child and he's the big white father. And he treats us all accordingly."

"And the others put up with it?"

"Of course they do," Simon answered, feeling more confident that his new version of the Head Office situation was being accepted. "We all get paid well. It's only me who thinks that having individual initiative crushed for money isn't worth it. They're all looking at today while I'm looking into the future. And if Chestertons carries on the way it's going, there won't be a business to worry about in the future."

"Have you spoken to any of the others? Gerald? Brian?"

"Who could I speak to?" Simon asked scornfully. "They're all onto a good thing. Gerald can't see a thing past the end of his nose, and Brian thinks he owes my father everything in the world."

"Then be patient," Della advised him. "Sit back and wait for the right opportunity. If the sales graph begins to slide, and it's because of all the reasons you've stated, you'll get your chance. Your father's not going to want to stay in the business for the rest of his life. He'll want to turn over the reins eventually."

"Sure. To Gerald." Simon's voice was sour. "After my father, my brother's the squarest man I know."

"Then put your ideas across properly," Della said. "Look at what I'm doing with the advertising presentation and learn something. Think a project through from beginning to end, iron out all the snags before you try to sell it. That way you'll be successful, because you won't get caught out by questions you can't answer."

The Pan American jet bringing Jonathan and Brian back from England landed at Kennedy Airport just after eight in the evening. While Jonathan was driven to the house in Great Neck by the company chauffeur, Brian took a taxi into Manhattan, using the journey time to prepare himself for the next confrontation with Thelma. Each time he geared his thinking in that direction, however, the memory of that night in London blocked out everything.

The anger and self-loathing which had assailed him had disappeared, leaving in its place an inexplicable feeling of curiosity. Had time allowed, Brian believed he would have returned to the public house, drawn there as if by a magnet. But the opportunity to do so had not presented itself; Jonathan had made dinner appointments covering their two remaining nights, so a second visit had been out of the question.

It was beginning to rain when the taxi dropped him off in front of the apartment on Central Park West, large drops which fell with more intensity as each second passed. Brian thrust a bill at the driver, grabbed his one suitcase from the seat and ran inside the lobby of the building. Opening the main door, he caught the elevator to his own floor, covering the short distance to the apartment in a few strides. Praying that Thelma was awake or sober, hopefully both, he pressed the buzzer. There was no answer, so he pressed again, holding down the buzzer. Still no sound came from within the apartment. With a feeling of weariness, like a man embarking on a familiar but despised journey, Brian fitted his key in the lock and turned it. The door refused to budge. He checked the key, then tried again, pushing against the unyielding door until he realized that the safety lock was also on, something neither he nor Thelma used unless they left the apartment empty.

Learning that his wife was out, Brian became optimistic. Perhaps she had made a sudden return to sobriety. On the other hand, she could just be out buying more gin; the pessimistic mood returned immediately. He opened the door and stepped into the apartment, knowing it was useless to call Thelma's name but doing so.

Leaving the suitcase in the hallway, he walked through the apartment. Thelma's bed was made, and the dressing table was clean—too clean, he suddenly thought. None of the junk which usually littered it was in sight. Quickening his pace, he walked into the den. The red typewriter was gone. All that remained on the desk was a single sheet of yellow paper. Anxiously he picked it up and began to read. The message was simple and very much to the point:

> Brian...I have had more than enough. I think we both have. Your life is here, mine is in Chicago. Since making the decision to return, I haven't touched a drop. That little tidbit of information is in case you're interested. I couldn't care less whether we get a divorce or not. If you want one that badly, you go to the trouble.

He read the note again, seeing on the second perusal that Thelma had not even signed it. There was no date on it either, but he figured she had written it on Monday, the day after he had left for England—maybe even while he was in that public house. He caught himself quickly; why should he even connect the two events?

Letting the sheet of paper drop onto the desk top, he sat down in Thelma's chair, uncertain what emotion he should be experiencing. Should it be a sense of loss, or should he be jumping with glee? His problems were solved, but he felt nothing. Her departure meant that little to him. Idly he looked at the trash can, empty except for a screwed up ball of paper. Opening it, he read the cable from Thelma's savings and loan bank in Chicago, advising her of the transfer of money to a bank in New York City. So she had wired for the money to get back. She'd been that desperate. Brian shrugged; it's probably for the best, he thought. It'll solve all our difficulties.

Eventually he stood up and tossed the cable back into the trash can. Then he began to unpack the suitcase and prepare for a return to work.

Della was surprised by the ease with which she sold Jonathan on her advertising presentation. And with him went Gerald, his mother and Brian. The only disturbing point was seeing Simon hesitate before openly approving her proposals, unsure before he knew which way the others were going to vote.

Again, the only stumbling block to the four-day promotion theme was Gerald's concern about regular customers feeling cheated after buying an off-price special at the normal price. But Della was ready with a convincing argument which, she claimed, would expand the company's business and influence.

"Do you accept charge cards in your stores?" she asked blandly, knowing that Chestertons did.

The question, completely out of context with the general tone of the discussion, seemed to hang in the air. Della looked from one person to the other, finally stopping at Simon. "Well?" she asked. "Do you?"

Gerald took it up. "The major ones, just like any other large retail company. But what's this got to do with what we were talking about?"

Della smiled sweetly, her brown eyes sparkling, enjoying the situation now that she knew she had it completely under her control. "Have you ever thought about starting your own credit scheme, Chestertons charge accounts?"

Jonathan cut in quickly, believing that the debate was deviating too far from the subject. "You're losing us all, Della. You're jumping around from one thing to the other with no apparent connection. Please get to the point."

"If you ran your own credit scheme, your account holders could receive special privileges," Della said.

"Such as?"

"Advance notice of all off-price promotions, for one thing," she replied. "That would kill two birds with one stone. You could persuade customers to become account holders, bringing extra money into the company, and you'd have no trouble with them feeling cheated over promotional-priced merchandise. Your best customers would all have an account, and they'd know all about the promotions well in advance."

Jonathan weighed Della's words carefully. "I assume you've done some research into charge accounts."

"Of course," Della answered brightly. "A considerable amount, in fact. I've made myself familiar with the results of several major studies on consumer buying habits. For instance, did you know that a customer who holds a charge card from a certain company is three times more likely to buy from that company in the future than he would be if he held something like an American Express card?"

"No, I didn't," Jonathan replied truthfully, taken aback by the depth of Della's presentation, admiring the way she was tying it all together. "Tell me what else I don't know."

"Customer loyalty is one of the main reasons for running your own account system if you're big enough," Della continued. "And I think Chestertons is big enough. Other reasons include increased purchasing because of the convenience of the card, but the most important thing is that your customers come back to you. You'd be surprised at how loyal they can be."

"What about bad debts?" The question came from Gerald.

"Obviously you'll have to operate a proper credit department," Della told him. "It will pay you time and again, though. Think about it. Why pay money to those credit card companies whose services you use when you can run your own operation? Every time a customer makes a credit purchase, the credit department is contacted to ensure that the account isn't overdrawn or the card presented isn't on the hot list, stolen from somebody else. Likewise, if a man wants to open an account, the credit department checks his credentials before authorizing the granting of credit facilities."

Miriam, who had offered no contribution to the meeting, content to listen, made her presence known for the first time. "You seem to have gone to extreme lengths, well over and above a simple advertising presentation."

Della faced her mother-in-law. "I knew the question of special promotions would come up. It's a perfectly valid anxiety, and I'm simply covering all the bases. My agency would very much like to have the Chestertons account."

When the meeting broke up, Simon walked Della through the store to the sidewalk, where he hailed a cab. As she was getting in, she looked hard at him.

"Learn anything?" she asked.

"What about?"

"About thinking something through," she replied, getting ready to close the door. "That, and having enough backbone to stand up for what you thought was fantastic the night before."

Before Simon could think of a reply, Della slammed the cab door angrily, glaring at him through the window. He shrugged his shoulders as he watched the cab pull away, heading toward the agency on Madison Avenue.

Jonathan had remained in the boardroom discussing the presentation with Gerald, Miriam and Brian. He had been impressed with Della, especially her knowledge of how effective a good credit scheme could be. He had looked into the possibilities of beginning a credit operation for the Chestertons group, but he had never considered it to be viable. Now, after listening to Della list the reasons for starting such a scheme, skillfully tying it in with the advertising presentation, he was having second thoughts. He was also having the greatest difficulty in suppressing his enthusiasm for his daughter-in-law.

"You know something?" he said. "That girl's got a shrewd head on her shoulders."

Gerald laughed at his father's enthusiasm. "So hire her. You've never been one to turn down competence."

Jonathan looked to Miriam, seeking another opinion. "Well?"

"Gerald's right. She's too bright to be wasted in an agency. If you're finally going to launch a proper advertising program, we need an advertising manager. Is there anybody better that you know of?"

Jonathan turned to his general merchandise manager. "What do you think, Brian? You're part of this as well."

No response was forthcoming from Brian. He remained in his seat staring blankly across the office at the far wall, a vacant look on his face as if he had not heard the question.

"Brian?" Jonathan raised his voice a fraction. "Are you with us?"

Seeing that Brian had still not heard, Gerald tapped him under the table with his foot. Brian jumped slightly in the seat, startled, looking around like a man rudely awakened from a deep sleep. "What's happening?" he blurted out. "What did I miss?"

Gerald and Miriam laughed, but Jonathan remained silent, concerned about the man. During the whole meeting, Brian had appeared to be deep in thought, his mind elsewhere, speaking only when a question was directed at him, never offering an unsolicited opinion. Jonathan recalled that he had acted strangely in London, but he put that down to being in a new city and the five-hour time difference. Now he began to feel seriously worried. He stood up, indicating to Miriam and Gerald that he wanted to be alone with Brian.

"Okay, what's the problem this time? Thelma again?"

"She's gone back to Chicago," Brian said listlessly.

"Is that good or bad?" Jonathan asked.

"I suppose it should be good, but it's a bit of a shock."

"Want a few days off?"

Brian walked around the boardroom, stopping to study the color photograph of the New York store behind Jonathan's desk, next to the large map of the United States. "No. I'll be all right. It just takes some getting used to, that's all, not having a drunk to clean up after when I get home each night."

The comment fell badly with Jonathan, but he chose to overlook it. "Just make sure you don't take her place," he warned, glad to see the smile which appeared on Brian's face at the remark.

"There's little chance of that," Brian said. "These past few months have almost put me off drinking altogether. If she'd stayed around, I'd have joined a temperance group. I even threw out the bottles she left."

"Bad memories?"

"No. She drank gin. I hate the stuff, scented water. Now if it had been Scotch," Brian said, winking slyly, "I might have kept it as a memento of a marriage."

Jonathan laughed loudly. "If it had been Scotch, I'd have been round your place to share it." He lowered his voice conspiratorially. "It's getting harder and harder to find a place where I can smoke and have a drink in peace these days."

In bed that night, Della remained cold and aloof, ignoring Simon's advances, turning away from him. She was aware of his hands, but she could think only of his actions during the advertising presentation.

"What the hell's the matter now?" he growled. "You're acting like you've been stuck in the freezer for the past month."

She replied to the question without moving, her back still to him. "If you were as forthright at the office as you are at screwing, maybe your father would have some respect for you."

As soon as the words were out, she felt Simon's hand stop moving across her stomach and withdraw. "That's nice language," he said. "Where did you pick it up, from your fancy friends at the agency?"

Slowly she rolled over to face him, the normally soft brown eyes blazing with anger. "Simon, you're the original gutless wonder. You haven't got the spine to say what you think when it really matters. When there's nobody around, you're the bravest man I've ever seen. But you're scared to say a word when it counts. If you've got what you consider to be a valid opinion, then say it. Don't sit there like a dummy waiting to see what everybody else is going to say.

"And never, never leave me again in a position like you did this afternoon, where I'm expecting your support and looking like a fool because you're not helping. Because you're too busy seeing what everybody else is doing—all your equal partners," she added bitingly.

He smiled in the darkness, finding amusement in her show of temper.

Reaching out suddenly, he grabbed her by the short hair, pulling her face to his own. "My valid opinion as of this moment is that I'm horny. And I'm stating it."

Della struggled in his grip, still furious with him, pushing at his chest, pummelling his shoulders with her clenched fists. The blows ceased as she wrapped her arms around him, dragging him onto her.

When it was over, she lay in the crook of his arm playing with the auburn hair on his chest.

"Simon?"

"Now what?"

"Why aren't you like that in the office?"

He glanced sideways at her. "There's nobody I fancy."

"You idiot," she mumbled, and fell asleep.

# 19

Sniffing the afternoon air appreciatively, Marilyn Chesterton could physically feel the imminence of spring. A slight chill remained in the air as a memento of winter, but the sun was high and the trees were beginning to bloom, pink and white clusters scattered haphazardly against the lustrous green foliage.

Clad simply in a white tennis outfit and an unzipped blue Adidas jacket, she dropped the racket and container of tennis balls onto the passenger seat of the red Alfa Romeo. Looking back at the house for a final time, she waved at Karen, who was being held in the window by the Filipino housekeeper. Then she slid into the driver's seat, eager to be on her way.

Even the car felt different to her touch. It's a summer car, she reasoned, and acts like it knows that the weather's finally broken, as if it's got a mind of its own and wants to go, to burn up the roads and hug the bends like it's designed to. She drove carefully onto the street, checking left and right before pulling out completely, slipping the clutch as she revved the engine. Joyously she let the clutch fully out, stamping her right foot down on the gas pedal, hearing the rear axle thump solidly as it took up the load.

Fortunately for Marilyn, there were no police radar checks on the eight-mile journey to the club. She raced along happily, ecstatic at being alive on this wonderful spring day, feeling as much a part of it as the welcome blossom on the trees. It would be her first visit to the club for more than a month; even the prospect of seeing Stan Jarvis seemed immensely appealing.

Swinging into the club's parking lot, Marilyn saw Jarvis's silver-gray XKE Jaguar sitting regally in its reserved parking space close to the clubhouse. She pulled in alongside, braking sharply at the last moment, enjoying the rough sensation of being thrown forward against the restraining shoulder harness. Getting out of the car, she saw Jarvis standing in the clubhouse entrance; he was grinning ruefully as she approached.

"Hi!" he greeted her. "Are you sure you want tennis coaching, not driving lessons?"

"There's nothing wrong with my driving," she answered a trifle primly.

"Nothing that a fatal accident wouldn't cure," he said. "You must have a lot of faith in your brakes to pull a stunt like that. Even I haven't driven that way since I was a kid hot rodding around the side roads in a '52 Chevy."

He examined her carefully as he spoke, openly taking in the well-shaped legs and thighs which never failed to arouse him. Some guys went for women in high-heeled boots, but to Jarvis there was no sight more sexually appealing than a pair of legs encased in nothing kinkier than white tennis socks; a tennis outfit gave a woman a look of virginal sweetness, although Jarvis could not remember the last time he had made out with a virgin.

"I've got faith in my brakes," Marilyn replied, "and in my driving ability."

"Maybe you have. Just make sure you don't hit the silver beast next to you if you do it again."

Marilyn turned around to look at Jarvis's Jaguar sports car. "Is that your most prized possession, Stan?"

Jarvis grinned again, preferring to let his facial expression answer the question. There was no need for words.

Marilyn walked past him into the clubhouse, putting her racket on a chair while she slipped off the Adidas jacket. "Are we playing indoors today, Stan, or can we go outside?"

"We'll take a look at the grass courts," he said. "It's been dry lately, and they're all marked out." He waited till Marilyn began moving toward the door which led to the outdoor courts, then called out after her.

"See what you think. I'll be out with you in a minute, after I get something from my most prized possession."

He watched Marilyn close the door behind her as she stepped out onto the grass courts; then he strode quickly into the parking lot. Checking to see that he was unobserved, he opened the driver's door of the red Alfa and released the hood catch. Reaching into the engine compartment, he loosened the high-tension cable from the coil to the distributor, leaving it in place but not fitted securely enough to make an electrical contact. Satisfied, he closed the hood, opened the door to the Jaguar and pretended to search for something in the glove compartment, slamming the door loudly when he had finished. On his way back to the clubhouse, he went over his actions, his reasons for immobilizing Marilyn's Alfa Romeo. If he wanted her—and Christ, did he ever want her!—he would have to create a scenario, a situation where everything would fall into place. First she would be furious when the car did not start, then grateful to him when he offered her a lift home. And finally . . . well, what woman wasn't impressed by riding in the aircraft-cockpit interior of a Jaguar sports car?

Marilyn was waiting for him on the grass court, bouncing a ball with her racket, impatience visible in every stroke. As Jarvis reached the sideline, she mischievously lobbed the ball across the net into the opposite corner, laughing as she watched him scamper across the grass to retrieve it.

Ten minutes later she was out of breath because of her long layoff, but enjoying the game nevertheless. She was also losing, but that was no worse than she had anticipated.

Jonathan fussed around the boardroom, straightening chairs, making certain that nothing was out of place. His meeting with Della, on the surface to accept her presentation, but really to offer her the newly created position of advertising manager, was still ten minutes off. Yet he was nervous. There was something about this young woman which made him feel uncertain. Was it that she was so competent, always appearing to have taken the unexpected into consideration? In Della's presence, when she began to explain her point of view in such a matter-of-fact manner, he felt about ten years old, a boy in school again. God knows, he thought for the thousandth time, why she had married Simon. But if anybody can sort him out, it must be Della.

The secretary rang through five minutes later to inform him that Della had arrived. Instead of waiting for her to be shown into the boardroom, as was his custom when receiving visitors, he walked into the reception area, where he found her talking to the secretary.

She kissed him on the cheek, as she always did, before preceding him into the boardroom. Jonathan tagged along in her footsteps, knowing that the secretary was regarding him strangely. Nobody else had ever kissed him publicly in the office, not even Miriam. And he realized he was grinning, feeling quite pleased with himself.

Della sat down and crossed her legs, the short gray skirt riding up marginally. She waited till Jonathan had made himself comfortable behind the desk before speaking.

"Are you ready to finalize the advertising?"

Jonathan reached into the top drawer and pulled out a cigar, stuffing it into the corner of his mouth, regarding her thoughtfully. "We liked your presentation," he said. "You know that already. But I'm afraid we don't want you to handle it."

Whatever shock she may have felt at hearing such a totally unforeseen statement, Della managed to keep it out of her face. "Is it because I'm family," she asked, "and you think it will interfere with my efficiency, my objectivity?"

"No, not at all. You're probably the most efficient and objective young lady I've ever met."

"Don't be condescending," Della interrupted.

Jonathan almost choked. "Efficient and objective person," he said. "Any better?"

"Much better, thank you."

"And I'm glad you're part of the family."

"Then what's the problem?" Della countered.

"There is no problem. Your agency can have the account. It's just that we'd like to have you on our side."

It took Della a few seconds to comprehend what Jonathan had said. "You want me to work for you? For Chestertons?"

"That's about the size of it." Jonathan took the cigar out of his mouth and laid it carefully in the ashtray, the soggy, chewed end turned toward himself, out of Della's sight. "You convinced me the other day that we need a proper advertising program, something which puts over a proper message each time. Something tying in directly with what's happening in the stores, as opposed to the institutional advertising we have been doing. You know that we left everything to the agency in the past. Now we realize that attitude was a mistake. You also convinced me, although I don't think you were doing it intentionally, to hire you as advertising manager before somebody else got a hold of you."

Della eyed the unlit cigar in the ashtray. "Do you want to light that thing?" she asked. "I won't tell anybody."

Jonathan had the gold Dunhill out immediately, lighting the cigar, inhaling luxuriously. "That's another reason I'd like you to be part of this company. You don't complain about my smoking. Now tell me what you think about the idea."

Her mind was made up already, but Della decided to keep Jonathan waiting. "Do you mind if I talk it over with Simon first? I think that's only right."

"Go right ahead," Jonathan encouraged her, puffing contentedly on the cigar. "But I'm telling you now that he'll agree."

"Is he in?"

Jonathan dialled his son's extension. The secretary answered, informing him that Simon was free. Replacing the receiver, he extended a hand in invitation to Della.

"Go right in. Just don't say anything about my smoking—otherwise your first paycheck'll get lost."

Della smiled warmly at her father-in-law. "Don't worry about it." She sniffed delicately, catching the aroma of the cigar. "You'd better turn on your air circulator before somebody else comes in, though."

She watched while Jonathan flicked a switch by the side of the door; the extractor fan in the ceiling hummed into life, starting slowly, then picking up speed, drawing the smoke upward.

Walking along the corridor to Simon's office, she rapped on the door and entered. He stood up and kissed her firmly on the lips, but she broke away, leaving him standing forlornly in the middle of the room.

"Now what did I do?" he complained.

"You mustn't carry on with the staff," she said with mock severity. "Gossip spreads."

Simon's mouth dropped open in amazement. "The staff? What staff? What the hell are you talking about?"

"Your father just offered me the position of advertising manager with Chestertons. He said he'd better grab me before somebody else gets the same idea."

Confounded by the news, Simon returned to his desk and sat on the edge, his head shaking in bewilderment. "Is that what you really want?" he asked.

"I don't think that's really a relevant question," Della replied, walking over to the desk. "Surely it's more a question of what you want."

"Come again?"

"If I'm here, Simon, you'll have at least one ally in the office. Together we can work to get something going for you, build you up. If you get a decent idea, we can pursue it properly."

The reaction she got from Simon was completely unexpected. He leered at her, pointing to the table which stood over the area of carpet where they had first shared their love-making the night he had met her at the Second Avenue singles bar. "I never thought you'd be in this office to discuss business," he said.

Glancing at the table, Della remembered the evening well. However, she failed to see anything humorous in the present situation. "That was a long time ago, Simon. I'm here now for a completely different reason. I won't have any power here when it comes to the actual crunch, but I'll certainly be able to sway things in your favor before they reach an ultimate decision. What do you think?"

"I think it's absolutely marvellous." He slid off the desk and went to the office door, locking it. Ringing through to his secretary, he told her that he did not want to be disturbed for the next hour. Then he looked at Della.

"Give me a hand moving that table, will you?" he asked.

Marilyn was pleasantly exhausted. Her legs felt like two sticks of pliable rubber, wobbling slightly as she walked back to the clubhouse, and her arms were dropping from fatigue. On the positive side, she believed she had acquitted herself with some degree of honor. After the month-long layoff, she had gone onto the court and given Stan Jarvis her best. She had lost, of course, but it was no disgrace. Even Jarvis was breathing heavily from his exertions; Marilyn saw this as a moral victory.

"Thank Christ you're the last one for today," the coach grunted, collapsing onto a chair. "That run-around has just about finished me."

Marilyn stayed for ten minutes in the clubhouse, sipping at a cold drink while she caught her breath. Jarvis joined her, drinking a beer nonchalantly while he waited for her to leave. When she did, he followed her as far as the door, shouting after her to mind his car as she drove away.

He stood in the shelter of the doorway, a feeling of anticipation building up inside him as he watched Marilyn walk unsuspectingly across the parking lot to the red Alfa Romeo; she turned to wave as she reached it. The sound of the engine turning over came clearly to him as Marilyn tried to start the car. The noise stopped, a pause of a few seconds; then it began again, the fruitless struggle of a starter motor trying to coax a dead engine into life.

Inside the Alfa, Marilyn pressed the gas pedal to the floor, holding it there for ten seconds to clear the flooded carburetor. The smell of gasoline was strong enough to make her nauseous when she released it. Turning the key again, she heard the engine crank willingly; still no spark caught. She tried again, several times, before removing the key in disgusted fury and getting out of the car. Helplessly she stood alongside the Alfa, staring futilely at the hood, hands on her hips as she wondered what to do.

Hearing footsteps on the gravel behind her, she turned around. "What's the problem?" Jarvis asked.

"It won't start."

Jarvis gave her a look of pained exasperation. "I can see that." Taking the ignition key from Marilyn, he slipped into the driver's seat and tried to start the engine. He tried three more times before getting out of the car.

"How do you open the hood?" he asked.

Marilyn pointed to the catch. He looked into the engine compartment, checking the high-tension leads from the spark plugs to the distributor, taking great care not to touch the coil cable he had loosened earlier.

"Doesn't seem to be anything loose," he volunteered.

Marilyn's fury at the car began to turn into anxiety. She had to get home. Gerald would be back by six-thirty, and she wanted to prepare dinner for him. The housekeeper could be entrusted to clean and occasionally look after Karen, but Marilyn insisted on doing the cooking. "What could it be?" she asked. "Do you know anything about car engines?"

"A bit." Jarvis unlocked the trunk of the Jaguar, bringing out a tool kit. "First we'll see if you're getting a spark," he said. "Won't take a minute."

Marilyn stood on the other side of the car, watching while he expertly fitted a plug wrench onto a tommy bar and began to unscrew the spark plug from the Alfa's number one cylinder. Holding the lead with a pair of insulated pliers, he fixed the plug into the end of the high-tension cable, holding it close to the cylinder head.

"Turn the engine over," he instructed Marilyn. "Try to start it. We'll soon see if we're getting anything."

Obediently Marilyn climbed into the car and turned the key. The engine cranked over while Jarvis scrutinized the end of the plug, watching for a spark to jump from the electrode to the metal of the cylinder head. He knew that he was showing unnecessary precautions by using insulated pliers. There would be no current coming down to the spark plugs from now until the end of the world unless the high-tension cable between the coil and distributor was fitted properly. But he took a certain pride in making the performance look authentic.

"Forget it!" he yelled, lowering his voice as Marilyn ceased her efforts. "You're getting nothing. Either your coil's no good or something's wrong with your distributor. Maybe your condenser's had it."

Marilyn got out of the small car again. "Now what do I do?" she asked.

"Call a garage. But Christ knows when they'll turn up."

"I've got to get home now. I can't wait here till some tow truck operator decides to show up."

"How far have you got to go?" Jarvis asked, knowing the answer already.

"About eight miles. Just this side of Manhasset."

Jarvis sighed deeply, signifying that he had made up his mind. "Give me a few minutes to clear up my things; then I'll run you home. It's not too much out of my way." He pointed to the Jaguar. "Lock your car and put your things in there. I'll be out in a little while."

Marilyn transferred her equipment from the Alfa to the silver XKE, closing the passenger door as she got in. She shot a furious glare at the little red car, cursing it for refusing to start, remembering how sprightly it had seemed on the journey out. And now, nothing. While she waited for Jarvis to return, she inspected the Jaguar's interior, deciding it was in keeping with her opinion of the tennis coach; discarded cigarette packs and two empty beer bottles were scattered across the small back seat, evidently thrown there to lie unheeded until he next had the car cleaned. The sight of the garbage brought a smile to Marilyn's face, making her forget momentarily the aggravation caused by the Alfa's refusal to start.

Jarvis returned ten minutes later, having taken his time deliberately. He mumbled a quick apology for being so long, then turned the ignition key. The Jaguar's powerful, six-cylinder engine burst into immediate, throbbing life.

"You should go out and buy a decent car," he said, grinning cockily at Marilyn. "Get rid of that piece of junk you're driving now. These English sports cars have got those flashy wop imports beat by a mile. Italian cars are like Italian women—all looks and pretty curves but no staying power."

"And you'd know all about that, I suppose."

"Sure would." Laughing loudly, he put the car into gear and let out the clutch with such fierceness that the back end of the Jaguar broke away. Steering into the skid, he corrected it perfectly, looking to Marilyn for some comment on his driving. She made none.

Passing through the parking lot exit, Jarvis swung right toward Manhasset, taking the engine revolutions right up to the red mark on the tachometer each time before changing gear. As he dropped his right hand from the wheel to change into third, he stole a glance at Marilyn's thighs, his heart quickening as he saw the muscles vibrating slightly with the movement of the car. He grasped the gearshift and thrust it savagely through the neutral gap into the third gear slot, jamming his foot down hard on the gas pedal, trying to figure out the right time to make his move, the exact psychological moment when Marilyn's resistance would be at its lowest, when she would be unable to ward off his advance.

Marilyn stared through the windshield, totally unaware of either Jarvis's covetous glance or the speed at which he was driving. She was thinking about the Alfa, puzzled why it would not start. Less than two weeks earlier it had undergone a major service in preparation for the coming warm months, when it would be at its most enjoyable, the roof folded back and the warm wind whistling through her hair. She had been looking forward to taking Karen out in the open car; she had even ordered a special seat for the baby. The minute she arrived home she would arrange for the dealer to pick it up from the club's parking lot. And, at the same time, she'd give him an earful that he would not forget in a hurry for doing such a poor job on the tune-up that the Alfa had broken down already.

So wrapped up in the mystery of the Alfa was Marilyn that she did not notice, as Jarvis changed up into top gear, how his hand strayed from the gearshift and brushed against her left leg. Jarvis took Marilyn's lack of hostile reaction as the green light. Less than thirty seconds later, as he changed down to take a sharp bend, he moved his hand away from the gearshift and held the back of his fingers against Marilyn's calf. He felt her move in the seat to look at him, but he continued to keep his eyes on the road.

"Stan." Marilyn's voice reached across the intervening space like the point of an icicle. "Take your hand off my leg."

He made no **move** to comply with the demand. Instead, he reversed his hand, moving it up so that the plam lay on Marilyn's thigh, his touch gentle but insistent. "Don't fool around with me, Marilyn." His voice was oozing with confidence. "You've been asking for this ever since you came to me."

Marilyn tried to move away, wriggling in the seat, making herself as small as possible. Jarvis kept his hand on her thigh. When she spoke again, the voice was perfectly modulated, pitched to sound like it had when she had taught school and was trying to bring order to an unruly class.

"You've got your signals all wrong, Stan. Get your hands away and take me home, and I'll forget all about this."

Jarvis laughed crudely, seeing her resistance as a kind of foreplay heightening his anticipation even more. "After all the trouble I've been to? No way. Just relax and enjoy it. You know you will."

"Trouble? Then it was you who fixed the car?"

"Nothing more drastic than loosening a wire." He began to slow down, heading for a side road which led into the woods, now even more confident that he was right about Marilyn Chesterton, that he had been right all along, that the full reward for his persistence would be paid in just a few more minutes. He felt his pants begin to tighten at the prospect, and he moved in the seat, digging down into his crotch with his left hand to relieve the mounting pressure.

As he braked the car to a halt where the side road petered off into a track, Marilyn galvanized herself into frantic action. She opened the door and leaped out, clutching her racket and purse, looking for a place to run, sanctuary. Laughing at the prospect of a pursuit, Jarvis pocketed the ignition key and followed her with an easy lope, closing in as she stopped to face him.

"Look around you," he invited. "Nothing but trees. What better privacy could we ask for? Making love as it should be done, right in nature's bosom. Come on, Marilyn,"—he adopted a cajoling tone—"we're both grownups, entitled to have a little fun."

He moved toward her, expecting no real resistance. He had called the game, dealt the cards, and now he wanted to cash in on his hand, take what was rightly his. And had he ever been mistaken before? Marilyn dropped the purse onto the ground. As Jarvis's eyes followed its downward path, seeing it as the first stage of her surrender, she suddenly swung the racket at his head with both hands. The edge caught him across the temple, splitting the skin. Staggering back, he clutched at the wound, feeling the blood on his fingers, warm and slippery. When he looked back at Marilyn, blinking in pain and surprise, all trace of laughter had disappeared from his face. In its place was a snarling mask of hatred.

"You goddamned bitch!" he hissed. "You'll pay for that."

Terror-stricken by the threat in Jarvis's eyes, Marilyn backed away. She held the racket out in front of herself like a two-handed sword, unable to believe that she could have inflicted such a frightening wound, simultaneously determined to duplicate it should the opportunity arise. As Jarvis circled warily, stepping forward in a feint, she swung the racket again. This time he was expecting the move and ducked; the racket whistled through the air like a whiplash, passing a foot over his head. He advanced again, watching cagily for the next swing, determined to charge Marilyn when she made it, taking advantage as she momentarily lost her balance.

Marilyn changed her tactics. She pretended to swing, then threw the racket into Jarvis's face, hoping for a lucky hit. Instinctively he punched out with his left hand, deflecting the racket over his shoulder, hearing it land in the brush behind him.

"Just you and me now," he whispered threateningly. "Nothing left to fight with, you stuck-up bitch."

Marilyn spun around to run into the woods, not knowing where she was heading, only acknowledging the overriding need to get away. She scrambled in her panic, slipping, losing her balance. Jarvis, with a sudden burst of speed, caught her within five yards, dragging her down to the ground in a football tackle, arms encircling her legs, sending her sprawling.

His breath was hot on her face as he turned her over and pressed down, holding her arms. She tried to fight, wriggling to free her arms, to claw at his face, but his superior strength easily overcame her.

Blood dripped down onto Marilyn as Jarvis sat astride her, his legs on either side of her body, his face looming over her own, hands pinning her arms to the ground. "You shouldn't have done that with the racket," she heard him say. "You're going to wish you'd never done it."

She felt her left arm released as Jarvis used his right hand to fumble with her jacket, feeling inside, grasping her breasts roughly through the tennis top. She tried to raise herself up. Jarvis withdrew his right hand and slapped her hard, backhanded, across the face, knocking her back—again, then a third time, rocking her head backward and forward against the earth. She cried out in agony, each scream being cut off by the next slap, then starting again. But it was not Jarvis's blows that were causing the pain. It was the jagged object on the ground which her head had struck, grating against her scalp as she reeled under the slaps.

Oblivious to Jarvis's frantic attempts to rip off her jacket and blouse, Marilyn moved her free hand to her head, feeling underneath, groping for the cause of her agony. Her fingers closed around a small rock, no larger than a baseball, pear-shaped with the narrow end tapering to a jagged, vicious point. Trying to calm her screaming nerves, she breathed in deeply, letting the air out of her lungs gradually, forcing her body to relax, lulling Jarvis into a false sense of security.

Feeling the body underneath him begin to soften, Jarvis experienced a surge of satisfaction. His head hurt like hell, and he was going to make this goddamned tease pay for that swipe with the racket. He was worried that the gash would leave a scar, marring his handsome features, but his preoccupation with Marilyn momentarily overrode that anxiety. Slowly, leisurely, he brought his face down to Marilyn's, smearing her chalk white skin with blood from the cut. His lips met hers, flaccid, unresponsive, and he moved his mouth down, using both hands to rip open the tennis top and claw at her brassiere.

He did not see Marilyn's hand come out from beneath her head. Nor did he see it come flashing toward his own head, the sharp point of the rock jutting out toward him.

He only felt the shattering sensation of blinding white fire as the rock was driven with all of Marilyn's remaining strength into his already injured temple.

Marilyn experienced a rush of barbarous elation as Jarvis straightened up like a man on the receiving end of a massive electrical shock, screaming in a frenzied spasm of pain, hands flying to his head. Energy flooded into her, adding strength to her arms, determination to her being. Raising herself on one elbow to get within range again, she smashed the rock into his head a second time, seeing his neck snap back with the force of the blow. A third time she struck him before she fell back onto the ground, the energy deserting her as suddenly as it had come; she was only dimly aware of the lessening pressure on her body as Jarvis collapsed and dropped away to one side.

The thought crossed her mind that perhaps he was dead—in which case there was no need to hurry.

# 20

As the Long Island Rail Road train thundered eastward from New York City, Gerald sat back comfortably, gazing out of the window, watching the scenery flash past, the newspaper he had bought at the terminal lying unopened across his lap. He felt contented with his father's decision to hire Della for the new position of advertising manager. It was a sensible move and would add strength to the overall marketing plan. There were no two ways about it as far as he could see; through either luck or a rare case of good judgment, Simon had married an incredibly bright girl.

At the station he got into the brown Ford Thunderbird and began the final stage of the homeward journey, eagerly anticipating the ritual pre-dinner drink. He expected to find Marilyn tired after her return to the tennis coaching sessions, and he was looking forward to an early night. Instinctively he took his left hand off the steering wheel to cover his mouth as he gave vent to an enormous yawn.

Parking the car, he entered the house through the small connecting door from the double garage and bellowed his normal greeting. "Marilyn! I'm home. Where's my drink?"

He waited in the hallway, listening for the familiar light footsteps followed by the appearance of his wife holding the silver tray. Ten seconds passed before he heard any sound, and then it was only Anita, the housekeeper.

"Where's Mrs. Chesterton?" he asked.

The girl rolled her brown eyes helplessly. "No come home yet from tennis," she replied hesitantly.

Apprehension flooded over Gerald immediately. He dropped the briefcase to the floor and picked up the telephone, flicking through the pages of the personal directory for the club's number, misdialling initially in his agitation. When he got through, the call was taken by the janitor.

Gerald identified himself, saying that his wife was two hours late in returning from a coaching session.

"Can you check if her car's still in the parking lot? It's a red Alfa Romeo sports car." There was a moment's pause. "That's right!" he snapped. "A little red car with a black soft top. Do you understand?"

Tapping his fingers in exasperation on the telephone table, Gerald waited while the janitor looked for the car. The information came back that the Alfa was still there, standing by itself in the lot; but the premises were closed and all the members had gone home. Gerald thanked the man brusquely and hung up, looking around powerlessly.

"Baby asleep," Anita said helpfully, failing to see what all the consternation was about.

Gerald stared at her, nodding abstractedly. Then he picked up the telephone for a second time. Anticipating the worst, he called the police.

Darkness had fallen by the time Marilyn regained consciousness. She eased herself up onto her elbows, shivering in the cold of the March evening. Her head felt light, spinning around and around as she tried to focus her eyes, unable to place the location, seeing only the threatening trees which surrounded her like an army of hostile troops. Her gaze fell to the ground, and her brain recoiled in horror as she identified the inert body of Stan Jarvis lying next to her, his arms spread-eagled like those of a man who had been crucified. Gingerly she reached out with her right hand to touch him, jerking away in fright as she came into contact with the cold skin.

The piece of rock was still in her left hand. As terrifying recognition dawned—and with it the memory of what she had done—she stared wide-eyed at it, willing her fingers to open. Her muscles refused to obey the instructions, and the jagged lump remained firmly clasped in her hand, its rough edges digging painfully into her skin.

A quick self-inspection revealed that her shorts, blouse and jacket were stained with Jarvis's blood, the spots now cold and congealed, turning brown. She looked at the injuries to his head and was shocked that anybody could bleed so much.

The call of an owl made her swing around in fright, its eerie hooting causing her to peer anxiously into the blackness of the woods expecting to see a wild animal bound out, its eyes yellow, mouth slavering rabidly. Nothing emerged; no movement stirred the peaceful ring of trees as they remained mute witnesses to what had taken place.

She stood up slowly, cautiously testing her limbs to ensure that nothing was broken. The events which had led to her being in this small clearing came flooding back: the car that would not start; Jarvis's friendly offer of a lift; the casual advance; then, when she had resisted, the assault—and this. She looked at the rock again, her blue eyes drawn to it by a morbid magnetism, unable to fully comprehend that she could have wielded it with enough force to split a man's head open, to kill him.

In the dim moonlight which filtered through to the clearing, she spotted her purse and tennis racket. She picked them up, looping an arm through the purse's strap, holding the racket to her breasts. Staggering numbly toward the road, she stopped at the silver gray Jaguar long enough to see that the keys were not in the ignition; Jarvis had removed them when he had begun to chase her, and she did not relish the prospect of searching through his pockets.

Ahead of her lay the road. She had seen two cars pass, their headlights cutting white swathes which could be seen through the trees. Still holding the purse and racket, with the rock clutched securely in her left hand, Marilyn continued walking toward the road.

Gerald was frantic. After reporting Marilyn's disappearance to the police, he had telephoned his father, putting him in the picture. Jonathan had promised to come over immediately. When he arrived, Miriam was with him, as patently worried as her husband was forcibly calm.

Gerald greeted his mother gloomily, feeling certain that her presence could do nothing to ease the situation. Before he could voice his misgivings, however, Jonathan sensed his son's thoughts.

"You try to stop her," he whispered. "It'd take the Sixth Fleet and more." He turned to Miriam, speaking gently. "Why don't you go upstairs with the girl and see the baby's all right?" He waited till she had left the room before he continued speaking to Gerald.

"Anything since you called me?"

"Nothing. The police haven't got back to me. They even said that somebody's not classified as missing if they're only two hours late. But they're keeping an eye out for her."

"What about the club?"

"There's nobody there but the janitor. He's the guy I spoke to when I first got home. I don't think he even knows how to spell his own name, so he's not much help."

"Do you want to go out and look?" Jonathan suggested, feeling it would be in their best interests to keep active.

Gerald shook his head resolutely. "We'd better stay here in case the police come up with something." He moved away from his father, talking quietly, as if to himself.

"It doesn't make any sense for Marilyn to run off like this. She's never done anything like it before without telling me about it. Dear God, please let nothing have happened to her. Please."

Several cars passed in both directions, their main beams lighting the verge along which Marilyn walked. None stopped for the figure in the open flapping jacket and shorts, her blouse torn all the way down the front, the racket clutched tightly, its strings like the front of a cage across her brassiere. Neither, for that matter, did Marilyn take any notice of the traffic which swished past her. Her legs moved automatically, her brain not knowing in which direction they were taking her. As the temperature dropped down into the low thirties, her teeth took up an incessant chatter.

If she could have seen herself in a mirror, Marilyn's reaction would have been one of acute disbelief, positive that the reflection which would have stared back was not her own. The normally well-groomed ash-blond hair was bedraggled, knotted in places, with pieces of broken twig and dried grass clinging to it. The blood which spotted her face and tennis outfit was cracked like a broken brown crust. Her skin was the color of alabaster, almost translucent; other than the dried blood spots, the only relief was the red of the two patches on her cheeks.

She breathed sluggishly, wheezing, gasping for air as she walked unseeing, stumbling blindly, staying on the grass verge by instinct. She did not hear the car pull up beside her, nor did she notice the headlights which illuminated the road ahead. Only when her name was called a second time did she stop.

"Mrs. Chesterton? Are you Marilyn Chesterton?"

Marilyn squinted in the direction of the summons. The indistinct blur gradually took on the familiar shape and color of a police cruiser. The door opened and a sergeant got out, walking toward her, his pace slow and measured, reassuring, not wanting to scare her.

"Are you Marilyn Chesterton?" he asked quietly.

She stared at him blankly for several seconds, his face going in and out of focus, advancing and receding. "Yes." Her voice was hushed. "I'm Marilyn Chesterton."

The police sergeant's face broke into a wide, friendly grin. "We've come to drive you home, Marilyn. Your family's very worried about you." He took her gently by the arm, guiding her into the back seat of the car, putting his hand on top of her head as she got in to keep her from catching it on the side of the car. Removing the purse and tennis racket from her grip, he wrapped a heavy plaid blanket around her shoulders.

"Can you tell us what happened?" the sergeant asked as his partner moved the car away from the side of the road.

Marilyn heard the question. She wanted to tell this police officer everything—that if he looked in the woods he would find a corpse, that she had killed a man. But her lips refused to form the words. She just sat silently in the back of the car, shivering less as the blanket brought warmth to her body.

Jonathan and Gerald sat in the living room drinking coffee which Miriam had made for them. Jonathan was craving for a smoke, the yearning becoming stronger as each minute passed. With Miriam in the house, however, he dared not light a cigar. Even the current emergency was no excuse in her eyes. Getting older's like being born all over again, he thought miserably. If you want to do anything enjoyable, you'd better make damned certain you don't get caught doing it.

Conversation between father and son had dried up completely. There was nothing to talk about other than Marilyn's disappearance, and that was a subject best left alone till definite news came.

As the minutes dragged by with no information, Gerald's fears became certainties. Visions of Marilyn lying in some secluded spot flashed before his eyes, chilling his blood. What the hell could have made her leave the car at the club? She always came straight home. Why had she chosen to do differently this time?

Feeling his father tap him on the knee, Gerald looked up, the images disappearing. Jonathan was pointing through the window into the street. A police car was parked outside the house, its red and white emergency lights flashing urgently, casting alternate shadows across the street and onto the fronts of the houses opposite; as he watched, the lights died, plunging the street into comparative darkness. The car doors were open, and two policemen were assisting a huddled figure from the vehicle. Gerald could not see the face, but the white socks and tennis shoes were identification enough. He ran from the room toward the front door, Jonathan following closely behind.

Flinging open the door, he raced out into the night, taking Marilyn from the policemen, holding her tightly, his eyes not seeing her dishevelled state. "Where have you been?" he cried. "We've all been worried sick about you."

"Just take her inside, sir," the police sergeant advised him. "She's in no fit state to answer any questions at the minute. And we've got a few of our own we'd like to ask."

Gerald helped Marilyn into the house, half pushing, half lifting her, laying her down with extreme tenderness on the living room couch, bending over her. The two police officers followed him in, one dropping Marilyn's purse and tennis racket on the hall floor.

Hearing the commotion from downstairs, Miriam left the baby in the housekeeper's care. When she entered the living room, she found her husband, son and two police officers clustered around the couch. Gerald was trying to get Marilyn to drink the coffee which had been made for him. Seeing Miriam enter, Jonathan broke away from the group.

"Go away for a few minutes," he urged her. "She's all right, thank God. Don't worry. Just leave us alone."

Miriam cast a long, anxious glance past Jonathan at the group surrounding her daughter-in-law. She felt Jonathan push her back into the hall gently but firmly. "Go on. You can come back later when she's feeling better."

"Can't I do anything?"

"Sure you can. Make some more coffee. That's the best thing you can do. The police would probably like some."

He closed the door and returned to the couch. Gerald, holding the cup in his right hand, was pointing with his left to the stains on Marilyn's face and clothes. "What's that?"

"Dried blood," the sergeant replied.

Gerald raised his head sharply, looking into the sergeant's eyes. "Is she hurt? I don't see any cuts."

"It's not your wife's, sir. Until she tells us any different, we can only assume that she was attacked and defended herself."

Jonathan continued to stare down at his daughter-in-law, a sense of relief passing over him as he watched the blue eyes open and try to focus on the white, looming faces. He dropped his gaze to the blood stains on her clothes, then to the object gripped so tightly in her left hand. It took him a moment to recognize what it was; then he tapped the sergeant on the shoulder.

"I think you'd better have a look at what she's holding."

The sergeant took Marilyn's hand, carefully prising open the fingers. He examined the rock closely before passing it to his colleague. Gerald watched the performance pensively.

"What is it?" he asked, realizing its importance by the care with which the police officers were handling it.

"At a guess I'd say it's the weapon, sir," the sergeant replied. "Whoever lost that blood"—he pointed to the stains on Marilyn—"got that way because of this chunk of rock."

"You mean that my wife could have hurt somebody?" Gerald asked incredulously, aghast at the possibility. "She hit somebody with..." The words died in his throat as Marilyn fixed him with her eyes, recognizing him. She tried to reach up, and he clasped her shoulders, pushing her back onto the couch, whispering to her to lie still. "It's all right," he assured her. "Don't be scared. You're safe now, you're home. Everything's all right."

Tears formed in Marilyn's eyes as she recognized Jonathan as well, but the presence of the two uniformed men aroused confusion. She gazed at them, bewildered, having no recollection of how they had found her and brought her home.

"Ask her what happened," the sergeant whispered to Gerald.

"Can't it wait, for Christ's sake?" he hissed.

"Please ask her, sir. It's important."

"Okay then," he agreed grudgingly. "Marilyn, where did all the blood come from? What did you have the rock for?"

Marilyn closed her eyes, trying to blot out the scene. "Stan Jarvis," she moaned. "The Alfa wouldn't start. He offered me a ride home. On the way he tried to..." Her voice faltered. "He tried to... you know."

"Ask her where this Jarvis has gone," the sergeant urged Gerald. "We'd better pick him up before he skips."

The question was unnecessary. Marilyn had heard the police sergeant's whispered words.

"He hasn't gone anywhere. He's lying in the woods with his head smashed in."

Then, as her memory vividly brought the scene to life again, she burst into tears.

After an hour, Marilyn was well enough to make a complete statement to the police, telling them exactly where Jarvis's body could be found. Gerald had called the family doctor, who had given Marilyn a sedative, promising that he would return on the following day, but stressing that he saw no cause for concern.

When the police had left, Gerald sat downstairs with his parents, still dazed by the turn of events. There were a thousand questions in his mind concerning the assault. What had made the man so sure of his ground? Had Marilyn done anything to lead him on? He despised himself as he considered the possibilities, but he needed to know the answers. Had Marilyn, seeking to relieve the monotony she had been complaining about, been enmeshed in a web of her own unintentional manufacture? Had she flirted with the man, no matter how innocently?

Whatever reason the tennis coach believed he had, he'd paid for it, Gerald thought ruefully. He'd sure as hell paid for it.

Miriam made him a light meal which he pecked at before pushing it aside, unable to eat. She looked at him anxiously as she removed the plate.

"Are you going to be all right," Jonathan asked, "or do you want us to stay the night?"

"Don't worry about me," Gerald replied, sitting on the edge of the couch, fidgeting nervously. "I'll be okay. You two go along home. I'll call the car for you."

The chauffeur picked up Jonathan and Miriam twenty minutes later. Gerald watched his parents leave, standing in the doorway of the house as the Rolls-Royce pulled away. He turned back inside, locking the front door. Walking upstairs, he found Marilyn fast asleep, her arms outside the blanket, breathing easily under the sedative, the color back in her face. Karen was also asleep, and there was no light or sound from the housekeeper's room.

After careful consideration, Gerald took his pajamas and a book to the guest room, preferring to spend the night alone and give Marilyn a peaceful sleep to help her recover.

Miriam was already in bed by the time Jonathan had finished his secretive smoke in the back garden of their home. Before entering the bedroom, he scrubbed his teeth religiously to get rid of the smell of tobacco, topping it off with a strong mouthwash. His mouth tingled to the point of burning, and his gums seemed to be raw, but he was certain that Miriam would not be able to detect any telltale smell on his breath.

Remembering that he had left his jacket in the kitchen, he retraced his steps, humming quietly. As he climbed the stairs again, the jacket folded over his arm, he found himself wheezing, having difficulty with his breathing. Damned cigars, he thought. Even my body's having a dig at me now. Reaching the top of the stairs, he paused, running a hand across his forehead, which seemed hot to the touch. He stayed on the landing for a minute, waiting while his breathing evened out. Then he entered the bedroom, sitting on the edge of the bed while he kicked off his shoes.

"Some times we're going through," he muttered to Miriam as he slipped into his pajamas. "Makes you wonder what's coming around the next corner."

"That was a terrible thing to happen," she replied. "Who would have thought that something like that could take place at the club? Marilyn was always saying that the membership was made up of the nicest people."

Jonathan slid underneath the sheet. "The membership doesn't include the staff." He would have said more, but a blast of pain smashed across his chest like a sledge-hammer blow, forcing him to sit up gasping, the sweat springing to his forehead. Gritting his teeth, he tried to control his breathing again, hoping that Miriam would not notice. But she did.

"What's the matter with you?" She raised herself, leaning across the gap between the two beds for a closer look. "Are you feeling all right?"

He waved a hand at her. "Relax. It's just the aggravation of the evening catching up with me—gas or indigestion." He remained propped against the headboard till the pain had passed, surprised at finding himself soaking wet with perspiration, his pajamas and the sheets clinging to him.

"See?" he said to Miriam, who was still watching him. "Nothing but gas. Now turn off the light and go to sleep."

# 21

Deprived of Thelma's presence, the two-bedroom apartment on Central Park West seemed deserted. Brian was far from regretful that his wife had decided to return to Chicago, viewing it as a welcome release from the hell he had been enduring. At the same time, however, he realized the impracticality of maintaining the large apartment solely for his own use. As well as unutilized, unnecessary space, there was the financial consideration; a one-bedroom apartment would be just as comfortable to serve his own needs, and certainly cheaper.

He had telephoned several agencies during the midday break, arranging appointments to view apartments during the evening. Now he prepared his papers for the Monday afternoon merchandise meeting, knowing gratefully that it would be over quickly; everybody was still too upset over what had happened to Marilyn to prolong meetings needlessly. Thankfully she had recovered from the assault and had been completely exonerated by the inquest. But Christ, he thought, what an ordeal for her to have to go through—first the actual assault; then her own actions, killing the tennis coach with the rock as she struggled to escape; finally the inquest forcing her to go through it all over again, dragging the facts out, making her show her deepest self for public view. He grinned spontaneously, picturing a similar situation happening to Thelma, wondering how she would respond. She was so perverse that she would probably jump at the opportunity, he decided; the coach would have to find a rock to beat her off with.

Briefly he scanned the minutes from the previous week's meeting. The concern which had been expressed earlier over the Mr. Simon shops, when Jonathan had told him to take over their operation from Simon, had all but disappeared. With the correct merchandise properly displayed, the boutiques were finally pulling their weight, although Simon took every opportunity to complain about the way they were being handled.

In keeping with Jonathan, Brian took little notice of Simon, listening to his grumblings before destroying them completely with well-chosen arguments. Only his mother seemed to have any inclination to listen to his ideas; even when she cast her vote in his favor, Miriam knew it was assisting a lost cause, as Jonathan always overruled him. And with Jonathan went Brian and Gerald. Brian liked Miriam, and he respected the way she tried to hold the family together by not letting Simon become a total outcast. In a way he found it amusing, childish even, the sort of action which gave a very human side to the running of a large corporation.

Gathering up his papers, Brian left the office and walked briskly to the boardroom, annoyed at finding himself the last to arrive. He nodded to the others before taking a seat next to Della, who was attending the meeting to explain how her proposed advertising program would operate. Brian recalled that the first ad would come out on the Wednesday of the following week, one layout and promotional garment for the East Coast, and carefully selected alternatives for the Midwest and West Coast. He was as interested as anybody in seeing the results.

Opening the meeting, Jonathan glossed over the previous week's results, as all categories had met budget. He went into greater detail when he reached reports from regional managers on personnel problems they were encountering, a high staff turnover leading to a lack of continuity in the stores. While his father spoke, Gerald scribbled down pertinent notes in a tiny scrawl in his desk diary; anything not related to merchandise came under his jurisdiction, and he liked to get onto personnel problems immediately. He had learned long ago that without a satisfied staff, there was no business. Or, as Jonathan had once explained it, with a good staff you can sell bad suits if you're so inclined; with a poor staff, you cannot even give away the Great Seal of the President of the United States.

As he wrote, half listening to his father, Gerald let his mind drift back to the confrontation he had steeled himself for with Marilyn. He had approached it cautiously, feeling his way, sensing that she was just as embarrassed about the incident as he was. Initially she had claimed that she had done nothing to lure Jarvis on; the Alfa Romeo had broken down, and she had taken him up on his offer of a lift. Gradually the story had changed, and it had been as he had suspected. Under his patient, gentle questioning she had admitted that she saw Jarvis as an egotistical schoolboy and that it had amused her to play up to him occasionally, seeing it as nothing more than a harmless flirtation, watching him rise to the bait like a well-trained dog. Gerald had accepted the story gratefully, feeling a vague measure of remorse that the man was dead, but relieved to know that Marilyn's involvement had been almost accidental. He knew only too well how bored and frustrated she had become, grasping at every chance to get out of the house. Perhaps she would be able to return to teaching in the near future, leaving Karen in the care of the housekeeper—providing that the housekeeper learned more English than she knew already. Maybe, he thought in a moment of levity, he could match up the housekeeper with the janitor from the club. Between the pair of them, they might be able to put out one coherent sentence.

When he had come to examine Marilyn the day after the assault, the doctor had tactfully suggested to Gerald that psychiatric help might be necessary to help heal the mental wounds left by the experience. Gerald's first reaction had been one of horror. The thought of Marilyn undergoing analysis, something which he felt belonged only in a situation comedy on television, filled him with acute dread. He had begged off on Marilyn's behalf, telling the doctor that he would only dream of using such an approach as a last resort.

Marilyn had come down the following afternoon, still dazed from the sedatives. They had talked then, Gerald having taken time off from the office to look after her. He was grateful that she could view the experience fairly objectively, but he was dismayed at her reaction to his touch. When he had reached out to console her as she talked of Jarvis, she had withdrawn sharply, her eyes opening wide, body shivering, shrinking back into the chair.

Following this, they had slept apart for a further three nights. Gerald made no attempt to force himself on Marilyn; he simply prayed that she would soften as the memories of that night in the woods faded. Otherwise—and he had shuddered at the prospect—perhaps the doctor's suggestion had been more accurate than he wanted to believe.

On the fourth night, Marilyn had come into the guest room at three in the morning, the flimsy nightdress billowing out behind as she walked, making a train, silhouetting her body. Without a word, as he had watched her from the pillow, she had pulled back the light woollen blanket and climbed into bed with him. When the housekeeper brought up coffee at six-thirty the following morning, she had been surprised to find nobody occupying the main bedroom—and even more taken aback when she found Marilyn and Gerald sleeping, cramped but peaceful, in one small bed in the guest room.

The meeting lasted for fifty-eight minutes—the first to ever go under an hour—a record-breaking fact that Jonathan insisted be included in the minutes to serve as a precedent for future meetings. Seeing an opportunity for an early afternoon, Brian returned to his office, cleared up an outstanding problem on suit deliveries from the distribution center to the West Coast stores, and left the building before anybody could detain him. He rode a taxi to the apartment management office which he had called earlier that afternoon, and by eight in the evening he had found a place which appealed to him, a one-bedroom apartment in Edgewater, New Jersey, facing upper Manhattan over the expanse of the Hudson River, a two-minute drive from the George Washington Bridge. The prospect of living outside the city delighted Brian. He realized it would entail an extra journey to the office each day, but he welcomed the opportunity of living away from the permanent helter-skelter atmosphere of midtown Manhattan.

Leaving a check to cover a month's rent with the superintendent as a deposit, Brian caught a bus back across the bridge from Fort Lee to Washington Heights and took the subway to Fifty-ninth Street, his nose wrinkling faintly in disgust at the condition of the train. When he got out at Columbus Circle, he passed a hot-dog stand; the sight of people eating suddenly reminded him how hungry he was. Since Thelma had left, he had taken to cooking again, enjoying the opportunity of experimenting with dishes, something he had not done since the early days of his marriage when it had still seemed like fun. Tonight, however, he fancied being waited on, wanting to relax after the hours of looking at apartments.

He ate in a small Italian restaurant on West Fifty-seventh Street, near the store, then began to walk across town, appreciating the improving weather, his coat open, hands in his pockets. He crossed Madison, Park and Lexington Avenues, eventually reaching Second Avenue near the Queensborough Bridge ramp across the East River. Knowing this to be an area densely populated by singles bars, he began to look along both sides of the street like an explorer in unknown territory, waiting for one that would tempt him. The first four he checked were almost empty. Passing them up, he continued north on Second Avenue, heading toward the Seventies. A bar on the opposite side of the road caught his eye. As he crossed over, two men came out of the bar laughing, sharing a joke. Interest mounting, he quickened his pace, catching the door before it had fully closed.

Once inside, his courage almost deserted him. He stood by the door, looking nervously into the premises. Four men were seated at the bar talking. Another dozen men were scattered around in groups of two or three, while the barman stood in front of his display of bottles polishing glasses. Brian took a deep breath and strolled as casually as he could to the bar, feeling several of the men turn to look his way and assess him.

"Johnny Walker Black," he said quietly.

The barman poured the drink without a word. He took Brian's five-dollar bill, pushing back the change. As Brian pocketed the money, the bartender returned to polishing his glasses, holding each one up to the light, squinting as he checked for spots. Brian muttered his thanks and sat down in the furthest corner from the door, making himself comfortable at a small table.

A minute passed during which he sipped uncertainly at the Scotch. He looked around. Nothing had changed. Occasionally one or other of the men would turn and glance in his direction—steady, appraising glances which he returned.

Brian began to wonder whether he had made a mistake. Since Thelma's departure, coming immediately on the heels of his experience in the London pub and his subsequent soul-searching, he had decided to be honest with himself, do what he felt was right. Now, as he sat alone in the corner of the bar totally ignored, he wondered if he had, in fact, taken the right course.

Finishing the drink, he went back to the bar and ordered a refill, surveying the nearest group while he waited, searching for some sign of recognition, of acceptance. One of the men, with curling blond hair, looked briefly before returning to his conversation. Dismayed that the evening was developing into one long anticlimax, Brian took the new drink back to the table, returning to idle pondering on his motives for seeking out such an establishment.

The opening of the street door interrupted his thoughts, offering a diversion from his fruitless self-interrogation. Looking across, he saw that three men had entered. One of them gazed around the bar; his eyes came to rest on Brian, and there was a mutual instant of surprised recognition. He broke away from his companions, walking quickly across to where Brian sat.

"Of all the faces I might have expected to see here, Brian, yours certainly isn't one of them. Hello and welcome."

Brian smiled sheepishly at the greeting, taking the offered hand hesitantly, shaking it. He had known Fletcher Austin for many years, and seeing the model in the environment of a gay bar gave him a shock which he managed to disguise. Certainly he had heard the rumors about the man, but he had dismissed them as idle gossip, tales that were spread by other models jealous of his success, aired again when there was nothing more interesting to talk about. With a slight feeling of amusement, he noticed that the model was wearing one of the Viscenzi designer label suits, a pale blue pinstripe three-piece which complemented his light brown hair and tanned skin admirably.

"Join me?" Brian asked.

Still shaking his head in surprise at the unexpected encounter, Fletcher sat down, tossing a pack of cigarettes and a lighter onto the table.

"What about your friends?" Brian asked. "Do they want to sit with us?"

Fletcher twisted his neck awkwardly to see that the two men with whom he had arrived had sat down in another part of the bar, not even glancing his way.

"It's the old story, Brian. Two's company and three's just an uncomfortable crowd. I was only tagging along for the ride, seeing what I could get up to. But never mind me, what are you doing here? I'd heard that you and your wife had come to a parting of the ways, but this is still unexpected."

Brian studied his drink, wondering how to reply. He could still protect his innocence by claiming that he had wandered into the bar by mistake, not knowing what it was, and had been interested enough to stay around and learn how the other half lived. "It takes some people longer than others to recognize themselves for what they are," he said eventually. "Guess I'm one of the latecomers."

"Better late than never, to coin a hackneyed phrase." Fletcher pointed to Brian's glass. "What are you drinking?"

"I'm okay," Brian protested.

Fletcher waved aside the refusal. "If I can't buy a drink for a man who can put plenty of business my way, then I might as well pack up and go home for the night—read a book, or do something equally desperate."

Almost reluctantly, Brian drained the glass and passed it across the table to Fletcher. He felt the Scotch beginning to take effect, loosening him up, spreading a pleasantly warm and contented sensation throughout his body; on top of the heavy meal, it was starting to make him feel at peace with the world. By the time Fletcher returned with the drinks, Brian had removed his light coat and opened his jacket, prepared for a far longer stay than had originally looked probable.

"To your new-found identity," Fletcher toasted, raising his glass. "May you live long to enjoy it."

Brian responded warmly, clinking his glass against the model's. "It sure as hell can't be any worse than the one I had."

Fletcher eyed him speculatively. "You're living in an enlightened age now, Brian. You're supposed to have a positive attitude, none of these negative vibrations. If you are something, be proud of it. Don't hide your light underneath a bushel when you're among friends."

The ease with which Brian had sought out the bar began to desert him again, just as it had done when he had first entered and realized what he was getting into. He felt apprehensive, nagged once more by doubts. Seeking an escape route, he changed the subject, trying to draw Fletcher into a conversation on the planned change of advertising policy at Chestertons.

"I don't know," the model mused. "I make my money from standing in front of a camera, making your shoddy suits look better than they really are for the benefit of a gullible public." His face split immediately into the famous friendly grin. "I'm kidding you," he added quickly, in case Brian took umbrage.

"Seriously, I don't bother thinking too much about the philosophy of advertising. I'm only worried about how I come out in the picture. It's a specialist's field—the model, the ad manager for the company, the photographer, etc. We all stick pretty much to our own areas."

"Do you know the girl who's running our show now?" Brian asked.

"Simon's wife, isn't it?" Brian nodded. "We've worked together a few times in the long distant past," Fletcher said.

"What do you think of her?"

Fletcher rolled the drink around his glass, eying it as he thought out his answer. "She's not my favorite person, if that's any kind of reply to your question," he said, suddenly becoming very earnest. "She's far from it, in fact."

"How come?"

"Because I'm sitting here talking to you right now. That's how come." Fletcher saw that Brian was puzzled by the answer and elaborated. "Della Sanchez, or Chesterton as she now calls herself, is one very shrewd lady. She is also a very straight lady, painfully so. The reason that little pipsqueak agency she used to work for hasn't wanted me for years is that she doesn't like gays. And she had a lot of influence around the place. I don't think she can bear to be around anybody in pants who doesn't want to crawl into hers."

Brian took a quick pull of his Scotch to hide his fluster at the model's reply. Christ, what was he getting into? Visiting a gay bar only to find out that Simon's wife had—or so Fletcher alleged—a mentality regarding homosexuals that went back to the Victorian era.

"So what will happen to you at Chestertons," he asked Fletcher, "now that she's handling the account from the inside?"

"That's a different story," Fletcher answered confidently. "The few accounts I lost at her old agency were the type of jobs any idiot could do— cigarettes, lip salves, bread and butter garbage. But nobody in this city models clothing the way I do. Old Jonathan would never let me go."

"I hope you're right," Brian said, feeling little of Fletcher's certainty; he had already seen some of Della's sharpness, her planning and execution.

Fletcher smiled disarmingly. "Of course I'm right. And she'll probably do a first rate job of advertising for Chestertons, once she swallows her pride about using me. She's bright, and she's got all her stuff together. You'll find that out next Wednesday when the first advertisement comes out."

Talking of the company made Brian once again feel on firmer ground. "Tell me the truth, what do you think of our merchandise?" he asked the model. "You see enough of our competitors' goods to know the score."

For answer, Fletcher pulled his jacket open to reveal the large Viscenzi label prominently displayed on the inside pocket lining. "I wear your suits," he said. "Isn't that reference enough?"

"Only because we gave it to you on top of the normal fee for the Viscenzi shoot," Brian retorted, grinning. "Give me a straight answer; how do we stand up?"

"The best for the price. I've modelled some real garbage in my time to keep old man wolf away from the door. Your stuff is far and away the best. Make you happier?"

Brian continued to discuss the business with Fletcher, pleasantly surprised to find the model extremely knowledgeable about the clothing industry. Many of the models Brian had encountered had only been interested in the financial reward which their looks and style brought them; they had neither interest in nor knowledge about the clothes they modelled. Perhaps that was what made Fletcher Austin the number one clothing model in the city.

Shortly before eleven, Fletcher stood up to leave. Brian, at a loss how to conclude the evening, also rose.

"How about coming up for a nightcap?" he asked, the words spilling out of his mouth before he could think about them.

Fletcher gave him the same cool, speculative look he had used earlier. "Sure," he agreed. "Why not?"

Jonathan was still suffering intermittently from the pain across his chest, a tight, constricting sensation, coming and going without warning, making breathing difficult. Additionally his left arm seemed to ache, and he suspected rheumatism.

Go to the doctor, Miriam had urged him at least twice a day. And at least twice a day he had refused. But when the discomfort continued, increasing and abating in an unpredictable rhythm, he began to get concerned. He had never bothered with regular checkups, only going when Miriam's nagging became unbearable and the doctor's pontifications on health seemed the lesser of the two evils. What hit other people would never dare to attack him. But...

Okay, he thought irritably. I'll keep Miriam happy. I'll go to the damned quack. And I'll get bawled out for smoking again because he'll spot it. And I'll be told that I can't drink any more. And no coffee, no sugar, no this and no that. And I'll say yes, yes, yes—and carry on just as I have been doing.

And for all that, the doctor will get a hundred bucks and nothing will change—except Miriam will be happy for five minutes.

# 22

The first new-format advertisement was greeted with a degree of trepidation at the Chestertons Head Office on West Fifty-seventh Street. Della brought in a copy of the newspaper when she and Simon arrived, only to find that other management members had done the same thing. As she took off her coat and sat down to study the advertisement, Jonathan rang through, asking to see her. She made him wait five minutes while she checked the copy scrupulously, an action she knew was unnecessary; but her inbuilt professionalism forced her to the task.

Pleased with the overall effect, she took the newspaper to the boardroom. Jonathan had his own copy on the desk, spread open at the Chestertons advertisement.

"Happy with it?" he asked. "Will we have customers breaking down the doors to buy those suits?"

"Give it some time," she cautioned him. "It's a four-day promotion, not a one-day special offer. I doubt if you'll see much traffic in the stores before this evening when people leave work. Your big selling times will come in the evenings and on Saturday."

Jonathan grunted and returned his attention to the newspaper. "And what happens next week? And the week after that? We can't keep putting things on special promotion. We'll be broke in no time."

"I thought we discussed all that," Della replied. "We do a four-day special promotion once a month, a different garment each time to pull in customers. This month it's a suit, an expensive piece of merchandise, so it's a big saving to the consumer. Next month it could be a sports coat, trousers, leisurewear, even something as small as a sweater."

"But what happens between the off-price ads?"

"I was coming to that. We use fill-ins during the other three weeks to keep the Chestertons name in the public eye. We'll have carefully worded fashion ads telling of new merchandise developments, painting a picture of today's market to keep our customers informed of what's happening on the men's wear scene. It will be almost like a regular article in the newspaper, except we'll be paying for it and it will feature only Chestertons. And if we have a slow selling line, we can do a special promotional advertisement; it was all in that final presentation I made last week."

"You're perfectly right," Jonathan apologized. "I must be getting absent-minded." He paused to unwrap an antacid tablet, popping it quickly into his mouth. "Absent-mindedness and indigestion—two things that God sends to plague you as you get older."

"Are you sure it's indigestion?" There was a trace of anxiety in Della's question.

"What else could it be? Either I ate in too much of a hurry, or Miriam's cooking isn't what it used to be."

"It's the first reason," Della suggested. "There's nothing wrong with the cooking."

Jonathan gave her a disgusted look which he tried to hold but could not; it changed after a second into a warm smile as he realized how fond he had become of his second daughter-in-law. "That's women's loyalty speaking. You're not supposed to take sides." He turned back to the advertisement for a final time, then straightened up abruptly, snapping his fingers. "The whole reason I asked you to come in here . . . I forgot about it completely."

"Oh?" Della's eyebrows rose a fraction. "What was that?"

"What made you decide to use a different model? I thought our regular guy always looked pretty good."

Della had been expecting the question; indeed, she was surprised that Jonathan had allowed himself to ramble onto other subjects before bringing it up. "I don't think Fletcher Austin's very good for the Chestertons image," she replied calmly. "Don't you approve of the model I used?" For this first advertisement, Della had taken it upon herself to arrange for new photographs to be taken, neglecting those which had been shot at the beginning of the season. She had selected a new model and shot the promotional garments again, sending revised plates out to the newspapers.

"I think this guy looks too young," Jonathan said. "Sure, he's got plenty of style, but he's somehow not us. What's wrong with Fletcher, anyway?"

"He's bent."

"He's what?" asked Jonathan, uncomprehending at first.

"Bent," Della repeated slowly. "Gay. Queer. Homosexual. A fag."

The deliberate way in which Della rolled out the expressions shocked Jonathan. He glared at the young woman, trying to intimidate her with his size. "So what? Even if it is true, it doesn't mean a damned thing to our customers. All that matters is that they think they'll look as good as he does if they buy the suits he's advertising."

Della stood her ground, not batting an eyelid, refusing to be cowed into surrender by Jonathan's bluster. "It's a personal thing," she admitted. "If we're in the business of selling men's clothes, we should have a man advertise them. Or would you rather I went back to him?" she added tactfully.

Jonathan mulled the question over in his mind. The antacid tablet had not done a thing for him, and he was feeling more uncomfortable with each passing minute. He badly wanted to belch, but each time he tried nothing happened; the pocket of painful gas stayed exactly where it was.

"Do whatever you like," he said gruffly. "It's your ball; run with it as you see fit." He stared in surprise when she stayed where she was. "Go on," he urged. "Take off and dream up some more winners for us."

"I'd like to see you about something else if you've got the time right now," she said.

Jonathan shifted uncomfortably, trying to ease the pressure in his chest. Damn it, he thought irritably. Why the hell can't I belch—after Della's gone, of course—and get rid of it?

"What is it now?" The impatience in his voice was unintentional.

"I think it would be in our best interests to do some sort of promotion for the Mr. Simon shops as well," she replied. "From what I've seen, we've got a lot of money tied up in them. Although we're beginning to make some headway, I think a good shot in the arm from some thoughtful advertising would do them the world of good."

Jonathan was about to reply that the shops had been advertised once before, months ago, with copy dreamed up by Simon. Offhand he could not remember the exact wording of the ad, only that it had been something about becoming a Mr. Simon man. The advertisement copy had rambled on at great length about a concept in dressing which had made little sense to anybody but Simon, who had claimed that the meaning was as clear as day. It had not mentioned any specific merchandise, merely the fact that being outfitted in the boutiques would turn a man into an altogether different, more attractive personality. The result had been a complete disaster, with very little new business directly traceable to the advertisement.

Then Jonathan remembered to whom he was talking—Della, Simon's wife—so he made no mention of the earlier ad.

"What have you got in mind?"

"A personal approach. An interview with Simon."

Jonathan knew that his mouth had dropped open in surprise and fought to bring it back to its normal state. "An interview with Simon?" he gasped. "What the hell's going on?"

Della remained perfectly calm in the face of Jonathan's open hostility to the idea. "If we put the message across on a personal level, a confidential talk from the man behind the boutiques, I think it would have a tremendous impact. It would create a positive link between the retailer and the customer."

Jonathan allowed Della's description of Simon as the man behind the boutiques to pass without comment; he was still amazed that she could be serious about such an advertising approach. He had seen this type of promotion done before, and he was certain that Simon was not the best person to be identified through it.

Unperturbed by the obvious pessimism on his face, Della continued speaking. "Think of this. We use a picture or two of Simon, very relaxed, and throw in six leading questions which will reflect the positive side of the Mr. Simon shops if they're answered properly." She saw Jonathan open his mouth to speak and kept right on going.

"The answers will be written by me, and we'll make up the most fitting questions for them. Don't worry about it. All we're going to do is explain the younger man's attitude toward the clothing he wears—and explain it in a way which will appeal to him and forge a link with Mr. Simon."

"Where's the money coming from?" Jonathan grunted.

"That's something else I wanted to bring up," Della said. "From what I've seen so far, you've never bothered with a proper advertising budget. You've treated it like a petty cash expenditure, having the ads placed as and when you felt like it and paying when the bills came in. In my office, I have a projected budget for the remainder of this season, and a complete one for fall-winter. You'll find it all makes a lot of sense and will pay you well in the long run. Do you not think so?"

Jonathan raised his hands in surrender. "Go. Do whatever you want. The more I hear from you, the more faith I have in you—after I see the results of this four-day promotion," he added with a wink.

Smiling triumphantly, Della left the boardroom. She turned left to go to her own office, then changed her mind, doing an about-face toward Simon's room. She had just won his first battle.

As she passed by the boardroom door, she heard what sounded like a loud belch from within. But she could not be sure.

Gerald stayed in the store till it closed at nine, watching with pleased interest as customers walked in and examined the suits which were featured in the advertisement. Special signs had been ordered to co-incide with the promotion; he thought it was effective, supporting the advertisement well. What he enjoyed most, however, was watching the salespeople, who came under his responsibilities as operations manager.

The Chestertons group prided itself on stocking only the best merchandise and hiring only the best salespeople to sell it; the three hours Gerald spent in the main store offered him ample testimony. As customers became interested in the suits on special offer, they were being persuaded to buy shirts and ties without even realizing it. One salesman in particular caught Gerald's attention, a man who had been with the company for six years and was slated for a certain managership when one became available. Gerald watched, fascinated, as the man helped a customer into a navy suit, leading him to a full-length mirror which was placed strategically close to a shirt display unit. As the customer checked his reflection, the salesman made a point of glancing at the shirts. He picked two from the rack, one blue, one cream, and held them against the suit the customer was trying on.

"These both go very well, sir. Which one would you prefer?"

Before the customer knew what was happening, he had agreed to buy both shirts and two ties to go with them. And when he left the store, he walked out with a smile on his face, certain that he had come away with a bargain.

Once, Gerald caught the salesman's eye and grinned. The man responded with a broad wink. "It's easy," he whispered in passing. "Never ask a question where the answer could be no. It's like taking candy from a baby."

"Has the ad helped?" Gerald asked.

"Ask me again when payroll hires a truck for my commission this week." The salesman walked quickly across the floor toward another customer who was looking at the off-price suits.

By the time he arrived home, Gerald was ready for bed. He had watched other people work, but the intensity of traffic through the store made him feel that he had been doing the selling. He was also happy. The advertisement had been a big attraction, and, just as important, he had seen that the salesmen were really on their toes, enjoying their work enough to put in one hundred percent and more. Hardly one customer had walked out with just a single purchase.

As he entered the house, Marilyn came out to greet him, the glass of Scotch balanced on the tray. He kissed her and took the drink, all in one sweeping motion.

"You're late," she chided him. "Three hours late. You could have called me, at least. Dinner's ruined, and you'll have to make do with an omelette."

"Have you had yours?"

"No. I waited for you. Anita's eaten and gone to her English classes, and I've been waiting here all alone."

"All alone and feeling blue?" Gerald asked, grinning at her over the top of the glass. "I got stuck in the store, and five minutes turned into three hours."

Marilyn took the empty glass he held out to her. "That busy tonight?"

"And how. That advertisement's pulling them in like flies around a garbage dump." He thought over what he had said, adding, "Hardly a good comparison, but it was something to see all the same."

"So you've got a bright sister-in-law," Marilyn said, walking into the kitchen. Gerald followed closely, grabbing her around the waist as she reached the sink.

"Not nearly as bright as my wife."

She turned and saw the laughter in his face. "What about your dinner then?" she asked.

"You told me it was ruined already. What difference is another hour or two going to make?" He laughed loudly and picked her up, hoisting her over his left shoulder in a fireman's lift.

"Mind your head," he called, walking through the kitchen doorway, heading for the stairs.

In the privacy of their bedroom, he stood in front of the king-sized bed and dropped her gently into the middle of it. She bounced twice as the mattress recoiled under the sudden attack. Then he was leaning over her, feeling himself falling, falling, falling into those crystal clear blue eyes.

"Are you sure I'm brighter than Della?" she teased him.

"Opposites attract, remember? It's an old physics law or something. I prefer mine to have blond hair and blue eyes."

When the telephone rang that evening, Brian was in the middle of packing fragile possessions in preparation for his move to Edgewater on the following weekend. Once he had made the decision to move, he could not wait to get out of his present accommodation. The apartment held too many memories of Thelma, the drinking, the rows, the downhill gallop to nowhere. It was as though the bitterness of their stay had permeated the walls, worked its way into the very structure of the building, a ghost which haunted the house of its demise for all eternity, seeking peace while spreading unease wherever it trod; the only way Brian could exorcise it was by moving out.

He had heard from a friend in Chicago that Thelma had returned to the city as if she had never left it, reverting to the shrewish romance writer she had once been with no visible effect from the drinking bout. So she was happy again, secure in the life she knew, and he was happy for her.

Reluctantly he put down the Wedgewood dish he had been packing so carefully and walked over to the telephone. He let it ring one more time before picking up the receiver.

"Brian Chambers."

The voice at the other end came back with a remarkably good impersonation of his own Chicago accent. "Fletcher Austin."

"What a lovely surprise," Brian burst out. "Are you coming over to give me a hand with the packing?"

"I hadn't planned to, but I will. There are a couple of things that I'd like to see you about."

"Such as?"

"That ad in today's paper, for one thing."

"And what's the other?" Brian asked.

"That ad in today's paper. I want to talk about it twice."

"What about the ad?" Brian asked. "It was the first one of the new kind, you know that. Gave us quite a good day apparently."

"It was a great ad," Fletcher agreed enthusiastically. "Absolutely marvellous. Except for one thing. I wasn't in it, and I think our friendship is worth an explanation why."

Brian breathed out slowly, a long, tired sigh. "Come on over and we'll talk about it," he promised.

Fletcher Austin arrived twenty minutes later. Brian opened the apartment door and led him into the living room. The model glanced inquisitively at the packing cartons, gently picking up a bone china ornament which Brian had bought in London.

"Like it?" Brian asked.

Turning it upside down to see the manufacturer's name, Fletcher said, "It's exquisite. Royal Doulton. Got any spare ones lying around that you don't want?"

"Keep it," Brian offered. "It's called the Balloon Lady, one of their more popular pieces."

Fletcher placed the piece carefully on the stereo set. "Thank you. Is it really a gift, or merely a salve for my injured ego?" He sat down in an easy chair and stretched out his legs. "What the hell happened with that ad, Brian? How come I wasn't used for this new promotion?"

Brian spread his hands helplessly. "Honestly, I didn't know they weren't going to use you. Nobody did, not even Jonathan, as hard as that may be to believe. We all saw the mock-ups of the new ad with you on them. But instead of using shots from our stock—and I only found this out today when the ad came out—Della went out and hired a new model. She had a complete shooting session with him."

The model regarded Brian evenly. "So what happens in the future? Do I get used again, or do I get shafted permanently in favor of this new character, or whoever Della decides to drag in?"

"I'll bring it up at the next meeting," Brian promised. "Just a casual mention about why we're not using you any more." He remembered the conversation in the Second Avenue bar. "You said she'd had you bounced in other places. Looks like she's doing it again."

"I would have thought that somebody"—he let the word hang— "would have stuck up for me at Chestertons. We've been together for a long time. Looks like I was wrong."

"Fletcher, we were all surprised by the ad this morning. Don't worry, I'll do what I can for you."

"I'd appreciate it," Fletcher said. He had been furious that morning on seeing the newspaper. It made no difference to his financial status how many times he appeared in the ads; once he had modelled the clothes during the preseason shooting, his job was over. But to find himself suddenly usurped in midseason by somebody else was a severe blow to his reputation, especially in a new type of presentation. That was adding a liberal dose of salt to a very raw wound. He had thought of calling Brian at the office, demanding to know what had happened, but he left it till the evening as being the more diplomatic course.

Brian would have to do something for him. With advancing age, Fletcher's once unassailable position as the leading male model in the city was nowhere near as secure as it had once been. There seemed to be a growing preference for slimmer guys, all skin and bones and tough-looking faces; he sensed he might be on the professional way out. Nevertheless, Fletcher Austin was determined to make the remainder of his stay as long and as lucrative as possible.

"Maybe I'd better change my ways and make a pass at her," he suggested. "The straight models who had her never complained about the experience."

"Neither did Simon," Brian said. "According to office rumor, he was making out with her for six months before they decided to get married."

"Each unto his own," Fletcher remarked philosophically. "Just see what you can do about getting that other creep bounced. I'm still number one, and I want back in those ads."

# 23

The doctor's voice was low-pitched, penetrating. He looked across his desk at Jonathan as he spoke, tapping the end of a yellow pencil on the desk for emphasis.

"Mr. Chesterton, I have such implicit faith in you that I'm certain the moment you walk out of that door you'll disregard everything I'm saying, just like you always do, and carry on as if nothing had happened. But I'm warning you—if you do it this time, you'll be signing your own death warrant."

Jonathan glared back, daring the doctor to say another word. He had gone through an hour-long examination which, as far as he was concerned, was an hour out of his life, an irreplaceable sixty minutes which could have been far better spent at the office. And to add insult to injury, he had to sit through another lecture from this damned quack.

The doctor paid no attention to Jonathan's painfully visible antagonism. He continued speaking, driving home specific points with the end of his pencil, a noise and action which became increasingly irritating to his patient.

"Is all that banging really necessary?" Jonathan asked finally. "Do you have to keep time with yourself like you're Leonard Bernstein?"

The tapping ceased immediately as the doctor opened his hand. The clatter the pencil made as it settled on the desk top acted on Jonathan's nerves like chalk screeching across a blackboard. He sat bolt upright, teeth clenched, jaw muscles standing out.

"Mr. Chesterton, your every action stresses what I'm trying to tell you. You're so caught up in your business that you're living on a virtual razor's edge. Pull out of it while you still can. Give it away, all of it. Let somebody else have the worry; otherwise your desk will become your coffin and your stores your memorial stone. Maybe that's what you really want. I don't know. I'm a medical man, not a shrink. But I still feel duty-bound to stop you trying to kill yourself.

"Maybe you think this whole thing is a big game, ignoring my advice to stop smoking, abusing your body in every way you can find. It's not a game. It's life itself." His hand edged out for the pencil again, stopping when he saw Jonathan's eyes following the movement.

"Stick to the diet I gave you last time, the one you've been ignoring. Remember it? But I tell you this. If you ever smoke another cigar or take another drink, you may as well jump in front of a train. Your heart can't take much more of what you're handing out, Mr. Chesterton. That indigestion you've been complaining about—that's not indigestion, that's angina; it's your heart sending out an SOS which you're disregarding completely. One day—and it's not far off—there won't be any more warnings, just a massive heart attack that'll blow you away like a leaf. Is that clear enough for you to understand?"

"Crystal clear," Jonathan replied coldly. "Now I'm waiting for you to call my wife and tell her to spy on me to make sure I behave myself."

For the first time, the doctor smiled. "Mr. Chesterton, you're absolutely incorrigible."

In a fraction of a second, Jonathan's mind spanned forty years, remembering when he had told his father the same thing. But the reasons were different. Jacob had only been exhibiting a pessimistic outlook on an event which was completely alien to him; he was not fooling around with his health.

"All right," Jonathan said, surrendering. "You win." With a dramatic gesture he reached into his jacket pocket and pulled out a cigar case, tossing it into the trash can by the doctor's desk. The doctor observed the performance with an amused glint in his eyes.

"Is this little show for my benefit, Mr. Chesterton, or are you really doing it for yourself?" Not expecting an answer, he bent down and scribbled out a prescription which he handed to Jonathan. "Take those if the pains come back. But you should be free of them if you follow my instructions. Stay away from alcohol and smoking—and the office when you can. There must be other people there whom you can trust."

Standing up, he escorted Jonathan to the door. As they shook hands in farewell, the doctor said, "I expect to see you again in six months without a trace of cigar smoke."

"How would you know if I've been cheating?"

"Very simply. Your wife will cancel your appointment because she'll be your widow. Good morning, Mr. Chesterton."

The simplicity of the statement struck Jonathan far more solidly than had all the figures and statistics which the doctor had thrown at him. As he waited for the elevator to take him down to street level, he was troubled to find himself shivering slightly. The doctor's parting words had brought him face to face with the reality of his own mortality, something which he had never acknowledged before. How could a man who had almost single-handedly built an empire like Chestertons be mortal? Yet now, as the doctor's farewell echoed in his mind, he realized he could be just that.

When he arrived at the office, he studiously collected his three metal ashtrays, dropping them into the trash can underneath his desk. He treated the action like a ceremonial rite, pausing between each one. Then he called Miriam, telling her of the examination results. Although she passed no comment, Jonathan sensed a righteous attitude and shortened the conversation to a minimum.

How the hell do I take it easy? he wondered, sitting behind the desk. There's a business to be run, and that overpaid cretin with a shingle wants me to walk away from it. He might as well have ordered me into a wheel chair or a senior citizens' home.

Looking at the wall clock, he was glad to see it was almost lunchtime. He rang through to Brian Chambers, asking what he was doing for lunch. Learning that Brian had nothing planned, Jonathan arranged to meet him in ten minutes.

Before leaving the office to keep his lunchtime appointment, Jonathan had second thoughts about his earlier deeds. He bent down and picked the three ashtrays out of the trash can, replacing them on the desk and table.

Della put the end of the pencil in her mouth, nibbling lightly on the wood while she read the words she had just written. Satisfied with the theme, she lifted her eyes from the note pad and looked across the living room at Simon, who sat watching her.

"Think you could have said this?" she asked, holding out the note pad to him.

Simon eased himself out of the chair and walked toward her. Scanning over the rough copy for the Mr. Simon advertisement, he digested the main points and disregarded the padding.

"Well?" Della insisted. "Could you?"

He read the copy again, this time more thoroughly. "Never in a million years," he said. "It's good, damned good."

Della was pleased. "That's why it's so important for Chestertons to have somebody around who's good with words. That sort of approach will pull people into the Mr. Simon shops. When that ad comes out, you'll be talking directly to every potential customer. You'll be telling him about changing trends and how you're interpreting them—why youth has accepted the role of fashion leader, and why all the bizarre styles of ten years ago have been toned down because of the current economic slump. Every person who sees this ad will think they've got a personal link with you. You'll establish a credible personality with the people you want to patronize the Mr. Simon shops. You're showing them you care. And, most important, you'll be getting the sort of exposure that nobody at Chestertons has ever got. After this comes out, you won't be a backroom boy any more.

You'll be acknowledged by the public as a leading member of the American men's clothing industry. That's what you want, isn't it?"

Simon nodded eagerly, seeing it all happen. "How did you get my father to go along with this?"

"The same way I've been telling you to go about things. Think a project through from beginning to end and present it in a logical sequence, nothing left unanswered, everything in clear black and white with no gray areas. Besides, ever since that first off-price advertisement came out, your father thinks I can do no wrong."

Simon dropped the note pad on the table. "Looks as though I've got my own public relations officer for nothing, just by marrying her."

"Not quite for nothing." She tossed the chewed pencil on top of the note pad, watching while it rolled to a halt. "You can pay me back by thinking before you open your mouth in the future. If I build you up, I don't want you wrecking everything by rushing in like a crazed bull in a china shop. When you're powerful enough within the company, then you can have your disagreements. But don't fly off the handle when you've got nothing to back yourself up with. You'll only hurt yourself that way, and my work will go down the tube."

The final sentence struck Simon as odd. "What do you mean by your work? The advertising program?"

Della's smile was positively beatific. "Hardly. At the moment I don't find it very glorifying to be the wife of the company's also-ran." Seeing the way he started, she laughed. "You're all equal partners after your father, remember?" Simon blushed at having the lie brought up again.

"It didn't take me long to find out how untrue that was," Della continued. "The only reason I took the job your father offered me was because of the chance I'd have to build you up. I want you to have the same respect as your brother Gerald. I want to be married to the most powerful man in the company."

Simon made no reply. He stood silently, trying to comprehend what Della had said. He was seeing a side of his wife he never knew existed. Ambition was one thing; he knew she had that. But to lay out in clear terms that she was maneuvering him toward the top because she thought him incapable of reaching it under his own steam cast a new light on her. Simultaneously, he was not displeased.

When he eventually spoke, he moved the subject to one where he felt more comfortable. "Coming to bed?"

"Not for the moment," Della replied. "There are a couple of other things I want to get done this evening." She smiled warmly at him, forgetting the earlier conversation. "Make my side of the bed warm, will you?"

Simon was laughing as he left the room.

Long after her husband had gone to bed, Della remained in the living room, thinking deeply about what had to be done at Chestertons if her ambition was to be fulfilled. The advertising did not concern her unduly; she could handle that blindfolded. She was more intrigued with her plans to elevate Simon from his position of handcuffed mediocrity to one of real power. Personalizing him with the Mr. Simon advertisement would help, but only marginally. No matter how the public saw him, there were still the other members of the board to be taken into consideration. Somebody must be persuaded to side with him. His mother did already, but that vote meant nothing, a cry in the wilderness. It had to be either Jonathan, Gerald or Brian. And even in her wildest optimism, she saw little to be hopeful about with any of those names.

It was after midnight when she stood up, yawning luxuriously. She placed the note pad in her attaché case to be taken to the office in the morning, then walked into the bedroom. Simon was asleep already, and she was amused to see that he lay on her side of the bed, face up. She undressed quietly, then tiptoed to the bed, leaning over the sleeping form. Pressing her mouth down on his, she forced his lips open with her tongue, feeling him come awake and reach out for her.

"I think we'll make quite a team if we play our cards right," she said, pulling away from him. "You and I—we'll be invincible."

Simon shook himself into full wakefulness. "Later," he said, dragging her down. "We'll talk about it later."

# 24

Della's star at Chestertons was in a meteoric ascendancy. Figures from the previous week's business showed a marked increase over projected budget, most of which was centered around the range of suits featured in the four-day promotion; other incidental increases were picked up from accessories sold with the suits. Telephone reports from regional managers stressed the need for more information on forthcoming special promotions so that the salespeople could have time to plan their selling strategy. Additionally, the first advertisement for the Mr. Simon shops was almost ready for insertion; the copy had been cleared by Jonathan, and space booked. Despite her air of professional detachment, Della could not wait for the ad to appear; she was certain that the exposure would increase Simon's prestige, making the venture into a two-edged sword.

Outlining her plans for forthcoming promotions, she looked around the boardroom's mahogany table, eying her listeners, holding a stare, gauging their reactions toward her suggestions. Jonathan, his chin cupped in his hands, listened intently, either nodding or grunting monosyllabically as she comprehensively covered each point, expanding on a subject when she thought fit. Simon, who already knew the contents of her delivery, doodled on a sheet of paper, occasionally looking up to smile encouragement at her. As if I needed it, she thought; nevertheless she returned the smile. Gerald appeared to be only half listening, glancing at his father every so often to see what he was doing, while Brian made copious notes of everything that was said. Finally Della looked at her mother-in-law, knowing that the older woman had little to say at these meetings but determined to make her feel important; there was no time like the present in Della's mind for laying the groundwork of a useful alliance.

When she had completed her summation of the projected campaign, Jonathan led off a discussion, beginning with his favorite topic. Where was the money going to come from? His arguments were halfhearted, however; he had seen from the results of the first promotion that the advertisement had more than paid for itself. To argue about money, though, was part of his function, and Della could see that he was enjoying the situation, questioning her budget proposals, pinning her down to specifics which she answered immediately.

"I'm satisfied," he conceded at last. "What about anybody else? Any questions?"

Gerald brought his head up, giving his whole attention to the meeting, sitting back, hands flat on the table. "I'm for it one hundred percent—with all the trimmings, nothing spared. The only question I can think of is why we never had a properly thought-out advertising program before."

Simon turned to look at his brother. "Because we never had Della before." He made it sound that everybody should have known the answer and that Gerald was simply displaying his ignorance by asking such a question.

The compliment gave Della a distinct sensation of pleasure. It was the first one which Simon had publicly thrown her way; an excellent example, she decided, of how his courage was improving under her skillful tutelage.

"Will there be anything else," she asked, running her eyes over the people sitting around the table, "or can we call it a day and get some work done?"

She stopped talking as her gaze came to rest on Brian. There was something about his demeanor which arrested her attention completely. He had been acting out of character the whole meeting, taking notes of her suggestions, something he normally never did. He was troubled, deeply so, and Della could sense that he was also uncertain about broaching the subject which was aggravating him.

"Brian?" Her voice was gentle, persuasive. "I can see you're not happy about something. Can we bring it out into the open now and thrash it out so we don't run up against any problems later on when they'll cost us money?"

Brian coughed quietly into his hand, embarrassed at being called upon. "Maybe it's because I'm a traditionalist," he began, "or maybe it's because I'm a downright reactionary, but I don't like to see change when I'm quite happy with things the way they are."

Unable to see clearly where Brian's stumbling words were leading, Della gave him an ungraceful shove. "You're not making yourself very easy to understand. Let's have it straight—what's bugging you, Brian?"

"The whole four-day promotion struck me as strange." The words flooded out before he could check them, before he could think of a better way of phrasing it. "I didn't recognize it as one of our ads at all. It could have been anybody's. There was nothing to identify it with Chestertons."

"It was the new format, that's all," Della explained. "It was very simple and, as you can see from the figures in front of you, very, very effective."

Silently Brian began to debate the wisdom of getting onto the subject. He had taken notes of everything Della had said throughout the meeting, hoping that some reference would be made to reinstating Fletcher Austin, wishing that another of the management group would bring up the subject of why the model had been dropped and release him from the responsibility of broaching it. But nobody had cared enough about the switch to mention it, and the only information he could pass back to the model would be negative.

"It wasn't the format," he told Della. "It was the choice of model. I've been so used to seeing Fletcher, uh, what's his last name?"

"Austin."

"That's right, Fletcher Austin. I've been so used to seeing him in our ads, ever since I was in Chicago way back when. This new guy strikes me as strange. And the public's used to seeing Fletcher. If they're looking for one of our ads, they're going to be looking for Fletcher—the two are inseparable. Using this other guy concerns me—whether it's good for our image. Chestertons customers identify with Fletcher. This other guy's going to throw them."

Della's right eyebrow twitched almost imperceptibly in an involuntary muscle spasm. Her face became rigid as she tried to control her surprise at witnessing Brian's totally uncharacteristic dive into the advertising side of the business.

"I thought we needed a change, a new face," she said mechanically, her mind racing ahead of the words. "I realize that I switched the photograph without telling any of you. It was done in a rush, and I apologize for my lack of concern. But I think that Chestertons has been using Fletcher Austin for far too long. Besides"—she laughed lightly, trying to make the matter appear to be of little value—"he is getting on a bit, and we have to look elsewhere. It's easier for a middle-aged man to identify with a young model than for young people to identify with a model who's approaching middle-age." She glanced quickly at Jonathan, wondering if he remembered her disparaging remarks about the model, and her reasons for wanting to drop him. Jonathan stared back morosely, his mind elsewhere. Looking at the other three listeners, she saw that nobody was paying much attention to the interchange.

"I don't agree with you," Brian persisted. "Fletcher portrays the elegance that's associated with Chestertons. The other guy's much too young. He looks terrific, sure, but completely out of place in our clothes and our ads."

Della yielded graciously, seeing no point in pressing Brian further; she could see he was flustered enough as it was. "All right, Brian. We've got Fletcher's shots for the remainder of the season, so we'll use them. Then we'll have a proper discussion on what we should do for the fall-winter campaign." Dismissing Brian, she looked around the table again, letting her gaze linger on Simon, wondering if he had read anything strange into the conversation with Brian. Simon had returned to his doodling, taking no notice of what was going on around him.

"Will there be anything else?" she asked quietly, exploring all the intriguing possibilities which had appeared with Brian's concern over the advertisement.

Jonathan stood up, signifying the end of the meeting. Della waited by the door for Simon, walking with him to her small office. She closed the door, locking it. Simon noticed the action with surprise, a grin forming on his face.

"Now?" he asked in amazement. "My office is much better if that's what you want."

"No, you idiot." She laughed all the same. "That's not what I want. What do you know about Brian?" she asked.

Simon shrugged. "He's a Chestertons man through and through."

"His personal life. Think about that."

"Separated," Simon said. "His wife's taken off back home, and he's jumping for joy about it. Apparently she was a bitch. Apart from that one piece of information, he's an incredibly boring man."

"Does he go out at all? Any women you know about?"

"Who the hell knows?" Simon asked in return. "Who cares?"

"I do," Della said, "because I think he's a fag."

"A what?" Simon shouted, controlling his voice only when he saw Della's fierce look of warning. "What makes you come up with a ridiculous claim like that?" he asked in an exaggerated whisper. "That's a hell of a statement to make."

"Why?"

"Because it is." Simon stumbled around for a more concrete answer. "He's too dull, that's why. His conventional attitude would never let him be one."

"Has he ever been overly interested in the advertising before?"

"Not really," Simon answered, thinking back. "He usually left it to the agency. That's been part of the trouble in the past. Nobody really cared a damn about it."

Della began to walk around the office, pacing back and forth, reminding Simon of a lawyer in a courtroom drama. He dropped his eyes to her legs, watching the calf muscles as she walked, forgetting about Brian, forgetting about the reason he was in his wife's office.

"Think about this," Della said, standing in front of him, waiting while he raised his eyes. "One, all of a sudden Brian becomes interested in who's doing our advertising. This happens right after I take the unprecedented step of dropping Fletcher Austin. Two, Fletcher, as I told your father when I explained why I didn't want to use him, is one of the biggest closet queens in town. I don't know whether the breakup of Brian's marriage has anything to do with this. It's immaterial. But two things have suddenly happened, and they have to be connected."

As outrageously impossible as it seemed, Della's argument began to make some kind of sense to Simon. His eyes opened wide, and his jaw dropped till he was gazing at his wife with a half-witted expression. "You think he's got something going with Fletcher Austin?" he asked, dropping onto a chair in shock.

Della patted him on the head. "Make your face straight, Simon. The Mongoloid look doesn't do anything for you." She waited while Simon resumed his normal pose, although his face was still tinged with disbelief. "Would you like to make a friend of Brian," she asked, "have him on your side?"

The stupefied look returned to Simon's face. "A friend of Brian? He can't stand the sight of me, and I hate his guts."

"But think how helpful he'd be with his own Sword of Damocles hanging over him." She saw the metaphor was lost on Simon and explained further. "Do you think he'd help you if his own reputation rested on it?"

"How do you plan on doing that?" Simon asked. "Walk into his office, tell him you know he's a fag—if he is—and demand his support for me?"

"Wrong, wrong and wrong again. First we make certain of our suspicions," Della said. "Secondly, when we are certain beyond any shadow of a doubt, you tell him."

"Me!" Simon exploded. "The whole thing's your marvellous brain wave. Why the hell should I have to do the dirty work?"

Della's tone turned cold. "If you don't know the answer to that, Simon, you'd better resign yourself to remaining a nobody in your own family's business. I'll make all the bullets you need, but you have to fire them."

She walked past Simon, who remained seated, thinking over what Della had told him. He glanced around as she unlocked the office door, leaving it open, the message clear.

The storm which had been threatening all afternoon broke as Brian left the office. He stood in the shelter of a doorway for ten minutes while he waited for an empty cab and watched the heavy raindrops pound down onto the sidewalk, washing the city's dust into the already overflowing gutters. Seeing a cab, he rushed to the curb, stepping back quickly as the driver spotted him and cut in, splashing fountains of water over where Brian had been standing.

Entering the apartment, he walked carefully around the packing boxes that would be making the trip to Edgewater on the weekend. He slumped into a chair, mentally drained by the confrontation with Della over the advertising program. He knew now that the meeting, with its witnesses, had been the wrong place to make inquiries about Fletcher's future; to compound that mistake, he had tackled it wrongly. He realized he should have taken an entirely different approach, like holding up the ad and saying there was something different about it, letting Della make the statement that they had changed models. It would then have been up to her to explain why she had made the change, not up to him to get into a twisted mess making her volunteer the information.

He was thankful that Della had not mentioned Fletcher's homosexuality as the reason, although she knew about it. Even if Fletcher had not told him so, Brian would have believed that Della knew; advertising people had a way of knowing which way their models were inclined.

Pouring a generous measure of Scotch to soothe his shattered nerves, Brian went over the situation again, taking a more positive viewpoint. With the assistance of the whisky, his opinion of the conversation with Della began to change. How could she guess anything from what must have seemed nothing more important than a chance remark? She could have no reason to suspect anything. He was a businessman and, like many, averse to change; he wanted to know why the models had been switched. Hadn't he made that clear enough?

Feeling more confident as he saw the situation in a less damning light, Brian poured another drink and took off his damp raincoat, throwing it over the shower bar in the bathroom. Walking back to the living room, he looked disinterestedly at the packages awaiting the moving men. He would be glad when he was living like a civilized human being again, with all his possessions where they belonged, neat and orderly. The boxes were a darned nuisance; instead of seeing the art objects he treasured, the boxes hid them from sight—and were a health hazard as well, if he did not look where he was going.

Draining the glass, he picked up the telephone.

Della waited patiently in the bright yellow MG Midget with the black hood. When she had bought the small sports car two years earlier, it had seemed ideal for the city; light, easily maneuverable and small enough to park on half a meter space. The fact that the suspension was not up to the strains imposed on it by the city's diabolically potholed roads did not deter her. Nor did the fact that the convertible top had twice been slashed open to allow access to valuables left on the seat. She just made certain, after the second occasion, not to leave anything in the car. When she had married and moved into Simon's apartment, he had laughed at anybody wanting a car in Manhattan. He was not, however, averse to using it himself when the opportunity arose.

From where she was parked, Della had a clear view of the entrance to Brian's building. During the hour she sat watching, more than two dozen people walked in or out, but there was no sign of the man she sought.

She had left the office long before Brian and had gone back to the apartment to fetch the car from its underground garage. When Simon had asked where she was going, she had simply smiled. From the apartment, she drove back to West Fifty-seventh Street, waiting for Brian to come out, following the taxi to Central Park West.

If her suspicions were correct, the conclusive piece of the puzzle should fall into place very shortly. And if not tonight, there would be another time.

Fiddling with the tuning control of the radio, Della found a station she liked and sat back to wait comfortably, humming softly in time with the music.

Fletcher Austin answered the telephone on the fourth ring. He had been expecting Brian to phone with the results of the advertising meeting and had waited for the call.

"It's Brian. How you doing?"

Fletcher grinned. "Fine. Yourself? What's the news from the palace?" He listened for the reply. "Okay. I'll be over in an hour. Just give me time to finish a few things."

He hung up and looked around the apartment. He had nothing to do, but he did not want Brian to get the idea that he would run over straightaway. So Brian was doing him a favor. Big deal. That's what friends were for—and they were more than friends.

Fletcher knew the straights laughed at the word "lovers" when applied to the gay community, but it fitted. And if something fits, wear it. Doing favors, that's what lovers were for.

Turning on the color television, he sat down to watch a news program, taking little interest in the events portrayed on the screen, merely seeking a way to pass an hour.

While he waited for Fletcher to arrive, Brian fidgeted around the apartment seeking things to do. He found nothing. Everything which could be packed away was already in one of the boxes. All that remained were his clothes and a few kitchen utensils which he was leaving till last.

Agitated that the model was taking so long, Brian brought out the bottle of Scotch and poured another large drink. He was about to swallow the spirit neat when he remembered Thelma's abrupt nose dive into a bottle. He poured some of the whisky back, adding two ice cubes to the glass and topping if off with tap water.

Thinking about Thelma made him realize how grateful he was that she had recovered. It was a selfish thought; if she had carried on in Chicago as she had in New York, she would have been unable to work and would have sought his help. Lifting the glass, he toasted her deliverance from alcohol and wished her success in the future—as long as that future never involved him.

When the bell to the downstairs entrance finally rang, Brian hurried across to the intercom and pressed the talk button.

"Who is it?"

"Fletcher, you peasant. Let me in."

Pushing down the door-release button, Brian counted to five and released it. He waited another minute before looking through the security spyhole in the apartment door, seeing the model approach from the elevator. He opened the door and greeted Fletcher warmly.

"Come inside. I've got some good news for you."

Fletcher entered the apartment and shrugged off his coat, handing it to Brian as if he were a cloakroom attendant. "I sincerely hope you have. There have been enough sarcastic comments about that blasted advertisement, and I'm looking like a fool. If it happens again, I'll be on the skids." He walked past Brian and picked up the bottle of Scotch. "May I?"

"Help yourself." Dropping the model's coat over a chair, Brian waited till Fletcher had poured himself a drink. "I found out today that you'll be used for the remainder of the season. I managed to squeeze that much out of Della."

"Tactfully, I hope." Fletcher sipped the drink thoughtfully, swilling it around in his mouth. "What about next season, though, and the season after that? If I wind up on the outside then, that's also no damned good to me."

"I've got you a reprieve for this season," Brian said. "If you want it taken any further, you'll have to make friends with Della, get her to see your point of view."

"And how would you suggest I go about that difficult task?" Fletcher asked sarcastically. "Screw her?"

"Simon might object."

"So might I," Fletcher said, laughing. Putting down the empty glass, he walked to the window and looked out over Central Park. "Give me a better idea."

Pressing a sixty-dollar Italian shoe down on the clutch, Della pushed the Midget into gear. She glanced into the mirror, saw that the road behind was clear and pulled out. The satisfied smile on her face reflected her inner contentment. First time at bat, and a home run, a grand slam to start the game with. What more could a player ask?

Simon was watching television when she entered the apartment. He heard the front door open but paid no attention, completely engrossed in the show; on the coffee table next to him was a half-eaten sandwich and a glass of milk.

Della walked up behind him, her footsteps deadened by the thick carpet. "Guess who?" she teased, putting her hands over his eyes, pulling back his head.

"Genghis Khan, and get your hands away!" he yelled. "I'm trying to watch a damned show."

Della continued to blindfold him, ignoring his outburst. "Guess again. And try Sherlock Holmes this time."

"All right," he said impatiently, "Sherlock Holmes. Now will you let me see, please?"

She dropped her hands and walked in front of him, blocking off his view of the television set. He looked up, beginning to get genuinely annoyed. "Della, please. I'm trying to watch a . . ." He stopped abruptly as his brain registered the import of her words.

"What do you mean by Sherlock Holmes? What have you been up to?"

"Sitting outside our friend's apartment building on Central Park West, waiting to see who turned up. And guess who did turn up."

"Fletcher Austin?" Simon ventured, his voice a mixture of hope and fear.

"The very same. What do you think of those apples?" She turned her back to Simon and walked to the television set. "May I switch this garbage off?"

"Go ahead," he told her, his interest in the show forgotten. "Did you see Fletcher actually entering Brian's apartment?"

"No. I only saw him go into the lobby of the building."

"That's not good enough," Simon protested quickly, suddenly frightened by the enormity of the scheme which was becoming apparent to him. He was uncertain whether Della's plot was technically blackmail, but it seemed to come horrifyingly close. "Fletcher might have been visiting anybody."

"There are exactly twenty-four apartments in that block," Della countered. "That's too much of a coincidence. As I see it, Brian telephoned Fletcher to tell him about our conversation this afternoon. Fletcher obviously must have been running scared that his days with Chestertons were numbered. So what better thing could he ask than for his boyfriend to check out the position?"

Simon remained pessimistic. "They might just be friends."

Della shot him a scornful look. "How many times do I have to explain this to you, Simon? Exhibit one, Fletcher's gay. Exhibit two, Brian's single these days. And exhibit three, they're seeing each other. What else could you ask for? A signed confession by the pair of them that they're indulging in a homosexual relationship?"

"It's all happening too quickly," Simon complained. "Everything's falling into place like a gigantic coincidence. I can't go in to Brian and lean on him with this. It's too circumstantial."

Della watched him impatiently. She had expected Simon to demonstrate a degree of uncertainty. "Leave it to me," she said. "I'll make the first break in his defenses. When I've probed them, you can finish off the job. When it comes to the actual blackmail,"—she watched Simon blink in horror at the word—"that's right, blackmail; when it comes to that, it has to be you who tightens the screw."

"Okay." Simon swallowed hard. "Just make damned certain that his defenses are down. I don't want to go walking into a solid brick wall."

Della ran the tip of her tongue slowly over her lips in anticipation. She wrapped her arms around Simon's neck, clasping her fingers, dragging his head down to her own level.

"His defenses will be down," she assured him. "Now how about some token of appreciation? I reckon I deserve it."

# 25

Jonathan finished drying himself off from the shower, tossed the wet towel haphazardly over the rail and stepped onto the bathroom scales, looking down eagerly at the glass-covered dial.

"Miriam!" His shout rolled right through the house, reaching clearly to the morning room where Miriam was making breakfast. "I've lost three pounds in the past week. How about that?"

Grinning hugely at the achievement, he slipped into a robe and walked out of the bathroom, padding downstairs in slippered feet. "Did you hear what I said?"

Miriam continued to set the breakfast table. "I heard. I couldn't help hearing, the way you bellow. And it's about time you started losing weight. Thank God you're finally listening to the doctor and not going your own foolish way any more."

The euphoria at losing the weight dropped away from Jonathan as he surveyed breakfast—half a grapefruit, a slice of toast, yogurt and a cup of black tea. It might be fun to see the scales, but it was no joke eating to get that way. Since his last visit to the doctor, Miriam had cracked down with a vengeance. She had kept him to the diet with a determination which surprised him; he had forgotten what a potato looked like. But, he admitted grudgingly, he felt better than he had for a long time.

"Paper come yet?" he asked, spreading a thin veneer of marmalade onto the toast.

Miriam sighed deeply. "I'll look for you." She returned a moment later, handing the morning newspaper to Jonathan.

Grunting his thanks, Jonathan opened the paper searching for the Chestertons advertisement. As Della had predicted, the ad was on page five, in a much better position than that accorded to the five other New York City clothing retailers who had taken space in the same issue. He hoped that Chestertons had similar positions throughout the country.

339

Slipping on reading glasses, Jonathan studied the advertisement. The heading block pleased him: "There are sports coats and there are Chestertons sports coats." Reading down, he noted the factual, low-profile copy style which Della had adopted. It spoke of the care taken in the jacket's construction, styling details, and—possibly most important—how it could be offered cheaply because it was made in Chestertons' own factory, eliminating the middleman's profit. What the advertisement did not, of course, point out was that Chestertons, through a complicated charging system, paid just as much as they would have had to pay an independent manufacturer for a similar piece of merchandise; the manufacturing and retail units operated completely autonomously of each other.

At the bottom of the advertisement, in sizeable bold type, was the main attraction. "For four days only, these sports coats will be offered at fifteen percent below normal price."

Turning to the illustration, Jonathan saw that Della had indeed reverted to using Fletcher Austin. Queer or not, the model looked terrific, he thought—a certain draw to customers. But the choice of models was Della's prerogative. Jonathan had the final say, as in all things, but he also believed in letting specialists get on with their job without undue interference. And the more he delegated, the happier he made Miriam.

Passing the newspaper across the table, Jonathan began to eat his breakfast, grimacing as the first spoonful of yogurt entered his mouth. God, he absolutely loathed the stuff. Baby's food it was, or for people with no teeth. What was wrong with a couple of fried eggs and three or four slices of toast? Yogurt, for Christ's sake!

He sensed Miriam looking at him, so he lifted his head from the plate and smiled at her. "Delicious," he said, licking his lips ecstatically. "Absolutely delicious. Don't know how I lived without it all these years."

Miriam glared at him and returned to the newspaper.

Brian read the newspaper on the bus from Edgewater to Port Authority in Manhattan. His heart leaped as he saw Fletcher's face staring out at him from the advertisement, the clear eyes seeming to search him out, the mouth curving in a slight smile which was meant solely for him. He glanced quickly at the man in the adjacent seat, wondering if his actions were coming under scrutiny. But his fellow passenger remained engrossed in his own newspaper, ignoring everything else.

Entering the office, Brian dropped the newspaper on the desk, opened at the advertisement. As he settled into the chair, there was a knock on the door.

"Come in," he called.

The door opened and Della appeared, a clipboard in her hand. Brian looked at her questioningly.

"Relax," she told him. "You haven't forgotten about an appointment—not with me anyway."

Brian looked relieved. "That's exactly what I thought had happened," he admitted. "You took me quite by surprise."

Smiling to put him at ease, Della walked to the desk and sat down opposite Brian. "I just popped in on an off-chance, to sound you out about doing some prestige advertising for the Viscenzi designer label line."

"You don't mean to promote them off-price, do you?"

"Perish the thought," Della said. "They sell too well to do that. No, I was just kicking around an idea for a Viscenzi advertisement which would help to establish a solid fashion identity for Chestertons. Only on the East Coast, though, as the majority of Viscenzi sales are there." She noticed the newspaper on the desk for the first time and pointed to the picture of Fletcher Austin.

"Are you happier with that ad?" she asked. "The reactionary in you must be pleased that Fletcher's back in favor for the time being." She spoke easily, the innocuous expression on her face giving the impression that she was bringing up the subject on the spur of the moment. But her eyes narrowed as she waited for Brian's reply.

For a moment he appeared confused. He blushed slightly, fumbling with the newspaper as he tried to hide his bewilderment. "I thought it was a great ad," he said. "Fletcher looks good, don't you think?"

"Not bad," Della conceded. "Not bad at all." She stood up and moved toward the door.

"Hey! What about the Viscenzi advertisement?" Brian called after her. "You said you wanted to discuss an idea with me."

Della swung around to face him. "It can wait. I've got a couple of other things to do first." She turned on her heel and walked out, leaving Brian to stare at the open door wondering what had been the purpose of her visit.

Outside, Della made straight for Simon's office. She found him drinking coffee while he perused the racing form.

"You seem happy for so early in the morning," he said. "Come and pick me a winner."

"I'll give you a certainty without even looking at your scratch sheet," she replied. "Brian Chambers. You should see what he looks like, now that his boyfriend's back in the limelight." She recounted the short meeting, telling Simon how the general merchandise manager had reacted. "Now it's up to you. I've made the opening. Go in there and give him hell."

Simon seemed distressed at the finality of her words. "I still don't like it. No matter what you say, we haven't got positive proof that Brian's involved with Fletcher. It just doesn't seem possible."

Della's patience left her completely. "Do you really want to remain a nobody all your life?" she snapped. "Because that's precisely what you're going to finish up as if you keep sitting on your ass hoping something will

342

happen. It'll only happen if you start the ball rolling." She glared at Simon, willing him to take the bait. When nothing happened, she added disgustedly, "I'll get you one more piece of proof—positive proof. If you do nothing after that, you deserve to be a glorified office boy."

"Now what are you going to do?"

"Do you still have that cassette recorder here," she asked, not bothering to answer his question, "the one with the phone attachment that you use for taping your calls to the bookmaker?" Simon opened a desk drawer, passing across the compact recorder. "Now get the switchboard girl in here for ten minutes," she said. "Make any excuse you like, just get her."

Simon looked startled. "Sheila? Whatever for?"

"Because I'm telling you to. I'm going back to see Brian one final time; then I'll tell the girl she's wanted by you. When she comes in, keep her busy for at least ten minutes. Do you think you can manage that?" she asked acidly.

"I suppose so. I can make up some garbage about not getting messages when I'm out."

"I'll send her in to you."

Della walked quickly back to Brian's office, knocked on the door and went inside. Again Brian seemed surprised to see her.

"Now what?" he asked.

Della affected a dizzy air. "I'm terribly sorry, Brian, but I'm rushing around so much that I forgot to mention something to you. Remember the other day when you said Fletcher Austin represented the kind of customer we're trying to attract?"

Brian nodded. "What about it?"

"I spoke to the agency about this ad,"—she pointed to the open newspaper which still lay on his desk—"and they tend to agree with you."

"So why did you come back?" Brian asked, perplexed, seeing no reason for Della's return.

"Just to tell you that. You were right. I'm sorry."

"Sorry I'm right?"

"No, sorry I made a mistake. See you later about that Viscenzi idea."

From Brian's office, Della went to the switchboard which served the Head Office lines. Sheila, the operator, looked up as she approached.

"Can you see Mr. Simon for a few minutes?" Della asked. "He's a bit concerned about some messages he didn't receive."

The girl looked worried. "I can't leave here," she explained. "There's nobody else to take over."

"I've done plenty of things in my time, including running a switchboard," Della assured the girl. "I'll hold the fort till you get back." Uncertain, the girl looked around her. "Go on," Della urged. "He's waiting for you. I can handle it."

The girl offered Della her chair. With a feeling of triumph, she sat down, laying the cassette recorder out of sight, familiarizing herself with the switchboard's simple layout; there were only twenty extensions and she foresaw no difficulties.

During the first two minutes she sat there, four calls came through which were routed automatically to their proper parties. A fifth call received no answer from the extension, so Della took it, writing a message neatly on the pad and tearing it off to join the pile of other messages. She felt a sense of satisfaction at performing the job efficiently, taking as much interest in it as she did in her normal work, seeing it as yet another challenge. The call she was waiting for, however, had not taken place.

"Cross-training yourself in case the advertising program goes bust?" a gruff voice asked from behind.

Frightened by the interruption, Della swung around. Jonathan was standing over her, grinning broadly at finding his daughter-in-law in the unaccustomed position of switchboard operator. "What happened to Sheila?" he asked.

"She had to go somewhere," Della answered glibly. "I've always wanted to find out how to cut people off in the middle of a conversation, so I volunteered to stand in."

"Just make sure you don't cut me off," Jonathan growled.

With an increasing sensation of alarm, Della noticed that the light beneath Brian Chambers's name had come on. There had been no incoming call, so Brian had to be dialling out. She glanced quickly at Jonathan, hoping her agitation at his presence did not show. He stared down, taking an interest in the workings of the switchboard.

"What does that do?" he asked, pointing a stubby finger at a red, transparent button.

"That's for holding," Della replied. For God's sake go back to your own office and leave me alone, she thought. She tried to smile, but the best she could manage was a very weak simper.

Jonathan shrugged his massive shoulders. "I'll leave you to it," he said. "I don't want to get blamed for the phones being screwed up. See you later about this morning's advertisement."

He walked away, and Della breathed an enormous sigh of relief. Making certain that he was out of sight, she picked up the receiver and listened in on Brian's call, pressing the suction contact from the recorder to the earpiece. When she heard Brian call Fletcher by name, she caught her breath, clamping her teeth over her lower lip in case the excitement was communicated over the telephone.

"See the paper this morning, Fletcher?"

"I'm looking at it right now," the model replied. "And I was about to call you. I'm in your debt."

There was a break in the conversation, and Della pressed the receiver closer to her ear, frightened of missing anything. Brian's voice came on again.

"She's been in to see me twice this morning—first time about some advertising campaign which she didn't mention in the end, then about me being right to want you in the ads. She even admitted she was wrong to drop you for that first one."

"She said that?" Fletcher asked, drawing out the last word. "Does that mean I'm in for next season?"

"That I don't know. You're on your own now, Fletcher. I just called to tell you what she said. Seriously, I can't push it too hard in case she gets suspicious. She's a sharp bitch, that one. But you know all about that already."

Della heard Fletcher's laugh. She bit her lip hard in indignation at being referred to as a bitch. The adjective sharp she rather liked.

"Maybe you're right, and I'd better make a pass at her," Fletcher cracked. "I suppose one has to sink pretty low at times to achieve certain objectives." He laughed again, completely unaware of Della's furious thoughts; if it was not for the chance of finding an ally for Simon, she would make damned certain that Fletcher Austin never appeared in another advertisement over which she had any influence.

She had heard enough. Replacing the receiver carefully, she unhooked the cassette recorder and waited for the switchboard operator to return. A minute passed, and she became annoyed that Simon was keeping the girl so long, yet realized that Sheila's absence was simply proof that Simon was doing a thorough job. She dialled his extension, telling him he could release the girl.

"You look flushed," Simon said as she entered his office.

She set the recorder down on his desk. "So would you if you'd listened in on that conversation." She rewound the tape, then pressed the play button, watching Simon's face as the tape played back. When the tape reached Fletcher's wisecrack about sinking low, Simon reddened and clenched his fists.

"I've got a damned good mind to punch that fag smack in the mouth," he muttered, looking at Della.

She laughed at his sentiment. "I don't want to have to clean up after you again, Simon. You might throw me out like you did the last time."

"I could take him out," Simon said confidently, disliking the sensation of having fun poked at him.

"Just because he's queer doesn't mean he wouldn't tear your head off your shoulders," Della pointed out. "Fletcher's got a very good build. He'd probably do a far better job on you than the bookmaker's friends. But the thought was nice anyway." She switched off the tape, watching curiously as Simon unclenched his fists.

"Now you've got all the proof you're ever going to need. I was right on target with those two."

Simon was paying only partial attention to Della's words. Deep down he had known all along that her instincts would be proved correct, but he still remained unhappy about using the information in the way that she wanted him to. He could, however, see no other way of attaining the power within the company that he had to have. If he had to do it this way, so be it.

"I'll see Brian later on," he promised Della. "I have to ask him about some purchases for the Mr. Simon shops, so I'll slip it into the conversation."

"Just make certain you do," Della said meaningfully. "You're standing on your own two feet from here on in. I'm not holding your hand any more."

Early in the afternoon, Simon collected some cloth samples and left his office. Popping his head around Della's door, he winked broadly at her, simultaneously wishing he felt as confident as he was trying to look. Then he walked to the general merchandise manager's office, dropping the fabric swatches onto the desk, making himself comfortable while Brian took a phone call.

The conversation ended, and Brian turned his attention to the visitor. Picking up the cloth which Simon had placed on the desk, he rubbed it between his fingers, a dubious expression on his face.

"Do you really think these linen looks are going to take off, Simon?" he asked. "The colors are very light. They're impractical, need a lot of care. The dry cleaning shops will do good business with them, but will we?"

"Sure we will. Haven't you read any of the articles in the trade press lately?" Simon asked in reply. "They're full of these looks. Every exhibition is showing them."

Brian stroked his chin thoughtfully, totally unconvinced by Simon's arguments. "I don't know. I realize that the Mr. Simon look is high-fashion, for young-thinking men, but I still reckon we'd be jumping in a bit early if we went with this stuff right now. Quite frankly, I'd rather let somebody else carry the ball for a little while, see how they make out before we commit ourselves."

"But think of the sales we'd lose if we let others get in ahead of us," Simon said earnestly, leaning forward across the desk. "Everybody would have the linen look but us."

"I'd rather see us lose a couple of sales in the beginning than be stuck with unsaleable merchandise," Brian said, steadying himself for what he saw as another fruitless argument with Simon. "I promise you, if I see these things taking off anywhere else, if I see a reasonable number of men in the street wearing them, I'll give you the go-ahead straightaway."

Simon took a deep breath, steeling himself for the crunch. "Just think of the advertisement we could run," he oozed, his eyes lighting up with enthusiasm. "Maybe we could even justify a four-color ad. One of these suits would look fantastic on Fletcher Austin, in either a pale salmon color or a mint green. With his coloring, it would be a winner from the word go."

The cloth samples dropped from Brian's hands. His head shot up, and he stared straight into Simon's eyes; this was the third time in one day that Fletcher Austin's name had been thrown at him out of the blue.

"What the hell do you mean by that?" he demanded, regretting the question immediately.

Simon did his best to look surprised by Brian's aggressive response. He could not, however, stop a smile from stealing across his face. God, that Della sure knew how to pick them. "It would look absolutely marvellous on him. That's all I said. Why are you getting so uptight all of a sudden?"

Brian dropped his eyes, feeling his stomach turn to lead; he felt a sudden need to go to the toilet, empty his bowels. "It's nothing," he said. "I just don't feel all that well, what with moving to New Jersey and everything that entails. Sorry I bit your head off."

"Forget it," Simon said grandly. "I know how hectic it can get when you're changing apartments, running around like a blue-assed fly." He began to chuckle good-naturedly as he gathered up the pieces of fabric, stacking them into a neat pile.

"I'll see you about these later, okay Brian?" He held up the pieces of cloth.

"Sure. I'd appreciate that."

Simon stood up and walked slowly to the door. As he was halfway through it, he turned back into the office, a hand resting on the door handle.

"Jesus, the way you acted just then, when I mentioned Fletcher's name, anybody would have thought you were having an affair with the guy. Catch you later!"

He slammed the door and was gone.

# 26

Brian was distraught. More than a week had elapsed since Simon's casual revelation that he knew all about the general merchandise manager's relationship with Fletcher Austin, yet the horror of possible exposure refused to depart. Steeped in middle-class tradition and taboos, Brian had lain awake at night and begged for sleep while Simon's laughing words echoed in his ears, going around and around in his head like a spreading migraine. He had gone off his food, not bothering to cook, eating out only when he remembered to. In the short time since Simon's visit to the office, Brian's weight had dropped from one-sixty to one-fifty-three, and as he stared in the mirror each morning while shaving, the eyes that stared back were hollow, lackluster.

Seeking some condolence, he had told the model that their relationship was common knowledge. The fact that so far only Simon and Della knew of it provided little comfort to Brian; if they so chose, they could pass the information around in a matter of seconds—and ruin him with the greater shame.

Instead of offering sympathy, however, Fletcher had looked on the whole incident with a degree of cynical amusement.

"It's just like being raped," he had told Brian. "Why fight against it when you can lie back gracefully and derive some enjoyment? You can't be any worse off by going along with what Simon wants. This way you'll be known as gay by a select few, and you'll still have your job and your self-respect. Go against him, and he'll leak it. You'll be known as gay by everybody, and you might not have your job."

After the seemingly innocuous comment about the linen suits looking great on Fletcher, and the subsequent disclosure, Simon had spelled out very clearly what he expected from Brian in return for secrecy—some support within the company for his ideas, nothing more, nothing less.

When Simon wanted something put through, Brian would go along with him, helping to sell Jonathan on the idea.

Alternatives had crossed Brian's mind. Go to Jonathan? To the police? The thoughts lasted for no more than a few seconds before shame drove them away. How could he possibly go to Jonathan and admit that he was having a relationship with the company's top model? In a soul-searching moment, Brian likened himself to Judas. Even his price had been money, though. Mine, he reflected, is the continuing privacy of a relationship which I was stupid to get into in the first place, with a person who finds the whole situation highly amusing and is in no way concerned about my feelings.

During any discussion with Jonathan, Brian found it difficult to look his friend in the face, this man to whom he owed so much—and this before a crisis had even been reached. Just thinking about the betrayal that must surely come any day made him feel ill.

At least Simon had been considerate—Brian laughed humorlessly at the word—considerate enough to promise that he would only enlist his support for matters of major importance. He would not use it frivolously, take advantage of the hold he had over him. No, mundane problems he would take care of by himself. Only for major decisions would he seek Brian's help. Brian knew from past experience that all of Simon's problems reached major proportions before they were sorted out—catastrophic even.

And the first major problem looked like being those linen suits which Simon was so intent on stocking for the boutiques. Despite reasoned arguments against their immediate purchase, Simon had remained adamant. His ego was at an all-time high following the appearance of the Mr. Simon personalized advertisement. He had become almost unreachable, boasting how he had been stopped in the street on twenty separate occasions by complete strangers who had recognized him from the ad and wanted to talk to him about fashion. He even had the temerity to have the advertisement blown up into a gigantic poster which he nailed to the inside of the office door directly opposite where he sat so that he could look at it whenever he lifted his eyes from the desk.

With the look and enthusiasm of a man leaving his cell for the short walk to the gas chamber, Brian, clutching the purchase orders for the linen suits which now bore his approval, wearily closed the door to his office. His stomach churned as he entered the boardroom. Jonathan was sitting in his customary position at the head of the table, talking quietly to Gerald, while Simon joked with his mother. As Brian took his seat, Simon looked up, but no expression betrayed whatever thoughts he might be experiencing about the coming meeting. He merely glanced at Brian, nodding curtly in greeting as he always did, before continuing his conversation with Miriam; whatever he was saying must have been funny, because his mother laughed.

Dropping his papers onto the table, Brian leaned back in the chair, staring ahead gloomily, waiting for the meeting to begin, and with it his first forced alliance with Simon.

Glossing over the Chestertons sales figures for the previous week, Jonathan concentrated on the Mr. Simon shops, which were experiencing a strong upswing. Della, who was not present at the meeting, had compiled a comprehensive report which linked the increase in boutique business directly to the advertisement which had featured Simon. Looking across the table at his son from time to time, Jonathan read excerpts from the report.

"Seems like your ugly mug does more good for the Mr. Simon shops than your knowledge of merchandise ever did," he commented.

Simon said nothing, simply holding his father's gaze, but Miriam looked at Jonathan crossly.

"Is this going to be a short meeting," Jonathan continued, hoping against hope that it was, "or is there anything else to discuss?" He laid down the report from Della and looked around the table, finishing with Simon, who had a hand half-raised. "Yes?"

"I sent you some suggestions about linen suits for the boutiques," Simon began. "I wonder if you've had time to study them yet and give me your reactions."

Jonathan riffled through the stack of papers in front of him. "Linen, linen, linen...ah, here we are." He found the three-page memo from Simon and glanced through it briefly, familiarizing himself again with the contents. "It's still a very fringe trend at the minute, Simon. Why do you want to jump in so quickly?"

"Because it's going to be a major seller. Everybody's talking about it, and I want us to be the first. Brenson and Selman has sent us some samples, and they look fantastic."

"Brenson and Selman again?" Jonathan screwed up his face in disbelief as he recognized the name. "Why in God's name are you dealing with them? We threw them out last time when you wanted to buy three hundred of their suits for the Atlanta renovation. Or don't you remember? They're schlock merchants, one hundred percent garbage, clothes that will fall apart in two seconds. If you're going to insist on linen and Brian goes along with you, buy from somebody else."

Simon stood his ground, confident as never before in a discussion with his father now that he knew he had an ally sitting alongside him. "Brenson and Selman has got the best merchandise for the price. They're a mile and a half ahead of everybody else for fashion detail. Linen's a plain fabric, so the fashion details are extremely important to the look. And I want those suits for Mr. Simon."

Looking away from his son, Jonathan eyed Brian. "Let's have your thoughts on this. You've got the final say on what merchandise goes into Mr. Simon. Tell my son that Brenson and Selman makes junk."

Brian's mouth went dry. His moment of truth had arrived, just as he had known it would, and found him wanting. He tried to speak, to back Simon up as he must; the words refused to come. Seeing Simon's puzzled glance at the lack of support, Brian slid the approved purchase orders wordlessly across the tabletop to Jonathan. By the time they were picked up, he had found his voice.

"I'll go along with Simon on this one. The samples we've had are pretty good. Like Simon mentioned, the fashion details are fine; the suits look terrific."

Holding the purchase orders in his left hand, Jonathan looked at Brian in amazement, the bemused cast of his face clearly asking if he had heard correctly. Then he lowered his eyes to the documents.

"One thousand suits," he whispered in shocked tones. "That's a hell of a size for an initial order. What's wrong with a hundred or so as a tryout?"

"We're getting"—Brian took a deep breath, closing his eyes for a moment, praying that he could complete the sentence—"much better terms this way."

"What about the better terms we'll get if we're stuck with the suits?" Jonathan asked. "We'll be eating them on better terms. Come on," he pleaded, "tell me it's all a joke, that you're pulling my leg."

Simon's intervention saved Brian from any more immediate distress. "It's no joke. Far from it. We're on a big upswing with the Mr. Simon shops, and I think we should hammer home the advantage while we've got this opportunity." He flicked a glance at Brian as he spoke, trying to see how his pressured ally was standing up to his first test. Brian's face was completely blank. He stared vacantly at the table, his left eye twitching as if he were suffering from a nervous tic.

Jonathan's normally gruff voice gave way to a low-pitched roar. "Hammering home a winning streak is one thing, but trying to pour crap into the boutiques is a different ball game altogether."

The words "ball game" made him suddenly think of Myron; the face of Miriam's brother flashed in front of his eyes. It took Jonathan a few seconds to associate the odd coincidence. He had been with Brian at the opening of the Chicago store when he had heard of Myron's death. Christ, what a time to think of that. Shaking his head roughly to dispel the image, he glared at Simon.

"I'd still feel a lot happier if you'd settle for an initial order of one hundred suits," he reiterated.

Simon started to say something, thought better of it and stopped. He looked to Brian instead. "You tell my father. He'll believe you sooner than me."

Jonathan's voice rose again. "That sort of talk's unnecessary, Simon. I'm just trying to get a straightforward assessment of the situation. That's all I'm after. Keep your wise remarks to yourself. We don't need them in this room."

Brian waited gratefully for Jonathan to finish. The outburst was to his advantage; he needed time to steady himself. "Simon's right," he said eventually. "If we take one thousand pieces, we get the best deal possible."

"But are you sure we can get rid of them once we've bought them?" Jonathan shouted. "That's what I want to know."

He felt the pain begin across his chest again, spreading into his left arm. Taking a deep breath, he forced himself to be calm. "That's all I'm trying to clarify, for God's sake. If we get stuck with a line in Chestertons, we can always spiff it or knock it down as a promotional special for a new store opening or something. We can't do the same thing with the boutiques. We don't have the Gellenbaum clearance outlets any more. What's bought for Mr. Simon stays there till it's sold for the regular price or tossed out onto the junk heap...with the guy who bought it," he added meaningfully.

Exasperated, he turned to Gerald, who had been watching the exchange with an air of detachment. "Let's have your two cents' worth."

Gerald spread his hands wide. "Don't get me involved in merchandise squabbles. I've got enough problems on the operations side to worry about without creating additional ones. Brian's your general merchandise manager. He's always done a good job for you, so let him get on with it."

If he had felt so inclined, Jonathan could have asked Miriam for an opinion. He was not up to it. Letting his head fall almost to his chest, he expelled great lungfuls of air through his lips in long sighs.

"Okay, Brian. One thousand suits for the initial order. And I just hope for your sake that Brenson and Selman has upped their quality. Meeting's over for today."

Simon was the first to push back his chair and stand. Grinning triumphantly, he looked down at his father's hunched figure and bowed formally from the waist.

"Thank you for your blessings."

Jonathan eyed him coldly. "Don't push your luck."

Brian walked quickly out of the boardroom and headed straight for the washroom. Locking himself in a cubicle, he leaned low over the bowl and brought up his lunch, gasping in pain as he continued to gag long after his stomach had emptied itself of its contents.

Ten minutes later, he felt well enough to return to his office. Simon was waiting when he arrived, toying with the electric pencil sharpener on the desk.

"There, that wasn't so difficult, was it?" he asked, as Brian flopped into his chair, sweat covering his face, his clothes sticking to his body. "And just like everything else, it gets easier with practice."

Brian made no effort to reply, and Simon added, "I bet it was like that with Fletcher the first time, wasn't it? Difficult. Getting any easier now?"

"You're a prick," Brian said.

"And that's something you'd know all about, isn't it?" Simon shot back, grinning maliciously.

"Just get the hell out of here," Brian snapped. "It makes me sick even to look at you."

# 27

It was shortly after midnight when Simon finally got to his double room in the Chicago hotel. Literature for the leisurewear exhibition he would be attending in the city was stacked neatly on the bedside table—press releases, merchandise photographs and a list of manufacturers who would be taking space at the show. Disregarding them for a moment, he picked up the telephone and asked the operator to connect him to his New York apartment.

It was a sleepy Della who took the call, covering a yawn. "Did you just get in," she asked, "or did you forget to call me till now?"

"I just arrived. There was a delay before we took off. I'll hit the show first thing in the morning, see if I can wrap everything up in one day and get home tomorrow night."

"Is there really anything there you want to buy," Della asked, "or did you just fancy some time away from the office?"

"I want to look around, that's all. Did anything happen after I left?"

"Brian was trying to get hold of you. Left a message with me that the first of those suits were going into the Mr. Simon shops."

"Did he look happy about it?"

"As happy as a zombie."

"Maybe he'll look happier when they start selling; he'll be able to bask in the reflected glory."

"That's what I told him," Della said. "He didn't look very impressed about it."

"He doesn't have to," Simon said. "As long as he does what he's told, that's all that matters."

Della yawned again. "Call me when you get back into New York," she said. "We're an hour ahead of you, and right now it feels like six." She hung up the phone, leaving Simon with a dead receiver.

Simon arose early the next morning, showered, had a speedy breakfast and was down at the show as it opened for business. He spent four hours walking around checking merchandise, exchanging phone numbers with a number of suppliers. He found it amazing to count the number of new companies which were showing their merchandise for the first time, avant garde clothes which attracted him like a magnet. Whichever booth he visited, he was treated like royalty as a vice-president of Chestertons and general manager of the Mr. Simon boutiques. It was a situation that Simon revelled in. Here he was an important man; it did not matter if he ordered nothing. Contacts were made at these shows, plans formed for future strategy, for a future when he would be more powerful within the company.

At midday he called the office, telling Della what he had accomplished. She seemed pleased, especially by the way he had been welcomed by the exhibitors. Returning to the show area, he noticed a small group of men clustered around one of the booths. He stopped by the rear, standing on tiptoe, trying to learn what the excitement was about. At the front of the crowd he could make out a ruddy-faced, middle-aged man with sandy hair covering his ears, who was speaking so quietly that Simon could hardly hear him. Every so often, a brief laugh erupted from the crowd, and Simon pushed his way through, eager to hear what was being said.

When he finally broke through to the front line, the man eyed him with a degree of amusement.

"Now here's a man who really wants to learn something about fashion," he joked. "And you've come to the right place."

Simon felt his face begin to redden, realizing he was being made the center of attention; it took him a few seconds to understand that the man was English, speaking with a highly affected accent which seemed to tone in with his looks. He was wearing a casual blue denim suit that was literally covered with orange decorative stitching, and from his shoulder hung a leather bag.

"I'm always interested in hearing what somebody's got to say," Simon ventured, unsure of himself.

"I was just pointing out that the suit you're wearing"—he nodded toward Simon's three-piece brown suit—"has only one place in today's market. On the city dump."

A gale of laughter swept around Simon. He looked around angrily, noticing that the men who were listening to the Englishman were all dressed casually; nowhere among them was a traditional suit to be seen.

"Don't take any offense, love," the Englishman continued. "You're in the majority at the moment. But someday soon—it may be five years, it may be ten—the traditional suit isn't going to be around any more." He opened the flap of his shoulder bag and pulled out a pack of Players cigarettes, offering one to Simon, who refused. "Are you an exhibitor or a visitor?" he asked, lighting the cigarette.

The crowd of onlookers, sensing that the show was over, began to drift away, leaving Simon alone with the Englishman. "I'm a visitor." He offered his business card to the man.

"Chestertons?" The Englishman's eyebrows rose in tribute. "No wonder you're wearing a suit. My name's Alan Constantine, by the way, formerly of the United Kingdom of Great Britain and Northern Ireland, now of the colonies." He offered Simon his hand. "Pleased to meet you."

Simon fell in step with Constantine as he began to walk along the aisle. "I've been into a few of your shops," Constantine said. "Your marketing plan's so conservative that it makes Ronald Reagan look like Eugene McCarthy in comparison."

"I'm responsible for the Mr. Simon boutiques," Simon tried to explain, not wanting to be tarred with the Chestertons brush; as far as the main company was concerned, he was forced to agree with Constantine.

"Even worse," the Englishman exclaimed. "You shouldn't have a suit in any of your shops. But you do, don't you?"

"What should I have?"

"Casualwear, man. What I'm wearing, not what you're wearing. The suit is dying. And the only reason it hasn't done the decent thing and buried itself yet is because of companies like yours which insist on trying to keep it popular."

Before Simon realized the direction in which they were walking, they were at the bar. He pulled out a ten-dollar bill and placed it on the counter. "What are you drinking?" he asked Constantine.

Constantine directed the reply at the bartender. "Large gin and tonic, and very easy on the tonic." He turned to Simon. "My thanks. You've got to admit it's cheap for a consultation fee."

Simon ordered himself a soft drink; then both men repaired to a table where Constantine lit himself another cigarette. While Simon watched the Englishman fumble with his shoulder bag as he replaced the pack, an idea began to form in his mind, unclear as yet, but a germ from which something solid could grow.

"How long have you been over here?"

"Two, three years," Constantine replied.

"What are you doing?"

"Free-lance consulting. Pays the bills till something comes up."

"What were you doing in England?"

"Ravaging women." Constantine burst into a highpitched laugh.

"In the clothing industry, I meant."

"Many things." Constantine closed his eyes. "Let me see. I'm forty-one years old, so that makes it twenty-three years ago that I decided to make my living out of this industry." He opened his eyes again, staring at Simon. Simon noticed that the eyes were a pale blue, very watery and rimmed with red; he put it down to drinking, just as he was certain that the man's complexion came from alcohol, not from a healthy outdoor life.

"I was in the trade press for a long time," Constantine said, "writing about this wonderful industry of ours. Then about eight years ago I talked a middle-of-the-road British manufacturer into hiring me as a fashion consultant. Three years ago they went bankrupt, and I was out of work, so I came over here."

"Why did they go bankrupt?"

"Because they carried right on making what everybody else was making—traditional garments. Only they weren't as good or as competitive as everybody else. Nothing to do with me," he added quickly, in case Simon thought it was.

"Have you been free-lancing over here the whole time?"

"No. To get my permanent resident status I had to have a job offer." He gave Simon the name of a clothing manufacturer who was known for extreme styling. "They kept me happy for about a year; then I went into business for myself."

"You live in Chicago?"

"It'll cost you another drink to find that out," Constantine replied, emptying the glass. He waited for Simon to return with a fresh gin and tonic. "I live in New Jersey. Top half of a house in Englewood Cliffs, where I work from."

"How often do you go into New York?"

"As little as possible. Why?"

"I'd like you to have lunch with me someday. And another guy, fellow called Brian Chambers; he's general merchandise manager for Chestertons. I think we might be able to work something out."

Constantine raised the glass in mock salute. "I'd be glad **to.** Like the true journalist I once was, I have never yet been known to pass up a free meal. Thanks for the drinks."

Before the flight left Chicago, Simon called Della and cajoled her into meeting him at the airport.

"What's so important?" she asked as he climbed into the Midget. "Couldn't you take a cab home without dragging me all the way up here?"

"I met a guy in Chicago, and he's going to help me big," he enthused. "Limey name of Alan Constantine. This guy has got brains, despite what he sounds like."

"Tell me about him," Della said.

Simon did, going over his conversation with Constantine, the way the Englishman saw the industry going, how it coincided so strongly with his own views. Della listened thoughtfully, driving almost automatically.

"How will you get your father to go along with it?" she asked.

"By using Brian. Constantine's going to call me next week, arrange a lunch date. I'm taking Brian along, and he'd better back me up on this guy or his ass will be in a sling."

"Oh, he'll back you up all right, Simon. The way you've got him now, he wouldn't dare do otherwise."

Realizing how true Della's statement was, Simon broke into a satisfied grin; he was still smiling when the car pulled off East River Drive at Sixty-third Street.

# 28

Gerald Chesterton sat in the living room of his Manhasset home, staring with a mixture of gloom and disbelief at the reports from managers of the stores where Mr. Simon boutiques were located. Marilyn had gone to bed more than an hour earlier; now he sat by himself trying to make some sense out of the confusion felt by the managers. Their means of expression differed, but the underlying message was the same—What the hell is going on at Head Office? Why are you sending us junk?

Tired, he rubbed his eyes and yawned loudly, not bothering to stifle it with a hand; there was nobody around to be polite for. He looked back at the reports again, reading them for a third time. Attached to each was a list of complaints from customers who had bought the linen suits which Simon had been so insistent upon ordering. The suits looked fantastic; the customers had no complaints on that score. They fitted well and gave a marvellous appearance. And right there the love affair ended. Seams split without any real stress, and the fabric wore badly, pilling in areas where it was rubbed, like the insides of the arms and legs.

Of six hundred and fifty suits sold across the Mr. Simon chain during the first month, more than three hundred had been returned by irate customers within the following month. And, to exacerbate the situation, Simon had arranged for more of the line to be distributed to the boutiques to fill up the gaps in inventory.

Gerald had first shown the reports to Brian, who had halfheartedly muttered something about giving the supplier hell. What had nagged at Gerald was how Brian could have so blatantly overlooked the quality angle in the first place, even claiming it was good when Simon had initially raised the subject.

When he had shown the reports to his father, Jonathan had snorted angrily and called Brian in immediately for an explanation, intent on getting to the root of the problem straightaway. As with Gerald, Brian had

358

simply said that he would call on the supplier and demand credit for returns. Furiously Jonathan had slammed a clenched fist onto the desk top, shouting that the damage had been done with the initial purchase, and why the hell hadn't anybody listened to him about the dangers of ordering so much to begin with? No amount of credit with the supplier was going to bring unsatisfied customers back into the stores. And if they were upset with Mr. Simon, the same feeling of disenchantment would run over to Chestertons. The linen suits, he had pointed out, had cost the company at least three hundred customers, plus those men who did not want to bring back the suits because they were too embarrassed to complain.

At one point during his stay in the living room, Gerald had drafted a reply to the store managers, ensuring them that the same situation would never happen again. He had torn up the letter less than a minute later, when he realized that he could not be certain it would never be repeated. He recalled that Brian had scrapped Simon's order for fill-ins, although he had not seemed happy to do it. Brian had kept on repeating that the suits were basically good and that Simon had been right to order them. Sure, Gerald thought. Right enough to lose us a bunch of good customers. And if it happened once, it could all too easily happen again. That was what Gerald found really frightening. He had witnessed poor buying before—it befell even the most selective retailers—but never to this extent, never to where the buyer went out, ignoring advice from all areas, and apparently ordered garbage deliberately. Because that was what it looked like to Gerald.

He stayed up for another two hours, running the situation through in his mind again and again, looking for a key to the puzzle, something he might have missed. Finally he was realistic enough to see that he would achieve nothing by staying up any longer; he was also tired enough to see it, barely able to keep his eyes open. Replacing the reports in his briefcase, he turned off the light and went to bed.

Jonathan was feeling more confused than angry. He was hurt, deeply so. The unquestioning faith that he had always placed in Brian—which till now had been repaid many times over—was beginning to bother him.

How could a man with a track record like Brian's suddenly get suckered into ordering junk like those linen suits? And from a company which had a reputation for dealing in junk? No matter which way Jonathan looked at it, he failed to find an answer. All of a sudden Brian's agreeing with Simon, he thought, and that's the biggest anomaly of all.

But where Gerald could not see a clear solution to the linen suit enigma, Jonathan had prepared a ruthless one. First thing tomorrow he would order the recall of every piece of Brenson and Selman merchandise—and dump it. The supplier would not take back the garments; that was too much to hope for. So he would cut his losses before they cut his throat.

"Your precious son," he muttered at Miriam as he climbed into bed. "See what a mess the genius has landed us in this time?"

"It's Brian's fault as much as anybody else's," Miriam replied, continuing to defend Simon. "Brian approved the purchase orders for the linen suits; he saw the samples and liked them. Those suits must have had some merit to them; otherwise he wouldn't have gone ahead and ordered."

"The pair of them must have been crazy," Jonathan grumbled. "Maybe working so closely with Simon has finally loused up Brian's judgment. Do you think Simon's stupidity could be contagious?"

He waited for an answer, but Miriam turned away, ignoring him. Angrily he reached across the space between the two beds and tugged at her blanket. "You haven't heard the latest, have you?" he demanded. "The pair of them want to hire a fashion consultant now, somebody to upgrade the image of the Chestertons stores. Screwing up Mr. Simon with those linen suits isn't enough for them. They want to do a job on the whole chain."

Miriam did not bother turning around. She continued to lie on her left side, staring at the dressing table in the bay window. "Would that be such a terrible thing?" she asked quietly. "If you could get in a good man, perhaps he'd have a beneficial effect across the company. You've carried the business on your own shoulders for far too long. Being a quality company isn't the be-all and end-all, Jonathan."

Her voice began to rise, despite a powerful effort to keep it down; Jonathan's constant sniping at Simon was wearing her patience thin, and she felt she had to fight back, to defend her son. Simon had tried his hardest, and the sales results had confirmed that his merchandising approach was right. She had heard about the returns; it was unfortunate, a problem which could be rectified by dealing with another supplier.

"Do you realize how long it's taken to build up this company," Jonathan suddenly asked, "to make it into the force it now is? You should. You were there at the beginning in Houston Street. You went through it all with me—the union, Gilbert, the war—everything. And you should damned well care. It's a lifetime of hard work, and now Simon's trying to wreck it within a year."

"Jonathan," Miriam pleaded, biting back tears. "Let it rest. He made a genuine mistake, that's all. Anybody could make it."

"Did I?" The question held an accusation. "Can you ever remember me making a foul-up like this?"

"No," she answered truthfully. "Look, you're mad at him, but have you ever stopped to think about how frustrated he must feel? Every time he tries to do something on his own initiative he gets his wings clipped."

Jonathan blew up. "Is it any damned wonder? Whatever he even looks at puts us in the hole."

"But this time he must have been right!" Miriam shouted back, stunning Jonathan with the ferocity of the words. "If Brian went along with

him, there must have been something to it. You're always saying you wish
you had more people like Brian, how much easier it would make your life.
So Simon must have known what he was doing. And look at the way those
suits sold. They were a success from the moment they went into the
boutiques."

Jonathan did not hear the last two sentences. "There's something to it,
all right," he muttered, feeling the fight drain out of him. "I just wish to God
I knew what."

Before turning out the light above his bed, he looked across at Miriam,
realizing the futility of the argument. She lay away from him, her shoulders
trembling; he could hear her quiet sobbing.

"I'm sorry," he said, reaching out to touch her shoulders. "You'd think
by now that we'd know we're too old to shout at each other and cry about
it."

He sat up in bed, looking at her for another half-minute before turning
out the light.

# 29

When Nino Viscenzi returned to the United States to review his range of designer label suits for the fall-winter season, the change he noticed in Chestertons was electrifying. The Viscenzi line was progressing satisfactorily; sales were well in advance of projected figures, and the suits being manufactured in the company's Buffalo plant were in keeping with the high-quality standards upon which he had insisted. But the general demeanor of the company startled him.

With Jonathan he walked through the main Chestertons store on West Fifty-seventh Street long after it had closed for the day. In surprise he stopped by a display of jeans, merchandised with a selection of heavy-buckled belts. Flicking the jeans disgustedly with his hand, he looked questioningly at Jonathan.

"What is this? What are you trying to do to your stores? Or have all your customers suddenly joined a rodeo show?"

"We've got a new direction," Jonathan explained, sounding unconvinced himself. "We're expanding our casualwear side."

Viscenzi studied his friend. "Agreed, there is a lot of money in the casual clothing market. But you still have to stay at your end of the scale. What you should be doing is showing expensive, well-made styles, corduroys, good denims, but not this trash. Certainly not"—he jabbed a finger at the rack—"jeans and Billy-the-Kid leather belts.

"What is happening here?" Viscenzi asked, placing his hands on Jonathan's shoulders. "The store seems to have gone slightly crazy. Are they all like this?" He felt Jonathan's shoulders sag beneath his touch.

"I'm being finessed," Jonathan replied. "Everybody suddenly knows how to run a store but me. I'm the only one who doesn't know how to buy any more."

"Please explain."

"We're keeping up with the times. We get the chance to buy some

362

immediate lines—high-fashion merchandise at cutthroat prices—so we take it."

Sadness showed on Viscenzi's handsome face. "Jonathan, Jonathan," he repeated softly. "This whole thing does not make any sense. When I last saw you, you had a wonderful group of stores. Even I was jealous of your success. Now everything seems to be wrong. Tell me, what is going on here?"

"Come to dinner and I'll be glad to bore you with all my troubles," Jonathan invited. "I cry better on a full stomach."

They ate in a restaurant near Viscenzi's hotel. Over dinner, Jonathan explained the Head Office situation. The designer listened attentively, asking Jonathan to enlarge on certain parts. When the meal was finished, Viscenzi leaned back and lit a Romeo y Juliet cigar. Through the wreath of smoke, he noticed Jonathan looking hungrily at the Havana.

"Would you like one?" he asked, offering a silver cigar tube across the table.

"I'm not supposed to," Jonathan admitted, "but if you don't tell anybody, I won't. I haven't seen one of those for longer than I care to remember, not since Kennedy saw Castro for what he was." Gratefully he accepted the cigar from Viscenzi, piercing the blunt end with a toothpick, rotating the sliver of wood to enlarge the hole sufficiently. He accepted a light from Viscenzi, then relaxed, luxuriating in the rich aroma.

"Who is responsible for this new direction of yours?" Viscenzi asked.

"Simon, of course. Somehow he got Brian turned onto his way of thinking."

"Brian?" Viscenzi could not mask his surprise. "He's as levelheaded as anybody. How could that brainless son of yours get him involved in such madness?"

Jonathan chewed on the end of the cigar, puffing gently, feeling comfortable with the familiar object between his teeth. "Beats hell out of me, Nino. But the best is yet to come. The pair of them conned me into hiring this character who calls himself a fashion coordinator, a merchandise genius."

"What is his function?"

"Goes around trade shows and steals everybody else's ideas, as far as I can see," Jonathan replied. "He's the one who's been arranging all this way-out gear in the stores."

Viscenzi leaned across the table and grasped his friend by the arm. "Jonathan, that merchandise on West Fifty-seventh Street does not even belong in the Mr. Simon shops. You have to do something, reestablish some semblance of order."

"Sure I have to do something. But what? Gerald and I are beaten at every turn. Miriam—you know how she feels about Simon—is firmly convinced that he's doing the right thing. She thinks he's finally showing what he can do, so she goes along with him. And what with Brian taking his side suddenly, Gerald and I, the allegedly sane voices in the company, are screwed whichever way we look."

"Who is this fashion coordinator?" Viscenzi managed to make the title sound like a medieval plague. "What is his name?"

"Constantine. Alan Constantine. Does it ring a bell with you?"

Viscenzi shook his head. "The name means nothing to me. Where did he come from?"

"He's a limey." Jonathan saw the puzzled expression on Viscenzi's face. "English," he explained quickly. "Used to be a business journalist over there on one of the clothing trade magazines. Then he managed to talk his way into some company or other as a fashion expert. From doing that he came over here. He was working freelance when Simon dug him up at some show in Chicago."

"And that trash in your stores is his work, the result of his fashion coordination?"

"That's it," Jonathan said. "I admit that we're getting some sales with the stuff, but what scares the hell out of me and Gerald is that we might frighten off our traditional customers, scare away those men who've spent good money in our stores over a number of years. If the avant garde crap was restricted to the Mr. Simon operation, I wouldn't be so damned worried. But this guy Constantine, with Simon and Brian backing him to the hilt, insists there is also a market for it among the more mature men, the guys who've always shopped at Chestertons."

Viscenzi gazed down at his brandy snifter, inspecting the amber liquid. "I would like to meet this man Constantine," he said at last. "Very much would I like to meet him."

"I can arrange that. Come into the office next Monday afternoon. We should be having a lulu of a meeting."

Viscenzi inclined his head slightly. "Jonathan, I promise not to use Italian slang if you will return me the same courtesy with the English language."

Jonathan grinned, the first time during the evening with Viscenzi that he had shown any expression of humor. "We'll be having a ding-dong battle," he said, "a real hell of a meeting."

"That," said Viscenzi, mirroring his friend's grin, "I understand perfectly."

Since Simon had gained influence over Brian, Della had noticed a distinct change in her husband. Where once he had been uncertain about following a course of action, he now exuded confidence. She was proud of him, proud of herself, too, for being the catalyst in his positive transformation. Slowly but surely, Simon was guiding himself toward a position of major power within the Chestertons group.

Thinking back to the time she had eavesdropped on Brian's conversation with Fletcher Austin, she felt no regret about her deceit. At other times, when she had inadvertently dialled into a cross line, she had always hung up immediately, not wanting to intrude. But the phone call that morning had been engineered carefully; it had been crucial to her plan.

Fletcher was still being used in the Chestertons advertisements, despite Della's deep-rooted feelings about the model. She felt it to be a small sacrifice for ensuring Brian's loyalty. Poor Brian, she thought in an unguarded moment; he's getting it in the head whichever way he looks—from Simon, who needs his support at the office, and from Fletcher Austin who wants his modelling career to continue forever. The eternal Peter Pan.

A genuine pang of sympathy for Brian crossed Della's mind, surprising her. She pushed it aside, realizing that she could not afford to be sorry for the man. His assistance, no matter how it was obtained, was too important for Simon's welfare.

She continued to think about Simon's increasing confidence as she drove the small MG, its top down, the wind whistling like a living thing around the lowered windows. Simon sat next to her, wearing light brown slacks and a white roll-neck sweater. From time to time he looked at her, observing the precise way she drove the sports car, arms locked straight as she gripped the steering wheel, the way he had seen professional racing drivers control their vehicles.

"Why does Constantine have to live in New Jersey?" he shouted above the shrieking of the wind and engine noise. "Why can't he be civilized and live in Manhattan?"

"Brian also lives in New Jersey," Della reminded him. "There." She pointed across the Hudson River to the apartment building which stood on the Jersey side. "You can even see his place from here."

"He's not civilized either," Simon retorted, sparing a moment to glance across the water, following Della's pointing hand.

Taking her concentration off the Henry Hudson Parkway for a split second, Della turned in the seat and grinned at him. "Stop complaining all the time. You're enjoying the drive, aren't you?" She waited till Simon nodded his head vigorously. "We have to see him this evening to make sure everything's set up for Monday's meeting. We can't afford to have any differing opinions among ourselves. The whole thing must be presented as a single unit so your father can't pick any holes in it."

Changing down into second gear, she joined the line of traffic forming to get onto the George Washington Bridge. The lessened wind noise gave her the opportunity to lower her voice. "What do you think of your father these days?" she asked.

"The same as ever," Simon replied caustically. Mimicking an airline captain's approach speech to his passengers, he continued, "In about ten minutes we will be touching down in the Chestertons Group boardroom on West Fifty-seventh Street. Thank you for flying with us, and please put your watches back five hundred years."

"No," said Della, who had heard the performance many times before.

"Not that. I mean his health. He doesn't strike me as looking very well lately."

Simon laughed roughly, without sympathy. "That's because he's no longer getting his own way within the company. My father is finally finding out, after decades of despotism, that there are other people at Chestertons who have something valuable to contribute. It's only his bad temper showing through, that's all."

Della got onto the bridge approach and speeded up. Steering the MG into the center lane, she took the upper level of the bridge, coming off at Palisades Parkway heading for Englewood Cliffs.

"What happens to the business if your father dies?" Della asked.

The question, completely out of the blue, astonished Simon. He had never thought of Jonathan dying; his father was like Manhattan itself—there for eternity.

"I don't know," he answered frankly. "It's a private business, so I suppose it would be split three ways—my mother, Gerald and myself. And there's Brian to take into consideration, of course. What makes you ask a question like that?"

Della kept her eyes on the road. "I told you before. He doesn't look well. You know what your mother said after his latest visit to the doctor, how he was warned about his health. He's lost quite a bit of weight since then, but he still looks seedy."

Simon said nothing for the remainder of the journey. He was preoccupied with his father. Now that Della had mentioned it, Jonathan had looked under the weather for the past month or so. He began to think seriously what would happen should his father die.

When they arrived at Constantine's house, Brian's red Impala was in the driveway, taking up all the available parking space. Della left the Midget in the road and rang the bell for the apartment which took up the top half of the house.

There was a sound of footsteps down the stairs; then Constantine opened the door, dressed simply in a pair of jeans and a gray sweat shirt, the front of which bore a heat-transfer print of Queen Elizabeth II. He smiled self-consciously as he saw Della and Simon staring at it in fascination.

"Have to fly the flag for the old darling sometimes," he explained lightly. "One must never forget one's humble beginnings, must one?"

He guided them upstairs into the living room. Brian sprang up from a chair as they entered; he was also dressed casually in light blue trousers, black slip-ons and an open-necked sport shirt.

"Drinkies, anybody?" Constantine asked. "May as well wet our whistles before we start."

The affected English accent, coupled with the supposedly esoteric language which Constantine adopted, grated on Simon's hearing, although he could see that Della was finding it amusing. After working with Constantine for a few months, Simon decided that if he had to choose between Constantine and Brian for who was the homosexual, his vote would go to Constantine. Brian looked and acted decidedly normal in comparison with this fruity Englishman. And no matter how much assistance Constantine could offer in the company, nothing would ever change Simon's opinion.

Constantine chaired the informal meeting. With the ever present gin and tonic balanced precariously on one knee, he rested a large note pad on the other, jotting down ideas as he talked.

"Point one. Now that we've finally got some decent casualwear into Chestertons, we have to expand upon it, increase our grip on the situation. This meeting on Monday is to discuss how we can build up on the base we've so far established, and to sort out the advertising program that will accompany the push. Does anybody see any problems in putting the whole casualwear concept across?"

Simon looked at Brian. The general merchandise manager bowed his head, staring morosely at the floor. He looked back to Constantine and shook his head.

"Fine. Personally I reckon the whole thing should go like grease through a goose." Constantine moved his attention to Della, who was sitting next to Simon, an attaché case resting across her knees as she waited to speak.

"I take it your side of the job is already finished, my dear."

Della patted the case confidently. "It's all there, everything we'll need on Monday. No need to worry."

Constantine smiled, the red face creasing up like an overripe apple. "Of course there isn't. I'm a great admirer of your professionalism." He turned to Simon. "And your suppliers are all ready to go? We can be guaranteed chain-wide delivery of those separates within two weeks?"

"No sweat. Brian and I have been in touch with them. They're happy to be dealing with us."

Brian came to life at the comment. "Surprised is the word I'd use—surprised as hell. They never thought they'd live long enough to get an order from Chestertons."

"He must needs go whom the devil doth drive," Simon said evenly. "If they're the suppliers who come up with the best offer, then they're the ones we're going to use."

Constantine sensed the flare-up of animosity between Simon and Brian; he had noticed traces of it before, during other meetings, but now it arrested his attention. "I thought you were all for this deal," he said accusingly to Brian. "We can't afford to have any dissension in the ranks at this stage, old sport. We're in too deep to pull out."

Brian did not even bother to look up. "I'm all for it," he replied quietly, "but that doesn't mean I have to put up with Simon's asinine remarks."

Simon gave him a withering glance. "Can it, Brian. It's bad enough listening to Alan pretend he's Montgomery at el-Alamein without you throwing in your two cents as well."

They continued talking for another hour, outlining the plan of action for Monday's meeting. Brian was the first to leave, claiming he had an appointment. Simon grinned maliciously, savoring the man's discomfort.

"Have a nice evening," he said blandly. "Get yourself in fighting trim for Monday."

They waited till Brian had slammed the front door before continuing the conversation. "What's the matter with him?" Constantine asked, rolling his watery eyes expressively. "Methinks there could be bad blood at the top."

"He has his moments," Simon said sourly. "Nothing that will cause any trouble, though. You can take my word for that."

Brian drove slowly from Englewood Cliffs to his apartment in Edgewater, four miles away. Fletcher Austin was sitting out on the balcony when he arrived, dressed in a pair of ragged Bermuda shorts and a T-shirt. He heard Brian enter the apartment but made no move to greet him; he maintained his position on the balcony, waiting for Brian to come out.

"How did it go?" Fletcher asked, staring out across the river at upper Manhattan, watching the lights of cars moving along the Henry Hudson.

"Just like usual," Brian replied. He walked to the edge of the balcony and leaned over, staring down at the parking lot five stories below.

"Don't do it," Fletcher warned. "Somebody will only have to clear up the strawberry jelly afterwards."

Brian turned around. "Don't worry yourself. I wasn't about to."

"But the thought has crossed your mind."

"Sure it has. What would you do if you were in my position?" Brian asked vehemently. "Wouldn't the same thought cross your mind? I'm betraying a friend. Surely you're not so insensitive that you can't see that."

Fletcher stretched out in the chair, enjoying himself as he noticed Brian staring at the action. "It means whatever you want it to mean, Brian. Look at the beneficial side of it. You're still in an extremely well-paid job and, just as important, you're helping me. Old Man Chesterton can't last forever, so you're getting in on the ground floor of the new dynasty. The clout that Simon has with you could very well turn out to be to your own advantage. Try to look at it that way."

Brian turned away, walking back into the apartment. "Sure," he muttered disgustedly. "Every time I go into the office I'm stabbing the greatest guy in the world right in the back. That's to my advantage all right. Makes me feel just marvellous, a real hero."

He heard the chair creak behind him as Fletcher stood; then he felt the model's hand on his shoulder.

"Everything's a compromise, Brian. Remember that. Look around you, from the top government official to the filthiest, most flea-bitten bum in the Bowery. Nobody can afford the luxury of living by definite standards any more. I'll give you any odds that Old Man Chesterton cut a few corners on the way up, compromised himself somewhere along the line to get where he is."

"I doubt it," Brian replied. "Jonathan Chesterton is one guy who never made a compromise in his whole life—not for anything or anybody."

But his words lacked any conviction. He felt that he was speaking merely to hear his own voice, hoping to find reassurance in it.

# 30

If Simon was surprised to find Nino Viscenzi attending the Monday afternoon meeting, he made no show of it. He knew that the Italian designer was due in the office, although he never expected him to be present at a meeting which had nothing to do with the designer label suits. He simply nodded to Viscenzi, who sat away from the boardroom table, and took his seat.

Gerald was seated already, the usual stack of paperwork piled in front of him: figures for the previous week's business for both Chestertons and Mr. Simon, plus reports from the regions.

Brian entered a minute later, talking to Della and Alan Constantine. They were followed immediately by Jonathan and Miriam. Viscenzi stood up as his friend entered, walking across the room to greet him.

"Now who is this fashion coordinator you were telling me so much about?" Viscenzi asked loudly. "I feel that I am in need of more education."

Jonathan indicated Constantine, who rose to his feet, uncertain about being called upon. "Alan, I'd like you to meet a very dear friend of mine, Nino Viscenzi from Paris. You may have heard of him," he added, very low-key.

As the name registered, Constantine flashed Simon a look which needed no interpretation—What the hell is he doing here? Simon shook his head briefly, signifying that he did not know.

"Mr. Constantine," Viscenzi said warmly, having noticed the visual interplay, feeling pleased that his reputation could have caused it. "I am delighted to meet you. My friend Jonathan has told me much about you." He grasped the man's hand and shook it vigorously. "Perhaps you would be kind enough to let me pick your brains afterwards. I understand that you have some very interesting theories on where our industry is heading, and I am always keen to hear new ideas."

Constantine appeared to be embarrassed by the attention he was receiving from the voluble Italian. "I'd love the chance to talk to you," he replied, extricating his hand with difficulty from Viscenzi's grasp, "but I'm afraid it will have to wait for a while. I'm rather busy today."

"Of course, of course," Viscenzi said understandingly. "I am only here in an unofficial capacity. It's far better than sitting outside, waiting till you have finished your meeting."

As Constantine sat down again, he felt Simon kick him under the table. Simon's face resembled a voodoo death mask, the hazel eyes gazing out balefully. "Go easy," he whispered. "I don't like it."

"What the hell's that bloody dago doing here?" Constantine hissed. Too late he saw Della, to his right, glaring at him, pure venom in her eyes; he remembered her Puerto Rican background and bit his tongue.

Jonathan covered the standard agenda quickly, keeping discussion on merchandise performance to a bare minimum. He knew there was a confrontation coming, and he wanted to get to it as speedily as possible. He listened to the last piece of store information, then pushed aside his copies of the reports with an air of finality.

"Right. Is there any more business?" Jonathan directed the question at Simon, knowing from which quarter any attack would come.

"Alan and I have an idea," Simon began.

"You mean you have an idea," Jonathan corrected him. "Alan's a big boy; he's old enough to speak up for himself."

Simon reddened slightly at the put-down. "If you prefer it that way," he acknowledged, "I have an idea about expanding the casualwear side of the Chestertons business. We've proved during the past couple of months that the more mature man—the traditional Chestertons customer—will happily buy this style of clothing if it's presented properly. Now I feel that the time is right to build upon that foundation."

Jonathan looked past Simon to Brian. I don't know why I'm bothering, he thought pessimistically, but I'll give it a try. "What about you, Brian? How do you see the market?"

Before replying, Brian flicked his eyes in Simon's direction; the action was not lost on Jonathan.

"Our direction is leading us that way," he said. "I think we're now big enough to dictate fashion, not follow it any more. It's our responsibility to tell men what they should be wearing, not fill up our racks willy-nilly with what the trends seem to be." He stopped talking abruptly as Viscenzi left his seat and strode toward the table.

"Nobody is big enough to dictate fashion as you have just suggested," the Italian said. "Not even"—he inclined his head in a mock gesture of modesty—"me."

Constantine tipped back his chair for a better look at Viscenzi. "Oh, come on, old sport." There was a smile on his red face as he chided the designer. "We all know that's a load of old twaddle. Look at the motor industry as an example. If GM, Ford and Chrysler got together and told the poor bastards in the street that all cars should have blue doors, white interiors and burlap seat covers next year, they'd all believe it and stand in line for the new models. Of course we're big enough to dictate fashion. We just haven't had the brains or the guts to do it in the past."

"We are not the motor industry," Viscenzi said slowly, "and your concept is totally wrong." He scrutinized Constantine's clothes while he spoke, his lips curling derisively at the blue cotton dungarees and roll-neck sweater. "Because you feel you have a subconscious need to dress like an automobile mechanic does not mean that you have to think like one."

Constantine was thinking of a sharp retort when he felt Simon kick him once more under the table; he said nothing.

"You do not jump from point A to point C without going through B," Viscenzi continued, turning his attention to the whole meeting. "Fashion trends are all part of the evolutionary process, one step to be taken at a time. If you believe a change is needed—and I, for one, see no reason for such a change within this company—you do it gradually. You introduce a new theme, but you do it quietly, letting it gain its own momentum as time progresses and your customers become accustomed to it. You do not have it shrieking for attention in the front of your store, scaring away regular customers while you search desperately for your new identity and patronage."

Listening to Viscenzi's mellow tones, Jonathan could not resist a broad smile. The Italian's words were like soothing music to his ear, reflecting his own thinking perfectly. Doubts which had assailed him before the meeting drifted away as the Italian's voice rolled on.

"Whose idea was it to put jeans and cowboy belts on display in the store?" he asked, his tone like that of a schoolmaster asking a culprit to own up. "Is anybody going to admit responsibility for that?"

Simon, who had been growing more furious as the monologue continued, jumped to his feet, pushing back the chair so roughly that it toppled to the floor.

"It was my idea!" he shouted, making no attempt to hold down his voice. "Mine and Alan's—and Brian's. And I don't see what goddamned business it is of yours. You have one specific job with this company, a contract to design a line of suits, nothing more. So you can keep your opinions about anything else to yourself. Nobody here is interested in them, because they're not wanted."

"Yes, they are. They most certainly are." The voice was Jonathan's, quiet, even, refusing to allow himself to be drawn into an argument. "Nino's opinions are probably the most valuable ones we'll hear in this room today." He swivelled in the chair to face the Italian, who had remained standing over the table, completely unfazed by Simon's angry outburst.

"Sorry about that, Nino," Jonathan said, apologizing deliberately on Simon's behalf. "Please carry on. I'm enjoying it."

Before Viscenzi could comply, Simon yelled across the table, "Don't make any apologies for me! I think it's about time we all found out exactly where we stand."

Viscenzi regarded Simon oddly, his mouth half-open as if he were debating whether or not to speak. "I know exactly where I stand, Simon," he eventually said; the smile he sent across the table did not contain the slightest trace of warmth or humor. "I never had to beg my father for money to keep me out of trouble with bookmakers or gangsters."

The awful memory of that day crashed into Simon like a bucket of ice-cold water. He staggered back, almost tripping over the upturned chair, his face drained of blood, lips moving soundlessly. Della, sitting opposite, looked shocked, remembering only too clearly the two men who had used her to gain entry into Simon's apartment that day. Even Miriam was upset, regarding Viscenzi through tear-clouded eyes, hurt that he could have so spitefully opened such an old and painful wound.

The designer paid no attention to any of them. He had said what he wanted to say; now he turned to Jonathan. "If you will excuse me, I will wait for you outside. Perhaps we can talk more amicably over dinner."

With Viscenzi's departure, Simon recovered his bravado. He glared at his father, pointing at the door through which Viscenzi had just passed. "He's had it with us. That man has done his last piece of work for Chestertons."

"Says who?"

"Says me!" Simon snapped. He looked around the table for support. Brian studiously avoided his gaze, while Miriam fidgeted uneasily, still upset over Viscenzi's statement. His glance fell on Gerald, who stared back with tired eyes.

"Go wipe your snotty nose," Jonathan told Simon. "And if you behave yourself, we'll get somebody to change your diapers for you."

An exasperated gasp came from Della, who had sat through the whole exchange without saying a word. "Can we please continue with this meeting?" she asked. "There has been enough said during the past two minutes that everybody will regret. Do you truly think it's in our best interests to compound it?"

Miriam smiled warmly at her daughter-in-law's suggestion. Jonathan saw the expression and grimaced; anything for a little peace and quiet, that was Miriam of late. As long as nobody bothered her, she was happy. Maybe that's the right attitude to have, he thought.

"Della's right," Gerald said. "Can we get on with this thing? It may as well be now as later."

Jonathan surrendered. "All right. Simon, if you can keep your opinions to the business at hand, would you explain what you have in mind?"

The room began to settle down as Simon went over his proposed buying plan. Jonathan listened patiently as his son defined the market he was trying to reach, the mature man who wanted to get away from the formal look in clothing for his leisure hours. It was obvious to Jonathan that Simon had worked hard on the presentation—too hard. Jonathan thought he could see Della's handiwork. Even in his most charitable mood, he could not credit Simon with such comprehensive research.

There was a definite market which Chestertons had hardly touched. Nino Viscenzi had said as much the other night when the two men had talked over dinner. But Jonathan remembered him adding that the company should not drop its standards to capture that market. Simon, however, had an argument to cover that as well.

"If we try to put the quality of our suits into casual garments, we'll defeat the whole purpose," he said earnestly, the earlier friction now completely forgotten. "The price will be so high if we insist on the same standards that our customers will buy these casual garments instead of a regular suit, not in addition to it."

Jonathan took the point, admitting it was well made. The whole objective of successful retailing, he knew, was to force the customer to make an extra purchase, not persuade him to buy one style in preference to another. Get him to buy both, that was the secret of success.

Alan Constantine, still smarting from being told that he dressed like a mechanic, joined in the discussion, taking it up from Simon in a logical sequence. "The whole trick to this sort of clothing is the fashion angle. If that's right, we're onto a certain winner. The garments don't have to be top-quality; their appeal will last a season, no more. Fashion's the important thing. And once you've got your customers onto this style of clothing for their leisure hours, there'a multitude of accessories to go along with it. You name it, everything's part of this concept. Carrying it to the logical conclusion, you can even portion off part of each store where you have the space and create a casualwear club, or something along those lines."

"We've already got shops within shops," Jonathan reminded him. "Mr. Simon has taken care of that."

"That's a separate thing altogether," Constantine said. "These would be a part of the regular Chestertons store, but set aside slightly. You break up the stores anyway, shirts here, knitwear there, suits at the back. So you break them up a bit more."

"How would you go about promoting such a new concept in leisure dressing?" Jonathan asked, knowing that a projected advertising program would have been worked out already.

Della took up the cue immediately. "Psychologists have assured us for a long time that men dress a certain way because they want to be noticed by women, a peacock syndrome if you like. It was always that way in Europe till maybe one hundred years ago, when women were the dowdier dressers."

"Go on," Jonathan said, realizing he was about to get another of Della's well-thought-out lectures. "I'm listening."

"It's only in this century that the opposite became true, with the austerity imposed by wars. Men all walked about looking like each other, and every suit was dark blue, dark brown or dark gray. But since the sixties, when Britain's Carnaby Street brought color back into men's clothing, men have had this desire for bright clothes again. I think we should take this into consideration with the advertising, use a peacock theme with women in the ads as a backdrop to the model." Opening her attaché case, she withdrew artist's impressions of the advertisements she favored.

Jonathan studied them curiously. Uncertain, he handed them to Gerald, who looked at them briefly before passing them along the table.

"Having women is one thing," Jonathan said, "but do they have to be that undressed?"

"You're selling leisurewear," Della reminded him. "The models are relaxing on a beach or by a swimming pool. How would you want them to be dressed? In raincoats?"

"Fair enough. But can we buy decently this time? No more linen suit fiascos. We want people to come back to us, certainly. But we want them back to buy, not to return merchandise and complain about it."

He directed the last comment at Brian and Simon, letting it hang in the air as he left the boardroom to see Viscenzi.

Jonathan ate dinner with Viscenzi that night; then both men returned to the office. The designer began to apologize for his sarcastic comment on Simon's gambling debts, but Jonathan waved it aside.

"It was the best thing you could have said, Nino. I only wish I'd thought of it," Jonathan told him. "Miriam would probably have divorced me, though. I wish you'd stayed right through to the end of the meeting. Then you could have seen how they all gang up on me. And Gerald's not much help. He's an administrative genius, but he doesn't know a great deal about the merchandise side, hasn't got any feeling for it." He laughed bitterly. "I'm beginning to feel like General Custer at Little Big Horn, and everybody else is an Indian or a spectator. By the way," he added, "did you ever get to speak to Alan Constantine?"

Viscenzi pursed his lips. "I caught him for a few minutes before he left the office."

"And?"

"He has an instinctive feeling for a certain level of the men's wear retailing industry, the very high-fashion end. But he does not have the faintest idea of the technical side. If you talk to him about so many stitches to the centimeter, he looks at you as though you were speaking a foreign language."

"Is there anything on the positive side?" Jonathan asked.

"He has this appreciation for the high-fashion mass market," Viscenzi replied. "I don't know what good that is to you, however."

Jonathan mulled over the information. "Another one of Simon's bright ideas," he muttered. "With Brian's backing, of course."

Viscenzi sat down, opening his jacket. "I may be wrong, Jonathan. Perhaps your son and Brian have something special in mind for which Mr. Constantine will be perfect. He knows his suppliers apparently. And I understand he drives a very hard bargain."

"That's the polite way of putting it," Jonathan said. "He screws them right into the ground. That's also no good, because they won't deal with us again in a hurry."

"Jonathan, when I saw you and Brian in London six months ago, you were both on top of the world. You were continuing to uphold the traditions on which your company was founded. Now, Simon has jumped from virtual obscurity, and Brian—to whom I gave more credit—is following blindly in his footsteps. What happened?"

"I don't know," Jonathan said wearily. "I honestly don't know. It started a couple of months after we returned from London. Simon got into a lather about some linen suits which he wanted for the Mr. Simon shops. Here,"—he walked across to a clothing rack against the opposite wall— "this is one of them. We shouldn't have gone near this junk with a ten-foot pole, but Brian backed Simon, so I let them get on with it. We got burned but good."

Viscenzi inspected the jacket, letting the trousers fall to the floor. Taking a tiny knife from his pocket, he looked inquiringly at Jonathan. "May I hold a post-mortem?"

"Sure. Go right ahead. You can't make it look any worse."

Expertly, Viscenzi slit open the shoulder and side seams and began to strip the jacket, examining each component as it came away. "There is a rule in grammar that two negatives make a positive," he said, tossing pieces of fabric onto Jonathan's desk. "Unfortunately, the same principle does not apply in clothing construction. Here, if you put trash on top of trash, you come up with a double dose." A thought occurred to him. "This garment did not come from your Buffalo factory, did it?"

Jonathan shook his head. "God forbid."

"God forbid is right. You see this?" He held up a length of thread for Jonathan to see. "Monofilament thread. I wouldn't touch it with a pair of gloves."

Jonathan's face was a picture of puzzlement, and Viscenzi smiled. "Your father would have understood better than you. The thread you use at Buffalo, that is multifilament, a number of separate strands wound together to make one. It comes in different colors for different shades of fabric, so you are forced to carry a substantial stock. Monofilament is supposed to be the ultimate answer to thread inventory problems."

"How come?" Jonathan asked, still perplexed.

"See?" Viscenzi said. "It's translucent and has only one core, like a fishing line. The manufacturers claim that because of its translucency it can be used for all colors, since it will blend in perfectly with the fabric, doing away with the expensive and time-consuming necessity of keeping comprehensive stocks of thread. The truth of the matter is, or so I have found, it shows up on all colors and matches perfectly with none. It also produces excessive wear on sewing machine parts, and, because of the single filament construction, wherever the end is cut it forms a tiny barb. Makes you feel like you've got fleas. It itches like mad if it breaks through the fabric of the garment you're wearing." He shuddered slightly to back up his observations.

"What else is wrong with the suit?" Jonathan asked, remembering Viscenzi's comment about a double dose of trash.

No immediate reply was forthcoming. Viscenzi continued opening the seams, searching. Finally he held up the left forepart. "Poorly fused canvas," he stated simply. "It's a poor quality canvas to begin with, and the fusing is inadequate."

Jonathan took the piece and scrutinized it. Where the canvas had been heat-fused to the top fabric, it had come away in several places, leaving the jacket susceptible to wrinkling when the canvas curled.

"Can you wonder why people complained?" Viscenzi asked. "Everything about the suit is bad—fabric, construction, the lot. Put something like this through a dry-cleaning machine just once, and you are left with a rag to clean the car."

Jonathan tossed the piece of fabric he was holding onto the desk to join the pile already there. "Want a job?" he asked Viscenzi. "I never realized how much I missed not having Jacob around."

"I told you that he and I were alike."

"Maybe that's why we get on so well," Jonathan said. "Perhaps I need to have a good technical man around the place to keep me on my toes."

"No, my friend. You will do very well by yourself. What is happening here now has happened in many companies. The younger man feels his power and, being surrounded by young people, forces his ideas across. The older man, yourself, suddenly feels himself being pushed to one side as something obsolete. But have no fear," Viscenzi said. "You will still be in charge the next time I come over." He gazed into Jonathan's eyes for a moment, communicating soundlessly. "You have to stay around for my sake. I fear that after today's episode, Simon and his friends will not be very receptive to my ideas."

"He wanted you bounced."

"And what happened?"

"You're still working with Chestertons."

"So I am. So I am," Viscenzi repeated wondrously. "You see, you are still the one who holds the real power in this company." He pulled out two silver cigar tubes. "Jonathan, surely you will not refuse the finest Havana?"

In his imagination, Jonathan could already taste the exquisite flavor of the cigar. He took one, uncapping the tube, waiting while Viscenzi finished using the solid gold clippers. Taking them, he snipped a groove in the end of the cigar, lighting it from Viscenzi's Dunhill.

"What I'd like now is a glass of brandy," Jonathan mused, "but I might be pushing my luck too far." He drew deeply on the cigar, feeling the smoke cool in his mouth, the rich aroma easing him. He blew the smoke in a column toward the ceiling, watching in fascination as it was sucked into the extractor, disappearing without trace.

"Moderation," he told Viscenzi. "That's the word, the key to everything. Just one cigar on the infrequent occasions you're here won't do me any harm."

Viscenzi nodded in agreement, his own cigar held loosely in his right hand. "Moderation," the Italian repeated. "I just trust that some other people see its benefits."

"So do I," Jonathan said, feeling more mellow with each puff of the Havana. "Too many people with too many extreme ideas have left the world a lousy place to live in."

He coughed as he said the last three words, a dry hacking cough, as though he were trying to clear his throat. Then his throat exploded as if his lungs were pushing their way up, forcing their way into his mouth. He snapped forward, coughing violently, choking, his eyes clouded with water, unable to focus.

Viscenzi jumped out of his chair and rushed over to Jonathan. He picked up the cigar from the carpet where Jonathan had dropped it, placing it in an ashtray. Straightening Jonathan in the seat, Viscenzi patted him on the back to clear his lungs. The deep resonance of the continuing cough frightened him, and he looked around for water. A door led off from the boardroom to Jonathan's private washroom. Leaving his friend, Viscenzi ran to the door, opened it and returned with a glass of water which he held to Jonathan's lips.

Slowly the coughing spasm subsided, leaving Jonathan wheezing weakly, tears streaming down his face, his heart pounding. He blinked as his vision cleared, wiping at his eyes with the backs of his hands.

"God doesn't want me to smoke," he said hoarsely, trying to joke about the incident. But Viscenzi refused to find anything funny.

"Are you feeling better?"

"Yeah, I will be. Just give me a couple of minutes to get myself together."

Shame flooded over Viscenzi as he remembered offering the cigar to Jonathan. "I'm a fool for giving you that cigar. And you're an even bigger fool for taking it."

Jonathan regarded his friend fondly. "Just don't tell Miriam," he croaked. "And make sure you get rid of those butts before we leave. I've got enough aggravation without her having a go at me as well."

# 31

The first phone call came through to Jonathan less than five minutes after he had arrived at the office. As his secretary was not yet in, he was obliged to take the call himself when the switchboard automatically routed it through to his extension.

"Yes? Hello?" What a way to answer the telephone, he thought. But at eight-twenty in the morning who really cares?

"Mr. Chesterton?"

"Yes."

"You are Mr. Jonathan Chesterton, president of Chestertons?"

Jonathan began to lose patience with the caller. "Yes again. What is this, some kind of guessing game?"

"Good morning, Mr. Chesterton. My name is Alexander Simes," the caller introduced himself.

Jonathan flicked through his mental file of names but could not place the man. "What can I do for you, Mr. Simes?"

"At this very moment I am looking at your advertisement in this morning's newspaper, Mr. Chesterton," Simes said. "And I think it is disgusting that a company of your reputation and integrity should stoop to this form of loathsome advertising."

Jonathan went rigid in his chair. "I'm sorry, Mr. Simes. I'm not following you. Could you hold on a moment while I look at the newspaper?"

He picked up the copy from his desk, still folded as it had been when he bought it from the kiosk near the store; the delivery boy had been late that morning, and Jonathan had not yet had a chance to read the paper. Flipping the corners of the pages, he came to the Chestertons advertisement for the casual clothing that had been discussed at the earlier meeting. What he saw took his breath away.

"Jesus Christ," he whispered, unable to believe what was printed on the page in front of him.

"Did you say something, Mr. Chesterton?" Simes enquired.

"No," Jonathan lied, realizing that he still held the receiver to his mouth. "I just coughed."

He continued to stare at the advertisement, his brain reeling with shock. This was certainly not the layout he had approved with Della; it was nothing like it. The first one, which he had thought to be borderline for good taste, was a kindergarten nursery rhyme compared with the one which faced him now. The casual clothing was shown, certainly, but its presence in the picture was almost incidental, a frivolity thrown in to fill up empty space. Fletcher Austin's attention was riveted on the girl who lay face up across his lap, clad only in the scantiest of bikinis, which left little to the imagination. One of Fletcher's hands rested under the girl's buttocks, while the other was poised above her breasts, fingers curved like the talons of a bird of prey ready to plunge and plunder.

The headline added to Jonathan's sense of shocked fury. "Chestertons... for those men who know what they want out of life."

"Mr. Simes, I'm at a loss for words. I don't know what to say. This whole thing has come as a complete surprise to me." It was all he could do to keep the rage out of his voice.

The caller's voice came back sharply, laden with blatant disbelief. "I find that rather difficult to credit, Mr. Chesterton. I am also in the retail business, and our advertising never appears in the media without approval of the management committee." Then came the words which Jonathan had been fearing, the whole reason behind the phone call.

"I have shopped at your New York store for the past five years, as has my son, Mr. Chesterton, because we thought your company offered excellent value and service. That is a practice which you can be assured we will no longer be continuing. Good morning."

Jonathan stared dumbfounded at the mute instrument in his hand, ready to smash it against the desk in anger. Almost a full minute passed before he could regain control of his emotions; then he replaced the receiver gently and stood up, intent on finding Della the moment she came in and wresting an explanation from her. He got no farther than three paces from the desk when the telephone rang again.

"Jonathan Chesterton."

The caller's name this time was Petersen, but the message was the same. Chestertons had lost another customer of long standing. By the time his secretary arrived, Jonathan had taken five more calls, all informing him that the stores would be losing business because of the advertisement.

When Della arrived shortly before nine, she found Jonathan pacing agitatedly in her office. Mistaking the signals completely, she smiled warmly at him, saying, "This is a nice surprise."

"Close the door," Jonathan ordered. When she had done so, he glared at her. "Just what the hell is the meaning of this?" he demanded, thrusting the newspaper toward her, jabbing at the advertisement with his forefinger.

Della stared at the page, then at Jonathan, uncomprehending. "It's the leisurewear ad."

"Are you trying to tell me that this is the one I approved? Because it damned well isn't."

For the first time Jonathan saw his daughter-in-law lose some of her composure. He welcomed it. "We didn't think it was eye-catching enough the way it was for the type of merchandise we wanted to promote," she began hesitantly. "So we decided to brighten it up a little bit."

Jonathan threw the newspaper down onto the floor between them; its leaves scattered across the carpet. "Who the goddamned hell is we? You and that idiot son of mine?"

"Simon is not an idiot!" Della shouted back.

Determined not to be outdone if it came to a shouting match, Jonathan raised his voice even more, bellowing across the office. "No? What would you call him then? A genius?"

Before Della could think of an answer, the door opened and the subject of the argument walked in. He looked in surprise from his wife to his father. "What's all this yelling about? I can hear you from the other end of the corridor."

Della jumped in first. "Your father doesn't like the ad," she explained, lowering her voice.

"You're damned right I don't like it!" Jonathan yelled, striding across the three yards separating him from Simon and Della. "And guess what? Neither did any of the dozen customers who've already called me up this morning to say that they're not buying their clothes here any more. Is that what an advertisement's supposed to do, drive people away?" He waited for an answer. Della put a hand to her mouth, unable to believe what Jonathan had just said.

"Gets right to you, doesn't it?" Jonathan added triumphantly. "What have the pair of you got planned for an encore? Another big surprise to lose us more customers?"

Simon held out a hand toward his father, palm forward, a traffic policeman's signal to halt. "Wait a minute. Do you know what kind of customers we'll lose because of that ad? I'll tell you—sixty-year-old ultraconservatives who spend all their time writing to newspapers and congressmen to complain about the way this country's being run."

Jonathan pushed Simon's hand aside and jabbed him hard in the chest with his finger, driving him back against the wall. "No. I'll tell you about the kind of customers we're losing because of that ad—people who come into our stores on a fairly regular basis and buy a lot of clothes to pay the salaries of fools like you."

Gradually Jonathan began to calm down, realizing that the display of temper, gratifying as it felt, could do him little good. "What the hell ever made you change that ad," he asked, his tone normal once again, "especially without telling me a thing about it?"

Della opened her mouth, but Simon motioned for her to stay quiet. "We felt the ad wasn't lively enough," he replied. "It needed some pizzazz, something to lift it into the realms of the merchandise we were showing."

"I'll ask you the same question again. Why didn't you tell me what you were planning to do?" The words came out between clenched teeth.

"Because we knew you'd react to it just the way you're reacting now," Simon said.

"Wrong!" Jonathan spat the word out. "I'm carrying on like this because the damage has already been done, and we're losing business left, right and center any time one of our customers opens a newspaper today. Before I would have just slung the pair of you out of the office and let it go at that." He stopped speaking long enough to draw breath.

"Who else was in on this irresponsible piece of lunacy? Brian? Your limey friend Constantine?"

Simon nodded.

"Well I'll tell you what you can do now. First you get hold of Constantine and tell him that his services are no longer required by this company; he'll get his severance pay in the mail. Then you can find Brian and send him in to see me. You,"—he pointed a finger at Della—"I don't know what I'm going to do with you. You can just thank your lucky stars that you're married to this idiot—that's right, idiot!—otherwise you'd be joining the late Mr. Constantine at the unemployment office."

Without waiting for a response, Jonathan stormed out of Della's office, slamming the door behind him. When he returned to the boardroom, his secretary informed him that three more customers had telephoned to express their displeasure with the advertisement, and that Gerald was waiting to see him.

Jonathan took the messages and walked into the boardroom, seeing Gerald standing in front of the desk. "And what did you know about this advertisement?" he asked his son. "Were you in with those idiots as well?"

Gerald shook his head in dazed wonderment. "I didn't know a damned thing about it till I opened the paper this morning. I think it's going to hurt us."

"It's done that already." Jonathan sat down, suddenly feeling exhausted, the strain of the row with Simon and Della catching up with him. Putting a hand to his chest, he could feel his heart hammering away. "Gerald, get me a glass of water, please." He waited till his son returned with the drink, then swallowed one of the nitroglycerine tablets the doctor had prescribed for him, washing it down.

"Feel better now?" Gerald asked anxiously.

"It's passing."

"I heard the row and came in here to wait for you," Gerald said. "Everybody heard it. You shouldn't carry on like that; you know it's bad for you."

"You and your mother both," Jonathan remarked disparagingly. But he was forced to admit that Gerald was right; he had no business getting involved in arguments, and he was a fool to ignore the advice. "What are we going to do about Brian and Della?" he asked his son. "Any bright ideas?"

Gerald looked confused. He perched on the corner of his desk, staring down at his father. "God knows," he finally said. "I don't think that Della's so much of a problem. She knows all the advertising angles, and she's done a good job for us up till now. She just went a bit too far this time, probably at Simon's instigation."

"I disagree with you," Jonathan said. "It's the other way around, if you ask me. Ever since they got married and she began working with this company, Simon's arguments have been much stronger, far more lucid. It's as though somebody's been coaching him in the subtle art of putting his point across."

Gerald gave a short, cynical chuckle. "That can't be bad, remembering some of his earlier efforts at communication. But Brian I honestly don't know about. There's something weird going on there. His wife split and went back to Chicago, and everything was fine for a while. Then it all went bang. Do you think it could have upset him that badly, thrown him right off balance?"

"No way," Jonathan said with a degree of certainty. "He was crying on my shoulder when his wife was here, how she was a drunk and it was getting him down. Then, when we came back from England, he found out that she'd gone back to Chicago. First thing he did was jump ten feet in the air and click his heels for joy. Something else has happened since then to make him throw in his lot with Simon like this."

"Maybe he sees you retiring in the near future and Simon taking over," Gerald suggested, not sounding as if he believed it himself.

Jonathan did not hear the comment. He sat chewing his bottom lip, thinking over the odd alliance as he had thought about it more than one thousand times. "It's got to be one of the great mysteries of the modern age. When Brian first took over the job of sorting out the Mr. Simon buying problems," Jonathan recalled, "they were at each other's throats the whole time. Now they're like a couple of mongrels in the street, sniffing around each other, doing everything together." Stuck for words, he cast his eyes around the boardroom, letting them rest on various familiar objects. Gerald waited patiently.

"I think we should see how many of these damned phone calls we get in," Jonathan said at last. "Then we can get together this afternoon and thrash the whole thing out. I tell you this though,"—his voice took on a resolute note—"by the time this afternoon's over, Della will have been yanked firmly back into line, and Brian will either be back on our bench or out on his ass."

He looked up at Gerald. "Set it up, will you? And make sure you're there."

Jonathan spent the lunch break with Gerald, walking around the main store, keeping an eye on the casual clothing displays which had been featured in the morning's advertisement. He was grateful to see some action, but there was nowhere near enough, in his own estimation, to compensate for the threatened withdrawal of patronage.

Gerald telephoned stores in the same time zone and found out that they had received similar complaints; wherever the advertisement had appeared, it had met with emotions varying from amazement to barely controlled disgust from Chestertons' regular customers.

Shortly before the meeting was due to start, Jonathan called Miriam to advise her of the situation; she had not even seen the advertisement, so he had to start from the beginning. Quite innocently she asked if her presence was necessary. Jonathan was aghast that she should want to attend. He saw the forthcoming meeting as a final showdown over control of the company, one time when he certainly did not want his wife to be there, what with her complete inability to see Simon through anything other than rose-colored glasses, failing as usual to separate him from Myron in her mind.

"Don't worry about it," he assured her. "It'll be quiet and civilized. No murders if we can possibly avoid them."

"Just make sure you don't get yourself all worked up," Miriam warned. "Remember what the doctor told you."

Jonathan groaned quietly; how could he forget? He had it rammed down his throat the whole time, if not from Miriam then from Gerald. "Yes, Miriam. I remember exactly what he said. I'll be as meek as a newborn lamb. I'm just going to throw a fit... quietly."

Gulping down a quick sandwich, he cleared his desk and made ready for the meeting. Before the others arrived, Jonathan laid a copy of the advertisement in front of each seat around the mahogany table, leaving blank the spot which Miriam occupied normally. Then he sat back to wait.

Gerald was first. He glanced around the empty table, smiling slightly as he noticed the copies of the advertisement. "I spoke to Ma a few minutes ago," he said. "She called me up and told me to keep an eye on you."

"Just sit yourself down," Jonathan said brusquely. "Save your speeches for later on when we might need them."

Brian was next in. He had been out all morning seeing a supplier and had only learned of the meeting a few minutes earlier when he had returned to the office. He looked at Gerald, then glanced quickly at Jonathan, who nodded tersely, indicating a seat.

A minute later Simon and Della entered, and Jonathan prepared to start the meeting, waiting for them to sit down before he began. When the door opened again to admit Alan Constantine, Jonathan froze in astonishment. But when he regained his self-possession, his voice rocked the room.

"What are you doing in this building?" he roared. "You don't work for Chestertons any more! Now get your ass out of here before I throw you out."

Constantine stood his ground as Jonathan's voice assaulted him like a physical force. His pale blue eyes flickered from Jonathan to Simon, expecting a defense against the onslaught. Simon acknowledged the glance and stood up, turning to face his father.

"Alan stays," he said forcefully. "He possesses both the experience and ability to help this company in the future. And I, for one, will not see you stand in our way." Finished, he sat down, pulling his chair into the table, motioning for Constantine to do the same.

Inch by inch, Jonathan stood up, utterly incapable of comprehending the mutiny which was taking place within the organization he had labored so long to build up. When he reached his full height, he leaned over the table, glowering down at Simon.

"If you find Constantine's company so appealing, maybe you'd like to go along with him. And while you're about it, take your wife with you. I've seen and heard enough today to know that Gerald, Brian"—he hesitated slightly as he said the name—"and I can run this company a damned sight better without your lunatic schemes."

Ten seconds passed during which no movement was discernible in the room. Incredulity crossed Jonathan's face that neither Simon nor Della nor Constantine had left yet.

"Go on!" he yelled. "What are you all waiting for? Get the hell out of here! Goddamn it!"

From the corner of his eye, he saw Gerald stand up and move swiftly toward him, the only person in the room to show any sign of motion. He felt Gerald's hand on his shoulder pushing him gently back into the chair.

"Take it easy," he whispered. "Getting yourself into a state isn't going to solve anything."

Reluctantly Jonathan took his advice. He lowered himself into the seat, continuing to glare along the highly polished length of the table. Simon and Della returned his gaze defiantly. Brian coughed self-consciously into his hand, turning his face away from the table, avoiding Jonathan's eyes.

The period of relaxation lasted for less than five seconds, the amount of time it took Constantine to pull out Miriam's chair and sit down at the table as if he belonged at the meeting. Sensing the impending explosion, Gerald tried to hold his father down in the seat, but Jonathan shrugged off the restraining hands, stood up and walked around the table. Standing menacingly behind Constantine, who looked up, suddenly worried at the prospect of violence, Jonathan grabbed the back of the chair and pulled it savagely.

"You don't hear too well, do you? I told you to get out of this building. Now do it!" He twisted the chair abruptly, sending Constantine tumbling to the carpet. Jonathan stood over him, feet planted either side of the prostrate body, daring the Englishman to do anything.

Carefully gauging the threat, Constantine slid away from underneath the threatening figure and stood up three yards away, dusting his clothes.

"What are you waiting for?" Jonathan asked. "Do I have to throw you out bodily?"

The confrontation was interrupted by Della. Forgetting the way that Jonathan had shouted at her that morning, she smiled sweetly at him, trying to defuse the inflammatory situation.

"I think you're being a little unreasonable about this," she said quietly. "Can't we all sit down and talk this out like civilized human beings?"

Instead of relieving the tension, Della's suggestion had exactly the opposite effect. Forgetting all about Constantine for the moment, Jonathan swung around on his daughter-in-law, using her as a target for his fury. "Civilized people don't run pornographic advertisements like we did this morning!" As he shouted the words, his breath came faster—short, shallow gasps as he began to gag. His legs started to buckle beneath his weight; the boardroom was upside down, then standing on its side as he swayed violently.

"Pa!" Gerald's scream echoed around the boardroom as he saw too late that his father had irretrievably overstepped the mark. He ran across to Jonathan, shoving aside Constantine to get to his father. Jonathan seemed to be collapsing, the great frame shrinking in on itself, a balloon punctured, deflating as the air leaked out. He staggered two steps, lurching to the side, clutching at the table to steady himself.

Gerald grabbed him with both hands, manhandling him to the nearest chair, easing him into it. He looked into his father's face and was horrified to see the white, straining features, the eyes rolling upward as Jonathan gasped frantically for breath. He tried to speak, to tell Gerald for a final time not to treat him like an invalid, but the blast of pain across his chest killed the effort; all that came out was a series of agonized wheezing sounds, grating whistles as he struggled to breathe.

Wild-eyed, Gerald looked around him. Nobody had moved, silent spectators to the drama in their midst. "For God's sake!" he screamed. "Somebody call an ambulance, a doctor. Don't just sit there like a bunch of dummies. Can't you see he's dying?" He began to feel through Jonathan's pockets, trying to find the small vial of nitroglycerine tablets, praying that it was not too late.

As if released from a trance, Brian jumped up and ran to the telephone on Jonathan's desk, frantically clawing at the dial as he tried to get the emergency number. Simon also stood, walking to where his father sat, looking over his brother's shoulder with an air of curious detachment. Della followed him, while Constantine remained standing where he was.

Gerald pushed Simon and Della out of the way. "Give him some air," he hissed, trying to force one of the tablets down his father's throat, then pulling off his tie, ripping open his shirt collar.

Eyes blurred by water and lack of oxygen, Jonathan tried to look around him, feeling annoyed that somebody was attempting to undress him. He was old enough to undress himself; why was somebody else doing it for him? His hands batted ineffectually at Gerald, trying to push him out of the way, make him stop pulling off the tie. On the periphery of his vision, he could vaguely make out three figures standing motionless, watching him. He blinked again, and his sight cleared for a moment; the three figures became definite. He recognized Simon and Della—and Constantine. With a final, almighty effort he pushed Gerald aside and staggered to his feet, a mortally wounded Goliath wanting one more opportunity to fight; the chair he had been sitting on toppled backward.

Jonathan pointed a wavering arm at Constantine, shouting with all his remaining strength. "Get him out of here! I won't have him in this room! In this building!"

Then he tottered forward three paces in Constantine's direction and collapsed, dropping straight down like a falling tree. The last thing he remembered was the dull pain as his face smashed into the carpet, his nose splitting like a piece of overripe fruit, his forehead crashing down like a hammer.

Gerald knelt down beside the body of his father, turning him over, feeling for a heartbeat, the faintest flutter that would show he was still alive.

There was nothing.

# 32

The doctor had left more than two hours earlier. Miriam lay asleep under a heavy sedative, while Gerald sat alone in what had been his father's den, the only room in the large Great Neck house where Jonathan had once been allowed to smoke his cigars in peace and quiet. Gerald replaced the telephone receiver, having just finished his second call. The first had been to make the funeral arrangements, which he had followed by calling Marilyn, who was looking after Karen in Manhasset.

His initial reaction to Jonathan's death had been one of numbness; he had remained kneeling by the prostrate body for almost five minutes, vaguely aware of other figures moving about the boardroom. Constantine had left immediately, followed by Simon, who had escorted Della away from the scene of the tragedy. Only Brian had remained, sitting at the table crying openly. When a doctor whose practice was in the same building officially pronounced Jonathan dead, the scene had not changed.

Now, late that night, Gerald sat in the den, his mind accepting the crushing blow, moving onto the next logical step, the fate of Chestertons itself. He would not be able to work for the next week, but neither would Simon. Gerald saw little comfort in that, however; he could no longer be certain that anybody was capable of running the business.

Three times during his deliberations he had tiptoed upstairs to check on Miriam; she slept soundly, the events of the day blotted out through merciful drugs. Miriam had received the news from him, diplomatically diluted, with no mention of the row. Simon had not been near the house, nor had he telephoned to learn how his mother was. Gerald could not even force himself to feel surprised by his brother's lack of consideration.

Again he went over the possible candidates at Head Office who could assume complete responsibility while he was away. The name of Brian Chambers kept recurring as an obvious choice, but Gerald failed to see how the man could be trusted with even the simplest task after the events of the past few months; it had been his unexpected, inexplicable alliance with

Simon which had caused the series of crises culminating in Jonathan's death.

With no other alternative, Gerald picked up the telephone a third time, prepared to put into operation the plan he had first decided upon. He checked his watch and saw that it was almost four in the morning; more than seven hours had elapsed since he had first entered the den. Estimating the time difference between the East Coast and Europe, he dialled zero, asking the operator to find out the number of Nino Viscenzi, on the rue Royale, Paris, and put him through.

While he waited for her to call back, he wondered how the Italian would view the favor he was about to ask.

Within three hours of receiving Gerald's telephone call, Nino Viscenzi was sitting in the first-class compartment of an Air France 747 from Orly Airport, Paris, to New York. He was slouched in the wide seat, dazed, the seat belt still fastened across his lap although the aircraft had reached its cruising altitude fifteen minutes earlier. The customary elegance was sorely missing; his shirt collar was open, revealing a gold Saint Christopher medallion, the silk tie awry. In his right hand was a glass of Courvoisier brandy. The snack which had been placed in front of him was untouched.

Viscenzi could still not believe the news. Not a month ago he had seen Jonathan alive and well. Certainly his friend had coughed badly while smoking the cigar, but he had been nowhere near death. The designer shook his head in bewildered sorrow; he felt a dampness in his eyes and dabbed at them with a silk pocket handkerchief.

Jonathan had been far more than a business associate in Viscenzi's eyes. He had been a true friend. Now he was dead, joining his father so soon. In the space of less than one year, Viscenzi had lost two friends, two men whom he had known for too short a time.

Why is it, he thought bitterly, that you only meet such people when there is so little time left to enjoy them?

A stewardess walked by and looked at him with a degree of concern. Viscenzi motioned for her to remove the food; he could stomach nothing solid.

"Some more brandy perhaps, sir?"

He glanced up at her, momentarily forgetting the reason for his hurried journey; he saw a pretty redhead with appealing freckles on her face. "Thank you. That would be very nice indeed." Then he reverted to staring at the seat in front, his mind on Jonathan again.

Unlike previous occasions, there was nobody waiting to meet him once he had cleared customs and immigration at Kennedy. He took a taxi from the airport, dropping his one suitcase on the seat beside him. Giving the driver the address in Great Neck, Viscenzi leaned back against the upholstery, feeling exhausted after the long flight for which he had been totally unprepared. As the taxi drew up outside the house, Viscenzi saw the black limousines waiting by the curb, the hearse closest to the front door, its rear open, ready to receive its cargo.

"This what you came for?" the cab driver asked. Viscenzi grunted an affirmative reply, feeling in his pocket for money. "Looks like you made it to the minute."

Viscenzi looked toward the house and then saw the door begin to open. Four men emerged, carrying the coffin between them. Behind it walked Simon and Gerald and other men whom Viscenzi did not recognize. Urgently he thrust a handful of bills at the driver and scrambled out of the taxi, not bothering to wait for change. Only when he had run three paces toward the house did he remember the suitcase. Turning back, he saw the driver holding open the door for him to retrieve it.

Gerald was the first to recognize him. Red-eyed and unshaven, he grasped the Italian by the hand, a look of relief on his face that Viscenzi had come so soon. Feeling his throat constrict, Viscenzi indicated the coffin which was being placed in the hearse.

"I am very sorry," he said quietly to Gerald. "There are no other appropriate words."

"It was marvellous of you to come, Nino. You must be feeling worn-out."

"Later I will have time to feel tired," Viscenzi said, making light of the three-and-a-half-thousand-mile journey. Seeing Simon, he shook his hand perfunctorily before turning his full attention once more to Gerald. "Where is your mother?"

Gerald pointed back to the house. "Inside. She's taken something, but she's still pretty badly shaken up."

Viscenzi shouldered his way ungracefully past Simon and the other mourners who were waiting while the coffin was loaded onto the hearse. He found Miriam sitting in the kitchen crying, while Marilyn tried to comfort her; there was no sign of Della.

A smile of recognition flashed across Marilyn's face as she noticed the Italian standing in the kitchen doorway. "Look," she said excitedly to Miriam, who was bent double, sobbing futilely. "Nino's come all the way from Paris to see you."

When Miriam looked up, Viscenzi fervently wished he was somewhere else. His stomach began to spin, and the tightness in his throat became worse. Miriam seemed to have aged ten years since he had seen her the last time; her eyes were sore from crying, and her face was a mass of lines. She tried to smile a welcome, and, disregarding his own discomfort, Viscenzi stepped forward quickly and kissed her lightly on the cheek.

"Come now," he chided her, forcing a smile onto his own face. "We cannot have you looking like this. You will scare everybody away. They will be too frightened to come to see you."

"He wouldn't look after himself," Miriam sobbed, looking directly into Viscenzi's soft brown eyes, but speaking to herself. "He just kept laughing at the doctors, saying they were fools. Cretins with a shingle he always called them. He thought he knew best, smoking, carrying on like he was still a young man. What could I do?" she asked helplessly.

Viscenzi took her hand in his, patting it gently. "There was nothing you could do. You did everything that was possible and made Jonathan a very happy man." Guilt flooded over him as he spoke the comforting words; he was haunted by the memory of the cigar he had given to Jonathan when they had last met, the Havana which had triggered off the coughing spasm.

Straightening up, he took Marilyn aside. "Where is everybody else? Della? Brian?"

Marilyn stared at him coldly, the blue eyes turning to ice at the mention of the names. "Your guess is as good as mine. There was a tremendous row in the office yesterday, caused by Simon. My father-in-law had his heart attack right in the middle of it; he just dropped dead."

"Does she know?" Viscenzi nodded toward Miriam, who was taking no notice of the conversation.

"No. Gerald kept it from her. He didn't want her any more upset than she was already." Marilyn recounted the events of the previous afternoon as told to her by Gerald. Viscenzi listened numbly, his eyes closed, feeling the tears well up behind the lids. His own words to Jonathan came ringing back: "The younger man feels his power and, being surrounded by young people, forces his ideas across." How simple the remark had been to make, how glibly it had rolled off his tongue. Only Jonathan had been unable to see the business in that perspective; he was a fighter, a scrapper right to the end, not about to let anybody put a plan into operation which he thought was bad for the company. And it had killed him.

Feeling a hand on his shoulder, Viscenzi opened his eyes and looked around. Gerald was standing beside him. "There's space in one of the cars if you want to come with. We're about to leave."

Viscenzi nodded. He turned back to Miriam, kissing her again, holding her by the hand.

"Be pretty for when I return," he said. "I do not like to see you looking like this."

Brian Chambers did not attend the funeral. He knew that he should, that his position within the company dictated such an action, but he could not bring himself to get dressed and pay the final, hypocritical tribute to Jonathan Chesterton.

Sitting alone in his apartment overlooking the Hudson River, he wept uncontrollably, letting the tears run down his cheeks untouched, as if their passage would wash away his guilt.

He had killed Jonathan; he was certain of the fact—killed him just as surely as if he had held a loaded revolver to his forehead and pulled the trigger. By siding with Simon to protect his own secret and reputation, he had destroyed a man who had once looked on him as a friend.

Holding his head in his hands, the tears dropping straight down onto his trousers, Brian thought over every action he had taken since Simon had compromised his role at Chestertons, making him into nothing more effectual than a puppet. Why didn't I have the guts to stand up to his blackmail? I'd have been exposed; other people would have known about my relationship with Fletcher. So what? I could have lived with it. And I could have made life damned miserable for Simon—if he had dared to say a word about it. But I couldn't see any of that in the anxieties of the moment. No, all I could think about was myself. Tunnel vision. Blinded. Totally unaware of the way I could have fought back.

He remained sitting for more than an hour. The dried tears made his skin feel taut, and his eyes seemed full of sand, painful even to blink. Finally he came to a decision; standing up, he walked purposefully to the bathroom, only too well aware of the direction he was taking and his reason for doing so. Opening the medicine cabinet, he surveyed the contents. His eyes flicked past the spare safety razor he kept in case the electric Norelco broke down, past the bandages and box of Band-Aids, past the after-shave lotion. They stopped at the bottle of sleeping pills prescribed for him by the doctor during one of the worst periods with Thelma. He unscrewed the cap and tilted the bottle; two pills fell into his waiting hand. Two? Not enough. Nevertheless he popped them into his mouth, swallowing hard as he continued his search. In the far corner of the cabinet his gaze was arrested by the familiar Bayer label on the full bottle of aspirin. Clutching the bottle tightly in his right hand, he went to the kitchen, where he filled a glass with water.

Then he began to swallow the aspirin tablets, four or five at a time, swilling them down with water, quickly gulping more, eager to be finished before he could change his mind.

Della felt a twinge of remorse at her father-in-law's passing, but no guilt. As far as she was concerned, neither she nor Simon had in any way been responsible for Jonathan's death. She had discussed the final, fatal meeting with Simon and Alan Constantine; they all agreed that Jonathan had died simply because he had not known when to let go.

While Gerald mourned openly for his father, with Simon as unwilling company, Della schemed. In cold, hard terms, the main obstacle to building up Simon as the major power within Chestertons had been removed. It was unfortunate. It was callous. And it was true. All that remained now was Gerald, and it was well known that his strength lay in administration, cold facts, the physical operating of the stores. He had always left the merchandise decisions to other, more experienced, more talented people.

Like Simon.

The funeral party returned to the house, a somber group. Gerald, without even thinking about it, sat down on one of the low wooden chairs brought in for the period of mourning. Simon looked depreciatingly at the small seat before settling down, demonstrating clearly to anybody who was watching exactly what he thought of the practice. Viscenzi pulled up a straight-backed chair and sat next to Gerald, speaking in lowered tones.

"I feel I should join you down there."

"How do you figure that?"

"Your father was like family to me. Jacob, too," Viscenzi explained. "I felt that I had known them both all my life. I grieve for Jonathan almost as much as you do."

Notwithstanding the sadness of the occasion, Gerald smiled warmly at the Italian's sincerity. "How long do you plan on staying in the States, Nino?"

Viscenzi shrugged. "There is no time limit. My business will run itself sufficiently well without my interference. Who knows,"—he chuckled meaningfully—"it might do even better without me there to confuse people." He studied Gerald carefully. "You mentioned on the telephone this morning that I could help you. What is it that you want me to do while I am in this city?"

Checking to see that Simon was not listening in on the conversation, Gerald leaned closer to Viscenzi, whispering into the Italian's ear. "Would you go into the office on my behalf till I get up from mourning? Keep an eye on things?"

"What could I do for you at the office? I know very little of your business, my friend."

Being termed a friend had a profound effect on Gerald; it placed him on a par with his father in Viscenzi's eyes. "Nino, please do it for me," he begged, gripping the Italian's hand. "While I'm away, I don't know what's going on down there. My father must have told you about some of the things that were happening." Viscenzi nodded slowly, remembering Jonathan's qualms.

"I'll give you my authority," Gerald continued. "Just go in and keep things under control till I get back. You know what I mean. No buying is to be done without your approval, no supply deals made. You're familiar enough with our operation to do that much." He searched the Italian's eyes, seeking an answer.

"I don't know," Viscenzi objected halfheartedly. "I am only familiar with the work that I did for Chestertons. Everything else would be new to me."

"Do it for my father's memory, Nino. Please."

Viscenzi felt the same tug he had encountered when he had first seen Miriam that afternoon.

"I will do it for your father's memory, Gerald," he said. "And for you as well."

# 33

From where he stood outside the lobby of Brian's apartment building in Edgewater, Fletcher Austin could look out over the swimming pool to see the Circle Line boat chug slowly past as it showed the sights of Manhattan to anybody interested enough in making the voyage. Beyond it, he could easily make out the Henry Hudson Parkway running along Manhattan's West Side, the cars cruising along it reflecting the late evening sun directly into his eyes.

Giving the boat a final look, Fletcher raised his hand to press the buzzer to Brian's apartment, letting it drop as the lobby door was opened from the inside by a tenant on his way out. Fletcher muttered his thanks and entered the building, just catching the elevator before the doors closed, riding it up to the fifth floor. Footsteps cushioned by the deep pile carpet in the hall, he strolled leisurely to the apartment and rapped his knuckles on the door. There was no immediate answer, so he rapped again, more insistently this time, becoming impatient as the summons remained unanswered.

The news of Jonathan's death had been given that morning in the *Daily News Record*, the trade newspaper which Fletcher read assiduously because it kept him in touch with the industry which rewarded him the most. The story had given him no small shock. He had worked as Chestertons' number one model for more years than he cared to remember, although of late he had needed to pressure Brian to maintain that lofty position. With the passing of Jonathan, who had kept the organization together with a hand of iron, Fletcher saw his future in anything but certain terms—especially so with Della taking over complete control of all advertising functions, as she most certainly would, including the choice of model.

Fletcher was well aware of the strong influence exerted over Brian by Simon because of the relationship with himself. Now that Simon would need no more reluctant allies to get his way within the company, Fletcher badly needed some reassurances on his own future.

Impatience gave way to anger as Fletcher banged on the door a third time, listening closely for footsteps from within. He put his ear to the door, hoping to hear a radio, any sound which might betray Brian's presence. There was nothing. He was about to turn back toward the elevator when he thought he could hear a faint noise, like the sound of somebody groaning in pain.

"Brian!" he yelled, pounding on the door with both fists. "Are you all right?"

The door of the adjacent apartment opened, and a middle-aged man stepped out, glaring at Fletcher. "What the hell's all this racket about?" he demanded. "You don't get out of here, I'll call the goddamned cops."

Fletcher did not bother answering. He could hear the groaning clearly now, a low mumbling noise which rose and fell. "Where's the super?" he snapped at Brian's neighbor. "Which apartment? What's his name?"

"It's 115, Mike Musiak. What's it all about?"

Fletcher spun around and raced back down the hall. The elevator was no longer on the fifth floor, so he used the stairs, leaping down them three or four steps at a time, swinging around on the handrail to gain extra leverage and speed as he came to each landing.

He reached the apartments on the first floor and began to check the names and numbers—115, Mike Musiak, superintendent; the tenant on the fifth floor had been right.

"No apartments for rent," the superintendent said as he opened his door and saw Fletcher standing outside. "Didn't you see the sign out front?"

Fletcher breathed in deeply, half from the exertion of running pell-mell down the stairs, half from temper. "I don't want one of your crummy apartments. I've got a friend in five-twenty, Brian Chambers. He's ill. Will you open the door so we can get to him?"

The superintendent eyed Fletcher suspiciously before remembering that he had seen the model in the building before. All the same, he had no desire to leave the comfort of his own apartment. "What makes you so sure he's ill?"

"Because he's not answering the door."

"Maybe he's out," the superintendent suggested. "How the hell should I know why he doesn't answer the door." His eyes narrowed. "How come you got into the building if he didn't answer?"

Fletcher squared his shoulders, reached out with both hands and grabbed the man by the front of the shirt, yanking him off the ground; his feet dangled in the air like those of a hanged man.

"Never mind how the hell I got in, turkey. I can hear the guy groaning inside the apartment. Now will you get the spare key and open the door for me, or do I use your thick Polack head to bust it down with?"

Fear showed plainly in the superintendent's eyes as he felt Fletcher's hands bunch even tighter around the fabric of his shirt. "Okay! Okay! Ain't no need to blow your cool. I just got to be sure, that's all. We've already had two burglaries in the block this month."

Fletcher relaxed his grip, and the man scurried back inside the apartment, returning a moment later with Brian's spare key. As he rode the elevator up to the fifth floor, he kept his eyes averted from Fletcher's face, not wanting to give this madman the slightest excuse for another show of force.

The neighbor was still standing by Brian's door, but he was no longer alone. A blowzy blond dressed in a faded pink housecoat was with him, and they were talking earnestly. Fletcher pushed them aside, making room for the superintendent, watching while he turned the key and pushed against the door. It opened for three inches, catching as the safety chain took hold. The superintendent turned to look helplessly at Fletcher.

"Maybe your friend's fallen asleep."

"Does that sound like he's sleeping?" Fletcher asked as an agonized cry came from within. "Get out of my way."

He stepped back a few paces and positioned himself so that his right shoulder was pointing in toward the door. Suddenly realizing what was about to happen, the superintendent held out a hand to stop Fletcher, while the two neighbors watched avidly, their mundane lives temporarily brightened by this drama on their doorstep. The superintendent's action was as futile as if he had been trying to stop a herd of wild elephants. His hand was brushed aside like a feather as Fletcher took three running steps and slammed his shoulder into the door, smashing it open. The chain snapped off, ripped from its mounting as the door flew back and crashed against the wall.

As it rebounded, Fletcher elbowed it aside and stepped into the apartment living room. He saw Brian immediately, sprawled out on the couch, his breath coming raggedly, the saliva which dribbled from his mouth staining the front of his shirt.

While the superintendent remained cowering in the doorway, with the two neighbors looking over his shoulder jostling for a better view, Fletcher ran across the living room. "Call an ambulance!" he yelled over his shoulder. "This guy's on his last legs."

He turned back to Brian, feeling his friend's wrist for a pulse. "What happened, Brian? Come on, everything's going to be all right. What did you do?"

"Aspirin." Brian's words barely reached Fletcher; he leaned over the body, putting his ear close to Brian's mouth. "Aspirin," he repeated, his face contorted in an agonized spasm. "A bottle full. And sleeping pills."

"How long ago?" Fletcher's voice was urgent. "Do you remember?"

"Hour. Maybe two. I forget. God . . ." Brian stiffened as another wave of pain clawed through him, tearing into his stomach, ripping him apart.

"My stomach's on fire. It's burning up." He coughed sharply, spraying Fletcher with a mixture of blood and saliva.

Fletcher ran into the kitchen, only vaguely aware of the blood-flecked saliva on his jacket. Disregarding the empty aspirin bottle on the drainboard, he filled a glass with milk and took it back into the living room. Lifting Brian's head, he forced the liquid into his mouth. Half of it spilled out, but he was thankful to see some stay down. Brian choked and spluttered while Fletcher laid him back on the couch, watching helplessly.

The superintendent returned from Brian's bedroom, where he had used the telephone to call for an ambulance. He stood over Fletcher, watching curiously while the model tried to force more milk down Brian's throat.

"Why the milk?"

"Because he's swallowed a bottle of aspirin," Fletcher replied out of the side of his mouth. "They're tearing away the lining of his stomach, and he'll die from internal hemorrhaging if we don't get proper attention soon. The milk may act as a temporary buffer. It's the best we can do till they get him to a hospital and pump his stomach."

He lifted his head and looked around, seeing the neighbors still standing in the doorway. "Get those rubbernecks the hell out," he snapped at the superintendent, "and try to keep everybody else away till the ambulance gets here."

Within ten minutes the ambulance arrived. Expertly the attendants strapped Brian to the stretcher, standing it upright in the elevator as they made their way down. Exhausted, Fletcher wiped his brow as he watched the elevator doors close. Then he went back into the apartment, closing the door and dropping onto the couch, too tired to move even when he remembered that he had found Brian lying there only minutes earlier.

Miriam was sleeping under heavy sedation when Nino Viscenzi visited the house in Great Neck the following evening. Marilyn let him in, leading the Italian into the living room, where Gerald sat alone. Viscenzi made no attempt to conceal his surprise when he noticed the empty stool next to Gerald.

Guessing the question that was about to come, Gerald said, "Simon will probably be along later for prayers."

"He doesn't stay here all day and sit with you?"

Marilyn answered for her husband. "I think we should be grateful that he only comes in the evening. He stays in his own apartment during the day. Or maybe he goes to the track."

Gerald stood up to stretch his legs, feeling cramped from the long hours of sitting on the tiny chair. "What happened at the office today? Any major catastrophes, or only minor ones?"

"Haven't you heard?" Viscenzi asked.

"Heard what?"

"About Brian Chambers—last night when he tried to kill himself."

Gerald had almost forgotten about Brian; he had not noticed his absence at the funeral, nor at the house during the first night of mourning. "He did *what*?" he asked incredulously. His astonished glance flew from Viscenzi to Marilyn, then back to the Italian; he did not care where the explanation came from just as long as he got one.

"I received a telephone call very early this morning," Viscenzi said, "from Fletcher Austin, the model. He wanted to speak either to you or your brother. I took the call and told him that I was standing in for you and handling all office matters."

"How does Fletcher come into all this?" Gerald was becoming more confused by the minute.

"Apparently he had an appointment with Brian yesterday evening to discuss some upcoming project. I did not ask what," Viscenzi answered. "He had arranged to meet Brian at his apartment. When he arrived, he found that Brian had swallowed sleeping pills and a bottle of aspirin tablets." The designer looked nonplussed that Gerald was unaware of the event.

"I automatically assumed that Fletcher would have called you as well," he continued. "Otherwise I would have let you know immediately. I am sorry."

Gerald sank down slowly onto the small wooden chair, feeling his way with his hands. "Oh, my God," he gasped. "What the hell is going on with these people?" He glanced up at Viscenzi, who was watching him with a worried expression in his brown eyes. "Did Fletcher tell you which hospital he was in, or his condition?"

Viscenzi pulled a sheet of paper from the inside pocket of his jacket. "Englewood Hospital. And his condition is satisfactory as of this morning. He is bleeding internally and will have to stay in the hospital for at least a week, maybe more, but he is out of danger."

Gerald put a hand to his forehead, trying to come to terms with the second tragedy, which had followed so closely on the heels of the first. "Why?" he asked. "Why? Why? Why? Why is all this happening to us?"

"I'll call them now," Marilyn suggested. "Maybe the hospital can tell us more." She left the room, closing the door quietly behind her.

Viscenzi allowed a minute to pass, waiting unhurriedly for Gerald to recover. Then he crouched down next to him. "I have to talk to you about the business. Do you feel up to it?"

"What's on your mind?"

"Many things," Viscenzi said. "But first, tell me what will happen to the Chestertons Group. Have any plans been made?"

"A long time ago. My father was a firm believer in his own immortality, but he was also worried about what would happen to the empire should something happen to him. Maybe he had visions of what's actually taken place."

"How do you mean?"

Gerald grinned dully. "Leaving us with all the internal conflict that's been going on." He paused as the door opened and Marilyn returned to the room. "Anything new?"

She shook her head. "Just as Nino said. Progressing satisfactorily. I had to lie and say it was his wife calling from Chicago."

The words made Gerald smile. "Hope the nurse or whoever took the call doesn't pass that on to Brian. If he thinks Thelma's checking up on him, he'll have a relapse. How about a cup of coffee and some sandwiches for Nino and me before we get swamped with visitors?" he suggested. He waited till Marilyn had left the room again, then turned back to Viscenzi.

"My father made only one will," he continued, reverting to the original conversation. "That was about four years ago. Everything's left to my mother. She's the boss now."

"Was that wise?" the Italian queried dubiously; he remembered Jonathan saying that Simon could always rely on Miriam's encouragement.

"About as safe as he could play it. My mother's harmless really. She only supported Simon because she knew he'd be outvoted anyway. She didn't want him to feel like Ian Smith in Rhodesia. At least, that was the case before Brian suddenly decided to switch camps."

The mention of the general merchandise manager sent Gerald's thoughts back to the suicide attempt. "I still can't believe he'd do a crazy thing like this. Why would he want to kill himself? He had everything made—a powerful position, a damned good income. He'd got rid of his bitch of a wife. What else could he want?"

"Perhaps there is something we do not know about," Viscenzi mused. "Every man has something to hide about himself."

Gerald thought about the statement, wondering what Brian's secret could have been, why it had driven him to try to perform the ultimate act. "You know something, Nino? You might just be right. Do you think it could have had anything to do with his change of attitude at the company?"

Viscenzi gave an expressive shrug of his shoulders. "Who is really to know? Perhaps one day we will learn. And then again, perhaps we will never learn what caused it." He stood up and began to pace around the room, a hand cupped to his chin while he thought. "If you should want it, Gerald, I am prepared to stay in New York for as long as you need me. I feel after today that I could probably help you until everything is straightened out."

Gerald's face brightened immediately. "We need somebody here. My mother trusts you; she'll listen to whatever you say. As she's technically in the chairman's seat at the moment, any assistance you can offer will be invaluable."

"Leave it with me, Gerald. I will talk later with your mother, when she is feeling better." He angled his head a fraction as the doorbell chimed. "Would that be your brother now?"

Gerald checked his watch; five after seven. "Probably."

"Then we will talk no more of business," Viscenzi said with an air of finality.

The living room door opened, and Marilyn showed in Della and Simon, following them with two cups of coffee and a plateful of sandwiches for Gerald and Viscenzi; she made no effort to offer anything to her brother-in-law or his wife.

Simon ignored Viscenzi completely, walking past him as if he were not there. He looked briefly at his brother and sat down in an armchair, crossing his legs. "Don't see any point in crippling myself till the visitors come," he said to Della, in reference to the vacant stool next to Gerald. "When there's somebody here to appreciate it, I'll put on a show."

Viscenzi's voice dripped acid. "Obviously your father's memory is not worth a little discomfort."

"What the hell are you doing here anyway?" Simon snapped back. He saw Della's look of warning reminding him of the occasion but took no notice. "You're not a member of this family, and I don't think you come under the classification of friend either."

"Your father was my friend. Your grandfather also. So is your brother."

"Well you're no damned friend of mine," Simon told him. "So don't go sticking your face into my business."

"Simon," Gerald cut in, "I think you'd better get used to seeing Nino's face around for quite a while—both here and in the office. He's offered to look after the whole show till everything gets settled."

Although Gerald spoke to his brother, he kept his eyes on Della. She swung around to her husband, her head swimming with what Gerald had just said. He did not catch the urgent, whispered phrases; he craned forward, eager to hear, but Della kept her voice too low to oblige him.

"What's wrong with Brian continuing to run the merchandise side of the company?" she asked. "That's his job, surely. He"—she pointed at Viscenzi—"has no call to get involved."

Della's question made Gerald realize what he had so far not taken into account. If he had not known of Brian's suicide attempt, then surely neither had Della and Simon. Fletcher Austin had called the office and spoken to Viscenzi, leaving the information with him, assuming that he would pass it on—which he had.

Although he regretted using the unfortunate circumstances as a surprise tactic, Gerald experienced a sense of elation as he prepared to confront Della with the news. "I'm afraid that's quite impossible," he said quietly, enjoying every word as he built up to his climax.

"Why is it impossible?"

"Brian can't do anything. He's in the hospital for at least a week, maybe even longer."

"What's the matter with him?" Simon asked, moving toward the edge of the armchair as if bracing himself for some bad news. "He was perfectly well when I last saw him."

"When was that?"

"At the meeting, when Pa had his attack."

"That was two days ago," Gerald said. "Yesterday evening he tried to commit suicide."

Della turned a chalky white. Slow step by slow step she retreated till the back of her left leg came in contact with Simon's armchair. She sat down, balancing unsteadily on the arm. Her hand went out to Simon, who took it in his own, twining his fingers around Della's.

Gerald felt Viscenzi nudge him. "Go on," the Italian whispered. "Ask them if they know anything."

Still speaking in the same level tone, Gerald continued, "Nino and I think he may have done it because he felt he had something to hide, something which might come out now. Can either of you two throw any light on it? Did he ever do anything to arouse your suspicions?"

Della moaned weakly. She raised a hand to her forehead, laying the palm against her brow.

"Simon," she said faintly. "Please take me home. I don't feel very well."

# 34

His stomach was aflame, filled with liquid fire, a tortuous burning pain which came and receded in agonizing waves, searing one moment, a dull, charred sensation the next. He groaned feebly, remembering all too clearly how he had earned the pain, the methodical way he had stuffed the aspirin tablets into his mouth, flushing them down with deep draughts of water, determined that none should escape.

He had been amazed at how long he had stayed in full possession of his faculties after emptying the bottle. But when the pain had started, he had forgotten about everything else. His whole being had centered around the gnawing ache in his stomach, an army of rats eating its way out, becoming more piercing with each passing breath. He had collapsed in agony onto the couch in the living room, drawing up his knees in a fetal position, gasping as the fire ate away at his stomach lining.

Fletcher Austin's dramatic entry into the apartment was nothing more than a dim memory—a hammering at the door, a pause, then a crash as the safety chain was blasted aside, and the blurred image of his friend moving swiftly across the intervening space to where he lay on the couch.

The pain came again, and Brian shifted awkwardly in the bed, seeking a less uncomfortable position. How long had he been here? For all he knew it could have been four hours. It could also have been four weeks.

Through the half-open Venetian blinds, Brian could see blue sky interrupted by a few fleecy cumulus clouds which scudded across his line of vision, pushed along by the strong breeze. The door to the private ward opened, and a nurse entered. She smiled professionally at him as she took the thermometer from the sterilized cup by the side of the bed.

"How do you feel today, Mr. Chambers?"

"What day is it?"

"Saturday. You've been here two days, since Thursday night." She held the thermometer toward him, its end inches from his mouth. "Open wide. Let's see how you're coming along."

403

Obediently Brian opened his mouth, feeling the thermometer being inserted underneath his tongue. "That's fine," the nurse said. "Hold it like that for a while." She regarded him strangely for a long moment.

"What made you do such a thing, Mr. Chambers?"

"Such a thing as what?"

The nurse appeared embarrassed to talk about it. "The aspirins," she said. "What made you take so many?"

Brian waited till the thermometer was removed from his mouth. "I had a terrible migraine."

The nurse laughed at the reply, relieved that he could talk about the suicide attempt. "You must be feeling better if you can make jokes about it." She checked the thermometer reading, recording it on the chart at the bottom of the bed. Wiping the instrument, she replaced it in the holder.

"That's an extremely painful way to go," she said. "Consider yourself very lucky that your friend found you when he did—and just in time."

Brian said nothing, but his mind was active. So Fletcher Austin had saved his life. And it had been Fletcher, albeit indirectly, who had made him think of taking it. All that remained now was Jonathan's death, brought about in part by his betrayal, an unwilling alliance designed to protect his own secret. Nothing's ever clear-cut any more, he thought despondently. There's no longer a one hundred percent cause of anything; everything's partially this or partially that, no certain blame to be apportioned anywhere.

So engrossed was he with the past few days that he barely heard the nurse tell him that visitors were waiting outside.

"Now don't go getting yourself all excited," she warned. "You've got to take it easy. And remember, there must be some people who care about you. It was a silly thing to do, right?"

Brian nodded halfheartedly. "I guess so. I guess it was pretty stupid of me."

The nurse left the ward, holding open the door for the visitors to enter. Brian propped himself up in bed, curious to see who would come to visit him. When he recognized Simon and Della, the feeling of inquisitiveness turned to one of anger which burned with the same intensity as his injured stomach.

Simon's voice was cheerful, a forced bonhomie which added fuel to Brian's loathing. "Hi, old buddy. We heard about your little accident from..." He stopped in mid-sentence, unwilling to say Viscenzi's name. "From Gerald. But the doctor says you've got nothing to worry about; you're going to make it just fine."

Brian gritted his teeth against the pain. "Get out," he hissed. "Just get the hell out of here, the pair of you."

Reasoning that a woman's voice would be more persuasive under the circumstances, Simon stood aside to let Della through. She sat on the edge of the bed, leaning forward confidentially.

"Brian, it's very urgent that we talk. Put aside your personal feelings for just a moment. There's a lot more at stake here than emotional grudges."

He lay back on the pillow, closing his eyes, trying to shut out the sight of Della. "What do you want from me now?"

"We know Jonathan was your friend," Della said, coating her words with such a believable veneer of sincerity that even Simon, who remained standing behind her, was amazed. "And we know you feel that you betrayed him. But you've got to realize that what you did, helping Simon, was for the greater good. It was obvious that Jonathan was not a well man. Even if that final argument over the casual clothing advertisement had never taken place, he could not have lived for much longer. Brian,"—she stressed his name, laying a hand on his arm,—"the man had a weak heart. It could have gone at any time. It was just unfortunate for us that it went during that meeting."

From the deepest reaches of his body, Brian found the strength to raise his voice. "Unfortunate for us?" he asked angrily. "What about unfortunate for him? Doesn't his death mean a damned thing to you?" He sat up in bed, shaking off Della's hand. "Don't you care about it, Simon? For God's sake, he was your father."

"Brian, please listen to me," Della entreated. "Believe me, we're all upset, but we have to face up to the future, to what is going to happen to all of us. Right now Gerald is engaged in a big power play; he's scheming to have Nino Viscenzi look after the merchandise side of the business until final arrangements can be made for the chain to carry on. He's had him come over from Europe just for that. He's usurping your authority at Chestertons, can't you see that? We all know we were on target for the company's good, and we don't want to see anything go wrong now." She looked back at Simon; he nodded almost imperceptibly, urging her to carry on.

"Please stay with us," she begged. "We'll see that you never want for anything. Just don't let us down now."

Brian placed both hands against Della and pushed her away from the bedside with a force that surprised her. She staggered back a few steps until Simon put out a hand to steady her.

"Get out of here. Just leave me alone." Reaching up, he rang for the nurse, determined to have her escort Simon and Della out of the ward if necessary.

Seeing the action, Della began to walk toward the door. "We'll be back, Brian. Please think about what we said. It's for your sake as well as ours—unless you don't care about our little secret any more."

With her arm through Simon's, she left the ward. Outside, they hurried to the parking lot where the small MG was standing. "Think he'll go along and stay quiet?" Della asked, starting the engine. "Or will he risk his own reputation by blabbing?"

Simon looked up at the hospital building. "I'll tell you what I think. He could have done us all a big favor by doing a better job with the aspirin."

"That's a wicked thought," Della chided him. "But under the circumstances it's perfectly allowable."

Nino Viscenzi sat behind Jonathan's old desk in the Chestertons boardroom. He had just telephoned his own company in Paris, informing his assistant that he would be away for at least a month. The man had been curious, and Viscenzi felt it only right to apprise him of the situation which had forced his prolonged stay in New York.

Now he studied merchandise and sales reports, compared them with projected figures, quickly familiarizing himself with the Chestertons system. After all, he thought, a retailer is always a retailer, no matter where his business is located or what commodity he deals in.

Fortunately the summer months are slow in the men's wear industry and, by careful delegation of responsibility to members of the Head Office staff, all vouched for by Gerald, Viscenzi had been able to keep the operation ticking smoothly. When Gerald returned the following week, they would be able to sit down and make plans for the immediate future. Unfortunately, or so Viscenzi considered, Simon would also be returning to the office.

Alan Constantine, whom Viscenzi had met briefly during his last visit to Jonathan, had entered the boardroom just once, to enquire about some reorders for the casual clothing program. Adopting his most arrogant demeanor, Viscenzi had ordered the Englishman to stall the supplier until further notice; there would be no ordering of merchandise till Gerald returned.

Constantine had stood in front of the desk gaping. "What do you mean, when Gerald returns?" he had spluttered. "It's Simon's decision what merchandise goes into the stores."

"As of this moment it is my decision!" Viscenzi had snapped. "And you will do as I say." He had pointed to the door. "That is the way out. Now please leave, as I have other, more important matters to attend to."

He had watched with satisfaction as Constantine had left, humbled. If he had his way, Viscenzi would fire the man immediately, seeing little use for his dubious talents in a company like Chestertons—or like it had been under Jonathan and would one day, he hoped, be again. But that would be exceeding his authority. He was helping out as a favor, running the operation until Gerald—the only member of the family he trusted implicitly—returned. Then Gerald could have the undoubted pleasure of dispensing with the man's services.

Taking a cigar from his pocket, Viscenzi sniffed appreciatively at the Cuban tobacco as he held a lighter to the end. Something seemed to nag at him, and he flicked the lighter closed, dropping it back into his pocket, the cigar still unlit. Then he realized what was wrong. Try as he might, he could never again smoke in this room. He crushed the cigar between his slim fingers, letting the shredded tobacco fall into the wastebasket.

The memory of Jonathan was too poignant in the boardroom to allow Viscenzi to smoke.

Miriam had cried herself dry. In the three days since Jonathan's death, she had stayed in bed almost the whole time, drugged heavily. When she came down on Saturday afternoon, she felt weak from the sobbing which had racked her body almost continuously during her waking hours.

In the kitchen she found Gerald and Marilyn sharing a light snack. They stood up as soon as she entered the room and helped her into a chair, fussing over her.

"Is anybody else here?" she asked.

"Only us," Gerald answered.

"Who's looking after Karen?"

Marilyn smiled at her mother-in-law's concern. "A neighbor. Don't worry; she's in good hands."

Miriam sighed. "You should be thankful you've got such good neighbors." She looked around as if puzzled by something. "Aren't Simon and Della here?"

"Probably at home," Gerald said quickly. "They'll be along later." He sought to change the subject immediately, not wanting his mother to be more upset than she was already by learning of the almost total split between the brothers. Additionally the news of Brian's brush with death had been kept from her.

"Everything will be all right," he said soothingly. "Nino's pinch-hitting for me at the office till we get everything back to normal again."

Over the top of his mother's head, Gerald saw Marilyn give him a sharp look at his use of the word "normal." A stupid thing to say, he admitted. How can anything ever be normal again for my mother with Jonathan gone? But Miriam said nothing; she sat silently at the kitchen table, smiling her thanks as Marilyn made her something to eat.

Viscenzi arrived an hour later, bringing a pile of paperwork from the office for Gerald to see.

"Any problems?" Gerald asked automatically.

"No. Things are quiet, for which I am grateful," the designer replied. "The store was quite busy, but it's Saturday, so it should be. What else can we ask?"

Gerald grinned wryly. "After the events of recent weeks, not very much, I suppose."

By Monday Brian felt well enough to get out of bed and walk around the small private ward. The pain in his stomach had decreased considerably as the injured tissues continued to heal; the doctor had told him that if there were no complications he would be allowed home within three or four days.

Neither Della nor Simon had visited him again. Apart from Fletcher, who popped in every evening for a few minutes, the only other visit he had received had been from a woman who belonged to some soul-saving society or other; he could not remember which. He realized that she had come because of his suicide attempt, although how she could have learned of it was beyond him. She had probed gently, asking seemingly innocent questions as she tried to find out what had caused Brian to take such a drastic step. The interview had amused him to a point, a brief respite from the continuing battle with his own conscience. He had handled the woman in a glib manner, leaving the machinations of the company out of the story he had told her. He had claimed that he had been upset by a friend's death, an easily checked fact, and had looked for a way out. The woman had seemed satisfied, and there were no further visits; nobody else was interested in saving his immortal soul.

During the days he lay in bed, Brian had time to think, exploring the problem from every angle, coming up with every possible solution. By continuing to side with Simon, he could ensure himself of both prestige and prosperity. In fact, the situation could be completely reversed. He would have influence over Simon, getting whatever he wanted by threatening to expose the blackmail that Simon had used. Fighting fire with fire—the idea had its merits, a certain poetic appeal.

But Brian also knew that he had lied for long enough. He had tried to kill himself, an act that still refused to strike him as outrageously as he knew it should. He understood why. Other people and what they might think of him were no longer of any interest to Brian; he decided that his own self-respect, if any could be redeemed at this late stage, was far more valuable than any monetary arrangement he could make with Simon.

When the nurse came in later that morning to take his temperature, Brian asked her for some note paper, an envelope, a pen, and a thirteen-cent stamp.

Then he sat down to write to Gerald.

# 35

Gerald paid scant attention to the heavy stream of traffic already on the Long Island Expressway as the morning's rush hour began to build up toward its peak. He rolled the Ford Thunderbird along the ramp, glanced quickly to his left and floored the gas pedal. The large, powerful car responded eagerly, surging into the outside lane as it headed toward the city.

As he maintained a steady seventy miles an hour, there were two thoughts predominant in Gerald's mind. The first was the letter from Brian Chambers which seemed to be burning a hole in his pocket; the second was what he would do with his brother when he saw him.

What a return to the office. Seven days of mourning for my father, then a race into the city, imagining with every revolution of the wheels how I'd like to take my brother's head in both hands and smash it with all my might against the closest wall.

A green Volkswagen Beetle hogged the outside lane, its small, rounded shape reminding Gerald of a snail dragging its home on its back— and moving at about the same damned speed. The driver seemed oblivious of the Thunderbird speeding up behind him, not bothering to look in his rearview mirror. Gerald held his hand down on the horn, blasting away with furious impatience, flashing his lights, his anger at Simon transferred for an instant to the Wolfsburg import. Come on, you idiot, he cursed the driver. Pull over and let me through so I can kill my brother five seconds earlier.

After what seemed like an eternity, but was really no more than five seconds, the Volkswagen signalled and moved out of the way, slipping neatly into a gap in the next lane. The Thunderbird flashed past, Gerald sparing a moment's concentration to shoot a withering glance at the driver. Then his mind returned to Simon.

Okay, I've never been fond of him, the spoiled brat with his crazy ideas for updating the company image. Sure, I've wanted to kick him in the ass a few times, especially during the past week when he didn't even bother turning up for prayers most nights. How many different excuses can I make to my mother? He's not well. Della's feeling sick. But I've never wanted to kill him before; this heralds a new all-time low in an already low relationship.

Gerald took his left hand off the steering wheel and felt inside the breast pocket of his jacket, running his fingertips over the torn edge of the envelope, caressing the letter inside. Poor old Brian. No wonder he was doing such an about face on company policy, throwing in his lot with Simon. We thought he was having a difficult time because that bitch of a wife had left him, and all the while it was that little bastard of my brother leaning on him, blackmailing him, extorting his support.

His brown eyes flicked to the dashboard clock. Twenty-seven minutes to nine. Only fifteen minutes earlier, when he was preparing to leave the house, he had been looking forward to returning to the office. Being cooped up for the past week while people came to offer their condolences had gotten to him in the end. Marilyn had been wonderful, he recalled. After they got up from mourning, she had insisted that his mother move in with them for as long as she wanted; they both felt uneasy about leaving her alone in the big house in Great Neck, haunted for her by the memories of Jonathan.

Nino Viscenzi had been a prime factor in helping to make the long week more bearable, acting as an escape valve when he dropped by the house in the afternoon or early evening with news of the company before taking a taxi back to his Manhattan hotel. At one time—Gerald could not resist smiling as he remembered it—he had offered the Italian the use of his car. Viscenzi had responded by looking at him as if he were insane.

"In Paris I drive with my heart in my mouth," the designer had said. "But in New York, no thank you."

Gerald had grinned at the Italian's expressive face. "It's nowhere near as bad as they make out," he had replied, feeling obliged to defend the driving habits of New York motorists.

"I wish to drive again with my heart in my mouth in Paris," Viscenzi had countered. And that had ended that conversation.

As he had opened the door leading to the garage that morning, Gerald had checked his appearance automatically in the full-length mirror. His hand moved to straighten the tie knot; if a clothing man can't look good, then who can, he remembered thinking.

Holding the door open with his right foot, he called back into the house, "Marilyn, I'm leaving. If it looks like I'll be late, I'll call you."

His wife's voice came from upstairs. "Just a minute. Karen wants to say good-bye."

Karen, poor kid. She's been through it this past week, shunted from house to house like a piece of flotsam, sleeping here, eating there; thank

God for friends and neighbors at times like this. He let the door swing closed and turned back toward the stairs. Karen came down, carefully navigating each carpeted step on all fours, her diaper-padded backside sticking up in the air toward him. For one long, delightful moment, Gerald forgot all about returning to the office, just wanting to stay in the house and play with his daughter, make it up to her for the neglect she had suffered during the past few days. He crouched down and lifted her high in the air, seeing Marilyn reflected in the child's fair complexion, which contrasted so strongly to his own dark skin.

"What have you got for me?" he asked, his lips forming an exaggerated kiss.

Karen studied him thoughtfully for a moment before leaning forward in his arms and sticking a wet kiss on his mouth. Pulling a handkerchief from his trouser pocket, he wiped his lips.

"I think you'd better brush up on your technique before you get much older," he advised Karen with mock severity. "Otherwise you're going to lose a lot of friends."

He closed the door quietly, knowing that his mother still slept in the rear bedroom. Let her rest; she needs it. She'd rather sleep an extra couple of hours than be woken up by me to say good-bye. Maneuvering the Thunderbird into the road, he saw the mailman coming. He rolled down his window and held out a hand.

"Anything that looks interesting?"

The mailman held up a bundle of letters in greeting. "How you doing, Mr. Chesterton?" He passed the mail into the car, waiting to see if Gerald wanted it dropped into the house.

He leafed through the envelopes quickly—bill from the telephone company, bank statement, something for Marilyn from one of her clubs. Not the tennis club, he was certain of that; she had not been back there since that night with Stan Jarvis. He came to the bottom envelope, plain white with a handwritten address and a New Jersey postmark. That looks like Brian's writing, he thought. Probably a letter of condolence. He felt guilty as he looked at it, knowing that he had not been to see the general merchandise manager while he was in the hospital. Brian would understand though.

Holding onto the New Jersey envelope, he passed the remainder back to the mailman, waiting in the car till it had been dropped off at the house. The mailman gave him a cheerful wave as he walked back to the street and continued his round.

Using his thumb, Gerald ripped open the white envelope and began to read the letter it contained. Disbelief, then numb horror surged through his mind as he scanned the three sheets of tightly spaced handwriting. He slumped back in the seat, his senses deadened initially, before reading the letter again, as if another look would change the contents. When the words registered a second time, the feeling of shock gave way to one of comprehension. Now he understood everything. All the weird events of the past few months took on a new, more significant meaning. Simon and his Brian, Svengali and his Trilby: one person singing through another's lips. All the answers, with the t's crossed and the i's dotted, were contained in Brian's tiny scrawl. And when Gerald laid his hands on Simon, it would take the greatest willpower in the world not to rip him to pieces on the spot.

He snapped back into the present with a physical jolt as the Thunderbird began to wander into the center lane and an angry driver leaned on the horn. He straightened out the front wheels and glanced in the mirror, seeing that the green Volkswagen was again in the outside lane, but now hundreds of yards behind as he pressed harder on the gas pedal, uncaring about unmarked police cars, radar traps and indignant drivers who were righteously maintaining the posted speed limit. Gerald had no thoughts of driving niceties; he was only interested in reaching the office as speedily as possible.

Forty minutes later, thankful that he had been caught in only one small traffic jam, he drove into the underground parking lot near the main store. Getting out, he tossed the keys to the attendant and hurried along the street to the store. Although the front door was unlocked to admit staff, the store was not yet open for business. Gerald nodded to the store manager as he walked through to the office complex.

"Simon in yet?" he asked the receptionist.

"No, Mr. Gerald." She was thinking of something to add to convey her sorrow at Jonathan's death, but Gerald's mind was already two steps ahead.

"Give me a call when he arrives, but don't tell him I'm here. Okay?" He turned toward his own office, then swung around. "Is Mr. Viscenzi in?"

"Yes. He's taken over Mr. Jonathan's old desk in the boardroom." The girl said the words slowly, as if the mention of the dead man was alien to her lips.

"Thanks. I'll be with him. Don't forget," he added as he began to walk away. "Call me when my brother arrives, but don't let him know I'm here."

Opening the door to the boardroom, Gerald saw Viscenzi standing in front of the map of the United States, studying the locations of the Chestertons stores. He heard the door open and left the map to greet Gerald.

"Welcome back. That is quite a memorial to one man's work," Viscenzi said, referring to the map.

"So is this," Gerald replied, reaching into his pocket for the letter. "Only it's not the same man. Read it."

Viscenzi put on a pair of horn-rimmed reading glasses and began to look at the sheets of paper. "What is this?" he asked, his voice hushed as the import became clear.

"Read it all. It gets better."

Viscenzi's look of shocked interest became more intense with each line he read. His mouth dropped open as he read aloud, his command of written English nowhere near as perfect as his flunecy with the spoken version. Finishing, he returned the letter wordlessly.

"What do you think of it?" Gerald asked.

"When did it come?"

"This morning, as I was leaving the house. Nobody else has seen it yet."

"It is the action of a criminal," Viscenzi said. "Simple blackmail, nothing else."

Gerald pulled out a chair and sat down at the mahogany table. "I sure as hell wish the old man was here right now," he said longingly.

"I, too, wish he was here," Viscenzi said. "But not, I think, for the same reasons. I miss Jonathan as a friend. I fear that you miss him as a guiding light."

Gerald looked up at Viscenzi with a new appreciation for the man. "You're so right. He'd know what to do in a situation like this. Me? I'm guessing."

"The point is, Gerald, what do you plan to do?" Viscenzi asked. "Will you turn your brother over to the police, which seems to be the correct action? Like I said, he has committed a crime."

"Are you crazy?" The prospect of police involvement horrified Gerald. "How on earth can I do a thing like that? Do you want to see me drag this whole mess out into the open? Believe me, Nino, there's nothing I'd like better than to see Simon get it. But you know damned well that I can't. There are too many other people's lives at stake, not least of all Brian's."

"Ah, yes. Poor Brian—the unwitting crux of this whole miserable matter," Viscenzi concurred.

When the telephone rang, Viscenzi moved toward it, but Gerald got to the desk first. He picked it up and was told by the receptionist that Simon had arrived.

"Was he by himself, or was Della with him?"

"He came in alone."

Gerald hung up and looked to Viscenzi for advice. "Do I see him here or should I go to his office?"

"You see him here," Viscenzi said without even having to think about the answer. "Make him come to you." He picked up some papers from the desk and began to move toward the door. "I will now leave you to your business, Gerald. Call me when you are through."

"Wait a minute!"

About to open the door, Viscenzi turned around. "Yes?"

"I'd like you to stay here with me. Remember you promised to hang around till we got things sorted out?"

"I don't recall including being a witness to the act of fratricide in my offer."

"There won't be any," Gerald assured him. He picked up the

telephone and dialled Simon's extension. "Simon, it's Gerald. Have you got five minutes to come by the boardroom? It's, uh, it's pretty important." He replaced the receiver before his brother had a chance to question the summons.

Viscenzi took up an unobtrusive position in the corner. "I leave center stage to you, Gerald. I will be nothing more than an observer."

Gerald nodded his agreement, impatiently pacing across the room while he waited for Simon to appear. When the door opened, the cool self-control he had been striving for deserted him completely. He spun around to face the door, obviously agitated. Simon entered, wearing a double-breasted blue suit, one of a range which he had bought from an English manufacturer for the Mr. Simon operation.

"Feels good to be back," he said, trying to inject some cordiality into the air. "Sitting at home gets to you after a while."

"Shut the door," Gerald told him. "We've got a few things to talk about."

Simon noticed Viscenzi leaning against the wall in the far corner of the room. "What about him?" he snapped, falling immediately onto the defense as he sensed something amiss. "What's he doing here?"

Gerald glanced at the casual figure of the Italian. "Nino stays. Right now he's an important part of this organization." He reached behind, feeling his fingers come in contact with the letter on top of the desk.

"Recognize the handwriting?" he asked, pushing the sheets of paper toward his brother.

"How should I know whose handwriting it is?" Simon snapped back. "I'm not an expert on calligraphy, and it's too early in the morning to play amateur detective."

"I'll go along with that," Gerald said evenly. "There isn't very much that you're an expert on—apart from a little blackmail now and again to further your own ends."

Simon's self-assurance fell away like a coat being removed, leaving him naked under Gerald's accusing glare. "What's that remark supposed to mean?"

With a slow, measured pace, Gerald moved away from his position by the desk. He walked across the boardroom and flashed out his right hand like a snake striking, grabbing Simon by the lapel before he could move out of range. With his left hand, he thrust Brian's letter into Simon's face.

"Do you know what this is?" he hissed. "It's a letter from Brian, written while he was in the hospital, telling me that he's resigning from the company—and why he's resigning."

The blood began to drain from Simon's face, leaving it ashen.

"In other words, it's an explanation of what's been going on in this company during the past few months," Gerald continued. His forced coolness began to desert him, and he found pleasure in succumbing to the mounting fury.

"Brian Chambers put a lot into this company, a lot of effort and a lot of time. He put in a damned sight more than you or your friends ever did. And you used him, wrecked him by finding out something nobody else even suspected and blackmailing him about it."

Simon tried using flippancy as a defense. "He should have been more careful about his private life."

"Nobody knew or gave a damn about his private life!" Gerald shouted. "How did you find out? Spy on him?"

"He gave himself away. Della and I saw it, just like we could see everything else that the rest of you were too stupid to notice."

"How?"

"All that fuss he made at the meeting when the first new-format advertisement came out, about Fletcher Austin being dropped as the model. We could see it a mile off that he had a more than professional interest in Austin's future."

Standing in the corner, Viscenzi sensed an impending climax to the confrontation. He straightened up and moved quickly towards the two brothers. He heard Gerald's scream of rage and reached out with both hands to pull him back. Before he could make contact, Gerald had flung himself on his brother, punching wildly. Simon staggered back under the furious assault, too surprised to make any move to defend himself.

Viscenzi dove into the fray, pulling Gerald off with difficulty, marching him forcibly to the opposite side of the room, holding him against the wall till he calmed down, a boxer waiting in a neutral corner while his opponent takes a count. He looked back at Simon, who stood up slowly, his nose and mouth bloody, dabbing at them with a white handkerchief.

"Get out," Viscenzi said. "And stay out. I will not be around the next time. Then he might kill you."

# 36

On hearing Gerald unfold the circumstances of Brian's defection within the company, Marilyn experienced two strong emotions—pity for Brian, and revulsion for her brother-in-law. Her flesh crawled as the sordid details emerged; each time Gerald mentioned Simon's name, she shuddered involuntarily.

"Your brother's a first-rate bastard with all the extras," she said, when Gerald had finished the tale.

"That's the worst you can think of?" He sounded surprised. "You used to be a teacher; surely you can come up with something a little better than that. Nino called him a criminal, which is pretty well where the whole thing's at. So don't you be shy about saying what you really think."

"How are you going to tell your mother?" Marilyn asked, thinking of Miriam sleeping peacefully upstairs.

Gerald appeared lost. "That's the toughest job of all. She's still in a state of shock over Pa's death. I hate to think what would happen to her if I unloaded all this on her. She doesn't even know about Brian trying to kill himself yet. God knows how this would affect her." He leaned forward and buried his face in Marilyn's breasts, feeling her cool hands on his neck as they massaged gently. His words were indistinct, filtered through the fabric of Marilyn's dress.

"How the hell did we ever allow ourselves to get into this mess? If word ever gets out, we'll be ruined."

Marilyn continued to hold him close for a minute, moving her hands over his head. Then she eased him back so that she could look into his eyes. "Your mother has to know, Gerald. Sooner or later she's bound to find out about all this. How would you want her to learn? From you? Or hear a distorted story from somebody outside the family which is going to make it even worse?"

Gerald shook her hands off. "She doesn't have to find out anything about it."

"Who else knows?"

"Me, you and Nino. Brian obviously. Simon, Della and perhaps Fletcher Austin."

"What about that creep Constantine?" Marilyn asked.

"I don't think so. Even Simon wouldn't have been stupid enough to spread it around. Anyway, one of the first things I did today was pay Constantine off and kick him out of the place. So he's out of it completely; we don't have to worry about him."

"Did Nino have any suggestions for keeping it under wraps?"

"One," Gerald said, recalling the conversation he had shared with the designer after the fight with Simon. "It amounted to blackmail of a sort."

"Simon to resign completely, otherwise you'd press blackmail charges?"

His wife's intuitiveness surprised Gerald. "Almost, only we can't instigate proceedings. It has to be Brian."

The problems which could arise from that course of action were abundantly evident to Marilyn. "The question is, would he? He'd have his name dragged through the mud."

"Not necessarily. Nino did come up with a pretty good idea, a bluff. We're going to the hospital later on this evening to see how Brian's getting on, and we'll bring it up then."

"Poor Brian," Marilyn murmured, feeling genuinely sorry for the man who had been one of the prime causes of the misfortunes. "Nobody's even been to see him. Nobody's cared enough."

Gerald looked down at his hands, trying to define his own feelings toward Brian. "What do you reckon I should do about Brian? Accept the resignation and let him go, make an end of it? Or should I tear up the letter?"

"That's for you to decide," Marilyn told him. "Whichever course you take, you'll always feel that you took the wrong one. But while you're making up your mind, always remember one thing."

"What's that?"

"He was more affected than anybody by your father's death, even more so than your mother. When he tried to kill himself, it wasn't because he was scared of what people would think of him; it was because he saw himself as being directly responsible for your father's death."

"Yeah, I suppose you're right," Gerald agreed wearily. "I'll try to figure out what the old man would have done."

When Gerald and Viscenzi entered the ward later that evening, Brian turned away, unable to meet their eyes. Gerald walked around the bed and stood between him and the window, blocking the patient's view, forcing him to look up.

"How are you feeling?" Gerald asked, keeping his voice light. "Are they treating you okay?"

Brian appeared puzzled by the questions. Following the letter, he had not expected a visit from Gerald; the most he had hoped for was the opportunity to slip away quietly, to start afresh somewhere else.

"They feed me all right," he said, "but if I get a headache they won't let me have any aspirin for it."

Gerald smiled at the retort. "Brian, we've got to speak to you about Chestertons. There's a lot at stake, and we need your help in the worst possible way."

"What help can I give?" He sat up in bed; the self-directed anger he had been experiencing urged him to reveal his innermost self. "How can you want anything from me after all I did? I helped to kill your father, Gerald. Can't you understand that? I don't know why you even bothered coming to see me."

"You're not to blame for my father's death," Gerald said quietly, feeling embarrassed at the outburst. He looked across the ward to see Viscenzi shuffling his feet awkwardly. "Brian, you were compromised into a situation where you had two choices, one of which you felt was quite impossible. You weren't able to know what was going to happen. How could you?"

Brian sat mutely listening to Gerald, his head bobbing up and down in agreement at the unexpected absolution.

"There is a way you can help us undo some of the havoc, though," Gerald continued. "Something has to be done about my brother, but we don't want a word of what's happened to get out, for reasons you should be able to understand."

"Your mother."

"My mother, for one. And other adverse publicity which would do the company little good."

"What do you want me to do?" The question was spontaneous, springing immediately to Brian's lips before he realized that he was trying to ease his own tortured conscience.

"Call Simon and get him up here right now. Don't tell him we're here. Just say you want to see him."

"It won't work," Brian objected. "I threw him and Della out of here the other day."

"What the hell were they doing here?" He glanced at Viscenzi; the Italian's look of surprise was as great as his own.

"Pleading with me to stay quiet," Brian replied. "If I did, Della promised me that I'd be in good with the company once things got straightened out again. She's the one who needs getting her head kicked in, not Simon. He's just stupid, doing whatever she tells him while he thinks it's his own idea. She's the schemer behind everything that's taken place."

"Never mind that," Gerald cut in, eager to hear everything about the visit. "What else did they have to say?"

"They tried to get me to go along with them by saying that he"—Brian pointed a finger at Viscenzi—"was usurping my authority at Chestertons and I shouldn't stand for it. They were figuring that Simon would have the upper hand, especially if I went along with them and said nothing. That was when I decided that the best thing for me to do was write to you."

Taking into account the events of the past few days, Gerald felt that he should have been more immune to his brother's—or Della's, as Brian had claimed—treachery. But again he was shocked.

"That's all the more reason for you to call them now. Tell them whatever you like. Lie like a politician seeking election, but just get them up here."

Without another word, Brian reached out for the telephone on the bedside table. Viscenzi stepped forward quickly and handed it to him.

Della's anxiety was evident by the way she drove to the hospital, her normally fluid handling of the little sports car disturbed by the sudden summons from Brian. Twice as she pulled away from traffic lights she stalled the Midget, letting up the clutch too soon and instantly becoming the target for horn-hitting motorists lined up behind her.

"What do you think he wants?" she asked Simon. "He's already told your brother all there is to know. What else could he want from us?"

"God knows," Simon replied. Tenderly he touched his face, which was still sore from the battering it had received. "Maybe he wants to say he's sorry."

Della did not think the comment worth answering. She concentrated on her driving, trying to ease herself back into the smooth rhythm she always enjoyed. The more she tried, however, the poorer her control became. Changing down to come onto the approach to the George Washington Bridge, she missed second gear altogether. The grinding noise from the gearbox startled her, and the protesting vibration from the gearshift made her withdraw her hand quickly.

"Watch out!" Simon reprimanded her. "There's no need to take it out on the damned car."

"Shut up, Simon. We've got enough problems without your asinine remarks."

Reaching the hospital, she was out of the car quickly, leading Simon into the building. Outside Brian's ward, they hesitated long enough to discuss the coming encounter.

"We'll see what he wants and get out as quickly as possible," Della said. "He's done his damage already, so there's no point in hanging around."

Her face was blank as she entered the ward, holding the door open for Simon, who followed her in. Only when they were inside the small room did either of them notice Gerald and Viscenzi, who were standing behind the door.

"What's going on?" Simon blurted out. He looked wildly around the ward and began to back toward the still open door. Viscenzi stepped in behind him and pushed the door closed with his foot, cutting off the avenue of retreat.

Gerald's voice cut across the ward. "Della. Simon. You were asked to come here by Brian because he has something important to say, something he wants you both to hear."

Brian fixed Simon and Della with a cold stare. "I owe it to myself to set the record straight," he said quietly. "I don't like leaving loose ends around for people to fall over, so I'm pressing blackmail charges against the pair of you."

The words had the effect of creating five seconds of pure silence. Simon stood perfectly still, transfixed with horror at the prospect of criminal proceedings. The vacuum was broken by Della, who gasped hoarsely, bringing a hand quickly to her mouth to cut off the sound.

Deep down, Gerald felt a primitive thrill of satisfied vengeance at their reactions. He had hated to use Brian as a tool, but it was a necessary step to protect both family and business. And now, this one moment of seeing his brother almost petrified with fear filled him with a joy the like of which he had never experienced.

Simon's mouth opened and closed as he swallowed hard. When he managed to regain some control, his voice was shaking, words spilling out unevenly. "Is . . . is there nothing else?" he quavered. "No . . . no other way? Surely there must be something."

Brian shook his head determinedly. "I want the pair of you to go through the same sort of hell you put me through. Do you think for one moment that I enjoyed selling your father out for your stupid power games? I hated myself every minute of every day. Now I want to see you two bastards sweat a bit. Nothing worse can happen to me, so what the hell do I care?"

Neither Gerald nor Viscenzi said a word. They stood against the wall, a silent audience to Brian's performance. Viscenzi felt that the man was actually enjoying the situation now that he had gotten into the role.

Seeing no mercy in Brian's eyes, Simon swung around to his brother. "Do something," he begged. "You can't let him go ahead with this and get me sent away. For Christ's sake, you're my goddamned twin brother. You don't want to see me in jail, do you?" The question trailed off into a pleading whine.

"Why should I help you?" Gerald asked, turning the screw even more, enjoying it. "You've been working so hard these past few months, maybe a rest in jail will do you the world of good."

Della, in an incredible testimonial to her inner strength, had regained her composure completely. She walked to the bed and stood over Brian. "Have you called the police yet, Brian?" she asked sharply.

"Not yet. I wanted you both to be here when I did it." His hand was poised over the telephone, when Viscenzi pushed himself away from the wall and began to speak, coming in perfectly on cue. His tones were cool and persuasive, reasoning, just as he and Gerald had planned they would be.

"Do you think it is prudent to drag the Chesterton name through the courts?" He directed the question at Gerald, knowing that Simon and Della were hanging on every word. "No good can possibly come of it, you know."

Simon felt a small surge of hope. He turned to look at Gerald, silently beseeching him to listen to the Italian's comment.

Viscenzi continued speaking, noticing that Brian's hand remained poised over the telephone. "Despite all that has happened, Gerald, I think there should be enough family spirit left to circumvent such a drastic action as involving the police and publicizing this whole unfortunate series of events."

Weighing the Italian's words very carefully, Gerald stared at Simon and Della, seeing the undisguised hope which burned deeply in their eyes, his brother far more so than Della's. "It's not my decision, Nino. Brian wants to do it; he feels it's the only way he can straighten himself out."

Simon could remain a listener no longer. "Anything!" he broke in. "I'll do anything you say. Just don't let him call the police." He swung around to Della. "Come on," he pleaded. "Tell them we'll do whatever they like."

Gerald raised his eyebrows in question. "Well, Della? Will you?" She nodded, an almost unnoticeable movement of the head. Gerald turned to Brian. "It's your game. Do whatever you feel you've got to."

Brian picked up the receiver immediately. Gerald saw the hope die in his brother's eyes and realized that the charade had been taken far enough. He motioned to Viscenzi; the designer gently but firmly removed the receiver from Brian's hand and broke the connection.

"Brian, before you go ahead and file your complaint, I want to speak to you," Gerald said. He looked at Della and Simon. "Would you two wait outside?"

When they left the room, Gerald spoke to Viscenzi. "How long do you reckon we should give them? Five minutes?"

"Make it ten. Let them feel uncomfortable for long enough."

"Okay, so what do we talk about for ten minutes?" Gerald grinned openly at the Italian, deriving enjoyment from the fear he had helped instill in his brother.

"Have you got any plans made for when you get out of hospital?" he asked Brian.

"I hadn't thought very much about it," Brian replied. "Go back to Chicago, I suppose. Pick it all up again somewhere else—or try to."

"Patch it up with Thelma?"

Brian looked up in surprise. "No way, especially not now."

"What about work? What are you going to do?"

"I don't know. Work's pretty well been the last thing on my mind. I guess you can understand that."

Gerald clearly recalled his final words to Marilyn, how she said that whatever course he took would always seem wrong in retrospect. And what would his father have done in a similar situation? What action would he have taken? Gerald knew immediately.

"That letter of yours, Brian—I was only interested in the part about Simon and the blackmail."

Viscenzi caught the gist of the statement before Brian did. He glanced curiously at Gerald initially; then an expression of approval crossed his face.

"Does that mean you still want me?" Brian asked. "Even after all this?"

"Let's just say we'll give it a try and see how it works out," Gerald said, not really certain what he wanted. "If we can pick up the pieces again, maybe it's the best thing."

Viscenzi coughed into his hand, signifying that the ten-minute waiting period was over. He opened the door to readmit Della and Simon. Simon had his head bowed, expecting the worst, but Gerald noticed that Della stared straight at him. He directed his words to her.

"To save further grief and embarrassment to this family, Brian has agreed not to press charges." A look of relief spread itself across Simon's face, and he lifted his head, a condemned man learning of his reprieve as the noose is placed around his neck. "There is, however, a condition," Gerald added.

Della's mask did not slip; she had been expecting a rider. "What is it?" she asked.

"That you both resign from Chestertons, and that Simon relinquish all claims he has against the company in his position as a vice-president."

Simon found his voice at last, prompted by what he saw as the injustice of the condition. "That's preposterous! What the hell am I supposed to do for a living? Beg for crusts? Or do you want to see me starve?"

"Starving's more than you deserve!" Gerald shot back. "But I'm not as big a bastard as you. I haven't had the practice or the instructor." He let his eyes wander from Simon to Della, wanting his sister-in-law to know that she was included in the statement. "You can have the three stores we picked up in San Francisco last year, as long as you take the Chesterton's name off the front. And that's a damned sight more than you deserve."

"San Francisco!" Simon exploded. "That's three thousand miles away, the other side of the world. What am I supposed to do out there?"

"Disappear—simply that. I don't care if you jump off the Golden Gate Bridge with a ton of concrete around your feet, but I never want to see your face in New York again. You'll just tell our mother that you've decided you'll be happier on the West Coast and you want to try building up your own operation in your own inimitable style." He smiled darkly, finding amusement in what he had to say next.

"You should have no trouble getting known. After all, you'll have the services of a top-notch advertising manager going with you. That must constitute a big help."

Seeing that Simon was about to continue his protest, Gerald cut him off quickly, tiring of the situation. "You can either accept the condition, or I give Brian the go-ahead. Take your choice."

Only Della saw through the play acting. "Even if Simon refused to do as you say, Brian would never call the police," she said confidently. "You couldn't afford to let him."

Gerald considered her words carefully. "Maybe not," he admitted. "But are you prepared to take that chance? That's what you've got to ask yourself."

Della regarded him coolly for a long moment, wondering how far she could have gone if it had been Gerald she had met that night in the singles bar on Second Avenue, and not his brother. All the way, she decided; there would have been no stopping them. But, as luck would have it, the right twin was already married, and she had to meet the wrong one.

"Well?" Gerald insisted. "Are you?"

"No," she finally said, pushing the thought regretfully from her mind. "I'm not."


Driving back to Viscenzi's hotel in Manhattan, Gerald asked the designer if he approved of the way he had handled the situation.

"Your blackmail was as good as your brother's," Viscenzi replied. "That's really all it was, Gerald. You even used the same lever—Brian. Your blackmail threatened to expose your brother's blackmail unless he did exactly as you told him."

"I'd like to think that my reasons were different."

"Oh, they certainly were," Viscenzi chuckled. "I approved of yours wholeheartedly, just as I approved of your offer to Brian. You don't throw twenty-five years of a man's life away like that. But now comes your first big test."

"What first big test? I thought I'd passed all the ones there were."

"You have a lot of responsibilities now, Gerald. With Brian's help—if it works out, and I think it will—you'll have to handle all the stores and keep an eye on the factory. You're suddenly left with very little top management."

"I know. How long are you prepared to stick around for?"

Viscenzi spread his hands wide. "I can give you a month at the very most. After that I must return to Europe to attend to my own business. Fortunately it is summer, so my presence will not be missed that greatly." He paused long enough to light a cigar. "Instead of the French Riviera, I will spend my summer vacation this year at the West Fifty-seventh Street Riviera." He changed position in the passenger seat so that he could look at Gerald while he spoke.

"I think you will do very well," he said sincerely. "You are the third generation I have known, and I have faith in you."

Gerald was delighted to hear Viscenzi's praise. "Nino, I'm not pumping for compliments, but why do you say that?"

424

"You are your father's son."

"Say again?"

"All the time you were thinking what your father would have done with Brian, right?" Viscenzi asked.

Gerald nodded, never taking his eyes off the road.

"I think you did what he would have done under the same circumstances," Viscenzi continued. "And in your position I could think of no greater encouragement."